MW01658541

THE BEST PLAYS OF 1922-23

AND THE

YEAR BOOK OF THE DRAMA IN AMERICA

Edited by

BURNS MANTLE

BOSTON
SMALL, MAYNARD & COMPANY
PUBLISHERS

"Rain," copyright, 1922, by John Colton and Clemence Randolph.

"Loyalties," copyright, 1922, by John Galsworthy.
Published by Charles Scribner's Sons, N. Y.

"Icebound," copyright, 1922, by Owen Davis.
Published by Little, Brown & Company, Boston.

"You and I," copyright, 1922, by Philip Barry.
Published by Brentano's, N. Y.

"The Fool," copyright, 1922, by Channing Pollock.
Published by Brentano's, N. Y.

"Merton of the Movies," copyright, 1922, by the Authors.

"Why Not?" copyright, 1922, by Jesse Lynch Williams.

"The Old Soak," copyright, 1922, by Don Marquis.
Published by Doubleday, Page & Company.

"R. U. R.," copyright, 1922, by Paul Selver.
Published by Doubleday, Page & Company.

"Mary the 3d," copyright, 1922, by Rachel Crothers.
Published by Brentano's, N. Y.

COPYRIGHT, 1923

By SMALL, MAYNARD & COMPANY
(Incorporated)

Printed in the United States of America

THE MURRAY PRINTING COMPANY
CAMBRIDGE, MASS.

THE BOSTON BOOKBINDING COMPANY
CAMBRIDGE, MASS.

CONTENTS

INTRODUCTION

IT is never an easy task to select ten plays for inclusion in this annual year book of the drama in America. It was harder this year than usual. First, because there were a greater number of dramatic plays from which to make the selection and, second, because many of them were of an even merit.

There were, according to our records, one hundred and ninety productions of new plays and important revivals made in the New York theatres between June 15, 1922 and June 15, 1923. Of these we had our choice of, say, one hundred and thirty-five.

Balancing one consideration with another we finally selected ten and put the others aside. "Why ten?" Arthur Hopkins inquired. "Why not nine? Or twelve?"

To which we could make no more reasonable answer than to say that, having started with ten, we disliked to break the habit, also that unless a specified number was agreed upon the selection would lose its zest as a game. "Why should it be a game?" continued Arthur. He is a most persistent person.

There is a strong probability, however, that our worthy publishers would object that more than ten would make too bulky a volume, and less than ten would be too few to satisfy our omnivorous public, which may be even now fairly storming the bookstalls and the libraries (particularly the libraries) in a mad quest for this, the fourth and latest issue of THE BEST PLAYS series, which started in 1919–20.

The season of 1922–23, as you will see by reference to the chapter devoted to a review of the season in New York, has been an unusual season in many ways. As we look back upon it now it seems to have been an exceptionally clean and stimulating season. True, there was, for the first time within recent history, a conviction in court of a manager and a company of actors charged with the production of what a jury described as an obscene and immoral play. But there were very few plays — even of the frothy, farcical type — that so much as ruffled the resentment of the purists. The bedroom farce, for instance, was conspicuously rare, so rare that we cannot now recall a single lace counterpane torn and trampled by a wandering husband, nor a single picture of a worried gentleman peeking out from under a Fifi's bed.

The ten plays from which we have taken excerpts, and which make up the body of this volume, are, we believe, representative of the season's worthiest offerings. The assumption of omniscience, as we have said before, is voluntary. We do not pretend to say there were no other plays just as good in the season's list. But we do say that these are the ten that, to our notion, reflect the most credit upon the playwrights who composed them, the producers who staged them and the public that indorsed them.

In any list of ten there are certain to be some about which all so-called authorities are agreed. There is, for example, no question this season about "Rain." Dramatized from a short story written by W. Somerset Maugham called "Miss Thompson" by two who were new to the profession of playwriting, John Colton and Clemence Randolph, it is readily conceded to be the most vitally alive and forcefully dramatic of the season's plays. In the writing it lacks the finish of Galsworthy's "Loyalties," and the epigrammatic brilliance of Barry's "You and I." But for sheer drama it stands alone.

"Loyalties," another of those nicely balanced dramatic discussions, in the writing of which John Galsworthy excels, may have owed its New York success partly to its racial conflict. But aside from an interesting theme it is a fine drama which quickly stabs and insistently holds the interest of its auditors. A sane, intelligent, humanly appealing story told in terms of a skillfully manipulated dramatic plot. And, like most of the Galsworthy output, it reads as well as it plays.

"You and I" invades, in a way, a new domestic field in the theatre. This is frankly the story of the higher middle class — the $40,000-a-year, two-car folk of New York's fashionable suburbs. It may be, so far as its dialogue is concerned, unnaturally brilliant. But it is basicly so human, its theme of the artist crying for self-expression in the soul of one who has felt, as the author puts it, "the heel of expediency on the neck of inclination," has so general an appeal, that it has quickly found not only the public for which it was written by its young author, Philip Barry, a Yale man who studied drama at Harvard, but a much larger public than either its producers or its reviewers believed it would attract.

Owen Davis' "Icebound" represents the one-time author of melodramas written for the cheaper circuits at his recent best. He emerged a year ago with a play called "The Detour" that was direct and simple and fine. He followed it this year with a study of the coldly calculating home folk of his native Maine, who are "icebound within and without" the better part of their lives. This won him the Pulitzer prize of $1,000 for the best play of the year. It represents a long and honest struggle on the part of Mr. Davis, handicapped by his earlier successes with plays of the "Bertha the Beautiful Sewing Machine Girl" type, and, though it plays better than it reads, it is a fine and honest native drama.

Channing Pollock's "The Fool" is frankly a sermon play, obvious in its mechanics and simple in its text. The hero is a young clergyman who tries to live as Christ might conceivably live were he on earth today.

He is badgered and buffeted by the church and doubted by the publicans, and his greatest triumph comes through God's staging a miracle to confound the sinners and reward a child of great faith. But for all its obvious adherence to theatrical conventions "The Fool" is effective dramatic entertainment, human and sincere, and greatly beloved of the public it was intended to reach.

Rachel Crothers' "Mary the 3d" is another of this author's sincere and interestingly analytical studies of American family life. Again the free and rebellious present-day flapper is her heroine, but before Mary the 3d there were the two Marys who were her mother and her mother's mother, and the contrast offered of their gradually changing viewpoints and methods, with the resulting reactions in each successive generation, is entertainingly set forth. Miss Crothers is inclined to scold a little and to view with alarm as an impatient outsider. But it will do neither the flappers nor the flappers' mothers a bit of harm to listen to her.

"R. U. R." is the novelty of the list. We included this dramatic fantasy for the same reason that we have selected others of the Theatre Guild's list of plays — because it best represents the taste of a theatre-going public that is constantly growing in America, particularly eastern America, and also because it most creditably represents the progressive continental drama. It is also good entertainment and, it seems to us, is as dramatically effective in the reading as in the playing.

"Merton of the Movies" and "The Old Soak" are representative American comedies which justify their popularity with the people. "Merton," sifted through three bright minds, cleverly satirizes the reactions of native youth to the lure of the movies, and tells a simple, human, amusing story doing it.

"The Old Soak" perfectly represents that typically American comedy drama in which the central character is the whole show because of the gentle humor, the quaint philosophy and the major virtues he commands to offset a certain definite but harmless shiftlessness and weakness of character. Rip Van Winkle was such a character, and Old Bill Jones of "Lightnin'" another.

The statistical record of the season again covers such facts as we believe theatre followers of the country will be interested in knowing. There are paragraphed synopses of nearly two hundred plays, with the casts of the companies playing them in New York, and the usual biographical data concerning the better known players.

The success of the three previous issues of THE BEST PLAYS encourages us to think these volumes are proving helpful as a record and interesting as a reminder of what the theatre has offered for the entertainment of playgoers in the seasons covered. The satisfaction of thinking so, at least, lessens the burdens of compilation.

B. M.

Forest Hills, L. I.
June, 1923.

THE BEST PLAYS OF 1922-1923

THE BEST PLAYS OF 1922-1923

THE SEASON IN NEW YORK

IF the particular theatrical season of which this volume is a record does not recommend itself to future historians of the theatre as the most notable of a generation, it should at least be given credit for being the first theatrical season in a generation that has not been described as "the worst in years."

It has been the writer's experience that theatrical seasons, taken by and large, average pretty evenly. There are usually three or four outstanding dramatic successes to which we delight to point with pride, a dozen individual achievements in characterization that serve to hearten both actors and critics, and enough musical comedy successes to satisfy the demand of those wearied merchants whom tradition credits with the support of the more trivial entertainment of the playhouse.

But it happens that, in addition to these familiar virtues, the current season can boast an event or two of first importance to the theatre the like of which even the old-timers cannot recall.

It will be remembered, for one thing, as the season in which no less than five Shakespearean revivals, so cast and staged as to command the interest and the respect of a public that has long flouted Shakespeare, were prominent on Broadway.

Two of the five — those popularized by Jane Cowl's Juliet and John Barrymore's Hamlet — ran over a hundred performances each, and a third, "The Merchant of Venice," with David Warfield as Shylock, reached ninety-two. True, the other two, Ethel Barrymore's revival of "Romeo and Juliet," and the National Theatre production of "As You Like It," ran faster toward the storehouse than they did toward a record, but they were worthy productions for all that.

The season of 1922–23 will also be historically checked as that in which the Moscow Art Theatre Company first visited these shores. No dramatic importation within this generation's memory has created the stir the Muscovites caused, nor the comment.

They naturally aroused great excitement among the thousands of Russians and their descendants now resident in New York. They stirred up the native play reviewers, who saw in their perfect ensemble playing evidences of the triumph of art over commercialism in the theatre. American actors and actresses became quite emotional in their admiration for the perfect "team work" of the visitors, and, finally, that large section of the lay public that is spontaneously affected by anything new and strange in the theatre arose, as the comedian says, "in a mess," and applauded wildly.

As a result the Russians were pretty generously praised and, in many instances, foolishly overpraised, in spite of which their success was honestly earned. Having played the rôles they presented here for a quarter century they have naturally attained a smoothness and perfection in characterization the actors of other nationalities would find it difficult to duplicate without similar training. And the fact that they played exclusively in Russian severely handicapped their critics. Taking their art more seriously these players were never inclined to cheat their audiences. But if they had been so inclined we doubt if any of their local critics could have caught them at it.

Aside from these unusual happenings the season was not distinguished by other outstanding events which we now recall. The summer period, between June 15 and the first weeks of August, offered little worth mentioning. There were two new colored vaudevilles, "Strut Miss Lizzie" and "The Plantation Revue," seeking to trade on the popularity of the successful "Shuffle Along," but neither got far. Michio Itow, a Japanese dancer, evolved an artistic mixture of dance, song and scenic art and took it to Richard G. Herndon for production. Mr. Herndon thought it might go if there were something in it to attract the less artistic element among summer playgoers. He thereupon engaged Raymond Hitchcock to combine forces with Mr. Itow and between them they produced a "Pinwheel Revue." There was, however, too much Hitchcock for the followers of Itow, and too much art for the followers of the ubiquitous "Hitchy." The "Pinwheel" whizzed wheezily for a week or two and was dead. Revised later in its original Itow form it enjoyed another fitful run, while Mr. Hitchcock took his portion of the entertainment into vaudeville.

A late June production was Georg Kaiser's "From Morn to Midnight," done originally as a subscribers' treat by the Theatre Guild. It proved sufficiently popular and inexpensive to suggest a regular engagement in an uptown theatre. Frank Reicher was the producer and played the leading part. He took charge of the moving and the play had a six-week run at the Frazee.

August was less active than Augusts have been, revealing but fifteen new plays in its thirty-one days. But several of these were good. Don Marquis' "The Old Soak," for one, started the twenty-second and ran through the season, for reasons you may be able to detect in the excerpts from the dialogue printed elsewhere in this volume. Being still under the influence of the mystery play craze we also had "Whispering Wires" and "The Monster" served early in the month. "Whispering Wires," an ingenious and shivery melodrama in which an unlucky gentleman is killed by telephone, caught the crowd's fancy and ran through the season.

Frances Starr made an early season bid for favor with an amusing light comedy called "Shore Leave," which David Belasco staged attractively at the Lyceum. It ran for one hundred and fifty-one performances, but just missed being as popular a success as Miss Starr had hoped for. George White, later than usual with his annual "Scandals," came in the twenty-eighth and stayed for ten weeks, and there was a satirical comedy, "The Torchbearers," written by George Kelly, an author of vaudeville sketches, that started off with such a rush it seemed destined for a season's run. It made good-natured sport of the affectation and pose cluttering up certain phases of the Little Theatre Movement, which limited its appeal, however, and though it lasted through one hundred and thirty performances in New York, it was not as sound a hit as anticipated.

Two of the outstanding successes of the month were George Cohan's amusing comedy exaggeration of stage Englishmen and stage Americans, "So This Is London," which is at the moment threatening to continue through the summer, and a musical piece, "The Gingham Girl," which was popular from August till May. "The Woman Who Laughed" laughed only for two weeks, a movie melodrama called "Lights Out" flickered and failed after a ten-day struggle and "Fools Errant," a well-written but somewhat studiedly conversational drama by Louis Evan Shipman, editor of *Life*, remained for eight weeks.

September was a busy theatre month, as usual, with twenty-three new plays offered. In the list were several that lived up to their fulsome heralding, which is the supreme test, and a number that were rather sensational upsets. John Galsworthy's "Loyalties" was not produced until late in the month, but it was for many weeks thereafter one of the much-discussed hits of the year. It moved on to Chicago after two hundred and twenty-one performances on Broadway. Ina Claire and Bruce McRae helped to make "The Awful Truth" one of the pleasantest of the season's light comedies, and a rather vivid melodrama, "East of Suez," was played successfully until Florence Reed, the star, quarrelled with the producer, A. H. Woods, and withdrew from the cast.

The upsets included Avery Hopwood's "Why Men Leave Home," one of the best of his comedies killed, wise showmen say, by the title; "The Endless Chain," written by another usually dependable author of plays, James Forbes, which failed after forty showings; "Spite Corner," which Frank Craven and John Golden had hoped would be another "First Year," but which gave up after three months; "Rose Bernd," a somber study from the German which Ethel Barrymore's fine characterization of the heroine could not carry past its eleventh week, and "La Tendresse," which even the combined strength of Henry Miller and Ruth Chatterton could not force through to a success.

This same month the Selwyns scored a Broadway failure with "The Exciters," William Harris, Jr., another with "Banco," and Sam H. Harris one with "It's a Boy," by the author of "Six Cylinder Love," which ran through the previous season. And each of them was sure of success. There were two or three musical shows that were well liked, notably one by Eddie Dowling, a recruit from vaudeville, called "Sally, Irene and Mary," and the annual "Greenwich Village Follies," which played practically through the season.

There were more successes than failures in October, or at least as many. These included Channing Pollock's "The Fool," Austin Strong's "Seventh Heaven," Irving Berlin's second "Music Box Revue," the Theatre Guild's "R. U. R.," the Shuberts' "Lady in Ermine," and another novel mystery, "The Last Warning." These all ran through until spring. "The Fool," which we have included in this volume, was slow to start, but gained a mighty impetus as it went along, and now promises to continue indefinitely; "Seventh Heaven" has an advance sale that will carry it through till fall and "The Music Box Revue" will likely play on until its successor is ready for rehearsals in October.

The newly organized Equity Players, whose advent as producers signalized the first attempt of actors to maintain their own theatre, began their season at the Forty-Eighth Street Theatre with a creditable production of a Spanish melodrama called "Malvaloca." Jane Cowl played the heroine, but no one appeared to care particularly for the play. This reception momentarily depressed, but fortunately it did not seriously dishearten, the producers.

Grace George, having had some success with "The Nest," translated another Geraldy drama from the French, which she called "To Love," and staged it with herself, Norman Trevor and Robert Warwick playing the three parts. The crowd voted it tiresome. W. A. Brady brought "The Insect Comedy," by the brothers Kapek of Czechoslovakia, over from Prague, renamed it "The World We Live In," gave it a handsome production and kept it playing for three months. "Six Characters in Search of an Author," a Pirandello novelty from Italy, was produced by Brock Pemberton to confound the morons, which it did. It was not, however, much of a financial success.

November is quite frequently the banner month of the theatrical year in the number and quality of its offerings. Producers who have what they consider a particularly good piece of theatrical property usually hold it until November. They argue, or so we assume, that by that time the summer vacationists are home and more or less settled in their minds, and that the first chill of winter has suggested the comfort of indoor amusements. There may be, however, a definite bond between temperature and temperament.

This particular November brought "Rain," the supreme dramatic triumph of the year, also "Merton of the Movies," one of the big comedy successes, and John Barrymore's "Hamlet," which started such an interesting revival of Shakespearean plays as New York has not boasted in a generation. There was a weighty drama from the French called "The Love Child" that continued for one hundred and seventy-one performances and two music plays that ran through the season, George Cohan's "Little Nelly Kelly" and a tuneful version of Frank Craven's "Too Many Cooks" renamed "Up She Goes."

On the other hand there were several spectacular failures.

"The 49ers," so called both because they performed on Forty-ninth Street, in the Punch and Judy Theatre, and sought to discover gold in a new form of revue, lasted only two weeks, even though they were backed by the wits of the town and country. Contributors to their program, which was a jumble of satires, burlettas and spoken pieces, included Ring Lardner, Montague Glass, Heywood Broun, Franklin P. Adams, George Kaufman, Marc Connelly and Robert Benchley, and they had such gifted players in the first cast as May Irwin, Roland Young, Beryl Mercer, Sidney Toler and Denman Maley. It was a clever program, but the multitude sniffed and would have none of it.

There was a melodrama called "The Bootleggers," aiming to expose and satirize the failure of the law's representatives to keep the city dry, which exploded after four weeks, and "The Romantic Age," a fine bit of sentiment, by A. A. Milne, lasted no longer.

The Equity Players, rebounding from their first failure, offered an upstanding American drama called "Hospitality" as their second bill, but because it was ruthlessly true to the home life it depicted, and not particularly pleasant entertainment, the crowd failed to support it and it was withdrawn after six weeks. The Theatre Guild also suffered a failure with a Milne comedy, "The Lucky One," which had one or two fine scenes but was, in the main, one of those intelligent, well-played, but depressing family dramas the American playgoer seldom approves. "The Texas Nightingale," a brightly written history of a temperamental Texas prima donna, written by Zoë Akins, was rather sadly cast and never quite human, passing out after four forced weeks, and "The Bunch and Judy" was the first of the elaborately staged Dillingham music pieces to suffer defeat at the Globe.

David Warfield arrived in December with "The Merchant of Venice," and before the month was over Ethel Barrymore had tried her "Romeo and Juliet." Neither of these fine players was particularly happy in these Shakespearean adventures. Warfield was accepted as an intelligent and interesting Shylock and racially a striking type. He also gave technically a finished and often a moving performance. But he fell below those standards of greatness with which tradition has credited former interpreters of the rôle and his public's support was not what had been expected. Ninety performances and he sent the handsome Belasco production to the storehouse to await next season's tour, when "The Merchant" may be played alone, or included in a repertoire of revivals.

Miss Barrymore had planned to play Rosalind in "As You Like it," but suddenly changed her mind and substituted "Romeo and Juliet." It was one of those unfortunate quick decisions that frequently affect the whole course of a player's career. Miss Barrymore's Juliet, often beautifully and sympathetically read, lacked the magic touch of youth or any simulated spirit of youth. The company, taking its cue as to mood and pace from her, consequently gave a heavy and uninspired performance. Four weeks later the revival was withdrawn, a failure.

It was in December, too, that the Selwyns came a cropper with their imported production, "Johannes Kreisler," in which an attempt was made to reproduce the shifting scenes of the movies in an acted drama. There were fifty odd scenes shown on a variety of stages, and through these a large company, headed by Jacob Ben-Ami, raced breathlessly. Whatever values the drama may have had were completely lost in the jumble of scenic novelties.

This was the month, too, that "The God of Vengeance," later to be declared a vicious and immoral play by a jury in court and withdrawn by court order, was first shown in Greenwich Village, where it ran for eleven weeks before the outraged authorities discovered it. The conviction of its producer and chief actors served to lessen the agitation favoring the appointment of a play censor. It also put a fear of the law in the hearts of several other producers given to taking chances with plays of questionable character.

"Secrets," a stimulating drama for the sentimentalists, started in December and, partly because Margaret Lawrence gave a superb performance as its heroine, ran through until June, and Peggy Wood found a winning music play in "The Clinging Vine," the book of which was written by Zelda Sears, for many years a favorite comedienne. The popular Fay Bainter, back after countless performances in "East Is West," could not pull "The Lady Cristilinda" past its fourth week, though it was in many ways excellent entertainment, and the happy authors of "Irene" failed to score with a sister music play called "Glory."

The third Equity play was a divorce comedy entitled "Why Not?" written by Jesse Lynch Williams (who won the Pulitzer prize in 1918 with "Why Marry?") and it proved not only the best, but the most popular of the actors' selections, continuing for one hundred and twenty-three performances before it was closed. There was also a colorful Mexican drama called "Gringo," well written by Sophie Treadwell, which was played for five weeks, and another of those "La Tosca" variants in which a reckless roué pursues a frightened heroine about a locked room, tearing her gown from off her shoulder and leering unthinkable things at her, until his heart valves close up. This one was called "The Masked Woman," and Helen MacKellar and Lowell Sherman, adept at this sort of thing, played in it for one hundred and seventeen performances.

Other December incidents were the appearance of Miss Billie Burke in a gorgeous setting arranged for her by her husband, Florenz Ziegfeld, and a pleasant but unimportant little play by Booth Tarkington called "Rose Briar," and the production by the Theatre Guild of Claudel's "The Tidings Brought to Mary." This was an impressive but somber miracle play that continued for four weeks. Leo Ditrichstein also came in from the road with Ben Hecht's "The Egotist," but only stayed six weeks, which may have been Mr. Hecht's fault, or Mr. Ditrichstein's, or ours.

January was distinguished by the arrival of the Moscow Art Theatre troupe, before mentioned, under the somewhat excited chaperonage of Morris Gest. The early performances, the first week being devoted to "Tsar Fyodor," were jammed with the élite, not to overlook the bon ton, among the city's playgoers. When the first curiosity was satisfied, there was still an enormous Russian and Russian-American public to be taken care of, with the result that the Muscovites probably played to more real money during their engagement in America than in all the twenty-five years of their life at the home theatre in Moscow. They toured as far west as Chicago and came back for a farewell four weeks in New York before sailing for home.

It was in January that "Will Shakespeare," written by Clemence Dane, whose "Bill of Divorcement" had been so successful the season before, was produced by Winthrop Ames. Beautifully written and handsomely staged though it was, the big public would have none of "Will Shakespeare," probably because it gave the impression of being more historical than human. It also exploded a generally accepted tradition that young Will's romance with Ann Hathaway was, sentimentally, a pleasantly romantic affair, and concluded eloquently as an impressive glorification of England which lost something of patriotic appeal in America. Whatever the cause, neither the fine speeches of the author nor the inspiring performance of Haidee Wright as Queen Elizabeth could save it, and after ten weeks of partly forced business it was withdrawn.

This was the month of Jane Cowl's appearance as Juliet, and the triumph of the Klauber-Selwyn production of the Shakespearean love tragedy. Everything that was heavy and slow-paced about the ill-fated Barrymore production was here spirited and youthful. The young people of the cast, the Romeo (Rollo Peters), the Mercutio, the County Paris and all the roisterers of Verona were young in fact. As a result the tragedy became the liveliest of melodramas and the audiences rose to it with enthusiasm. This, added to the fact that Miss Cowl is easily the most beautiful and most gifted of the Juliets of our day, carried the production through one hundred and sixty performances at the Henry Miller Theatre. With Juliet as the cornerstone of the classical repertoire she now plans to build up (she will add Shakespeare's Cleopatra and Viola next season), there is every reason to expect this actress will, within the next decade, take position as the first actress of the native theatre.

This same month "Polly Preferred," a lively and amusing comedy of the motion picture world, with

Genevieve Tobin playing the heroine, earned a popular success; there was a comedy called "Give and Take," with the comedians Louis Mann and George Sidney as rival partners in a fruit canning business; a successful musical comedy called "Caroline," with Tessa Kosta, produced by the Shuberts, and Guthrie McClintic tried a homely and true little American comedy by Lewis Beach called "A Square Peg," which deserved success, it seemed to us, but missed it, probably because it was another of those unpleasantly analytical domestic dramas that depress the other "square pegs" who see them.

Three of the plays that we have chosen for the ten best of this volume were produced in February. The first was Owen Davis' "Icebound," which won the Pulitzer prize; the second, Philip Barry's "You and I," which would have made a strong bid for that honor if we had been one of the Pulitzer committee, and the third, Rachel Crothers' observant criticism of modern family life, called "Mary the 3d."

Ethel Barrymore, who refused to be whipped by the failure of her Juliet, returned to the sort of comedy she does best in a play by Alfred Sutro called "The Laughing Lady," and was immediately re-established in the hearts of her adoring public. The Theatre Guild produced the weird and undramatic Ibsen poem, "Peer Gynt"; the Kennedys, Edith Wynne and Charles Rann, re-emerged at a series of special matinées, playing a miracle play written by Mr. Kennedy called "The Chastening"; and Laurette Taylor took a glorious tumble in a piece made from Fanny Hurst's "Humoresque." Miss Taylor's performance as a Jewish mother was a fine bit of characterization, but the Jews did not think she was Jewish and the Irish did not admire her for trying to be. "Humoresque" lasted but four weeks.

March brought "Roger Bloomer," a weirdly impressionistic drama of adolescence written in the continental manner by John Howard Lawson, a young American of Jewish parentage. The Equity Players courageously staged it with a good cast and with many scenes skillfully manipulated. But the public was never quite able to grasp the idea that struggled for expression through the play and it was soon withdrawn. Later it was revived in Greenwich Village and continued there for a month or six weeks.

There was disappointment this month in the quick failure of Sacha Guitry's "Pasteur," which Henry Miller produced at the Empire. A fine play, historical, biographical and frequently dramatic, but foreign to American playgoers, to whom Pasteur was little more than a name. Mr. Miller gave in the titular rôle as fine a performance as he has ever given in his long career, but still there was no response at the box office, and two weeks later "Pasteur" was gone.

Lowell Sherman, having suffered senility and heart failure in "The Masked Woman," took to drugs in "Morphia" and increased the good impression he lately has been making as a character actor with a future. David Belasco brought Lionel Atwill in from the road with a Guitry comedy called "The Comedian," quite actorish, having to do with the love adventures of an aging matinée idol, but interesting and well played. It stayed on for eleven weeks.

The Theatre Guild produced "The Adding Machine," written by the Elmer Rice who wrote "On Trial," another impressionistic study on an American theme — that of the overworked, underpaid, socially rebellious unfortunates whose mental sufferings through the daily grind are as likely as not to drive them to murder. The hero of this adventure, killing his employer, is executed, passes on to the Elysian Fields, finds them not altogether to his liking and is finally ejected from heaven and sent back to earth that his soul may be more fully seasoned.

Producer Brady imported a Pinero fantasy written in the Barrie manner, called "The Enchanted Cottage," wherein, through the eyes of love, the ugly and misshapen see themselves not as they are but as they would like to be. It was a shade too fine for the crowd and ran but eight weeks. Pauline Frederick, hugely successful with an artificial play called "The Guilty One" on the road, brought it to Broadway and was a four-week failure, despite the interest her picture following took in her appearance in the flesh.

April brought Cyril Maude over from London in a machine-cut dramatization of "If Winter Comes," in which bungling Mark Sabre got on Mabel Sabre's nerves in the first act, went to war and came home again in the second, protected Effie Bright and her child in the third, was tried and tortured by the coroner's jury in the fourth, and finally rewarded with the love of Lady Tybar. The book's public, added to that which rightly holds Mr. Maude a most engaging comedian, kept the Hutchinson story going for five weeks, at the end of which time Mr. Maude produced a new comedy called "Aren't We All?" by Frederick Lonsdale. This one scored the biggest success the comedian has had in America since his "Grumpy" days.

Alice Brady, returning from the cinema fields to try a melodrama called "Zander the Great" at the Empire, with the idea of establishing it for picture use later, awoke the morning after the first performance to find herself with a popular play on her hands. Being the simple and theatrically effective story of a motherly maid servant who adopts a baby boy and travels with him in a flivver across country in search of his lost father, "Zander" quickly found an interested public, and is likely to run through the summer.

Otherwise the month revealed little of interest except the sincere attempt of Augustus Thomas to interest the Producing Managers' Association in a National Theatre movement. They gave him $25,000 to work with and he produced "As You Like It" with a cast headed by Marjorie Rambeau, A. E. Anson, Ian Keith, Margola Gillmore and many others. But the conditions were not right and the venture failed. On the twenty-third the Theatre Guild made its last production of the season with Shaw's "The Devil's Disciple," which pleased the subscribers and continued well into the summer.

May was livelier than usual, thanks largely to the continued cool weather. There were eighteen new productions and important revivals, which is an unusual number for what is practically the closing month of the season.

An interesting incident was a Little Theatre tournament, organized by Walter Hartwig and indorsed by the Drama League of New York. Twenty Little Theatre units from the Metropolitan district, having their home theatres within twenty miles of Manhattan, took part, each paying an entrance fee and presenting its best one-act play. Four plays were given each night for five nights. A committee then selected the three considered best and these were repeated at the Saturday matinée and given prizes of $100 each. They were played again Saturday night and the best of the three was awarded a David Belasco trophy, which is to be retained for a year. The tournament, it is expected, will be an annual affair.

The Ethiopian Art Theatre of Chicago also tried to interest Broadway in its work this month, presenting "Salome," "The Chip Woman's Fortune" and "The Comedy of Errors" at the Frazee Theatre. The colored players were graciously received by small audiences and generous critics, but only stayed two weeks. It appeared a general impression that the Ethiopian artists, to be assured of success, will have to divide their repertoire — presenting negro folk plays, which they do admirably, for the entertainment of white audiences, and making such selections from the white man's drama as may appeal to them for presentation in their own theatres for their own people.

The Equity Players, facing a deficit at the end of their experimental season in play production, staged all-star revivals of Sheridan's "The Rivals" and Paul Kester's "Sweet Nell of Old Drury," thus recovering a part of their losses. Laurette Taylor was the volunteer heroine of "Sweet Nell," and Francis Wilson the Acres of "The Rivals." "Sun Up," a Carolina folk play, attracted favorable attention as the month closed, being tentatively tried and found worthy.

The Players' Club, continuing its recently inaugurated custom of reviving a classic once a year, staged "The School for Scandal" for the good of the drama and the treasury of the club. Ethel Barrymore was the Lady Teazle, John Drew the Sir Peter and the Surfaces were played by McKay Morris and Charles Richman. It was a stunning cast and the revival was both socially and financially successful.

Finally came "The Passing Show of 1923" at the Winter Garden and the season, so far as this record goes, which is to June 15, was closed. An unusually good season, as intimated, with one hundred and ninety plays to its credit and a higher percentage of hits than usual.

THE SEASON IN CHICAGO

By Sheppard Butler

Dramatic Editor *Chicago Tribune*

THE outstanding thing about the "best plays of 1922-1923" in Chicago is that there were no "best plays." No play of serious import or striking value as entertainment made any deep impression on the midwest metropolis; none attained the degree of appreciation that was expected for it. Chicago audiences were perverse, and a disappointment. So, since Mr. Mantle in a previous volume has indicated that his title might properly read "The Best of the Successful Plays," the paradoxical sentence which opens this paragraph would seem to stand.

Consider what happened to Clemence Dane's "A Bill of Divorcement," a somber thing, no doubt, but as fine and forceful and compact a drama as reached Chicago during the year. It languished for a fortnight of its original engagement and then was ordered out of the theater which it occupied. Allan Pollock, its chief player, believed in it, however; he bought the production, brought it back to town after a week elsewhere, and installed it on his own hook in a little upstairs out-of-the-way playhouse, determined to prove that it would find an audience. He hung on doggedly for seven weeks, losing all the time, and finally gave it up. It was a brave and pitiful adventure — on the human side rather the most arresting event of the season.

Galsworthy's keen play of "Loyalties" had a sorry time of it, too. There was no one to come to its rescue, as Pollock tried to do for "Divorcement," and it remained but four weeks, to meager patronage. Two or three visiting producers happened to be in Chicago when "Loyalties" left, and contemplated the catastrophe at close range. They threw up their hands in despair, professing themselves completely at a loss as to what the provinces want.

Frank Craven's capital comedy, "The First Year," came loaded with hosannas from the high places in the east, and had an odd experience. The piece settled down to stay out the season, but it soon appeared that something was wrong. The expected capacity audiences didn't materialize. At another theater Winchell Smith and Tom Cushing's "Thank-U," which New York had found no great shakes of an entertainment, was running along coincidently and to steady profit. The two plays, vaguely similar in content (both were "small town" comedies) and sponsored by the same manager, developed a race, with the wiseacres eagerly watching. And the lowly "Thank-U" remained twenty-two weeks to "The First Year's" eighteen!

So it was with most of the things which trailed clouds of glory into the loop. Not all the New York successes were failures here; some had sizable runs. But in no case did the Chicago public perform according to Hoyle. It was most disturbingly oblivious to the fiat that a Broadway triumph means a triumph everywhere else.

Ernest Truex went away broken-hearted because "Six-Cylinder Love" had only indifferent success. Miss Helen Hayes told me "it made her so mad" that people didn't come to see "To the Ladies!" The blithe comedy of "Kempy" managed only six weeks. "Bulldog Drummond," with H. B. Warner playing the title rôle vastly better than another played it in New York, had forty-eight performances. Two months more than satisfied the demand for Mr. Arliss and "The Green Goddess," and Mr. Drew and Mrs. Carter, with Somerset Maugham's "The Circle," outstayed their welcome in the same period. Four weeks sufficed for Milne's "The

Dover Road"; Andreyev's fantastically lovely "He Who Gets Slapped" lingered twice as long, with Richard Bennett scolding scant audiences in curtain speeches every night.

Without doubt an inhospitable and perplexing season, disturbingly provocative of speculation as to why it was so. The managers pondered this reason and that, coming upon nothing definite except in one direction. They encountered a suddenly increased and articulate resentment over the matter of altered casts. "He Who Gets Slapped," for example, brought a large company of players wherein Mr. Bennett himself was the *only one* of the original group. Every rôle except that of the title was played by a substitute. Those who saw the Theater Guild's fine presentation in New York will have an inkling of what the change must have meant.

This, of course, was an extreme case. Most of the managers played fair, but some of the innocent suffered with the guilty.

Still, there were successes. If "Loyalties' " unhappy four weeks seems a reproach to Chicago, contemplate the heartening case of Mr. John Willard's "The Cat and the Canary." It came at the beginning of September and stayed the season through — thirty-six rousing weeks, the longest run of the year. To be sure, the piece was more a compendium of tricks and surprises, in the manner of Hanlon's "Superba," than a serious venture in playwriting. But it was a play.

And there was William Hodge. He wrote a long-winded and saccharine treatise on right living, called "For All of Us," brought it to town, and was egregiously laughed at for his pains. The play seemed doomed; those who owned the theater in which it was housed wanted Mr. Hodge to take it away.

He demurred. A manufacturer from Elgin, he said, had seen "For All of Us" and wanted to bring his employees in a body to be edified and uplifted as he had been. A minister was preaching the play to his flock; an old lady had loved it. So Hodge ignored the critics and other hard-boiled frequenters of the showshops, and went after the church folk, the patrons of lectures, and those who, in other centers, keep the Chautauquas prosperous. He built up a following of his own, achieved the second longest run of the season (twenty-eight weeks), and took oodles of money away with him. When Channing Pollock's "The Fool" comes to Chicago it may find a town that doesn't need any further regenerating at all.

To get down to statistics, the year brought Chicago eighty-seven entertainments in its standard theaters. Of these sixty-five were dramatic and twenty-two of the musical variety. It is noticeable that the proportion of plays steadily increases year by year, while the number of musical shows diminishes. Last season there were forty-nine plays and twenty-nine diversions with tunes. Evidently the expense of venturing this far from home with a musical production causes the managers to stop and ponder.

In the matter of plays, however, the entrepreneurs have been showing a sudden and rather startling affection for the city by the lake. Not only have they sent their New York successes; after neglecting us for years as a scene of theatrical experiment, they have come back with a rush to seek our opinion on new offerings. Of the season's sixty-five plays, twenty-four had their first important showing here.

This was pleasant, but not an unmixed blessing for the playgoer, for, as usually happens, the experiments yielded rather more chaff than wheat. There are certain advantages, in the theater, in sitting at the second table. You are not offered so many bad plays.

The first venture of any consequence was the staging of "The Guilty One," for Miss Pauline Frederick.

This was a lurid, emotional affair which kept Miss Frederick wringing her hands over a murder for two hours and a half, only to be brought up with a bang against a trick ending. It was rather a silly play, but the movie fans adored seeing the star "in person," and both here and in the towns to which she afterward went Miss Frederick did measurably well.

Leo Ditrichstein came next, bringing the play by Ben Hecht, Chicago novelist and ex-newspaper man, which, after much travail of spirit, they decided to call "Under False Pretenses." New York saw it later as "The Egotist." Came then Zoë Akins, with a comedy entitled "Greatness" and Miss Jobyna Howland to play its leading rôle, and that, too, went valiantly to New York, with its name changed to "The Texas Nightingale." The Hecht play was treated gently here; Miss Akins' piece was an abject failure. Neither seems to have caused any profound stir in New York, though I am told certain critics still mutter in their sleep that "A Texas Nightingale" was a great comedy.

Miss Nance O'Neil, faithful to Jacinto Benavento since her success with "The Passion Flower," tried another of the Spaniard's plays, "Field of Ermine." This proved tiresome and ineffective, and was quickly discarded.

Miss Elsie Ferguson submitted James Bernard Fagan's "The Wheel of Life" in January, but it brought her no great happiness. Here she plunged into melodramatic adventures in India, designed apparently to have an atmospheric vividness like that of Mr. Archer's "The Green Goddess." The play, however, lacks the snap and crackle and drive of "The Green Goddess"; where it should be stirring, it is somber and turgid in its effect. Its theme is illicit romance, culminated at a moment when both parties are beleaguered in a remote mountain fastness and expect to die. It may be rewritten for a New York showing in the fall.

Saddest of the unfortunate experiments here to be recorded is, I should say, that of Mrs. Fiske with "The Dice of the Gods." Its central figure, that of a blithe and witty aristocrat fallen into seedy circumstances through the ravages of the morphine habit, was a characterization of blinding brilliance in the actress' hands. But a central figure is not enough, and the fabric of the play which surrounded it fell woefully apart. No doubt suspecting this, Mrs. Fiske nevertheless journeyed on from Chicago to New York. And "The Dice of the Gods" is now a memory.

The month of February seemed to mark a turning point in the fortune which attended dramatic initiative here. Better things began to come.

A new play called "Peter Weston" arrived, with Frank Keenan, reclaimed from the films, as its star. It is the work of Frank Dazey and Leighton Osmun (the former is a son of the Dazey who wrote "In Old Kentucky") and tells in conventionally theatrical fashion the story of a granite-souled father whose iron will leads him to blundering disaster when a series of calamities overtakes his children. The play is old-fashioned, melodramatic, and a little preposterous; its value lies in the opportunities it gives for forthright, thumping histrionism. An excellent company took full advantage of these in Chicago, with Mr. Keenan carrying things to a terrific finish in a final scene of collapse and spiritual breakdown closely akin to that played by Lionel Barrymore in "The Claw." Of the two, Mr. Keenan's, I think, was the more human and therefore the more stirring performance. "Peter Weston" ran twelve weeks, until summer drove it away, and high hopes are held for its future.

March brought Samuel Shipman's "The Crooked Square," something about the wicked lure of Broadway, full of dependable incitements to laughter and tears and centering upon a hapless maiden from the country, acted here by Miss Constance Binney. Chicago was noncommittal about "The Crooked Square"; Mr. Shipman will see what New York thinks in the fall — without Miss Binney's assistance.

"Two Fellows and a Girl," an airy comedy by Vincent Lawrence, also was disclosed in March. It is light of texture and its title is sufficiently descriptive, since it has to do with courtship, marriage, and a droll disposition of the eternal triangle. Good acting carried it quickly into favor and its owner, Mr. George M. Cohan, thinks that he has in it a highly valuable property.

Close on the heels of the Lawrence comedy came "Light Wines and Beer," Aaron Hoffman's contribution to the irreverent literature about Mr. Volstead and his works. This is a happy frameup, not to be taken too seriously as drama, involving the adventures of two saloonkeepers, one of whom becomes a prosperous bootlegger while the other finds penury and Pharisaical satisfaction in "dry" fanaticism. Joseph Cawthorn and George Bickel were the protagonists of the fable in Chicago, which explains what kind of a play it is. Cawthorn has left the cast, but there will be somebody else. Also, there will be a new title — probably "The Good Old Days."

In April Booth Tarkington and Harry Leon Wilson's "Bristol Glass" was produced, with Frank McGlynn, Gregory Kelly, and Miss Ruth Gordon in the rôles of chief importance. The comedy has a Maine setting, and takes a kindly fling at certain amusing phases of family pride, bringing into conflict a group of patrician Philadelphians and a stern New England ménage, each equally haughty and each comically oblivious to the other's claim to importance. Of course romance in the second generation runs through the piece, negotiating a difficult course to a happy ending. A mellow humor pervades the tale, but it is not the Tarkington-

Wilson combination at its best. Chicago found it rather ineffective entertainment.

These were the high lights among the new offerings. Sandwiched in among them were other things of varying importance — a mystery play called "Zeno," pleasantly calculated to curdle one's blood with its mingling of murder and spiritualistic fakery; "The Rear Car," notable as being the most completely idiotic of the thrillers; one of Mme. Petrova's highly colored essays on feminism; "Steve," a romance crammed with hokum for Mr. Eugene O'Brien, of the movies, and enough more, mostly failures, to make up the total of twenty-four, as aforesaid. In the matter of mere length it was a notable list, inasmuch as Mr. Mantle's last year's volume recorded only four original productions for Chicago.

The remaining plays of the season were sent us from New York. What happened to some of them is set forth at the beginning of this chapter. The rest were mine-run, good and bad, the procession of their arrival interrupted by nothing uncommon except the vivid incident of the Moscow Art Theater's three weeks' visit in April. The amazing Russians were somewhat neglected at first, but their engagement wound up in a blaze of glory.

If it be necessary to select the ten best plays of 1922–1923 in Chicago, I should name them thus, taking into account not alone their literary quality, but the way in which they were acted and the general effectiveness of their presentation:

"A Bill of Divorcement."
"Six-Cylinder Love."
"The Circle."
"Loyalties."
"The Green Goddess."
"The First Year."
"Kempy."

"Captain Applejack."
"Peter Weston."
"Peter and Paula."

Of these, the first three are included in Mr. Mantle's last year's list and the next, "Loyalties," in his list for the present volume. Chicago saw "R. U. R." and "Why Not?", which also appear within these covers, but the opinion here, if one may say so, is at variance with that of the Atlantic seaboard. The Capek play, a stimulating thing to read, seemed to us to lose half its savage irony in the acting, and to dwindle and slump strangely. "Why Not?", after a brilliant start, went to pieces, we thought, in the last act.

Concerning "Peter and Paula," mentioned herewith, it may be explained that it is the Molnar play which was known in the east as "Fashions for Men." It had only moderate success in Chicago, as elsewhere, but those who saw it found it a most delectable and beguiling comedy.

The year's musical entertainments may be dismissed with a sentence. The successes here were successes of former seasons in New York, and the best of them were "Sally," the first "Music Box Revue," Al Jolson's "Bombo," and the Ethiop "Shuffle Along."

An interesting postscript to the season is taking form as I write. Much has been said in Chicago about emulating such ventures as that of the Theater Guild in New York, but for the most part the plans have got no farther than tea and talk. Now, with the benign encouragement of Mr. William A. Brady, two Chicago managers are feeling their way toward a guild by the novel method of getting started first and talking afterward.

They have produced a play called "Chains," by Jules Eckert Goodman, giving it a good cast which includes the names of O. P. Heggie and Miss Helen Gahagan. It is a treatise on morality and conventions, badly constructed, but being carried into popularity by Miss Gahagan's fine acting. On the managers' desks are piles of manuscripts and in the managers' hearts hopes of putting on more plays. They propose to try something else and, if the enterprise gains any real footing, to go out later on and see about subscription lists.

At the moment the thing seems to have promise, but, of course, it may all have come to naught by the time these lines reach print. We shall see.

RAIN

A Drama in Three Acts

By John Colton and Clemence Randolph

THERE is a story back of the production of every play, and the story back of "Rain," which happens to have been the most consistently popular dramatic success of the season of 1922–23, is especially interesting.

"I read the story, 'Miss Thompson,' upon which 'Rain' is founded, as it appeared in the *Smart Set*," writes John D. Williams, the producer. "I thought it the greatest example of modern realism I had ever read. But I did *not* think it contained material for a play. I did *not* buy the story for purposes of dramatization. Some time after reading it, I met John Colton, who told me that he had happened to be in San Francisco when the proof sheets of 'Miss Thompson' were sent to W. S. Maugham, its author, for corrections. Maugham was busy at the time and asked Colton to correct the proof sheets and mail them back to the *Smart Set.* As Colton thus read the story, in galley form, he, and he alone, was struck with the idea that it contained material for a great play. Colton there and then told Maugham his belief that the story could be refashioned for the stage. Maugham's answer was that he could not see any play in the story of 'Sadie Thompson,' looking at the material from any point of view. But he concluded by telling Colton to do what he wished with the material.

"Colton then came east and sat down with Miss

Clemence Randolph to remold Maugham's story for the stage. When he had written half of the first act — on yellow sheets in lead pencil — he showed it to me and it was then that I contracted to buy the play. Half of the first act, as written by Mr. Colton and Miss Randolph, was proof enough that a great play would result from the magical touch of these two young dramatists who could quicken Mr. Maugham's plot and characters into an exceptionally vivid and dramatic stage representation."

With the play finished the search was not for the manager who would offer the best terms as a sharing partner in its production, as Mr. Williams further explains, but for the actress best suited to play the part. Happily, after a lapse of weeks and the consideration of many promising young leading women, Sam H. Harris suggested that, inasmuch as he had Jeanne Eagles under contract and no play for her, Mr. Williams might like to consider her for the rôle. Mr. Williams was delighted, and proceeded with the staging of the play. He chose the cast, directed the rehearsals, timed and trained the intermittent rainstorms that are so impressive a feature of the production, and offered "Rain" at the Maxine Elliott Theatre on the night of November 7, 1922.

Within the week the advance sale was enormous, and, so far as the records show, there was not a vacant place in the theatre at any performance during the succeeding six months. And "Rain" is still continuing at this writing.

This drama is not to be numbered with the pleasant plays. It is, to the contrary, distinctly unpleasant in certain of its phases. But it is what the experts know as "big" drama. It cuts deep into the life from which it is sliced, as "Anna Christie" did, and it is equally true to itself.

The locale is the port of Pago Pago, on the island

of Tutuila, in the South Seas. The scene is the semi-public living room back of the general store and hotel run by one Joe Horn. "It is to be presumed," records the author's description, "that this hotel store is a frame building of two stories, with broad verandas on both floors, and a roof of corrugated iron. It stands on a little incline a short distance from the wharf at which the steamers touch. Aside from the government buildings and a small U. S. Naval Station, it is the only occidental building on this tiny island in the South Seas."

The section of the living room which we see is dingily furnished with European rattan and disorderly remnants of cotton rep. There is a dilapidated large wicker arm chair in which the trader, Joe Horn, habitually reclines, besides one or two upright chairs of the same pattern.

Against the back wall we have a maroon-plush sofa of the species middle-class housekeepers were once wont to call elegant.

The time is the present, and the rainy season is about to set in south of the equator. For the moment, however, "at the lifting of the curtain the scene is bathed in a tense sunlight of an early morning." There are the sounds of natives singing as they work in the near distance. One or more of these cross the empty stage, carrying fruit into the store. Ameena, Joe Horn's native wife, seeking a momentary breathing spell, sinks into Joe Horn's favorite chair, filling it completely — even too completely, seeing Ameena weighs in the neighborhood of two hundred and fifty pounds.

Griggs and Hodgeson, young American Marines stationed on the island, bustle in to spread the exciting news that the boat's in — that there are cigarettes — white man's cigarettes — aboard her, and that the Horns had better get busy and "break 'em out" pretty pronto. But Ameena can do no more than pass them on to Joe, and Joe, dragged from the store, refuses to be hurried.

Horn, the trader, is an American in his early fifties.

His indolent life has permitted him to take on somewhere near three hundred pounds of flesh, and he moves ponderously. "He is superbly lazy and the cares of the world have no part in his life. His idea of happiness is to slump into his huge arm chair and bury himself in a book. He is a natural philosopher, satisfied to let a busy world take its way while he, secure in his own little peaceful kingdom, simply lives from reading to reading and meal to meal. He is dressed usually in gray dungarees and a soft white shirt invariably open at the collar. Apparently the only exercise he gets is fanning himself."

The impatience of the lads willing to walk a mile or two for a proper smoke has little effect on Horn. He holds with amiable persistence to his arm chair and to the philosophy of Dr. Samuel Johnson. "Great works," said Johnson, "are not accomplished by strength alone, but by perseverence. He who walks three hours a day will, in seven years, circle the globe." . . .

There is a party coming up the hill from the wharf, headed for the store. Evidently they are off the *Orduna,* which has docked. And they look to Ameena like "mee-sion-arry!" "God damn — I run!" says she, evidently holding her own opinion of salvation's outriders.

The visitors are Dr. and Mrs. McPhail and Mrs. Davidson. "Dr. McPhail is a man of perhaps forty-five, rather gray at the temples, and one whom you would instinctively trust." Mrs. McPhail is a colorless, agreeable little woman of thirty-five. Mrs. Davidson "is a religiously withered creature. Age about forty. Her hair, which is dark, is drawn straight back from her forehead and finished in a mid-Victorian knot, all of which serves to accentuate her sharply determined features. . . . Her entire life is devoted to Mr. Davidson's dictates."

The McPhails are on their way to Apia. The

Davidsons are headed for another of the islands of the group, Mr. Davidson being a missionary. They are to transfer at Pago Pago from the *Orduna* to a schooner, and pending the reshipping of their baggage they have come to Joe Horn's place for a bite of lunch.

MRS. MCPHAIL — I must confess I rather dread the rest of the trip on the schooner — this must seem almost like home to you, Mrs. Davidson.

MRS. DAVIDSON — Oh, no, we still have ten days on the schooner after we leave you at Apia — I'm sorry you're getting your first impression of the South Seas from this island though.

MRS. MCPHAIL — Why?

MRS. DAVIDSON —It's far below the moral standard. The steamers touching here make the people unsettled — then there's the naval station — that's bad for the natives — (*sighs*). Yes — they say it's almost a hopeless task for the missionaries here —

MRS. MCPHAIL — Really?

MRS. DAVIDSON — Your husband's coming is most timely, Mrs. McPhail. Mr. Davidson was saying only last night that for once the Institute sent the right man for the right job. Disease conditions here are terrific!

MRS. MCPHAIL — I suppose we'll be stationed in Apia several months —what's it like there —

MRS. DAVIDSON — It's a dreadful place — the British own it, you see — the missionaries haven't as much power as they ought to have. The natives do very much as they like and the place is overrun with American prostitutes —

MRS. MCPHAIL— How horrible!

MRS. DAVIDSON — But Pago Pago here is under the American flag and it's almost as bad they say. You know what I was telling you yesterday. Have you told Mr. McPhail yet?

MRS. MCPHAIL — About what their marriage customs used to be? Yes.

MRS. DAVIDSON — What did he say?

MRS. MCPHAIL — Well, he never says very much, but I am sure that he thought it was perfectly awful.

MRS. DAVIDSON — About what the old men and the old women used to do? About the common house? About the festivals?

MRS. MCPHAIL — I — tried — to —

The woeful depravity of the natives and their general need of a constant surveillance by missionaries is still uppermost in Mrs. Davidson's mind when Sadie Thompson enters. Sadie was a fellow passenger with the Davidsons and McPhails on the *Orduna*, although she was traveling second class. She, too, is on her way to Apia. None of the first-cabin passengers paid much attention to her, but Mrs. Davidson remembers that she had danced outrageously with certain of the ship's officers at the captain's ball the night before.

Sadie comes up from the wharf gayly escorted by Quartermaster Bates himself, a ruddy-faced little cockney of forty who imagines himself quite a hit with the ladies. She is a "wind-blown creature, the victim of her own good humor, fond of life and taking its rebuffs smilingly. She is not more than five feet six, slender and overly rouged, in fact her face, while showing traces of a hard beauty, is a walking advertisement for cosmetics. She wears a lace coat and a salmon-color dress which fairly shriek. White-topped shoes, each with a tassel dangling from the top, a wide-brimmed straw hat topped by a huge purple plume complete her engrossing costume. She is ready at all times to be friendly. The only persons she can't understand are those who do not like a wildly good time."

SADIE — So I'm to be parked here, am I, dearie?

BATES — Yes, make yourself right to home, Sadie. How do you do, Mrs. Horn; how's Joe?

MRS. HORN — 'Allo, Quartermaster — Joe be damn fine.

BATES — How's all the kids? No new ones since my last trip?

MRS. HORN — (*looking at Sadie*). Mebbe you bring wife back this trip?

BATES — Get that, Sadie,— she thinks you're my wife.

SADIE — Why, do I look that weak of intellect? Should I marry the little husband of all the world?

BATES — (*turns to Mrs. Horn*). This is my friend, Miss Sadie Thompson — this is Mrs. Horn,— Sadie. (*Turns towards the Marines.*) Sadie, meet the U. S. A.

SADIE — That's right. Good boys. Join the Navy and see the world. (*Turns towards O'Hara.*) Hello, Handsome — when did you leave Kansas?

GRIGGS — Oh, man! The lady's got your number, Tim.

HODGESON — Ha! She got you that time, kid.

SADIE — (*Turns towards Griggs and Hodgeson*). Say you couldn't mistake it, you got a Corn Belt baby stare that screams. I mean it kindly, don't get sore.

HODGESON — He's very shy, Miss, don't mind him.

O'HARA — Shut up! You half whittled pin —

GRIGGS — He is liable to bite, Miss — better keep away.

O'HARA — Stow that blab, or I'll —

SADIE — Don't hurt 'em, Handsome. I came from Kansas once myself, as fast as I could hoof it — how are you?

O'HARA — Fine — very pleased to meet a lady. (*Griggs and Hodgeson howl with laughter.*)

SADIE — What's the matter with these two colts? They act as though they had too much oats — bad thing to jump 'em from milk too fast. Young things like that should be put to grass first. I'm a farmer's daughter, so I know.

BATES — Sadie, let me introduce you to two of the ladies who were on board the *Orduna* — (*starts to lead Sadie towards Mrs. Davidson and Mrs. McPhail who are seated at the dining table*).

SADIE — (*grasping Bates by the arm and jerking him back.*) Pull yourself together, little one — pull yourself together. (*Looking at Mrs. Davidson.*) No, now that I've got my bearings, I think I'll go back into the sunshine. Who is coming with me? You, buttercup?

While Sadie is being guided about the island by her new friends, the Marines, the Rev. Alfred Davidson, missionary, arrives with some rather important news. A case of cholera has been discovered aboard the schooner that is to take the Apia passengers on, and the chances seem excellent that the boat will be held in quarantine for several days. "Mr. Davidson is a tall man, bushy-haired, penetrating eyes and brows continually drawn as though trying to pierce the thoughts of those to whom he is speaking. He is rather high-strung and nervous. He speaks in a deep authoritative voice. In everything he says he exhibits his relentlessness toward the sinner. He is dressed in a loosely fitting black alpaca suit. He wears always a white soft-collared shirt and a stringy black bow-tie."

It may be possible, thinks Davidson, to get the governor's permission to have the schooner proceed after the cholera patient has been removed. He goes now to see what can be done about it. Meantime the women, Mrs. Davidson and Mrs. McPhail, are looking over Horn's available rooms with an idea of making the best of such housing arrangements as they are compelled to, which leaves Dr. McPhail and Horn to get better acquainted.

HORN — You are not a missionary,— I can see that.

MCPHAIL — No, I'm not a missionary — you're right.

HORN — Can't exactly place you though.

McPHAIL — McPhail's my name, I'm a doctor.

HORN — Much better — for this relief, much thanks.

McPHAIL — You sound prejudiced —

HORN — Prejudiced? Oh, no. Damn fine people,— missionaries. Got plenty of good friends among 'em. Some traders are afraid of them, but I've always found them all right — my only objection to 'em is — well they're kinda shy on humor.

McPHAIL — Is that a necessary qualification for the job?

HORN — It helps in any job.

McPHAIL — Persuading your neighbors to believe what you believe is a serious business, friend!

HORN — Certainly got to have a single track mind for it —

McPHAIL — Just so. There's no place for the light touch in reform.

HORN —Now that's a word I can't listen to without spitting. It's my belief that these reform folks fighting public depravity are only fighting their own hankering for the very indulgences they suspect in others —

McPHAIL — Just so! They chase you with a hatchet because they like a drink too,— is that it?

HORN — Shouldn't wonder. I hear life's terrible back home in the States now.

McPHAIL — How so?

HORN — Everybody being made to behave.

McPHAIL — Yes,— we live in the day of the new commandment —"Thou shalt not commit enjoyment."

HORN — Say,— I saw it coming twenty years ago — that's why I left Chicago — I wanted peace. Gad — I found it too — nothing like it, brother. Friend, you behold here the last remnants of an earthly paradise — look yonder — see where the mountains touch the clouds of Heaven? Then tell me how it shall benefit the scheme of my quarrel with the missionaries.

McPhail — Yes, I can see how the bleak civilization might be a little out of place — sort of like a school ma'am waking up in a harem, what?

Horn — Yeah, take these Islanders, Doctor. They are naturally the happiest, most contented people on earth — they ask nothing of life, save to be allowed to sing and eat — dance and sleep — thinking gives 'em a headache — the trees and the sea give 'em all the food they want — so they don't have to fight — they are satisfied with their gods of wind and ways — then along comes Mr. Missionary in broadcloth and spectacles and tells 'em they're lost souls and have to be saved whether they want to or not.

McPhail — Thoughtless of man not to develop a soul without losing the Garden of Eden.

Horn — You're a real philosopher, Dr. McPhail.

McPhail — Call me, rather, an observer of life.

Horn — Ditto, brother — an observer of life who sees the joke.

Griggs, O'Hara and Hodgeson are back with Sadie, bringing her few belongings nondescriptly wrapped. The rain has soaked them pretty thoroughly, though a sail cloth has served Sadie as a raincoat. She is still cheerful, however, even when she hears that she may be marooned in Pago Pago for two weeks. "Two weeks?" she mutters incredulously. "Well, what can't be helped can't be helped, as the canary said when the cat swallowed it." She is not the one to worry. "I never fret," she assures them. "Make the best of things today — they're bound to be worse tomorrow," is her philosophy.

They find her a place to camp in an old storeroom on the first floor, seeing all upstairs quarters have been appropriated by the McPhails and Davidsons.

Sadie is for having a party. It would cheer everybody up. She has a bottle of hooch that a friend had given her before she left Honolulu, and a little nip of that wouldn't do any of them any harm. The Marines believe her. Under her direction they open the bundles and find the bottle. Also a phonograph. Sadie had brought that along for company, seeing you never can tell when you are going to be lonesome. They have their drink, from the bottle, it being a waste of time to look for a glass. Soon the phonograph is grinding out a jazz tune, and Sadie and Hodgeson are dancing wildly to an appreciative audience — when in comes Mrs. Davidson.

MRS. DAVIDSON — Young woman!

SADIE — (*to Hodgeson*). That's right — you got the swing of it now.

MRS. DAVIDSON — Young woman, have you no respect for the Lord's day?

SADIE — What?

MRS. DAVIDSON — Young woman, this is the Sabbath.

SADIE — Are you speaking to me?

MRS. DAVIDSON — I am just reminding you that this is Sunday.

SADIE — Let's see, — right you are, yesterday was Saturday. (*Continues dancing.*)

MRS. DAVIDSON — I protest — I protest — this must stop.

GRIGGS — Ah, are we disturbing you?

SADIE — (*bending away back as Hodgeson leans over her while both shimmy*). Oh, I love that step.

MRS. DAVIDSON — Whether I have been disturbed or not, is of no consequence. There are six days in the week to dance, if you must dance. (*Hodgeson and Sadie stop dancing.*)

SADIE — 'Nuff said — the complaint's registered. We'll withdraw to my private suite, if you have no objections, Mr. Horn.

HORN — No objection — as far as I am concerned.

SADIE — All right, boys, — pick up everything, come on, we are moving. Here, little one, I'll take the hooch. Well, my little army. (*Turns towards Horn — Marines and Bates exit to room.*) Drop in later if you feel like it, Mr. Horn — always glad to see you.

Mrs. Davidson is properly horrified. Mr. Davidson, she is quite sure, will not approve such goings on. A common woman like that, under the same roof with respectable people!

And Mrs. Davidson is right. Mr. Davidson does not like Sadie's party. He has the governor's word that nothing for the present can be done about moving the schooner. Probably they will all have to stay there for two weeks. The thought disturbs him more and more as the sounds of revelry continue to burst through the thin partitions of Sadie's room.

MR. DAVIDSON — This girl, you say, was on the *Orduna?*

MRS. DAVIDSON — Yes — but Dr. McPhail has met her — he can tell you more than I can.

MCPHAIL — (*trying to divert his mind*). She isn't anybody of any importance — I am interested, Davidson, in your theory of disease.

DAVIDSON — I believe any disease tendency can be brought under control just as any weakness of the moral structure can. (*An uproar from Sadie's room.*) Music of this sort is demoralizing, isn't it?

MCPHAIL — (*ignoring the noise from Sadie's room*). Your theory would be easy, Mr. Davidson, if any of us were — ever could be — certain of ourselves —

DAVIDSON — I disagree with you — why can't we be certain of ourselves?

MCPHAIL — Because in each and every one of us are hidden blights — erratic formation — undiscovered infirmities — none of us can ever be sure of ourselves until the moment of ultimate pressure —

A blast from the *Orduna's* whistle, forewarning those ashore of her departure, stops the party momentarily. Sadie and her Marine friends come to the door of the girl's room to see Quartermaster Bates off. They are all a little excited with drink, and Bates has what is known technically as a comfortable edge. They finally get him pushed off the porch and are returning to the room when Sadie and the missionary come face to face. For a moment they stare, a little curiously, a little defiantly at each other. And then, as the roisterers continue on into the room, Sadie is heard to say: "There's a guy out there who gave me the dirtiest look —" They close the door. Soon the phonograph and the laughter begin again.

DAVIDSON — How long has this sort of thing been going on.

MRS. DAVIDSON — All morning.

MR. DAVIDSON — Where did those Marines come from?

MRS. DAVIDSON — They just appeared from nowhere — in her wake. If there's to be two weeks of this, I don't know what we shall all feel like at the end of it. (*Mr. Davidson suddenly starts and looks towards Sadie's room.*) Alfred, what's the matter?

MR. DAVIDSON — Of course, — it has just occurred to me. This woman is out of Iweili —

MRS. DAVIDSON — Iweili — Iweili — the thought came to me when I first saw her, but I dared not speak it.

MRS. MCPHAIL — What do you mean by Iweili?

MRS. DAVIDSON — The plague spot of Honolulu — the red light district.

MRS. MCPHAIL — Oh! — Oh! —

MRS. DAVIDSON — It is obvious that she has come out here to carry on her trade.

MCPHAIL — I think you're wrong. She has a position waiting for her in Apia.

DAVIDSON — I am not wrong — I know the look of

Iweili. I went there once, — she is as clearly out of Iweili as though the fact were written in scarlet letters on her brow.

McPHAIL — (*mildly*). Still one has no right to assume a thing like that unless —

DAVIDSON — (*growing more feverish in his speech*). I tell you I went there — to reach it, we went down side streets near the harbor — in the darkness — across rickety bridges,— through deserted roads — then suddenly you came into the light of its shame.

McPHAIL — (*as though to dismiss the matter and a trifle impatiently*). We can easily imagine the sort of place it was, Davidson.

DAVIDSON — A broad street divided into two parts — here the motors park and the saloons thrive — and beyond this street lay other streets — and in those streets are rows of twin bungalows — little houses neatly painted — lining straight lanes — laid out like a garden city. Picture it. Spruce, systematized, orderly — arrayed for sin.

McPHAIL — (*Almost as though he were talking to himself*). Thus is even the search for purchased love systematized, regulated nowadays.

DAVIDSON — Men wandered about, looking at the women who sat in their lighted windows — men of all nations — American sailors — soldiers from the regiment quartered on the island — white, black, and Japanese, Chinese and Hawaiians, all silent, oppressed.

McPHAIL — (*philosophically*). All desire is sad.

DAVIDSON — It was a crying scandal of the Pacific, yet it was impossible to avail against it. You know the usual arguments of the police, that vice is inevitable, consequently, the best thing to do to control it is to localize it. The truth is that they were paid — they were paid by the saloon-keepers, by the bullies,— paid by the women themselves — but, thank God, at last they were forced by public opinion to do something.

McPhail — Yes, I read about it in the paper —

Davidson — For once, a new Mayor dared to live up to his election platform. Iweili with its sin and shame ceased to exist on the day that we arrived in Honolulu. The whole population was brought before the Justice — (*Sadie's laugh is heard again*) — and this girl is one who probably managed to escape. (*Turns and starts for Sadie's door.*)

Mrs. Davidson — Alfred, what are you going to do?

Davidson — What do you expect me to do? I am not going to have this house turned into a brothel, I am going to stop it.

With a determined stride he reaches the door of Sadie's room, pulls it open and enters. A moment later the sound of a crashing of furniture is heard; the phonograph, evidently pushed off a table, suddenly ceases its strident tune; there is shouting and muffled cursing, above which the Rev. Davidson's voice is heard yelling: "Scarlet woman!" A second later the doors are burst open and the missionary is pushed violently into the room and falls in a heap on the floor. "There," shouts O'Hara, towering over him, "if you know what is good for you, get out and stay out." Davidson gets to his feet and faces Sadie, glaring menacingly at her. And she glares as wildly back at him.

Sadie — Well, who do you think you are? My God! (*To boys.*) The nerve of them. Perhaps he thinks that's funny. (*Sadie and the Marines give Davidson one last look and turn back into her room, and close the door. Davidson stands staring at the door — then turns and exits up stairs.*)

Mrs. McPhail — What will he do?

Mrs. Davidson — I don't know — only I wouldn't be in that girl's shoes for anything in the world. (*Sounds in Sadie's room of the phonograph starting up again and men's voices laughing as the curtain falls.*)

ACT II

It is late afternoon, two days later. The scene is the same. The rain has ceased for the moment, but it rains intermittently all during the action of the play, now softly, now in a veritable downpour that rolls in miniature cascades off the awning covering the porch.

Dr. McPhail is in from a two-minute walk; can't get very far, he finds, walking in "hot pea soup." Horn, the storekeeper, knowing the climate better, is sitting comfortably in his old armchair, sipping the native *kava* and indulging his vision of the philosophical and practical life.

There is, Joe Horn has concluded, too damned much misdirected energy in the world. And that's what starts all the throat-cutting. For instance: What right has Missionary Davidson to be hounding Sadie Thompson, as he has been doing? What right has he to demand that she be turned out of the Horn establishment, merely because he (Davidson) does not approve of her? She may, and again she may not, have come from the red light district of Honolulu —

HORN — I don't know and I don't care. What if she is — we've all crossed thresholds we don't brag about. Just because she has a few gaudy rags and a bum phonograph, and is a little too live to let live, what right has he to conclude that she's out of Iweili? The whole trick in thinking is — what sort of vision you have. If you have a low horizon, God pity you. Davidson has that. This girl hasn't any. That's why I like her. Poor thing — Davidson has sort of got her wondering.

MCPHAIL — How so?

HORN — She's wondering what he's up to. You notice when the boys came around last night to see her, she took them out to the porch pretty quick and talked to them there —

MCPHAIL — Yes — I noticed that — and it wasn't the

most cheerful sort of an evening, either. What with the rain and everything, we'd all been happier, I think, if she'd been in her room with her friends.

HORN — She felt it too, she knows if she gets put out of here, there's no place else for her to go.

MCPHAIL — Why?

HORN — Nobody'll take her in — if they know the missionaries have their knives out for her. He's been to the governor, too, to have her sent back to the States.

MCPHAIL — What did the governor say?

HORN — I dunno, she's got wind of that, too.

MCPHAIL — You know, I felt rather sorry for her last night, after her Marine friends left. She went into her room without looking at any of us. Just as we were ready for bed, she started her phonograph. Somehow it sounded dismal — like a cry for help.

"Suddenly Sadie's phonograph starts, raspingly." McPhail and Horn look at each other understandingly. Outside the rain comes down in torrents again. "Hard business, trying to cheat one's loneliness," observes McPhail. The rain is plainly getting on his nerves, too. He is as jumpy as a cat.

The phonograph stops as suddenly as it began. A second later Sadie opens the door of her room. Her manner is gay enough, but it is evident that she is desperately in need of companionship, and that she is worried. All afternoon she has been playing solitaire trying to decide what she would have for supper, "tunny fish or beans — and beans won." And then she played beans against tomales, and tomales won — and she is on her way to the store to buy a can. Still, there is no hurry. Perhaps they wouldn't mind if she sat down for a nice little chat about Greenland's icy mountains, or something.

It is evident that Sadie is interested in but one subject of conversation, however — and that the Rev. Davidson.

She has been keeping the Marines pretty well behaved since the night Handsome O'Hara had pitched the missionary out on his head. Been entertaining them on the side porch, mostly. But apparently this has not satisfied Davidson. Now she is eager to hear from O'Hara how far the missionary has gone. That he has made some sort of appeal to the governor of the island she knows. And he has reported O'Hara to his officers for drinking. The nerve of him!

HORN — Oh, I guess O'Hara can take care of himself —

SADIE — Well, so can I — if that Davidson gets gay with me again, I'll tell him who his mother is! — Possibly he don't know —

HORN — Miss Thompson — I'd be careful —

SADIE — God give me strength! If that old sin buster minds his own business I'll mind mine — but if he's looking for trouble, I'll see he gets it plenty. (*Pauses — looks toward McPhail.*) Well, anyway, there's no hard feeling between any of us, is there? I wouldn't say that Doc over there has been exactly chatty. (*McPhail, who has been saying nothing, turns and dismisses any unpleasantness with a wave of his hand. Sadie turns to Horn.*) Where do you keep your canned tomales, old pardner?

HORN — On the shelf — by the door. (*Voices of Mrs. McPhail and Mrs. Davidson are heard off stage.*)

SADIE — Ha! methinks I hear the winds of religion whistling down the chimney! — Wherefore the low hussy frolics off to buy her dinner.

Mrs. Davidson is greatly worried about her "Alfred." He has not slept much since — since the unpleasantness they all know about. And when Alfred can't sleep, neither can she. Alfred has been going out a great deal in the rain, and that isn't good for anyone. But when

Alfred is on the Lord's work there is no stopping him. He is very forgiving and understanding, but he has no mercy for sin.

The Rev. Davidson comes out of the rain a moment later, and again refuses to change his wet garments, despite his worried wife's entreaties. He can but smile indulgently at her urging, and gently put her aside.

DAVIDSON — (*placing his hands on his wife's shoulders and speaking tenderly*). My wife! Like Martha — thou hast troubled thyself about many things — and mostly about me! When I was broken and weary, it was she who would read to me from the Bible until peace came to me like sleep to a child. And when at last she would say, "We will save them in spite of themselves," then I would feel strong again and answer, "Yes, with God's help. I will save them — I must!"

MCPHAIL — Save who?

MRS. MCPHAIL — The natives, Robert!

DAVIDSON — You see, they were so naturally depraved, we had to teach them what sin is. We had to make sins out of what they thought were only natural actions —

MCPHAIL — Make sins?

DAVIDSON — Yes, we had to make it a sin, not only to commit adultery and to lie and thieve — but to expose their bodies, and to dance and not to come to church. I made it a sin for a girl to show her bosom and for a man not to wear trousers —

MCPHAIL — How did you manage to standardize those sins?

DAVIDSON — Obviously, the only way to make people realize that an action is sinful is to punish them if they commit it.

MCPHAIL — Ah! I see.

MRS. DAVIDSON — Mr. Davidson instituted fines.

MCPHAIL — You fined them, eh?

DAVIDSON — I fined them if they didn't come to church. I fined them if they danced. I fined them if they were improperly dressed. I had a tariff and every sin had to be paid for either in money or work. At last, I made them understand —

MCPHAIL — Didn't they ever refuse to pay?

DAVIDSON — How could they —

MRS. DAVIDSON — (*trying to impress the McPhails with Mr. Davidson's power*). You must remember, in the last resort — Mr. Davidson could expel them from the church membership.

MCPHAIL — Did they mind that?

DAVIDSON — Yes. They couldn't sell their copra. When the men fished they got no share of the catch. It meant something very like starvation. Yes, — I may say, they minded quite a lot.

On one occasion, the missionary admits, it had been necessary for him to "break" a trader who had defied him, and to send him back to Sydney completely crushed in spirit and body. If —

The phonograph in Sadie's room begins ripping out another tune. It brings the girl smartly to their minds again. What is the Rev. Davidson going to do about her? He must, he admits, give the girl every chance — but — He thinks, perhaps, if they don't mind leaving him alone he had better have a talk with Miss Thompson alone. He sends Ameena to call her.

DAVIDSON — Sadie Thompson, I have brought you out here to offer you a gift.

SADIE — You want to give me something?

DAVIDSON — Yes.

SADIE — Well, I'm glad of that — I'm pretty short in cash.

DAVIDSON — The gift I am offering you is the infinite mercy of our Lord.

SADIE — What's the idea?

DAVIDSON — Your problems can be solved in only one way and that way is going to affect the whole future course in your life.

SADIE — I don't know as I've got any problems.

DAVIDSON — The time has come for you to make your choice.

SADIE — I can't see why I rate all this attention from you.

DAVIDSON — Those who have the key of salvation offered them and fail to open the door must be destroyed.

SADIE — Oh — I see what you mean, but don't you worry about me, I won't get destroyed. (*Turns and starts for her room.*) I guess I'll go back to my supper, I'm hungry.

DAVIDSON — You are hungry, but not for mortal food. You are hungry for the bread of the spirit.

SADIE — You know, Reverend Davidson — you mean right by me and I mean to be grateful. Just between ourselves I thought you were out to get me on account of that little trouble we had the other evening. And I have been wanting to apologize —

DAVIDSON — You mistake me — but I don't think wilfully —

SADIE — They all told me you were sore,— but I didn't think a man as big as you would hold a grudge over a little misunderstanding.

DAVIDSON — (*attempting to change the conversation and coming to the point for which he had asked Miss Thompson to come into the room*). For some time past you have lived in Honolulu, haven't you?

SADIE — Yes, I had a job there.

DAVIDSON — What kind of a job?

SADIE — Well, part of the time I had sort of a singing job — my voice isn't so awful if you don't listen too hard.

DAVIDSON — Before you went to Honolulu, where were you?

SADIE — Where do I come from, you mean?

DAVIDSON — Yes, where do you come from?

SADIE — Well, I was born in Keneshaw, Kansas,— my folks got the California fever, so they sold the farm and bought a little ranch outside of Los Angeles — Ma died and Pa and I didn't get along so well together so I went to 'Frisco. And I was working there at the time I went to Honolulu.

DAVIDSON — (*continuing his attitude of a lawyer cross-questioning a witness*). What made you go away to Honolulu?

SADIE — I — I don't know — I wanted a change, I suppose.

DAVIDSON — (*sternly*). You had your own soul in trust and you failed — it is now my business to show you the way to redeem it. You can choose one of two paths.

SADIE — (*much spirit*). What's the second choice?

DAVIDSON — Destruction!

SADIE — Destruction stuff, eh!— ches — ches! (*Looking intently at Davidson.*) And you — what are you going to do?

DAVIDSON — (*with an air of finality*). My duty, Sadie Thompson — I shall not let you go on to Apia!

SADIE — (*springing from chair and fairly screaming at Davidson*). Now I get you! All that stuff you were spilling about salvation was just a bluff. You've been to see the governor about me, haven't you? You're gunning for me and aiming to kill.

DAVIDSON — Be silent! Are you ready to put away your sins — to pray for forgiveness? If you are not, be it on your own head!

SADIE — (*turning from him*). Hey — hey —

DAVIDSON — (*in a firm accusing voice*). Sadie Thompson — you are an evil woman — you have come here only to carry your infamy to other places — you are a harlot out of Iweili!

SADIE — (*shouts*). You're a liar!

DAVIDSON — Look at me!

SADIE — (*menacingly advancing toward Davidson*). Who in Christ's name do you think you are — calling me names! You listen to me — you lay off me or it will be the worse for you, see?

DAVIDSON — The devil in you is strong, Sadie Thompson — he has claimed you for his own.

SADIE — You take care of your own devil, and I'll take care of mine — old tidbit!

DAVIDSON — (*raising his eyes and speaking fervently, hands clasped before him*). Lord, hear thou my prayer —

SADIE — You Biblebacks don't fool me! Make me over your way, would you? Get my scalp to hand to the Lord? You just try it. (*Davidson suddenly grasps Sadie's arm.*)

DAVIDSON — Kneel, Sadie Thompson — God is waiting.

SADIE — Let go of me.

DAVIDSON — (*trying to force Sadie to her knees*). This is your last chance.

SADIE — Let go of me. (*Breaks from Davidson's clutch and steps back.*) Hah, you make me laugh — you mealy mouthed hymn hound. (*Spits in Davidson's face.*) That's what I think of your bunk!

DAVIDSON — (*stands and glares at Sadie*). You are doomed, Sadie Thompson!

The rain comes down again, as the Rev. Davidson rushes off the porch, all but knocking over the approaching O'Hara in his madness to hurry his campaign for the redemption of Sadie's soul.

O'Hara is not as exercised over the threats of Davidson as Sadie is. Things, according to Handsome, is bound to work out some way. What if they do stop her from going to Apia? She could go back to the

States, maybe. But that appears to be the last thing Sadie wants to do. The thought of it worries her much more than anything the Rev. Davidson has threatened. She doesn't want to go back to the States — or to Honolulu, either.

She might try Sydney, suggests O'Hara. Sydney's a nice place. Work's easy to get. He's going to Sydney himself in six weeks — soon as he gets rid of his chevrons. He's got friends in Sydney, too. Biff and Maggie. Biff was an old army buddie, and Maggie — well, Mag is another regular girl just like Sadie. They'd oughta be great friends, Sadie and Maggie.

SADIE — Baby boy! One of the reasons I like you, is you don't see yet why I get the tall top hat from friend Biff's wife.

O'HARA — Maggie's not the kind of female you're meaning. They're mighty happy and comfortable now — Biff and Maggie are — though all the croakers said they'd never make out. I guess no girl who hadn't been on the rocks herself would have risked Biff. Sixteen years in the Marines don't put much polish on a guy's finger nails — and I guess no guy who didn't know the mill would have risked Maggie either. It's funny, ain't it, how those who kick up the highest, settle down the hardest?

SADIE — Do you mean this Maggie was sorta gay before Biff came along?

(*Rain suddenly comes down in a deluge.*)

O'HARA — Yeh, they were both nuts over each other from the first. It never mattered to either of them that they met in Iweili — us guys in the Marines are pretty rough, and knowing the worst to begin with ain't the worst way to begin — what?

SADIE — (*jumps from her chair, crosses room*). My God! Hear that rain come down!

O'HARA — Yep — it sure is falling — I wouldn't want

to persuade you if there was some one you was looking forward to seeing in Apia.

SADIE — No — I'm not looking forward to Apia with any mad, wild joy —

O'HARA — If you do go to Sydney, Sadie — I'll be hoving in sight in a few weeks. Not that that might mean so much to you, maybe.

SADIE — I haven't got so many friends, Handsome, but what I could do with one more. (*Pauses and looks earnestly at O'Hara.*) You're an awful funny fellow.

O'HARA — I guess I'm the dumbbell king all right.

SADIE — (*slowly*). I thought I knew most all there was to know about men, until you came along — but — say — have they any kids —

O'HARA — Who?

SADIE — Those friends of yours in Sydney.

O'HARA — Oh,— I was thinking of something else. Yeah — they got two. (*And as Sadie turns and walks away.*) How about it —

SADIE — (*turns, faces O'Hara*). About what?

O'HARA — Changing your route and going to Sydney, anyway?

SADIE — (*spiritedly*). Sure,— why not? I guess no one can stop me! God! Me jumping with the shakes and nervous as a witch just because of that miserable crumb of a Davidson! Sure, Handsome, I'll go to Sydney —

There is a new light in the girl's eyes as she walks away, but it has little chance to flame. The Rev. Davidson is a quick worker. A native bearing a letter from the governor has at the moment come from the porch. And the letter orders the deportation of Miss Sadie Thompson on the next steamer sailing for San Francisco.

"He's going to send me back to 'Frisco," wails Sadie, finishing the letter; "I won't go back to 'Frisco — there's reasons I can't tell you. I've got some rights, haven't I?"

Handsome assures her that she has, and now's the time for her to tell them to the governor. If she'll tell him she wants to go to Sydney instead of San Francisco probably he'll let her do it. In a moment Sadie has dashed into her room to get a cloak to cover her and O'Hara is throwing on his slicker to take her to the governor's house, when Davidson walks up the steps. Sadie meets him as she comes tearing back from her room.

SADIE — . . . So you're back, are you? You low-down skunk, what have you been saying to the governor about me?

DAVIDSON — I've been hoping to have another talk with you, Miss Thompson.

SADIE — (*advancing toward Davidson*). You miserable snail snatcher. I wouldn't talk to you if you and me were the only people left on earth. That's what I think of you, coming to me with all that guff you spilled about salvation — then going and having me deported on top of it — you low-lived bastard —

O'HARA — Sadie — for God's sake —

DAVIDSON — (*taking a step towards stairs and closely followed by Sadie*). I am indifferent to the abuse you think fit to heap on me, Miss Thompson —

SADIE — You know what you've been and done — filling the governor up with a lot of lies about me — and now this comes and I've got to beat it on the next boat —

DAVIDSON — (*endeavoring to pass Sadie and walks toward footlights, still closely followed by Sadie*). You could hardly expect him to let you stay here under the circumstances —

SADIE — What did the governor know or care about me until you went and hauled your hooks into me?

DAVIDSON — I admit that I urged the governor to take the only step consistent with his duty.

SADIE — (*losing control of her anger*). Well, was I doing you any harm — was I?

DAVIDSON — You may be sure if you had, I would be the last man to resent it —

SADIE — You don't think I want to stay in this rain hole, do you?

O'HARA — Sadie — Sadie, you're only making it worse. (*O'Hara grasps Sadie's arm and starts her toward the veranda. She breaks from his grasp and turns back toward Davidson, a wildly infuriated creature.*)

SADIE — You — you — you dirty two-faced mutt! I'll bet when you were a kid you caught flies and pulled their wings off — I bet you stuck pins in frogs — just to see 'em wriggle and flog, while you read 'em a Sunday-school lesson. I know you! You'd tear the heart out of your grandmother if she didn't think your way, and tell her you were saving her soul, — you — you — psalm-singing son — of — a —

Before she can complete the speech O'Hara has rushed Sadie out of the room. The Rev. Davidson is shocked, but satisfied. It is his duty to stand the ravings of the sinful. But he corrects them in the end, as he explains to McPhail. Not many but bend before his power if he sees fit to exert it. The governor, for instance, was of a mind to let Miss Thompson stay on three or four days until the Sydney boat could take her on. But the Rev. Davidson reminded him that it would do him no good politically if a complaint were to go to Washington of how he managed the affairs in the island, and the governor promptly issued the order of deportation to the States.

A moment later the Rev. Davidson and Mrs. Davidson are reading their daily Bible chapter. The rumble of their voices can be heard from their rooms upstairs.

O'Hara brings Sadie back, and asks Dr. McPhail to

do what he can to cheer her. She's not feeling very well. But it isn't a physical illness that has overcome Sadie. It is the fear of being sent back to the States. The governor has said she can stay over for the Sydney boat, if the Rev. Davidson will agree. Perhaps if Dr. McPhail puts in a word for her with the missionary he will let her stay —

Dr. McPhail is willing to do all he can. And he does speak to Davidson. But the missionary is adamant. And suspicious.

DAVIDSON — Why doesn't she want to go to San Francisco?

MCPHAIL — (*placidly*). I didn't inquire — and I think one does better to mind one's own business.

DAVIDSON — (*as though to a child*). You mean this interference for the best, Doctor, but my mind is made up.

MCPHAIL — (*belligerently but with dignity*). I know you haven't asked me, but, if you want to know what I think — I think you are harsh and tyrannical —

DAVIDSON — I'm terribly sorry you should think that of me, Dr. McPhail, believe me my heart bleeds for that unfortunate woman, but I cannot find it in my conscience to change the decision. If the governor wishes to do so on his own account, that is his business —

MCPHAIL — (*pointedly*). He won't — and you know why!

DAVIDSON — Please don't bear malice toward me because I cannot accede to your wish — I respect you very much, Doctor — and I should be sorry if you thought ill of me —

MCPHAIL — I have no doubt you have sufficiently good opinion of yourself to bear mine with equanimity —

DAVIDSON — (*as though to laugh it off*). Well, that's one on me.

The Rev. Davidson returns to his Bible reading above stairs and Sadie is left disconsolate below. Nor can any of the kindly meant words of the others rouse her. Even Horn's bottle of *kava,* though she drinks from that, fails to register. Dr. McPhail's offer to see the governor himself cheers her for a moment, but he is soon back with the word that the governor cannot be reached.

Solemnly the party seats itself at dinner. The Rev. Davidson says grace. On the porch Sadie paces up and down, up and down, evidently seeking the courage to speak. Finally she comes into the room and approaches the missionary. Hesitantly, but earnestly, she apologizes to him. She is sorry for what she said, sorry for all that happened. But, for God's sake, let him not send her back to San Francisco.

Pressed for a reason for what seems to be a very strong fear of returning to the States, Sadie admits finally that it is because she wants to "go straight" and she knows that she cannot in San Francisco. There is a politician there who will know when she returns, despite everything she may do to elude him. All the boats are watched, and —

Davidson — Do you mean to tell me every boat coming into the port will be watched on the chance you are on it? (*Mr. and Mrs. McPhail and Mrs. Davidson exit.*)

Sadie — Yes — yes — that's it!

Davidson — Come, Miss Thompson, these evasions are getting you nowhere. Why are you afraid to return to San Francisco?

Sadie — I've told you — I keep telling you —

Davidson — Yes, and now I will tell you why you are afraid to go back. You have told me lies — now I shall tell you the truth. This politician you fear is a politician with a uniform and he wears a badge — what you are afraid of is the penitentiary —

Sadie — Oh!

DAVIDSON — Is that it — the penitentiary?

SADIE — I was framed but I got away before they caught me. They'll nab me the moment I step off the ship. Give me a chance — one chance —

DAVIDSON — I'm going to give you the finest chance you've ever had —

SADIE — You mean — I don't have to go back?

DAVIDSON — You said you wanted to go straight. If that is true, you must repent — you must atone to God. When you want me, Sadie Thompson — call for me. I will stand ready. I will help you. (*Davidson turns and walks out veranda. Sadie watches him go and then suddenly calls out.*)

SADIE — Rev. Davidson — Rev. Davidson! (*Rev. Davidson returns to room and stands facing Sadie.*) Rev. Davidson — you're right. I am a bad woman. But I want to be good — but I don't know how. So you let me stay here with you and show me what to do, and no matter what it is, I'm going to do it.

DAVIDSON — No, you can't stay here, you've got to go back to San Francisco. You've got to serve your time.

SADIE — You mean to say if I repent and want to be good, I still have to go to the penitentiary?

DAVIDSON — Yes — you've got to go —

SADIE — But if you send me back there — that would be my finish —

DAVIDSON — No, it will be your beginning —

SADIE — But I was framed I tell you,— I was framed —

DAVIDSON — Innocent or guilty — you must serve your sentence — it's the only way you can prove to God that you are worthy of his mercy —

SADIE — Innocent or guilty — what kind of a God are you talking about. Where's your mercy. No, Rev. Davidson, I guess that repentance stuff is off.

REV. DAVIDSON — Was it ever on?

SADIE — Whether it was or not — it's off now. The way you figure God out, he's nothing but a cop!

DAVIDSON — You've got to go back to San Francisco . . .

SADIE — Straight orders from your private heaven, eh, — I can see now that your God and me will never be shipmates — and the next time you talk to him, you tell him this: Sadie Thompson's on her way to hell.

DAVIDSON — Stop! This has gone far enough —

SADIE — (*hysterically*). No, it hasn't gone far enough! You've been telling me what's wrong with me — now I'll tell you what's wrong with you. You keep yelling at me — be punished!— Go back and suffer! How do you know what I have suffered? Or why I'm the scarlet woman? You don't know and you don't care! And you call yourself a Christian — you're nothing but a miserable witch burner — that's what you are — you believe in torture, that's what you do — you believe in torture — you know you're big and strong — and you've got the law on your side — and the power to hang me — all right! But I'm going to tell you this — I've got the power to stand here and tell you — HANG ME AND BE DAMNED TO YOU!

(*As Sadie finishes her tirade, she rushes madly to her room and slams the door. The curtain falls.*)

ACT III

It is early evening of the fourth day following the last scene. The rain is still beating persistently upon the roof of the Horn store. Inside an old ship's lamp hung in the center of the room casts a circle of reddish light on the floor. The corners are in shadow.

The Horns are having a more or less quiet five minutes to themselves, the trader doing most of the talking. The others are attending a native festival, the beating tom-toms of which can be heard. Intermittently Horn is interrupted by the calls of Sadie Thompson. Sadie is in her room, weakened, it transpires, by four days of struggle with the devils which the Rev. Davidson has been trying to cast from her sin-ridden body. She is calling now for the missionary, that his prayers may dispel the creeping fear in her heart.

From the barracks — more specifically from the brig, in which he has been confined for four days — comes O'Hara. He has suspected that something was going on at Horn's, and he has had a feeling that Sadie needed him. Now, from Horn, he learns that his suspicions were correct. For four days the Rev. Davidson has been praying with and for Sadie, until he's got her "beached with his psalm stuff." "Beached and delirious," according to Horn.

O'Hara — He took damned good care to get me stowed away before he started, didn't he? — Well, I beat him to it tonight —

Horn — How did you get out?

O'Hara — Walked out through the mess window — Griggs and Hodgeson helped me — good boys — both of them — they ought to be here any minute now.

Horn — (*searchingly*). Hm! What's doing, O'Hara? You arouse my curiosity.

O'Hara — If I was you I'd ease off to bed with my old lady — and not have any curiosity.

Horn — (*amusedly*). You would,— would you — and why would you do that?

O'Hara — I'd do that —so's I wouldn't get blamed for anything — in case anything happened. (*Horn considers the above speech for an instant, then looks at Ameena in a childishly annoyed manner. Motions for her to leave the room.*)

Horn — Run along, Ameena — sounds like another row is starting. (*Ameena rises and exits into store.*)

Most unlucky day of my life — that day the *Orduna* came into port. I like comfort — for five days now this whole household has centered on that tormented Thompson girl in there, while Davidson and Old Nick wrestled for her soul — It's got me nervous!

O'HARA — Well, you cheer up — it won't center around her much longer!

HORN — A lot you know about it — safe in the brig all week! There hasn't been such a casting out of devils since the first chapter of Exodus. The last vestige of mortal sin lurking in that poor critter's heart has been torn out — the Sadie Thompson that blew into my hotel a week ago — isn't any more. Wait till you see her.

O'HARA — Ain't keeping anything from me, are you?

HORN — Wait till you see her, I tell you —

O'HARA — (*rushing over to Horn*). What's he done to her — tell me quick —

HORN — My boy, it'll make you sick to look at her. She's like a victim all trussed up to sacrifice to some bloody idol —

O'HARA — Hell!

HORN — Maybe you've read of those fierce prophets of old, scourging their votaries with rods — eh? Well, I got one of 'em in my hotel — Yep! In the hereafter if I meet one of these prophets out of Israel I'll know him when I see him.

O'HARA — What — ?

HORN — At that I'm kind of sorry for Davidson. He's changed. There's something wrong with his eyes — they don't look right to me. They flash kind of funny —

O'HARA — (*nervously*). God! What's she doing now — sleeping?

HORN — I haven't heard her yell for Davidson for at least ten minutes — so let's hope so —

O'HARA — (*with a burst of determination*). Get her out for me! I'll tend to the rest of this —

HORN — Gladly, gladly — my mind's a blank save for one fact: Tomorrow Miss Sadie Thompson will be on the high seas —

O'HARA — You bet she'll be —

Horn calls Sadie, retrieves his bottle of *kava* and quietly steals away. As Sadie opens the door and stands framed in the half light she "is a pathetically wan and beaten creature. She is dressed in a bathrobe now past its glory. Her hair is frowsy and her entire attitude is that of one who has been thoroughly crushed." O'Hara is appalled at her appearance. To him she looks "awful sick," which gives speed to his plans. Everything is arranged, he tries to tell her. She is to pack her bags as hurriedly as she can before the Davidsons and the others get back from the native festival. Griggs and Hodgeson will tote her bags to a junk lying just off shore. In an hour she will be sailing for the Samarkind Islands, where she can pick up the Sydney boat.

But she can't understand. Did Mr. Davidson say she was to do this? He didn't, O'Hara admits, but she is to do it just the same.

SADIE — (*appreciatively*). It's mighty fine of you to go to all this trouble for me —

O'HARA — Fine! — Fine — nothing. This ain't one small bit what I'd like to do for you — if I got the chance —

SADIE — You're doing this — it kinda makes me wanta cry — but —

O'HARA — What's the but — ?

SADIE — I can't do it —

O'HARA — Why can't you do it?

SADIE — Because I'm going through with what I've got to go through with —

O'HARA — Are you afraid of Davidson? He'll never get hold of you again — I'll see to that —

SADIE — No — no — that isn't it at all — ! It would be awful hard for me to make you understand what's come over me. I can't understand myself. Remember that day — Handsome! — It seems one hundred years ago — that day the governor's letter came — I lost my nerve — ran around like a chicken with its head off. By'n'— by — I got a little calmer and I could think — and I thought I'm just rattled. I thought I'll try and fool him so I told Reverend Davidson a lie — as to why I didn't want to go back to 'Frisco — but he saw right through me — he looked right into me. He knew — he knew — I felt a big net was catching me — nothing was any use — I tried again — I called him back and told him I was a bad woman — and I wanted to repent — that was a lie — I didn't think I was bad so there wasn't anything to repent about — I had almost figured out things for myself — I thought, some folks have luck — some haven't — all folks can't be alike anyway — who knows what's good or bad? Nobody. So I just let things go at that — and did not think too much. Anyway I told him I'd repent — he said if that was true I'd have to go back to be punished — I lost my head again and I talked to him something terrible. He didn't seem to mind. He followed me into my room and asked me if I would kneel down and pray — I was so desperate I said yes. Oh, Handsome — Handsome —

O'HARA — All right — all right — go ahead and spill it all — you'll feel better.

SADIE — He knelt down and began to pray — prayed for a long time — I did not pay any attention at first — the rain was coming down — and the mosquitoes were humming — I was kind of numb — I suppose — a great fear was catching at my breath — then letting go — He prayed for hours and hours — I was awful tired — but all at once I found myself listening — sort of in spite of myself — and suddenly I found myself out in a big — bright — beautiful place — seemed all my life I had been in a fog and hadn't known it — and I was sort of happy — I knew I could be saved if I wanted to repent — and then it came — I did feel sorry for the life I had led — there was nothing phony about it — I wanted to repent! — I saw myself just as I was — Oh — God! — Oh, God!

O'HARA — Sadie — this stuff ain't making you happy — you don't realize — it ain't yourself. You've got to forget all about Davidson and come with me —

SADIE — You don't know what you're saying — you've no idea what you're saying —

O'HARA — They're not going to send you back there — with no one to take care of you. In Sydney — in a few weeks you'll have me — remember what I told you about Biff and Maggie?

SADIE — You don't understand — I've got to go back and serve my time — I've got to be punished for the life I've led — then God will forgive me. It's the sacrifice I've got to offer up. Oh — if it would only begin — it's the waiting for it to start that's so terrible. The world is a dangerous place, Handsome — on all sides of us there are terrible things — you've got to be pretty strong to live at all — Yes — it will be much easier in the penitentiary.

O'HARA — (*starting to his feet*). What d'ye mean — the penitentiary?

SADIE — When I get back to 'Frisco — I've got to go to the penitentiary for three years —

O'HARA — (*almost breathlessly*). Good Christ!

But nothing that he can say will move her. True, she was "framed" for the offense for which she is to be sent to prison, but the Rev. Davidson says that doesn't matter. "He says it's God's way of letting me settle for everything else," she tries to explain; "he says I've got to accept an unjust punishment by man as a sacrifice to God."

And when O'Hara tries to urge her she pushes him away and cries loudly and fearfully for the Rev. Davidson to come and save her, as though she doubted her own strength. Griggs and Hodgeson appear as promised, also eager to serve as life-savers. By way of making the trip pleasant for her, and the day's wait for the Sydney boat interesting, Hodgeson has brought his pet monkey as a present. And she ain't got no idea how entertainin' a monkey can be.

They have her clothes tied in bundles before she knows it, though she continues to call loudly for Davidson. And O'Hara's pleas are eloquent. She'll be in Sydney, soon, away from all her trouble. She'll be with Biff and Maggie, and after a bit he will come, and she'll become Mrs. Tim O'Hara, and they'll start afresh like two pals, 50-50. He is coaxing, cajoling, pleading with her and is just about to pick her up in his arms and carry her away when the Rev. Davidson strides into the room.

DAVIDSON — Here I am — Miss Thompson —

SADIE — Oh — oh —

DAVIDSON — (*looks with angry reproach at O'Hara*). It seems I got here just about in time, Miss Thompson. All evening I had a peculiar feeling you were in danger — it was almost as though God were whispering in my ear to hurry back —

O'HARA — Sadie — Sadie — don't pay any attention to him.

DAVIDSON — I'm sorry for you — O'Hara. What you are trying to do is a serious offense.

O'HARA — (*heatedly*). What you're trying to do would make a hyena cry.

DAVIDSON — You are trying to abduct Miss Thompson. You have made an attempt to defeat the law — it's likely to go hard with you. (*During the ensuing conversation both men become more menacing in their attitude.*)

O'Hara — That's my lookout — God, what kind of a man are you, anyway? Picking on this poor kid here. Getting her so she's half crazy. Sending her back to where she's got to go to prison — you're one fine specimen, Davidson! I'll say that for you. They don't make your kind every day!

Davidson — You are a reckless, headstrong man — O'Hara — you are given to loud language and strong drink. Your officers apparently have no control of you. You are breaking barracks now — and attempting a high-handed crime. You defy the authority of State and God. You cannot go on the way you're going — and I shall see to it that you don't!

Sadie — (*to O'Hara, with a quaint wistfulness*). But you don't see what I see. I was nobody — now I'm somebody. Reverend Davidson has shown me! If it hadn't been for him I could have gone through my whole life not knowing. It's a wonderful thing to know you've been made of some account — the only thing I don't understand is how it happened to come to me!

O'Hara — (*with a sudden realization that his efforts to induce Sadie to leave with him have come to naught*). Is that the way it is — honest — Sadie?

Sadie — That's the way it is.

O'Hara — (*in a boyishly hesitant manner*). What do you want me to do?

Sadie — I don't want you to do anything, except just not say anything more.

O'Hara — All right; I'll tell the boys to bring your things back. If you and me never see each other again I want to say this: I'll never forget you — ever.

Sadie — Good-bye —

Davidson — (*soothingly*). My poor child, it was not your fault. Far down the beach I heard your cry for help —

Sadie — O'Hara is an awful simple fellow — he thought he was helping me. You see — he doesn't understand. I couldn't bear to think of him suffering and in trouble — it's all right for me — it was coming to me — but I wouldn't want it to come to O'Hara.

DAVIDSON — Can't you see that indirectly you are responsible for the finest thing that could happen to O'Hara. He is to have his chance — just as you had yours!

SADIE — (*in a voice of a child*). Can't — can't — what's coming to me do for both of us?

DAVIDSON — No one can pay another's reckoning — each one must pay his own —

SADIE — Yes — but you told me — maybe I can't understand rightly yet — you told me Christ took the punishment for all of us — when they crucified Him —

DAVIDSON — Sadie — Christ saved the world for us, but each of us must bear his share of the cross — it wouldn't be fair to leave the whole weight on His shoulders, would it?

SADIE — When you're around — everything seems clear — everything seems all right — that old life I led — that doesn't seem to belong to me — that was someone else. When I feel like that — Reverend Davidson — does it mean I'm redeemed?

DAVIDSON — (*very tenderly*). Yes, Sadie — in the last few days you have become very close and dear to God — he has tested you and found you true. Tonight he sent the devil to tempt you. Once your soul lay like a stagnant pool in the deepest pit of the deepest valley — tonight it is cleansed — glorified —

SADIE — (*starts toward her door and pauses wearily*). If I'm afraid and can't sleep — will you pray with me?

DAVIDSON — Yes — when I hear you call — I will come —

The McPhails and Mrs. Davidson are back from the festival. They find Davidson standing, a little exalted, staring at the door of Sadie's room. A great happiness has come to him, he tells them. He has had proof that

Sadie Thompson has been reborn. "I have been privileged to bring a lost soul into the loving arms of the Lord." McPhail, however, is still skeptical. He can't see how any man, least of all a man carrying on the Lord's work, should want to send a helpless creature back to three years in an American prison.

But Davidson is thrilled with the glory of his victory. Too filled with it to follow the rest to bed. He must have time to commune with the flaring inner spirit that has taken command of him, and despite Mrs. Davidson's protest he goes again into the rain.

MRS. DAVIDSON — (*to the McPhails*). He prayed with Miss Thompson, last night, until she went to sleep. It was nearly three o'clock when he came upstairs. Then he threw himself down in the bed, exhausted. But he only slept in snatches. He has strange dreams that puzzle him — he'll have a breakdown if he doesn't take care —

MCPHAIL — Heaven knows, I pity Miss Thompson, but all we non-Biblical people seem to be utterly helpless in the matter —

MRS. DAVIDSON — I never saw Mr. Davidson so wrought up before. Last night he kept crying out in his sleep —

MCPHAIL — Is that so?

MRS. DAVIDSON — This morning he told me he had been dreaming about the mountains of Nebraska.

MCPHAIL — The mountains of Nebraska? That's odd!

MRS. DAVIDSON — I don't believe anyone but myself realizes what an enormous amount of emotional force my husband puts into his work.

MCPHAIL — Work seems to be the only outlet for his tremendous energy — he should look out.

MRS. DAVIDSON — The Lord's work is Mr. Davidson's life! On our wedding night Mr. Davidson explained to me his ideals of our marriage. He believed it should be a union free from earthly indulgence, devoted entirely to the salvation of others —

McPhail — A noble doctrine, Mrs. Davidson — but to a medical man like myself, everyday experience proves that flesh and blood are not things apart from the spirit. Frankly — natural emotions can never be denied, only disguised —

Mrs. Davidson — You are quite wrong. Both Mr. Davidson and I have high views on matters commonly accepted as part of human nature. I can safely say our marriage is entirely a contract of the spirit —

Mrs. McPhail — And obviously a happy one. All marriages are happy where people have the same ambitions.

Mrs. Davidson — You are right. It was hard working alone — and would have been harder as we grew older. I had been a missionary in China. I met Mr. Davidson at a congress in Boston we were both attending. It was agreed we were to come out to the islands, which my imagination had pictured in glowing colors. Perhaps I had looked forward to a marriage of another sort — like all women. I believe — I — wanted children. But that was long ago. Sometimes I wonder a little — two people as isolated and solitary as Mr. Davidson and myself. (*She rises suddenly.*) But no! Mr. Davidson is right! There is only one course for those who work for others, immolation of self, and sacrifice of all. Good night!

The women retire to their rooms. McPhail lingers for a word with Horn. Things that he has heard and seen puzzle him.

McPhail — I say, Horn, did you ever go through Nebraska on a train?

Horn — Twenty years ago —

McPhail — Notice the mountains?

Horn — Mountains! Molehills you mean.

McPhail — Call them what you like. They rose from the plain abruptly, remember, rounded, smooth —

Horn — Yep. What of it?

McPhail — Didn't it strike you that they were curiously like a woman's breast?

McPhail goes upstairs. "Horn pauses for a moment, gazing after McPhail. Then he turns and looks at Sadie's door. Again reflects and then turns out the hanging lamp, and goes into the store. Far off come the sounds of a native tom-tom, while, intermittently, come the plaintive wails of reed instruments, the rain increases its downpour, while through a rift in the clouds a shaft of moonlight finds its way into the room, shedding a ghastly ominous pallor on the door to Sadie's room."

The curtain is lowered briefly. When it rises some time has elapsed. A cold, threatening early dawn is beginning to throw weird shadows across the room. The rain is falling heavily. Afar off can be heard the continuing beat of the tom-toms. Sadie's door opens slowly and "she appears holding a lamp in her hand. She is a sickly pale. Her hair is tousled mussily about her head. Her entire facial expression seems to indicate the haunting fear of an unknown dread. About her she has a grey-white dressing gown, the folds of which seem to accentuate her forlorn appearance. She takes a hesitant step into the room and then slowly, holding the lamp before her, makes her way to the foot of the staircase. She pauses and calls up the stairs: "Reverend Davidson! Reverend Davidson!"

Getting no answer she makes her way unsteadily to Horn's chair and huddles herself despondently in it. The Rev. Davidson finds her thus as he enters from the veranda. She couldn't sleep, she tells him, and she was frightened by her thoughts. He, too, has been troubled.

DAVIDSON — (*as though under terrific strain*). Out there in the rain — I walked, and wondered too. The darkness was full of eyes — I saw things I never saw before. I looked into the awful groves of Asteroth, where Solomon went to find the secrets of joy and terror. I saw Asteroth herself — I saw Judas. Sadie — you don't have to go back to San Francisco.

SADIE — (*looking searchingly into his face*). I don't have to go back — what do you mean?

DAVIDSON — (*he has a peculiar hoarseness in his voice*). Just that — you don't have to go back. (*Leaning toward her his voice full of emotion.*) You are redeemed!

SADIE — (*unheeding the change in Davidson's tone*). What other sacrifice could I offer — that is all I have got to give. I only hope I will be able to go through with it right.

DAVIDSON — From now on you will be strong — no more fear. (*He now speaks as though in ecstasy.*) Beautiful — radiant — you will be one of the daughters of the King. (*He is bending over her and speaks in a reverent whisper.*) That's what you are now, Sadie — one of the daughters of the King — radiant — beautiful.

SADIE — (*looks again into his face, a wistful smile seems to give her face a madonna-like appearance*). Am I? (*She picks the lamp from the chair arm and rises. Slowly walks toward her door and then pauses and turns back to face Davidson.*) Pray with me Rev. Davidson — when you pray, everything seems all right.

She turns and goes into her room. Davidson stands as though hypnotized and watches her go. For a brief moment he seems to gain control of his emotions, then strides towards her door and stops abruptly outside it. Suddenly his head droops, his hands clasp convulsively and a bitter struggle between Davidson, the man of God, and Davidson, human creature, seems to take place. His head and shoulders now square and with studied deliberation he grasps the handle of Sadie's door, opens it and steps inside, slowly closing the door after him. The rain is now almost a cloudburst and its relentless beating seems to suggest that it has won a victory.

There is another lapse of hours. The stage is now bathed in the sunlight of early morning. Two natives are bending over the veranda railing, intent on some action below. A native policeman enters. He is looking, excitedly, for Horn, whom he brings from the store, and to whom he has communicated his own excitement. Horn quickly summons McPhail. O'Hara comes in search of Sadie. She is still in her room. If she is asleep let her sleep. Horn and McPhail rush out of the house. They are gone but a moment.

On the beach below they have found the body of the Rev. Davidson. He had cut his throat and thrown himself into the sea. Native fishermen had seen him. He has been dead, the doctor thinks, about two hours.

They hesitate to call Mrs. Davidson. And yet she must be told. When she comes she seems to have sensed the tragedy. Coolly she asks where she is to go. They lead her out towards the beach.

Suddenly from Sadie's room the raucous tones of the phonograph break forth. It is uncanny. They can't understand. Someone must stop her playing the infernal thing. If she knew —

Suddenly Sadie appears in the doorway. She "is once more dressed in the gay finery with which she had made her appearance in the first act. Her face is rouged, but for all of her joyous attire there is an odd cynical atmosphere which seems to cling to her."

SADIE — Surprised to see me — all dolled up, eh! Well, why not? Had to put on my best, didn't I, this gay and glorious morning? Besides you know, I'm radiant — beautiful — Ha — ha — ha! Could not believe my eyes when I saw the sun. Do I feel fine? I do! I would race you down the beach if it wasn't for these pesky heels.

O'HARA — Sadie — for God's sake turn off that phonograph —

SADIE — And why, for God's sake, should I turn off my phonograph?

O'HARA — They'll be back any minute.

SADIE — Who?

O'HARA — Mrs. Davidson —

SADIE — (*apparently once more herself and sure of her own ability to manage her own affairs*). And why should I turn off my phonograph because Mrs. Davidson is coming back? (*Snarling sneer has crept into her voice.*) I am not concerned with what Mrs. Davidson thinks nor for that matter with what your Reverend Davidson thinks. My advice to him is to pin on his wings and try the air —

O'HARA — (*to Horn*). Get that phonograph turned off quick.

SADIE — Stay out of that room, Old Horn — that phonograph stays on —

O'HARA — Sadie — something has happened —

SADIE — Yes, you're right — something has happened. You men! You're all alike! Pigs — pigs! I wouldn't trust any of you —

O'HARA — (*hurt*). Sadie!

SADIE — No offense to you in that last remark, old pal — and I'm going to Sydney if that invitation still holds good —

O'HARA — You bet it does — Sadie. Davidson has killed himself.

SADIE — What?

O'HARA — They found him on the beach this morning in the water with his throat cut —

SADIE — (*she speaks slowly and a remarkable change*

seems to come over her). So — he killed himself? Then I can forgive him. I thought the joke was on me. I see it wasn't —

McPhail — (*enters from the veranda and excitedly speaks*). What the devil are you doing? Stop that damned machine — Mrs. Davidson is coming.

Sadie — (*weakly*). Yes — stop it — stop it —

Horn goes to Sadie's room and stops the phonograph and re-enters, pausing by Sadie's door. Mrs. Davidson enters, followed by Mrs. McPhail, who goes and stands beside her husband. Mrs. Davidson walks to Sadie —

Mrs. Davidson — I understand, Miss Thompson. I am sorry for him — and I am sorry for you. (*She crosses to the stairway and pauses at the foot. Her shoulders shake convulsively. Her head is bowed. After an instant's pause she mounts the stairs. Sadie has watched her go and turns and faces the lights.*)

Sadie — I guess I'm sorry for everybody in the world. (*O'Hara crosses and stands by Sadie's side. She turns her face toward him.*) Life is a quaint present from somebody — there's no doubt about that. (*Little sob works its way into her voice.*) It'll be much easier in Sydney.

THE END

"YOU AND I"

A Comedy in Three Acts

By Philip Barry

THIS is the ninth "prize play" to be written by those students of playwriting who have worked with Prof. George Pierce Baker in his "47 Workshop" class at Harvard, and the eighth to be produced. Thomas P. Robinson's "The Copy," which was awarded the prize in 1921, was accepted for production by Oliver Morosco in New York, but shortly thereafter Mr. Morosco's firm was in temporary difficulties necessitating a reorganization, and "The Copy" was put aside.

Later Mr. Morosco abandoned his plan to offer the annual $500 prize to the Baker students and Richard G. Herndon, another New York manager, took his place. Professor Baker, Mr. Herndon and Walter Pritchard Eaton were named as the committee to make the selection. Fifty plays were submitted, and from these the committee chose Philip Barry's "You and I." It was produced by Mr. Herndon in the Belmont Theatre, New York, February 19, 1923, and sprang into immediate popularity, continuing through the remainder of the season.

"You and I" is an epigrammatic play of the type usually classified as a society comedy, written in the mood and manner of that trio of English dramatists, Oscar Wilde, Arthur Wing Pinero and Sidney Carton, who contributed so notably to the English and American stage twenty years ago, and whose only American competitor at the time was the late Clyde Fitch.

It is about seven o'clock of a late September evening, 1921. The scene is the library of Maitland White's summer home in Westchester county, New York — "a huge, motherly sort of room that pats your hand as you come into it and tells you to sit down and be comfortable with the rest of us."

Offstage, right, some one is playing the latest dance tune, the some one, as you guess a moment later, when she bursts a little angrily into the room, being Veronica Duane. Veronica, whom no one thinks of calling anything but "Ronny," is "about nineteen, slim, of medium height, with a decidedly pretty, high-bred face, lovely hair, lovely hands, soft, low-pitched voice — whatever she may be saying. Heredity, careful upbringing, education and travel have combined to invest her with a poise far in advance of her years. She has attained the impossible — complete sophistication without the loss of bloom. Her self-confidence is an added charm — free, as it is, from any taint of youthful cocksureness." She is dressed becomingly in what are probably known in this section of Westchester as sport togs.

Ronny is followed by "Ricky" (otherwise Roderick) White. Ricky, wearing the suit he golfs in, has quit smoking the pipe he carries in his hand and "looks just a little bit scared." "He is a well set-up, thoroughly nice boy of about twenty-one. High color, hair carefully brushed, a disarming smile." The elder White had once declared Ricky and Ronny to represent "The cream of their astonishing generation."

The reason for Ricky's being a bit frightened presently is revealed as the result of a liberty he has just taken with Ronny. She had looked up at him, adoringly, he thought, as she played the piano, and he had kissed her full upon the mouth, which has irritated Ronny excessively. Not that she was not pleased; or that she was taken completely by surprise. Some day she knew Ricky might grow that bold. Some day she expected, vaguely, that he might even propose to her. As next door neighbors they had practically grown up together.

But her irritation of the moment apparently is caused by what she is pleased to consider an utter lack of judgment and consideration on Ricky's part.

RONNY — On the fifteenth of October you're going abroad for three years. For the love of Pete, why couldn't you have held out just two weeks more? Then you'd have gone, and I'd have forgotten you. And that would have been all there was to it.

RICKY — In a pig's eye.

RONNY — I tell you it would! And now — after *this* — oh — a sweet winter I'll put in, getting over you!

RICKY — (*genuinely dismayed*). Getting *over* me . . . ? Gosh, I don't want you to do *that!*

RONNY — (*ironically*). No. I'll sit around doing basket-work, while you and your little playmates at the Beaux-Arts scamper up and down Paris.

RICKY — (*grandly*). I am going abroad to study architecture — not to go on parties.

RONNY — Show *me* a student on the Left Bank who doesn't study life! Thanks, Rick. By spring you will be but a memory.

RICKY — But — but Ronny — can't you get it into your silly head that I'm *really* in love with you? I'm — you've — oh, damn it — *won't* you marry me?

RONNY — Ricky! (*Shakes her head with conviction.*) Uh-uh. It's awfully nice of you. But I couldn't wait three years for the Prince of Wales.

Which Ricky accepts as discouraging proof that it is "a fat lot" she loves him. Such, however, is not Ronny's reason at all. Things are not as pleasant as they might be in her home for one thing, and promise to be little if any better until she is "settled." Furthermore Ricky has always meant to be an architect and she has no intention of standing in his way. As Ricky sees it there is no reason why she should. He can still be an architect and marry her. He can, for the sake of the better wage, go into his father's factory temporarily. Then he can study nights and drift into architecture gradually. For the matter of that it would be no great calamity if he should get into business and stay there. "Father dished painting to marry Nanny. And do you suppose he's ever regretted it? Look at them!"

It is a persuasive argument and a moment later they have plighted their troth, as the saying is, and are calling upstairs to "Nanny," who happens to be Ricky's absurdly youthful but still quite wonderful mother, to relay the grand tidings to her.

Nancy White, who presently appears at the head of the stairs, "is a young forty, medium height, with a slim, girlish figure, lively, whimsical brown eyes, dark brown hair and a charming manner. Despite her poise one feels that her age is merely 'put on'— that she will never really grow up." She accepts their news with a show of genuine interest in them, but with suggested misgivings as well. She settles them finally on the sofa and draws an armchair up before them.

NANCY — Now, you two precious idiots, we'll talk this over.

RICKY — (*lowly, to Ronny*). Isn't she immense?

NANCY — I thought the fact of your living next door to each other for twelve summers would act as an anti-toxin.

RONNY — (*timidly*). It came as a shock to me, Mrs. White.

NANCY — I dare say. But of course this is quite out of the question. You're nothing but children.

RICKY — (*shaking his head reprovingly*). Gosh, Nanny — that's awfully old stuff.

NANCY — Roderick — be kind enough to reserve your infantile comments. (*Ricky subsides.*) Nothing but children. It is beautiful, my dears, but quite, quite ridiculous.

RICKY — Pardon the interruption — but how old were you, when *you* became a married maiden?

NANCY — That has nothing to do with it!

RICKY — (*indulgently*). I know — but just as a matter of record. . . .

NANCY — (*with dignity*). I was — ah — nineteen. But —

RICKY — You mean a couple of weeks past eighteen. What're you, Ronny?

RONNY — I'll be twenty in December. Big girl.

RICKY — Check. And how about Dad?

NANCY — He was a great deal older than you are!

RICKY — Your memory's failing, Nanny. He had me just four months.

NANCY — (*ironically*). I don't want to be sordid — but what *do* you expect to live on?

RICKY — Query: What did *you* live on, darling?

NANCY — (*a little confused*). Why — ah — I had a little of my own, and your father worked.

RICKY — (*with a gesture*). 'S a perfect equation!

RONNY — I've about two thousand a year from Aunt Isabel's estate. Dad's promised me a house.

NANCY — (*to Ricky*). And may I ask what you intend doing about your architecture?

RONNY — (*leaning forward*). You and I both, Mrs. White. . . .

RICKY — Quiet, child — let me manage this. I'm going like a breeze. (*To Nancy.*) Well, you see, I'm going to pass that up, and —

NANCY — (*really troubled*). But —

RICKY — Oh — maybe not for good. Maybe, by and by, when we get on our feet. . . .

NANCY — By and by! Somehow — that sounds vaguely reminiscent to me. Unless you do it now, you'll never do it!

RICKY — Well, really — what if I don't? I mean, you told me that father wanted to paint, or something

— but you and he were married at twenty-one and eighteen respectively, and he went into business, and stayed there. What I mean is, it seems to me that you two have made a pretty good go at it.

"We have made an uncommonly good go at it," Nancy admits. "But—" She still has her own reasons for wanting them to be very sure they are doing right before they go ahead with their plans. She does not doubt they love each other. "I've never given a happy hang for any one else," Ronny confesses; "I'd simply — lie down and die for him," and she thinks — perhaps — it will be all right — somehow. But — there is still a but.

It is after Ronny has gone to dress for dinner that Nancy takes her son more completely into her confidence. From a drawer of her desk that is bulging with slips of paper she hands him a few. They are sketches and bits of sketches that, over a period of twenty years, she has found in her husband's pockets whenever she has given his clothes to the valet to be pressed. The elder White is also given to experimenting in murals — which is why the wall by the telephone has to be repapered so frequently.

It may be possible for Ricky to have both the architecture he has always been eager to study and the girl he loves — and again it may not be possible. It may seem simple now — but what of that later time?

NANCY — . . . when you're forty or so, you may look on love as a kind of captivating robber — who chatted so sweetly, as he plucked your destiny out of your pocket. . . .

RICKY — (*gaily*). There you go again! Ask dad — he knows! (*A whistled tune is heard from the hall upstairs.*)

NANCY — (*rapidly*). You may suddenly feel choked

off — thwarted — in the one really big thing you could have done. Then — though you love her dearly — you'll resent Ronny. You'll try not to let her see. If she loves you, she can't avoid it. Or even you yourself may not know quite what's wrong. You may simply find, all at once, that you are very empty, very unhappy.

RICKY — But *Nanny* — look how happy father is!

(*The whistle draws closer.*)

NANCY — You can't tell much by a whistle, son. . . .

Maitland White, who is "Matey" to his intimates in this generously nicknamed family, "is forty-three, about five feet ten, and golf and squash have kept him in the pink of trim. He is not particularly handsome, but with a face and smile that win you immediately. There are a few grey hairs, which Nancy or the barber will pull out next week. To look at him, you might think him any one of a number of things. You guess that it is business, and you know that he is successful. His hands — long, slender and restless — and a kind of boyish whimsicality in him are all that betray the artist."

For the moment Maitland is too much taken with a Watteau print he has brought home for Nancy's room to pay much attention to his son, at the moment bursting with news of his engagement to Ronny. But finally Ricky succeeds in getting the news across. First, he tells his father he expects to marry Miss Duane, and second, that he also expects to give up temporarily his planned career as an architect. It is a harder blow for Matey to assimilate than it was for Nancy. He is quite stunned by it, in fact. And yet his attitude is kindly and sympathetic.

MATEY — Look here, old fellow, this is a little confusing. Would you mind telling me more about it?

RICKY — Why — there isn't a great deal to tell, sir.

It's just that we're — very much in love, and want to be married as soon as we possibly can. I figure that if I go to work now, by spring everything will be rosy.

MATEY — What do you plan to do?

RICKY — Same as you, The Warren Company. Caught you, sir — you thought I'd say, "sell bonds."

MATEY — And your architecture goes by the boards, eh?

RICKY — Why should it? I can study evenings, and Sundays, and finally — (*Matey laughs mirthlessly. Ricky is injured.*) Well — I *can*. . . .

MATEY — Ricky — our method of upbringing for you and Jean has allowed room for very few "Thou-shalt-nots." I'm not going to start ordering you about now, but there are a few things, that — as an older man — I want to remind you of —

RICKY — (*quietly*). Yes, dad. . . .

MATEY — I have my own eyes, and the word of your masters at school and college, to tell me that you have a considerable gift for building-design. You love the work, and you're unusually well suited for it. You need technique, and a background — and you need them badly. Three years at the Beaux-Arts will give you the best there are. . . .

RICKY — But Ronny —

MATEY — (*a little exasperated*). If Ronny won't wait for you, there'll be another girl just as charming, later on. . . .

RICKY — Oh, dad. . . .

MATEY — I want to tell you, son, that the most important thing in a man's life is his work — particularly when he has an equipment such as yours. It's hard to get going; for a while you need absolute independence — freedom to think only "I — I — I — I and my work." After marriage that's no longer possible. From then on "it's you and I" always — with the "you" first, every time. "You and I."

RICKY — Sound grammar, anyway.

MATEY — Don't think I'm speaking idly! And don't make the mistake either of underrating the suffering a flouted destiny can send you. There's a course you feel cut out to take. Step off it now — and you'll regret it as long as you live.

RICKY — But — I simply can't give up Ronny.

MATEY — (*brutally*). In my opinion, any man who sacrifices his career for the sake of a girl hasn't the backbone of — a cup-custard. (*Nancy's head drops a little. Ricky glances at her apprehensively.*) And any girl selfish enough to permit —

RICKY — Dad —

MATEY — What?

RICKY — Isn't that a bit rough on mother?

MATEY — (*puzzled*). Rough on — what do you mean . . . ?

NANCY — Don't be silly, Ricky.

MATEY — But . . . ?

NANCY — (*matter-of-factly*). I must go and dress. (*To Ricky.*) You'd better come too.

MATEY — Just a moment, dear — Rick, it's sheer nonsense to think you can manage two occupations. One or the other must go. You —

RICKY — I'm afraid it's no use, father. I've thought it all out, and my mind's made up.

Etta, who happens to be an unusually attractive maid, announces the arrival of Mr. Warren. Warren is the G. T. Warren who is president of Matey's manufacturing firm and he is to spend the week-end with the Whites. "He is about fifty-five, and partially bald — a short, plump little man with a ready smile. He has the conceit of most self-made men, but in his case, it is made amusing by his naïveté. He is, in the business vernacular, always 'on his toes,' and literally exudes prosperity and good nature. He speaks rapidly, and with conviction." He greets his host and hostess with an assured affability and matches small talk with the effervescent Ricky as best he can. To the young man's suggestion that another White is ready for the firm Mr. Warren reacts with enthusiasm. It is an age of business and he is quite sure Ricky is acting wisely in giving up his plans for European study. He is ready to put him through the Warren mill any time he is ready to start. The Whites try guardedly to dissuade their son from making the plunge too suddenly, but just now he is of no mind to listen to them.

With Ricky and Warren gone, full of plans, Matey confesses that he feels a bit done up. He probably should take the vacation that every one, Nancy most of all, is urging upon him. And yet with the market as uncertain as it is, and the chance that Ricky will yet be made to see the light and decide to go on with his studies, any long vacation is out of the question.

Through the open door at the right Geoffrey Nichols is heard approaching. "Geoff" is an old, old friend of Matey's, a college chum, an usher at the White wedding. But they have not seen each other for the better part of twenty years. While Matey has been getting on in business Nichols has been acquiring some little fame as a writer of popular fiction. As he enters now "he is distinguished in appearance and attractive — the air of a cosmopolite without the vice of obtruding it. For a successful literary man his affectations are few."

Nichols is in town only for a few days, preliminary to sailing for Europe. He spends much of his time in Europe. "I'm a veritable flea for travel," he confesses. "London is my old lady — Paris my mistress — and Rome — ah, Rome — my saint in décolleté!" He is happy at being able to have a few hours with the Whites, and amusingly reminiscent in recalling the years when they knew each other better. With Nancy gone to dress for dinner the men come seriously to the inevitable comparison of their respective lives.

NICHOLS — (*reflectively*). And yet at twenty, we were much the same. Twenty — the incendiary age, Matey! I was going to set the world on fire with my novels — your match was a paint-brush.

MATEY — And I gave up my painting to marry Nancy Lyon. . . .

NICHOLS — While I forsook sweet Kitty Nash, to wed an ink-pot. A pair of jilts, we two! Well — what do you think of your bargain?

MATEY — I've come out the winner, Geoff!

NICHOLS — And so have I!

MATEY — (*laughing*). Impossible! I've a happy home — sufficient leisure — a regular income — two fine, spoiled children — and a wife that's a simple miracle. Trump them, if you can!"

NICHOLS — (*gaily, with the gesture of laying cards on the table one by one*). The world's my home — every hour of my time is my own — I'll match my income with yours any day! And for your last three items, I say what Bacon said: "A man with wife and children has given hostages to Fortune!"

MATEY — But old Lady Fortune has done me rather well.

NICHOLS — Oh — she has her favorite slaves. But freedom's the thing old chap. As Shaw said to me one day last April — dash it all — what *was* it he said? At any rate, it was simply convulsing.

MATEY — But how on earth have you done any work?

NICHOLS — Work? Why, every new experience is material. "Copy" we call it. Wherever I go, my typewriter follows. No worries, no responsibilities — just *life* — the one life I have — spiced and succulent.

MATEY — While I — day after day — "Nine to five — nine to five."

NICHOLS — Those words are the business man's epitaph.

MATEY — (*determined to be sprightly*). Oh — one has one's moments, even a business man.

NICHOLS — (*watches Matey a moment*). Matey — as I remember, you showed amazing promise. I've known artists with wives — with children, even. Why, in the name of Raphael, didn't you go on with it?

MATEY — (*a little wanly*). Well, you see, Nancy and I married ridiculously young — neither of us rich, but both of us accustomed to a certain standard of living — a regular income became pretty much of a necessity —

NICHOLS — (*thoughtfully*). And you put it off. Tsch — what a shame —

MATEY — (*reluctantly*). Perhaps — I don't know. Sometimes when I look back, and think that I haven't yet done the thing I wanted to do — my forty-three years seem rather futile and misspent. It's been particularly salty today — my son Roderick, for whom I've expected . . . Oh, well, it's the old story over again; expediency's heel on the neck of inclination.

NICHOLS — But some phases of your life must be very interesting. Now business for instance —

MATEY — Geoff, business is a dump for dreams . . . I believe that every fourth man in it has something shut down in him. You can see it in their faces. Some wanted to paint, like me — some to write, to sing — to be doctors, lawyers. God bless me, even preachers! But expediency ordered it otherwise. And now most of them will die in the traces, poor devils . . . die of market reports — Babsonitis — hardening of the soul —

NICHOLS — (*sagely*). Ah, yes — as some one says, "Most men lead lives of quiet desperation."

MATEY — (*softly*). "Quiet desperation." By the Lord — here's one who's fed up with it. I've a good mind to chuck business *now* — and go to painting! (*Nichols looks somewhat alarmed — this is being taken too seriously.*)

NICHOLS — You're not serious . . . ?

MATEY — So serious that the turn of a hair would decide it.

Nor does all Nichols' sound reasoning dislodge Matey's conviction that fate, having been unkind to him, should at least be given a chance to offer some sort of compensation. What has the manufacture of soap, face creams and cosmetics — which he reluctantly confesses to Nichols is the Warren line — what can such a business offer a man who hungers to be painting?

It is in this mood that Nancy finds him when Nichols has gone. And though she tries tactfully to lead him out of it she does not succeed. Finally, a little desperate, she demands the truth from him.

NANCY — Matey — you sweet old thing — what *is* the matter?

MATEY — Oh — nothing —

NANCY — Dear — it seems to me that you have about everything that a person could desire. We've — most of the good things of life — health — position — enough money — and a happy family. (*She hesitates.*) And we've — each other. Nor is ours the tame, settled love most people have at forty. Some blessed good fortune has kept the keen edge on it. I love my children — but compared to you — oh, Matey! I fancy — there's more woman in me than mother. . . . You have been unusually successful in your work. What more could any man ask than *you have* . . . ?

MATEY — Oh, Nanny, Nanny. (*Impatiently, but with intense suffering.*) Nanny, Nanny, *Nanny* — what *do you* know about it! (*Nancy catches her breath sharply, holds it a moment and then lets it go.*)

NANCY — (*almost in a whisper*). I suppose — you know — it — just about knocks the heart out of me, to hear you say that. . . . (*She waits for a response. None comes. She clenches her fists, and throws back her head, in pain — turns to him.*) Oh — this *can't* be you and I! (*A moment's silence.*) Maitland — as you love me — there's something I want you to do.

MATEY — What is it?

NANCY — (*directly*). Leave business for a year. Get leave of absence, if possible. Otherwise, resign. . . .

MATEY — (*affecting to be puzzled*). But — my dear — *why* . . . ?

NANCY — (*with an impatient gesture*). Oh — *please!* Do you think I've had all these years of you — to be fooled by pretense now? I've known for a *long* time that you weren't happy — and why you weren't. But I've *not* known — quite how much it meant to you. I want you to devote the year to painting.

MATEY — (*with amused tolerance*). It's a nice idea, Nanny, but — (*his gesture includes the house, the cars, the servants*).

NANCY — (*rapidly — closer to him*). We'll give up the apartment. We'll stay out here over the winter. One car — and run it ourselves. We'll keep Katie and Etta — and let the others go. I'll do the upstairs myself. Ricky will be in business — no longer an expense. My own income will be enough to dress Jean and pay her school bills. . . .

MATEY — (*uncertainly*). You understand — I've very little outside of my salary?

NANCY — Little — but plenty for us. We'll economize in everything. (*Looks at lighted lamps with a smile.*) We'll — even be careful about the electric lights. The front attic can be made into a studio. . . .

MATEY — (*laughing*). It sounds too delightful! But impossible, of course —

NANCY — What's the matter — don't you dare?

MATEY — People would think I'd lost my mind.

NANCY — (*scornfully*). People!

MATEY — (*slowly*). I suppose they wouldn't have to know. But G. T. —

NANCY — (*quickly*). Tell him it's — personal research work.

MATEY — And if the research finds nothing?

NANCY — Matey — if you don't still think the bird in the bush worth any two in the hand, you might as well die.

Matey permits himself, half-willingly, a little wonderingly, to be carried on by Nancy's enthusiasm. It is possible the experiment might be made — if this and that could be arranged. But — there are so many things to be considered. For one, what would he do for models? He would naturally want to do portraits, and models, brought to the country, while he was brushing up, would be expensive.

But Nancy has a ready solution for that problem. There is Etta, the maid. An unusually beautiful girl, Etta. And, with proper inducements, Etta could undoubtedly be induced to pose. Yet, even after Matey studies her for the first time as a possibility and is convinced she might serve, Etta is not so sure it would be a proper business for a young woman.

NANCY — (*to Etta*). If you will consent to remain here in the country with us this winter, and pose for a few hours each day —

ETTA — (*gently*). I am sorry, ma'am. (*Turns to go.*)

NANCY — Just a moment! I'll increase your wages, and help you with your work.

ETTA — (*firmly*). No, ma'am. I could not consider it. Not for all the money in the world.

NANCY — (*frankly puzzled*). But — I don't understand. Would you mind telling us why? (*Etta hesitates. Peers at Matey.*) You may be quite frank.

Etta — Well — I do not like to say nothing, but the man of the house, in the third last place I was in, made advances that was — advances that *were* — most unwelcome. You know how careful a girl has got to be — 'specially when nature has blessed her with looks like mine. I can usually tell by their eyes. (*She tries to get a look at Matey's. He looks up at her, then rises suddenly, and goes to window.*) I am not saying nothing against Mr. White. So far, he has behaved like a real gennulman. But if I should forget myself to the extent of — oh, you know what artists are — they, and sailors —

Nor is Etta easily won over. She knows artists — "women to them are as tinders to the flames," she insists. "There's the Hearst of it, Matey," Nancy explains. But Etta is won finally, after she has been reassured that none of Mr. White's gennulman friends will be permitted to gaze openly upon her charms while she is posing. She will always be modestly and becomingly draped, Nancy promises, and the experience will enable her to learn much that every real lady should know.

They decide not to tell Mr. Warren of Matey's determination to resign until later. Ronny comes back, looking very pretty in a new frock. She may have a "plain face, but she's a nifty dresser," Ricky admits. Etta summons them to dinner as the curtain falls.

ACT II

It is late afternoon of a day in spring seven months later. The scene is the attic, converted into a studio for Matey's use, access to which is gained from below through a stair well at back.

"Matey, in smock, with a small daub of paint on his cheek, is busily painting at his easel. Etta poses in the throne-chair. She wears a simple, exquisite afternoon dress, and a small string of pearls at her throat. Her hands rest in her lap. Her hair is dressed most becomingly, and the transformation into a charming lady of unusual grace and beauty is quite complete."

Matey has had some little trouble with Etta as a model. She will sneeze at inconvenient moments and so far she has been unable to settle her features into just the expression the artist has been trying to catch. The portrait, however, is nearing completion, and by one last heroic effort, during which Matey appeals feelingly to his model's imagination by the recital of a most interesting fairy story in which she, as a grand lady in Fifth Avenue society, is the heroine, he manages to put the few finishing touches to the mouth that he has been struggling for. With a whoop of joy he grabs Etta from her throne and they are dancing wildly about when Nancy comes up the stairs.

She, too, is properly impressed with the success of the picture, and a little happily tearful over Matey's enthusiasm. But a moment later she unwittingly uncovers a flaw in the amber of her Matey's happiness. She has brought him his mail, which he has not even glanced at for days. And in the mail there is news from his broker of a serious break in the market. Matey's stocks are down—'way down. And there is a chance they will go lower. And although he takes the blow philosophically and bravely, it still is a blow to both of them.

Ricky joins them. He is dressed as a troubadour and carries a guitar. There is to be a fancy dress party at the Duane's that night at which the engagement of Ricky and Ronny is to be gaily announced. Warren is coming out, and Geoffrey Nichols, who is back from Europe.

Ricky has been getting on famously at the Warren plant. He is not exactly wild about the work, or the future it promises — but he is game. And he will have Ronny. One can't have everything.

It is plain that he still thinks of his architecture, however, and of the plans he had made, though he artfully tries to conceal that fact. It comes out later when he and Ronny are alone, and she discovers him carrying a first edition of Mossgrave's "Architecture and ye Associated Artes" in his pocket. His enthusiasm over this treasure that he has picked up in an old bookstore hits home with Ronny. It forces a culmination of her suspicions — that it would be unfair to marry Ricky and permit him to give up the career he is so ready to sacrifice for her. She is troubled with this thought when from out the book slips a piece of paper bearing a free-hand sketch of plans for a small house on it. Ronny picks it up.

RICKY — Here — lay off! That's not finished yet! (*Starts to take it.*)

RONNY — What is it?

RICKY — It's a plan I was making for our new diggings. Now you know what made me late for dinner last night. (*Ronny's face lights up.*)

RONNY — Tell me about it!

RICKY — (*The paper has a free-hand sketch on it of the plans of the house with cellar, downstairs, upstairs, top floor, on the top half of paper. The bottom half a drawing of the stables and kennels.*) (*Explaining.*) You see — I wanted something we could add on to — the way dad and Nancy did to this. First comes the cellar — for the furnace and things. Downstairs: hall, living room, dining room — that little hole is the library, kitchen — out back, servant's quarters above. Upstairs: four bedrooms — yours and mine, and two guests' rooms. Three baths. Top floor: small storeroom and playroom. . . .

RONNY — . . . For us . . . ?

RICKY — (*solemnly*). For our progeny.

RONNY — Isn't it big! How many do you think there ought to be?

RICKY — Oh — conservative — three or four. . . .

RONNY — (*thoughtfully*). Well — I'll see what I can do. . . . (*Indicating the stables, etc.*) What's that?

RICKY — (*with additional enthusiasm*). Ah — here's the real work! Look, Beau'ful — the stables — miniature reproduction of Charles the Second's at Windsor. And this is the kennels — just like some I once saw for St. Bernards at a monastery near St. Moritz.

RONNY — (*regards him oddly*). They're more interesting than the house, aren't they?

RICKY — Ever so much. You see it is one of my pet convictions that you can make any building beautiful, even a cow shed, without in the least contradicting what . . . (*He regards her in surprise.*) Dearest! What can be the matter with you? You look like the very devil —

RONNY — (*confused*). I — ? Why —, I —. Don't be a fool, Rick. (*Her hand brushes across her eyes. She sighs, shakes her head, and laughs shortly.*) I'm — just simply in a fog over tonight. . . . (*Ricky regards her dubiously for a moment, then becomes matter-of-fact once more.*)

RICKY — Oh say. (*He rises putting book in pocket, takes up the guitar.*) I don't want to muff that troubadour stunt. Slip me the dope again, will you . . . ?

RONNY — (*lifelessly*). It's not my idea, you know. It's mother's. We're to have supper on the south terrace at twelve. When they're all seated, you amble up below the second story window, and begin. (*Ricky begins thrumming and singing, gaily. As he does so, Ronny holds the slip of paper, looks at it.*)

RICKY — List to me, Lady Love, hark to my plea.
Love hold'th no bounty so precious as thee,
Flown my heart's gayety, lovelorn my life,
Sad and desolate I, save I have thee to wife.

— and then you press a red, red rose to your lips, and toss it lightly to me, and I catch it in my teeth, or something, and *Voila!* (*Chord.*) Kitty is out of the bag!

RONNY — (*slowly*). And — suppose — instead, I just — turned away — and shut the window, would you be sad and desolate?

RICKY — On the contrary I should execute a few choice clog steps and sing:

Be she fairer than the day
Or the flow'ry meads in May —
What care I how fair she be
If she be not so to me?

(*During the song Ronny has rolled the plan together into a small roll and placed the engagement ring on it.*)

RONNY — (*quietly, after a pause*). Is that the way you'd really feel — do you think?

RICKY — (*gaily*). Sure!

RONNY — (*softly*). I'm glad. Because I — don't —

RICKY — (*still strumming, softly*). Don't what?

RONNY — Don't love you, Rick. (*Ricky looks at Ronny, appalled and then laughs. His thrumming continues throughout the next few speeches — an accompaniment to the conversation.*)

RICKY — (*scoffing*). No — that's why you're marrying me! (*Plays again.*)

RONNY — (*rises*). It's — why I'm *not*. . . .

RICKY — (*not to be taken in*). Too late now, old thing —

RONNY — It's — just this side of —too late. . . . (*Pause, Ricky is trying bravely to smile.*) I — *mean* it, Ricky —

RICKY — (*with difficulty; his smile comes and goes, and comes and goes. He stands guitar against chair*).

Ronny — please find some other way to — ride me. I'm — you're —I — you see, I'm such a fool about you, that I can't — play up to this.

RONNY — (*speaking in a small voice*). It breaks me into little pieces — but I mean it.

RICKY — Ronny — you — you simply *can't*. . . .

RONNY — (*turns to him*). Do — you remember that day last autumn — what I told you about father and mother — ? (*Ricky tries to speak, but nods instead.*) How I said I was going to marry the next nice person I was — fond of? You were the nice person, Ricky. (*Shakes her head, sorrowfully.*) Oh — the nicest one! And I thought surely I'd love you. But — I don't. And I can't — just *can't* go through with it, without —

RICKY — (*looking away. Speaking with effort*). I — don't know what to do. I don't know what's expected of me. I don't quite understand it. Nearly — but not quite. I can't believe that you — (*closer to her*) — you've simply got to tell me some more about it. . . . (*There is a sound at the stairs, Ricky glances over his shoulder. His voice lowers.*) Hell — Nichols, I suppose. . . . (*Goes to stairs and looks down.*) . . . The playroom — quick!

It is Etta, come to dust the room, and not Nichols. But Nichols follows a moment later, and mistaking Etta, still dressed as the lady of the model, for one of the earlier guests, he is quite charmed with her. And she, flattered no end by his mistake, does her best to live up to what she has come to believe a lady would do under the circumstances. She fools him so completely that, before Nancy's coming interrupts them, Nichols has asked her to motor with him on Thursday, and to dine. He suspects his mistake a moment later when Nancy shows him Matey's painting and he recognizes the likeness to Etta. But he says nothing.

The painting, Nichols agrees, is amazingly clever,

in so far as he is able to judge. "It's such an extraordinary fine likeness, I suspect it's not great work," he says. "He may be merely — clever with a brush — as I am clever with a typewriter." But Nancy hopes it's not just that. The question now is how is the picture to be exhibited — and sold.

NANCY — If only someone would want it at once.
NICHOLS — Has he done anything else?
NANCY — Just a few sketches. It was difficult, getting under way.
NICHOLS — Such a different life — quite natural. Last autumn, I did my best to dissuade him. Frankly — how do you think he likes it?
NANCY — Oh, underneath, I think he's been very, I think he's been happier.
NICHOLS — Good; you know apart from my personal interest — to me Matey is Everyman.
NANCY — How do you mean precisely?
NICHOLS — My gardener kept me occupied for twenty minutes this morning telling me what a splendid carpenter he would have made — and means to make still. (*He laughs shortly.*) He's sixty-three.
NANCY — (*thoughtfully.*) I see. But is it the same?
NICHOLS — Maybe not. How have you weathered the change?
NANCY — I've tried — Oh, I've tried so hard! (*With a little shudder.*) It's shameful, the way prosperity softens one.
NICHOLS — (*incredulously*). *You — ?*
NANCY — (*nodding*). It's a little pathetic, you know, to find you're the sort of person whose conception of a real sacrifice consists in managing with two servants, instead of five.
NICHOLS — Nonsense! Sacrifice is relative. You suffer as much from lack of luxuries as another woman from lack of meat.

NANCY — Maybe. But it's rather disconcerting to reach down into your — depths and touch bottom so quickly.

NICHOLS — Matey's not faltering, is he?

NANCY — No — only a trifle worried. The family budget does it. It's not precisely bulging. And today — poor dear — he's had such upsetting news — (*with a wry smile turns to Nichols*). Someone at a directors' table said, "Please pass the dividends."

NICHOLS — What a bore. (*Thoughtfully*). I wonder if I couldn't —

NANCY — (*with a grateful smile*). No — he wouldn't let you. When it comes to taking help, he's the rankest of egotists!

NICHOLS — But — (*A thoughtful pause. He looks at the portrait. His face lights up.*) Nancy — I've an idea! This portrait — it's really charming. Now Mrs. Carhart is having her usual drove of twenty or so up for the week-end. There are certain to be a few wealthy patrons of art among them, and —

NANCY — (*rises — excitedly*). Geoffrey!

NICHOLS — I'm sure that if I asked her, she'd hang it in her drawing room. One of them might want to buy it. At any rate — they'd talk — and it would be a fair test of its worth. The only difficulty is, that if they damned it, Matey would be so cast down that —

NANCY — You darling! Listen. He won't have to know anything about it! He's going into town on the 4.51 — coming out again later in the evening. . . .

NICHOLS — Yes?

NANCY — Yes — Can't we take it over right after he goes — and have it back before 9.30? They'd have plenty of time to see it. . . .

NICHOLS — I don't know why not. But — if it wasn't a go, some one of them might speak about it afterwards. . . .

NANCY — But they won't know who did it! You see

— it isn't signed! Say it's the work of an unknown painter — a protégé of Matey's — just in case — (*turns to portrait*). Oh, it's not quite dry. Suppose we had an accident with it?

NICHOLS — That's not likely — wrap it carefully. I'll drive over now and see her — come back for you about 5.30 —

Matey interrupts them and they are at some pains to allay his suspicions. He feels they have been cooking up some sort of a conspiracy. He has no real hint of their plans, however, and is pleasantly buoyant with Geoffrey, despite the financial worries he is shouldering.

When Ricky comes from the playroom, and is alone with his father, he reports Ronny's decision not to marry him. He is pretty badly cut up about it, but he won't have his father say anything unkind to Ronny. She's feeling pretty rotten about it, too. Ronny comes in before Ricky can get away. For a second their eyes meet, and then Ricky dashes down the stairs.

RONNY — (*hesitantly*). Mr. White —

MATEY — (*kindly — moves toward her*). Yes, Ronny. . . .

RONNY — Ricky — told you? (*Matey nods, unable completely to hide his scorn.*)

MATEY — You don't love him, h'm — ?

RONNY — (*passionately*). Love him. Oh — if a year ago someone had told me that I'd ever love anyone as I love Rick now, I'd have — (*She cannot go on.*)

MATEY — Then I fail to see why you've —

RONNY — I'll tell you why. If I told him, he'd just laugh me out of it. Give me your word no one else shall know — no one at all. . . .

MATEY — (*after a pause*). Very well — my word.

RONNY — I'm standing between Ricky and the thing he wants to do. That's plain. If I don't marry him, he'll go abroad and study as he should. *You* know what it means to him. *You* know he *must* be what he's cut *out* to be!

MATEY — You dear child. . . . (*He picks up her hand and touches his lips to it.*)

RONNY — (*taking it from him at once*). Oh — please — that's *Ricky's* trick!

MATEY — You're very brave, Ronny, and very fine — but it's useless, because —(*She shakes her head violently.*) We can't afford to send him abroad, now. (*Ronny straightens up, puzzled and shocked.*)

RONNY — Wha—a — a — t . . . ?

MATEY — I am not a rich man. I depend largely upon my salary. It stopped when I left business.

RONNY — But you've *something* — and I only need half of what I have a year. Take the other half — put it with whatever *you* can. I'd be happier — *much.*

MATEY — My dear. . . . But there's been bad news, you see. I've almost nothing, now — not even enough for Nancy and me.

RONNY — (*cruelly*). Then why don't you go back to business? (*Matey flinches, in spite of himself.*)

MATEY — One has — certain obligations to oneself — you know. (*Ronny squares off — a cold fury.*)

RONNY — I've just taken my heart and (*with a gesture of breaking it between her hands*) done *that* with it. For him — for my Ricky. And you can stand there talking about yourself. Aren't you his father? Aren't you responsible for him?

MATEY — (*genuinely moved, but smiling a little*). You are telling me I've given hostages to Fortune?

RONNY — (*impatiently*). I don't know anything about "hostages." I just know that there's something big in Ricky, that's got to come out. You can help him — and because you *can* you *must.* He's your son — you've let yourself in for it. (*This is too much; Matey's spirit is up at last.*)

MATEY — Listen to me; your reasoning's very bad. You say I'm responsible for Ricky. All right — I'm responsible for bringing him out of nowhere into a very lively, very interesting world — for giving him twenty-one years of every advantage a boy can have. Now why shouldn't I think of myself for a while?

RONNY — When all that time you've been teaching him to love something aren't you bound to stick by him till he shows what he can make of it?

MATEY — He had his chance.

RONNY — And now that it's gone, must he wait till he's — forty, or so — for another? (*This shot tells.*)

MATEY — (*doggedly*). Why not? That's what *I* did.

RONNY — So — you want everything — to be for him — just as it's been for you —

MATEY — (*sharply*). Please! Please!

RONNY — Only *you* had Mrs. White in its place. He'd have nothing: I'd feel like a thief. You're used to doing what you don't want to. He's not. He'd be just — empty.

MATEY — He can quit now — and do what he wants on his own.

RONNY — And so he would! But could he go abroad? Could he be all he might be?

MATEY — That's up to him.

RONNY — It's up to — Oh, we *can't* argue, can we? What makes my reasons right for me, is just what makes them wrong for you.

MATEY — That's the old and the young of it, Ronny.

RONNY — (*swiftly*). But there's one thing we jibe on.

MATEY — Yes.

RONNY — Both of us love Ricky. What you won't do for duty, you *will* do for love!

MATEY — (*with a gesture toward his painting*). Do you know how I love this?

RONNY — Not half so much as Ricky! He's your son. He'll come first!

MATEY — (*whimsically*). You haven't convinced me, Ronny. But you've reminded me that there's a very cruel law that rules most men's destinies.

RONNY — (*an avalanche*). *Not* only *man's!* (*She shuts her eyes in pain, swallows hard, shakes her head as if to shake something out of it, and then raises her chin sharply. Nancy appears at the top of the stairs, carrying a large piece of brown wrapping paper and a ball of cord.*)

NANCY — Matey — your train. . . . (*Ronny wheels about and confronts Nancy. For a moment we feel that she is about to attack her as she attacked Matey. But when her voice is heard it is the voice of a heart-broken little girl, trying her best to be spunky to the end.*)

RONNY — Doing anything special Monday morning?

NANCY — (*puzzled*). Why, no. . . .

RONNY — If I may, I want to come over —

NANCY — Do. . . .

RONNY — And cry on your shoulder.

NANCY — But what has happened . . . ? (*Ronny flings her last words over her shoulder as she goes down the stairs.*)

RONNY — I'll be in about eleven! (*Nancy, bewildered, looks after her for a moment and then turns to Matey.*)

NANCY — Matey — what *is* it . . . ?

MATEY — (*grimly*). A joke on me — one of fate's funniest. . . .

MATEY — (*Matey crosses toward the stairs, shaking his head and laughing softly and bitterly.*) Laugh, my dear — laugh at me. . . .

(*Nancy is gazing at him intently as the curtain falls.*)

ACT III

It is nine o'clock the same evening. The scene is still the studio. There are the remains of a buffet lunch on a long table at back, and through the window may be seen the faint glow of Japanese lanterns swung for the party in the Duane's garden.

Nancy and Geoffrey Nichols are hurrying as quietly as possible to get Matey's picture back on its easel before Matey himself returns from town and misses it. The picture has been to Mrs. Carhart's and back, and there is a rumor to the effect that it has found a purchaser. Mrs. Carhart is to phone particulars within the half hour.

She is much too old to be as excited about anything as she is about Matey's possible success, Nancy insists, but she does her best to keep hold of her nerves. She is thankful for one thing — the dinner had gone off beautifully, with Ricky playing up to the situation manfully, and even humorously, for all his heart was leaden.

Now Matey has come — a little late because his train had decided to be "more local than usual"— but in fairly good spirits.

NANCY — How did you find things in town?

MATEY — Pretty bad. It took another slump today. I told Hubbard to sell four hundred shares at ten o'clock Monday. Well — no use grousing over it, I suppose.

NANCY — Not the slightest. Let's forget it till we *have* to think —

MATEY — That's been our method with most disagreeable things, hasn't it?

NANCY — Um.

MATEY — And we've marched along pretty damn splendidly, haven't we?

NANCY — (*nodding*). I'm so glad contentment hasn't caught us — and wrapped us in cotton-wool. We'll never be quite content, you and I. So we'll never be dead until they shut our eyes, and fold our hands.

MATEY — And even then I dare say our spirits will go

on poking about the heavenly shrubbery — looking for birds that may be there!

NANCY — Darling — it's the way to live. (*Another furtive glance at the stairs.*) But it plays simple havoc with your nerves. . . . (*Suddenly.*) Matey — tell me you love me.

MATEY — Child! I abominate you.

NANCY — Ah — very satisfactory.

Now Nichols is back from the telephone. Mysteriously he summons Nancy to the head of the stairs and there they hold a loudly sibilant conversation.

NICHOLS — Ssss-s-s-s — Pss – ssh — Pscpssch —

NANCY — Not *really!* But I never *heard* of anything so remarkable!

MATEY — (*approaching them*). Here — what's this? Why not include the smaller nations in the conference?

NANCY — (*motioning to him behind her back*). Go away! (*They whisper more earnestly. Matey returns to the sofa.*)

MATEY — What *have* you two got up your sleeves?

NICHOLS — (*over Nancy's shoulder*). A white rabbit, now. It *was* a white elephant.

MATEY — Hmm — sounds more like a wild turkey, to me. (*Nancy and Nichols join hands, and keeping perfect step march over to a position in front of Matey. Matey speaks to them indulgently.*) Yes, my little ones — what can I do for you?

NANCY — (*at once timid and exultant*). Maitland — Geoff and I have something to tell you. . . .

MATEY — Fancy that, now. (*Nancy turns imploringly to Nichols.*)

NANCY — I *won't* have my biggest moment ruined by such crass stupidity.

NICHOLS — Really, old son — we've three columns of news.

MATEY — Um. Newspapers bore me.

NANCY — (*in desperation*). Matey — we've sold your picture.

NICHOLS — Not quite *sold*, but —

NANCY — At any rate, we've got an offer for it.

MATEY — Well, well — isn't that nice? (*He sighs.*) Come on — we might as well get it over with: Who has made the offer? (*Nancy appeals to Nichols. He laughs.*)

NICHOLS — The truth is, that we don't *know* who!

NANCY — Well — we took the portrait over to Mrs. Carhart's. Geoff had arranged with her to hang it in her drawing-room, and show it to everyone before dinner — said it was by a protégé of yours. Then, just before you arrived, her chauffeur brought it back, and with it a message saying that she'd phone before nine-thirty. That was Geoff's call, and —

MATEY — (*confused*). But — who — ?

NICHOLS — That's what we don't know. It was her butler who phoned. Said she was sending the — prospective purchaser here to see me now.

NANCY — And it's probably either Kendall or the Ewings! They were both there. And it's an out-and-out offer —

NICHOLS — A handsome one, Matey — four thousand dollars.

MATEY — Four thousand dollars — for the work of an unknown modern?

NICHOLS — I made him repeat it three times. Not, of course, that I doubted its worth. . . .

MATEY — Oh no — certainly not — of course not. But — (*in sudden buoyancy*). I say! — He must have *liked* it, h'm . . . ? (*He gathers Nancy to his side with one sweep of his arm, and grasps Nichols' hand.*) Oh — you bully good people! I wouldn't trade you for any other two on earth!

Matey tries not to be too jubilant. And he tries to

feel sure his work has been bought by some one who knows painting. He is, at first, ready to make a little ceremony by signing the portrait. Now that it's sold, and on its merits, there is no need for continuing the artist's anonymity. But Nancy advises against it. Everything looks all right — but there is still a chance there "might be a slip —'twixt the offer and the cheque." So the ceremony is postponed.

For the moment they are all in high spirits — until the appearance of Ricky reminds them of his unhappy adventure with love. Ricky has come to tell Nancy that Ronny wants to talk with her.

NANCY — I — don't think I care to see her now. . . .

RICKY — Off that, dearest. If Ronny wants to change her mind, why that's her privilege. I'll expect you to be just as nice to her as you possibly can be. And by that, I don't mean any of your well-known politeness at ten below zero. . . .

MATEY — I haven't yet told you how sorry I am about this.

RICKY — (*smiling*). Oh — it's not everyone has *your* luck getting married.

NANCY — Come here, Rick — (*He goes to her and she takes his face between her hands and kisses him.*) Tell Ronny to come up. (*Ricky hugs her, drops his head upon her shoulder for a moment, and then looks up, smiling brightly.*)

RICKY — Thanks, old precious — thanks. (*He goes out.*)

NANCY — Matey — he makes me ache all over.

MATEY — Our own good fortune seems nothing when I think of it.

NANCY — He'll get over it, of course — they always do. But a thing like this takes the sweetness out of a boy. It hardens him — makes him shrewd — metallic. (*Exclaims in pain.*) Oh — the poor darling! (*Flam-*

ing into anger against Ronny.) And all along I've thought that Ronny's air of inconsequence was merely an overlay to many things fine, and true —

MATEY — My dear — it *is* —

NANCY — This looks it, doesn't it? — This parody of love!

MATEY — It's hardly that, Nanny. And you must be very careful with her.

NANCY — (*coldly*). And why should I be?

The coming of Ronny interrupts her. She, too, is dressed for the party. "She wears a long dress of peacock blue satin, brocaded with silver, a silver girdle and silver slippers. Binding her hair is a slim bandeau of pearls. It is the costume of a seventeenth century court. She looks considerable older — a charming woman of, say, twenty-six." Matey is struck by the picture she makes.

MATEY — Van Dyck might have painted you.

RONNY — I wish he had. I'd like it better — if I were — just stuck up somewhere. . . . (*To Nancy.*) I hadn't a chance at dinner — I wanted to be sure that — you weren't hating me too much —

NANCY — I'm afraid I am very old-fashioned. Forgive me — but I find it difficult to regard jilting with anything but — distaste.

MATEY — (*an entreaty*). *Ronny — ?*

RONNY — All right — only Ricky mustn't know.

MATEY — (*to Nancy*). Ronny told me something this afternoon. She told me a number of things. One of them was the motive for what she has done. She loves him very much. Rightly or wrongly, she felt that she was keeping him from the thing — from a perhaps notable career. So she broke her engagement, and gave him a trumped up reason for it.

NANCY — (*incredulously*). She could do *that!* When I — ? Oh — (*She stands with her head bowed.*)

MATEY — (*he must say something*). No doubt she's placed too much importance upon it. She's — (*Nancy turns to Ronny.*)

NANCY — Ronny — I think I am one of the few mothers who consider the girl their son loves really good enough for him.

RONNY — (*barely audible*). You're very kind. But —

NANCY — (*with a gesture asking her to come to her*). Please. You make me feel very little. You are doing something that I, years ago, hadn't the courage to do. (*Ronny looks from her to Matey. Then realizes what she means.*)

RONNY — Oh — it's not at all the same, you know.

NANCY — I think it very much the same — (*Pause.*) But I don't know what to advise you. I've — had a happy life, my dear. . . .

MATEY — And so have I, Ronny — a very happy one. (*Nancy glances at him, gratefully.*)

NANCY — It's — doubtful now, whether we *could* send Ricky abroad. . . . (*Ronny looks at Matey, who looks away.*) . . . Even if he would consent to go. And it may be that you and your love could mean —

MATEY — Could mean — much more than anything else could — without them.

RONNY — As I see it, that's not the point —

MATEY — But the more I think of it, the more certain I am that —

RONNY — It's no good arguing, Mr. White. I'm sure I'm right. And you know what a stubborn little mule I am. . . .

NANCY — You've told your mother?

RONNY — That it was off? Yes. Told both of them. Father won't speak to me, and I left mother eating aspirin tablets. (*She laughs shortly.*) It's a great life.

Ronny will not listen to their sympathetic suggestions

that she may be making a mistake. After all — they *have* been happy — despite the fact that Matey had given up his career, they insist. And why shouldn't she and Ricky — But Ronny's mind is made up — that Ricky shall have his chance, and the best chance they can give him, whatever the cost to her. . . .

G. T. Warren finds the climb to the studio pretty stiff. You hear him puffing his way up the last flight of stairs under protest, and when he meets Nancy at the top he is greatly surprised. He had expected St. Peter!

G. T. has come from the Carhart's dinner. He has been wildly curious to discover what Matey has really been doing with himself. It is all right for a man to take a rest — but it isn't resting after the first six weeks — it's rotting — so far as he is concerned. However, he did not come to talk vacations.

NICHOLS — Oh yes — Mr. Warren saw the portrait, Matey — (*Dance music begins to be heard faintly, from the Duanes'.*)

MATEY — (*easily*). That's right — you were at the Carhart's, weren't you? Amusing chap — this protégé of mine. A bit erratic, of course — you know painters.

WARREN — Um.

MATEY — Oh — oh — by the way — did you hear Ewing or Kendall say anything about coming over?

WARREN — Here? No. And listen — those fellows make me tired. You should have heard them pulling your friend's picture to pieces. All about "dim cherry-askure" and "flat composition"— and all that highbrow rot. Blind as bats — both of 'em! Missing the greatest thing about it! White — I want to tell you that that picture has human interest appeal!

MATEY — (*bravely*). You — found it interesting?

WARREN — Enough to pay four thousand dollars for it!

NANCY — (*quietly*). You — are the prospective purchaser, Mr. Warren? (*Nichols returns to window. Matey nods his head reflectively, staring at the floor.*)

MATEY — H'm — very generous offer, very —

WARREN — You bet I am! Why, it's the sweetest face I ever saw! (*Rises and crosses to easel.*) This it? Ah — if that doesn't give trumps to all the Old Masters *I've* ever seen — I'll — I'll — (*He gazes at the portrait with a rapt expression, Matey brings himself heavily to his feet. Nancy edges closer to him, watching him.*)

MATEY — You say — Kendall and Ewing and the others — didn't think so much of it?

WARREN — Bah — they make me sick!

MATEY — They make *me* — a little sick. . . .

It is a blow to Matey, this "victory." Nancy, sensing his hurt, quietly grasps the hand he has swung behind his back, and soon the awful truth is revealed to them. Warren has bought the picture "to personify the Warren line," to advertise his soap and cosmetics as a unit in a monster advertising campaign, such as Matey had always insisted should be done. To do the trick, all this picture needs is a nine-point script line reading, "*The Warren Line is Purity Itself*" written across the bottom.

MATEY — Instead of the painter's signature. Yes — I can see it. G. T.— you're not aware of it — but in a way you're— uncannily like God. . . .

WARREN — (*after a pause. Surprised, then amused*). Me . . . ? God — ? Ho! Ho! Thanks for the compliment. Wonder if it wouldn't be better to put something in her hand. (*Regarding the picture.*) Art department could retouch it in — a bunch of flowers . . . or a can of talcum —

NANCY — I think, Mr. Warren, that its great charm is its — refreshing freedom from artifice —

WARREN — Well — you ought to know. You're a

woman. And it's women we want to reach. (*To Matey.*) Make the cheque out to you?

MATEY — You'd better wait. The — artist may not care to have it used for advertising purposes. I'll let you know Monday. . . .

WARREN — (*laughing*). What? Temperament? (*He goes to table and writes cheque.*) Wave this under his nose. If he's as poor as most artists, he'll soon forget his highty-tighty notions — and tell him I want to see him about doing two or three more, in different poses. Same price. . . .

MATEY — (*directly*). That, I am certain he will not consent to.

NANCY — (*softly*). Ah — you *brick!*

NICHOLS — Bravo!

WARREN — (*to Nancy*). What's that?

NANCY — I was speaking to my husband.

WARREN — Oh! (*Etta enters with a note for Matey. Warren leaves cheque on table, and rises.*) You watch — he'll come around. He'll —

MATEY — It is — the *face* you like, isn't it?

WARREN — Certainly. I don't know anything about the technique, or whatever you call it — (*Etta passes Warren, unnoticed by him.*)

MATEY — I think perhaps we — can find the model — and some proficient — *commercial* artist can do her in other poses.

WARREN — Suits me. Say now — before I go — there's one more thing —

ETTA — (*giving Matey envelope*). A message for you, sir — and *thank* you, sir.

MATEY — (*gravely*). All right, Etta. (*Etta turns to go out.*)

WARREN — (*continuing*). I'm not too well pleased with the way the Chicago — (*As she passes Warren, Etta looks up at him. He stops speaking abruptly, and his mouth drops open in amazement. He turns and *watches her as she goes out. He looks again at the portrait, then wheels about quickly, and explodes.*) White — there's something damn queer about this whole thing. Did *you* paint this picture?

MATEY — (*smiling*). G. T.! — Imagine me an artist!

WARREN — (*suddenly his face lights up in complete understanding*). Now I see it! *That's* why you left! You knew we had to advertise. You knew I couldn't find what I wanted. So you got a big idea — worked it out by yourself — and then sprang it on me! What a fellow you are!

MATEY — It's a pretty explanation,— but quite erroneous, quite —

NICHOLS — Oh, agree with him, Matey — what's the odds?

MATEY — You're quite wrong —

WARREN — Dammit, right or wrong, I want you back, and now that I've OK'd your advertising plans, you ought to be on hand to manage 'em — Well, what do you say?

MATEY — I don't know. I'll tell you that on Monday, too. If I should come back — would you agree to my having Fridays and Saturdays free the entire year round — to devote to a — hobby of mine?

WARREN — Absolutely!

MATEY — I'll think it over, and let you know.

Matey is helped in that heart-wrenching decision by a letter that comes from Greg Kendall, as good a judge of painting as any man he knows. It is "a bit of a facer," this letter, but Matey insists that Nancy shall read it to him, every word.

"Ewing and I have had a lively discussion concerning the portrait painted by your protégé," writes Kendall. "Ewing insists that it is of no consequence, but I cannot bring myself wholly to agree with him. . . . I find the technique above the average, and the brush work distinctly promising. My main objections hang upon a certain inflexibility in treatment. We do not expect a painter's early work to be individual, but such rigidity is as ominous as it is uncommon. Unless your young friend is content with a place in the ranks of the agreeably mediocre, he should devote the next three or four years to the most painstaking study under a good European master. This may, or may not, be his salvation."

There are crumbs of comfort in that letter, Matey finds. Kendall did like his brush work, and that is important. Again the hope flares in him that, with a little tutoring in town, and his Fridays and Saturdays to do with as he will —

But Nancy is not for compromises. He is not one to do things by halves. Let him go abroad, and study, seriously. They can manage somehow. They can sell the place, if necessary.

But Matey will not listen to her. Already another plan has shaped itself in his mind, a plan in which Ricky figures importantly. Now Ricky, having been summoned, comes bounding in, again strumming the guitar. He is making a brave show of high spirits, but he feels, as he frankly admits, "like holy hell."

MATEY — Rick,— how'd you like to — go abroad — as you planned? (*Ricky glances at him quickly.*)

RICKY — What! (*A thoughtful pause.*) Take the wherewithal from you? No — thanks a lot — but it can't be done. I'll manage all right in some New York office.

NANCY — That's the you in him speaking, Matey. (*Matey thinks rapidly for a moment.*)

MATEY — But I've good news for you. When you

were born, your grandfather took out an endowment policy in your name. You're supposed to get it when you're thirty — a yearly income of about two thousand for a term of five years.

RICKY — But — I'm only —

MATEY — Hubbard's the executor. This afternoon he told me that it can come to you now — provided I consider you old enough to expend it properly.

RICKY — Gosh, dad — that's knockout news —

MATEY — And if you and Ronny are careful, it's enough to take her with you, together, you'll have four thousand a year, you'll do better work than you would if you had more —

RICKY — But Ronny doesn't —

MATEY — Let me finish! Son — the happiness of a man's family can mean a lot to him — a tremendous lot. So if you've something you feel it's your destiny to do — something out of the beaten track — unusual, difficult — you'd better begin your married life doing it —

NANCY — (*quietly*). And if you don't?

MATEY — The chances are it will never be done. (*Ricky looks from one to the other, bewildered.*)

RICKY — But listen —

NANCY — (*to Matey*). Then what — ? (*For a moment Matey's head sinks. He lifts it again, smiling.*)

MATEY— Why — then I suppose — you turn philosopher.

NANCY — Philosophy — to fill an empty heart. It must be rather dreadful. . . .

MATEY — It *would* be — if one's heart *were* empty. But when it's full already — well — habit has a way of changing destinies, don't you think? (*He laughs lightly.*) How's that — for philosophy?

With a rush Ricky is off to find his Ronny, and Matey and Nancy are left facing each other with something between a great sadness and a great hope between them. The fine story Matey has made up for his son Nancy knows to be untrue.

NANCY — His grandfather did nothing of the sort.

MATEY — I know he didn't. But he wouldn't have taken it from me — not for both of them.

NANCY — Are you certain — you're acting wisely?

MATEY — Wisdom has nothing to do with love, my dear.

NANCY — (*a stilled voice*). Matey — if this is failure, it's a kind I've never seen before.

MATEY — (*brightly*). Why — you talk as though I'd given it up entirely! Didn't you hear me arrange with G. T. for time to —

NANCY — (*with a hopeless gesture*). Week-ends . . . ?

MATEY — Um. And by and by when Ricky's on his feet, and Jean is married — (*Nancy buries her head on his shoulder.*)

NANCY — (*pitying him with her whole heart*). Oh — *Matey* — you'll be nearly fifty!

MATEY — You call that old?

NANCY — (*clinging to him*). I don't like the look of this — at all. . . . (*Matey holds her to him, staring fixedly into space over her shoulder. The orchestra at the Duanes' begins to play a waltz. His face brightens.*)

MATEY — (*as briskly as he can*). Well — if we're going to the dance, I'd better get into costume. (*He blows out the candles, and Nancy turns out the lamps leaving the room lighted only by the moonlight, which faintly illuminates the small windows, and flows strongly through the great dormer upon the portrait and upon Nancy. A shaft of pale light lights the stairs from below. Matey takes one last look at the portrait and then goes to Nancy.*) What hideous disguise have you got for me?

NANCY — The usual — a matador.

MATEY — No! Tonight I shall be something different.

NANCY — But there isn't anything!

MATEY — Yes, there is — (*He picks up his smock and holds it out for her to see.*) I am going, my love — (*The smock envelopes him now, and he turns to give Nancy a full picture, as he stands there a parody of himself and his hopes*) — as an artist! (*Nancy's hand goes out to him in a little vain protest. He takes the red Spanish beret from the animal's head on the wall and sets it jauntily upon his own. He lifts "Genevieve" from the hobby horse, and takes Nancy's arm through his. The three cross toward the stairs, Matey with his head high — "Genevieve" on one arm, Nancy a tragic figure on the other — whistling the waltz with the orchestra.*)

THE END

LOYALTIES

A Drama in Three Acts

By John Galsworthy

"LOYALTIES" had created something of a sensation in London before it was bought for America by Charles Dillingham, and the bidding for it was rather lively. And yet, being distinctly British in tone and setting, there was some reason to doubt that it would prove a success in America.

For the first few weeks following its production at the Gaiety Theatre the evening of September 27, 1922, Mr. Dillingham had cause to question the soundness of his judgment in bringing the play over, but soon interest in it began to grow and within the month there was a steady capacity demand which continued, practically, through until spring.

No other play of the year created quite as interesting or quite as freely indulged a discussion as to the merits of its argument. The leading character, Ferdinand De Levis, is a young Jew, eager to make his way socially in London. Therefore his assertion of his reasonable deserts, contrasted with the explanations of his social "superiors" justifying their own varying attitudes, makes for an always interesting, and frequently impressively dramatic, story.

At Meldon Court, near Newmarket, the Charles Winsors are entertaining a house party during the racing season. The opening scene is Mr. Winsor's dressing room, the hour about eleven thirty at night. It is a plainly furnished room, with a balcony window—similar in form and appearance to a string of other bedrooms strung along a hall in the same left wing.

The party has scattered to its respective rooms. The Winsors, about to retire, are recalling casual impressions of the day. Lady Adela, for one thing, doesn't know exactly how to take young De Levis, who, Winsor admits, is a bounder for luck, and rich as Crœsus. Not only had De Levis won two races that day, but his bridge luck in the evening had been unusual. And he looked "exactly as if he'd sold me a carpet when I was paying him," reports her ladyship. Which, according to Winsor, isn't surprising — seeing the young Jew's father had been a carpet wholesaler in his day.

WINSOR — Ronny Dancy took a tenner off him, anyway, before dinner.

LADY A.— No! How?

WINSOR — Standing jump onto a bookcase four feet high. De Levis had to pay up, and sneered at him for making money by parlor tricks. That young Jew gets himself disliked.

LADY A.— Aren't you rather prejudiced?

WINSOR — Not a bit. I like Jews. That's not against him — rather the contrary these days. But he pushes himself. The General tells me he's deathly keen to get into the Jockey Club. It's amusing to see him trying to get round old St. Erth.

The Dancys have the room next the Winsors, Lady Adela explains; De Levis is in the room beyond them and Margaret Orme at the end of the hall, "with only one bath to wash the four of them!" Which is one of the mistakes made with the left wing when it was built.

Lady Adela has just gone to her own room when there is a knock on Winsor's door and young De Levis appears. He is "clad in pyjamas and flowered dressing-gown. He is a dark, good-looking, rather eastern young man. His face is long and disturbed."

The facial disturbance of the moment is caused, it transpires, by De Levis' discovery that he has been robbed of nearly a thousand pounds in Bank of England notes.

He had that day sold his Rosemary filly and the bookie who bought her had paid him cash. He had the money in his wallet. When he was getting ready for bed he had taken it out, counted it, put it back and shoved the wallet under his pillow, while he went to have a bath. When he returned, fifteen minutes later, he had found the money gone and the wallet stuffed with shaving papers, though his door was still locked as he had left it.

The Winsors are stunned, and secretly resent De Levis' veiled suggestions that possibly some of the other guests may know something about it. Anyway, a thousand pounds is a lot of money and he would like to have it back.

WINSOR — Look here, De Levis! This isn't an hotel. It's the sort of thing that doesn't happen in a decent house. Are you sure you're not mistaken, and didn't have them stolen on the course?

DE LEVIS — Absolutely. I counted them just before putting them under my pillow; then I locked my door and had the key here. There's only one door, you know.

WINSOR — How was your window?

DE LEVIS — Open.

WINSOR — You've got a balcony like this. Any sign of a ladder or anything?

DE LEVIS — No.

WINSOR — It must have been done from the window, unless someone had a skeleton key. Who knew you'd got that money? Where did Kentman pay you?

DE LEVIS — Just round the corner in the further paddock.

WINSOR — Anybody about?
DE LEVIS — Oh, yes!
WINSOR — Suspicious?
DE LEVIS — I didn't notice anything.
WINSOR — You must have been marked down and followed here.
DE LEVIS — How would they know my room?
WINSOR — Might have got it somehow.

The butler, Treisure, is called and questioned. He furnishes, in addition to a none too subtle sneer or two at De Levis' accusation, what he believes to be complete alibis for all the servants.

The other guests are told. They are all a little shocked at De Levis' insistence upon pressing the charge, particularly his determination to see that the police are called.

General Canynge, "a slim man of about sixty, very well preserved, intensely neat and self-contained," is, however, of the opinion that under the circumstances that is the only thing to do. But even De Levis can see how distasteful the action is to Canynge and Winsor. Suddenly his anger flares.

"You seem to think —" he begins, hesitates, and continues: "What was I to do? Take it lying down and let whoever it is get clear off? I suppose it's natural to want my money back?"

"Canynge looks at his nails; Winsor out of the window," as Winsor assures the young man he perfectly understands.

Margaret Orme, "a vivid young lady of about twenty-five in a vivid wrapper," and the Dancys, come in. To Miss Orme the adventure is simply gorgeous. The Dancys, however, take it more seriously. Mabel Dancy is "a pretty young woman with bobbed hair, fortunately, for she has just got out of bed, and is in her nightgown and a wrapper."

WINSOR — Awfully sorry to disturb you, Mrs. Dancy; but I suppose you and Ronny haven't heard anything. De Levis' room is just beyond Ronny's dressing-room, you know.

MABEL — I've been asleep nearly half an hour, and Ronny's only just come up.

CANYNGE — Did you happen to look out of your window, Mrs. Dancy?

MABEL — Yes. I stood there quite five minutes.

CANYNGE — When?

MABEL — Just about eleven, I should think. It was raining hard then.

CANYNGE — Yes, it's just stopped. You saw nothing?

MABEL — No.

DANCY — What time does he say the money was taken?

WINSOR — Between the quarter and half past. He'd locked his door and had the key with him.

MARGARET — How quaint! Just like an hotel. Does he put his boots out?

LADY A. — Don't be so naughty, Meg.

CANYNGE — When exactly did you come up, Dancy?

DANCY — About ten minutes ago. I'd only just got into my dressing-room before Lady Adela came. I've been writing letters in the hall since Colford and I finished billiards.

CANYNGE — You weren't up for anything in between?

DANCY — No.

MARGARET — The mystery of the grey room.

DANCY — Oughtn't the grounds to be searched for foot-marks?

CANYNGE — That's for the police.

DANCY — The deuce! Are they coming?

CANYNGE — Directly.

A moment later Inspector Dede is announced, and the second scene shifts to De Levis' bedroom.

The setting is the same, though the furnishings are different from those of Winsor's room. Here, for the benefit of the inspector, De Levis again goes over his story of taking his money from his suit-case (where he first had hidden it in a shoe), putting it under his pillow, locking the room and going to the bath, followed by his discovery of the robbery a quarter of an hour later.

The inspector's cross-examination and his deductions are alike ponderous and amusing. He questions the servants, inspects carpets and fittings with his magnifying glass, tries all the keys of adjoining rooms, to the further humiliation of the Winsors, and finally gives it as his opinion that "the thief walked in before the door was locked, probably during dinner, and was under the bed. He escaped by dropping from the balcony — the creeper at that corner (*pointing to the left*) has been violently wrenched. I'll go down now," he continues, "and examine the grounds, and I'll see you again. Good-night, gentlemen."

Winsor accompanies the inspector, and they are barely out of the room before De Levis turns quickly to General Canynge with the somewhat startling assertion that he (De Levis) knows the thief.

CANYNGE — The deuce you do! Are you following the inspector's theory?

DE LEVIS — That ass! (*Pulling the shaving papers out of the case.*) No! The man who put those papers there was clever and cool enough to wrench that creeper off the balcony, as a blind. Come and look here, General. (*De Levis points stage right.*) See the rail of my balcony, and the rail of the next? (*He holds up the cord of his dressing-gown, stretching his arms out.*) I've measured it with this. Just over seven feet, that's all! If a man can take a standing jump onto a narrow bookcase four feet high and balance there, he'd make nothing of that. And look here! (*He goes out on the balcony and returns with a bit of broken creeper in his hand, and holds it out into the light.*) Someone's stood on that — the stalk's crushed — the inner corner too, where he'd naturally stand when he took his jump back.

CANYNGE — That other balcony is young Dancy's, Mr. De Levis; a soldier and a gentleman. This is an extraordinary insinuation.

DE LEVIS — Accusation.

CANYNGE — What!

DE LEVIS — I have intuitions, General; it's in my blood. I see the whole thing. Dancy came up, watched me into the bathroom, tried my door, slipped back into his dressing-room, saw my window was open, took that jump, sneaked the notes, filled the case up with these, wrenched the creeper there for a blind, jumped back, and slipped downstairs again. It didn't take him four minutes altogether.

CANYNGE — This is outrageous, De Levis. Dancy says he was downstairs all the time. You must either withdraw unreservedly, or I must confront you with him.

DE LEVIS — If he'll return the notes and apologize, I'll do nothing — except cut him in the future. He gave me that filly, you know, as a hopeless weed, and he's been pretty sick ever since, that he was such a flat as not to see how good she was. Besides, he's hard up, I know.

CANYNGE — It's mad, sir, to jump to conclusions like this.

DE LEVIS — Not so mad as the conclusion Dancy jumped to when he lighted on my balcony.

CANYNGE — Nobody could have taken this money who did not know you had it.

DE LEVIS — How do you know that he didn't?

CANYNGE — How do you know that he did?

DE LEVIS — I haven't the least doubt of it.

CANYNGE — Without any proof. This is very ugly, De Levis. I must tell Winsor.

DE LEVIS — Tell the whole blooming lot. You think I've no feelers, but I've felt the atmosphere here, I can tell you, General. If I were in Dancy's shoes and he in mine, your tone to me would be very different.

CANYNGE — I'm not aware of using any tone, as you call it. But this is a private house, Mr. De Levis, and something is due to our host and to the *esprit de corps* that exists among gentlemen.

DE LEVIS — Since when is a thief a gentleman? Thick as thieves — a good motto, isn't it?

CANYNGE — That's enough! Now, look here! I have some knowledge of the world. Once an accusation like this passes beyond these walls no one can foresee the consequences. Captain Dancy is a gallant fellow, with a fine record as a soldier; and only just married. If he's as innocent as — Christ — mud will stick to him, unless the real thief is found. In the old days of swords, either you or he would not have gone out of this room alive. If you persist in this absurd accusation, you will both of you go out of this room dead in the eyes of society: you for bringing it, he for being the object of it.

DE LEVIS — Society! Do you think I don't know that I'm only tolerated for my money? Society can't add injury to insult and have my money as well, that's all. If the notes are restored I'll keep my mouth shut; if they're not, I shan't. I'm certain I'm right. I ask nothing better than to be confronted with Dancy; but, if you prefer it, deal with him in your own way — for the sake of your *esprit de corps*.

CANYNGE — 'Pon my soul, Mr. De Levis, you go too far.

DE LEVIS — Not so far as I shall go, General Canynge, if those notes aren't given back.

With the accusation flatly made there is nothing to

do but send for Dancy. General Canynge explains to the captain that they are all trying to avoid the scandal spreading and questions him as to his having any theories. Dancy is as much in the dark as any of them. He had not heard anything of the sale of De Levis' filly at the tracks and cannot suggest anyone who might have known of it. He turns quickly at the suggestion of a sneer in De Levis' voice, but General Canynge, putting his hand on his arm, restrains him. as Dancy turns quickly and walks out on the balcony.

The inspector can find no trace of footprints below the window, nor marks a ladder might have made. It's a bit of a puzzle, he admits. He will take the numbers of the missing bank notes, if he can get them from the bookmaker who bought the horse at the track, and follow the trail from that end.

In the recapitulation of evidence running through Winsor and Canynge's minds after the inspector leaves, one ugly fact stands out to confront them.

"Winsor," says the General, "Dancy's sleeve was wet!"

It had been raining about the time De Levis is positive his money was taken. But surely there must be some explanation for Dancy's having been out in it. Meantime, De Levis must be kept quiet. They call him from the window.

CANYNGE — (*with cold decision*). Young Dancy was an officer and is a gentleman; this insinuation is pure supposition, and you must not make it. Do you understand me?

DE LEVIS — My tongue is still mine, General, if my money isn't!

CANYNGE — Must not. You're a member of three clubs, you want to be member of a fourth. No one who makes such an insinuation against a fellow-guest in a country house, except on absolute proof, can do so without complete ostracism. Have we your word to say nothing?

DE LEVIS — Social blackmail? H'm!

CANYNGE — Not at all — simple warning. If you consider it necessary in your interests to start this scandal — no matter how, we shall consider it necessary in ours to dissociate ourselves completely from one who so recklessly disregards the unwritten code.

DE LEVIS — Do you think your code applies to me? Do you, General?

CANYNGE — To anyone who aspires to be a gentleman, sir.

DE LEVIS — Ah! But you haven't known *me* since I was a boy.

CANYNGE — Make up your mind.

DE LEVIS — (*after a pause*). I'm not a fool, General. I know perfectly well that you can get me outed.

CANYNGE — (*icily*). Well?

DE LEVIS — (*sullenly*). I'll say nothing about it, unless I get more proof.

CANYNGE — Good! We have implicit faith in Dancy.

There is a moment's encounter of eyes; the General's steady, shrewd, impassive; Winsor's angry and defiant; De Levis' mocking, a little triumphant, malicious. Then Canynge and Winsor go to the door, and pass out.

DE LEVIS — (*to himself*). Rats!

The curtain falls.

ACT II

Three weeks later four members of a prominent London club are playing bridge in the card room. They are Lord St. Erth, "an old John Bull," and prominent in the direction of the club's affairs; Augustus Borring, "an essential clubman"; General Canynge and Charles Winsor.

The talk is desultory, the game ditto, until De Levis' name is mentioned. The filly he had from Dancy for practically nothing and sold for the thousand pounds of which he was robbed has just won the Cambridgeshire stakes at nine to one, and the gossip is that De Levis is pretty well cut up about it. The fact that he has also been blackballed by another club has not added to his peace of mind.

Presently Major Colford, "a lean and moustached cavalryman," bursts into the room. He has come from the billiard room — where he has just heard De Levis revive the story of his lost money and openly make the assertion that it was Captain Dancy who had robbed him at Winsor's.

With the approval of Lord St. Erth, General Canynge sends for De Levis. Dancy also is reported in the club and the General asks that he be diplomatically kept within reach until something is done about the De Levis charge.

That young man sends word back to General Canynge that he has nothing to add to what he has said before, and is summarily re-summoned. "Kindly tell him," instructs the General, "that if he wishes to remain a member of this club he must account to the committee for such a charge against a fellow member."

When De Levis does come in he is in a "highly-colored not to say excited state."

De Levis — Well, General Canynge! It's a little too strong all this — a little too strong.

Canynge — (*calmly*). It is obvious, Mr. De Levis, that you and Captain Dancy can't both remain members of this club. We ask you for an explanation before requesting one resignation or the other.

De Levis — You've let me down.

CANYNGE — What!

DE LEVIS — Well, I shall tell people that you and Lord St. Erth backed me up for one club, and asked me to resign from another.

CANYNGE — It's a matter of indifference to me, sir, what you tell people.

ST. ERTH — (*drily*). You seem a venomous young man.

DE LEVIS — I'll tell you what seems to me venomous, my lord — chasing a man like a pack of hounds because he isn't your breed.

CANYNGE — You appear to have your breed on the brain, sir. Nobody else does, so far as I know.

DE LEVIS — Suppose I had robbed Dancy, would you chase him out for complaining of it?

COLFORD — My God! If you repeat that —

CANYNGE — Steady, Colford!

WINSOR — You make this accusation that Dancy stole money in my house on no proof — no proof; and you expect Dancy's friends to treat you as if you were a gentleman! That's too strong, if you like!

DE LEVIS — No proof? Kentman told me at Newmarket yesterday that Dancy did know of the sale. He told Goole, and Goole says that he himself spoke of it to Dancy.

WINSOR — Well — if he did?

DE LEVIS — Dancy told you he didn't know of it in General Canynge's presence, and mine. (*To Canynge.*) You can't deny that, if you want to.

CANYNGE — Choose your expressions more nicely, please!

DE LEVIS — Proof! Did they find any footmarks in the grounds below that torn creeper? Not a sign! You saw how he can jump; he won ten pounds from me that same evening by betting on what he knew to be a certainty. That's your Dancy — a common sharper!

Canynge — (*nodding towards the billiard room.*) Are those fellows still in there, Colford?

Colford — Yes.

Canynge — Then bring Dancy up, will you? But don't say anything to him.

Colford — (*to De Levis*). You may think yourself damned lucky if he doesn't break your neck.

But De Levis is calmly defiant. He knows that he is "marked for Coventry," but there will be some satisfaction in taking Dancy with him. It is Lord St. Erth's conclusion that he must be a very rich man. "A jury is likely to take the view that money can hardly compensate for an accusation of that sort."

When Dancy and De Levis again face each other Lord St. Erth repeats to Dancy De Levis' charge. Dancy replies with an offer to settle the matter "with any weapons, when and where he likes." An invitation that De Levis sneeringly declines, and one that St. Erth admits cannot settle anything. If De Levis will not retract, the courts must be appealed to. De Levis is ready to argue, but not to retract.

De Levis — If you were downstairs all the time, as you say, why was your door first open and then shut?

Dancy — Being downstairs, how should I know? The wind probably.

De Levis — I should like to hear what your wife says about it.

Dancy — Leave my wife alone, you damned Jew!

St. Erth — Captain Dancy!

De Levis — Thief!

Dancy — Will you fight?

De Levis — You're very smart — dead men tell no tales. No! Bring your action, and we shall see.

(*Dancy takes a step towards him, but Canynge and Winsor interpose.*)

St. Erth — That'll do, Mr. De Levis; we won't keep

you. (*He looks round.*) Kindly consider your membership suspended till this matter has been threshed out.

DE LEVIS — (*tremulous with anger*). Don't trouble yourselves about my membership. I resign it. (*To Dancy.*) You called me a damned Jew. My race was old when you were all savages. I am proud to be a Jew. *Au revoir*, in the courts.

There is a tone of triumphant defiance in his voice as he leaves the room. A little worried, the others take up the subject of court action, and are somewhat puzzled by Dancy's lack of eagerness to press it, for the honor of the club, if nothing else. "I might prefer to look upon the whole thing as beneath contempt," ventures the Captain, as he leaves them. Only Colford is strong in his defense of the accused.

WINSOR — Colford! (*A slight pause.*) The General felt his coat sleeve that night, and it was wet.

COLFORD — Well! What proof's that? No, by George! An old school-fellow, a brother officer, and a pal.

WINSOR — If he did do it —

COLFORD — He didn't. But if he did, I'd stick to him, and see him through it, if I could.

(*Winsor walks over to the fire, stares into it, turns round and stares at Colford, who is standing motionless.*)

COLFORD — Yes, by God!

The scene changes to the sitting room of the Dancy's flat. Mabel Dancy is there, hearing for the first time the story of the De Levis accusation against her husband. Margaret Orme is relating the scandal with gusto and obvious effect. Little Mrs. Dancy is quite bewildered. In the first place it is so utterly silly, and, in the second, why had her Ronald failed to take her into his confidence? She must telephone him — and have him home at once.

While she is telephoning Lady Adela Winsor calls. It is quite evident from her manner that she shares something of the doubt of her husband regarding the Dancy defence and is not at all sure what the outcome of a suit for defamation of character might be.

It is Miss Orme's opinion, however, that it would be at least "frightfully thrilling!" and that as a witness she would look wonderful in black georgette with an ecru hat.

Lady Adela — Oh! Why did I ever ask that wretch De Levis? I used to think him pathetic. Meg — did you know — Ronald Dancy's coat was wet? The General happened to feel it?

Margaret — So that's why he was so silent.

Lady A.— Yes; and after the scene in the club yesterday he went to see those bookmakers, and Goole — what a name!— is sure he told Dancy about the sale.

Margaret — (*suddenly*). I don't care. He's my third cousin. Don't you feel you *couldn't*, Adela?

Lady A.— Couldn't what?

Margaret — Stand for De Levis against one of ourselves?

Lady A.— That's very narrow, Meg.

Margaret — Oh! I know lots of splendid Jews, and I rather liked little Ferdy; but when it comes to the point —! *They* all stick together; why shouldn't we? It's in the blood. Open your jugular, and see if you haven't got it.

Lady A.— My dear, my great grandmother was a Jewess. I'm very proud of her.

Margaret — Inoculated. (*Stretching herself.*) Prejudice, Adela — or are they loyalties — I don't know — criss-cross — we all cut each other's throats from the best of motives.

Yet, Margaret is frankly at sea herself. She knows Dancy to be one of those restless souls who simply can't live without danger. She hunted with him — and she has seen him do many mad things for the sheer delight of the risk. Then, too, she knows the Captain to have had something of a past. He always has been attractive to women — and right up to his marriage —

Mrs. Dancy is back, and shortly Captain Dancy. A little embarrassedly the callers withdraw.

Dancy's excuse for not having told his wife was his hope that, seeing De Levis again, there might be some chance of forcing him to withdraw the charge. He is disgusted with the whole thing. If she will go with him he is ready to cut the whole thing and get out to Nairobi — and let people think what they will. "I don't care a damn what people think — monkeys and cats! I never could stand their rotten menagerie!" he growls. And what satisfaction can a court action give them?

But Mabel cannot take that view. It would be too much like running away. No, the only thing they can do is to stay and fight — and find the real thief.

"Suppose I'd been accused of stealing pearls? . . . I might, just as easily. What would you think of me if I ran away from it?"

"All right," he agrees; "you shall have a run for your money. I'll go and see old Twisden!"

There is a knock at the door. It is De Levis. Mrs. Dancy begs that she be permitted to talk with him first, to which Dancy hesitantly agrees. De Levis has called, he explains, to see Captain Dancy, who, he understands, has been looking for him. He would not like the Captain to think that he (De Levis) is afraid of him.

To Mrs. Dancy's assertion that he is robbing her husband of his good name, and to her plea that, knowing his charge to be false, he withdraw it, De Levis remains cold.

MABEL — Mr. De Levis, I appeal to you as a gentleman to behave to us as you would we should behave to you. Withdraw this wicked charge, and write an apology that Ronald can show.

DE LEVIS — Mrs. Dancy, I am not a gentleman, I am only a — damned Jew. Yesterday I might possibly have withdrawn to spare you. But when my race is insulted I have nothing to say to your husband, but as he wishes to see me, I've come. Please let him know.

It is Captain Dancy's idea that he can in some way force De Levis to sign an apology. He presents it to him now, as a sort of final threat. But still De Levis stands firm. "I will sign nothing!" he says. "The charge is true; you wouldn't be playing this game if it weren't. You'll hardly try violence in the presence of your wife, and if you try it anywhere else — look out for yourself — "

"Get out of here, you swine!" shouts Dancy.

De Levis "stands a moment, irresolute," and then smilingly takes his leave.

A moment later the Dancys, his wife's reiteration of her faith in him, even though all the world may think him guilty, ringing in the Captain's ears, are on the way to the lawyer's.

ACT III

The scene is the office of the solicitors, Twisden & Graviter, Lincoln's Inn Fields. Graviter, the younger member of the firm, is in charge. Mr. Jacob Twisden is at court. The Dancy–De Levis Case has been on for several days. The town has been ringing with reports of it and the papers have been filled with the accounts.

These have attracted the attention of a Mr. Gilman, grocer, and he has called to consult with Mr. Twisden.

At Mr. Graviter's suggestion, seeing he can get nothing out of the grocer himself, he decides to wait.

The trial, as Mr. Graviter reports to Winsor and Miss Orme when they call, has been progressing favorably. Sir Frederick, who has it in hand, is pretty well through with Dancy's witnesses. He has decided at the last minute to call General Canynge, who had not previously been subpœnaed, and Winsor is a little worried.

He admits as much to Mr. Twisden a minute or two later. It rained that evening at Meldon. The General happened to put his hand on Dancy's shoulder and it was damp. And he is such a George Washington — the General. "If they should ask him, of course he would tell."

But the solicitor is not inclined to consider that particular bit of evidence serious. Of course, if Mr. Winsor feels he should warn Captain Dancy to have an explanation ready there should be no harm. . . .

The grocer Gilman has called, as he explains to Mr. Twisden, "from a sense of duty, sir, and also a feelin' of embarrassment." He had recently given change for a fifty-pound note which bore a serial number corresponding to those published by the police as having been stolen from Ferdinand De Levis.

He had it, explains Mr. Gilman, from an old customer, an Italian wine salesman named Ricardos, and in order that things might be set right, and that he might do what he could to help Captain Dancy, whose plight has excited his sympathy, Mr. Gilman has not only brought the recovered note to Mr. Twisden, but he has brought Mr. Ricardos as well.

GILMAN — As I told you, sir, I've been followin' this case. It's what you might call piquant. And I should be very glad if it came about that this helped Captain Dancy. I take an interest, because, to tell you the truth, (*confidentially*) I don't like — well, not to put too fine a point upon it — 'Ebrews. They work harder; they're more sober; they're honest; and they're everywhere. I've nothing against them, but the fact is — they get *on* so.

TWISDEN — (*cocking an eye*). A thorn in the flesh, Mr. Gilman.

GILMAN — Well, I prefer my own countrymen, and that's the truth of it.

Mr. Ricardos is quite as eager to do whatever is right as is Mr. Gilman. But his position is a trifle more complicated, and he begs a private interview with Mr. Twisden.

During this interview Ricardos admits that he had the fifty-pound note and others from a certain gentleman, a particular friend of his daughter's, in payment of a debt of honor. Pressed for the name of the gentleman he admits, reluctantly, that he was Captain Dancy, "a man of honor," to whom he had but to speak once or twice before he got the thousand pounds to which he considered his daughter was entitled.

With the truth in hand the firm of Twisden & Graviter is pretty severely shocked. Yet there is nothing to do but face it. Sir Frederick must be told before he goes on with the case. "Complete confidence between solicitor and counsel is the essence of professional honor," as Twisden explains.

Mrs. Dancy calls, groping eagerly for a word of hope. But there is little to be hoped for from the expressions of the solicitors, though they try to cheer her as best they can. As she leaves, Twisden starts off to get in touch with Sir Frederic and apprise him of the situation confronting them.

The curtain falls to indicate the passage of the night.

The next morning at ten thirty Dancy is in his lawyers'

office. He has come to learn just what Winsor has been hinting at in saying that he should be prepared to explain General Canynge's testimony if the matter of his wet coat sleeve be brought out in the testimony.

Reluctantly Twisden tells him of the visit of Ricardos and the recovery of the notes. Dancy takes the news standing and admits his guilt. He had stolen De Levis' money in a moment of bravado — to satisfy the debt of honor he owed the Ricardos girl — and to keep his wife from learning the truth.

Twisden is sympathetic and understanding. Of course Sir Frederick has but one course to follow. He will withdraw from the case the moment the court sits. But there is something he believes Dancy can do. In all probability the court will order the issuance of a warrant. There is still time for Dancy to get out of the country and avoid further humiliation. There's a war on in Morocco — why couldn't the Captain go there?

Dancy is flustered by the suddenness of the calamity that faces him. He thinks perhaps if he has a little time he can think a way out. He withdraws to an inner room. From here he overhears Canynge and Colford when they call to demand of Twisden an explanation of Sir Frederick's withdrawal from the case. Canynge is cut up about it; that isn't his idea of professional etiquette, and Colford is angry. Margaret Orme comes to offer her pearls to pay De Levis — if that will help save Dancy. But the lawyer convinces her it will not.

Dancy enters the room without their seeing him. When they turn to him he tells them he has partly made up his mind. He is going home first to clear things up with his wife. After that . . . he doesn't know. Canynge also urges him seriously to consider the Morocco suggestion as a way out. Dancy is not sure he can consider it — but he accepts a letter from the General that may help him if he decides to go.

Before he can leave De Levis is announced. He has

come, he explains, to do what he can to help straighten matters out.

DE LEVIS — (*moistening his lips*). Yes. I came to say that — that I overheard — I am afraid a warrant is to be issued. I wanted you to realize it's not *my* doing. I'll give it no support. I'm content. I don't want my money. I don't even want costs. Dancy, do you understand? (*Dancy does not answer, but looks at him with nothing alive in his face but his eyes.*)

TWISDEN — We are obliged to you, sir. It was good of you to come.

DE LEVIS — (*with a sort of darting pride*). Don't mistake me. I didn't come because I feel Christian; I am a Jew. I will take no money — not even that which was stolen. Give it to a charity. I'm proved right. And now I'm done with the damned thing. Good morning!

"He makes a little bow to Canynge and Twisden, and turns to face Dancy, who has never moved. The two stand motionless, looking at each other, then De Levis shrugs his shoulders and walks out. When he is gone there is a silence."

The curtain falls.

The scene changes to the Dancys' sitting room. Dancy has completed his confession to Mabel. It is the end, he says. But she will not give up. She will go with him — anywhere. He is on his knees before her, kissing her hand in gratitude for her loyalty.

DANCY — (*getting up and speaking*). It was a crazy thing to do; but, damn it, I was only looting a looter. The money was as much mine as his. A decent chap would have offered me half. You didn't see the brute look at me that night at dinner as much as to say:

"You blasted fool!" It made me mad. That wasn't a bad jump — twice over. Nothing in the war took quite such nerve. (*Grimly.*) I rather enjoyed that evening.

MABEL — But — money! To keep it!

DANCY — (*sullenly*). Yes, but I had a debt to pay.

MABEL — To a woman?

DANCY — A debt of honor — it wouldn't wait.

MABEL — It was — it was to a woman. Ronny, don't lie any more.

DANCY — (*grimly*). Well! I wanted to save your knowing. I'd promised a thousand. I had a letter from her father that morning, threatening to tell you. All the same, if that tyke hadn't jeered at me for parlour tricks! — But what's the good of all this now? (*Sullenly.*) Well — it may cure you of loving me. Get over that Mab; I never was worth it — and I'm done for!

MABEL — The woman — have you — since — ?

DANCY — (*energetically*). No! You supplanted her. But if you'd known I was leaving a woman for you, you'd never have married me.

Dancy admits there is danger of prosecution, of prison, in fact, and Mabel adds her pleas that he get away as soon as possible. She will come to him some way.

MABEL — Whatever happens, I'll go on loving you. If it's prison — I'll wait. Do you understand? I don't care what you did — I don't care! I'm just the same. I will be just the same when you come back to me.

DANCY — (*slowly*). That's not in human nature.

MABEL — It is. It's in *me*.

DANCY — I've crocked up your life.

MABEL — No, no! Kiss me! (*A long kiss, till the bell again startles them apart, and there is a loud knock.*)

DANCY — They'll break the door in. It's no good — we must open. Hold them in check a little. I want a minute or two.

MABEL — (*clasping him*). Ronny! Oh, Ronny! It won't be for long — I'll be waiting! I'll be waiting — I swear it.

As the bell rings a second time Dancy goes into the inner bedroom. For a moment Mabel is able to hold the officers back. But soon they are trying the bedroom door and demanding entrance.

There is the noise of a lock being turned. And almost immediately the sound of a pistol shot in the bedroom. Mabel rushes to the door, tears it open, and disappears within, followed by the inspector, just as Margaret Orme and Colford come in from the passage, pursued by the constable. They, too, all hurry to the bedroom door and disappear for a moment; then Colford and Margaret reappear, supporting Mabel, who faints as they lay her on the sofa. Colford takes from her hand an envelope, and tears it open.

"Dear Colford," it reads, "This is the only decent thing I can do. It's too damned unfair to her. It's only another jump. A pistol keeps faith. Look after her, Colford. My love to her, and you."

"Margaret gives a sort of choking sob, then, seeing the smelling bottle, she snatches it up, and turns to revive Mabel."

INSPECTOR— (*re-entering*). This is a very serious business, sir.

COLFORD — (*sternly*). Yes, Inspector; you've done for my best friend.

INSPECTOR — I, sir? He shot himself.

COLFORD — Hari-kari.

INSPECTOR — Beg pardon?

COLFORD — (*he points with the letter to Mabel*). For her sake, and his own.

INSPECTOR — (*putting out his hand*). I'll want that, sir.

COLFORD — (*grimly*). You shall have it read at the inquest. Till then — it's addressed to me, and I stick to it.

INSPECTOR — Very well, sir. Do you want to have a look at him?

Colford passes quickly into the bedroom, followed by the inspector. Margaret remains kneeling beside Mabel. Colford comes quickly back. Margaret looks up at him. He stands very still.

COLFORD — Neatly — through the heart.

MARGARET — (*wildly*). Keeps faith! We've all done that. It's not enough.

COLFORD — (*looking down at Mabel*). All right, old boy!

THE END

"ICEBOUND"

A Drama in Three Acts

BY OWEN DAVIS

A PLAY by Owen Davis called "The Detour" was a *succes d'estime* of the 1921–22 season. It told a simple story of life on a Long Island farm, and was the first attempt Mr. Davis had made to write a character comedy of the type.

Encouraged by the reception of "The Detour" he set to work on a play of New England life. "I am now turning toward my own people," he wrote in his foreword, "the people of northern New England, whose folklore, up to the present time, has been quite neglected in our theatre. I mean, of course, that few serious attempts have been made in the direction of a genre comedy of this locality.

"Here I have at least tried to draw a true picture of these people. I am of their blood, born of generations of northern Maine, small town folk, and brought up among them. In my memory of them there is little of the 'Rube' caricature of the conventional theatre. They are neither buffoons nor sentimentalists, and at least neither their faults nor their virtues are borrowed from the melting pot, but are the direct result of their own heritage and environment."

It was not an easy play to sell, after it was written. Producing managers, with considerable reason, shy at serious drama. But "Icebound" was finally bought by Lewis and Gordon, Chicago producers, who later sold an interest to Sam H. Harris in New York. The play was produced at the Harris theatre, February 10, 1923, and ran until May. It was not one of the big popular successes, but it was promptly accepted as a human and worthy drama that enriched the repertoire of the native theatre. And in the early spring it was awarded the Pulitzer prize of $1,000 as the best American play of the season.

At the opening of "Icebound" the Jordan clan has gathered at the old Jordan homestead near Veazie, Maine. It is late November, 1922. Through the windows at back "one may see a bleak countryside, the grass brown and lifeless, and the bare limbs of the trees silhouetted against a gray sky." The room in which the Jordans are gathered, being the parlor, is "as drab as the lives of those who have lived within its walls. Here we have the cleanliness that is next to godliness, but no sign of either comfort or beauty, both of which are looked upon with suspicion of being sign-posts on the road to perdition."

The Jordans are gathered because the head of the family, the mother and grandmother of those assembled, is dying in the front bedroom upstairs. They have come dutifully to pay their last respects, but as the old lady respects none of them she has neither asked to see them, nor would she know them, in her present condition, if they were to go to her.

The Jordans include Henry, the next of kin, "a heavy man of fifty; worn by his business cares into a dull sort of hopeless resignation; Emma, his wife, a stout and rather formidable woman of forty with a look of chronic displeasure; Nettie, her daughter, by a former marriage, a vain and shallow little rustic beauty; Sadie, a thin, tight-lipped woman of forty, a widow and a gossip; Orin, her son, a pasty-faced boy of ten with large spectacles; Ella, a maiden lady of thirty-five, restless and dissatisfied."

The silences that fall upon the group are a bit oppressive, broken by the sniffles of young Orin, obviously suffering from a cold in the head, and the somewhat ostentatious sighs and loyal attempts at tears on the part of the women. You have the feeling that the Jordans are, in their secret minds, agreed that Mother Jordan is at least a little inconsiderate in not dying according to a prophesied schedule. Henry is anxious to get back to his store before closing time, and the others have their various duties and their several anxieties. None, however, would think of leaving, none, in fact, would dare to leave that gathering before the expected crisis has been passed.

Dr. Curtis comes down from the sick room. He has nothing — encouraging or otherwise — to report. Mrs. Jordan is about the same. He is sending Jane to the drugstore, and leaving Hannah, the hired girl, in the sick room. They are the women he feels he can best depend upon for the careful nursing that may yet pull the old lady through. Dr. Curtis has relied mostly on Jane, during Mrs. Jordan's illness. She is a distant relative, a girl of twenty-four, named Crosby. "A plainly dressed girl of quiet manner, she has been 'driven into herself,' by the lack of sympathy and affection. She speaks usually in short sentences, and has cultivated an outward coldness that in the course of time has become almost aggressive."

Jane is much hated by the Jordans because of Mother Jordan's apparent preference for her company. "It's my place she took," Ella explains, bitterly; "in my own mother's home. I'd been here now but for her."

Emma — Just as soon as you're head of the family, Henry, you've got to tell her she ain't wanted here.

Henry — Well — I don't know as I'd want to do anything that wasn't right, she's been here quite a spell.

Sadie — Eight years.

Emma — As soon as your mother's dead, you'll send her packing.

HENRY — (*hopefully*). Grandmother lived till eighty-four. All our folks was long-lived, nothin' lasts like it used to — poor mother!

ELLA — Of course she'll divide equal, between us three.

HENRY — (*doubtfully*). Well, I don't know.

SADIE — (*rises and puts arm around Orin*). Orin is her only grand-child, she won't forget that.

HENRY — (*pats Nettie on the shoulder*). Nettie there, is just the same as my own. I adopted her legal when I married Emma.

EMMA — Of course you did. Your mother's too just a woman to make distinctions.

NETTIE — Yes, and the funny part of it is, grandma may leave me a whole lot, for all any of you know.

ELLA — Nonsense! She'll divide equally between us three, won't she, Henry?

HENRY — (*sadly*). She'll do as she pleases, I guess we all know that.

ELLA — She's a religious woman, she's *got* to be fair.

HENRY — Well, I guess it would be fair enough if she was to remember the trouble I've had with my business. I don't know what she's worth — she's as tight-lipped as a bear-trap — but I could use more'n a third of quite a little sum.

ELLA — Well, you won't get it. Not if I go to law.

EMMA —It's disgusting. Talking about money at a time like this.

HENRY — I like to see folks reasonable. I don't know what you'd want of a third of all mother's got, Ella.

SADIE — (*to Ella*). You, all alone in the world.

ELLA — Maybe I won't be, when I get that money.

SADIE — You don't mean you'd get married?

EMMA — At your age?

ELLA — (*Nettie gives a little giggle*). I mean I never had anything in all my life. Now I'm going to. I'm the youngest of all of you, except Ben, and he never was a real Jordan. I've never had a chance, I've been stuck here worse than if I was dead, fifty times worse. Now I'm going to buy things — everything I want — I don't care what — I'll buy it, even if it's a MAN.

The Jordans explode with laughter at the suggestion, but quickly remember the unfitness of the time and the place for thoughtless merriment. Back to the consideration of their own affairs they are reminded of an absent brother — young Ben Jordan, the black sheep and long the favorite of his mother. They are not greatly worried about Ben, however. He is a fugitive from justice, the only Jordan who's disgraced the men of the family in more'n a hundred years, as Henry explains. "He stands indicted before the grand jury for some of his drunken devilment. If he hadn't run away like the criminal he is, he'd be in the State's prison now down to Thomaston. Don't talk *Ben* to me, after the way he broke mother's heart and hurt my credit."

NETTIE — I don't remember him very well; mother thought it better I shouldn't come around last time he was here, but he looked real nice in his uniform. (*Emma and Henry look reprovingly at Nettie.*)

SADIE — It was his bein' born so long after us that made him seem like an outsider. Father and mother hadn't any children for years and years. Of course, I never want to sit in judgment on my parents, but I never approved of it, it never seemed quite — what I call proper.

NETTIE — Mother, don't you think I'd better leave the room?

SADIE — Not if half the stories I've heard about you are true, I don't.

HENRY — Come, come, now, no rows. Is this a time or place for spite? We've always been a united family, we've always got to be, leavin' Ben out, of course. You can't make a silk purse out of a sow's ear.

Orin doesn't see just why anyone should want to make a silk purse out of a sow's ear, even if it could be achieved. Grown folks are frequently a little silly to Orin. . . .

Jane is back with the prescription, and she has brought Judge Bradford with her. The Judge has been the Jordan solicitor for years. It is in his safe that Mother Jordan's will at the moment reposes. He could, if he would, set at rest many of the doubts and questionings that are afflicting the Jordan clan, but he is as tight-mouthed as a country lawyer can be. They learn little from him — either about their own chances or Ben's. Old Mrs. Jordan had been heard many times to say that she would cut the latter off, and she has always been a woman of her word. And then, without warning, Ben Jordan walks in, "with a smile of reckless contempt."

"He is years younger than any of the others; a wild, selfish, arrogant fellow, handsome but sulky and defiant. His clothes are cheap and dirty; he is rather pale and looks dissipated. He doesn't speak, but stands openly sneering at their astonishment."

ELLA — Ben!

JANE — (*quietly*). I'm glad you've come, Ben.

BEN — (*contemptuously*). *You* are?

JANE — Yes, your mother's awful sick.

BEN — She's alive?

JANE — Yes.

BEN — *Well* — (*Looks contemptuously about*). Nobody missing. The Jordans are gathered again, handkerchiefs and all.

HENRY — You'll be arrested soon as folks know you've come.

BEN — (*scornfully*). And I suppose you wouldn't bail me out, would you, Henry?

HENRY — (*simply*). No, I wouldn't.

BEN — God! You're still the same, all of you. You stink of the Ark, the whole tribe. It takes more than a few Edisons to change the Jordans.

ELLA — How'd you get here? How'd you know about mother?

BEN — (*looks at Jane*). She sent me word to Bangor.

SADIE — How'd you get to know where he was?

JANE — (*quietly*). I knew.

HENRY — How'd you come, you don't look like you had much money.

BEN — She sent it. (*He nods toward Jane.*) God knows it wasn't much.

ELLA — (*to Jane*). Did mother tell you to — ?

BEN — Of course she did.

JANE — (*quietly*). No, she didn't.

HENRY — You sent your own money?

JANE — Yes. As he said, it wasn't much, but I didn't have much.

BEN — (*astonished*). Why did you do it?

JANE — I knew she was going to die. Twice I asked her if she wanted to see you, and she said, "No."

HENRY — And yet you sent for him?

JANE — Yes.

HENRY — Why?

JANE — He was the one she really wanted. I thought she'd die happier seeing him.

ELLA — You took a lot on yourself, didn't you?

JANE — Yes. She's been a lonely old woman. I hated to think of her there, in the churchyard, hungry for him.

Ben, softened a little by the recital, is ready to go to his mother, but it is too late, according to Jane. She would not know him. He is of a mind to go, anyway, and when Henry tries to stop him is ready to fight his way up the stairway. He hasn't come there, standin' a chance of arrest, says Ben, to be told what he can and cannot do by Henry. As he starts for the stairs again and Henry tries to stop him, he gives that worthy a push that sends him reeling against a wall table, which falls with a crash, just as Dr. Curtis comes down the stairs, protesting and horrified at such an unseemly scene. Mother Jordan has heard their voices and been disturbed. . . . A moment later she is dead.

The announcement is a shock, even though the Jordans are well prepared to receive it. The judge and the doctor, who have known the old lady all their lives, feel it as such a death is felt in a restricted community. . . . There is nothing anyone can do. . . . All arrangements have been anticipated.

JANE — Hannah and I will attend to everything, Henry. You might come over for a minute this evening and we can talk things over. I'll make the bed up in your old room, Ben, if you want to stay.

EMMA — (*looks at Jane coldly*). Now, Henry Jordan, if she's all through givin' orders, maybe you'll begin?

ELLA — Well, I should say so. Let's have an understanding.

SADIE — You tell her the truth, Henry, or else one of us will do it for you.

HENRY — (*hesitates*). Maybe it might be best if I should wait until after the funeral.

ELLA — You tell her now, or I will.

JANE — Tell me what?

HENRY — We was thinkin' now that mother's dead, that there wasn't much use in your stayin' on here —

JANE — Yes?

HENRY — We don't aim to be hard, and we don't want it said we was mean about it — you can stay on here, if you want to, until after the funeral, maybe a little longer, and I don't know but what between us we'd be willing to help you till you found a place somewheres.

JANE — You can't help me, any of you. Of course, now she's dead, I'll go; I'll be glad to go.

ELLA — Glad?

JANE — (*turns on them*). I hate you, the whole raft of you, and I'll be glad to get away from you. She was the only one of you worth loving, and she didn't want it.

EMMA — If that's how you feel, I say the sooner you went the better.

HENRY — Not till after the funeral. I don't want it said we was hard on her.

JUDGE — (*quietly*). Jane isn't going at all, Henry.

HENRY — What's that?

ELLA — Of course she's going.

JUDGE — No, she belongs here in this house.

HENRY — Not after I say she don't.

JUDGE — Even then, because it's hers. (*Looks at Jane.*)

SADIE — Hers?

JUDGE — From the moment of your mother's death everything here belonged to Jane.

HENRY — Not everything!

JUDGE — Yes, everything — your mother's whole estate.

The resulting explosion is devastating to sensitive nerves. Ben receives the news with a bitter, cynical shout of glee. Henry can't believe it. There must be some explanation! His mother must have given some reason for such action. She must have said something!

She said many things, Judge Bradford agrees, but he doesn't like to repeat them. Still, if they insist — which Henry does —

JUDGE — Very well. The day that will was drawn, she said to me: "The Jordans are all waiting for me to die, like carrion crows around a sick cow in a pasture, watchin' till the last twitch of life is out of me before they pounce. I'm going to trick them," she said, "I'm going to surprise them, they're all fools but Jane — Jane's no fool."

BEN — (*bitterly*). No — ha-ha-ha! Jane's no fool.

JUDGE — And she went on — (*Turns to Jane.*) She said, "Jane is stubborn and set, and wilful, but she's no fool. She'll do better by the Jordan money than any of them."

ELLA — We'll go to law, that's what we'll do.

SADIE — That's it, we'll go to law.

HENRY — (*to Judge*). We can break that will, you know we can.

JUDGE — It's possible.

HENRY — Possible! You know, don't ye. You're supposed to be a good lawyer.

JUDGE — Of course, if I *am* a good lawyer, you can't break that will.

Each of the Jordans is to receive $100 from the estate. The rest of it goes to Jane. None of them can understand it, though it is Emma's opinion that it is a judgment on the lot of them for being a stuck-up, snobbish crew. "You the salt of the earth — you Jordans! You paupers!" she flings at them as she takes her daughter and her still stunned husband out of the house.

" 'Crow buzzards' mother called us," echoes Ben, as the last of them go. "The last of the Jordans — crow buzzards! And that's what we are!"

He is still bitter when the Judge reminds him that he had better think of getting away before the sheriff is after him. He can't stay in Veazie, he should know that. "I signed the warrant for your arrest myself," the Judge explains. "It has been over a year since the grand jury indicted you for arson."

The Judge has no intention of giving Ben up, but

that he is there is bound to be known and he is certain to be jailed if he stays around. Ben is ready to get out. He would like to look upon his mother first, if Jane will let him, which she does.

JUDGE —(*as Ben disappears up the stairs*). And she left him nothing. Just that hundred dollars, and only that because I told her it was the safest way to do. Sit down, Jane. I thought he was her one weakness, but it seems she didn't have any.

JANE — No.

JUDGE — She was a grim old woman, Jane.

JANE — I think I could have loved her, but she didn't want it.

JUDGE — And yet she left you everything.

JANE — I don't understand.

JUDGE — She left a sealed letter for you. It's in my strong-box. You may learn from it that she cared more about you than you think.

JANE — No.

JUDGE — There was more kindness in her heart than most people gave her credit for.

JANE — For Ben and the Jordan name, that's all. I don't understand and I don't think I care so very much. It's been a hard week, Judge.

JUDGE — I know, and you're all worn out.

JANE — Yes.

JUDGE — It's a lot of money, Jane.

JANE — I suppose so.

JUDGE — And so you're a rich woman. I am curious to know how you feel.

JANE — (*looks at Judge — half smiles*). Just tired.

When Ben comes from the death room he is visibly affected. The sight of his mother, her expression unhappy, even in death, has disturbed him. "Crow buzzards! God damn the Jordans!" he shouts. The thought of the misery they have all had a hand in causing the dead woman unnerves him.

There is a sharp ring at the bell. A moment later Jim Jay, the sheriff, has entered the room.

JIM — I'm sorry, Ben. I've come for you.

JANE — What is it?

JIM — I've got to take him, Jane.

BEN — (*turns fiercely*). Have you?

JIM — (*quietly*). I'm armed, Ben. Better not be foolish.

JANE — He'll go with you, Mr. Jay, he won't resist.

JIM — He mustn't. You got a bad name, Ben, and I ain't a-goin' to take any chances.

BEN — I thought I'd get to go to her funeral anyhow, before they got me.

JIM — Well, you could maybe, if you was to fix a bail bond. You'd take bail for him, wouldn't you, Judge?

JUDGE — It's a felony. I'd have to have good security.

JANE — Could I give bail for him? I'm a rich woman you said just now.

JUDGE — Yes.

BEN — So you're going to go bail for me. You want all us Jordans fawnin' on you for favors. Getting her money ain't enough. Well, by morning, the buzzards will be flocking around you thick. But I won't. You're goin' to hear a lot about how much folks love you, but you ain't goin' to hear it from me.

JANE — (*turns to him quietly*). Why did you come here, Ben, when I wrote you she was dying?

BEN — Why did I come?

JANE — Was it because you loved her, because you wanted to ask her to forgive you, before she died? Or was it because you wanted to get something for yourself?

BEN — (*hesitates*). How does a fellow know why he does what he does?

JANE — I'm just curious. You've got so much contempt for the rest, I was just wondering. You were wild, Ben, and hard, but you were honest. What brought you here?

BEN — (*sulkily*). The money.

JANE — I thought so. But when you saw her you were sorry, but even then, the money was in your mind — well, it's mine now and you've got to take your choice. You can do what I tell you, or you'll go with Mr. Jay.

BEN — Is that so? Well, I guess there ain't much doubt about what I'll do. Come on, Jim.

Ben thinks better of his decision the nearer he gets to the door. Arrived there he turns back to learn more of Jane's terms. She will go on his bond, she tells him, on the one condition that he will do as she says until his trial is called. That probably will not be before the spring term of court, a matter of four or five months.

JANE — You'll stay here till then, Ben; you won't leave town! You'll work the farm; there's plenty to be done.

BEN — Be your slave? That's what you mean, ain't it?

JANE — I've been about that here for eight years.

BEN — And now it's your turn to get square with a Jordan.

JUDGE — (*to Ben*). You heard the conditions? Shall I make out the bond?

BEN — Yes. (*Jane looks at him for a moment, then turns to window.*)

JANE — It's snowing.

JIM — Thought I smelled it. Well, nothing to keep us, is there, Judge?

JUDGE — No. (*Starts to write bond with rusty pen.*) This pen is rusty.

JIM — I was sorry to hear about the old lady. It's too bad. But that's the way of things.

JUDGE — (*writes*). Yes.

JIM — Well — it's early for snow. Not but what it's a good thing for the winter wheat.

The curtain falls.

ACT II

Some months later several of the surviving Jordans are gathered in the sitting room of the homestead. "This room," explains Mr. Davis, "shows some traces of a family's daily life, and to that extent is less desolate than the parlor. Although the stern faith of a Puritan makes no concession to the thing we have learned to call good taste, the old-fashioned simplicity seen in such a room as this has resulted from poverty, both of mind and purse, and has nothing akin to the simplicity of the artist. As a matter of fact your true descendant of the settlers of 1605 would be the first to resent such an implication. To them the arts are directly connected with heathen practices and any incense burned before the altars of the Graces still smells of brimstone."

Ella, the spinster, is hemming towels at the sewing machine. Sadie and her son Orin have just come in. Nettie is waiting for her father and mother, who presently arrive. They are all there to ask some favor of Cousin Jane.

If Ella had $200 she could buy a partnership in a dress-makin' business. Sadie needs money to pay her rent. Henry must have a note for $500 endorsed or suffer many humiliating experiences. Nettie can't go to Nellie Hamlin's Christmas party without a new dress.

But all the pleas, however artfully expressed, fall on deaf ears with Jane. She has helped and helped until she is wearied of ever doing any of them any good. And she is bound to prove herself worthy of Mrs. Jordan's trust by conserving the principal of the estate.

Since the night of his agreement to do as Jane tells him, Ben has worked the farm — a little resentfully, but capably, and with secret pride in the results he has achieved. He finds the "crow buzzards" in the sitting room, when he comes in from the barn, and is at no particular pains to conceal his contempt for them. Nettie he thinks a "good kid," but she is the only one to whom he is more than half civil, unless it is Jane. Whatever Ben's personal feelings toward Jane may be, he openly resents the Jordans' constant nagging and pestering of her. He's against that.

BEN — There's one way out of your troubles — one thing you could all do for a change — instead of making Jane pay all your bills — I wonder you haven't any of you thought of it.

HENRY — What could we do?

BEN — Go to work and earn something for yourselves.

SADIE — Like you do, I suppose.

EMMA — The laughing stock of all Veazie.

ELLA — Everybody talking about it — anywhere you go.

NETTIE — Jane Crosby's white slave — Jane Crosby's white slave.

BEN — They call me that, do they?

ELLA — (*to Nettie*). Why can't you ever hold your tongue?

BEN — I've been a damn fool — I'm through.

HANNAH — (*enters. To Ben*). She wants you.

BEN — Jane?

HANNAH — Yes.

BEN — I won't come.

HANNAH — There'll be another row.

BEN — Tell her I said I wouldn't come.

HANNAH — She's awful set you know when she wants anything.

BEN — You tell her I won't come.

HANNAH — (*as she goes*). Well, I don't say I don't hanker none to tell her, but I'd rather be in my shoes than in yours.

SADIE — (*to Ben*). Well, I must say I don't blame you a mite.

EMMA — If the Jordans is a lot of slaves, I guess it's pretty near time we knew it.

HENRY — She'll turn you over to Judge Bradford, Ben. He'll lock you up. It ain't going to help me none with the bank — a brother of mine being in jail.

BEN — So, they're laughing at me, are they, damn them.

NETTIE — She's coming. (*A pause and Jane enters followed by Hannah who looks on eagerly.*)

JANE — I sent for you, Ben.

BEN — I won't budge.

JANE — (*wearily*). Must we go through all this again?

BEN — I ain't going to move off this stool to-day. You do what you damn please.

JANE — I'm sorry, but you must.

BEN — Send for Jim Jay, have me locked up. Do as you please. Oh, I've said it before but this time I mean it.

JANE — And you won't come?

BEN — No.

JANE — Then I'll do the best I can alone. (*Takes chair from table and carries it up to highboy. Stands on chair and gets bottle of medicine out of cabinet.*)

BEN — (*to Jane*). What do you want with that?

JANE — It's one of the horses. I don't know what's the matter with her. She's down in her stall just breathing. She won't pay any attention to me.

BEN — Old Nellie?

JANE — Yes.

BEN — What's-cha got? (*Takes bottle from her hand and looks at it.*) That stuff's no good. Here — if you hadn't spent five minutes stalling around I might have had a better chance. (*He rushes out.*)

HANNAH — I allus said it was easier to catch flies with honey than it was with vinegar.

Now the Jordans have gone, made miserable by Jane's refusal to meet their respective needs. Of course, Emma admits, there is always the poorhouse, if the worst comes. . . .

Ben is back from "fixin' up old Nellie." Working with the horse has driven all recollection of his resentment at being called a "white slave" out of his mind. Ben likes animals. Hates to see them suffer. "I guess it's mostly because they ain't to blame for it," he figures. "I mean what comes to them ain't their fault. If a woman thinks she's sick until she gets sick, that's her business. If a man gets drunk he's got to pay for it, and he ought to. Animals live cleaner than we do, anyhow, and when you do anything for them,— they've got gratitude. Folks haven't." The more Ben thinks of it, the more he feels that he'd like farming. Leastways he would like to be around in the spring.

JANE — You'll be a big help.

BEN — I'll be in prison. (*Looks at Jane who drops head, and continues sewing.*) You forgot that, didn't you?

JANE — Yes.

BEN — What's the difference? A prison ain't just a place. It's being somewhere you don't want to be, and that's where I've always been.

JANE — You liked the army, didn't you?

BEN — I s'pose so.

JANE — Why?

BEN — I don't know. There was things to do and you did 'em.

JANE — And someone to tell you what to do.

BEN —Maybe that's it. Somebody that knew better than I did. It galled me at first but pretty soon we got over in France and I saw we was really doing something. Then I didn't mind. I got to doing what I was told and it worked out all right.

JANE — You liked France too, didn't you?

BEN — Yes.

JANE — I'd like to hear you tell me about it.

BEN — Maybe I'll go back there sometime. I don't know as I'd mind farming a place over there. Most of their farms are awful little but I don't know but what I'd like it.

JANE — Farming is farming. Why not try it here?

BEN — Look out there. (*Points out of window.*) It's like that half of the year — froze up — everything — most of all the people. Just a family by itself maybe — just a few folks good and bad — month after month — with nothing to think about but just the mean little things that really don't amount to nothing but get to be bigger than all the world outside.

JANE — Somebody must do the farming, Ben.

BEN — Somebody like the Jordans, that's been doing it generation after generation. Well, look at us! I heard a fellow in a Y. M. C. A. hut telling us how nature brought animals into the world, able to face what they had to face.

JANE — Yes, Ben?

BEN — That's what nature's done for us Jordans. Brought us into the world half froze before we was born. Brought us into the world mean an' hard so's we could live the hard, mean life we have to live.

JANE — I don't know, Ben, but what we could live it different.

BEN — They laugh over there and sing, and God knows, when I was there they didn't have much to sing about. I was at a rest camp near Nancy, after I got wounded. I told you about that French lady with all those children that I got billeted with.

JANE — Yes?

BEN — They used to sing right at the table and laugh. God, it brought a lump into my throat more than once, looking at them and remembering the Jordans.

JANE — I guess there wasn't much laughing at your family table.

BEN — Summers nobody had much time for it and winters, I guess you know —

JANE — Yes.

BEN — Just a few folks together, day after day, and every little thing you don't like about the other rasping on your nerves till it almost drives you crazy. Most folks quiet because they've said all the things they've got to say a hundred times. Other folks, talking, talking, talking about nothing. Sometimes somebody sort of laughs and it scares you. Seems like laughter needs the sun same as flowers do. Icebound, that's what we are — all of us — inside and out.

Jane does not agree with him — altogether. She can remember when she came to the Jordans to live that she laughed — laughed a lot, and was happy. She was just fourteen then, and Ben remembers she was a pretty little girl. But that's all. . . . He remembers France better, and she urges him to tell her again of his experiences in the army — especially the one about the dinner the French family with whom he was billeted gave him the night he left them.

BEN — It was a fine dinner — but it wasn't that. It was their doing so much for me. Folks like that. I sort of pictured them lots of times since then.

JANE — Go on.

BEN — All of the young ones laughing and happy, and the mother too, laughing and trying to talk to me, and neither of us knowing much about what the other was saying. (*Both laugh.*)

JANE — And the oldest daughter — the one that was most grown up?

BEN — She was scared of me somehow — but I don't know as ever I've seen a girl like her before or since.

JANE — Maybe it was that dress you told me about. Seems to me you don't remember much else about her. Not so much as what color her hair was — only just that that dress was blue.

BEN — (*very thoughtfully*). Yes.

JANE — Sometimes you say dark blue.

BEN — I guess so.

JANE — And then I say dark — as something I point out to you, that isn't dark at all — and you say, "No, lighter than that."

BEN — (*absentmindedly*). Sort of blue.

JANE — Yes, sort of blue. It had lace on it too, didn't it?

BEN — Lace? Maybe. Yes, lace.

JANE — There's more than one blue dress in the world.

BEN — Like enough. Maybe there's more than one family like that lady's but I'll be damned if they live in Veazie. Well, I might as well run out and see how the old mare is gettin' on. (*Goes to medicine chest, takes out bottle, starts for door.*)

JANE — You've got to shovel those paths for the clotheslines yet.

BEN — I know.

JANE — Well, don't forget.

BEN — It ain't likely you'll let me.

Ben is no sooner out of the room than Jane has romped gaily to the sideboard and taken out a box with a new blue dress in it. A blue dress with lace on it. Hannah catches her admiring it, and a part of her secret must be told. "It wouldn't be fair for me to wear it just yet," Jane admits. "It'll be like I'd sort of set a trap and I don't want it that way. Just now it seems like I might have a right to wear it pretty soon. I've been waiting a long time, Hannah — ever since I was a little girl, and it scares me to think that maybe I'm going to be so happy."

It being her birthday Jane thinks she is justified in doing a little something to brighten up everybody. They can at least have a special dinner and a cake, and —

She hurriedly puts the blue dress away in the sideboard, and shoves the empty box under the table when she hears the bell. Judge Bradford is calling. Jane is particularly anxious to talk to the Judge. She wants him to promise, among other things, that he will get Ben off — that he will fix it so the boy will not have to go to prison.

The Judge is hardly prepared to do that. For one thing it would be compounding a felony. For another — well, as a judge of the circuit court he could hardly mix up in such a proceeding. But — for Jane — of course the Judge would do almost anything for Jane.

JUDGE — You — you love Ben — Jane?

JANE — When you told me that day that Mrs. Jordan had left me all her money — I couldn't understand. Do you know what was in that sealed letter you gave me, the day after she died?

JUDGE — No.

JANE — I want to read it to you. (*Takes out portfolio, takes out letter and reads*):

"*My dear Jane:* The doctor tells me I haven't long to live, and so I'm doing this, the meanest thing I think I've ever done to you. I'm leaving you the Jordan money.

Since my husband died, there has been just one person I could get to care about — that's Ben, who was my baby so long after all the others had forgotten how to love me, and Ben's a bad son and a bad man. I can't leave him the money — he'd squander it, and the Jordan money came hard."

JUDGE — Poor woman. It was a bitter thing for her to have to write that.

JANE — (*continues reading*):

"If squandering the money would bring him happiness I'd face all the Jordans in the other world and laugh at them, but I know there's only just one chance to save my boy. Through a woman who will hold out her heart to him and let him trample on it as he has on mine."

JUDGE — Jane!

JANE — "Who'd work and pray and live for him until, as age comes on, and maybe he gets a little tired, he'll turn to her, and you're that woman, Jane. You've loved him ever since you came to us, although he doesn't even know it. The Jordan name is his — the money yours, and maybe there'd be another life for you to guard. God knows it isn't much I'm leaving you, but you can't refuse it because you love him. I'm a wicked old woman. Maybe you'll learn to forgive me as time goes on. It takes a long time to make a Jordan." (*Drops letter on table.*) Then she just signed her name.

JUDGE — Is the damnable thing she says there, true?

JANE — Yes, Judge.

JUDGE — And you're going to do this thing for her?

JANE — No — for him.

JUDGE — (*rising*). He isn't worth it.

JANE — I guess you don't understand.

JUDGE — No. (*Starts to put on overcoat and muffler.*)

JANE — You can't go like that — angry. You have to pay a price for being a good man, Judge. I need your help.

JUDGE — You mean — he needs my help.

JANE — Yes, and you'll have to give it to him if what you said a little while ago is true.

JUDGE — (*after a pause*). It *was* true, Jane. I'll help you.

The Judge is on his way to the village and Jane thinks she will walk along with him. There are some things she wants to buy for her birthday "party"—a blue ribbon, for one thing, such as the girls in France wear in their hair.

With Jane and the Judge gone Ella and Nettie come down from upstairs. They may not have been spying, but they are much amused at Jane's apparent interest in the Judge. Still, he probably is the best she could expect to do in Veazie. . . .

Now they have found — first, the empty box, and then the dress in the sideboard drawer. It is a prettier dress than either of them has ever seen before — just such a dress as Aunt Ella has wanted all her life; just such a one as she might have bought for herself if the Jordan money had been left to those to whom it rightfully belonged. "Some folks would say a dress like that wasn't decent," admits Ella; "but I wouldn't care. Not if it was mine."

It is just such a dress, too, as Nettie would love to wear to Nellie Hamlin's party. They are still admiring it when the bell rings. Ella goes to the door. Nettie, still fascinated with the dress, starts to put it back in the drawer, hesitates, and finally runs out of the room with it.

Young Orin was ringing the bell. His mother had told him he was not to act as though he belonged there any longer, and he had come, formally, as it were, to bring Jane a note.

Jane, back from the store, discovers the note to be the expected request that she pay Sadie's rent. Being happy herself, Jane writes the check; and another check for two hundred dollars and gives it to Ella, that she may buy an interest in the dressmaking business. The shock is great to Ella, but she survives it. Dressmakin', come to think of it, ain't much of a business, anyway.

Neither does Ben find Jane's gay spirits particularly infectious. He's tired, he has chilblains, and he's going to prison in the spring. So far as he can see there is not much joy in life. Briefly, Jane feels the depression of his mood.

JANE — I'm lonesome to-night. We always made a lot of birthdays when I was a girl.

BEN — Some do.

JANE — Your mother didn't. She found me once crying, the day I was fifteen. I remember how she laughed at me.

BEN — All the Jordans have got a sense of humor.

JANE — She wasn't a Jordan — not until she married your father.

BEN — When a woman marries into a family, she mostly shuts her eyes and jumps in all over.

JANE — Your mother was the best of the whole lot of you. Anyway, I think so.

BEN — I know it. I always thought a lot of her in spite of our being relations.

JANE — She loved you, Ben.

BEN — She left me without a dollar, knowing I was going to State's prison. And what I'd be by the time I got out.

JANE —Maybe some day you'll understand why she did it.

BEN — Because she thought you'd take better care of the money than any of the rest of us.

JANE — And you hate me because of that — the way all the rest of the Jordans do.

BEN — Sometimes.

JANE — I suppose it's natural.

BEN — But I ain't such a fool as Henry. (*Looks around. Notes it is getting dark. Goes to bracket lights and turns two on.*) — and the women folks. They think you took advantage and fooled her into what she did. I thought so at first — now I don't.

JANE — What do you think, Ben?

BEN — She watched you — she knew you were worth more than all of us in a lump. I know it too, but someway it riles me worse than if you wasn't.

JANE — That's silly.

BEN — Don't you suppose I know what you've been doing to me? Trying to make a man out of me? Trying to help me? Standing up to me and fighting me every day. Trying to teach me to be decent? Working over me like I was a baby or something and you was trying to teach me how to walk? Getting me so upset that every time I don't do what I ought to do, I get all het up inside? I never was so damned uncomfortable in all my life.

JANE — And I never was so happy.

God may have known what he was about when He made women, Ben admits, but he is not sure. He gave them all the best of it, anyway. But Jane takes issue with him on that statement. He may think she has been having an easy time of it, but she hasn't. It has not been easy trying to keep the old farm paying for itself. "The Jordans have been taking their living out of this soil for more than a hundred years," she says, "and never putting anything back."

"Just themselves, that's all," admits Ben.

And the pity of it is that something could be done with the old place if anyone would take hold of it.

He is sure of that — and Jane is sure he is the man for the job. But he has only a month before he will have to be going to jail.

BEN — I'm as good as convicted as I sit here. I've only got a month.

JANE — Then help me for that month. We could plan how to start out in the spring. I've got books that will help us and I could get more. We could do a lot.

BEN — If you want me to, I'll help you as long as I'm here.

JANE — Will you shake hands on that?

BEN — What for?

JANE — Oh, just because we never have.

BEN — We ain't going to change everything, are we?

JANE — One thing. We're going to be friends. (*Ben turns and takes her hand awkwardly.*)

BEN — You're a good sport. Game as a man — gamer maybe.

JANE — (*rising*). And now for the surprise.

BEN — The what?

JANE — You'll see. I want you to sit right here until I open these doors.

BEN — (*looking into the fire*). I wasn't thinkin' of movin.'

JANE — Just sit right there.

BEN — And do what?

JANE — Think.

BEN — What of?

JANE — Oh, anything — so long as it's pleasant. Of the spring that's coming.

BEN — In the prison down at Thomaston.

JANE — Of France, then — of the family that was so good to you — of the beautiful lady — of the daughter if you want to, the one that's most grown up. Just shut your eyes and think till I come back. (*Goes through dining room door.*)

Ben is still looking after her, wonderingly, when the hall door opens and in steps Nettie — wearing the blue dress and looking a picture in it. Turning at her call Ben is startled, then fascinated, by the picture. He rises and stands looking at her.

BEN — You sort of scared me, Nettie. I just been talkin' about France and pretty things, and women dressed like you are now. I never saw you before somehow. Why, you're a woman, Nettie! I never knew that you'd grown into a woman.

NETTIE — Of course I had — you stupid.

BEN — God, how sick I am of women dressed in black. Of folks that wear mourning on their backs and not inside of them.

NETTIE — I knew you'd like it. I put it on for you. Then I waited out there till I knew she'd gone.

BEN — If you knew how sick I was of just seeing ugly things.

NETTIE — (*takes step toward Ben*). You've been in trouble, Ben. I'm so sorry for you.

BEN — I give up — beat.

NETTIE — Oh, Ben.

BEN — (*comes close to Nettie*). Then you came — you pretty little thing.

NETTIE — Oh, Ben. You've been lonesome.

BEN — You don't know how lonesome — nobody knows. You pretty little kid. All dressed in blue, so soft and warm.

NETTIE — (*Ben takes her in his arms*). Don't Ben!

BEN — You pretty kid.

NETTIE — Just one then. (*Ben kisses her and as he does so, Jane enters through the dining room door and sees them.*)

JANE — (*bursting into room*). Supper's ready — (*Sees Ben and Nettie embraced and stops. Nettie disengages herself from Ben's arms.*)

NETTIE — I'm ashamed about wearing your dress, Cousin Jane. It was so pretty, I'll take it right off.

JANE — You needn't. I guess I don't want it any more. Supper's ready, Ben.

The curtain falls.

ACT III

Two months later the Jordans are again draped about the parlor as they were the day of Mother Jordan's funeral. They have gathered on this occasion at Jane's request. It is early spring and through the windows the prospect is less dreary than in the fall. The room has been brightened somewhat, too, by the removal of the slip covers that formerly hid the furniture. The Jordans are a little resentful of this change. The parlor never was a cheerful room, Ella admits, but as Henry says, "A parlor's a place where a person's supposed to sit and think of God, and you couldn't expect it to be cheerful." It is Sadie's idea that the Boston lady, lately arrived in the neighborhood, who is building a house without any parlor at all is going to have some planning to do when the first of her kinfolk dies.

The Jordans are also possessed of a great curiosity to know why Jane has asked them to come there. To meet Judge Bradford, she said. But why? Jane has been acting mighty queerly of late — snappin' everybody's head off every time any of them says anything to her. Especially Nettie. And Ben. But Ben, for some strange reason, isn't as resentful as they would expect him to be. He has just joined the group and flares out at them for their criticism of Jane.

"There ain't one of you here fit to tie her shoes," he tells them. "And I ain't. The only difference between us is I ain't worth much and I know it, and you ain't worth nothin' and you don't."

The affair between Ben and Nettie has come to nothing. They had been seen walking out together several times — but, as Nettie admits, she just couldn't bear the thought of people's laughing at her — after Ben went to jail. And he wouldn't try to get out of going to jail.

Judge Bradford arrives before Jane, but she quickly follows. And soon the Jordans know why they have been called. Jane wants to tell them of Mother Jordan's letter.

JANE — It was like she left me all her money in trust, so I could keep it safe until the time she was hopin' for came, and in a way it did come, not quite like she wanted it, but near enough so I can give up a burden I haven't strength enough to carry any more.

JUDGE — Let me finish, Jane. (*To the Jordans.*) Jane has asked me to draw a deed of gift, making the Jordan property over to Ben.

HENRY — Ben!

BEN — Why?

JANE — She wanted you to have it.

BEN — Why didn't she leave it to me then?

JANE — She was afraid to trust you.

BEN — Well?

JANE — You've learned to work, you'll keep on working. The Judge told me the wisest way to do this was to ask you all here and tell you about it — that's why I sent for you.

HENRY — You mean to say my mother wanted him to have it all?

JANE — Yes.

HENRY — I am a religious man, but there was a time when even Job gave up.

EMMA — Henry!

HENRY — So — all our money goes to Ben — and he can't even buy himself out of prison.

JANE — (*after a pause*). Ben isn't going to prison.

BEN — Why? Who's to stop it?

JUDGE — (*after a look from Jane*). Kimball agreed not to press the charge against you. It seems that there were certain extenuating circumstances. A motion has been made for a dismissal of the indictment, and it won't be opposed.

BEN — Why did he? Who fixed this thing?

JANE — Judge Bradford did. (*She looks at Judge.*)

BEN — You mean I ain't going to have to go to jail? I ain't got that ahead of me? I can stay here now? And do things — things I haven't dared to think about lately? Now I'll be here when spring comes. (*Nettie goes to Ben and takes a step. Hesitates and goes up to window. There is a pause.*)

HENRY — Well, Ben, so you got the money. I guess maybe it's better than her havin' it. After all, blood's thicker than water. We'll help you any way we can and — er — of course you'll help us.

BEN — What did you say, Henry?

HENRY — I said, of course you'll help us.

BEN — Why will I?

HENRY — We're brothers, Ben. We're all Jordans.

BEN — What was we when I got back from France? There was a band met us boys at the station. I was your brother all right, that day, only somehow, in just a little while you forgot about it. I was a Jordan when I was hidin' out from the police, and all that kept me from starvin' was the money Jane sent me. I was your brother the night mother died and you said you wouldn't go my bail.

ELLA — You ain't going to be hard on us, Ben?

BEN — I'm the head of the family now, ain't I? And you can bet all you've got I'm going to be a real Jordan.

One by one he puts them in their several places, according to that decision, and then he weakens enough to agree to endorse Henry's note — not because he loves Henry, but because it would not do him (Ben) "much good at the bank havin' a brother in the poorhouse."

He is still considerably puzzled by Jane's action and her attitude. He can't understand why she gave him the Jordan property if she didn't have to, as Judge Bradford agrees she didn't. And he can't understand why, having given it to him, she insists upon leaving.

If she wants to clerk in a pulp mill in Old Town as she says, all right. But there's no good reason why she should be leaving the house just when he will be needing her most — with all the new farm machinery and everything to order! Jane, however, is firm and goes upstairs to gather together her unpacked things. Ben stands gazing after her, a little stunned and pretty mad, while Judge Bradford looks on, his disgust thinly veiled.

BEN — Well — that's a lesson to me. Oh, she's a good woman. I ain't denyin' that — but she's fickle.

JUDGE — You're a fool, Ben.

BEN — I been doin' kitchen police around this town for quite a spell now, Judge, but from this day on I ain't going to take that sort of talk from anybody.

JUDGE — I assure you that you won't have to take any sort of talk at all from me. (*He starts for the door.*)

BEN — I didn't mean that. I don't want you to think I ain't grateful for all you've done for me.

JUDGE — (*coldly*). I have done nothing for you.

BEN — If it wasn't for you, I'd want to die. That's what I did want. I was afraid of that prison, just a coward about it. Now I'm a new man with a big life openin' out ahead of me — I've got everything in the world right here in my two hands, everything — and I owe it to you.

JUDGE — I am very glad to say that you don't owe me anything. I don't like you, I haven't forgiven you for what you did to your mother's life. Nor, for a worse thing, one you haven't brains enough to even know you've done. Don't be grateful to me, Ben, please. I think nothing could distress me more than that.

BEN — You've been a good friend to me.

JUDGE — I haven't meant to be. As I said, I don't like you. I haven't any faith in you. I don't believe in this new life of yours. You made a mess of the old one, and I think you will of the new.

BEN — No matter what you say, you can't get away from me. I'll be grateful till I die. But for you, I'd have gone to that damn prison.

JUDGE — But for Jane.

BEN — How Jane?

JUDGE — How Jane? Jane went your bond the day your mother died. Jane took you in and taught you how to work, made you work, taught you through the one decent spot in you; something of a thing you'd never know, self-respect. Worked over you, petted you, coaxed you — held you up — then you hurt her — but she kept on. She went herself to Kimball, after he had refused me, and got his help to keep you out of prison — then, against my will, against the best that I could do to stop her, she turns over all this to you — and goes out with nothing — and you ask, "How Jane?"

BEN — Why? Why has she done this, all this, for me?

The Judge is too disgusted to reply. Without further comment, he grabs his hat and stalks out the door, leaving Ben puzzled and in deep thought. He is roused by Jane's coming downstairs dressed for her trip to Old Town and carrying her hand-bag.

She tries to say good-bye to Ben, but he refuses to shake hands with her before he has certain things straight in his mind. First, why has she done all the things she has done for him? Why did she get Kimball to let him go? Why did she turn over to him the Jordan property when she didn't have to? Why did she send him her last cent so he could come home when his mother was dying? Why did she go on his bail?

JANE — Why do you think?

BEN — I don't know — I sort of thought — sort of hoped —

JANE — (*bravely*). It was because I was so fond of her.

BEN — Oh! (*Turns away disappointed.*)

JANE — You're forgetting, I guess, how long we were alone here — when you were in France — then the months we didn't know where you were, when the police were lookin' for you. She used to make me promise if ever I could I'd help you.

BEN — Well — all I got to say is you're no liar.

JANE — Good-bye. (*She turns to go.*)

BEN — Wait. (*Closes door.*) Let's see that letter you said she left you.

JANE — No. I won't do that. I've done enough — you're free — you've got the money and the farm.

BEN — They ain't worth a damn with you gone — I didn't know that till just now — but they ain't.

JANE — It's sort of sudden, the way you found that out.

BEN — Oh, it don't take long for a man to get hungry — it only takes a minute for a man to die — you can burn down a barn quick enough — or do a murder. It's just livin' and gettin' old that takes a lot of time. Can't you stay here, Jane?

Ben's pleading is rough, but direct. Nettie? Nettie never meant anything to him, really. He was lonesome and she was a girl and pretty. He wanted to kiss her and he did. That was all there was to that. And that isn't his idea of love.

Love? He doesn't even know the meaning of the

word, Jane assures him. But he means well. She is certain of that. And there is good in him, deep down, if he will try to reach it. Again she starts to go.

BEN — And so you're going to break your word?

JANE — (*hurt — turns*). Ben.

BEN — I don't know what 'twas you promised mother, but you've broke your word. No man ever needed a woman more'n I need you, and you're leaving me.

JANE — That isn't fair.

BEN — It's true, ain't it? Truth ain't always fair. You ain't helped me none, you've hurt me — worse than being broke, worse than bein' in jail.

JANE — It don't seem like I could stand to have you talk like that.

BEN — What you done, you done for her. I didn't count, I never have — not with you.

JANE — When you've been trying to do a thing as long as I have, it gets to be a part of you.

BEN — You done it all for her — well — she's dead — you'd better go.

JANE — Maybe I had, but if I do it will be with the truth between us. Here's the letter she left for me, Ben — I got a feeling somehow like she was here with us now, like she wanted you to read it. It's like she was guiding us from the grave — read it.

BEN — (*reads*). "*My dear Jane:* The doctor tells me that I haven't long to live and so I'm doing this, the meanest thing I think I've ever done to you. I'm leaving you the Jordan money. Since my husband died there has been just one person I could get to care about, that's Ben, who was my baby so long after all the others had forgotten how to love me. (*He mumbles the letter to himself, then brings out the words.*) Hold out her heart and let him trample on it, as he has on mine." (*Slowly he breaks down sobbing bitterly.*)

JANE — Don't Ben —

BEN — Look what I done to her. Look what I done.

JANE — (*hand on his shoulder*). Oh, my dear — My dear.

BEN — I did love her, more'n she thought, more'n I ever knew how to tell her.

JANE — (*kneels beside him*). It wasn't all your fault — you were a lonely boy — she never said much — she was like you, Ben, ashamed to show the best that's in you.

BEN — (*bitterly*). The best in me. I ain't fit that you should touch me, Jane — you'd better go.

JANE — Not if you need me, Ben, and I think you do.

BEN — I love you more'n I ever thought I could — tenderer — truer — but I'm no good. You couldn't trust me — I couldn't trust myself.

JANE — Spring's coming, Ben, everywhere, to you and me, if you would only try.

BEN — Can a feller change — just 'cause he wants to?

JANE — I don't want you changed. I want you what you are, the best of you, just a man that loves me — if you do love me, Ben?

BEN — Can't you help me to be fit?

JANE — I'm going to do the thing I always meant to do. Good times and bad, Ben, I'm going to share with you.

BEN — God knows I —

JANE — Hush, Ben — I don't want another promise.

BEN — What do you want?

JANE — You said I was a good sport once. You shook hands on what we'd do to bring this old place back — there's plenty to be done.

BEN — Do you think there'd be a chance for us?

JANE — Yes — a chance. I'm going to have my little time of happiness — weeks — months — a year. After that maybe you'll break my heart as you did hers, but I'm going to stay.

BEN — A good sport. (*He takes her hand.*) I'll say you're all of that. (*Hannah enters.*)

HANNAH — If you ain't careful you'll miss that train.

BEN — That's just what I want her to do.

HANNAH — You ain't going?

BEN — She ain't never going, Hannah.

HANNAH — You going to marry him?

JANE — Yes.

BEN — You bet your life she is.

HANNAH — I guess you'll be mighty happy. Marriage changes folks — and any change in him will be a big improvement. (*She takes Jane's bag and exits. Jane and Ben laugh.*)

THE END

"WHY NOT?"

A Comedy in Three Acts

By Jesse Lynch Williams

THE experiment of the Equity players in the establishment of a producing theatre has been commented upon in an earlier chapter in this volume, and need not be repeated here. It is enough to say that the third play of their season was the first to achieve popular approval. This was Jesse Lynch Williams' divorce comedy, "Why Not?" which was produced at the Forty-Eighth Street Theatre, December 25, 1922.

Even this play, wisely chosen and splendidly produced though it was by the Equity folk, did not prosper as those who were enthusiastic about it felt it should. Which frequently happens in the case of the "smart" play. It ran for eight weeks to moderate takings.

Mr. Williams is fond of the play title that propounds a query. Some years back, you may recall, he offered "Why Marry?" which was awarded the Pulitzer prize as being the best American comedy of that year.

"Why Not?" is in no sense a sequel, save that it does treat divorce with something of the same philosophic levity, superimposed upon a soundly reasoned protest against existing divorce laws and the accepted conventions surrounding the correction of marital mistakes.

"A comedy of conventions," Mr. Williams calls his play. "The two married couples in this play," he states further, "although there is a touch of phantasy in their behavior, are of a sort often met in life, though seldom on the stage. Intellectually, neither low-brow, nor high-brow. Socially, neither low-life, nor high-life— that is, they are not in the least smart, though they doubtless would be classified as society people, if they got into the newspapers. They are simple, gracious gentle-folk; too well-born, well-bred and well-disposed toward one another and the world to think much about intellectual or social position. Nor do they talk about My Sense of Humor — and thus demonstrate how little they possess. Indeed, they are rather old-fashioned. They even go to church. Nevertheless they are all good. The incongruity of this atmosphere helps to make the fun of their fantastic predicament. For this is a comedy of *human nature* versus *human institutions*."

In the library of the William Thompsons' country place, which is *not*, as the author is at particular pains to specify, on Long Island, Mary Chadwick, housemaid, is trying to help Leonard Chadwick, butler, walk and talk like a perfect representative of his station.

Mary Chadwick is a "lovely wife of about thirty-five with the low voice and quiet manners of breeding; intelligent, not brilliant. She has common sense and directness. A capable person without much 'art feeling.' "

Leonard Chadwick, a little older, is a "poet, but a 'regular fellow' despite his rather beautiful, sad eyes. Gifted, but handicapped by trying to be practical. At making money, a failure; at making love, a success. But for years he has conscientiously avoided being irresistible."

At learning to be a butler Leonard is awkward, not to say hopeless. Yet Mary is patient with him. They have, it develops, accepted these lowly positions so that their twelve-year-old daughter, Molly, may have the benefit of the country air. Leonard is a good poet, but not what used to be known as a good provider, and his practical wife has hit upon this scheme of their devoting themselves to service as a way out for the summer. "Parents don't belong to themselves," she explains; "they belong to their children. Molly could not have stood another summer in the city."

Leonard agrees that the plan is a good one and promises well. They have been engaged for Mrs. Thompson by Jane Davidge, "the usual maiden aunt who stays with the children while the master and mistress spend the usual months in the south."

The Thompsons are still away. It is Leonard's conclusion that they belong to the "new cars and second-hand ideas" set, the "great and glorious aristocracy of wealth." But Mary is willing to give them the benefit of the doubt. It is no secret in the servants' hall, however, that Mr. Thompson lives in the east wing and Mrs. Thompson in the west wing.

The discovery that they have bought both volumes of Leonard's poetry, however, quickly convinces that young man that they must, indeed, be people of taste. Not only are the books prominent upon the library table, but they have been most expensively rebound.

LEONARD — (*glancing through book*). Why, Mary! It's marked. These people actually *read* my stuff.

MARY — (*indifferently*). Which ones?

LEONARD — The love sonnets.

MARY — Oh, yes, the ones you wrote to me. (*She keeps on working, he absorbed in book.*) Leonard, while you were still a poet, I never liked to ask, but now that you're a butler, just what did you mean by "the brown and red of the waiting autumn woods." You proposed to me in a subway station.

LEONARD — What *I* never understood is why you accepted me. God knows I couldn't dedicate any butlers to you — merely books. (*Closes the book, tosses it on table.*)

MARY — You seemed so lonely and sad. I thought you needed me . . . women do so want to be needed, poor things.

LEONARD — And you seemed so young and brave. I wanted to protect you. (*He shrugs and laughs.*) Like the way I have protected you? Parlor maid?

MARY — Besides, you were just getting over one of your many golden *girls*. I thought it about time you had a wife of your own. I apologize for ruining your life, butler.

LEONARD — Mary, of all the women I ever loved there was only one I really wronged.

MARY — (*stops work and looks up*). Oh, Leonard, *you* were never dishonorable.

LEONARD — I married her. (*He kisses her hand.*)

Molly, back from school, finds her parents in the library. It is lonesome at the lodge, she explains, and it is not easy for her to understand being treated as one of the "servants' children." She is a beautiful little girl of thirteen, "unmistakably high bred," a suggestion heightened by her delicate frailness. Molly is ready to accept her parents' adventure as a sort of lark, but she is a little rebellious when they tell her that she is not supposed to play with Master Billy, the fourteen-year-old son of the Thompsons, but rather with the chauffeur's boy. But, as Molly has noted, Master Billy has a pony, and, besides, the chauffeur's boy is rough. He pulled her hair when they were coming home from school.

Right there Leonard wants to quit being a butler. He is willing to take whatever may happen to him, but no chauffeur's boy is going to be impertinent to his daughter. A summons from the front doorbell, assisted by Mary's tact, quiets his temper, however, and the Chadwick family resumes its position as the serving staff.

The caller is Churchill Smith, a "successful family lawyer, a bachelor, elderly, worldly, baldheaded and respectable — when watched. But he has a roving eye.

Being a lawyer he thinks he 'knows human nature.' " Mr. Smith has called to see Miss Davidge and he is inclined to be peevish over the discovery that Leonard, however capable a butler he may or may not be, is certainly a most impertinent young man. Leonard has dared to criticize Mr. Smith's taste in the selection of pink roses and yellow orchids for the same bouquet. The tactful Mary is able to keep the situation from reaching a climax, thanks partly to the fact that the "roving eye" of the lawyer has noted the freshness of her complexion and the comehithersome look in her eyes. He is quite distressed when she returns the tip he presses into her hand with the suggestion that he has committed another error in taste.

Smith and Miss Davidge have planned a tour of neighbouring greenhouses, but before they are started in walks Evadne Thompson and her young son. Evadne is back from the South suddenly and without her husband because, she explains, she was homesick for young Billy. But she is barely through the explanation when in walks "Big Bill," the husband. He had stuck it out a few hours without her, he explains, and then followed after. However, with Smith and Miss Davidge on their way to the greenhouses, the truer part of the story comes out.

EVADNE — Why did you come back?

BILL — To apologize, darling.

EVADNE — Sweet of you, dear. Perhaps I should apologize to *you*.

BILL — Can't blame you for skipping out, Evadne.

EVADNE — Blame my inadequate training. If I had a daughter, I would write out practical suggestions like books on golf and bridge: "What to do when your husband gets drunk."

BILL — Darling, don't say "drunk."

EVADNE — But, dearest, you *were* drunk.

BILL — It's not a nice word for a woman like you to use.

EVADNE — It's not a nice thing for a man like you to do.

BILL — I'll never do it again, Evadne.

EVADNE — So I've heard you say, Bill.

BILL — I mean it this time.

EVADNE — You always do.

BILL — Always? It's not often.

EVADNE — Not often, Bill but oftener. You didn't find it necessary to get *drunk* before you got *married.*

BILL — Just forgive me this once more. (*He holds out his hand. Evadne takes it.*)

EVADNE — Oh, I can always do that much, but I'd like — to do more.

But when he starts "the customary conjugal kiss appropriate to the occasion Evadne draws back." There is no use, she explains. There is no one to see and they would get no credit for this little acted bit of marital felicity. And Evadne is tired of the game of pretense they have been playing before their friends the last several years. They don't love each other, she tells him; they know they don't love each other and she doesn't see why they should not be truthful for a change.

Bill can't quite get her point of view. Not love each other? How ridiculous! "We must love each other. We most solemnly promised." "But we don't love each other," Evadne replies; "we most solemnly lied." Which forces Bill to the conclusion that it is high time for direct action of some sort.

BILL — Look here, Evadne. Why did you ever marry me anyway?

EVADNE — For the same reason that you married me. I didn't marry my mate, the man I loved, so I married the man I *told* myself I loved.

BILL — *Now* I see what you're driving at. Very well. You know how I detest it, but I can't *blame* you — if you want a — a divorce, Evadne. Tell me the truth.

EVADNE—(*after a pause*). First, tell *me* the truth. Is there any other woman?

BILL — There is not!

EVADNE — I was afraid of that.

BILL — You needn't be, I may drink but —

EVADNE — I was afraid there *wasn't.*

BILL — Afraid there *wasn't?* Oh, I understand. But there's plenty of other ways to get divorced.

EVADNE — No, still you don't understand. We never *do* understand each other, dear. Divorce is quite as detestable to me as to you. But if there were only some woman, some good woman, who could love you and bring out your best, not your worst — but as there isn't — (*Smiles sympathetic understanding.*) Why dear old Bill — (*Pats his arm.*) Do you think I'd turn my fellow victim loose, as things are now?

BILL — Well, that would put an end to your unfortunate marriage.

EVADNE — Would that put an end to your unfortunate drinking?

BILL — Evadne, what a little thoroughbred you are! You mean to say, if I cared for some one else —

EVADNE — Provided she were worthy of you.

BILL — You'd sacrifice yourself for my sake? Then you do love me.

EVADNE — (*cheerfully*). Not in the least, dear. If I loved you, I'd scratch her eyes out.

BILL — Oh, why *can't* we love each other! You're such a fine little thing. I admire you so. *I* don't see why I can't love you. *Honestly* I don't.

EVADNE — But as you can't, you've often thought how nice it would be if I were comfortably dead.

BILL — Evadne! How dare you attribute such thoughts to me!

EVADNE — Oh, I've had the same thoughts about you. Many married people have such thoughts.

Still Bill can't understand. Evadne has always been a good wife to him. However, if she does not love him, and is only staying married for his sake, the only decent thing he can do is to get unmarried for her sake.

But Evadne will not listen to that. There is only one person who would have any influence in making her consider a divorce, and that one — her son. Alcohol doesn't "make an ideal atmosphere for rearing children." But until it becomes a question of helping Billy, there will be no question of separation.

Big Bill and Little Bill are gone. Evadne has picked up a volume of Leonard Chadwick's poems. Her back is turned to the new butler as he enters to spread the tablecloth. He carries the table over near the sofa, and as he sets it down the noise attracts Evadne's attention. She turns, and as Leonard raises his head slowly, in apology, they stare directly into each other's eyes. For a second or two neither can speak. Then Evadne, "in growing agitation, which she controls," and in a low voice admits: "I had begun to think this never was going to happen."

LEONARD — Fifteen years.

EVADNE — No, not fifteen till October.

LEONARD — (*nodding*). The seventeenth.

EVADNE — So you have not forgotten, Leonard?

LEONARD — You were brown and red that day, Evadne, like the trees in your father's woods.

EVADNE — You remember that old sport suit? I still have it.

LEONARD — You still wear it?

EVADNE — No, out of fashion now — so much can happen in fifteen years.

LEONARD — Yes, fashions do change, don't they? (*Indicates own costume, but she has looked away.*)

EVADNE — (*change in manner, coming down to earth again*). You are a house guest of Miss Davidge?

LEONARD — I? No. Are you?

EVADNE — I? No. I live here.

LEONARD — You *live* here? (*He laughs, stops, laughs again as the irony of the situation sweeps over him.*) Well, I imagined a million manners of meeting, but never one quite like this. So *you* are the mistress of the house.

EVADNE — You didn't know that this was my house?

LEONARD — You didn't know that this was your butler?

EVADNE — My what?

LEONARD — I live here, too. I'm your butler. (*She smiles, perplexedly. He indicates his costume. She shakes head, can't understand.*) Many of your guests wear evening clothes at tea time, Evadne?

EVADNE — Seeing you put time and clothes out of my mind. Isn't this all a dream?

LEONARD — Pretty real to me.

EVADNE — Come, sit down. I'll try to understand. (*She sits, and indicates a place for him.*)

LEONARD — Butlers don't sit. Come to think of it, I never saw a sitting butler in all my life, did you?

EVADNE — Butlers obey.

So Leonard sits on the sofa, near to her, and is happy. And Evadne is happy to have him near. Yet both are consciously constrained in their exchange of reminiscences. He tells her of his many failures — principally of his failure as a provider for his family. "I could support myself on poetry," he explains, "or my wife on verse, or my child on rhymes, but there was only one of me and three of us. I couldn't do all three at once."

So he went into business — and hustled. But, someway, that didn't work out either. And finally — but

Evadne insists upon the whole story — from the beginning.

LEONARD — (*picking up book*). Well, not long after I read of your marriage —

EVADNE — That's not the *beginning*, that's the *end.* Start with that day in the woods.

LEONARD — *That* was not the beginning, Evadne, *that* was the end.

EVADNE — Why was it the end, Leonard? Why did you run away from me?

LEONARD — Don't you know why?

EVADNE — I've wondered why for fifteen years, Leonard. You had let me think you —rather liked me.

LEONARD — *Liked* you! (*Restrains himself.*) Well, you might call it that.

EVADNE — Didn't you guess that I — liked you?

LEONARD — That's why I ran away. (*She looks at him in tender amaze.*) You were so enormously rich, and I was too romantically poor.

EVADNE — And it never occurred to you that I was willing to share your poverty.

LEONARD — (*with a laugh*). You! You wouldn't have known how to be poor.

EVADNE — But you could have taught me.

LEONARD — But that would have been selfish. You could live on a tenth of the interest of your *income.*

EVADNE — I see. You consider it more honorable to marry a woman you can support than one you can love? You are what is called a gentleman.

LEONARD —I am what is called a butler, and the woman I married has to support herself.

EVADNE — Poor Leonard.

LEONARD — Poor is right.

EVADNE — Dear Leonard.

LEONARD — Dear is nice — well?

EVADNE — Oh, nothing, but — I'm glad you liked

me, anyway. All these years I was afraid you didn't.

LEONARD — Ah, Evadne, all these years —

EVADNE — You never once cared to see me?

LEONARD — Cared? I never once dared!

EVADNE — I'm glad that was it.

LEONARD — Though I'm afraid if you had ever asked me to come —

EVADNE — *I* never dared, Leonard.

A moment later Evadne learns for the first time that the new maid is not only the new maid, but Leonard's wife as well, and the meeting of the two is interesting. Mary comes, bringing the tea things, and Leonard, with his best butler manner, takes the tray from her so she will have one hand free to greet her mistress as Mrs. Chadwick.

Mary and Evadne get on famously. They are soon admiring each other extravagantly, and wondering why Leonard has never told either of the other in all the fifteen years he has been married. And now it transpires that Mary is also well acquainted with Mr. Thompson. "As soon as you said Evadne I knew it must be Bill's Evadne," she explains, "despite that portrait."

The situation grows complicated. Evadne insists that the Chadwicks shall remain as her guests. The Chadwicks are equally insistent that they prefer to remain as her servants. They need the jobs. Before a settlement can be effected Bill is back, and Churchill Smith and Jane. They, too, are naturally puzzled by the not altogether conventional actions of the new butler and maid, and Smith has not forgotten that Leonard was impertinent to him earlier in the day. Bill is distressed by the news. He must speak to Leonard. He must insist upon an apology. Servants cannot be permitted to be impertinent to house guests.

Evadne saves the situation, so far as Leonard is

concerned, by reminding Bill that the new butler, so she has been given to understand, is famous for his cocktails. And both Bill and Smith, absorbed in the preparation of a "Chadwick Cherub," known to every consistent clubman, forget the matter of the affront and expected apology.

The meeting of Bill and Mary is less romantic than that of Leonard and Evadne. After all they are practical citizens of the world. They are not poets and dreamers. Mary has come to take out the tea things. Bill looks up quickly and catches sight of her.

BILL — Mary! Good heavens! Has that cocktail gone to my head! Mary! It's fifteen years!

MARY— Well, Bill, we got it. I told you we would.

BILL — Got what?

MARY — Woman's Suffrage!

BILL — So you did.

MARY — You said we wouldn't.

BILL — So I did. What a silly thing to quarrel over, Mary.

MARY — Oh, it wasn't only that. It was what you said about the church.

CHURCHILL SMITH — The church. Which church?

LEONARD — "The" church. (*Puts tray of cocktails on table.*)

BILL — Her father was an Episcopal rector, her grandfather was a bishop, and one of her English ancestors, an archbishop.

MARY — And you are still a Presbyterian, Bill?

BILL — Certainly.

MARY — So you see it wouldn't have done.

BILL — But your husband, he can't be a churchman — he's a poet. (*Mary nods.*)

LEONARD — Sure — an Episcopalian — poet.

BILL — We were very young in those days, Mary. Ah, Mary, those days!

BILL — Of course you know you two can't be our servants, you're our guests.

LEONARD — Thank you so much. Can't afford to be guests. No money to tip the servants with.

MARY — Unless you pay us a month's wages in advance.

JANE DAVIDGE — You ought to, if you dismiss them without notice.

SMITH — (*about to go*). I shouldn't think you'd want to be a butler.

MARY — But he *never* does what he *wants* to do. He's a married man.

SMITH — Do you want to be a parlor-maid?

LEONARD — She never does what she wants to do, she's a poet's wife. I know it would be hard on you at first; ordering us about and all that, but it's wonderful what you can do when you have to! Mary has learned to order me about.

BILL — But *I* couldn't stand having Mary in *my* house — as a servant!

MARY — Bill always was tender-hearted. We'll have to leave, Leonard.

LEONARD — Then all your careful training is for nothing, Mary. Just our luck.

BILL — Of course I am going to get you a position more worthy of you.

LEONARD — But I've never proved worthy of any position I ever got except bar-tender. Come, Mary.

EVADNE — Wait! There's a cottage here on the place, down by the woods — our children could know each other — and then you could write, Leonard, write.

LEONARD — That's sweet of you, Evadne, but quite impossible. We'll have to go.

BILL — (*hesitates, delicately*). You wouldn't mind accepting a loan from us, would you?

MARY — Not in the least, if we could ever pay it back. We couldn't.

BILL — Well, what if you couldn't? Come — please!

LEONARD — I don't mind being your temporary butler, but your permanent debtor! Thank you so much.

Not even for the week end will the Chadwicks agree to stay on as guests, though Evadne adds her pleas to those of Bill. She knows they stand on dangerous ground, but she is eager to help. "My miserable money has ruined my life," she says to Leonard; "won't you let it redeem yours?" But Leonard thinks it quite bad enough to let his own wife help support him, without taking money from another man's wife.

In this mood they leave him. On the desk is a revolver that Churchill Smith had left for Jane to frighten burglars with. It occurs to Leonard that this may point a way out. He writes a note to Mary and is preparing to make it possible for her to collect his life insurance, with the gun to his head, when in she walks. A perfectly silly proceeding, she considers it.

MARY — Leonard, you ought to be ashamed.

LEONARD — Oh, I'm used to being ashamed.

MARY — You wouldn't do that.

LEONARD — But you see this butler thing was my last chance.

MARY — But think of Molly and me.

LEONARD — But you see, my life insurance is my last asset.

MARY — If you really love me, Leonard —

LEONARD — But you see, I don't.

MARY — You don't love me?

LEONARD — 'Fraid I never did, Mary. (*Mary cries gently.*) Oh yes, I do. Of course I love you. You know I do.

MARY — I know you *don't*, dear. I've known it all along.

LEONARD — Is that so? I thought I'd fooled you. Isn't that funny?

MARY — To think that you are willing to lie and even die for such an unworthy wife! I don't love you either.

LEONARD — (*wakes up*). Mary! *You* don't love *me?* Well, I'll be damned. Why, I thought of course you loved *me.* Just like a man, isn't it? But you've been such a good wife to me, Mary.

MARY — And you've been such a good husband to me, Leonard.

LEONARD — Same reason, I suppose — trying to make up for it.

MARY — Why, if we'd really loved we'd have hurt each other's feelings.

LEONARD — (*nodding*). But we didn't have any feelings deep enough to hurt. Queer, isn't it? Well, we had our chance. Missed it. Hard luck. Doesn't much matter now. *But our daughter's got to have a chance.* That's why I'm doing this. For her, not you.

MARY — But you're not going to do it. I won't let you.

LEONARD — Come, come, my dear, mustn't be sentimental. Got to look at these things practically.

MARY — (*indulgent smile*). Practically? What you propose is sheer poetry, dear.

LEONARD — Poetry! You always say I'm not practical. I'm sick of it — Oh, very well, name a more practical plan and I'll abandon mine. *That's* a fair proposition.

MARY — You promise?

LEONARD — Yes, if you'll agree to mine in case you can't.

MARY — I agree.

It is Mary's argument, first, that the life insurance would soon be eaten up; second, that for her to marry again, to "sell" herself to support Leonard's child, would be unthinkable, and, third, that if either of them should get out of the way she should be the one to go. There would be plenty of rich women for him to marry.

In the midst of their struggle for the revolver and each other's permission to die, Evadne returns. She is much calmer than they, however, for she happens to know the revolver is not loaded. And she is quite sure that they "are both perfectly silly and perfectly sweet." But, she says, there is another way out of the tangle they find themselves in. There is such a thing as *divorce!* And such a thing as *alimony*. Alimony even from an impoverished and impractical poet — if he chooses his second wife wisely. Mary is delighted with the idea. Let Leonard pick out a rich second wife and everything will be fine. But Leonard is horrified at the mere suggestion. He marry for money? He sacrifice honor, self-respect, decency?

EVADNE — If you are a real man and not a mere gentleman, you will acknowledge that such a relationship without love is worse, far worse for a woman than a man. Oh, Leonard! And you a poet!

MARY — Besides, it would be rather interesting for him to woo another woman. He hasn't tried it for so long. He's conscientious. But it'll all come back to you, Leonard. (*Leonard in speechless chagrin, turns his back.*)

EVADNE — Meanwhile Bill and I have planned to take a congenial crowd on a cruise to the South Seas, and he wants to talk to you about it. You'll find him in the trophy-room, dear.

LEONARD — Mary! Wait! This thing, Mary! You do it, please!

MARY — Sorry, darling, but the courts don't grant alimony to husbands — only to wives. You are utterly impractical! (*Exit Mary in triumph. Leonard alone with Evadne cannot look at her.*)

EVADNE — Don't think this is easy for *me*. But your life is at stake — I know just the girl for you, and I am going through with this if it kills me.

LEONARD — After scorning the woman I loved, abandon the one I respect! Marry some poor little victim I despise. And you — (*Turns and looks at Evadne.*) You of all women in the world, my go-between. Oh, Evadne!

EVADNE — Let me tell you about her first.

LEONARD — I do not care to hear.

EVADNE — She has more money than the one you scorned.

LEONARD — Oh, Evadne, please!

EVADNE — She will love you to the end.

LEONARD — I would despise her from the beginning.

EVADNE — I believe you will like her looks.

LEONARD — I am never going to see her.

EVADNE — Oh, she is coming on the cruise.

LEONARD — Then I am not going.

EVADNE — Oh, yes you are. She adores every line you've written.

LEONARD — I could never write another.

EVADNE — But it's your duty to write. The world needs poetry. Sacrifice yourself.

LEONARD — (*with finality*). No. I'm done with duty, I'm sick of sacrifice. I've had enough of this rotten world. (*Comes close.*) Come what may, cost what it will, I love you, Evadne, always you. And I shall not, cannot be untrue to you again.

EVADNE — For fifteen long years I've waited to hear those words. Oh, Leonard, can't you see, don't you understand, I am the one I meant.

LEONARD — (*in amazement*). You! You!! You!!!

EVADNE — You won't despise her, will you?

LEONARD — But, but — you're already married!

EVADNE — So are you. You aren't the *only* one who can get divorced. (*She holds out her hands. He hesi-*

tates. She puts her hand on his shoulder. Smiles.) Are you going to scorn me again because I'm richer than ever?

LEONARD — (*enfolding her*). No, my beloved, I've got you at last and I shall never, never let you go. But don't you see? This means happiness, so it must be wrong.

EVADNE — It also means duty, so it must be right.

LEONARD — But my wife! Your husband! It's so unfair.

EVADNE — Of course. We must go and confess at once. (*Mary and Bill enter. They look very seriously from one to the other. Jane enters.*)

BILL — Evadne! (*He turns from her to Mary. She takes his hand.*)

MARY — Leonard, we have come to announce our engagement, dear.

The curtain falls.

ACT II

Aunt Jane, having been, for the moment, rendered speechless by the turn the Chadwick-Thompson affair has taken, has collected herself sufficiently to telephone for Churchill Smith. He, being a lawyer, will, or at least should, know what to do.

Now Churchill has come and is listening to Aunt Jane's report. There is not much in it to give him cheer. All four of the contestants have acted perfectly delighted with the new arrangement. Evadne, reports Aunt Jane, had calmly met Mary's announcement of her "engagement" to Bill with the statement that she and Leonard had also "found great happiness" and were themselves engaged. And Bill, in place of throwing Leonard out, as Churchill would expect any he-man to do, had merely looked relieved and congratulated him.

JANE — All four of them seemed relieved, Churchill; and so brimful of pure happiness —

SMITH — Pure?

JANE — I mean impure happiness, that there was no room for the proper passion of jealousy.

SMITH —But they have no business being happy — they're married.

JANE — But they have no business being married, they're to be divorced.

SMITH — Divorced? Not in our family. Oh, it's this sudden meeting after years — gone to their heads. Bill's always tender-hearted, Evadne's always romantic; but they're good — all of 'em are good; self-respecting, self-controlled, self-sacrificing. Nothing modern or selfish about any of them. I'll soon bring them to their senses.

JANE — Then you had better be quick about it.

SMITH — Quick? They haven't skipped out already?

JANE — No, they're dressing for dinner, the poet in Bill's wing, his wife in Evadne's. But the closed car has been ordered for eleven o'clock.

SMITH — Oh-ho — elopement, eh? Evadne with the poet?

JANE — No. Bill ordered the car.

SMITH — Oh, Bill to elope with the poet's wife?

JANE — No; the poet's wife stays with Evadne.

SMITH — Then who goes with Bill?

JANE — The poet.

SMITH — What! Bill going to elope with the poet?

JANE — Nobody is going to elope with anybody. But they thought it would not be quite proper to stay under the same roof with either wife, now that each is engaged to the other's wife, so the two husbands are going in town and the two wives are to remain here and begin divorce proceedings at once. They want you to dine here and fix it up for them.

SMITH — I? Oh I'll fix it up all right. They are not going to get divorced.

JANE — How'll you prevent it?

SMITH — Oh, you'll see.

The engaged quartet goes blithely on, however, satisfied that the new arrangement will guarantee each party to the change happier than either he or she has ever been before. When they meet before dinner Leonard hooks up the gown Mary has borrowed from Evadne, regaling her the while with his greater love for his recovered mate, while Mary reassures him that to be married to Bill will fill her cup of joy quite to the brim. And yet, as Mary says, "It does seem too good to be right."

LEONARD — Mary — are you quite sure you never really loved me?

MARY — I am now — quite, quite sure.

LEONARD — Mary — we don't have to lie about *anything.*

MARY — No. We can tell the truth about *everything.*

LEONARD — Then, I think — I ought to tell you — I am feeling a slight — just a *slight* — polygamous pang.

MARY — Thank you, dear, for the delicate compliment. But you have gained character enough through monogamy to restrain it — The triumph of civilization. Now aren't you glad you've been good? For now you deserve Evadne.

LEONARD — Oh, no, I could never be good enough for *that,* Mary.

MARY — You used to have awful regrets for being good.

LEONARD — Why, Mary! How well you know me.

MARY — It was the chief regret of your married life.

LEONARD — No, my chief regret has always been that I didn't marry Evadne. Of all the women I loved before marriage, Evadne is the only one I loved *after* marriage.

MARY — Was she — indeed!

LEONARD — Yet of all the women I loved, she was the only one I never *told* I loved. That's what the poem's about, Mary.

MARY — Leonard!

LEONARD — Yes, dear?

MARY — I too feel a little pang.

LEONARD — You, too! Oh, I'm so sorry — No! Glad! These two little flaws in our happiness were all that we needed to justify it. Now at last I feel *sure* that we are doing right.

MARY — We must help each other to be true to them, dear. Here they come. Good-bye, Leonard.

LEONARD — Good-bye, Mary. The last kiss. (*She puts hand on his shoulder, he kisses her chastely on forehead and they separate.*)

Bill and Evadne enter. Again there are mutual congratulations, with Bill noticing the gown Evadne has loaned to Mary for the first time, though his own wife had worn it often, and Leonard raving over the picture that Evadne makes in her dinner gown.

At Bill's bidding Leonard makes another shakerful of the celebrated "Chadwick Cherubim" with which to toast the happy pairs. Only the return of Churchill, grown increasingly long-faced, and Aunt Jane, put so much as a slight damper upon the celebration.

They are a little undecided as to whether they should make the announcement of their intentions to Churchill before dinner or after. Before dinner would spoil his appetite, but after dinner might give him indigestion. Evadne directs the decision. First she sees that the cocktails are served at the instant they are most needed to divert Churchill's attention from his intended lecture on the sacredness of "duty," and then she shoos them all into the dining room before he can resume.

The curtain is lowered briefly. When it rises dinner is over and coffee, cigarettes and good advice are being taken in the drawing room. Churchill, who evidently has been holding forth for some time, is in possession of the floor. We catch him in the middle of a speech.

CHURCHILL — Moreover, marriage is not for the selfish benefit of the individuals concerned, but for the social benefit of civilization, which is still more concerned. The family is a unit of the state, the fundamental institution of society. At any sacrifice, the family must be saved!

LEONARD — Right. At any sacrifice the family must be saved. That's why we were driven to divorce. (*Smith, too angry for utterance, splutters.*)

BILL — Told you it'd give him indigestion. (*Jane throughout tries to agree with both sides, nods and smiles to each in turn.*)

EVADNE — Can't Leonard do more for civilization as a poet than as a butler?

MARY — Or an impractical suicide!

BILL — How'll it help the family for Mary and her child to starve to death?

MARY — Or for Bill to drink himself to death?

LEONARD — Why should our innocent children suffer for our mistakes?

EVADNE — Why should we all be miserable when we can all be happy?

MARY — Wasted, when we can all be useful?

BILL — What's the sense, Churchill? What's the sense?

SMITH — But how about your marriage vows. "Whom God hath joined together."

EVADNE — But God didn't join Bill and me together. Man did.

SMITH — What?

EVADNE — Man's semi-civilized ideas about money and matrimony. The world, not God, persuaded Bill and me that we'd make what the world calls a "*suitable match.*"

LEONARD — (*beside Evadne*). God did his best to join *us* together.

BILL — (*beside Mary*). And Mary and me.

LEONARD — Why else should God grant us humans the divine gift of love? This is what he intended in the first place. We disobeyed God.

SMITH — (*regaining his good humor*). Then pay the penalty.

LEONARD — We *have* paid the penalty — fifteen years' imprisonment.

SMITH — But marriage is a life sentence.

BILL — To be commuted by divorce — released for good behavior.

MARY — And that's all there is to it.

But, as Lawyer Smith a little testily points out, it is not all there is to it. Men can't trade wives as simply as that. Even if the law could be gotten around it would mean social and financial ruin. Bill would be thrown out of his firm.

To which Bill replies that he has little fear of that. His partner is getting a divorce himself. "But that's different," insists Smith. "A perfectly proper divorce — seduced the governess — perfectly proper — but you people — you're all good people, you have no cause for divorce."

Nor can they convince him that they are right. They may want a divorce, they may, as they say, have ceased to love each other, but the hard fact remains that their case would be thrown out of court for collusion. The law isn't interested in love or hate — it "is only interested in legality."

So they all try to concentrate on "cause." Non-support is suggested, and put aside. There is no chance of either Mary or Evadne proving, even if their respective husbands have failed to support them, that either of them ever wilfully sought to avoid his responsibilities in this particular.

They consider cruelty, and for a moment see in that charge a solution to the problem. Bill might strike Evadne in the presence of witnesses. But when he tries to do so, even with Evadne's urging, he can't bring himself to deliver the blow — and Leonard is sure he would have shot him if he had.

They simply won't consider statutory grounds, the only cause accepted in the state in which they live, because neither husband is willing to break his fifteen-year record of respectability by that sort of collusion. They had rather respect themselves than respect the law if it comes to that.

Finally they hit upon desertion. That would be a happy compromise. Let the two wives take the children and go to Reno. The husbands will stay on in Evadne's house, looking after each other, until the divorces are granted. It takes a little explaining, especially to Evadne. She doesn't quite see why the wives, in order to be deserted, have to do the deserting, but she is finally convinced, and it is agreed the wives will prepare to start immediately. They will wake up the children, take them to town for the night, do whatever shopping they think is necessary in the morning and start for Reno on the earliest possible train.

Left alone the husbands struggle with the minor problem of ordering train presents for their mates. Bill is not yet familiar with Mary's tastes, nor Leonard with Evadne's. They finally effect a second compromise by writing each other's lists.

Now the wives are dressed and ready to start when still another problem presents itself. The church enters in. Lawyer Smith is back to ask them how they are going to settle that. Mary is a devout Episcopalian. And, as Smith points out, "the Episcopal church will not marry even the innocent party to a divorce for desertion."

MARY — What grounds does the church require?

SMITH — Well — er — it's a word used frequently in the Bible and the prayer book, but not in such polite society as this. (*The four spouses exchange glances and drop them.*)

LEONARD — Speak up. You mean that either I've got to be untrue to my wife, or she's got to be untrue to her church? (*Smith nods.*) Then, of course, Mary —

BILL — Then, of course, Mary, you'll have to be a Presbyterian pro tem. It will be just as good a marriage in the eyes of the world and the eyes of the law.

MARY — This world and its laws mean nothing to the church. It's a matter of conscience, Bill. I must be married in the true church or not at all.

BILL — Oh, she'll come around.

LEONARD — You don't know this side of her, Billy. The weight of family tradition a church complex —

EVADNE — Think, Mary, think.

BILL — Think, Mary, think.

MARY — The church thinks for me. I must obey.

BILL — (*takes Leonard apart*). Don't you love your wife enough to be unfaithful to her?

LEONARD — No; I don't love her at all, but for fifteen years I've been true to her and I am not going to break my record now, simply to let her get married in a church I don't believe in.

BILL — But look here! If *we* don't get married, how are *you* going to get married? It's all up to you, old man.

LEONARD — (*to Mary*). For fifteen years I've lived for you, lied for you, and today would have died for you, but I'll be damned if I'll sin for you.

BILL — But come, you'll never see Mary again. You're under no obligation to be true to your wife now.

LEONARD — But, I tell you, even if I could bring myself to be untrue to my wife, I cannot, shall not, will not be untrue to *your* wife.

SMITH — But you don't have to be untrue to Bill's wife.

ALL — What?

SMITH — Not to her, *with* her, or else the church won't marry Bill.

EVADNE — Really, Cousin Churchill, I think your jokes have gone far enough.

SMITH — This is not a joke, this is a canonical law. (*Opens book and reads.*) "Canon Thirteen. Of Marriage and Divorce. Section eleven. No minister shall unite in marriage those divorced save for the cause of adultery."

LEONARD — (*takes Evadne's hand*). This woman and I — will not be driven into sin, even by the church!

EVADNE — That's final.

BILL — My God — then the whole thing's off.

SMITH — Yes, the whole thing's off. The church has not driven you into sin, it has kept you out — the sin of divorce. Good night. It was a daring move, but I knew my people.

For a moment there is a "ghastly silence." All four are plunged into hopeless dejection. Bill, unable to stand the strain, makes for the sideboard that looks like a bookcase and pours himself several drinks of whisky. Leonard sinks down into his chair a beaten "agnostic," an epithet Mary hurls at him to bolster her own conviction that she is doing the right thing. Downstairs the children come trooping with their wraps on. They, at least, are ready for the adventure.

MOLLY — Why, mother, you said we'd all be happy now.

BILLY — Oh, come on, hurry up.

MOLLY — Aren't we going?

MARY — No.

JANE — Then what will you do? (*No answer. To Leonard.*) Let your wife and daughter starve? (*No answer. To Evadne.*) Let your husband drink himself to death?

EVADNE — What should we do?

JANE — There's only one thing left to do.

EVADNE — What do you mean?

LEONARD — Do what the church requires?

JANE — (*to Mary*). My dear, for the children's sake, for their fathers' sake, for the sake of morality, you must forswear the church of your ancestors.

MARY — I cannot be a Presbyterian.

JANE — You don't have to be a Presbyterian.

ALL — What's that!

JANE — Get married by the Mayor!

MARY — Bill! That makes it all right — We'll do it.

EVADNE — Come, children!

JANE — Of course, divorce is the only way to save the family.

The curtain falls.

ACT III

It is late summer of the following year. The scene is again the Thompson library, slightly rearranged. For one thing a piece of tapestry now hangs over the door leading to the east wing. "Bill's books are replaced by others differently bound, and Leonard's portrait now hangs in the frame formerly filled by Bill's."

Churchill Smith and Jane Davidge are calling. It is their first visit since the happy consummation of the divorces and the remarriages that followed. Miss Davidge has just returned from a trip to Europe. To Jane it is all very sweet — "True mates . . . mismated . . . remated . . . an ideal divorce." Leonard is succeeding as a poet, at last, and Bill has quit his hard drinking and settled down to hard work. The children, too, are happy "with everything that money can buy," each little dear also enjoying "the spiritual blessings of a happy home."

But Smith is still doubtful. True, everything seems to be working out wonderfully — but — Bill has been forced out of the Douglas firm as he (Smith) predicted and Douglas has been managing Evadne's estate so badly that Evadne has been forced to close the east wing. Furthermore, all four of the ideal divorcees have been snubbed by the best people, including the Douglases. And the brazenness of it! At that very moment Evadne and Mary are lunching together at a nearby inn, where Mary and Bill have been spending their vacation "not half a mile from *his* former wife and *her* former husband," while Bill and Leonard are out on the golf links! "An ideal divorce!" he snorts. "It's idyllic!"

As though to prove him right Bill and Evadne at the moment briskly enter the room from the garden. Their manner might easily suggest to a suspicious person that they were up to something. Evadne is the first to recover from her surprise at finding Jane and Smith there, and she covers her own embarrassment by bantering Churchill. Is he trying to commit social suicide by coming to see them? What will the Douglases think of him? The nice, pure, socially elect Douglases, who have been among the first to snub the "ideal" divorces since they fixed up their own quarrel — with the seduced governess nicely installed in a handsome Riverside Drive apartment. "Mrs. Douglas is a devout churchwoman. She forgives even that for the children's sake," boasts Smith. The children should appreciate being reared "in an atmosphere of sin and mutual contempt," thinks Evadne.

With the Thompson-Chadwick children, it transpires, the situation is different.

BILL — (*to Smith*). Don't let me hurry you, but I'm due at the Inn at three o'clock. (*To Evadne.*) Sunday afternoon, I always take the youngster out riding in our — I mean, your — woods.

JANE — Your own youngster?

BILL — No, Mary's, of course.

EVADNE —Leonard's, of course. And Leonard always plays tennis with mine.

SMITH — With Bill's.

BILL — Of course.

EVADNE — Of course.

JANE — Quite a coincidence. But why not spend Sunday afternoons with their *own* youngsters?

EVADNE — Against the law. (*Almost together and*
BILL — Contempt of Court. *quite matter-of-fact.*)

JANE — To see their own children.

SMITH — The custody of the children was awarded to the mothers.

JANE — So each father is blest with the *other's* little *dear*. How sweet!

SMITH — The fathers are granted possession of the children twice a year, one month in every six.

BILL — But this is the close season.

JANE — The close season?

EVADNE — Until Christmas. Then Billy goes to his father for a month's visit and Leonard's adorable little daughter comes to us.

JANE — No doubt the change does them good — the darlings!

EVADNE — Leonard calls it the semi-annual swap.

SMITH — You are utterly shameless!

But it also appears the division of the children is not working out altogether satisfactorily. Bill misses his son more than he likes to admit. Even now he is sneaking away from Mary for a little visit with Billy before he is obliged to give the boy up again till Christmas, and he is deeply hurt when he finds that Billy is out playing tennis with his stepfather. It strikes him Leonard is a little unfair — playing tennis with Billy before three. He (Bill) never rides with Leonard's little girl before three. Furthermore he doesn't want Billy to grow up a tennis player. He wants to make a golfer — and business man — of him. But —

EVADNE — The courts gave the custody of the children to the mothers. *You* no longer have *anything to say about it.*

BILL — But Evadne. . . . I can't see him now till Christmas.

EVADNE — Oh, Bill, I'm sorry I said that.

BILL — All my fault, Evadne. A first husband has no right to damn a second husband.

EVADNE — No, my fault. A wife should never praise her second husband to her first.

BILL — Oh, you can't praise Leonard too much for me. Why, my dear, if it weren't for him, we'd still be having scenes like this every *day.*

EVADNE — Yes, for a minute there, it was quite like old times, wasn't it, "darling"?

BILL — Horribly like it, "sweetheart." But Evadne, suppose your present husband were as fond of children as I am?

EVADNE — Suppose he were, he has Billy. And Billy is such an unusual boy.

BILL — You bet he is, and your husband can see him every day whereas I, his own father — (*Going.*) Oh, well, I'll take a ride with Leonard's daughter.

EVADNE — (*indicates note still in her hand*). Wait,

Leonard says they'll be back in time for tea. Why don't you stay? Molly won't mind, just once.

BILL — Oh, Molly's a good little sport, but suppose her mother found out, she might guess the real reason why I spent my vacation here.

EVADNE — Hasn't Mary guessed it was to be near Billy?

BILL — I told her it was to be near the golf club. If Mary ever knew how much I miss the boy, it would make her very unhappy. She wants me to have everything, so I let her think that I am perfectly content with her little girl.

EVADNE — Well, that oughtn't to be difficult. Molly is a darling — she reminds me so of her father.

BILL — Just like her mother. But I'm damned if I'm going to wait six months every time I want to see my own flesh and blood.

As he steps out into the garden he turns back suddenly. If he had the time he would hide, but before he can do so Leonard and Mary enter. Mary is "radiant in a well-fitting sport suit. Love and success have wrought changes in Leonard, too. He is less tentative, more self-confident."

Mary's discovery of her second husband visiting his first wife does not surprise her in the least. As it happens she has been urging him for some time to talk with Evadne about resuming the management of her business and accepts that as his excuse for being there. It is the first time the four of them have been together since the divorce. Leonard thinks they really should be more neighborly. To Churchill Smith, however, the suggestion simply means that the divorce arrangement is not as happy as the contracting parties would like to pretend. He believes that secretly each of them would like to be married again to his or her old mate.

Churchill finds further confirmation of this thought when Evadne confesses that Leonard is about to sell the motion picture rights to his poem, "The Queen's Quest" (the buyers intending to change the title to "Passionate Females"), for $20,000, fifty per cent of the price paid his publishers, and Mary promptly advises him not to sign any such contract. No author of Leonard's standing should give up half his rights, Mary insists. Proving again that Leonard needs a practical person always near. It is plain to the lawyer that Evadne really needs Bill back to manage her estate, and Leonard needs Mary to direct his affairs. Quite soon, he thinks, they will be seeking a way of resuming their old relations, as he has predicted from the first.

Still Leonard maintains his attitude of being tremendously interested in the boy Billy, and flouts the idea that he cannot do as well by him as his own father could.

A moment later, with the room clear, Leonard is making a telephone "date" with a mysterious "dear" who is to meet him at the usual time and place while Evadne is taking her afternoon nap. But Evadne is wakeful that afternoon and catches Leonard before he can complete his arrangements. He is forced to indicate to her that he is eager to be alone with his writing.

EVADNE — (*approaching him as he sits at desk*). Make you happy to write?

LEONARD — On the contrary, it makes me write to be happy, and you make me happy.

EVADNE — Oh, how nice. Shame to waste it on your wife. By the way, I'm glad you're to see more of Mary.

LEONARD — Mary? Oh, you mean about contracts?

EVADNE — I'm not much use that way.

LEONARD — You sweet thing! What's the use of contracts when you can't write?

EVADNE — Well, you can't! When I stay here and gabble. (*She starts off, comes back, bends over him.*) Still no regrets?

LEONARD — (*laughs*). But I'll begin to think you have!

EVADNE — Oh, I have! A big one. That such a beautiful thing can't last.

LEONARD — Can't last? Why can't it?

EVADNE — Too perfect. Can't. . . . No, it simply *can't.*

LEONARD — "Where the apple reddens, never pry,
"Lest we lose our Eden, Eve and I."

EVADNE — And you're *sure* there's nothing you want outside our garden of Eden?

LEONARD — What more could I want? I have you. (*He takes her face in his hands and kisses her. She pats his hand and goes.*) Have a good nap.

EVADNE — Do some good work.

She blows him a kiss as she exits. The next moment Molly comes bouncing through the garden doors, calling her father in stage whispers, so as not to arouse the house. Now she has caught him hiding playfully behind the screen and dragged him to the sofa, where she is sitting on his knee, fixing his crooked tie. It is plain that "Leonard adores his daughter," and that she "coquettes with him, as daughters sometimes do."

MOLLY — Such a mean father, to keep me waiting outside your door like a little dog!

LEONARD — Oh, now, I couldn't help it. Your Aunt Evadne was here.

MOLLY — But I like Aunt Evadne so. Doesn't she like me?

LEONARD — Of course she does. Everybody likes you. But she must never know how much I like you. That's *our* secret.

MOLLY — Mother knows our secret. She doesn't mind.

LEONARD — Yes, but you see, your mother knows that you're an unusual child.

MOLLY — Billy knows our secret; so does his father.

LEONARD — Yes, but Billy and his father have the same secret. I take Billy to the base ball games and the movies because Uncle Bill agrees to take you. Then nobody is the wiser when we trade children.

MOLLY — Uncle Bill says Billy is an unusual boy.

LEONARD — Yes, *two* unusual children.

MOLLY — Billy and I think we have two unusual fathers. Billy and I were talking about our mothers and fathers today. We think you were all so fine and honest about the divorce.

LEONARD — About the — what a generation!

MOLLY — We decided that our parents are the only members of your generation that we really respect.

LEONARD — Well, I'm glad you approve of us.

MOLLY — But we don't. It isn't like our fathers to deceive our mothers.

LEONARD — Oh, but that's necessary.

MOLLY — No, it's sentimental. Where is Billy?

LEONARD — Out in the squash court. (*Molly gets up.*) Oh, don't go. (*Leonard rises.*)

MOLLY — I'll bring him in here.

LEONARD — Molly, I can see him every day. But this is my last chance to see you.

MOLLY — It's Billy's last chance to see his father. Uncle Bill is coming here.

LEONARD — What! Again?

MOLLY — He said you could have me only if he could have Billy. We must play fair, father.

LEONARD — Unusual fathers is right! I'll bring Billy.

They have a happy time of it, these fathers and the

children they have in a measure sacrificed to their happier marriages. Nor is it easy for the children to understand the need of all the deception. Why don't they just own up; why don't they tell Mary and Evadne that they have been getting 'round both the mothers and the law by these secret meetings with their own children.

BILL — Oh, no! This affair has gone too far to confess. You see mothers aren't like fathers, Billy, they're jealous — even the best of them.

BILLY — Oh, I see what you mean.

LEONARD — Good thing we're not jealous, Bill.

BILL — You bet. Evadne tells me you're going to make a poet of him.

LEONARD — Bill, I suppose you and Molly ride together every day out in Jersey.

BILL — Oh, yes. . . . Of course I'm not jealous, but . . .

LEONARD — Of course not, but I know what you mean.

BILL — But sometimes when you're playing tennis couldn't you just remind him — Hell! You know what I mean — tell him his father is a regular fellow.

LEONARD — On one condition. . . . Will you be on the level with me, too? (*The fathers shake hands.*)

MOLLY — Billy, was your father always so crazy about you?

BILLY — No, when he had a right to see me every day, he seldom paid any attention to me.

BILL — You're a darn liar!

BILLY — Oh, we're congenial now that I'm grown up. But when I was young I used to bore him to death. "Now run out and play, Billy."

MOLLY — I know. When I was young father used to call me a damn nuisance.

LEONARD — Molly!

MOLLY — Don't be sentimental, father. I was a

damned nuisance. . . . We lived all huddled up in a horrid little flat, and father used to rush in half crazy — "How do you expect me to write poetry with that baby squalling in the next room?"

A knock on the door startles them. Bill and Molly rush to hide in the garden. Leonard and Billy assume studious positions at the table, as though Leonard had been correcting Billy's composition.

Evadne has come to tell Leonard she is on the way to the Inn to see Mary. Discovery threatens. When she is gone the husbands plan that Bill shall take a short cut through the grounds and be home to prevent any revelations when the mothers begin comparing notes as to the absences of their respective children. But before they can do anything, Jane Davidge and Churchill Smith are again discovered descending upon them.

Bill and the children hide behind the screen. Leonard seeks nonchalantly to interest the callers. He is only partially successful. Churchill, having overheard Leonard arranging the telephone rendezvous with his "dear," and noticing the suspicious unsteadiness of the screen, is determined to expose the whole thing. Leonard, he charges, has been carrying on shamelessly with his first wife.

Leonard's guilty actions are proof that there has been something suspicious going on, and when he frankly admits there is a "she" and that he loves her, Churchill is convinced he will at last prove the whole business of collusion and divorce a complete failure. He would pull over the screen and make the exposure immediately, but he determines to let Evadne, returning from her visit to Mary, do that. Seeing Evadne coming, Leonard, too, dashes back of the screen.

"My poor child," Smith calls to Evadne; "prepare yourself for the worst, but remember it's for the best. Leonard has confessed all — and here she is —"

Mary has followed Evadne into the room as Smith pulls over the screen, "exposing the children in the guilty embrace of their own fathers. The culprits cower, huddled together for mutual protection, waiting for the blow to fall."

EVADNE — (*advancing with Mary upon the fathers*). So this is how you see your former wives — you wicked deceivers.

MARY — And to think we cannot trust our own husbands to chaperone our own children from their own fathers!

SMITH — It's quite against the law.

MOLLY — Forgive my father. I *love* him and he loves *me*.

EVADNE — So do I — you two darlings. (*She embraces father and daughter.*)

SMITH — Quite against the law, I tell you.

BILLY — (*leading Mary to Bill*). Father and I — so congenial since the divorce. (*Mary embraces father and son.*) What did we tell you? *They* don't mind.

BILL —You don't mind our seeing them — say, once a week?

MARY — Once a day!

EVADNE — All the time.

JANE — What wonderful wives — they want their husbands to have everything — even their own children.

SMITH — No! . . . You must respect the law!

BILL — Nobody respects the law, Churchill. Get around it again someway, like a good lawyer.

There is only one way, according to Smith. "You got divorced for the children's sake. Do it again. *Remarry* for the children's sake." But they all laugh at him. "Which will you sacrifice?" he shouts at them; "your offspring or your selfish love?"

And when he has them all properly reduced to a

contemplative silence, thinking that, after all, they probably will have to abide by the court decrees, he has another brilliant idea. Let the children decide! "And from the verdict of these innocent little ones you dare not appeal!"

"But 'these innocent little ones' belong to a generation which looks facts in the face. They place their fathers' hands in their stepmothers' hands . . ."

BILLY — (*to Smith*). Call me "innocent little one" if you like, but I'll be darned if I want a rotten home with father drunk and mother crying.

MOLLY — We want happy parents.

SMITH — Billy! Don't you want your own father to live with you here in this fine big house? (*Molly whispers to Billy.*)

BILLY — You bet. Tell them our plan, (*to Molly as he gets house plan*). Well, you and your mother and my father can open up this old wing —

MOLLY — And you and your mother and my father can keep on living in this wing.

SMITH — What! What's this?

MOLLY — And our families can share expenses and save money.

SMITH — But — but — you don't understand.

BILLY — And we can see both our parents every day —

MOLLY — And each other and each other's parents! And so can they. And we'll all be happy here together!

SMITH — (*turns to parents*). They can't do this. Tell them.

EVADNE — Why not? Just as private as an apartment house.

MARY — More so — all this neutral ground between.

LEONARD — Why, it's just the thing!

BILL — We'll do it! The home is sacred. And the law can't touch us.

ALL PARENTS — (*joyously*). Yaha! The law can't touch us, the law can't touch us!

SMITH — But nice people won't understand.

LEONARD — Nice people never do — let 'em rave.

JANE — Churchill! They must do it for the children's sake. "From the verdict of these innocent little ones they dare not appeal!" (*Raises her hand in benediction.*) Bless you my — parents.

THE END

"THE FOOL"

A drama in four acts

BY CHANNING POLLOCK

TEN years ago Channing Pollock wanted to write a play in which the leading male character should try to live as Christ lived, or as Christ might conceivably live in this day and age. During the ten years that followed he made various attempts to set about it, but he did not get it finally on paper until a year ago. "The Fool" is the result.

The play was first taken in the summer of 1922 to Los Angeles for a series of trial performances with Richard Bennett playing the name part, supported by the Morosco Stock Company. Here, according to the reports that floated eastward, the play's reception was uncertain. Mr. Pollock's faith, however, remained unshaken.

October 23, 1922, "The Fool" was produced in New York, at the Times Square Theatre, under the direction of the author and the Messrs. Selwyn, and with James Kirkwood, late of the cinema, playing the lead. Again the attitude of many reviewers, and apparently of many who saw the play, was not altogether favorable, and for three weeks the fate of "The Fool" again hung uncertainly in the balance. The fact that it was frankly a sermon drama seemed to militate against it. About that time, however, thanks largely to the persistent efforts of Mr. Pollock to interest the public he knew would like the play if they could be drawn into the theatre to see it, the tide turned. Within another fortnight the theatre was packed at every performance, and this success continued for the remainder of the season.

The first scene of "The Fool" is played before the chancel of the Church of the Nativity in New York. Just in front of the communion rail stands a huge Christmas tree, which at the moment is being decorated and piled high at its base with gifts for the children of the Sunday school who will attend the Christmas Eve exercises. The ladies of the church are attending to this work with such enthusiasm as they can command. One, Daffodil ("Dilly") Gilliam, being young, is a little rebellious. She certainly had no intention of giving up an engagement with "the best fox-trotter in New York" to "do a shimmy" with the ladder on which she is uncertainly perched. And another, Mrs. Thornbury, an attractive divorcée, feels the atmospheric repression of the place terribly; so much so that she would gladly "give her left arm for a cigarette." . . .

Mrs. Gilliam, "Dilly's" mother, is also ready to confess a somewhat unsettled and unhappy state of mind. Though she gives all her thought and much of her time to the service of others she has, so far, received precious little reward. Just the other day she had sent helpful thoughts from the Bible to all Mr. Gilliam's employees, and the very man who had received "Be Content With Your Wages" had gone right out and organized a strike. And now, to add to her irritations, the Star of Bethlehem, which is to decorate the top of the Christmas tree, simply won't light.

There are other visitors. Mrs. Tice and Jerry Goodkind among them. "Mrs. Tice has just entered middle age, and refuses to shut the door behind her." Jerry Goodkind is a typical son of wealth, blasé, cynical, and admittedly ungodly. "He can be very ugly when he wishes, and he is always sufficiently determined to get what he wants, though he gets it usually by showing the urbane surface. Jerry would describe himself as a 'kidder.' He is thirty-five, sleek, well groomed, and perfectly satisfied with himself. His most engaging point is a perpetual smile."

By the women of the church, particularly those with marriageable daughters like "Dilly" Gilliam, Jerry is looked upon as a great catch. But so far as Jerry is concerned, he flirts with them all and takes none of them seriously — none except Clare Jewett. It was Mrs. Tice's promise that Miss Jewett would be found at the church that had lured Jerry there, according to Mrs. Tice. And Miss Jewett, just now, is wrapping parcels in the choir room.

The conversation is desultory until Dr. Wadham, the rector, enters the room. The rector "is not the stage clergyman. On the contrary he is a very pleasant and plausible person — plausible because he believes implicitly in himself. He has passed sixty and has a really kind heart. But he has had no experiences with life, and he has never been uncomfortable."

Now the talk becomes rather quickly centered on young Daniel Gilchrist, the assistant rector, who recently has been taking active command of the church work. Mr. Gilchrist is young, and rather inclined to be radical. Mrs. Tice, for one, has been commissioned by Mr. Tice to speak to Dr. Wadham about the tenor of the Gilchrist sermons of late. Mr. Tice had promised a check for $5,000 to beautify the parlor of the parish house, and the very next Sunday Mr. Gilchrist had preached pointedly from the text about the rich man entering the kingdom of heaven, looking directly at Mr. Tice during practically the whole sermon.

"Do you know what he said, doctor?" demands Mrs. Tice. "He said all this 'decking the church' was making an accomplice of God. He said we couldn't take credit to ourselves for returning a small portion of our *ill gotten gains!*" And that "Charity wasn't giving away what you didn't want."

Mrs. Gilliam is in hearty accord with Mrs. Tice's

criticism of young Gilchrist and Jerry Goodkind is convinced the young rector is "a nut."

"Personally, I'm very fond of Mr. Gilchrist," qualifies Mrs. Gilliam. "His father had stock in our stores. But I don't think he's a good influence. This used to be a really exclusive church. Now, whenever Mr. Gilchrist preaches, there's such a crush of undesirable people in the galleries you can hardly get to your pew. We don't have that trouble with Dr. Wadham!"

Clare Jewett has come from the choir room, her arms filled with more packages for the tree. She is smartly dressed — "though in a fashion that suggests thought rather than expenditure; and pretty, in spite of a certain hardness." . . . Now the others have left, and Clare and Jerry are alone.

CLARE — It's funny to find you in church.

JERRY — Why? My father's the senior warden.

CLARE — (*laughs and takes up a parcel*). Whatever else you inherit, Jerry, it's not likely to be religion!

JERRY — Religion doesn't trouble the old man much — except Sundays. I came here to see you.

CLARE — Why?

JERRY — You've been avoiding me.

CLARE — Nonsense! Come help me with these parcels.

JERRY — I want to talk to you.

CLARE — That's just it, Jerry. You always want to talk to me, and always to say something I don't want to hear.

JERRY — Why not?

CLARE — (*simply, but not very surely*). I'm in love with someone else!

JERRY — You're *what?*

CLARE — (*looking defiantly into the mocking face close to hers and, this time, with conviction*). I'm in love with someone else!

JERRY — You're in love with Clare Jewett!

CLARE — You're very rude. I'm *engaged* to Mr. Gilchrist, and he loves me, and believes in me, and your sense of decency and fair play —

JERRY — Inherited from my father?

CLARE — . . . should keep you from proposing to a woman who's going to marry . . .

JERRY — You're not going to marry Mr. Gilchrist. What's the use bluffing? We've known each other since childhood. You know I'm not going to give up anything I want because it belongs to somebody else. And I know you're not going to give up what *you* want — comfort and luxury — for a crazy man who wears his collar hind-side before!

CLARE — Jerry!

JERRY — Now that's admitted, let's go on.

CLARE — Mr. Gilchrist isn't exactly poverty-stricken!

JERRY — No; he got quite a lot of money from his father. You like him and when you said, "Yes," you thought you were getting somebody you liked, and all the rest of it, too. But something's gone wrong with Gilchrist, and you know it!

CLARE — Why do you say that?

JERRY — Because, if you didn't before, you heard this afternoon, I saw you standing in the door. And I'm going to tell you a few things more!

CLARE — I don't want to listen!

JERRY — Maybe — but you will! Do you know that your young trouble-hunter has given away nearly one-tenth of his capital in three months?

CLARE — No, and I don't believe it!

JERRY — All right; ask my father! The old man has his money in trust! Gilchrist won't touch his income from Gilliam Groceries, because they're profiteering, and he's preaching such anarchy that both wardens are coming this afternoon to complain to Dr. Wadham! I don't want you to throw yourself away on a raving bug!

CLARE — And your advice is —

JERRY — Marry me. I'm a nice fellow, too — and I can give you what you really care about. You're over your ears in debt, without any chance of paying up — or cutting down. And you are, shall we say, twenty-nine in October? I know what it cost you when your father died, and you had to come down a peg. You don't want to keep on — coming down, *do* you?

CLARE — And so — you advise me to marry you?

JERRY — Yes.

CLARE — (*looking at him squarely and significantly*). Knowing all I *do* know about you?

JERRY — I don't see how *that* concerns you.

CLARE — It proves you don't love me.

JERRY — I want you, and I'm offering marriage to get you.

CLARE — You haven't said one word of love.

JERRY — I've said: "What's the use bluffing?" I'm no movie hero — and no crazy dreamer. I'm a little shop-worn, perhaps — maybe, a little soiled — but I'm sane, and I'm solvent. You're good-looking, and smart, and a lady. You'll help my standing and I'll help your credit. For the rest — we needn't bother each other too much. . . . What do you say?

CLARE — I say it's — *revoltingly* — sordid!

JERRY — (*looks at her an instant*). All right! (*Takes out his watch.*) You think it's sordid at three forty-five on Christmas Eve. Well, keep your ears and your mind open, and see how you feel in the morning. My telephone's six nine four two Rhinelander — and this is the last time I shall ask you! (*Puts his hand on the knob.*)

CLARE — Wait! (*He turns back.*) Whatever you believe of me, I love Mr. Gilchrist!

JERRY — Rhinelander six nine four two.

CLARE — And, what's more, I'm going to marry him!

JERRY — Rhinelander six nine four two.

CLARE — Jerry, I think you're the most detestable person I've ever known in my life!

JERRY — (*laughing*). Rhinelander six nine four two!

The wardens gather. First, Jerry's father, George Goodkind. "Goodkind is much like any other successful business man you might meet — and like — at dinner. He is brisk and economical of time, but pleasant, and, unless his interests are involved, extremely amiable. He does what he conceives to be his duty by his family, his community and his God, and feels that all three should appreciate it."

The second is Charlie Benfield. "Benfield is fifty, and a 'rough diamond.' He is self-made and proud of it, though nothing really good — nothing of education or refinement, or knowledge and appreciation of fine things — has gone into the making. He is arrogant, domineering, used to having his own way, and to sweeping aside obstacles."

Goodkind is principally concerned over the Christmas sermon young Gilchrist has declared he will preach — a sermon about the garment workers' strike. As it happens, neither he nor Benfield is interested in clothing, but they are interested heavily in West Virginia coal mines, and down there they are on the verge of the biggest walkout in their history. Any encouragement the men might get now — Besides, the labor problem's none of the church's business. That's what Gilchrist has got to be made to understand.

DR. WADHAM — I have told him . . . frequently.

GOODKIND — And what's the answer?

DR. WADHAM — He says every problem ought to be the church's business, and that, until the church becomes a power in live issues, it isn't a power in life!

GOODKIND — He won't listen to reason?

DR. WADHAM — No.

GOODKIND — Then he'll have to listen to something else. If he persists about this Christmas sermon — (*Barnaby enters. Goodkind turns impatiently.*) What is it, Barnaby?

BARNABY — There's a man out there wants to see Mr. Gilchrist.

GOODKIND — What kind of a man?

BARNABY — (*indifferently*). A poor man. I think he's a Jew.

GOODKIND — Whoever heard of a poor Jew?

DR. WADHAM — Mr. Gilchrist isn't here.

BARNABY — I told him that, but he won't go away. I wanted to ask had I better send for the police?

DR. WADHAM — Oh, I wouldn't do that!

BARNABY — Why don't he go over to the synagogue instead of hanging around a Christian church. Mr. Gilchrist gave this fellow his overcoat. I suppose he's come back for the gloves!

DR. WADHAM — Tell him I'll speak to Mr. Gilchrist. (*Barnaby shakes his head despairingly and exits.*)

GOODKIND — Well, there you are, and what I wanted to talk about privately is . . . what's got into the boy? Has he gone crazy?

DR. WADHAM — I've asked myself that. I've asked myself if what he saw in France —

GOODKIND — Exactly. A lot of young fellows go off the handle and start out to reform the world, but this lad has run through twenty thousand dollars in less than three months!

DR. WADHAM — In addition to his salary?

GOODKIND — Yes. I could understand if he'd spent the money on himself, but he hasn't! He's given it away! Gilchrist's father was my first partner, and I got the boy in here, and I feel responsible for him. As trustee, I can refuse to turn over another penny of his principal, and, as senior warden, I can demand his resignation from this church. But I want him to have every chance. Tell him if he'll get a grip on himself, and reconsider tomorrow's sermon — Here's Benfield!

Benfield is even more bitter than Goodkind, and more inclined to take immediate and drastic action. "All I got to say now is: Gilchrist leaves this church or I do!" is his attitude. And it is while he is repeating this very definite conclusion that Daniel enters the room quietly, and stands in the shadows by the door. If the star of Bethlehem at the top of the Christmas tree could throw a few flashing gleams of light about, they might have revealed him, but the star is still not working.

"You can decide which of us is the most valu'ble to your church!" he hears Benfield shout. "Because I tell you again — and straight — this church ain't big enough for Gilchrist and me!"

Daniel is smiling as he steps forward into the light. "A church that isn't big enough for two little men, Mr. Benfield, must be somewhat crowded for God!" he says.

"Daniel is thirty-three. He was a football hero at college," his playwright biographer says of him, "and he shows it. He was a gentleman before he went to college and he has been one ever since, and he shows that, too. What he doesn't show is what one expects in a 'reformer'— narrowness, hardness, something forbidding. An ascetic, beyond doubt, self-denial has only made him trim and fit. The goodness that shines in his face is partly good humor. He has honest eyes, with fire in them, and there is strength and zeal back of that — strength and zeal that will leave their mark later. As yet his exultation is chiefly in his smile. His great gift is charm — and sympathy. At this moment he wears no overcoat, and is glowing from the cold."

Mr. Benfield is somewhat disconcerted by the entrance of Daniel. With a grunt of disapproval he shuffles into

Dr. Wadham's office where he can continue his criticism of the church's interference in his personal affairs in a friendlier, or at least a more understanding, atmosphere.

Alone with Daniel, Dr. Wadham seeks with such diplomacy as he can master to warn his young assistant of the danger in which he stands.

DR. WADHAM — Daniel, you're in trouble.

DANIEL — Doctor, I'm used to it.

DR. WADHAM — This time it's serious. I've warned you often. I don't see how you can have been so blind.

DANIEL — I haven't been blind.

DR. WADHAM — Then you don't care for your position in this church.

DANIEL — There's only one thing I care for more.

DR. WADHAM — And that is?

DANIEL — To be worthy of it.

DR. WADHAM — When you're as old as I am, Daniel, you'll understand that being honest doesn't necessarily mean being disagreeable.

DANIEL — Doesn't it mean — telling the truth?

DR. WADHAM — Do you know the truth, Daniel?

DANIEL — Yes; don't you? Doesn't every man — in his heart? And if we want to keep it in our hearts, and never think about it or look it in the face, shouldn't someone pry open the door and cry: "Behold!" . . . I didn't tell them anything they didn't know, Doctor. I don't know anything they don't know. I just reminded them —

DR. WADHAM — (*exploding on the last word*). That we were heathen!

DANIEL — That we were Christians, and every man our brother, and that we were sitting, overdressed and overfed, in a Christian church, while our brother froze and starved — outside — in a Christian world!

DR. WADHAM — That isn't fair! These good people have given —

DANIEL — *Given* — what cost them nothing! Frumpery and trumpery and diamond stars! That's how all of us give — what we don't need; what we don't even want! You're a good man, Doctor, and, honestly, what would you say tomorrow if your wife told you she'd sold her rings, and given the money to the poor?

DR. WADHAM — Why, I —

DANIEL — You'd say she was crazy!

DR. WADHAM — But there's no necessity —

DANIEL — Oh, yes, there is! There'll be people lying in the parks tonight. What would Mrs. Tice say if I invited them to sleep in her pew?

DR. WADHAM — That there's no reason why she should share dirt and disease!

DANIEL — Exactly! We may believe in the brotherhood of man, but we *know* about germs! We're not sure what is truth, but there's one thing we *are* sure of, and *mean* to be sure of, and that's our own comfort! You know that, and I know it, and they know it — but we mustn't say it! All right; in God's name, what *are* we to say?

Dr. Wadham is not quite sure, but he would suggest that Daniel change his Christmas text to "Glory to God in the highest — and on earth, peace, good will toward men."

"There are many kinds of peace —" he seeks to explain, but Daniel stops him.

He will preach, he says, from the text: "And Peter followed afar off!"

"We all follow — afar off," he has observed. And he has been wondering if it would not be possible for all of us to come closer to Christ.

DANIEL — What would happen if anybody really tried to live like Christ?

DR. WADHAM — (*shaking his head*). It can't be done.

DANIEL — Isn't it worth trying? Men risk their lives — every day — in experiments far less worth while. We've had centuries of "fear, and hate, and greed"—and where have they brought us? Why not try love?"

DR. WADHAM — How can you make them try?

DANIEL — By showing that it would work.

DR. WADHAM — It *won't* work, Daniel. It's a beautiful ideal, but it won't work. Times have changed, and things are different. Life isn't as simple as it was two thousand years ago. The trouble with you, Daniel, is that you're not practical.

DANIEL — I wonder.

DR. WADHAM — And the great need of the church is practical men. We mustn't take the Scriptures too literally. We must try to interpret their spirit. And, above all, we must please our congregations, or we shan't have any. And then what becomes of our influence? Better fall back on my text for tomorrow, Daniel.

DANIEL — I can't.

DR. WADHAM — At least, you must promise not to discuss the strike.

DANIEL — I can't do that, Doctor.

DR. WADHAM — Or else let me take the pulpit.

DANIEL — I *won't* do that!

(*A pause.*)

DR. WADHAM — Very well! Preach your Christmas sermon, and afterward —

DANIEL — Yes?

DR. WADHAM — I think you may find a greater field of usefulness elsewhere. I'm sorry, Daniel. I know you've been very happy in your work here. I know how failure hurts. But you saw it coming, and you wouldn't turn aside.

DANIEL — (*he looks up with flashing eyes*). The man who turns away from his vision — lies!

Clare's return from the choir room interrupts them,

and Dr. Wadham takes himself away to the warden's meeting with such dignity as he still controls.

CLARE — . . . Got anything on your mind, Dan?

DANIEL — (*quickly*). What do you —

CLARE — I mean anything special to do?

DANIEL — Oh! No.

CLARE — Take me home.

DANIEL — (*he beams.*) *I'm* getting *my* Christmas present early! (*Gets his hat.*)

CLARE — Where's your coat?

DANIEL — Outside. That is — I lent it to a friend. Oh, I've got another — somewhere!

CLARE — But you can't go out without a coat. (*Looks at wrist watch.*) Anyway, I told the taxi man to come back at half past four. That's the worst of not having a car. Well, we may as well sit down! What's the matter with you, Dan?

DANIEL — Nothing important.

CLARE — There will be if you insist on going around without an overcoat! (*Looking at him narrowly.*) You're too generous. (*He is miles away.*) I say you're too generous. How are we going to be married if you go on giving things away?

DANIEL — (*laughs*). Is generosity a fault in a husband?

CLARE — That depends. Is it true you've been giving away — well — large sums of money?

DANIEL — Who told you that?

CLARE — A little bird. (*He laughs.*) And that you've refused to take part of your income?

DANIEL — Little bird tell you that?

CLARE — Yes.

DANIEL — Must have been a cuckoo!

CLARE — Is it true?

DANIEL — About the money? Yes.

CLARE — Why?

DANIEL — Well, there's the strike, and a good deal of unemployment, and I've got so much. Why — *I've* got *you!*

CLARE — Let's not talk about it now. Yes, let's! — You're so changed. I hardly know you. We don't seem to want the same things any more.

DANIEL — What do *you* want, Clare?

CLARE — I want to be happy.

DANIEL — That's exactly what I want!

CLARE — How can anybody be happy without money?

DANIEL — How can anybody be happy *with* it? Anyway, do you think people are? Happier than the people who just have enough?

CLARE — In our day and age there's nothing worse than poverty! There's nothing more degrading than having to scrimp, and save, and do without, and keep up appearances! I've tried it . . . ever since father died . . . and I know! I can't do it any longer, and I won't!

DANIEL — Clare!

(*She turns away, and comes back somewhat calmer.*)

CLARE — I don't want to quarrel with you, Dan. I just want you to be sensible . . . I love you, but I love the good things of life, too. I like to be warm and comfortable.

DANIEL — You can be sure of that.

CLARE — But that's only the beginning. I want good clothes, and furs, and my car, and money to spend when I like. I want my own house, and my own servants, and a husband who amounts to something. I'm no different from other women of my class.

DANIEL — I hoped you were.

CLARE — A year or two ago people thought you were going to be a bishop. Today you've made an enemy of every influential man in the church. All that may be very noble, but I'm not noble, and I don't pretend to be.

I don't feel any call to sacrifice myself for others, and I don't think you have any right to ask it!

DANIEL — I do ask it, Clare.

CLARE — You mean you're going on like this?

DANIEL — I mean I can't give you expensive clothes, and servants, and a big house, while all about us people are hungry.

CLARE — What do you propose to give me?

DANIEL — A chance to help.

CLARE — To help wash the dishes, I suppose, in a three-room flat in a side street!

DANIEL — And to visit the sick, and befriend the friendless.

CLARE — A charming prospect!

DANIEL — It really is, Clare. You don't know how happy we can be with work, and our modest plenty. There's so much to do — and they won't let me do it here. We've got to get *near* the people in trouble, and we can't with a big house and all that. I don't think we shall come to a three-room flat. (*He smiles.*) We'll have five or six rooms, and our books, and each other.

But that is not Clare's idea of what her married life should be, and before she leaves she has given him back his ring.

For a moment Daniel stands looking at the ring. From the choir room there come the strains of "Hark, the Herald Angels." He crosses to close the door, and as he does so he hears a step behind him. He turns and can vaguely make out the form of a man who has entered from the street and stands in the deeper shadows. He is the man to whom Daniel has given his overcoat earlier in the day.

DANIEL — Who's there? . . . Are you looking for someone?

POOR MAN — Yes.

DANIEL — I'm the assistant rector . . . Mr. Gilchrist.

POOR MAN — I know you, Mr. Gilchrist.

DANIEL — Oh, yes, I remember. You're the man who was cold. Can I do anything more for you?

POOR MAN — I think you can.

DANIEL — Let's have it then.

POOR MAN — Perhaps I can help you, too.

DANIEL — In what way?

POOR MAN — In my way.

DANIEL — My poor man, I wish you could! (*His despair impels him to confide in anyone.*) I was so sure of what I wanted to do, and now I begin to wonder if it can be done!

POOR MAN — It has been done.

DANIEL — But in this day — in this practical world — can any man follow the Master?

POOR MAN — Why not? Is this day different from any other? Was the world never practical before? Is this the first time of conflict between flesh and spirit? If it could be done then, why not now, and, if it was ever worth the doing, why not now?

DANIEL — But how?

POOR MAN — We have been told how.

DANIEL — "Take no thought of the morrow. . . . Sell whatsoever thou hast, and give to the poor. . . . Love thy neighbor as thyself. . . . Bless them that curse you, do good to them that hate you." But if a man did those things today, people would think him mad!

POOR MAN — What does it matter?

DANIEL — He would lose everything!

POOR MAN — And gain everything!

DANIEL — What good can one man do?

POOR MAN — Why don't you try?

DANIEL — The Master tried, and they crucified Him!

POOR MAN — Did they? And if they did, what does that matter? Is a man dead whose ideal lives? "Ye crucified me, but I am with ye always, even unto the end of the world!"

DANIEL — In God's name, who are you?

POOR MAN — I am a Jew!

"As he speaks, slowly the tree and everything beneath it is illuminated by the star of Bethlehem. The light, dim at first, grows stronger and stronger, its rays revealing sanctuary and picking out the points of the cross on the altar. But where the *Poor Man* stood is nothing. There is no one there. The spirit — if spirit it was — has disappeared. The man — if man it was — has gone. Daniel gives a cry, and, as he does so, the light is extinguished, and suddenly, to the music that has been heard faintly through the door during this scene, the full choir sings: 'Hark, the Herald Angels Sing.' "

In black darkness the curtain falls.

ACT II

It did not take the church trustees long to decide that Daniel Gilchrist was far too radical a young man to preach in their church. He was dismissed practically at the close of the Christmas Day services.

But there was a sort of string to the dismissal. George Goodkind, because of his liking for Daniel and the sense of obligation he felt as his guardian, undertook to continue him in the work in which he was interested, and sent him as a sort of harmonizer wherever the Goodkind employees were grumbling or rebellious.

"I didn't hire him because I was sorry he got fired out of the church," Goodkind explained to Charlie

Benfield; "and only a little because I knew his father. I hired him because he had theories, and I wanted to try them out. . . . Yes, and the remarkable part of it is that sometimes they work. They worked up at that power plant. A year ago I wouldn't have taken it as a gift. Gilchrist applied a little soft soap, and . . . with all the increased wages and decreased working hours the plant is making money now for the first time. . . . There's something in Gilchrist."

Ten months after the church episode, on an evening in November, the Goodkinds have been entertaining informally at dinner. After dinner word is brought to them that Max Stedtman, from the Goodkind mining properties in West Virginia, is in town with a committee of disgruntled workmen and would like to have a conference. He is sent for.

There has been trouble in West Virginia, and Gilchrist has been down there trying to settle it. What progress he has made is indicated by a telegram recently received. "Everything settled if you accede to rational conditions."

"Rational conditions," suggests Jerry Goodkind, summoned by his father, with Benfield, to meet Stedtman in the library, means nothing less than surrender. He, for one, will be damned if he will consider any such idiotic action.

Stedtman, who arrives ahead of the committee, is a "conciliator," an employer's spy; a member of an organization that worms its members into unions and then proceeds to "handle" any situation that may arise. To honest men he is what is known as a "rat." And Stedtman naturally is against Gilchrist, who has gone around talking compromise.

"Compromise ain't no way to settle a strike," he tells the Goodkinds. "Givin' 'em confidence! Why, we got a couple o' hundred representatives among the workmen tellin' 'em they got no chance. We got special police clubbin' 'em every time they try to hold a meeting. You wouldn't believe what we done down there in the way of harmony!"

The two other members of the committee arrive. They are Joe Hennig and Umanski, a giant Pole. Umanski is the honest member. Hennig, Stedtman figures, can be "reached." He's got a pretty wife — and men with pretty wives need money to keep 'em satisfied.

Neither of the Goodkinds nor Benfield can understand what the men are striking for, they tell the committee. The work's there and the pay is as high as the market demands. Let them take it or leave it. What's the matter with them, anyway?

Umanski, the Pole, undertakes to answer.

UMANSKI — I work twelve hours — every day—thurty years — got nothing.

BENFIELD — Why should you have? An untrained man —

JERRY — You don't even know English!

UMANSKI — How I gonna learn English — work twelve hours a day?

JERRY — Nobody asked you to take the job! Nobody asked you to come over here! You're not an American!

UMANSKI — I was American.

JERRY — When?

UMANSKI — When I fight in the war.

JERRY — (*flustered, turning to Goodkind*). We're not getting anywhere. We've been over this a dozen times!

GOODKIND — What do you want?

UMANSKI — I wanna chance to learn! I wanna chance to live! I wanna chance to see . . . sun!

JERRY — Wha'd' ya mean — *son?*

GOODKIND — *Your* son?

UMANSKI — God's sun. I never see him. Go to mines — him not up. Work in mines — him not see. Go home — him gone. Got baby five years ago. Never see *him*. Go to mines . . . *him* not up. Come back — *him* sleep. Go home one day — *him* gone.

GOODKIND — Dead?

UMANSKI — (*bowing his head*). My wife say: "Good! Not such many to feed!"

JERRY — When you worked you had enough to eat, didn't you?

UMANSKI — Yes. Work twelve hours a day and got enough to eat — so can work some more. Always work. Get up — work — come back — sleep — get up — work. Never got time to talk to wife — never got time to talk to nobody — never got nowhere. Never save nothing.

JOE — (*whining*). It ain't fair!

(*Jerry takes out his gold cigarette case.*)

UMANSKI — That little box — what you pay for him? (*Jerry turns, not deigning to answer.*) Ah, I know, gold. You pay more for him than I got for swing pick thirty years. Me and six families — we live in one house you own. We got one room upstairs; two down cellar. Sleep there. Eat — cook — wash upstairs. See nothing but brick yard, and clothes hang up to dry. Wife — she carry water from yard. Me — I carry potato peeling out front. Him rot. If I don't like that, I quit — and starve!

JERRY — You want to live on Fifth Avenue!

BENFIELD — And *then* you'd find something to kick about!

UMANSKI — If I don't like other man's will. Other mans take my job. I got little girl twenty years old. Awful nice little girl. Got gold hair. Got blue eyes. Her take sick. She sorry she's sick. She wanna go church. She ask me: "Pop, buy me new dress for church. Buy me pretty pink dress." Where I get him? We hire doctor once, and he say: "Air — sunshine — milk — eggs!" Where I get air — sunshine — milk — eggs? Got no job. My little girl, she cough, and cough, and one night she die. I tell you we got right to quit! We got right to hang together! We got right to fight — to live — and, by God, we gonna fight — we gonna live — we *gonna* — by God!

"The music stops. In the same short instant there is a patter of applause; more music — lively this time — and, bursting into the room, Dilly runs into Umanski. *She* has gold hair; she has blue eyes; and what is more: *she* has a new dress. It is a 'pretty pink dress,' too, and its owner wears jewels worth the ransom of a dozen Umanskis. Then . . . Umanski looks at her; then covers his face and with a great sob, drops into a chair. Stedtman puts his arm about the man's shoulders. Goodkind stares at him sympathetically."

. . . .

Nothing comes of the conference — nothing except the strengthening of the Goodkind-Benfield determination to fight it out.

Daniel misses the meeting with the committee. By the time he arrives the workmen have left. In the library he finds Clare, now married to Jerry, and a little miserable at the moment because her husband has just given her *another* sable scarf. She knows what that means — that he has done something he is ashamed of.

She brightens when Daniel comes in. She is glad to find him looking well and as though he were happy in his new work. It means much, she knows that. Her father-in-law has told her that if he succeeds in settling the West Virginia strike, it will mean promotion — and a huge salary. He must not give that away. . . .

CLARE — You don't really seem to have lost anything by giving up your church.

DANIEL — No. Queer as it seems, sometimes I think I've gained . . . in opportunity.

CLARE — (*pensively*). Perhaps one *might* have eaten one's cake and had it, too.

DANIEL — Clare!

CLARE — You frightened me so that night, with the bugaboo of poverty. Don't you think there might have been a compromise. Something half way.

DANIEL — Why open wounds that are beginning to heal?

CLARE — Yours seem quite healed.

DANIEL — And you have everything you want?

CLARE — Yes.

DANIEL — You see . . . I *was* selfish . . . to ask you to give up the things that count so much with you for those that count with me. . . . Afterward, when I knew you were to be married . . . I was afraid for you . . . and I was wrong again. You're happy . . . and I'm honestly glad!

CLARE — Are you . . . honestly . . . happy?

DANIEL — Honestly.

CLARE — In just helping others?

DANIEL — In just helping others.

CLARE — I don't understand that.

DANIEL — You will . . . some day . . . and so will all the world!

Their visit is interrupted by Jerry, who "has added two or three brandies to a generous allowance at dinner," and is sullen and quarrelsome. He resents finding Daniel and Clare together, resents the thought of what he believes to be their still existent love for each other. Most of all he resents Clare's attitude toward the sable stole as a conscience gift and her present pointed questioning of him.

JERRY — . . . I don't propose to be made a blackguard before strangers!

CLARE — Dan isn't a stranger. And I don't want to make you a blackguard. Only . . . since you've insisted on the truth . . . Dan, when *did* my husband leave Black River?

DANIEL — I haven't seen him since Thursday.

CLARE — No.

DANIEL — As a matter of fact, I wasn't —

JERRY — Oh! . . . Where were you?

DANIEL — At the mines.

CLARE — Is that the truth?

JERRY — Of course! It's the truth, and if it wasn't, I don't see that you've any right to ask questions! I haven't done anything that wasn't in the bargain! I haven't done anything every man doesn't do!

CLARE — Every man . . . perhaps . . . but one!

JERRY — Gilchrist! My God! Now we've got it! If you'd only married him! He's good, because he says so! You ought to've been here a minute ago . . . when the company detective warned us not to mention Gilchrist to Joe Hennig!

DANIEL — You mean —

JERRY — I mean Pearl Hennig!

DANIEL — Pearl Hennig? Why, *you* — you *know* that's not true!

CLARE — *I* know it's not true!

JERRY — Do you?

At this moment the voices of Stedtman and Hennig are heard in the adjoining room. They are quarreling and Stedtman is evidently trying to dissuade Hennig from entering. They burst into the room and Hennig, in a passion, faces Daniel and demands to know what he has done with Pearl. Daniel doesn't know where Pearl is. The last time he saw her she said she was going to her sister's. But Hennig has a wire from the sister saying Pearl isn't there. Furthermore, under Jerry's cross-questioning, Stedtman declares he saw Gilchrist and Pearl together a day or two before in Black River.

JOE HENNIG — (*starting for Gilchrist*). I knew it! I'm gonna kill you!

JERRY — No, you're not. You're going to keep quiet.

But you wanted the truth, and you've got it. I've known it all along. (*To Clare.*) Now do you think I was lying?

CLARE — I don't know. I don't understand.

JERRY — Oh, yes, you do . . . only you won't admit it!

CLARE — I suppose that's it.

DANIEL — Clare! I don't care what anyone believes but you!

CLARE — I'll believe you, Dan, if you'll only explain.

DANIEL — I —

JERRY — I forbid you to speak to my wife!

CLARE — Go on, Dan.

JERRY — I forbid you to speak to my wife!

DANIEL — (*to Jerry*). If I hadn't anybody to think about but *you!*

They glare at each other. Suddenly, Jerry lifts his open hand, and strikes Dan across the mouth. Dan starts to retaliate, but controls himself, opens his clenched hands, and lowers his head.

CLARE — Dan; you're not going to take that?

DANIEL — I have nothing to say.

CLARE — I didn't think you were a coward. You see, I was wrong about everything. (*She sweeps out of the room.*)

. . . .

Daniel's meeting with the elder Goodkind and the submission of his plan to settle the strike is, for Daniel, no more happily concluded. The millionaire employer is ready to admit that strikes are costly; that it would be much better to keep the men contented, to give them a real interest in their jobs, but it can't be done by giving them more wages, because the more they get the less they want to do for it.

"When you tell a man he's going to have the same reward, whatever he does — not because he's got ability, but because he's got a union card — down goes the standard, out goes incentive, and to hell goes the whole social structure!"

"Right!" agrees Daniel.

"That's why I'm fighting the unions! Not because I want to starve the man who works, but because I want to fire the man who doesn't . . . *and* reward the man who does! I want to give every man a good reason for doing his best! You can talk equality and democracy all you like, Dan, but the minute the average man isn't afraid of being fired he isn't afraid of being workless! . . . The minute you take away incentive — the chance to get *this* — (*indicating his home*) — that minute you reduce the world to a common level of common indifference and common futility!"

To all of which Daniel most heartily agrees. But when a moment later Goodkind finds similar phrases in Daniel's proposed "rational" settlement of the Goodkind strike he rebels vociferously. "Refer all disputes to arbitration! Divide one half of the profits, over and above a fair dividend, pro rata among the men, according to wage and length of service?" The idea disgusts Goodkind. He's got the strikers licked and he purposes to keep them licked.

Benfield also would take a hand. He'd like to have Gilchrist remember that he is working for them, not for the miners. What the —

GOODKIND — Wait a minute, Benfield. We've all lost our heads! Daniel and I have just been over all this and he admitted I was right.

DANIEL — Right as far as you went, but you only went part way! You have a right to a profit on your idea, and your investment and the labor you put back of it! The public has a right to coal, and transportation, and all it needs and pays for! But, above everything else, the workman who works honestly has a right to something more than the barest kind of a bare living and it can all be done if you don't sink everybody's rights to accumulate a fortune you don't need and can't see! . . . All the argument on earth can't make you *all* right so long as there's a Umanski in the world!

GOODKIND — If these people succeed there's no limit to what they'll do!

DANIEL — If they fail there's no limit to what you'll do!

GOODKIND — There's no good transferring control from the intelligent few to the ignorant mob!

DANIEL — There's no good in anything so long as we fight each other like beasts, instead of helping each other like brothers! There's no hope anywhere except in the Great Teacher, and the understanding that what He taught was not only good morals, but good sense and good business!

BENFIELD — Highfalutin' nonsense!

GOODKIND — Daniel doesn't realize what he's costing us!

DANIEL — What?

GOODKIND — Millions!

DANIEL — Oh, is that all?

BENFIELD — All?

DANIEL — Am I costing you one cigar? Am I costing you one blanket for your warm beds, or one stick of furniture from your comfortable homes, or anything else you'll ever miss? I'm taking nothing from you, and I'm giving thousands of men like you a chance to live!

GOODKIND — (*angrily*). You're costing yourself your last chance of success!

DANIEL — I don't want your kind of success! I'm through! I give you back your job, as I gave you back your church, and I give you twenty-four hours to sign that agreement!

GOODKIND — If I do, you're finished!

DANIEL — I am when you've signed!

GOODKIND — If you walk out of that door you're throwing away the chance of your life!

DANIEL — I'm keeping my soul!

BENFIELD — You Judas!

GOODKIND — You damned fool!

DANIEL — Good night!

He closes the door behind him.
The curtain falls.

ACT III

In October, 1920, Daniel Gilchrist is conducting "Overcoat Hall," a sort of mission of his own founding in lower New York. With so much of his remaining capital as he could worry out of George Goodkind he has bought a pair of those old brownstone fronts that once proudly represented the residential aristocracy of Manhattan Island, and converted them into a combination clubroom and meeting house for all who are either interested in, or in need of, their shelter.

His assistants are few, and voluntary. Chief among them Mary Margaret, "a child of fifteen and pathetically pretty," who is obliged, because of her twisted legs, to propel herself about Overcoat Hall with the aid of a pair of rubber-tipped crutches.

Mary Margaret is one of the few of his newer friends who not only believes implicitly in Daniel and his work, but seems able to grasp something of its spiritual significance. Grubby, who was a hansom driver until hansoms went out, and then took to drink until drink went out, is a faithful hanger-on at the hall, but in his heart he is convinced Daniel is a nut. And Mack, another confessed down-and-outer, who has just come in to see what arrangements he can make about getting one of the overcoats he has heard some guy is giving away, is of a mind with Grubby.

MACK — Don't he try to reform you?

GRUBBY — Naw! The way he talks, you'd think you was as good as him. He says to me, the other night, he says, "You're a good man, Grubby," he says. "You're strong and healthy," he says, "and if you learned to drive a taxi, all the best people in New York would be telephoning for your cab. I'll lend you the money," he says. Gee, he almost had me started!

MACK — What's the catch!

GRUBBY — I don't know.

MACK — There must be graft in it somewhere.

GRUBBY — If you ask me, I think the poor gent's got a few nuts in his nose-bag. A little bit batty. That's what *I* say!

MARY MARGARET — And that's what you got no right to say, Grubby!

GRUBBY — (*to Mack*). Mary Margaret.

MARY MARGARET — He's been good to you, ain't he?

GRUBBY — That's why we think he's nutty. What's he do it for?

MARY MARGARET — 'Cause he loves you.

GRUBBY — What for?

MARY MARGARET — God knows! (*She has brought a cup and saucer with other utensils, and is clearing and setting a place at one end of the table.*) After seven o'clock now, and the meeting half an hour, and he ain't had a bite since morning!

MACK — Where is he?

MARY MARGARET — He went to see a man that killed himself. (*Mack laughs.*) I mean . . . tried to. It was in the papers this afternoon, and Mr. Gilchrist says: "I want to talk to that man." (*Mack's interposition has brought his words to her mind, and reflecting on them, she explodes.*) Graft! Why he didn't have the rent money yesterday, and he was desprit! He ain't had money to get himself a pair of shoes, and nobody helps him, or comes near him, but you bums that roast him behind his back!

An early visitor this particular October day is George Goodkind. For some time he has been curious as to what Daniel has been doing. Recently he has been stirred to resentment by reports from Jerry that Clare has been paying rather frequent visits to Overcoat Hall. Also he is tired of seeing Daniel continue to waste money on tennis and handball and bath-tubs for those who are unable to appreciate such things, and he has come to see what can be done about it.

Goodkind has been waiting some few minutes when Daniel arrives, and his disgust has been increasing by the minute. Now he is witness to the crowning idiocy of his visit. Mack, stealing out quietly without having had a chance to talk to Daniel about the overcoat, decides to help himself to one on the rack. But the rack falls and Mack's intention is revealed. Whereupon Daniel chides him gently, but gives him the coat.

"You couldn't steal it," he explains to the astounded Mack. "It's your coat. You asked for it and I gave it to you. When you've worn it . . . into a good job . . . come back and help me give another to some one who needs it as you do."

"Well, I'll be damned!" explodes Goodkind. "He won't come back. Not one in ten would come back!"

"All right," answers Daniel. "That coat cost twenty dollars. If one in ten *does* come back we've made a man for two hundred dollars. Isn't it worth the price?"

To which Goodkind replies that it may be, if a man has the price — which Daniel hasn't. Furthermore he is not likely to get it — not the way he's been acting. First, there is the matter of Clare's visiting Overcoat Hall. That will have to be stopped.

DANIEL — I've asked her not to come again.

GOODKIND — And *he's* asked her . . . but she's coming when she likes. She says so. Because she's in love with you . . . God knows what women see in your kind of man! There was Pearl Hennig —

DANIEL — Please!

GOODKIND — Oh, my son told me! And I hear . . . in the neighborhood . . . that you've worse women than that running here! Women of the streets!

DANIEL — Not many. They're welcome, but they don't come.

GOODKIND — Well, that's *your* business! And if your neighbors get sick of having a resort of this kind in their midst, and drive you out, *that's* your business! But my son's wife —

DANIEL — Is *her* business!

GOODKIND — And his! Only Jerry's in no condition to settle the matter! He's broken down from worry and overwork, and you're partly responsible, and that puts it up to me! You can take this as a final warning! If you see Clare again, I'll act, and I'll act quick! That's all! Good night!

DANIEL — Oh! Mr. Goodkind!

GOODKIND — Yes?

DANIEL — How about the money?

GOODKIND — You've had what's coming to you!

DANIEL — But that's *nothing!* I pay half that for these crazy houses! And I've gone terribly in debt fitting them up!

GOODKIND — With baths and tennis courts!

DANIEL — People must have baths.

GOODKIND — These dirty immigrants!

DANIEL — The dirtier they are, the worse they need 'em. I want to show them how to live, and I want to show other people . . . that you don't have to make a pig-pen to make a profit!

GOODKIND — Are you making a profit?

DANIEL — Enormous. And, to go on, I've got to have twenty-two thousand dollars.

GOODKIND — Oh, is that all? Twenty-two thousand dollars to go on making a fool of yourself: Well, you won't get it!

DANIEL — Not even as an advance?

GOODKIND — Not a penny!

DANIEL — Don't drive *me* to —

GOODKIND — To what?

DANIEL — To ask for an accounting!

GOODKIND — To ask for — *what?* Now listen to me! I've stood all I'm going to stand! You've run amuck! You've become dangerous to yourself! . . . and . . . me . . . and the neighborhood! You're going to stop it, and you're going to stop it now!

DANIEL — That's your mistake.

GOODKIND — Is it? A year ago you gave me twenty-four hours to sign a paper, and I did it, and it cost me two million dollars! Tonight I give you thirty minutes to shut up this place, and quit seeing my daughter, and if you won't do it —

DANIEL — As I won't!

GOOODKIND — I'll be here inside of half an hour with a doctor!

DANIEL — And then?

GOODKIND — Then we'll file a petition to have you declared incompetent!

DANIEL — Mr. Goodkind, you don't mean that! You don't mean that because I'm trying to help —

GOODKIND — Help . . . whom? Strikers and street women and general riff-raff! And you don't even help them . . . because nobody *can!* And, if you could, and did, how in the name of God would that help the community? If I find you're still crazy in half an hour, I'll *say* you're crazy, and *I'll prove it!* Think it over!

As he rushes from the room he all but knocks over Umanski, the striking Pole, who has become one of

Daniel's most successful experiments. He has been studying and learning much. He works now "eight hours on the docks and six hours on myself," as he explains, and the results are apparent. But Goodkind has no time to take note of the change. . . .

Mary Margaret brings in the coffee and Grubby follows with the sandwiches. It is supper time, but Mary Margaret always has a time of it making Daniel stop working long enough to eat. . . . Mary Margaret is a little exalted today. She is wearing a pair of "solid gold" slippers that she took from a barrel of clothes a lady had sent to the mission, and they make her almost think she's Cinderella, sometimes.

DANIEL — If you believe it . . . you *are*.

MARY MARGARET — I guess believin' ain't never goin' to make *me* dance.

DANIEL — You can't tell — if you believe hard enough.

MARY MARGARET — That's what you said before, and I've tried, but somehow it don't work.

DANIEL — That's the very time to go on. If we stop, just because it don't work, that isn't faith.

MARY MARGARET — No; I s'pose not.

DANIEL — And faith moves mountains. Once upon a time there was a woman who'd been sick twelve years.

MARY MARGARET — What was the matter with her?

DANIEL — I don't know. But there was a Man in that city who said He could even make the dead rise. And everybody laughed at Him . . . as they would today. But the woman didn't laugh, and one morning, when He was passing her house, she got up and followed Him . . . just to touch the hem of His cloak. And what do you think?

MARY MARGARET — I dunno.

DANIEL — She was cured. And the Man said —

MARY MARGARET — I know. "Thy faith hath made thee whole."

DANIEL — That's right.

MARY MARGARET — Could God do that for me?

DANIEL — Yes.

MARY MARGARET — It would be an awful big favor.

DANIEL — But if he doesn't, you must go on. If faith doesn't heal our hurts, it helps us to bear them. And that's almost the same thing, isn't it?

MARY MARGARET — Yes.

DANIEL — Like believing you're Cinderella.

MARY MARGARET — Yes.

DANIEL — We can't decide what we want, and then be angry and doubtful because it doesn't happen our way. Because all the time it's happening His way. The only thing we can be sure of is that He knows what's best.

MARY MARGARET — That's right. You mean, if God wants me to be well, some day he'll make me well?

DANIEL — If you believe hard enough.

MARY MARGARET — And if He don't?

DANIEL — Then *that's* right . . . if you believe hard enough.

MARY MARGARET — I will, Mr. Gilchrist.

That night proved the most exciting of any Overcoat Hall had ever experienced. First, Pearl Hennig, who had successfully eluded the search of her husband the past few months, rushed in to warn Gilchrist that Joe was in town and searching for him. Joe had taken to drink lately and was openly accusing Dan of having spirited Pearl away. Worse than that, he was saying that Overcoat Hall was no more than a blind and that Daniel was using it to shield his way of living on women.

Daniel refuses to consider Joe's threats seriously. He even upbraids Pearl for not having stuck to her job, which was to bring Joe through, decently. And he refuses flatly to phone the police for protection.

Before Pearl can leave the door opens and Clare enters. She, too, is excited and the sight of Pearl Hennig does not serve to quiet her. Alone with Daniel Clare frankly confesses that she has left Jerry and come to him in the hope that he will let her stay. Jerry, drink-soaked, his health gone and his mind going, has grown increasingly impossible. Today he not only struck her, but openly accused her of having been Gilchrist's mistress, and made the threat that to even matters he was going to send Gilchrist to the insane asylum.

CLARE — I love you! I need you! I've always loved you, and needed you, even when I lied to you, and myself! This is our last chance for happiness! I've been blind, and stupid, and cruel, but it isn't too late! Take me, and hold me, and we'll both forget!

DANIEL — Forget?

CLARE — Forget everything. Won't you take me, dear?

DANIEL — No!

CLARE — Don't you want me?

DANIEL — No!

CLARE — That's not true! You love me! You've always loved me! Look at me and deny it if you can!

DANIEL — I don't deny it! I love you!

CLARE — Then take me!

DANIEL — I love the good in you . . . the good you're trying hard to kill! I love you because you're big enough to do what's right!

CLARE — What *is* right?

DANIEL — Go back to your husband.

CLARE — I'd rather die!

DANIEL — I'd rather you died . . . than *this!*

CLARE — Oh, you fanatic! You blind fanatic!

DANIEL — I love you!

CLARE — Love! You don't know what love means! You're only half a man!

DANIEL — And I'm praying to God, with all my strength, to save us from the other half!

CLARE — For what?

DANIEL — For you . . . and Him . . . and for *my people!* (*Off right Mary Margaret is heard singing, softly, "I'm a Pilgrim, I'm a Stranger."*) For the little girl out there.

CLARE — And for them you'd send me back to degradation?

DANIEL — That little girl's known degradation you and I will never know. And she's singing. Her constant companions are poverty and pain . . . and she's singing. She's crippled. She may never walk again, and she can say God's will be done. She believes in me. I can't disappoint her, and the rest. I'm going on with my job, and you're going back to yours.

CLARE — You mean Jerry?

DANIEL — Yes.

CLARE — You think *that's* God's will?

DANIEL — I know it is your job. You took it with your eyes open. It's up to you to see it through.

CLARE — Must I go on forever paying for one mistake?

DANIEL — Somebody must pay for our mistakes. That it was wrong to make a bargain doesn't make it right to break the bargain when we get tired of it.

CLARE — I don't know what to do.

DANIEL — Play the game. Go back to that poor, mistaken man lying across the foot of your bed — his mind going and his health gone. Bear your punishment and help him to bear his. That's your duty!

CLARE — Duty! Duty! Duty! What about happiness?

DANIEL — There *is* no other happiness. Oh, don't you see, my dear, *that's* been your *great* mistake? You're always crying — you and the world — "I want to be happy!" Happiness is service. Happiness is clean living, and clear thinking, and self-forgetfulness, and self-respect!

CLARE — And love?

DANIEL — Love *isn't* all. Not the love you mean. You said, "Take me, and we'll both forget." Could we have forgotten promises unkept, faith disappointed, aspirations unrealized? No, my dear, love isn't all; nor even happiness. There's something bigger, and better, and more important, and that something is — *duty!*

CLARE — The world doesn't think that!

DANIEL — That's what's wrong with the world!

CLARE — You want me to go back?

DANIEL — I want you to be right!

CLARE — Well, then . . . I'm going through. I'm going back, and play the game . . . with you in my heart always. You don't forbid that, do you?

DANIEL — You are in mine always.

CLARE — And this isn't good-bye. Sometime . . . somewhere . . . in this world, or out of it . . . there must be a moment . . . and a place to retrieve mistakes . . . Good night.

DANIEL — Clare . . . good night.

CLARE — And . . . thank you.

Clare has gone. The outer door slams. Then a cab door — faintly. Daniel sinks . . . tired with the effort of renunciation. Then he comes down slowly, and drops on the bench in front of the table. Mary Margaret enters, singing "I'm a Pilgrim" in a high key, to march tempo, keeping time with her crutches. . . .

Soon the neighbors are gathering for the evening meeting, and Mary Margaret helps receive. . . . Now Pearl Hennig is back, more excited than before. She has seen Joe, and his gang. She has heard them telling of what they are going to do to Overcoat Hall — and its phony man of God. Daniel stands ready to receive them as, a moment later, they burst through the door, an unruly mob of them, shouting the oaths of excited men.

Umanski stops them. With a grip of Joe Hennig's shoulder he sends that excited young mobster to his knees, and releases him reluctantly on Daniel's order. Hennig is the spokesman. Gilchrist is a cheater, he shouts; a low thing, living on the wages of women! No wife is safe anywhere within reach of Overcoat Hall! He knows, because his wife has been a victim! She says she's workin' in Macy's. What she's workin' is Sixth Avenue, and Gilchrist put her there.

Pearl admits a part of the charge. She lied to Gilchrist about Macy's. She is on the street.

Hearing her the crowd grows unruly. They press forward now. But Daniel stands his ground, with his hand on Pearl's shoulder. Whatever she has done she has not lost him as a friend, he tells them.

In a moment the crowd is hurling itself forward. Umanski is beaten back. A woman rushes to the window to shout for the police. At the end of the room to the left, just at the edge of the platform, Mary Margaret is praying aloud. Above the curse of the mob her shrill voice rises: "Our Father which art in heaven —"

Again the mob attacks and Gilchrist falls. George Goodkind appears in the door and forces his way through. Let everybody stand back, he demands. They need have no further fear of Gilchrist. He will be in an insane asylum before night.

Again above the crowd's jeers the voice of Mary Margaret in prayer: "Save him, Oh, God — "

GOODKIND — Leave him alone! You can't beat a crazy man!

PEARL — Mr. Gilchrist ain't crazy! He ain't a man! Ain't you seen what he just done to me?

A WOMAN — Hire a hall !

PEARL — Ain't you heard? I lied to him, an' he give me another chance, an' *I'm gonna take it!* He ain't no man! He's a saint! I tell you he's like God!

A VOICE — Where's his wings?

JOE — (*sneeringly*). Like God!

JIMMIE — That's blasphemy.

JOE — That's what it is, an' that's what he's been tellin'

'em! Ain't it . . . you . . . Grubby? Didn't he tell you that, Jimmie? Didn't he tell you he was a son of God?

THE GANG — Sure he did! That's right!

JOE — You see, that's what he's told 'em all! That's how he gets 'em! Didn't you tell 'em you was a son of God?

DANIEL — I am!

THE GANG — He admits it! (*A girl.*) And I'm Mary Magdalene! Pipe Mary Magdalene! Son of God!

DANIEL — So are we all! In you . . . and me . . . and all of us . . . deep down . . . is something of Him! We may try to hide it . . . or kill it, but, in spite of ourselves, we *are* divine!

THE GANG — Chuck it! Hell! Cut the gab! He's crazy! Come on; smash the place!

TONY — If you're a son of God . . . save yourself! If you're what you say . . . give us a sign!

Now the mob fights furiously to reach Gilchrist. Suddenly Umanski is overpowered and Daniel is struck down. Fighting like a demon Umanski clears a path through the crowd to his fallen benefactor, and as Gilchrist is revealed, a tiny trickle of blood running down his face, Mary Margaret ceases her praying and rises to her feet. Haltingly she walks toward Daniel. Suddenly the mob's attention is attracted to the child by the piercing scream of a woman.

MISS LEVINSON — Mary Margaret! Where are your crutches?

MARY MARGARET — I don't know! I kin walk! I kin walk! Mr. Gilchrist! Oh, Mr. Gilchrist!

PEARL — I told you! I told you he was a saint!

UMANSKI — You wanted a sign — *look!* Down on your knees — you damned murderers! God's in this room! Down on your knees!

One by one and two by two, the awestruck mob obeys. Joe is lying senseless, but his cohorts, crossing themselves, have seen a miracle.

The curtain falls.

ACT IV

Two months later Daniel and Mary Margaret are getting ready for another Christmas Eve celebration in Daniel's study above the clubrooms of Overcoat Hall. It is a peaceful Christmas Eve with them. Mary Margaret, grateful "to God and Mr. Gilchrist" for the miracle that cured her, has spent her pennies for a highly colored print of "Mama's Treasure" for Daniel, which she brings to his rooms that he may receive it from her hands rather than from those of whatever Santa Claus happens to have charge of the tree.

Which prompts Daniel to an even exchange, and Mary Margaret's present is brought forth — a child's set of beaver furs — "the most beautifullest" set that Mary Margaret has ever seen.

There is a caller. It is George Goodkind. He has dropped in only for a moment "on business." Jerry is waiting for him below in the car. The sight of Mary Margaret without her crutches reminds him. He wishes Daniel could perform a miracle on Jerry like that.

GOODKIND — Had a doctor look her over?

DANIEL — Three of 'em.

GOODKIND — Any opinion?

DANIEL — Three opinions.

MARY MARGARET — They said *he* didn't do it, and you seen him!

DANIEL — Ssh! They all say she suffered from hysterical paraplegia. Hysterical paralysis. One says she was cured by shock — you know; the riot. Another says it was suggestion . . . believing . . . which is another way of saying faith, isn't it? The important thing is that she's cured!

Mr. Goodkind has come to offer Daniel Jerry's job as general manager of the Goodkind properties. Jerry is ill. He has had to give up work, and there is more trouble at the mines. "We had a working compromise on your agreement," Goodkind explains, "and everything was all right. But we began figuring that we could make more money and the men walked out and flooded the mines." If Daniel will agree to take charge —

But Daniel can't. Not even for $100,000 a year. His work, as he sees it, is in Overcoat Hall, and even a hundred thousand dollars cannot buy him anything that he wants and has not got — shelter, food, friends, contentment.

But, demands Goodkind, is he a success?

DANIEL — Are you? What is success? Money? Yes; that is what our civilization tells us. Money! But where has that brought us? Only to the elevation of the unfit . . . the merely shrewd and predatory. All around us we see men of wealth who have nothing else . . . neither health nor happiness nor love nor respect. Men who can get no joy out of books, or pictures, or music, or even themselves. Tired, worried men who are afraid to quit because they have no resource except to make money — money with which to buy vulgar excitement for their own debased souls. Why, Mr. Goodkind, I have an income that you wouldn't suggest to your bookkeeper. But I have peace, and health, and friends, and time to read, and think, and dream, and help. Which of us is the rich man?

GOODKIND — But if everybody lived your way, what would become of the world's work?

DANIEL — Living that way is my contribution to the world's work. Another man's might be selling shoes, or writing plays, or digging ditches. Doing his job doesn't prevent any man from doing his bit. "From every man according to his ability to every man according to his needs." And every man who gives his best must find his happiness.

GOODKIND — I'm afraid there wouldn't be much progress . . . living your way.

DANIEL — That's the second time you've spoken of my way. It isn't *my* way. It's the sum total of all that has been learned and taught. You, and Jerry, and the others, have called me eccentric, and a fool, because I'm trying to walk a path trod hard by countless feet. Was Christ eccentric? Was Confucius a fool? And how about Buddha and Mohammed? What of Saint Bernard, and Saint Teresa, and Saint Francis of Assisi — of Plato, and Zeno, and Lincoln, and Emerson, and Florence Nightingale, and Father Damien, and Octavia Hill, and all the saints and scientists, and poets and philosophers who have lived and died in complete forgetfulness of self? Were they fools? Or were they wise men and women who had found the way to peace and happiness? Were they failures? Or were they the great successes of all time and eternity?

GOODKIND — God knows!

The door opens and Jerry Goodkind enters. He is a dying man. "He drags his legs with difficulty, and his speech is thick, but he is still cynical and defiant."

A suggestion of the old patronizing sneer curls Jerry's lip as he greets Gilchrist, and there is an echo of the old defiance in his trembling voice as he reports that although he is not so damned well at the moment, he will be all right as soon as he can get time to run down to Palm Beach. Clare's been a brick to him. Neither he nor his father is quite able to understand what has come over her, so eager has she been to do all that she can for Jerry.

But what of Gilchrist? The same old nut, Jerry can see that. "God," he wheezes; "some failure you've made out of your life! Wheels — by God, wheels!"

At the door the elder Goodkind turns. Jerry is stumping uncertainly down the stairs. Gilchrist stands in the glow of the firelight, the picture of strong, confident, contented manhood.

"I wonder if you're the failure, after all?" he says, as he goes out.

Daniel turns to the window, throws up the sash, and draws back the curtains. In the distance church chimes are beginning "Hark, the Herald Angels Sing." He stands looking up at the heavens, his left arm akimbo. Mary Margaret, feeling the cold air, draws her "beautifullest" furs closer about her and then slips her head through Daniel's arm and nestles closely to him.

Mary Margaret — Mr. Gilchrist! Is that the star of Bethlehem?

Daniel — I wonder.

The chimes swell out as the curtain falls.

THE END

"MERTON OF THE MOVIES"

A Comedy in Four Acts

BY GEORGE KAUFMAN AND MARC CONNELLY

(Based on the novel of the same name by Harry Leon Wilson)

GEORGE C. TYLER produced the first of the Booth Tarkington-Harry Leon Wilson plays, "The Man from Home," fifteen years ago, and both authors have been grateful admirers of his showmanship ever since.

It was natural, therefore, that Tyler should have first call on Mr. Wilson's "Merton of the Movies" when it came to a question of dramatizing that classic satire of the cinema. The stage rights were passed while the story was still running serially in the *Saturday Evening Post.*

For the work of transferring the comedy to the stage Mr. Tyler selected George Kaufman and Marc Connelly, the young collaborators whose two comedies, "Dulcy" and "Ladies First," had the previous season brought them to prominence. Later Hugh Ford, the stage director, joined the group, acquiring a half interest in the play and taking charge of its staging.

"Merton," produced at the Cort Theatre, New York, November 13, 1922, immediately took its place with the most popular plays of the season and is still popular at this writing, after practically eight months of continuous playing.

In adapting the story the Messrs. Kaufman and Connelly were wise in not permitting the obvious satire which is the tale's foundation to dominate the plot, which is homely and basicly human. They pick up the hero, Merton Gill, while he still is serving the customers of Amos Gashwiler's general store in Simsbury, Illinois, as general clerk. His passion for the movies is the subject of sly gossip, and he stands in a fair way of becoming a town joke, especially since Charles Harper swears he has seen Merton down in the Gashwiler pasture as early as six in the morning talking to the Gashwiler horse and posing for a picture with his arms around the unsuspecting beast's neck.

Gashwiler himself has noticed that Merton finds it increasingly difficult to keep his mind on his work Saturday nights, when there is always a new movie at the local theatre, and he suspects that his young helper is spending a good part of his income on the pictures.

Merton feels that he can afford to take the criticism of the Simsbury folk lightly. Having consecrated his life to a great career he cannot afford to let the reactions of small minds affect him, even if he were conscious of them.

This particular Saturday night he feels unusually sure of his position and his ultimate victory. His savings are mounting up, the "stills" that the village photographer has made of him in the various sartorial outfits he has managed to buy out of his fifteen-dollar-a-week salary are satisfactory, and he thinks he will soon be ready to start for California. Tessie Kearns, the village milliner, has brought the prints from the photographer and admired them with Merton, especially the one taken in a dress suit in which Merton's resemblance to Harold Parmelee, "perhaps the greatest star in a certain type of part the screen will ever see," is decidedly marked.

MERTON — . . . Of course, I don't intend to imitate him (Parmelee), anyway. When I begin acting professionally, I intend creating my own particular types.

MISS KEARNS — Have you made up your mind yet when you're going?

MERTON — Pretty soon now. I've got two hundred and seventy dollars. I figure in another month or so — I'll have a clear three hundred.

MISS KEARNS — And then you'll go out to California?

MERTON — The minute I get three hundred. I've got about all the clothes I need now. They can't say I haven't the equipment. I've got western suits, automobile clothes, a polo suit — 'n'everything!

MISS KEARNS — (*depressed*). I'll be sorry to see you go — in a way, Merton. But I know you're going to be a big success as an actor.

MERTON — Well, I've been working hard at it. But I guess I'm still pretty far from perfect.

MISS KEARNS — Nonsense! You took all that *correspondence course*, didn't you?

MERTON — It was funny, my thinking I knew everything before I took that course. Did I show you their certificate?

MISS KEARNS — (*reading*). All engraved!

MERTON — You bet.

MISS KEARNS — "Film Incorporation Bureau, Station N., Stebbinsville, Kansas." It's a wonderful *name*, you took, Merton! (*Reads from certificate.*) Clifford Armytage.

MERTON — I picked it myself.

MISS KEARNS — It sounds so real. You're an actor now, all right. Only I had no idea you might be going so soon.

MERTON — Just the minute I get three hundred.

MISS KEARNS — It'll be pretty quiet here.

MERTON — You ought to come out too, Tessie. That's the place for a scenario writer.

MISS KEARNS — Not on what the millinery business is paying.

MERTON — You know a photo playwright ought to be right on the ground just as much as an actor. All the world-famous authors go out there, Rex Beach, Elinor Glyn, Maeterlinck, and Rupert Hughes —

But Tessie is not altogether convinced. Having never sold a story she feels that she is not quite world-famous as yet. But Merton is confident she will get on. Some one is sure to buy her "Passion's Perils." All the great artists of the screen have had to be patient. Even the great Beulah Baxter. Miss Beulah is Merton's movie ideal, and it is her appearance in the latest installment of the serial, "Hazards of Hortense," that he has missed this Saturday night. Miss Kearns is telling him about it.

MERTON — I'll bet she was wonderful. What was the menace?

MISS KEARNS — They got the cabin surrounded by wolves and then set fire to it. It was harrowing. I don't blame you for admiring her. She's certainly fearless.

MERTON — The wonder woman of the silver screen, *I* call her.

MISS KEARNS — One time tonight she fought a wolf, hand to hand.

MERTON — Gee!

MISS KEARNS — I thought for a minute it was a double — it was so daring.

MERTON — Well, you can get *that* idea out of your head. I told you what she said at that personal appearance in Peoria. She said, if she ever used a double in "Hazards of Hortense" why, she'd feel she wasn't keeping faith with her public.

MISS KEARNS — Oh, it must have been wonderful, being virtually face to face with her.

MERTON — It was, and very inspiring. Why, she just *swayed* that audience.

MISS KEARNS—Mr. Gashwiler never found out *why* you went to Peoria, did he?

MERTON — No, but if he did I wouldn't hesitate to admit it. Miss Baxter is a great influence in my life. That Elmer Huff got me a little sore just now.

MISS KEARNS — Why what — what did he do?

MERTON — Nothing, really. But Miss Baxter's name almost came up in the course of conversation. If he'd have spoken lightly of her, I'd have lost control of myself. Say, Tessie, wouldn't it be wonderful if — when I went out there — I got a chance to work with her in a picture?

MISS KEARNS — I hope you do, Merton.

MERTON — Gee!

MISS KEARNS — Well, I'll be getting along — You know, Merton, in a way I'm just as glad you didn't see the show tonight. They had another of those comedies.

MERTON — Jeff Baird's? She'd be revolted if she knew her work was on the same bill. Here's a wonderful artist, on one hand, trying to do better and finer things all the time, like "Hazards of Hortense," and alongside of her they put a cheap thing like one of those Jeff Baird comedies. Was the cross-eyed man in it again?

MISS KEARNS — Yes, he was.

MERTON — It's enough to discourage a *real* artist.

MISS KEARNS — Still, there were times when I could hardly keep from laughing.

MERTON — They oughtn't to allow them to be made.

MISS KEARNS — No, I suppose not. (*Gathering up pictures and magazines.*) Well, good night.

MERTON — What's that — *Silver Screenings?*

MISS KEARNS — Yes, I've finished with it — if you want it.

MERTON — Thanks. Mary Pickford is beautiful, isn't she? (*Looking through it.*) Here's an interview with Harold Parmelee! (*Studying the picture.*) I've got a cap something like that.

MISS KEARNS — It's an awful good piece about him. I liked it where he says — (*She looks over at the story to refresh her memory.*) Ah —

MERTON — (*reading*). "Hard work and the constant striving toward an ideal. . . ."

MISS KEARNS — (*turns page*). No — here at the *end.*

MERTON — Ah! About his *wife!* (*Reads.*) "She is not only my best pal, but my severest critic."

MISS KEARNS — It's a lovely tribute.

MERTON — And to a splendid woman. . . .

Now Tessie has gone and Merton starts to close the store. He shuts the street door and pulls down the shades. From the windows he takes two wax dummies that have been on display, a female figure dressed in checked gingham and labeled, "Our Latest for Milady, only $6.98," and a male wearing a raincoat with a guarantee, "Rainproof or You Get Back Your Money," clinging to it. Rather a villainous looking person, the raincoat gent, and as Merton leans him against the counter he sneers, as Harold Parmelee might do, "You cur!"

From under the counter he pulls a small trunk that holds his personal belongings, and from the trunk takes the wallet containing his savings, to which he adds another fifteen dollars. As he does so he notices a sombrero. Placing this jauntily on his head he closes a small window and then, dramatically turning out the hanging lamp and plunging the room in deep darkness, save for the moonlight and a small handlight at the end of the counter, he acts out a picture scene as it might have been written, playing all the characters.

"One — a — little — kiss," he hisses as the villain dummy.

"Ah, God in heaven, is there no help at hand?" he screams, as the gingham lady.

And then, as the hero, he calmly takes command of the situation himself. "Just a minute, my friend. . . . I trust I am not too late, Miss St. Clair? Yes, it's me — Buck Benson, at your service, ma'am. I suppose this — this gentleman has been annoying you? Oh, he has, has he? (*Turning to villain.*) Now, curse you, you shall fight me in American fashion, man to man! Viper though you are, I hesitate to put a bullet through your craven heart —"

In another minute he has grabbed the raincoat dummy and is wrestling heroically with it toward the counter. "Now, you dog, we shall learn whose body goes over yonder cliff —" He is holding the dummy helpless above his head and seems about to throw it savagely behind the counter when the door opens and Mr. Gashwiler appears. He had heard the "riotin'" upstairs, and wants to know what it is all about.

Mr. Gashwiler assumes from the appearance of things that Merton must think he is actin' in grand op'ry, or somethin', and he's pretty mad about it. But Merton's apparent earnestness impresses him. Still, he can't stand for any cowboys around his grocery store, and he can't stand for any more of this movie studyin'.

MERTON — You don't mean that, do you, Mr. Gashwiler?

GASHWILER — I *certainly do.* There's a limit, Merton, I can't afford havin' anybody around whose spare time ain't spent in something worth while.

MERTON — And you don't think movies are?

GASHWILER — I certainly do not.

MERTON — Well, then I'll leave, Mr. Gashwiler — right now.

GASHWILER — You'll what?

MERTON — I'll leave; I'm going out to California and — enter the films — I was going in a month, but I'll go right away.

GASHWILER — To — to — California?

MERTON — Yes, sir.

GASHWILER — To be an actor?

MERTON — Yes, sir, and I'll succeed, too.

GASHWILER — Now 'tain't likely — a boy from Simsbury.

MERTON — Lincoln walked four miles for a book.

GASHWILER — Yes, but you ain't studying for President. You're tryin' to get into somethin' that nobody I ever heard of succeeded in.

MERTON — Well, just the same, Mr. Gashwiler, I'm going to *follow my star.*

GASHWILER — All right, Merton, if that's what you want to do, then I'm to go right ahead and get somebody else?

MERTON — (*pause*). Yes, sir.

GASHWILER — You got much money?

MERTON — Two hundred and seventy dollars.

GASHWILER — (*almost gets money out of pocket, changes his mind*). Well I — I hope you make a big success of it, Merton — Good night.

MERTON — Thank you, Mr. Gashwiler — and I'm sorry about the dummies.

GASHWILER — That's all right, you didn't hurt them none. (*Looks at Merton.*) I can't just make you out, Merton, you're a nice boy, one of the nicest I ever knew, but, I guess you're just crazy. (*Merton looks after him for a second, then moves male dummy and starts the phonograph. It is a Walter Camp Daily Dozen record. He follows the instructions of the voice from the phonograph.*)

MERTON — Some day we shall meet again. (*Phonograph.*) This time your life has been spared. (*Another pause; Merton changes his tactics and begins to address an imaginary interviewer.*) You ask me to tell the readers of your magazine to what I owe my success. Hard work, young lady. Hard work and the constant striving toward an ideal to give the best that is in me to the public. Perhaps I owe most, however, to Mrs. Armytage, my wife. She is more than a wife. She is my best pal, and, I may say, my severest critic. (*He stops the machine, and blows out the lamp. He pulls the cot from under the counter, takes money out of pocket, gets purse from under pillow, places the money in purse and puts the purse back under the pillow. He kneels beside the cot in the moonlight.*) Oh, God, make me a good movie actor! Make me one of the best! For Jesus' sake, Amen!

The curtain falls.

ACT II

Three weeks later, in the waiting-room outside the Holden lot in Hollywood, several "extras" are gathered. The room is bare, furnished only with a long bench along one wall. "There are but two doors, one at the left that leads to and from the outside world, and one at the right that leads on into the mysteries of the lot. On this latter door is a sign — 'No Admittance Except on Order.' "

There is another sign warning the "artistes" that costumes should be returned promptly and that the company is not responsible for damage to wardrobe furnished by the artists. The advice is also offered that "Talent Checks" should be cashed promptly.

Over a small window are the words "Casting Director," and back of the window a busy young woman is engaged a good part of the time with a busier telephone. The message she most frequently delivers, both in the phone and to eager callers, is: "No, no — nothing today!"

Occasionally she directs incoming actors to the stages

on which they are to work. Camera men and directors move in and out; the directors, nervous, irritable, superior individuals, seeking to shield themselves from the pestiferous actor-insects by an assumed indifference. Thus, the aging and somewhat seedy, but still dignified, Lester Montague, once an actor of the legitimate theatre, attempts to interrogate the director, Sigmund Rosenblatt, as to the prospects for early employment.

MONTAGUE — If I might — make so bold —

ROSENBLATT — (*to camera man*). Got to be a retake on them Chinatown scenes — the fan-tan game.

FIRST CAMERAMAN — Yes, sir.

MONTAGUE — Mr. Rosenblatt —

ROSENBLATT — (*he notices Montague*). What is it?

MONTAGUE — If by any chance the scenario calls for a real actor —

ROSENBLATT — All full up. (*He walks away.*)

MONTAGUE — You may recall that I played a desperado when you were taking —

ROSENBLATT — Oh, yes — what's the name?

MONTAGUE — Montague. Lester Montague.

ROSENBLATT — Haven't got a thing. (*Turns away.*)

MONTAGUE — I was with you in "The Little Shepherd of the Bar Z." That was the working title. I believe it was released as "I Want More Children."

ROSENBLATT — Well. Water stuff next week. Can you swim?

MONTAGUE — (*proudly*). Of course, I am an actor.

ROSENBLATT — Well! We'll see —

It is the first day Merton Gill has discovered the waiting room. He comes in now, somewhat awed by the surroundings but excited and eager. Nerving himself for the ordeal, he speaks to the casting director. Is this where the actors are selected? She glances at him casually and repeats the familiar: "Nothing today. Sorry."

Not knowing what else to do Merton wanders over near the door that leads to the lot. He would go on through, but the doorman stops him. So he stands around, awkwardly, observing the geniuses as they move and speak. He catches a glimpse of Bert Chester, the famous cross-eyed man of the Buckeye Comedies, and overhears the engagement of a man sufficiently bow-legged to let a hog slip between his knees and is disgusted. He tries again to pass the man at the lot entrance, but unsuccessfully. Again he wanders, a little helplessly, back to the casting director's window.

MERTON — (*trying to attract the woman's attention*). Excuse me —

CASTING DIRECTOR — My Lord — you again.

MERTON — I just wanted to ask you —

CASTING DIRECTOR — (*not unkindly*). There's nothing doing, and you can't go in.

MERTON — I know, but — if there were — something doing — you'd know about it first, wouldn't you?

CASTING DIRECTOR — Yes, next to Jesse Lasky.

MERTON — Well, then, you wouldn't mind if I waited here a while, would you? Just in case — there was something?

CASTING DIRECTOR — Help yourself, but, there's only two companies shooting on the lot.

He is back on the bench again when he is attracted by the conversation of a young woman of the movie soubrette type who has just come in. She is talking with Lester Montague, the actor, who is back, thinking there may be a chance for him in "Rich Men's Mistresses," if they still need a rich man or two. The girl is Montague's daughter, and they are comparing their job-hunting experiences.

GIRL — . . . I've been in every studio in Hollywood

in the last hour and a half. Covered 'em so fast they thought I was a tourist!

MONTAGUE — Conditions *are* discouraging.

GIRL — (*powders nose*). Tell me they're going to shoot some Arab stuff at the Consolidated tomorrow, but I says, No, thanks — I've been bit by my last camel.

MONTAGUE — Still any employment would be grateful in times like these.

GIRL — (*sighs*). Well, you can go to it if you want to. Besides, I'm getting too beautiful for the films. Baxter's jealous of me already.

MONTAGUE — (*on his feet*). You said the Consolidated, I believe?

GIRL — (*observing Merton, and answering with divided attention*). Huh? Oh! Yah, but look out for those camels. They sink a pretty tooth.

MONTAGUE — Oh, I know a remedy for camel bites.

GIRL — Hello, Newcomer! (*This to Merton.*)

MERTON — (*caught by her mention of Baxter, but feeling a vague animosity toward the Montague girl*). Oh — excuse me, but —

GIRL — Sure.

MERTON — Did you — you didn't mean Beulah Baxter, did you? That was jealous, I mean?

GIRL — Jealous? Last time I starred with her she said she'd quit cold if I kept on arriving in a different automobile every day. Had to *sell* my third assistant Pierce-Arrow.

MERTON — But nobody ever stars with Beulah Baxter —

GIRL — Well, I wasn't really starred. My parents wouldn't let me.

MERTON — They wouldn't? —

GIRL — Nope! Too young!

MERTON — Ah!

GIRL — *New* on the lot, ain't you?

MERTON — No, not exactly.

GIRL — Didn't remember seeing you before. Still, they come and go.

Merton is interested, but a little disgusted as well. Something tells him the Montague girl can't really take her art seriously when she makes so light of it. He hears her now telling the casting director that she could have gone on in a harem tank scene over at the Bigart, but they wanted her to dress like a fish and it happens that she is "built more like home folks." Still, she is hoping her dad will find something soon. If he doesn't, and goes on sitting around home making "old Kentucky bourbon in thirty minutes, he's going to see some moving pictures that nobody else can."

But the thing that convinces Merton finally that the Montague girl is wrong is her conversation with the famous Henshaw, who comes looking for his star, Harold Parmelee. Merton, overhearing the name, does his best to look as much like Harold as possible, but the great director does not notice him. He pauses to listen to the Montague girl, however, when she addresses him with the proper deference.

GIRL — Oh, Commander!

HENSHAW — Yes, yes?

GIRL — Could you — could you give me just a minute, please?

HENSHAW — Well, I'm very busy, very busy, but —

GIRL — Well, you see, it's this way, Commander. I got a great idea for a story, see, and I was thinking who to take it to, and I thought of a lot of them, and I asked my friends, and they all said, "Oh, take it to Mr. Henshaw, because he's the one director on the lot that can get every ounce of value out of it," so I thought — but of course if you're busy —

HENSHAW — I *am* busy, but then I'm always busy.

They run me to death here. Still, it was very *kind* of your friends, and of course —

GIRL — Thank you a thousand times, Mr. Henshaw. (*She assumes a worshipping pose.*) It starts off kind of like this. You see, I'm a Hawaiian princess —

HENSHAW — The character's an Hawaiian princess.

GIRL — Oh, excuse me. Well, anyway, I'm this Hawaiian princess, and my father, old King Mauna Loa, dies, and leaves me two thousand volcanoes and a billiard cue. Now —

HENSHAW — Ah — just a minute. A billiard cue?

GIRL — Yes, sir — And every morning I have to go out and ram it down the volcanoes to see if they're all right. Now then —

HENSHAW — What are you *talking* about —

GIRL — The *villain* is very wealthy and owns one of the largest ukelele plantations on the island —

HENSHAW — Tush, tush! Absurd; absurd; (*Walks toward casting director.*) Any word yet?

GIRL — Oh, dear, well, of course, I knew it was crude —but no one ever listens to you until you break into the magazines. "Really, really, said Miss Montague—termed by many as the most beautiful woman in the world — I am at a loss to understand why the public should be so interested in me — what can I say to your readers — Oh, please, please go away and leave me to my books and my art —"

Henshaw is irritated beyond words by such flippancy, and Merton is himself inclined to resent it. He tries now to tell the great director that he knew the girl was wrong about the volcanoes and the billiard cue. It couldn't be done. Anybody who knows anything about the practical side of moving pictures would know — But Henshaw merely brushes him aside as he might a black fly and turns to his assistants. The delayed Parmelee arrives and Henshaw takes up with him the matter of revising the story of "Robinson Crusoe." It is the director's idea that they should give Friday a white sister with whom Crusoe can fall in love. "In that way," he assures his workers, "we can get the sex into it."

As they start away Merton decides he should introduce himself to Harold Parmelee — first as one of his staunchest admirers and, second, as one who has been told that there is a certain striking resemblance. Perhaps if Mr. Parmelee will look at him he will see there is a resemblance —

But Mr. Parmelee cannot be bored by such silly stuff and leaves rather abruptly. Again the boy turns to the casting director. Nor will he be squelched when she repeats sharply that there is nothing doing and that he can't go on the lot. As he turns away he imitates Parmelee's exit, his gestures and his mincing walk. The casting director concludes from this performance that he must be a regular actor, and is prepared to register him.

CASTING DIRECTOR — I suppose your trunks are coming?

MERTON — I suppose you mean my — costumes?

CASTING DIRECTOR — You're new, aren't you?

MERTON — Well, I am now, but I won't be.

CASTING DIRECTOR — Have you registered?

MERTON — Madam?

CASTING DIRECTOR — Have I got your name and address?

MERTON — Oh — no.

CASTING DIRECTOR — You *are* new. (*She has picked up a pencil.*) Come on.

MERTON — Ma'm?

CASTING DIRECTOR — What's your name? You've got a name, haven't you?

MERTON — Clifford Armytage.

CASTING DIRECTOR — Come again.

MERTON — Clifford Armytage.

CASTING DIRECTOR — Clifford Armytage? Well, why not? Address?

MERTON — Two thousand four hundred and sixty Oakdale Avenue.

CASTING DIRECTOR — Line of parts?

MERTON — Huh?

CASTING DIRECTOR — What's your line?

MERTON — Oh! Well, that's what I was going to show you. (*He draws out the art photographs and gives them to her.*) You see, those'll give you a pretty good idea. I mean, that's —

CASTING DIRECTOR — Oh, my goodness. (*Inspecting.*) You don't mean these are all the same person?

MERTON — (*proudly*). They are, though.

CASTING DIRECTOR— My goodness, what do you think of that. . . . Cowboy, and — society man, and — now don't tell me that's you on the horse!

MERTON — Yes — well, of course, I just wanted you to see what I could do. Of course, I wouldn't expect big parts to begin with. I'm willing to work hard and sacrifice in the beginning.

CASTING DIRECTOR — You'll sacrifice all right.

MERTON — Because it's only out of hard work and sacrifice that the finer things come, and you take Beulah Baxter or Harold Parmelee, or any of them, and they all started that way.

CASTING DIRECTOR — Say, you're a regular bug, aren't you?

MERTON — Say — say — does Beulah Baxter — does she ever come in this way?

CASTING DIRECTOR — Sure — mostly.

MERTON — Right along here?

CASTING DIRECTOR — Just like a mortal.

MERTON — (*turns and surveys the room, worshippingly, then turns back to the window*). Is — is Beulah Baxter married?

Casting Director — Well now, let me think. I never can remember.

Merton — She's the little wonder woman, all right. I'll bet you she sacrificed, before she got up to where she is.

Casting Director — *I'll* say she did. . . . (*At telephone.*) Yes — yes, I understand — Stage eight, all right.

Merton — I don't suppose it would be possible to get in her company some time — ?

Casting Director — Now, listen, son, I might not be able to get you *anything* for a long, long time. . . .

Merton — Oh, I don't mind — struggling. The only thing is — I want to do something really significant, and not just mere comedies.

Casting Director — Well, I'll remember you. And I can always reach you at two thousand four hundred and so forth —

Merton — Yeh, only — during the day I'll be right here.

Casting Director — (*gives him a look*). All day?

Merton — Yeh.

Casting Director — Aren't you ever going to try the other studios?

Merton — Oh, no!

Casting Director — Well, I'd ought to enjoy that.

The Montague girl is back with Jeff Baird, the comedy king, and insists on introducing her new friend, Merton, to him. Merton acknowledges the introduction, but is not happy. Even so slight a contact with the producer of slapstick stuff is repugnant. It is Merton's wish to do "something of a finer nature than mere comedies," he assures Mr. Baird. "And I would not even entertain an offer to associate myself with them," he adds. If Merton's decision is final, Baird admits, it certainly messes up his plans.

Again the Montague girl tries to find out just what it is that is troubling this new "trouper." What, for instance, has he against Jeff Baird's comedies? They degrade art, Merton frankly tells her.

GIRL — *What* art?
MERTON — (*with dignity*). The art of the motion pictures.
GIRL — You haven't been around here long. Huh?
MERTON — I — I don't care to discuss my — private affairs.
GIRL — All right, kid. Only take an old trouper's word for it — it's a tough game. Work is few and far between, and when it does come, it's generally pretty cheesy. You take even an old timer like Pa. Last month he got a job in a moonshining play.
MERTON — You mean where the revenue officer falls in love with the moonshiner's daughter?
GIRL — That's it. Well, anyhow, Pa gets this job and they won't stand for the crepe hair, so he has to go and raise a garden. Gives a month to raising it — all his spare time — and what happens?
MERTON — I'm sure I don't know.
GIRL — After four days' work they go and have him killed off. Pa goes around for a week and tries to rent the garden, but by that time nobody was doing anything but Chinese pictures. That's what you're up against in this game, kid.
MERTON — But I couldn't raise a beard anyhow.
GIRL — (*a pause*). You win! . . . Still afraid of me, ain't you?
MERTON —Oh, no I'm not.
GIRL — Well, don't you be. I'm just a poor mug, the same as you, only I've been at it a little longer, that's all. I like you.
MERTON — (*very fussed*). Well, it isn't — I don't want you to think I don't appreciate —

GIRL — That's all right. You're a nice kid, only you're awful green. Don't think I talk to all of them like this, but somehow there's something about you that made me do it. If you want anybody to pilot you around, maybe introduce you at the other studios —

MERTON — Oh, no — thanks. I — I'm going to work just at this studio if you don't mind.

GIRL — What's the big notion?

MERTON — Well, you see — what I want — I mean, this is the company where Beulah Baxter is, and I figured —

GIRL — Say kid, look at me. You haven't gone and fallen in love with a picture, have you?

MERTON — I — didn't say that.

GIRL — I *know* you didn't, but I'm awful quick.

MERTON — It is merely that I am a great admirer of Miss Baxter's art, and regard her as the wonder woman of the silver screen.

GIRL — Honest?

MERTON — You — of course you were only joking about starring with her, weren't you? Because she doesn't ever have anybody. She doesn't even have anybody even double for her, the way some of them do when it's dangerous.

GIRL — Oh!

MERTON — So I thought if I could only get with her company, I mean no matter how small a part it was, why I thought I'd rather do that than go to one of the other studios and maybe work with somebody who — whose ideals weren't as fine as hers.

GIRL — I see.

MERTON — You — you don't know of anybody whose ideals are as fine as hers — do you?

GIRL — No. She's got the finest set of ideals on the lot.

There is another phone call for the casting director,

and this time they do need actors. Henshaw has begun to shoot his revised "Robinson Crusoe" and wants nine extras on stage six at eight thirty the next morning, all in evening clothes. Merton is chosen as one of the nine, and given his ticket. Opportunity has at last assumed a beckoning attitude and young Mr. Gill is greatly excited.

MERTON — (*to the casting director*). Say, should — should I have my breakfast before I come in the morning?

CASTING DIRECTOR — It might not be a bad idea.

MERTON — (*to the Montague girl*). We're to have breakfast first, before we get here.

GIRL — Those who *can* eat.

MERTON — (*stands in sheer excitement for a moment, his eyes sparkling. Finally looks at his watch*). It's about two o'clock now. That's — not so long, is it?

GIRL — No time at all.

MERTON — I mean, if I go to bed early, why, that'll make the time pass so much more quickly.

GIRL — (*to the casting director*). I didn't think it was possible.

MERTON — What?

GIRL — Nothing.

MERTON — (*his face alight with a new idea — rushes to the window*). I — I'm working here now!

CASTING DIRECTOR — So?

MERTON — You remember before I asked if I could go in, and you asked if I was working here? Well, now I am! (*He waits in suspense for the decision. The casting director looks up at the Montague girl, who nods.*)

CASTING DIRECTOR — Why, sure. Help yourself. (*Hands him card.*)

MERTON — (*in a trance, and unaware that the girl is the one to be thanked*). Thanks. (*He starts to walk toward the door at the right, when doorkeeper stops him, then suddenly, with considerable of a flourish, a footman enters. Merton stops to feast his eyes upon this strange proceeding.)* (*To the girl.*) Who is it?

GIRL — I think it's a friend of yours.

MERTON — Not — you don't mean — Beulah Baxter? (*Then Baxter followed by her maid enters, crosses and exits — followed by the maid and the first footman and Merton, who has watched every move, slowly follows.*)

The curtain falls.

ACT III

A week later Stage No. 6 on the Holden lot is set for the big society scene in Director Henshaw's version of "Robinson Crusoe." The cameras are placed, the Kleig lights are on, and Muriel, the leading woman, is being filmed in one of the minor episodes.

At one side, Harold Parmelee, the star, with his Japanese valet, fusses with his satin lounging robe, and at the edges of the set the nine extras engaged for the society scenes are grouped. Merton, who has, without thinking, sunk into the canvas-backed chair plainly marked "Mr. Henshaw," is half hidden by one of the extras. He comes to light quite suddenly a moment later when Henshaw, during an obvious mental strain, backs up suddenly in search of support and sits plump into Merton's lap. The great director would like to murder this fresh young extra, but he desists, and Merton is as covered with chagrin as his makeup will permit. A moment later, with the help of his assistants, Henshaw has recovered his shaken senses and is again in the midst of explaining the scene to Parmelee.

HENSHAW — Yes. He has a whole lot of guests —

society people. And he turns on them and bawls them out — there's a big kick for you, Harold — and says he's going to go some place and live alone. The simple life — see? And somebody says, "Oh, like Robinson Crusoe?" Only, we introduce it natural — with the book on the table. (*Takes book from table.*) And he says, "Yes — that's just what he's going to do — live on an island like Robinson Crusoe." Then he drives them all out, and settles down in a chair to think. He takes up the book — begins to look through it, and here's the big kick. (*Rap on table.*) He *dreams* he's Robinson Crusoe. (*Book down.*) (*Weller indulges in a long low whistle, implying that the majesty of the idea is too much for words to express. Henshaw turns to him.*) Like it?

WELLER — Big stuff, Chief.

PARMELEE — Ah — how about the scene — ah — you know, the scene in the book about — fifteen men on a dead man's chest? Do you show that later?

HENSHAW — I don't just remember that. As a matter of fact, I just skimmed that passage.

PARMELEE — Well, I thought that would be rather a good scene, you know, the — dead man, and all that.

HENSHAW — Yes, I thought that was in Monte Cristo.

WELLER — I don't think that is in Crusoe.

PARMELEE — Well, I remember as a child —

MONTAGUE GIRL — Excuse me, Mr. Henshaw.

HENSHAW — Yes — what is it?

GIRL — I think that's from Romeo and Juliet.

HENSHAW — Oh, yes, the court scene. Well, now we'll start presently. I've got to think it over — I want to get just the right atmosphere. How'll we begin?

To aid in the working out of this mighty idea Henshaw calls for the violinist. He had rather have a harp, but as the musician has not thought to bring one he is forced to do the best he can with the violin. To the strains of a Venetian air he paces the floor, thinking. The violinist follows. Merton keeps as close to the heels of the latter as he feels it safe to get. The music has its effect and Henshaw is soon able to continue with the scene.

"Camera!" he shouts, and, as the machines begin to grind: "That's the stuff — you're dead tired — you've been dancing till six o'clock — you're sick of the whole game — nothing means a thing to you — you're all in — you're tired — save it!"

"Save it!" officiously repeats Weller, the assistant.

And the thing is done.

Now Henshaw has discovered that "Robinson Crusoe" is a very old book, and he thinks the best way to introduce it will be for one of the guests to come upon it casually as it is lying on the table. He calls for volunteers, and Merton is the first to respond.

"All right, you'll do," agrees the director. "You find the book on the table, see? It's 'Robinson Crusoe' and you're a little surprised — it isn't the book you'd expect to find on a gentleman's table. Then you say: Ah — (*puzzled*). Let's hear that subtitle, Weller."

" 'I see you are a bookworm'," reads Weller.

"Splendid! Then, Harold, you say — what is it — ?"

"Yes, that is 'Robinson Crusoe'," reads Weller. "A fascinating romance, and one of the greatest stories ever written. There are times when I envy him."

"Exactly! Now run through that. There's the book — see? You come down casually and discover it — Stand back, you people. Don't crowd!"

Merton tries it, but not successfully. He is embarrassed and awkward and the more casual he tries to become the more awful he appears. Henshaw tears his hair. Again Merton tries, arriving finally at the table, and picking up the book with a start as though he had been struck. "It's a book! Not a rattlesnake!" shouts Henshaw. "Didn't you ever see a book before?" "Yes, sir," meekly answers Merton. But no one believes him, except the Montague girl, who has drifted into the scene from one of the other stages.

"I think if you give him another chance he could do it," she suggests.

Henshaw wearily agrees, but Merton is a little worse than before the second time. Henshaw will have no more of him. He's so worn by the experience, in fact, that he is forced to quit for the day. His nerves are simply ragged. The company is dismissed and told to report next morning at 8.30, in the same costume — all except Merton. "I need a different type for this sort of thing," Henshaw tells him. "Mr. Weller will give you your pay order." And he refuses, despite the boy's pleading, to discuss the matter further.

Now the actors and the camera men have all gone. Only Merton and the Montague girl are left on the set.

GIRL — It's — it's all right, kid. That doesn't mean anything. You'll get lots of bumps like that.

MERTON — No, thanks, I —

GIRL — The big bum's crazy, that's all. But don't let it do anything to you. They — they can't put you down, can they?

MERTON — I'm not — down.

GIRL — Of course you're not.

MERTON — I didn't know what he meant — when —

GIRL — Who does?

MERTON — When a person's making their first appearance and all — why —

GIRL — Sure. I know. Why, the first time they aimed a camera at me I thought there was bullets in it.

MERTON — But still it *was* my chance, and I had to go and — fail.

GIRL — Fail? Just because of a little thing like that? Why, you're going to succeed big. All you need is — confidence.

MERTON — Is it?

GIRL — That's all most of them have.

MERTON — (*eager*). I bet I could have done it next time.

GIRL — I know! Don't you worry about him. Why, he even fired Parmelee once.

MERTON — He did? I know I could act the way Parmelee does if I — practiced enough.

GIRL — Of course you could. The only thing is — (*she stops*).

MERTON — What?

GIRL — Well — sometimes it takes a long while before you really — that is, before they give you a chance.

MERTON — Oh, I *want* a struggle.

GIRL — (*quickly*). Yah, but — if it should take a while — I mean, before you — well — are you fixed all right — for it? Money, I mean?

MERTON — (*turning away*). Oh — yes.

GIRL — (*watching him narrowly*). That's good. *Say*, maybe I can get you a job over at the Bigart next week.

MERTON — Oh, no, thanks. You remember — I want to work only at this studio.

GIRL — Still sticking to that idea, eh?

MERTON — Oh, yes. Yes, indeed. Do you think — do you think there'd be any chance of my getting into her company — Miss Baxter's, I mean?

GIRL — Well, I wouldn't work with her just yet, if I were you.

MERTON — You wouldn't? Why not?

GIRL — Oh, I don't know. I just wouldn't.

MERTON — Oh, but I want to. That's one of the things I came out here for.

GIRL — Well, if that's what you *insist* on doing —

MERTON — I bet if I got with her I could learn how to act.

GIRL — And you're — you're sure you've got plenty of money?

MERTON — Oh, I don't care about that. I mean, what does money matter when — when — you just watch me. (*Boast.*) I'll practice, and some time when I'm acting with Miss Baxter, why, Mr. Henshaw will come along, and —

GIRL — Well, there's nobody can say you're not *trying.* (*Pause.*) Coming?

MERTON — Oh, no. I don't want to go off the lot — just yet. I mean — (*he looks involuntarily at the table and book*).

GIRL — Suit yourself. Sure, you're not *coming?*

MERTON — Not — just yet.

GIRL — Well — will I find you around — some time?

MERTON — Oh, yes, I'll be on the lot.

GIRL — That's good. And — so will I — if — the time ever comes when you need me. So — long.

MERTON — So long.

Merton, left alone, quickly rearranges the book on the table. He plays the book scene over again, with pathetic eagerness. He walks down the stage, as before, picks up the book; then he pauses, and brushes away a tear, he keeps at it, goes up again, as he picks up book again. The curtain falls.

The second scene, a week later, is in another section of the Holden lot, set for the taking of a night scene in one of Beulah Baxter's serials. The forepart of a two-masted schooner looms up in the foreground, cradled in a canvas tank of real water and a realistic assortment of waves. Sigmund Rosenblatt is on hand to direct the shooting of the scene, and the beauteous Beulah is standing by to be ready if needed.

A strange young man has been hanging around the Baxter company all week. He is there again, Felice, Miss Baxter's maid, reports, and she doesn't know what to do about it. Perhaps if Miss Baxter would speak to him and tell him how he is getting on her nerves he would go away. The idea appeals to Beulah and she calls the stranger out of the shadows. Merton approaches her eagerly.

BEULAH — You've been following me around for a week, and now it must stop.

MERTON — But — all I wanted was —

BEULAH — What *do* you want? That's what I'd like to know —

MERTON — Oh, I — I only thought if you'd just let me be around —

BEULAH — Oh! —

MERTON — Are you going to do the scene on the ship tonight?

BEULAH — I suppose so. But tell me, you've seen me in my pictures, is that it?

MERTON — Oh, yes, — and I think you're wonderful.

BEULAH (*pleased*). You don't say so.

MERTON — You're — you're my ideal — practically.

BEULAH — Really? Won't you sit down?

MERTON — Do you remember — when you made that personal appearance — in Peoria — I don't suppose you saw me — I was right in the front row, though — and I was the one that — opened the door of your automobile, afterwards.

BEULAH — You did? (*Laughs.*)

MERTON — Yes. Of course I wouldn't expect you to remember me. It was — May 19.

BEULAH — And you — you've been following me because you —

MERTON — Well, it's because I just wanted to see you — actually taking a picture — and especially here on the ship — and I thought maybe if there was ever —

ROSENBLATT — All right — come on, let's get at this. And Beulah, you get out — you only interrupt me!

BEULAH — Is that so?

ROSENBLATT — Yes, *it is!* I'd have been finished long ago if you hadn't bothered me all the time.

BEULAH — It isn't my fault if you always do things wrong.

ROSENBLATT — What do you mean by that?

BEULAH — Exactly what I say. There hasn't been a thing all week —

ROSENBLATT — Oh! for God's sake, SHUT UP —

MERTON — (*unable to stand it any longer*). I beg your pardon.

ROSENBLATT — What?

MERTON — But, you're forgetting yourself.

ROSENBLATT — What; what's that?

MERTON — You forget that there are ladies present — and I must insist that you apologize. (*Beulah breaks into laughter.*)

ROSENBLATT — Apologize? (*To Merton.*) For God's sake, get away from here — get out, I've got enough trouble without you — Get out.

MERTON — All right, I'm going, but, be careful how you treat this lady — because I'm not going very far —

Both the Montagues are in the ship scene of Beulah's picture. The girl is doubling for Miss Baxter for the jump from the ship into the sea, and the elder Montague is playing the beast who drives her to it. And, warns Beulah, let the Montague girl understand she will have to do a better jump than she did in the tenement scene; the Baxter reputation is at stake and cannot be trifled with.

Now the scene is set. The rain is started. The lights are thrown on. The lightning flashes. The cameras click. And out of the cabin, along the rail of the heaving ship the Montague girl, wearing the wig and makeup of Beulah Baxter, steals fearsomely, making for the forward part of the ship; at which moment Merton strolls for the first time into the light.

"There is nothing debonair about him just at present. He has been sleeping on the lot for a week, most of the time in his clothes. He has not shaved for four days. Nor eaten for two. The result of his starvation is that his thoughts are jumbled and confused, and most likely to pour forth irrelevantly. He is, in fact, almost on the edge of delirium."

Jimmy, from the Rosenblatt office, stands holding a blanket that is to cover the Montague girl when she comes from her plunge. Merton speaks to him.

MERTON — I just want to feast my eyes on her — the wonder woman of the silver screen.

ROSENBLATT —All right, now look behind you into the cabin — you think he is going to follow you. That's it! Come on. Come on along that rail. Steady — give us your face. We're taking it. Turn your face to the camera in the flashes of the lightning. That's it — Now Montague come on — all right, now you see him — you're frightened — go ahead now — watch her give it to him. (*Montague girl jumps as Montague fires.*)

MERTON — Gosh!

ROSENBLATT — All right, let it go at that; throw on the guide light, that's all — (*Effects are thrown off and the rain stops.*)

MERTON — Gee, she's coming up right here.

JIMMIE — Sure she is. (*Merton falls back a few steps, awe-stricken. There is a pause, then the Montague girl climbs up out of the water. Jimmy throws the coat over her.*)

GIRL — (*not seeing Merton*). Yes, sir! The bird that said they'd heated the water was just an ordinary liar!

MERTON — (*swept off his feet*). Wh-wh — what?

GIRL — (*peering at him*). Hello, trouper. (*There is both surprise and concern in her voice.*) Haven't seen you for a long time. How's everything — all jake?

MERTON — Why — why — (*He looks into the water.*) How do you come to — isn't Beulah Baxter — ?

JIMMY — Miss Montague's *doubling* for her. Don't you ever know that —

GIRL — (*regretfully*). Jimmy.

JIMMY — (*dully*). Huh?

MERTON — Why—why—no—no! She doesn't ever have anybody — I heard her say so her own self! (*Jimmy, with a shrug, walks out of the circle of light, but does not leave the stage.*)

GIRL — I'm sorry, kid, but it had to come out sooner or later. I don't like to bust up any dreams, but I've been doubling for her all along.

MERTON — (*nearly hysterical*). No — she wouldn't do it! I don't believe it — Why, she's the most wonderful — (*He grows incoherent.*)

GIRL — Take it easy, trouper. And — ah — let me take a look at you. You know, I haven't seen you for a week. Sure everything's all right? (*Merton nods, unable to answer.*)

MERTON — (*with difficulty*). I . . . I've been all right. (*Desperately.*) I've really got to get back on — location. (*He starts to go.*)

GIRL — Hold on — don't hurry. If you go *I'll* be along. (*He pauses; the girl turns to Jimmy.*) Oh, Jimmy!

JIMMY — Yes, Miss Montague.

GIRL — Run over and get two cups of coffee and about four of those sandwiches.

JIMMY — Right!

MERTON — Not — anything for me, thank you.

GIRL — Oh, I know — that's for Jimmy and me.

MERTON — So, then, if you don't mind, I'll be getting back.

He has been doing "miner stuff," he tells her. That accounts for the "garden" he has been raising. But he doesn't want to talk about himself. He wants to know about Miss Baxter. It can't be possible she hasn't been "keeping faith with her public," as she said. That, the Montague girl assures him, coldly, is what they all say. Furthermore, Miss Baxter is married to Sig Rosenblatt, her director, and Sig is her fourth — "since she began to count." Also all the hazards in the Baxter serials have been taken by her double — the ride across the canyon in a bucket, the automobile plunge off the bridge, the time she crept along the ledge of the tall building — all Montague and not Baxter. The news fair sickens Merton. He is so completely crushed he tries to get away without so much as a mouthful of food. But he doesn't deceive his little friend.

GIRL — (*with determination*). Sit down. It was a grand performance, kid, but it didn't fool mother for a minute. Have a sandwich. (*This time Merton takes the sandwich; he eats it voraciously — in about three bites. No word is spoken — but when the sandwich is finished the girl simply hands him another.*) Hey! Slow up for the curves. (*It goes like the first — still without a word. He seems to expect a third.*) You've got to start easy. Have some coffee. (*He takes it. He calms down a little.*) When did you eat last?

MERTON — (*in a whisper*). I can't remember.

GIRL — (*Looking at his clothes*). You haven't been home? (*She drinks coffee.*)

MERTON — (*beginning to find himself*). I — I didn't have any money — except what I got that day.

GIRL — With Crusoe?

MERTON — (*nods*). It lasted till — a couple of days ago.

GIRL — (*puzzled*). But if you didn't go home —

MERTON — I — I been right on the lot.

GIRL — For a week?

MERTON — (*another nod*). I was afraid if I went off it I couldn't get back on again. So I — I found a cabin they'd put up, and — there was a bed in it, and then when they tore that down, after the fight, why there was a picture when a girl was told to come home — her mother was dying, and I waited, and pretty soon they showed the mother and she was in a bed. That night after they'd all gone I — slept there.

GIRL — (*shaking her head*). Well, you're certainly made of the stuff that gets there — where'd you come from?

MERTON — Simsbury, Illinois. But I always wanted to be a picture actor. I used to go to see — (*His voice changes.*) — Beulah Baxter — whenever they showed one of her pictures — and Harold Parmelee, and all of them. And I read where they were trying to do something bigger and finer, and I thought if *I* came out here — well, it's worth sacrificing to do something worth while — don't you think?

GIRL — (*with an excited nod*). Go on. Don't ask *me* anything.

So he tells her of his correspondence course in the Stebbinsville, Kansas, school, and the diploma he was given; and of how he had saved up two hundred and seventy dollars and started in search of a career. As evidence that he was not all wrong in having confidence in himself he produces the art studies of himself and the horse and the dress suit. It is the pictures that excite her strangely.

GIRL — Wait a minute! Kid, this one is great — positively great!

MERTON — (*pleased*). Do you think so?

GIRL — "Yours truly, Clifford Armytage," but — (*She looks from Merton to the photograph.*) There's — there's something here and I can't put my finger on it. It — it reminds me of somebody. (*Merton pleased, waits for her to guess.*) Somebody I've seen lately — somebody that — I've got it! Harold Parmelee!

MERTON — I hoped you'd notice it! That's what I want to do if I can — like he does — really serious things that — that will help uplift the screen art — I mean big things in a really big way, and —

GIRL — (*looking at him as though transfixed*). Kid!

MERTON — Yes?

GIRL — Turn your face that way! (*He does so.*) Now toward me again! It's positively great — even with the lace you can't miss it!

MERTON — Huh!

GIRL — (*intensely excited*). Trouper! (*She whisks out some bills, from around neck.*) I want you to take this, go home and get all cleaned up and some food inside of you and come back and meet me here at nine o'clock in the morning. Got that straight?

MERTON — Oh, I couldn't accept —

GIRL — That's all right! I'm only lending it to you, and you're going to pay me back. You're going to be a big success — I got something all planned out. God help me!

A minute later she has sent Merton home with Jimmy, found Jeff Baird and outlined her big idea to him. There's a million dollars in Merton Gill, if he is handled right. Let Jeff take him and play him in a Buckeye comedy as an imitation Harold Parmelee and he will kid the life out of Parmelee without ever knowing he's funny.

BAIRD — (*as it dawns on him*). He looks wonderful, but can we put it over?

GIRL — Yes, but not if he knows it's a comedy. He hates comedies.

BAIRD — It's taking an awful chance.

GIRL — We can fix it easy.

BAIRD — But it's a bear of an idea. You're sure he doesn't know he's funny?

GIRL — He doesn't know anything's funny. You've got to put him absolutely serious in one of those screams of yours, with Bert Chester's cross-eyes and he'll be immense!

BAIRD — But suppose he finds out?

GIRL — That's the only thing I'm afraid of. We've got to keep it from him for a while, that's all. He's got a trusting way of looking at you that's sort of got me, and if he ever finds out I did it I couldn't stand — it. He's a nice kid, but he certainly looks like the second plume on a hearse.

BAIRD — (*noticing Merton, who has returned with Jimmy*). Psst!

GIRL — (*in a quick, tense undertone*). Do you think he heard?

BAIRD — I'm not sure.

MERTON — I think I forgot to thank you for that money —

GIRL — Oh, that's all right. You remember Mr. Baird, don't you — Jeff Baird?

BAIRD — How are you, kid?

MERTON — Oh, yes.

BAIRD — Well, you're going to *work* for me, now.

MERTON — What?

GIRL — Surest thing you know.

BAIRD — I'm going to give you a *real* chance and in *real* pictures.

MERTON — (*to girl*). But he . . . only makes . . . comedies.

GIRL — Comedies? I should say not! Why he's —

BAIRD — Well, I used to make comedies, but I'm through with them. From now on I'm going to make serious pictures.

MERTON — Serious pictures? (*To the girl.*) Is he — honestly?

GIRL — Why — yes.

BAIRD — Of course I may make a comedy once in a while, but I'm anxious to enter a bigger field.

MERTON — Oh, I'm awfully glad. You're sure you mean . . . regular serious ones?

BAIRD — Yes, indeed!

MERTON — Significant — I mean?

BAIRD — That's the word, exactly.

MERTON — And — and you want me to — come with you?

BAIRD — You bet I do! You've had a wonderful recommendation. (*He glances at the photos.*)

MERTON — (*to the girl*). You did it all! You did it all! It's everything I ever hoped for. It's my great opportunity. I've always dreamed about it, and now you've made it possible. You've opened the door for me.

GIRL — (*more than willing to be thanked*). That's all right.

MERTON — (*back to Baird*). And — and Mr. Baird, too! You're going to make serious pictures at last. I — I'm awfully glad to hear that. (*He shakes Baird's hand.*) I'll give you of my best, my very best, and *oh!* I certainly congratulate you, I certainly congratulate you!

The curtain falls.

ACT IV

A few weeks later Jeff Baird has succeeded in filming two Buckeye comedies with Merton featured as a burlesque Harold Parmelee without Merton's suspecting the truth.

The deception, however, is becoming less and less secure. The other comedians in the Baird troupe are having a hard time keeping their faces straight, and there is a certain amount of gossip trailing about the studio. Baird takes occasion to warn his players — especially Bert Chester, the cross-eyed man, that nothing must be permitted to reach young "Armytage," by way of smile, wink, gesture or spoken word, that will in any way give the trick away.

Now the Montague girl is beginning to worry. This morning she has come with Merton to the Baird studio. There is one scene that has to be retaken in order to get Merton's spurs in the closeup, and the girl is worried sick for fear he will discover what Baird is doing with him.

GIRL — I'm scared, Jeff. More than I was at first, even.

BAIRD — Why, it's a cinch.

GIRL — Maybe it is. But I'm scared anyway.

BAIRD — What's the matter with you? There's no danger. He still thinks he's playing in a serious Parmelee drama and if you *told* him it was a Buckeye comedy he wouldn't believe you.

GIRL — I just watched him out there, waiting. I never felt so guilty in my life. He was so trustful, Jeff. He really believes in his heart he's doing a big, vital drama and —

BAIRD — He's getting good money and you've saved his life.

GIRL — I'm wondering whether anybody could have forced him to take that money if he'd known what he was doing. When I think of him coming all the way out here to Hollywood, so innocent he doesn't know a close-up from a censor; and of our making a Buckeye comedy out of him without him knowing it —

BAIRD — Say, you're not getting emotional, are you?

GIRL — What?

BAIRD — I say, you're not falling for this kid?

GIRL — I don't know. What do you think?

BAIRD — I don't know — yet.

GIRL — If you find out I wish you'd tell me. I never felt this way before. You know, he came out here with a lot of ideals and he's lost one or two of them already. And when I think of that look in his eyes —

BAIRD — Still, he's got to find out some day — hasn't he?

GIRL — I suppose so.

BAIRD — Well, then, let nature take its course.

GIRL — I wonder just what that'll be, Jeff? Is it going to knock him out, or will he bounce? And I was also kind of wondering whether he'd ever speak to me again.

Merton is made up for a cowboy part, with all the accoutrements — chapps, sombrero, spurs, guns, quirt, etc. He has acquired a certain trick poise in his weeks of rehearsing, and evidently takes his art even more seriously than before.

MERTON — Mr. Baird, there's something I want to — talk to you about.

BAIRD — Sure.

MERTON — I — I don't like to say anything about anybody that isn't fair, Mr. Baird, but —

BAIRD — I want to hear any complaints, Merton.

MERTON — Well, it's — Mr. Bert Chester.

BAIRD — Yes?

MERTON — Yes. I think he's taking his work pretty lightly, Mr. Baird.

BAIRD — How do you mean, Merton?

MERTON — Well, inasmuch as you let him keep on acting in spite of his cross-eyes — I mean because of his sick mother, and all that — I don't think he ought to laugh when people are doing serious work.

BAIRD — Oh, you mean this morning? For a minute *I* thought he was laughing, too. Then I saw it was just an old lip trouble he's had for years. It's a sort of nervous tickling he gets. He apologized to me and asked me to apologize to you. I guess he was afraid you'd laugh at him — he *is* kind of ridiculous, with all his ailments.

MERTON — I wouldn't have laughed.

BAIRD — No, I know you wouldn't. But he's just terribly sensitive. However, if you want me to —

MERTON — Oh, no. I wouldn't hurt his feelings — for worlds.

BAIRD — Don't let it worry you any more, then.

MERTON — But while we're on the subject, Mr. Baird —

BAIRD — Yes?

MERTON — I think I ought to have a little better support in my new picture.

BAIRD — Oh, better support, eh?

MERTON — Yes. And — ah — I think it's time for me to do something different from Harold Parmelee.

BAIRD — Oh, sure, you're right.

MERTON — Besides, I was watching one of Parmelee's pictures the other day, and — I don't think he's quite as good as he used to be, Mr. Baird.

BAIRD — That so?

MERTON — Yes. Of course it may just be that my viewpoint is changing, but I think he's falling off a little. Mind you, I think he's still good, but —

Mr. Henshaw interrupts him. He has come to protest against Baird's too frequent and lengthy use of the projection room. But Merton takes advantage of the visit to recall himself to the great director's mind. It is just possible that Mr. Henshaw does not remember the occasion of their last meeting. Mr. Henshaw is quite sure he doesn't.

"That," Merton assures him, "was one of my earlier struggles. You must have thought I was pretty green that day, when I didn't know how to walk down to the camera or anything. I guess I *was* pretty green."

"Yes, yes — I remember. What are you doing now?"

Before Merton can answer Baird has succeeded in pantomiming Henshaw not to give the joke away, and another ticklish situation is saved.

"Some day — some day you and I will have many a good laugh over those days, Mr. Henshaw," prophesies Merton, putting his hand familiarly upon the Henshaw shoulder. "Awfully glad you dropped in. So long."

He goes on into the studio for the retake. Baird and Henshaw exchange significant glances as he disappears. The curtain falls.

The second scene is the living room in Merton's boarding house, a comfortable, old-fashioned home run by Mr. and Mrs. Patterson.

It is the morning after the first showing of the picture in which Merton and his spurs are featured and he has not been home all night. The Pattersons are worried, though Mr. Patterson is sure the boy is doing nothing more serious than a little bustin' out in celebration of his enormous hit. Mrs. Patterson is hopin' he won't go to dissipatin' just because he is a success.

There is a phone call from Miss Montague. She seems quite worried about Mr. Armytage, too. He must have been doing something unusual, Mrs. Patterson decides. However, if he *was* celebratin' he certainly was entitled to it, seein' the way the papers had praised him in their writeups.

Merton finally appears, practically led by the protecting hand of Jimmy, the office boy. He is crushed and weary, having walked the streets the most of the night trying to forget the awful shame of the picture. No one can cheer him. Jimmy has been telling him every five minutes for twelve hours that he had made the comedy hit of his life and that the people had fairly laughed their heads off at him.

MERTON — You give them the best and finest that's

in you, and they laugh! That's a *hit.* Jeff Baird meant it to be funny! So did she!

JIMMY — Well, it *was* funny.

MERTON — I'll never trust a woman again.

JIMMY — Good morning.

MERTON — (*stares into space, sees paper. Reads*). "The funniest newcomer in the realm of comedy." (*Tosses paper aside.*)

MRS. PATTERSON — *Well,* good morning!

MERTON — Good morning.

MRS. PATTERSON — I'm certainly awfully glad you got home. We were worried about you!

MERTON — I'm — all right.

MRS. PATTERSON — Congratulations!

MERTON — What?

MRS. PATTERSON — Congratulations on your big success!

MERTON — Oh!

MRS. PATTERSON — (*laughing*). My, my! I don't think we ever laughed so much in our lives as we did last night. And I just want to tell you how proud we are of you. (*Merton starts for the stairs.*) Now, can I get you some breakfast?

MERTON — No, thanks, I'm not a bit hungry.

A stranger calls. He is a Mr. Walberg and he comes from Bigart. He, too, wants to congratulate the new comedian and to tell him how good he is.

WALBERG — . . . I saw your picture last night, Mr. Armytage. Is it definitely certain you're going to stick with Baird?

MERTON — No.

WALBERG — That's fine. You're new to pictures, I understand.

MERTON — Yes.

WALBERG — Well, don't do like a lot of other comics

and try to do straight stuff. You know how far you'd get.

MERTON — I know how far I *got*.

WALBERG — You stick to comedy, because you've got everything. Why, you've got the best low-comedy face I've seen in ages. It's got genuine pathos, more pathos than Parmelee, the guy you were kidding. And you've got the gift of the world in knowing just how to kid bad acting. Frankly I don't believe you could ever make the grade in a serious picture. I candidly don't believe you could register if you imitated a *good* actor. But you've got pathos, pathos and acting — plus. I don't have to tell you that. You and Baird found out your limits and have started you off on what God meant you for.

MERTON—(*hardly able to stand it*). Mr. Walberg, I—

WALBERG — Now, hold on! Now, there's only one thing the matter with you. . . . *You're too good.* Parmelee makes hokum and the public wants hokum. *You* make satire, which is over the heads of most of the public. Take a beautiful woman like Beulah Baxter. She can't act. She probably wouldn't know two and two made four if she didn't get it by gossip. You're different — you've got intelligence. Now, how about doing some stuff for us?

MERTON — You mean — you mean — comedies?

WALBERG — Certainly.

MERTON — (*decided at last*). I wouldn't think of it.

WALBERG — You mean you wouldn't come with Bigart at all — on any proposition?

MERTON — That's what I mean.

WALBERG — Wouldn't three hundred a week interest you?

MERTON — (*after gulping*). No.

WALBERG — Three fifty?

MERTON — No.

WALBERG — Four hundred!

MERTON — No. (*Walberg gets up, takes his hat, looks at Merton, then crosses to the street door.*)

WALBERG — Well, you're certainly a tough egg, but we'll have you with Bigart yet. Yes, sir, even if Mr. Strausheimer has to come here *himself* — Good day.

Again Miss Montague telephones, but Merton will not talk to her. If she calls, he tells Mrs. Patterson, she is to be informed that he has another engagement.

The next one is Mr. Gashwiler, from Simsbury. He is all excited over the success of his former employee. He and Mrs. Gashwiler just happened to be tourin' the Golden West and by a miracle dropped in on the new picture.

"Well, I guess I laughed about as much as anyone," Mr. Gashwiler reports. "Merton, I never knowed what I was talkin' about when I said you hadn't ought ever try to get into the movies. Why, you're funnier than anybody I ever seen. Wait'll we get back to Simsbury. That place is going to have a plate. Yessir. A plate. 'Here worked Merton Gill.' If I have any influence that town's goin' to honor her illustrious son the way he ought to be honored. I'm goin' to have a brass plate made for the front of the store."

There's talk, says Mr. Gashwiler, that Tessie Kearns is thinking of coming to California. But Merton, beginning to rise above his depression, advises against it.

"No," says he, seriously. "It's a pretty stiff game, the movies. You've got to have a certain amount of what they call hokum to get your scenarios over. Tessie's an awfully nice girl and all that, but I don't think she could get away with it. It might break her heart."

It is while Mr. Gashwiler is still there that the Montague girl arrives, and Merton has no time to get away. When they are alone they face each other wonderingly for a second. Then Merton, assuming a cheering, even bantering, attitude, "embarks on a fine piece of acting."

MERTON — Well?

GIRL — Well? You've seen the picture. Shoot!

MERTON — (*smiling*). All right. I've certainly kidded the life out of all of you.

GIRL — What!

MERTON — I've certainly kidded the whole crowd of you. You thought all along that I thought it was a serious picture, didn't you? You and Baird thought you had me kidded all along, didn't you? Ho, ho! A serious picture with a cross-eyed man doing comedy stuff all around me every minute. I thought it was serious, did I? *Yes,* I did! Like fun!

GIRL — (*sits*). Just say some of that again!

MERTON — Didn't you people know that I knew what I could do and what I couldn't do? Didn't you s'pose I knew as well as anybody that I've got a low-comedy face and that I couldn't make the grade in a serious picture? Of course, I've got real pathos, but anyone can see I couldn't imitate a good actor. I can imitate a bad actor fine, but not a good one. Didn't you and Baird ever s'pose I found out my limits and decided to be what God intended me to be? Satire — (*rising*) — that's what I'm doing — and it's over the heads of most of the public. Why, they tell me that I was funnier than that cross-eyed man ever was in his life! And what happens this morning?

GIRL — What happens?

MERTON — Nothing, except that people are coming around to sign me up for four hundred dollars a week. Why, this Bamberger from the Bigart Company comes in before I'm really up this morning asking me if I won't go with his company, and . . . why . . . (*He breaks off as he notices her steady gaze.*)

GIRL — So you know everything, do you? You know you look just too much like Parmelee so that you're funny? (*Merton is hit.*) I mean you, that you look the way Parmelee would if he had brains?

MERTON — Certainly. Parmelee. Why, Parmelee's got nothing but hokum in his pictures.

But he can't play-act any longer. He breaks down now, and goes quickly to her. Now he has sunk down on the floor beside her and buried his face in her lap, sobbing. She comforts him with the same maternal solicitude she showed when he discovered the duplicity of Beulah Baxter.

GIRL — . . . There, don't you worry. Mother's got you and she's going to never let you go.

MERTON — (*sobbing*). It's like that night on the lot when I found out about you and Beulah Baxter and you were so —

GIRL — There, there. Don't you worry. Did he have his poor old mother going for a minute? Yes, he did. He had her going for a minute all right. But he didn't fool her very long, not very long, because he can't ever fool her very long. And he can bet a lot of money on that.

MERTON — I didn't see at first how I ever could live down what I saw last night. I guess I didn't understand some way.

GIRL — Don't worry, honey. Mother knows what's what, and she'll tell you all about it in good time.

MERTON — You think I ought to — keep on — making comedies?

GIRL — You will as long as I last. (*There is a whistle, three sharp blasts, outside.*) That's a friend of ours. He said he wanted to see you, if you were feeling . . . well.

MERTON — (*gaily*). There's nothing the matter with me.

The caller is Jeff Baird. He, too, is a little anxious at first. But Merton's manner soon reassures him and he is happy. The picture is a knockout, and as for these Bigart people, or any others, offering big salaries for Merton — no chance.

"Oh, I turned them down," announces Merton. "I know my place is with you, Mr. Baird. And I want to put everything I can into comedies. I want to give the best that's in me, because I realize that that's where you and God intended me to be."

"That's the talk," and Baird jauntily throws an arm about his young star's shoulders. "In three years we'll be giving you a salary that'll knock the eye off the ones Parmelee and those other swifts get."

"Still," Merton admits, "the public wants that hokum. Why, you take Beulah Baxter, for instance. She's nothing more or less than a high grade moron. Why, she wouldn't know two and two was four if she didn't hear people talking."

There is still another visitor that morning. A stranger to Merton, but known to Miss Montague, a man who has been wandering mysteriously about the studios of Hollywood for several days. Now he comes to call upon the new comedy star.

GIRL — Kid, meet Mr. John Wheaton, former Secretary of Agriculture, now head of the Motion Picture Industry.

MERTON — How do you do? Won't you sit down?

WHEATON — No, thanks, I've only got a minute.

MERTON — I'm glad to know you. I've seen you around.

WHEATON — And I'm proud to know you. It's men like you that the motion pictures need, Mr. Armytage.

MERTON — Oh, it's awfully good of you to say so.

WHEATON — Yes, indeed. You're going to help us a lot. This is not a one man fight, Mr. Armytage — I must have the help of all of you if the motion pictures are to be put upon a higher plane.

MERTON — Yes, sir. That's — that's what I want to do if I can. I mean, put them up higher, where —

WHEATON — My idea, exactly. We must strive ever upward, or there is no progress.

MERTON — Yes, sir.

WHEATON — Some time I'd like to get together with you, for a serious talk.

MERTON — I'll be delighted.

WHEATON — I'd like to hear your ideas. And now I'm sure you'll pardon me — I'm addressing some exhibitors.

MERTON — Yes, sir.

WHEATON — Good day.

Now they are alone, and growing conscious of the fact that neither has had any breakfast. It is just before Mrs. Patterson goes to prepare the meal that the telephone rings rather persistently. Mrs. Patterson answers The call is for Mr. Armytage and is from the *Silver Screenings Magazine*. Merton, with the becoming dignity of a celebrity newborn, walks to the phone, and as he rests his elbow gracefully on the table, the Montague girl leans protectingly over him, in a way directing the interview.

MERTON — Hello. Yes. This is Mr. Armytage.

GIRL — By the way, your name's going to be Merton Gill from now on.

MERTON — Is it? Hello, yes. This is Mr. Armytage. That isn't my regular name though, you know. . . . What? Gill. . . . G — I — L — L. . . . yes. Merton. . . . That's right. I don't know why your readers should be interested in me, however. Oh, just hard work, I guess. I've struggled and sacrificed to give the public something — what? No, I'm not yet, but I'm going to be. (*Looks to the girl.*) Miss Montague. Yes, that's the lady. Oh, I should say so. More like a pal. And I might also add she's my severest critic.

THE END

"THE OLD SOAK"

A Comedy in Three Acts

By Don Marquis

AS typically American in form and content as any play the season of 1922–23 produced was "The Old Soak," offered by Arthur Hopkins at the Plymouth Theatre, August 22, 1922. Here is another comedy drama that, trivial in itself, conventional to the point of inviting the sneer of the so-called intellectuals of the theatre group, still offers the multitude such satisfying entertainment that it not only attained great popularity, but held it through the season.

Usually these American comedy dramas (*vide* "Lightnin'" and "Peg O' My Heart") are humorous monologues strung on a thin thread of plot. But, thin as it is, this plot invariably is concerned with the recognizable problems of native domestic life. The centralized character, too, is always a human of humans, possessed of a native wit that permits him or her to score off all the smart puppets set up in opposition.

Clem Hawley, the amiable "Soak" of Mr. Marquis' play, has not quite so definite a sentimental appeal as had Bill Jones or Peg, but he commands much of their lovableness of character, and a timely philosophy respecting the drink habit that endears him, particularly in these days of trial, to all those with "a feelin' for liquor."

Mr. Marquis first introduced "The Old Soak" in a column of comment and humor he wrote for the *Evening Sun* of New York, and later transferred to the *New York Tribune*. He is representative of all the genial alcoholics, all the winning failures, all the domestic derelicts with weak characters but good hearts, who have both blessed and infested the world from the days of Bacchus to those of Volstead.

As we meet him in the play he is living with his wife, Matilda, the typical patient martyr of the drinking man's household; Clemmie, his son, and Lucy, his daughter, in the Baycliff, L. I., cottage that has been their home for many years. The children are in their early twenties, and both work in New York.

The home is like those that are handed down from one New England generation to another, losing something of both character and freshness with each transfer. There are "God Bless Our Home" mottoes on the wall, with a few "sugary Gainsboroughs and Romneys" to fill in. A cheap piano, a fireplace with an old-fashioned brass fender surrounding it and an old-fashioned clock ticking contentedly on the mantel. Both a family photograph album and a huge family Bible decorate the center table.

Matilda and Cousin Webster are at checkers, Cousin Webster being the village banker and leading upright citizen of Baycliff. Lucy, expecting her young man, Tom Ogden, who sells bonds in town, is trying to tidy up the room a bit.

The conversation, as frequently happens when Cousin Webster is seeking to refresh his knowledge of how low the Hawley family fortunes are sinking through the general worthlessness of Clem, reveals the exact state of affairs Cousin Webster expected to discover.

Lucy's young man hesitates to ask her to marry him, naturally, as Matilda explains, because of the "Old Soak" — that's what the village is callin' Clem. And Clem doesn't seem to care. He wasn't so bad before prohibition, but now he's been so busy huntin' liquor he can't seem to find any time to work. He hasn't done a thing since he sold his garage business, six months back, but hang around Jake Smith's hotel a'drinkin' and a'gamblin'.

Now he is about out of funds again and lately he has been tryin' and tryin' to borrow Matilda's Midland Express Company stock, left her by her father and which she has clung to tenaciously in the expectation that some day it will make them comfortable, if not rich.

Cousin Webster is pleasantly sympathetic. He might, if he were asked, take Matilda's stock off her hands — as an accommodation. It would be better for him to have it than to let Clem coax it away from her. But she thinks she will hold onto it for a while. It is only a hundred shares, but her father had faith in it, and so has Lucy's Tom, who knows something about bonds.

And then Clem comes in, a generally mussed up, flannel-shirt specimen of humanity with a winning smile. His approach, as usual, is heralded by his singing the few bars of "Rock of Ages" which persistently stick in his memory. He never gets far with it, but he is always starting out bravely enough to sing the entire hymn. Which, considering everything, irritates Matilda excessively. She mentions it now, as soon as the greetings are over.

MATILDA — I'd think you'd be ashamed to sing *that* song!

OLD SOAK — Why so, ma? I never had nothin' against the old-time religion. Three things I always held by — the old-time religion and calomel and straight whiskey. They got more kick in 'em than any of these here new-fangled notions. Don't you think so, Webster?

COUSIN WEBSTER — (*primly*). I'm no authority on drinking, Clem. I have always heeded the injunction to beware of the wine cup.

OLD SOAK — Well, so have I,— I always bewared of wine and beer and them soft drinks. I always stuck to hard liquor.

MATILDA — Yes, Clem, you've stuck to hard liquor more than you have to hard labor.

OLD SOAK — Hard labor! A man can't set down to rest in under his own vines and fig trees without some one brings up the subject of labor. Tom, do you mind if I ask you a question?

TOM — Not if you don't mind me not answering it.

OLD SOAK — Tom, I'll leave it to you — is this world a jail, or ain't it?

TOM — There's a catch in the question somewhere, I refuse to answer it.

OLD SOAK — You'd think this world was a jail that the human race was sentenced to, the store some folks set by hard labor. Always and forever the same question: Why don't you labor? Why don't you work?

MATILDA — Well, Clem, why don't you?

OLD SOAK — Ain't I always been a good pervider to you, Matilda? Ain't I pervided you with a couple children to work for you? Besides, the good book says —

MATILDA — You! Talking of the good book!

OLD SOAK — Why not, Matilda? I know it from cover to cover, Matilda, and it was wrote for sinners, wasn't it? Well, I'm a sinner, ain't I?

MATILDA — You are!

OLD SOAK — You bet your life I be! I'm a regular mammal of iniquity, to hear your prohibition friends tell it, I am!

TOM — But what does the good book say?

OLD SOAK — The good book, Tom, says for the weary husbandman to toil not neither for to spin, for all such is vanity, vanity, vanity and vexation of the spirit.

Tom and Lucy are off to look at the new moon and, it may be, see a movie. Clem is in for a lecture. He is, Matilda intimates, a lazy good-for-nothing. But Clem is inclined to argue the point. No one knows how much time he gives up to thinking. Hours at a time he just sits and thinks and thinks about his inventions — inventions that some day are going to make them so rich he'll be carrying hatfuls of hundred dollar bills around with him. Even now he is working on a "DEE-vice" that is likely to revolutionize transportation — a DEE-vice that can not only be used on airyoplanes, but on automobiles or "onto purty nigh everything that's got wheels onto it or machinery into it."

Cousin Webster does not think much of any "DEE-vice" that Clem might invent. As a matter of fact Cousin Webster does not think much of anything or anybody around the Hawley place, unless it is Clemmie. Clemmie, he admits, is a smart boy to have done so well with the insurance company for which he is working.

Now Cousin Webster is leaving, refusing Clem's cordial invitation to have a little drink before he goes. "My interests don't run that way, Clem," he says. "No," answers Clem, kindly but pointedly, "they run to prayin' on Sunday and foreclosin' mortgages on Monday, don't they Web?"

Left to drink by himself Clem extracts a bottle of liquor from the fireplace and pours himself a liberal portion. Standing with his foot on the fender rail he raises his glass to his own reflection in the mirror. Memory carries him back to the old days when the "poor man's club" at the corner was his favorite hangout.

Old Soak — How about you, Old Timer, have one? (*Answers himself as if another person were speaking.*) Well, Old Scout, as long as it's you, I don't care if I do! (*Takes bottle from fireplace.*) Never knowed me to refuse one yet, did you, Old Timer? (*His foot on brass fender as if it were rail of bar; drinks.*) How! (*Throughout this episode Clem addresses persons who are not there, drinking with one after another, and answering in character of old time barroom habitués, the mantel having become a buffet bar.*) Fellers, we'll have one in honor of my invention. Got the best little patent you ever seen! It's to be used onto these here submarines.

Well, sir, I hope that invention of yourn makes a million dollars! . . . Thank you sir, thankee, sir! Hope you get an invention of your own that makes *you* a million dollars! (*Bowing right and left, touching glasses; turns as if to bartender.*) Al, ask that little red-headed feller down there by the end of the bar if he won't join us. . . . Come on, stranger! You mustn't be down on your luck! . . . I misremember your name, but I seen your face here before. . . . Never say die, stranger! S'long as there's a bunch of good scouts, it's a good time! (*Fills glass; hobnobs with different persons; sings a line of "It's always fair weather when good fellows get together." Drinks.*) Hey? What? One on the house? Well, Al, I really hadn't orter have another one . . . but seein' it's you, Al! Jest one more . . . Al! This is my last one! Got to be goin' home. . . . Wife's got dinner on the table an' everything . . . you know how women is!

Clemmie interrupts his father's visit with the reflections of the mirror. Clemmie is not pleased, but he is used to seeing his father drink and just at the moment he is considerably worried over his own problems. Clemmie needs money — needs it badly and right away. Clem Senior would like to give it to him, but unfortunately his own affairs are not in a very good way. When he gets his invention workin,' of course it will be different. But it is Clemmie's idea that nothing will be different so long as the liquor holds out.

OLD SOAK — Liquor, Clemmie, can always be got by them that have a feelin' for liquor. It ain't so much a question of cash as a question of the kind o' person you be. There's Cousin Webster. His mind's set on money, and money tags after him and crawls into his lap like a pet kitten. And here's your dad. Your dad just nacherally finds liquor flowin' his way. What you want with extry money, Clemmie?

Clemmie is not prepared to say, but, being pressed, he admits it is a business opportunity that has come his way. It isn't, as his father suspects, anything to do with "buyin' chocolate drops and perfumery for some of them strange women the good book speaks about."

Mrs. Hawley interrupts them. She is, as usual, quick to take Clemmie's part. She has always spoiled him, his father insists.

OLD SOAK — You've petted him, Matilda, till he's got no moral staminy or will power left.

MATILDA — And you have!

OLD SOAK — (*trying to honey up to her as he begins speech*). Of course I have, Matilda! (*She turns away.*) What do you think kept me drinkin' if 'twasn't my will power? I been nagged and prayed against for thirty years to make me quit, and there was times I really wanted to quit but my will power always held me to it. (*Going towards door.*) You honey up to her, now e-wee lamb, and mebby you can coax some money out of her for that business opportunity of yourn — I'm gonna look up some business friends myself.

Clemmie's mother is anxious about his needing money, and she hasn't any to give him. It hurts her to have him cross about it. She trusts him, of course, but it would break her heart if he ever were to get like his father. Some way she feels that she has failed father. She has not been strong enough to keep him away from evil associates and he is easily led. That is why she wants her son to be sure he chooses his friends carefully. Lately he has not been keeping very good hours, and she doesn't know the people he spends his time with or where he goes. It is Clemmie's idea that to get along in business a fellow has to cultivate business associates. That's what he is doing. And he needs money to take advantage of his opportunities. As a matter of fact he needs money now because he is planning to get married. He has met a "peach of a girl" named Ina Heath. Ina is — well, she is a kind of an artist, and a mighty clever one. His mother will think so, too, when he brings her out, some day. Mrs. Hawley is a bit doubtful about Ina, never having seen her. She fears the girl may think Clemmie's folks are terribly old-fashioned. Clemmie tries to reassure her. Naturally he would like to get rid of a few of the wall mottoes — and kinda keep his father out of the way when she does come. But — he's sure his mother will like her.

MATILDA — . . . If you love her and she loves you, that is all I ask. Your wife will be as dear to me as if she were my own daughter — When do you plan to marry, Clemmie?

CLEMMIE — As soon as we can, mother. A little money right now would mean so much to me! (*Coaxing her, petting.*) There's that express stock, mother.

MATILDA — (*it hurts her to refuse; but she is gently firm*). Father told me to hold on to that. And so does Tom.

CLEMMIE — (*petting her*). I'll pay the money back in a month or two. Mother, I've sort of *counted* on that stock!

MATILDA — You'll have to let this chance go, Clemmie, and save your salary for the next one.

CLEMMIE — You won't do it, mother?

MATILDA — I can't, Clemmie — We'll be needing it for a payment on the house. Don't worry dear, there'll be another chance.

CLEMMIE — I suppose so.

MATILDA — Are you going to stay home this evening?

CLEMMIE — I suppose so.

MATILDA — That's good, it's been a long time since we've had one of our old-time evenings together at home.

Cousin Webster has come back to have another talk

with Matilda about buying her Midland Express stock. He finds Clemmie all wrought up over his failure to raise any money. In desperation Clemmie turns to Cousin Webster and asks him for a loan. The banker is interested, but wary. He would like to know more about the trouble Clemmie is in. Has he tried to get an advance at the office? Funny, his firm won't help him when the chances of profit are so sure.

COUSIN WEBSTER — . . . See here, Clemmie, you've held part of the story from me. (*Clemmie turns from him with a gesture of despair.*) Clemmie, I hope you're not short in your accounts!

CLEMMIE — (*explosively*). *Yes!* (*Then dejectedly.*) Now, damn it, you know!

COUSIN WEBSTER — I'm mighty sorry to hear this, Clemmie, mighty sorry.

CLEMMIE — (*taking hold of his coat*). Listen! I'm . . . I'm in a hell of a fix! If somebody doesn't come across with the cash in six or eight days it . . . it means jail!

COUSIN WEBSTER — Jail? That's terrible, Clemmie! Terrible! Why do you say six or eight days?

CLEMMIE — The auditor's due in a week or so.

COUSIN WEBSTER — How much are you short?

CLEMMIE — Two thousand dollars. But with twelve or fourteen hundred I can play my tip . . . and square the shortage . . . and repay the loan.

COUSIN WEBSTER — You've got it all figured out like a Napoleon of finance!

CLEMMIE — (*appealingly*). You won't throw me down, Cousin Webster!

COUSIN WEBSTER — Clemmie I've always been a believer of the golden rule in business. I do by others as they do by me, and they always ask *me:* "Have you got any collateral?" Have *you,* Clemmie?

CLEMMIE — No.

COUSIN WEBSTER — And no way of getting your hands on any?

CLEMMIE — No.

COUSIN WEBSTER — I think we ought to take your mother into our confidence.

CLEMMIE — No! no!

COUSIN WEBSTER — There's that Midland Express stock of hers . . . it'd just about fix you up, Clemmie.

CLEMMIE — I told you I'd been to her! She won't let me have it.

COUSIN WEBSTER — But, if she knew the trouble you were in . . . jail, and everything!

CLEMMIE — That's what she must never know! She must never know that I . . . was short in my accounts.

COUSIN WEBSTER — Well, if you won't tell her, you won't. But if you *could* get her to change her mind and lend you that stock, I'd give you thirteen hundred dollars for it.

CLEMMIE — (*dejectedly*). She'll not change her mind.

COUSIN WEBSTER — She might. She might. You might find it in your hands yet. . . . You've got your mother's power of attorney, haven't you?

CLEMMIE — Yes. I attend to all her business for her — payments on the house and everything. Why do you ask?

COUSIN WEBSTER — If she were to change her mind I could buy the stock from you, without bothering her with any of the details. You keep coaxing her, Clemmie, keep coaxing her, and you'll get hold of that stock yet — Clemmie, are you pretty sure of this market tip of yours?

CLEMMIE — Yes. It's straight, from the inside.

COUSIN WEBSTER — All market tips are chances. But in a case like yours, I suppose a man has got to take chances.

CLEMMIE — This tip is no chance; it's a sure thing;

it's as good as cash in the bank — if I had the money to play it!

COUSIN WEBSTER — If you *did* find the stock in your hands you could use it and have it right back in the clock there almost before Matilda realized she'd lent it to you, couldn't you? You're a young fellow with a lot of brains, Clemmie, and I'm not afraid you won't pull yourself out of this hole . . . a man will do a lot of hard thinking when he sees jail staring him in the face. You think up a way to get that stock from her, Clemmie, and you're all right. (*Goes over to clock.*) The way you folks keep all your papers in this clock case is scandalous. You ought to bring 'em over to the bank. (*With stock in hand.*) I don't see why she wouldn't lend you this. (*Webster looks at him keenly and then puts stock back in clock case.*) I did want to see your mother again, but maybe she's gone to bed. I can see her tomorrow. (*Hand on Clemmie's shoulder.*) Well, Clemmie, I hope everything turns out all right . . . and I'm sure it will. And when you do borrow that stock of hers, bring it to me. I'll pay you *fourteen* hundred dollars for it. Good night.

CLEMMIE —Good night.

Left by himself Clemmie is drawn irresistibly toward the clock. The logic of Cousin Webster's suggestions appeals to him, but he tries to overcome the temptation to take the stock. Suddenly he makes up his mind, opens the clock and reaches for the stock, just as Nellie, the hired girl, comes in. Nellie is a cheerful soul, but she resents what she accepts as Clemmie's personal allusions when he addresses her as "Little Rosebud." Nellie is conscious of a slightly red nose that suspicious people might attribute to drinking. She is ready to quit her place by the time Clemmie is through making sport of her. She's only stayed anyway on Mr. Hawley's account. He's the only person in the house with any kindness in his heart.

With Nellie returned to the kitchen Clemmie struggles briefly with his determination to "borrow" Mrs. Hawley's stock, then suddenly reaches for it, puts it in his pocket and hurries out of the room, as his father comes in.

A moment later Nellie returns. She sticks her head in the door, and finding Hawley alone calls softly to him. She has come to announce a friend. "Al" has called. And Al has brought with him some new hootch he has just made. On Clem's invitation he brings it in. None of them, however, is anxious to take the first drink of it. It may be all right, but there are some chances self-respectin' folks can't take.

"I don't want to hurt your feelin's, Al," Clem explains. "But I'm scared of this homemade stuff. It may be all right to take the grease spots out o' rugs with, but it ain't for the human digestive ornaments to fight against. . . . No, Al (*as Al offers to take the first drink*), you've been my favorite bartender for twenty years. It's got to be tried on some dumb beast first, like these doctors does with guinea pigs."

At Nellie's suggestion they agree to give Peter the first drink, Peter being Nellie's pet parrot in the kitchen, and Nellie goes to treat Peter. There is a drink to be had, however. Clem produces his bottle from the fireplace, and the two old cronies are soon visiting contentedly. Clem seats himself contentedly at the table and Al, once more the friendly bartender, waits on him.

AL — What will *you* have?

OLD SOAK — What would you advise, Al?

AL — How about a milk punch, sir?

OLD SOAK — Too much like vittles, Al. There's times when I can't bear the thought of vittles.

AL — Yes, sir, I can understand how you feel about vittles. How about a toddy? A toddy brings the stomach back to life right gradual, sir, without a shock.

OLD SOAK — There's water in a toddy, Al.

AL — Yes, sir, you don't want to be catching cold in your stomach this fall weather. How about a little straight whiskey?

OLD SOAK — Make it Bourbon, Al.

AL — (*pouring*). No sooner said than done.

PARROT'S VOICE — (*off stage*). It's always fair weather! It's always fair weather!

OLD SOAK — That's Peter, he's had his drink.

AL — He seems to like it, too. (*Both drink.*)

OLD SOAK — It ain't fitten for humans, tho, only for beasts, and insects, Al. Here's looking at you. I kind o' miss the old time barroom, with all them pictures on the walls and brass cuspidors to cuspidate in and fixin's, like Solomon in all his glory. (*Fill glasses again.*)

AL — What I miss is the genteel company. It was an education to a bartender just listenin' to some of the discussions —

OLD SOAK — Remember the songs the boys used to sing when they got a little jingled? (*Singing together.*) . . . "Darling I am growing old, silver threads among the gold. . . ."

AL — And them songs about home and mother!

OLD SOAK — Them songs used to make a better man of me, Al.

AL — There ain't any classy society anywhere, any more.

OLD SOAK — If I was a moneyed man, Al, I'd hire you to come wherever I went and fix drinks for me.

AL — (*drinking*). Here's hoping you strike it rich.

OLD SOAK — Mebby I will, too. That invention of mine is comin' along.

AL — What is it, Clem?

OLD SOAK — It's a DEE-vice, Al. To put onto these here elevators in city skyscrapers.

PARROT'S VOICE — (*off stage*). It's always fair weather!

OLD SOAK — Peter certainly likes that hootch . . .

but I can't understand an old time bartender like you makin' it.

AL — I always got hopes the next batch will turn out right. (*Pours a drink.*)

OLD SOAK — (*refilling his glass*). Hope's a fine thing. But it don't gurgle none when you pour it out of a bottle. What this country needs is a little more charity — Here's looking at you. (*Nellie comes in, swinging cage with parrot in it.*) 'S matter?

HIRED GIRL — Oh, Mr. Hawley, I've thought for ten years that Peter here was a gentleman parrot.

OLD SOAK — Ain't he? What's he done?

HIRED GIRL — I gave him two drinks of that hootch and he — Mr. Hawley — he laid a egg!

The party is well organized and a pleasant time is being had when Matilda breaks in upon them. Gradually the strains of their close harmony, devoted to "Sailing, sailing, over the bounding main," die away. Nellie sneaks back to the kitchen with as much dignity as the circumstances permit and Al quickly follows, leaving Clem to face the music.

Matilda is pretty mad, as any woman might be to find her house "turned into a barroom." And she will not listen to Clem's pleas that she be a little more gentle with him. Nor to his garrulous promises that he is yet going to cover her with silks and diamonds — as soon as he gets his ideas working properly. "Thirty years of it!" she mutters wearily, as he quietly takes his bottle and escapes. . . .

Tom and Lucy are back from their walk. And they have news for Matilda. They have decided to get married. Matilda receives the announcement with mingled feelings. She likes Tom — but married life, as she knows it, is not a risk she can joyfully recommend to her daughter. They are at pains to promise her that their life will be different — and that she shall share their happiness with them, and soon she is happy again, and glad for them.

Now she can give Lucy the present she has been saving for her — her grandmother's pearl brooch — the one she was married in. Lucy shall be married in it, too. She goes to the clock to get it.

The door opens and Clem Hawley, "pretty well intoxicated," lurches into the room. Tom and Lucy draw back from him, but Matilda, intent upon her search, does not see him. Clem stumbles into the room, looking for his hat, which is on the piano. Suddenly Mrs. Hawley realizes that the stock is gone, and as she turns, the suspicion that Clem has taken it assails her. Knowing he is in bad, Clem recovers his hat and staggers toward the door, humming his few bars of "Rock of Ages" to cover his retreat. Mrs. Hawley sinks wearily into a chair and bows her head in her hands. Tom and Lucy turn to her.

LUCY — There, there, mother!

TOM — Come, Mrs. Hawley! It's not so bad as all that! (*They both think she is weeping merely because of the Old Soak's condition.*)

MATILDA — It's worse than you know!

LUCY — Why mother, what is it? What else has happened? Tell me, mother?

MATILDA — (*head on table*). Oh, I can't tell you! I can't tell you!

The curtain falls.

ACT II

The scene is still the living room of the Hawley cottage. The time a few days later. Clem Hawley, sitting dejectedly in front of the fireplace, is trying to find solace in a smoke. But the cigar he lights he finds bitter to his taste. From the cache behind the fireplace he takes out his bottle. It is empty. With a sigh he replaces it. He sits down again and lights his pipe. Even that does not satisfy him. He is an unhappy man.

Nellie passes through the room with a shopping basket on her arm. From it she takes several packages and puts them on the table. Clem stops her and takes an apple from the basket, but one bite of it convinces him that *that* is not what he wants. With Nellie gone to the kitchen he rummages among the packages and finds a bottle. Surreptitiously and with a gleam of hope he pulls the cork and pours a little liquid into his hand. But one smell is enough. It is Matilda's hair tonic.

When Nellie comes again, in answer to Mrs. Hawley's call, Clem whispers to her. Where is "the bottle of unrighteousness Al left the other night?" "Peter drunk it," confesses Nellie. . . .

There is coldness in Mrs. Hawley's attitude. When Lucy comes from the city Clem speaks to her about it. Why does Matilda treat him "more so" than usual? Lucy tries to dissemble, but in the end she is obliged to confirm Clem's suspicions. It is the disappearance of the bonds that is worrying Mrs. Hawley. Clem's feelings are outraged. How could Matilda think that of him? Perhaps Lucy, too, thinks he took them. Lucy does not think he could have done it — unless. Clem knows. Unless — he had been drinking. But even that explanation hurts him. When Mrs. Hawley comes back into the room he speaks to her about it.

OLD SOAK — (*soberly*). Ma, you're thinkin' things of me you hadn't orter think.

MATILDA — Clem, these last few years I don't know what to think of you.

OLD SOAK — You don't trust me any more, Matilda.

MATILDA — You haven't *let* me trust you, Clem.

LUCY — Oh, dad! Mother — (*Intent on each other, they disregard her.*)

OLD SOAK — Where money was concerned, I always been all right.

MATILDA — Where money was concerned, you've been — careless.

OLD SOAK — I been a good spender, when I had it.

MATILDA — And sometimes when I had it!

OLD SOAK — Matilda, you don't believe it!

MATILDA — Clem, I don't *want* to believe it.

OLD SOAK — Matilda, don't you believe nothin' that hurts you that much to believe! (*Pets her; she frees herself.*)

MATILDA — No! Don't try to wheedle me. If you try that I'll *know* it's true. That's always been your way! To honey up to me and make me believe black's white. And I've always let you because —

OLD SOAK — Because you kind o' liked it, Matilda?

MATILDA — I never liked — staying mad at you. (*He makes for her but she stops him.*) No! Not this time! You've hurt me too much this time.

OLD SOAK — Then you *do* think — you really think —

LUCY — (*interrupting*). No, no dad! She doesn't — Mother, tell him you don't! (*Matilda is unresponsive except for a gesture of hopelessness.*)

OLD SOAK — (*watching Matilda*). Yes, she does, Lucy! And it looks as if there wasn't anything to do but *let* her think it till she gets *through* thinkin' it. . . . I'm gonna go! . . . I'm gonna get me a job somewheres — or something. . . . The good book says there ain't any use wastin' your sweetness on the desert air! I'm gonna pack. If it was some men this kind o' treatment would drive 'em to drink. (*He goes up the stairs.*)

LUCY — Mother, don't you care for him at all?

MATILDA — Yes. Too much. I always have — too much.

LUCY — Will he really leave?

MATILDA — He'll come back — when his money's gone. He always has. And I've always forgiven him.

LUCY — And you can't — now? (*Matilda does not reply.*) If he goes, that will make things — worse — Mother, I'm going to tell him he mustn't go!

MATILDA — No! Maybe he *will* get a job, when he has spent everything he has. And a job will be good for him. Oh, Lucy, he's my bad boy — my bad little grown-up boy. And I've never known how to manage him. If he wants to leave now — let him go!

Lucy continues to plead with her mother not to let her father go, but Mrs. Hawley is firm. She can't trust him now. He's been spending a lot of time at Jake Smith's and he may have gambled his money away, or paid old gambling debts with it. Men are always particular about their "debts of honor." The money was probably nearly all gone before he got it.

So Clem prepares to leave. He telephones Jake Smith first. He is coming over to be a star boarder for a while. And he'd like to take a truck-driving job or something, if there's one handy — just while he is working on his "DEE-vice." "It's shapin' up, Jake, it's shapin' up fine. Huh? My invention? It's a deevice, Jake, a DEE-vice — to handle heavy trunks with, and things like that."

A moment later he asks Matilda to help him separate his things from Clemmie's before he goes. He wouldn't like to have anyone think that he would take anything out of that house that didn't belong to him. . . .

Before Clem can get away Ina Heath calls. Ina is Clemmie's girl. She is a flashily dressed young woman of the soubrette type, and wears a typical Broadway makeup, including an expensive fur coat. The coat, she explains, was a gift from Clemmie. In some amazement she takes in the rather shabby furnishings of the room.

OLD SOAK — Clemmie never said much about me, did he?

INA — Why — no — not much.

OLD SOAK — Nor anything else around here, I'll bet — I seen you was sort of jolted when you came in.

INA — Why, Mr. Hawley, it's a — nice little dump.

OLD SOAK — Good enough for poor folks. That's a humdinger of a hat you've got on. Clemmie give you that too?

INA — N-no. He helped me pick it out though.

OLD SOAK — (*admiring her*). Clemmie's quite a picker, I'll say. (*She is flattered.*) You know, Clemmie sort of takes after me in his notion of what looks good to the human eye.

INA — He's a chip of the old block, eh?

OLD SOAK — Uh-huh! Heredity runs in our fambly. You ain't one of these flappers the papers has so much to say about?

INA — Suppose I were?

OLD SOAK — You ain't. Your hair ain't bobbed.

INA — But if I were, Mr. Hawley?

OLD SOAK — The good book says to beware of the bob-haired woman, for in the end she biteth like a serpent and stingeth like an adder. I better tell ma you're here.

Mrs. Hawley's greeting is affectionate when she is told who Ina is. She kisses her and gets lipstick on her cheek when the salute is returned. Having come from the kitchen, where she has been baking a pie, she gets flour on Ina's gown, which flusters her. But, of course, Ina will know more about such accidents after she has gone to housekeeping for herself. But Ina isn't going to keep house. Not much. "You see, a Jane in my profession hasn't got the time to fuss with garbage pails and dumb waiters," she explains.

From which it develops that Ina is a dancer—and rather a nifty dancer at that— having been "the first Jane that ever pulled a Fiji shimmy in a cabaret." But a shimmy, Clem hastens to inform Matilda, is not what she is thinking of.

MATILDA — So you're a dancer, my dear?
INA — I'll say I'm a dancer!
MATILDA — But you'll give that up, of course.
INA — (*shocked at the thought*). Give up dancing! My Gawd! Kiss my little kicks good-bye just when they're hopping me into the big-time! I'll say I won't!
MATILDA — But, you'll have to have a home! Clemmie's always had a home — and — if there are children —
INA — Children! Take it from me, Mrs. Hawley, there won't be any kids!
MATILDA — Oh!
INA — You see, a dancer can't afford to have children. Her figure is her fortune.
MATILDA — (*charitably*). Perhaps in time, my dear, you'll grow to feel differently about it. Sometimes women do. And Clemmie — must want — of course I haven't discussed it with him.
INA — Naturally *I* haven't.
MATILDA — Clemmie is the kind of boy who would want a home and children.
INA — I never got quite that slant on Clemmie.
MATILDA — My dear, a mother knows her own boy better than anyone else possibly could.
INA — (*who knows better*). You think so?
MATILDA — My dear, we shan't disagree! I know you love Clemmie better than anything else in the world, or you wouldn't think of marrying him. And so do I. And we're going to get along together and love each other for Clemmie's sake.

The meeting of Lucy and Ina is something of a shock to Clemmie's sister, and to Tom Ogden, too. But they succeed in making the best of it. Ina's presence is also an unpleasant surprise to Clemmie, when he finds her there. She purposely had not told him she was coming. She wanted to see for herself what sort of an "estate" he had led her to believe he was supporting on Long Island. Why had he been "stringing" her about everything, she would like to know.

CLEMMIE — I didn't string you.

INA — Clemmie, you're an awful little liar. (*He protests.*) Oh yes, you are! You never said in so many words that your people had money and a swell place — but you got it across.

CLEMMIE — Money? Is that all you care for?

INA — No! I care for a bird being on the square with me.

CLEMMIE — I wouldn't have had a look in if I hadn't spent money on you.

INA — You know that's not true, Clem.

CLEMMIE — You wouldn't have married me, unless —

INA — (*interrupting*). I haven't married you — (*She lets it sink in.*) Not yet!

CLEMMIE — You're going to — throw me down?

INA — You threw me down when you lied to me — listen! Get me right! I played around with you because I liked you for a pal. And I let you spend money on me because you threw the bluff you had plenty of it! But marriage is something else again. If you need your coin to help keep this place going, spend it here. I wouldn't rob an outfit like this — nor marry into it, either. (*Telephone rings; as he moves over to answer it she says:*) Where did you get it, anyway, the coin you've been blowing on me?

Her answer comes over the phone, for at this moment Clemmie's broker calls to say that Clemmie has been wiped out. The market had taken a severe turn for the worse, so far as Clemmie's investment was concerned, and as there was no more money on hand to margin it, the original sum was lost. Clemmie is inclined to be a little hysterical over the incident, and to blame it all on

Ina. But that young woman stoutly refuses to accept the honor.

Even his confession that he has taken money at his office and that he will face a jail sentence as soon as the auditor examines the books fails to excite her sympathy. He may have done it for her, as he says, but it is her opinion that when a man steals it is because he is that kind of a man. Nor do Clemmie's wild denials move her to any great show of pity. When she departs, however, she leaves her fur coat on a chair. "Maybe you can get something on this," she suggests.

Going out, Ina passes Clem coming in. Silently she points to Clemmie, bowed in grief, indicating that the boy is in trouble.

Suddenly Clemmie jumps up and starts for the stairs, as though he had come to a definite decision. Clem stops him. Whatever's wrong he doesn't intend that Clemmie shall "pull any fool stunt," or add any more worries to Matilda's overburdened lot.

And then Clemmie confesses the full extent of his sins — of how he had taken money at the office, and later the Midland Express stock, hoping to get out of the hole he was in. And now, not only is everything gone, but on the market the express stock has advanced. He has not only robbed his mother of her faith in him, but of her chance for the competence she had hoped some day to own.

CLEMMIE — Oh, I've been a fool! I've been a fool!

OLD SOAK — Your mother thinks *I* took that stock.

CLEMMIE — Oh, dad, I've been — rotten.

OLD SOAK — I've had my own times of feeling like a wormy apple. When I look at you, I know what she thinks of me.

CLEMMIE — But I never thought that *you'd* be blamed. I meant to put it back, and she'd thought it was just mislaid. (*Rises hysterical again.*) I'll tell her.

OLD SOAK — Wait! Don't tell her nothin'— yet. You've always fooled her and we've got to study to keep her fooled, about you — as long as we can — they don't know yet, at your office?

CLEMMIE — The auditor will be there day after tomorrow.

OLD SOAK — I wonder if Cousin Webster could help us out.

CLEMMIE — No!

OLD SOAK — You're mighty positive.

CLEMMIE — I went to him first. It was him that I sold the stock to.

OLD SOAK — Webster Parson? Did you hock it or sell it?

CLEMMIE — I sold it to him for fourteen hundred dollars.

OLD SOAK — How could you sell it? It was in her name.

CLEMMIE — Mother had given me power of attorney, so I could attend to business for her, because — (*Stops, confused*).

OLD SOAK — Because she didn't trust *me*, huh? Did Web know how you got that stock?

CLEMMIE — He thought mother lent it to me.

OLD SOAK — You never can be too sure what that fox is thinkin.' If we could find out some way to take care of your office, we'd let things here stay — the way they are.

CLEMMIE — Dad, I've been rotten — but I'm not that rotten. I let her have a wrong opinion of you when I was sure I'd pay it back — but now that I know it's gone —

OLD SOAK — Quit thinkin' of yourself and me! Our feelings don't amount to a damn. It's her that matters! Besides this thing ain't all your doin's, anyhow,— it's part mine.

CLEMMIE — Yours?

OLD SOAK — I'm your dad, and if I hadn't been — the kind of man I've been — you mightn't be the kind of boy you are. I never been exactly one of the twelve apostles, Clemmie, and you're — my son. You're one of my chickens that's come home to roost — singed.

CLEMMIE — It was my doings, alone.

OLD SOAK — Alone? I'm thinkin' that things don't work that way, Clemmie — nobody can do things, all alone — folks and their dads is all — all mixed up together — pardners, and can't help it.

CLEMMIE — I'm a weak pardner.

OLD SOAK — Yes, you've got a dish rag for a spine — and mine ain't been much stiffer than an oyster. I ain't much prouder of me, Clemmie, than I am of you — and the Lord knows I ain't proud of you at all. I orter licked you more when you was a kid. I might 'a' licked some of myself out of you, and then you'd 'a' had a chance in life. I might be just as useless as you are, if I had a father like yours. You can't help what was put into you afore you was born. And you've always seen me livin' loose and easy, too. As you sit there sniffling, Clemmie, you're the damnedest lesson I ever had — you poor miserable little whelp, you!

CLEMMIE — I *am* miserable. I'm in hell!

OLD SOAK — You and me got a right to be in hell, Clemmie. That addition was opened up for settlers like us.

CLEMMIE — Oh, Dad, if I get out of this mess I'll go straight the rest of my life!

OLD SOAK — I wish I was young and ignorant enough to promise that!

CLEMMIE — I'll go straight! I'll start right — I'll tell her now! (*Attempts to rise.*)

OLD SOAK — (*pushing him back*). No, you won't. From now on, you'll do what you're told to do. What she thinks of me, that's past all hopin' for. But what she thinks of you — mebby part of that can be saved for her, yet.

A moment later Clem has an idea. He calls Cousin Webster on the phone, and finding him out, leaves word that the banker shall call him as soon as he returns. Then he sends Clemmie away to prevent any chance of his weakening and telling his mother the story. "I don't want to crowd any more moral advice into you than your system's fitten to hold," he tells his son, "but if I was in your fix I'd go get drunk, myself."

The "Old Soak's" next trial comes when he meets Tom and Lucy. They are a little more vitally concerned in Clem's leaving the house than may appear, for if Clem goes Lucy cannot marry Tom and leave her mother alone, nor does she feel that it would be fair to Tom to ask him to take over the responsibilities of the family. If they could get Clem to insist that he did not take the stock, Matilda would not let him go. But at the moment Clem is in no position to assert his innocence, which convinces them that he must be guilty, and turns them, too, rather sharply against him.

Clem is rather low in mind when Nellie puts her head in the door to whisper cheerfully: "Mr. Hawley! Al's here!" and what's better, Al brings good news. Under the circumstances, Clem is convinced he could use a little good news. This news Al produces in a flask. It is the best stuff he has yet been able to get.

OLD SOAK — What millionaire you robbed?

AL — (*mysteriously*). Clem, I made a connection. Uh-huh! I'm in right! Makin' deliveries for a couple of under cover birds that's gettin' it from the bonded warehouse. Oodles of it!

OLD SOAK — *How* they gettin' it?

AL — These prominent and respected fellers always know how to work them things. It'd surprise you to know who's backin' me — one of the most prominent and respected citizens in town.

OLD SOAK — (*uncapping bottle*). Al, I had a hard day.

AL — What way?

OLD SOAK — Every way, Al. It's been goin' all wrong today. Especially that invention of mine. The good book says that hell is paved with good inventions. I ain't had a drink in two days.

NELLIE — Nor me, neither, Mr. Hawley, and I'm feelin' kind of down and out myself, I am.

AL — What's the trouble with you, Nellie?

NELLIE — (*eyeing bottle*). It's Peter that's the trouble. (*Sniffling.*) Peter, he's gone, Mr. Hawley, he is. He's d-d-dead!— seriously dead! It happened a half hour ago. I think it was his constitution undermined itself with that hootch Al brought here the other night; and I never will forgive myself, I won't. But he kept coaxin' and coaxin' for it that pretty that I couldn't refuse him. " 'Salways fair weather, it is," he'd say, and then I'd give him a drink of it. And then he'd cock his head onto one side and say: "Nellie was a lady," thankin' me, he was. And he kept drinking of it and drinking of it that-a-way till he deceased himself with it. He called out to me about a half an hour ago, he did. "Fair weather," he says, and then he laffed. Only he didn't laff natural, Mr. Hawley; he laffed kind of puny and feeble like there was somethin' furrin' weighing on his stomach. "I can't give you no more, Peter," I says to him, "for there ain't no more," I says. Then he stretched his neck out and bit the wire on his cage and squaked and he says in a kind of a sad voice: "Nellie was a lady, she was," he says. And them was the last words he ever give utterings to, Mr. Hawley. (*She leaves, weeping.*)

AL — Why don't you take a drink, Clem?

OLD SOAK — (*pours into cup*). I been sort o' playin'

with my thirst, Al — like they might tease one of them lions in the old times afore they flung a martyr to him. (*Drinks; feels his stomach.*) Way down inside of me, Al, there's somethin' warm wakin' up. Mebby it's hope. Mebby it's more discouragement gettin' ready to turn and rend me. (*Drinks again; pauses; feels his stomach.*) Blessin's on that prominent citizen of yours! I can feel that warm spot spreadin'! It *is* hope! (*Tenders bottle to Al.*)

AL — It's all yours.

OLD SOAK — (*pocketing flask*). Al, you're a human being!

Again Clem is picking up his suitcase preparatory to leaving home for Jake Smith's place when Matilda stops him. There is something very like tears in her voice as she tries gently to persuade him not to go, but she seems to hope she will not be weak enough to ask him to stay. She thinks, perhaps, she has said more than she should about his being out of work, and she is sure that they will be able to get along all right, with Clemmie and Lucy's help. Besides, there won't be anyone at Jake Smith's to look after him at all, like warning him to put on his woolens. But, Clem assures her, that does not so much matter. He never has been able to wear the scratchy stuff, though she had been trying to make him for thirty years.

MATILDA — Oh, Clem, I can't bear to think of you — looking around for jobs here and there. And that's what you'll be doing. Whatever money you've got will — will go — Oh, I can't think of you going about — looking for work like that — this winter. Oh, Clem, whatever you've done — (*He checks her.*)

OLD SOAK — Don't tell me whatever I've done I can stay here, Matilda! I wouldn't want a pardon wrote for me for something I hadn't done. And I wouldn't look to be acquitted for something I had done.

MATILDA — (*She is puzzled by his words.*) You mean — what do you mean — ?

Before she can finish Clem picks up the suitcase, which is not securely fastened, and it bursts open, permitting an assortment of things to fall in a heap on the floor. There are shirts, ties, collars, socks, etc., mostly wadded up as though they had been hurriedly and carelessly packed. There is also a corkscrew among the trinkets, and an old photograph which Matilda finds among the socks. Clem glances a little sheepishly over her shoulder as she studies the photograph.

MATILDA — Why — that was taken — (*Pauses.*)

OLD SOAK — On our wedding trip. You was a pretty little girl then, Matilda.

MATILDA — I didn't know you — had one of these.

OLD SOAK — I always kept it on account of Niagara Falls bein' took in the picture along with us.

MATILDA — Girls wore bangs then.

OLD SOAK — And bustles, too. And look at the high standin' collar, Matilda. That's the only time in my life I ever wore a high standin' collar.

MATILDA — And a Prince Albert coat. I remember — I made that into an overcoat for Clemmie when he was four years old.

OLD SOAK — The little rascal! I recollect how he looked in it. I bought him his first sled that year.

MATILDA — It was broadcloth.

OLD SOAK — I remember peelin' that coat off and tellin' that hack driver I'd throw him into the Falls if he didn't quit trying to overcharge me.

MATILDA — And the rice dropped out of your pocket then.

OLD SOAK — Uh-huh! And him and me both laughed at that and didn't fight.

MATILDA — Yes, and you paid him the overcharge after all! (*She hands him the photograph.*)

OLD SOAK — You — you ain't got one of these pictures, Matilda. I'll — I'll leave this one here for you. (*She does not take it. He fumbles with it awkwardly.*) Well, good-bye, Matilda.

MATILDA — (*suddenly bursting out*). Oh, Clem, you mustn't go! I was wrong! I was wrong! I know that I was wrong! You mustn't go! (*He stands wavering.*)

OLD SOAK — No — Matilda — I — won't tell you — that!

MATILDA — I'm sorry, Clem. (*She puts her hands over her face and goes up the stairs, quietly sobbing.*)

NELLIE — Dinner's ready!

OLD SOAK — I guess there ain't no appetite around this house tonight. (*Telephone rings. Old Soak picks up receiver.*) Hello — is that you, Web? This is Clem — Web, I want to see you. You wait there till I come, do you hear? (*He hangs up the receiver with a snap, turns towards audience pulling at belt and tightening it, bracing himself and assuming a determined manner.*) I got to gird my loins, like the good book says. (*He picks up his suitcase and goes out.*)

The curtain falls.

ACT III

A half hour later that afternoon, after banking hours, Al, the bootlegger, is calling on the silent partner of his new connection, Webster Parsons, in the latter's bank. They are sitting inside the cashier's grille, which also serves Parsons as an office. It is Cousin Webster's idea that he should have this one talk with Al, in order to impress upon him the importance of his doing all his future business with others.

COUSIN WEBSTER — You will take your orders from

Jake Smith. I know nothing about the business he's engaged in.

AL — Jake's got the understanding all three of us was in the bootleggin' game together, and him and me calls you our silent pardner.

COUSIN WEBSTER — Bootlegging? I don't understand you at all. I am lending Jake Smith money to extend his trucking business. What he hauls in his trucks is no concern of mine.

AL — That's a good line of talk, boss; and if I could kid myself along that way I guess I'd feel like a prominent and respectable citizen myself. Here's you and me, both bootleggers —

COUSIN WEBSTER — Hush! Don't use that word!

AL — See here, boss, you want to be a little bit chummier with me, if we're going to get along together and make money for all of us. You got the money and the political connections, and Jake's got the trucks, but me, I got the experience. I know practically every drinkin' man in Nassau county. If I was to drop out of this deal, you'd have a hard time gettin' hold of another bird like me. You go ahead and kid yourself all you want to, but when you talk to me you talk like one bootlegger to another.

COUSIN WEBSTER — I meant no offence, Al.

AL — I ain't mad. I'm just tellin' you. You got nuthin' on me that I ain't got on you. We're both runnin' the same risks.

COUSIN WEBSTER — Risks?

AL — Uh-huh. You can't fix anything so there ain't some risks.

COUSIN WEBSTER — Did anybody see you when you came in?

AL —Johnnie Peters and one or two others, mebby. But there's nothin' to that. I might be lookin' for a job or something.

COUSIN WEBSTER —Johnnie Peters, the town constable?

AL—Uh-huh. And my advice is to fix Johnnie. Johnnie drinks like a fish himself, but that wouldn't keep him from makin' a pinch for the glory and credit of it. He works with the revenuers — he helped 'em raid that roadhouse over by Hempstead Harbor last Saturday night.

COUSIN WEBSTER — Jake Smith can attend to him.

AL — You got to do right by people if you want 'em to do right by you. Now me, I'm honest, and if we get into any trouble I'll stick by you as long as you stick by me. But I won't stick any longer.

COUSIN WEBSTER — I wouldn't go back on you, Albert.

AL — You wouldn't dast to, boss. (*Taking flask from pocket.*) And now that we know where we stand, pardner, let's have a drink on the bargain.

COUSIN WEBSTER — (*waving it away*). I never drink.

AL — There's no one here to see you but me. You don't mean to say you don't really like it?

COUSIN WEBSTER — I have never taken a drink in my life.

AL — You're just turnin' bootlegger for the money, and not on account of a friendly feeling for liquor, boss! Well, I'll be darned!

The rattling of the outer door announces the arrival of Clem Hawley, and as Cousin Webster lets Clem in he ushers Al out with a loud: "I don't know of any job right now, Al, but you might look in in another day or two," to excuse the somewhat suspicious character of the visit. It is not enough, however, to fool Clem, even if Al did not wink wisely at him as he passed. The identity of Al's "prominent and respected citizen partner" is no longer shrouded even a little in mystery.

Cousin Webster is a bit startled at Clem's attitude, particularly when he begins to talk of the errand that has brought him to the bank — an errand, as he explains, having to do with money and trouble.

COUSIN WEBSTER — Clem, you're acting — strange. You've been drinking too much.

OLD SOAK — You don't need to be worried because I've been drinkin', Web. When I'm drinkin' I get good-natured, Web. . . . Why, if I was to take a notion to choke you, I'd do it in a perfectly good-natured way.

COUSIN WEBSTER — (*daunted somewhat, not knowing how to handle him*). Stop your fooling, and tell me what you want.

OLD SOAK — I want money, Web. I come to talk about money and trouble. Trouble that is, and trouble that's likely to come, Web. Matilda's in trouble. She's in worse trouble than she knows about.

COUSIN WEBSTER — What kind of trouble?

OLD SOAK — Through Clemmie. You know what Clemmie's trouble is. But Matilda don't know. And she don't know he took her stock. And she ain't gonna know, Web, because you an' me are gonna keep Clemmie's trouble away from her. If she found out, about him, it would just be about the end of the world for her. That stock closed today at a hundred and twelve, Clemmie sold his mother's shares to you for fourteen hundred dollars. I'm here, Web, for the other ten thousand.

COUSIN WEBSTER — Ten thousand? Are you crazy, or joking?

OLD SOAK — Mebby I'm jokin,' Web, mebby. I was readin' in the papers the other day about a mean joke some fellers played on a country banker. He'd been missin' for four — five days and when they found him he was all doubled up — and jumbled together and crammed inside one of them big safes. There wasn't anybody but him knowed the combination, and when they got him out he was a sight — it was a safe jest like that one.

COUSIN WEBSTER — I don't see anything funny in that story.

Old Soak — Neither did the banker — Web, I'm waitin' here patient for what you owe Matilda.

Cousin Webster — I owe Matilda!

Old Soak — Web, there's no use us two beatin' about the bush. If you didn't sell that stock at the highest price today, you will the first thing in the morning. You knowed it was goin' up. You knowed the fix Clemmie was in, and you took advantage of it to get hold of that stock cheap. More'n likely you tempted Clemmie to take it.

Cousin Webster — It was a perfectly legal transaction. He had her power of attorney.

Old Soak — Legal? Of course it was legal. That's the difference between you and Clemmie. You always done your stealin' legal, an' now you're president of a bank. And he, the poor little sucker, is in line to go to jail. You don't mean to say you'd see Clemmie go to jail?

Cousin Webster — He's made his bed and he'll have to lie on it.

Old Soak — S'pose he's made his mother's death bed, too? Will she have to lie on that? Web, your soul is so small that if there was a million souls the size of yourn in a flee's belly they'd be so fur apart they couldn't hear each other holler.

For twenty minutes Cousin Webster tries to wiggle out of the situation in which Clem holds him. He argues and pleads and threatens — only to be met with the shrewd philosophy of a new "Old Soak" in search of justice, and the repeated suggestion that the finding of a dead banker or two every few days is such common news it no longer startles anyone.

Cousin Webster — I've always hated the kind of thing you've stood for.

Old Soak — Hatin' things is what makes you bilious,

Web. There's two different roads to failure, and you've come one of them and I've come the other.

COUSIN WEBSTER — You and your son have failed because of what you've been.

OLD SOAK — That's true, Web. But what you been? If you was to be discovered hangin' dead on this here cord in the mornin' there wouldn't no one grieve. (*As he speaks he makes loops in the cord, and acts the scene out.*) Your clerks would come in and see you a-swingin' and a-swayin' there and one of 'em would say: "Well, the old coot's hung himself!" and the other would say: "I guess his conscience finally got next to him," and the first one would remark: "He must 'a' climbed onto this stool and put the cord around his neck and kicked it down"; and the other one would say: "I wouldn't 'a' minded jerkin' that stool from under his feet myself." (*With rapt manner.*) I can see you there, now, Web, a-swayin' and a-swayin' with your knees hittin' against the desk when the cord spins round!

COUSIN WEBSTER — You're threatening me! You've been threatening me ever since you came in here!

OLD SOAK — I wouldn't call it exactly a threat, Web. I'd call it a pointed invitation. . . . You come across with that money, Web.

Once, after maneuvering himself into position to get hold of the phone Cousin Webster tries to call the Baycliff police, but Clem cuts the telephone cords and brings a new pallor into the face of the banker by his careless brandishing of the office shears.

"I'll have you put behind the bars for this night's work," hoarsely threatens Cousin Webster.

"I won't go behind the bars for nothin' I've done *yet,*" calmly replies Clem. "But I may go behind the bars for somethin' I'll do *soon*. . . . I was readin' in the paper the other day about some fellers that took a country banker and rammed him up one of them chimbleys. It kind o' cracked his joints in spots. Nobody knowed he was there till they built a fire a week later."

Again Cousin Webster seeks to save himself by a ruse. He knows that outside the window, within sound of his voice, Johnnie Peters, the Baycliff constable, is standing. Suddenly he throws up the window and calls lustily for Peters.

But when Peters answers both the banker's nerve and his voice fail him. "Johnnie, we got somethin' for you," calls Clem, passing out some of Al's whiskey. And then he whispers defiantly to Webster: "Tell him now! Tell him I'm robbin' the bank! Mebbe Johnnie'd like to catch a bank robber and bootlegger both at one haul."

"This is blackmail," snaps Cousin Webster, angrily.

"Blackmail an' robbery an' anything else you want to call it," agrees Clem. "I don't care. Do I get Matilda's money?"

As a last resort Cousin Webster, pretending to open a money drawer, manages to get around to a drawer in which he knows the cashier's revolver is kept. But before he can get hold of the gun Clem quietly advises him to leave it alone. ". . . Web, you stick to the bootleggin' business — it may make a man of you yet. . . . You better put that gun away, Web. . . . I was readin' in the paper the other day about a country banker that went into the bootleggin' business, and some revenuers took him —"

"How will you have it? A check?"

"No, thank you, Web. Bills! Hundred dollar bills! A hundred of 'em."

And while Cousin Webster is working the combination of the safe and taking out the money Clem keeps him safely "covered" with his old cob pipe. It looks like a gun — thrust through the pocket of a coat, and the clicking sound that Webster may have heard was made by a patent cigar lighter in the same pocket.

"See that cute little trick, Web?" queries Clem, exposing the lighter a moment later; "Al gave me that."

He is singing "Pull for the shore, sailors, pull for the shore," and waiting for Matilda's money as the curtain falls.

A few minutes later Matilda, Clemmie and Lucy are sitting in the Hawley living room. Clem's continued absence worries them. That he has gone for good Matilda feels sure, and she is more conscience stricken than before, since she has heard Clemmie's confession that it was he who took the stock. She is angry and crushed in spirit. The son in whom she has taken such pride has disappointed her. The daughter in whose marriage with Tom Ogden she had begun to take pleasure has sent Tom away because she, too, is ashamed of the "Old Soak."

". . . He isn't half the man that your father is," she tells Lucy. And when the latter starts to reply she will not listen. "Don't answer me back! You haven't appreciated your father, either of you. You've treated him as if he weren't as good as you. But he's better! He's a thousand times better!"

Her fury and resentment are so real her children draw back from her, surprised and startled.

"Oh, I know that I was hard on him," she continues, more gently. "But I was hard on him because I loved him! He was willing to take the disgrace to save me . . . while I was unjustly accusing him. Oh, I am ashamed! Ashamed of myself, and of both of you. He is better, I tell you, than any of us, and we have been blind, and haven't seen it! It would serve us right if we never saw him again! He would have gone on to his grave, letting me think my son was innocent just to save me pain!"

Tom Ogden comes back to settle his part of the argument by informing Lucy that, no matter what her father has done, he intends to marry her. And a moment later Clem is heard singing "Rock of Ages" as he comes up on the porch.

Now he has entered the room and made straight for the table. Taking off his hat he begins to pour out hundred dollar bills until there is quite a pile of them.

OLD SOAK — All of you wonderin' where that money come from, ain't you? None of you ever thought that invention would amount to anything, did you? You act as if you didn't believe me, ma!

MATILDA — (*smiling*). I don't, Clem.

OLD SOAK — That comes of not having any business head on you, Matilda. Women never has any business head. You got to leave it to men for business ability. Well, I'll tell you the honest injun truth, Matilda. That money didn't come from my invention at all. That money come through my bein' a darned smart business man, watchin' the papers and keepin' in touch with things, and knowin' what's what generally. Matilda, that there stock of yourn that's been layin' round the house for two or three years really was worth somethin' after all! I knowed it, but your cousin Webster wouldn't believe it. Says I to Web, the other day: "Web, that stock's gonna go up!" "Ain't no such thing," says your cousin Webster. "Web," says I to him, "you trust my business judgment . . . that stock's goin' up, and there's a chance to make some money for Matilda off'n it." "She won't sell it," says Web, "I've asked her." "Web," says I, "We'll just put up a joke onto Matilda. I'll sneak that stock out and we'll sell it for her, and turn the money over to her, and surprise her. And that's what I done, Matilda. . . . You got a little bit fussed over missin' it, but I never minded that any an' . . . Matilda —

MATILDA — (*interrupting, gently*). It was all a surprise you planned for me, was it, Clem? You and

Cousin Webster? Did Clemmie know anything about it?

OLD SOAK — (*beginning promptly*). Not a word. . . . (*Becoming confused.*) That is, right at the start he didn't. Later, we had to go to Clemmie for advice, Web and me did, and Clemmie gave it to us. Yes, sir, Clemmie manipulated the market for us, like you read about in the papers. He spent considerable money doin' it and Web and me agreed that a couple thousand of this ought to go to Clemmie for his services. Clemmie, come on over and pick yourself out a couple of thousand — that's for manipulating the market.

MATILDA — Clem, you're an awful old liar!

OLD SOAK — Me, ma? Well, I guess mebby I ain't so honest as some folks.

MATILDA — I don't believe a word you've been saying.

OLD SOAK — Well, now, Matilda, the truth is . . .

MATILDA— (*interrupting, wooing him by her manner*). Clem, in all our thirty years of married life you never have deceived me, and you don't deceive me now. Clem, I know. (*He acts embarrassed and ashamed. She comes toward him, and at the same instant Lucy and Tom rush for him; all hug him simultaneously.*)

OLD SOAK — There, now, I never seen such a darn family!

Nellie pokes her nose in the door to announce that dinner, having been ready for an hour, is "plumb ruined." But no one cares. Tom suggests that they all go to the inn for dinner.

They file out, happy in the solution of all immediate problems, with everybody beaming except Clemmie, and he looking as cheerful as his mother can make him with her expressed forgiveness and a new vote of confidence. Clem is about to follow when Nellie again sticks her head in the door and calls, softly: "Oh, Mr. Hawley! Al's here!"

Clem stops, and wavers. Al appears cautiously in the doorway, with a flask in his hand.

"Clem, what's keeping you?" calls Matilda from the porch.

"Just a little message from Cousin Webster," answers Clem, as he takes the flask from Al, puts it in his pocket, and follows after the family.

THE END

"R. U. R."

A Fantastic Melodrama in Four Acts

By Karel Capek

BEGINNING its fifth season at the Garrick Theater, October 9, 1922, the Theatre Guild offered a continental novelty written by Karel Capek and called "R. U. R.," which is a trade abbreviation of the longer name, "Rossum's Universal Robots."

This fantastic melodrama, a story of the world's repopulation with artificial beings, proved much to the liking of Guild subscribers, and though it did not achieve the popularity of either Molnar's "Liliom," the Guild's importation from the Hungarian stage of two years before, or that of Andreyev's "He Who Gets Slapped," brought over from Russia the season before, it proved popular enough to stand transplanting, in November, to the Frazee Theatre, where it ran until early spring.

The author, Karel Capek, is a young Czechoslovakian philosopher born in upper Bohemia in 1890. He has written a few other plays, and numerous poems and short stories. "R. U. R.," however, is the first of his stage works to attract general attention.

It is a weird drama, a sort of socialistic satire, into which all sorts of symbolic meanings may be read by the spectator possessed of an active and sympathetic imagination. It projects the discovery of and experiments with a formula by which human beings, perfect in all ways except their lack of souls, are manufactured by the thousands, and it follows the results of the experiment to an acceptable, if not altogether reasonable, conclusion.

The first scene is in the central office of the factory,

which is located on an island considerable distance, it is assumed, from the more heavily populated centers, and dependent, therefore, upon infrequent communication with the world by ship.

The office is a plainly, though comfortably, furnished interior. At a central desk an executive is dictating to an odd-looking female seated at a typewriter. An ideal stenographer in that she listens attentively until the full letter is dictated, and then swiftly types it, without pausing for correction or erasure or further instruction. Her movements are mechanical and her mind evidently as impressionable as the wax cylinder of a dictaphone.

One letter is to a firm in Southampton, England, explaining that the Rossum Company does not undertake to guarantee goods damaged in transit. Another to an agency in New York, acknowledging receipt of an order for five thousand Robots (the artificial humans), and suggesting an exchange of hard and soft coal to be sent as cargo on the transport that is to take the Robots back. A third goes to Hamburg, Germany, acknowledging an order for fifteen thousand Robots, the efficient Germans being apparently the heaviest buyers of the mechanical workers, even thus early in their manufacture.

The office routine is interrupted by the announced arrival of a young woman with a card from the company's president. She is, it transpires, Helena Glory, the president's daughter, an attractive, serious-minded girl in her early twenties, and she has come upon a tour of investigation.

Harry Domin, the executive in charge, is glad to stop his work to show Helena every courtesy. Visits of attractive lady humans to Rossum Island are not frequent, and when Helena raises her veil young Mr. Domin appears in considerable danger of being bowled over by her beauty. He recovers his poise in time, however, to resume his official status. Anything that she would like to know he will be glad to tell her, though she must give her word not to divulge any of the secrets concerned with the manufacture of Robots that she may happen upon during her investigation.

DOMIN — But first, would you like to hear the story of the invention?

HELENA — Yes, indeed.

DOMIN — (*reciting mechanically*). It was in the year 1920 that old Rossum, the great physiologist, who was then quite a young scientist, took himself to this distant island for the purpose of studying the ocean fauna, full stop. On this occasion he attempted by chemical synthesis to imitate the living matter known as protoplasm until he suddenly discovered a substance which behaved exactly like living matter although its chemical composition was different. That was in the year 1932, exactly four hundred years after the discovery of America. Whew!

HELENA — Do you know that by heart?

DOMIN — Yes. You see physiology is not in my line. Shall I go on?

HELENA — Yes, please.

DOMIN — And then, Miss Glory, old Rossum wrote the following among his chemical specimens: "Nature has found only one method of organizing living matter. There is, however, another method, more simple, flexible and rapid, which has not yet occurred to nature at all. This second process by which life can be developed was discovered by me today." Now, imagine him, Miss Glory, writing those wonderful words over some colloidal mess that a dog wouldn't look at. Imagine him sitting over a test tube, and thinking how the whole tree of life would grow from it, how all animals would proceed from it, beginning with some sort of beetle and ending with a man. A man of different substance from us. Miss Glory, that was a tremendous moment.

HELENA — Well?

DOMIN — Now, the thing was how to get the life out of the test tubes, and hasten development and form organs, bones and nerves, and so on, and find such substances as catalytics, enzymes, hormones, and so forth, in short — you understand?

HELENA — Not much, I'm afraid.

DOMIN — Never mind. You see, with the help of his tinctures he could make whatever he wanted. He could have produced a Medusa with the brain of a Socrates or a worm fifty yards long. But being without a grain of humor, he took it into his head to make a vertebrate or perhaps a man. This artificial living matter of his had a raging thirst for life. It didn't mind being sewn or mixed together. That couldn't be done with natural albumen. And that's how he set about it.

But the elder Rossum's efforts at imitating nature proved a failure. He spent years on the creation of a dog that turned out a sort of stunted calf and lived but a few days. Then he began on man. The world is familiar with the experiments that followed, but what the world doesn't suspect, according to Domin, is that old Rossum was really mad. "The old crank wanted actually to make people," he explains. . . . "He wanted to become a sort of scientific substitute for God. He was a fearful materialist, and that's why he did it all. His sole purpose was nothing more nor less than to prove that God was no longer necessary."

But again old Rossum failed. After spending ten years on the making of a man, his first subject lived only three days. Then along came the younger Rossum, who was an engineer. "He was a wonderful fellow, Miss Glory," enthuses Domin. "When he saw what a mess of it the old man was making he said: 'It's absurd to spend ten years making a man. If you can't make him quicker than nature you might as well shut up shop.' Then he set about learning anatomy himself."

They quarrelled a lot, the two Rossums, and finally separated. In due time the father died and the son went on with his now successful experiments. His first important step was to consider man's anatomy from the viewpoint of a practical engineer. And what man needed, young Rossum quickly decided, was a general overhauling, with the idea of cutting out of him all superfluous organs, dimensions, senses, etc.

DOMIN — So young Rossum said to himself: "A man is something that feels happy, plays the piano, likes going for a walk, and in fact, wants to do a whole lot of things that are really unnecessary."

HELENA — Oh!

DOMIN — That are unnecessary when he wants, let us say, to weave and count. Do you play the piano?

HELENA — Yes.

DOMIN — That's good. But a working machine must not play the piano, must not feel happy, must not do a whole lot of other things. A gasoline motor must not have tassels or ornaments, Miss Glory. And to manufacture artificial workers is the same thing as to manufacture gasoline motors. The process must be of the simplest, and the product of the best from a practical point of view. What sort of worker do you think is the best from a practical point of view?

HELENA — What?

DOMIN — What sort of worker do you think is the best from a practical point of view?

HELENA — Perhaps the one who is most honest and hard-working.

DOMIN — No; the one that is cheapest. The one whose requirements are the smallest. Young Rossum invented a worker with the minimum amount of requirements. He had to simplify him. He rejected everything that did not contribute directly to the progress of work — everything that makes man more expensive. In fact, he rejected man and made the Robot. My dear Miss Glory, the Robots are not people. Mechanically they are more perfect than we are, they have an enormously developed intelligence, but they have no soul.

HELENA — How do you know they've no soul?

DOMIN — Have you ever seen what a Robot looks like inside?

HELENA — No.

DOMIN — Very neat, very simple. Really, a beautiful piece of work. Not much in it, but everything in flawless order. The product of an engineer is technically at a higher pitch of perfection than a product of nature.

HELENA — But man is supposed to be the product of God.

DOMIN — All the worse. God hasn't the least notion of modern engineering.

But young Rossum then proceeded also to grow ambitious. He wanted to create a race of giants twelve feet tall. They proved a terrible failure. Their limbs were continually snapping off, and for no apparent reason. So that formula was abandoned, and normal sized Robots only were made thereafter. At the moment these are being made in several grades. The best of them live about twenty years. By that time they are pretty well used up, Domin admits.

There is Sulla, the typist, for example. Sulla is a fine grade Robot. And so is Marius, an office clerk, who now brings in a couple of the coarser Robots that Helena may note the contrast. The common fellows are as strong as small tractors, have average intelligence and are excellent for street cleaning and such jobs. The finer Robots can be taught almost anything and depended upon absolutely.

But Helena is not convinced. She has found Sulla both an interesting and well informed conversationalist. She won't believe that she is a Robot.

HELENA — Oh, that's absurd! Sulla isn't a Robot. Sulla is a girl like me. Sulla, this is outrageous! Why do you take part in such a hoax?

SULLA — I am a Robot.

HELENA — No, no you are not telling the truth. I know they've forced you to do it for an advertisement. Sulla, you are a girl like me, aren't you?

DOMIN — I'm sorry, Miss Glory. Sulla is a Robot.

HELENA — It's a lie!

DOMIN — What? (*Rings.*) Excuse me, Miss Glory, then I must convince you. (*Enter Marius.*) Marius, take Sulla into the dissecting room, and tell them to open her up at once.

HELENA — Where?

DOMIN — Into the dissecting room. (*To Helena*) When they've cut her open, you can go and have a look.

HELENA — No, no!

DOMIN — Excuse me, you spoke of lies.

HELENA — You wouldn't have her killed?

DOMIN — You can't kill machines.

HELENA — Don't be afraid, Sulla, I won't let you go. Tell me, my dear, are they always so cruel to you? You mustn't put up with it, Sulla. You mustn't.

SULLA — I am a Robot.

HELENA — That doesn't matter. Robots are just as good as we are. Sulla, you wouldn't let yourself be cut to pieces?

SULLA — Yes.

HELENA — Oh, you're not afraid of death, then?

SULLA — I cannot tell, Miss Glory.

HELENA — Do you know what would happen to you in there?

SULLA — Yes, I should cease to move.

HELENA — How dreadful!

DOMIN — Marius, tell Miss Glory what you are.

MARIUS — Marius, the Robot.

DOMIN — Would you take Sulla into the dissecting room?

MARIUS — Yes.

DOMIN — Would you be sorry for her?

MARIUS — I cannot tell.

DOMIN — What would happen to her?

MARIUS — She would cease to move. They would put her into the stamping mill.

DOMIN — That is death, Marius. Aren't you afraid of death?

MARIUS — No.

DOMIN — You see, Miss Glory, the Robots have no interest in life. They have no enjoyments. They are less than so much grass.

The story of the manufacture of Robots grows more and more fascinating as Helena's investigation continues. Out the window she can see rows on rows of them laying brick. Through the windows of a great counting house other thousands are at work on the books of the firm. And they never know when to stop work unless they hear the whistle.

DOMIN — . . . In two hours I will show you the kneading trough.

HELENA — Kneading trough?

DOMIN — The pestle for beating up the paste. In each one we mix the ingredients for a thousand Robots at one operation. Then there are the vats for the preparation of liver, brains, and so on. Then you will see the bone factory. After that I'll show you the spinning mill.

HELENA — Spinning mill?

DOMIN — Yes. For weaving nerves and veins. Miles and miles of digestive tubes pass through it at a time.

HELENA — Mayn't we talk about something else?

DOMIN — Perhaps it would be better. There's only a handful of us among a hundred thousand Robots, and not one woman. We talk about nothing but the factory all day, every day. It's just as if we were under a curse, Miss Glory.

HELENA — I'm sorry I said you were lying.

The company's executives are introduced. They, too, are pleased to meet the president's daughter, and doubly pleased because she is a beautiful woman. Helena finds herself suddenly the object of their most solicitous attention. The situation puzzles her. Had Domin not said that all the company's officials were Robots? These men seem strangely like humans. Yet so did Sulla. Suddenly Helena is inspired with the thought that this is an appropriate time for her to state her real mission in coming to Rossum Island. Surely the way they are treated must distress them. It does her. It's terrible. The whole of Europe is talking about it, and she has come to see for herself. And she has found conditions a thousand times worse than she had dreamed. She cannot understand how they can put up with it.

ALQUIST — Put up with what?

HELENA — Good heavens, you are living creatures, just like us, like the whole of Europe, like the whole world. It's disgraceful that you must live like this.

BUSMAN — Good gracious, Miss Glory.

FABRY — Well, she's not far wrong. We live here just like red Indians.

HELENA — Worse than red Indians. May I, oh, may I call you brothers?

BUSMAN — Why not?

HELENA — Brothers, I have not come here as the President's daughter. I have come on behalf of the Humanity League. Brothers, the Humanity League now has over two hundred thousand members. Two hundred thousand people are on your side, and offer you their help.

BUSMAN —Two hundred thousand people! Miss Glory, that's a tidy lot. Not bad.

FABRY — I'm always telling you there's nothing like good old Europe. You see, they've not forgotten us. They're offering us help.

DR. GALL — What help? A theatre, for instance?

HALLEMEIER — An orchestra?

HELENA — More than that.

ALQUIST — Just you?

HELENA — Oh, never mind about me. I'll stay as long as it is necessary.

BUSMAN — By Jove, that's good!

ALQUIST — Domin, I'm going to get the best room ready for Miss Glory.

DOMIN — Just a minute. I'm afraid Miss Glory is of the opinion that she has been talking to Robots.

HELENA — Of course.

DOMIN — I'm sorry. These gentlemen are human beings just like us.

HELENA — You're not Robots?

BUSMAN — Not Robots.

HALLEMEIER — Robots, indeed!

DR. GALL — No, thanks.

FABRY — Upon my honor, Miss Glory, we aren't Robots.

HELENA — (*to Domin*). Then why did you tell me that all your officials are Robots?

DOMIN — Yes, the officials, but not the managers. Allow me, Miss Glory: this is Mr. Fabry, General Technical Manager of R. U. R.; Dr. Gall, Head of the Psychological and Experimental Department; Dr. Hallemeier, Head of the Institute for the Psychological Training of Robots; Consul Busman, General Business Manager; and Alquist, Head of the Building Department of R. U. R.

There is a laugh, rather than any show of resentment, at Helena's mistake. Nor are the managers worried when she confesses that she has come to make trouble for them. They are used to visiting reformers — reformers representing every known organization of progressives and radicals in the world. And they have made not the slightest impression upon the Robots. The mechanical people remember everything they hear but it doesn't mean anything to them.

Helena might, as a representative of the Humanity League, which was organized, she confesses, to liberate the Robots — she might possibly bring them all the benefits of civilization, but what good would it do the Robots? They have no physical appetites, no sense of right or wrong, no feeling of happiness or sorrow. They've no will of their own, no passion, no soul, no love.

Occasionally a Robot will exhibit a kind of defiance, Hallemeier admits. Now and again they have been known to go off their heads and start smashing things. "Robot's cramp," the managers call the disease, and it is necessary to send those afflicted back to the stamping mill at once. Evidently such outbreaks indicate a breakdown in the mechanism.

It is Helena's opinion that, to the contrary, such outbreaks may be caused by the birth of a soul in the automatons. But the managers are incredulous. Souls are not likely to indicate their presence by the gnashing of teeth.

HELENA — Perhaps it's a sort of revolt. Perhaps it's just a sign that there's a struggle within. Oh, if you could infuse them with it!

DOMIN — That'll be remedied, Miss Glory. Dr. Gall is just making some experiments —

DR. GALL — Not with regard to that, Domin. At present I am making pain-nerves.

HELENA — Pain-nerves?

DR. GALL — Yes, the Robots feel practically no bodily pain. You see young Rossum provided them with too limited a nervous system. We must introduce suffering.

HELENA — Why do you want to cause them pain?

DR. GALL — For industrial reasons, Miss Glory. Sometimes a Robot does damage to himself because it doesn't hurt him. He puts his hand into the machine, breaks his finger, smashes his head, it's all the same to him. We must provide them with pain. That's an automatic protection against damage.

HELENA — Will they be happier when they feel pain?

DR. GALL — On the contrary; but they will be more perfect from a technical point of view.

HELENA — Why don't you create a soul for them?

DR. GALL — That's not in our power.

FABRY — That's not in our interest.

BUSMAN — That would increase the cost of production. Hang it all, my dear young lady, we turn them out at such a cheap rate. A hundred and fifty dollars each fully dressed, and fifteen years ago they cost ten thousand.

The increased and steady manufacture of Robots, they tell her, is certain to revolutionize the world, to create a new and a more wonderful civilization than has ever been known. In five years —

BUSMAN — . . . Why, in five years' time I'll wager —

HELENA — What?

BUSMAN — That the cost of everything won't be a tenth of what it is now. Why, in five years we'll be up to our ears in corn and everything else.

ALQUIST — Yes, and all the workers throughout the world will be unemployed.

DOMIN — Yes, Alquist, they will. Yes, Miss Glory, they will. But in ten years Rossum's Universal Robots will produce so much corn, so much cloth, so much everything, that things will be practically without price. There will be no poverty. All work will be done by living machines. Everybody will be free from worry and liberated from the degradation of labor. Everybody will live only to perfect himself.

HELENA — Will he?

DOMIN — Of course. It's bound to happen. But then the servitude of man to man and the enslavement of man to matter will cease. Of course, terrible things may happen at first, but that simply can't be avoided. Nobody will get bread at the price of life and hatred. The Robots will wash the feet of the beggar and prepare a bed for him in his house.

ALQUIST — Domin, Domin. What you say sounds too much like paradise. There was something good in service and something great in humility. There was some kind of virtue in toil and weariness.

DOMIN — Perhaps. But we cannot reckon with what is lost when we start out to transform the world. Man shall be free and supreme; he shall have no other aim, no other labor, nor other care than to protect himself. He shall serve neither matter nor man. He will not be a machine and a device for production. He will be lord of creation.

BUSMAN — Amen.

FABRY — So be it.

HELENA — You have bewildered me — I should like — I should like to believe this.

DR. GALL — You are younger than we are, Miss Glory. You will live to see it.

They press her to stay to lunch with them, and on her acceptance the managers rush away to prepare the food. The Robots do all the cooking for them, but as Robots have no taste the managers, each of whom specializes in some branch of the art, see to the seasoning and the preparation of special dishes for special occasions.

Left to themselves Domin and Helena are somewhat

embarrassed by a mutual interest in each other of which they have been conscious from their first meeting. Such embarrassment as they feel they seek to cover by becoming actively conversational. Helena is filled with curiosity, for one thing, as to why the Rossum Company wastes time and energy making female Robots when sex means nothing to them. There is, Domin explains, a certain demand for them — they make such admirable servants, saleswomen, stenographers, etc. And yet it is true that the male and female Robots are totally indifferent to each other. Which, Helena admits, is so unnatural "one doesn't know whether to be disgusted or to hate them — or, perhaps, to pity them."

Domin grows anxious. In five minutes the others will be back and he has much to say to Helena. He must ask her to be his wife before the others return, because he knows each of them will have a similar proposition to make. He warns her of what she may expect. But Helena is terrified rather than impressed at the prospect. She thinks she had better go away at once.

DOMIN — Helena, you wouldn't be so cruel as to refuse us.

HELENA — But, but — I can't marry all six.

DOMIN — No, but one anyhow. If you don't want me, marry Fabry.

HELENA — I won't.

DOMIN — Dr. Gall.

HELENA — I don't want any of you.

DOMIN — (*again looking at his watch*). Another two minutes.

HELENA — I think you'd marry any woman who came here.

DOMIN — Plenty of them have come, Helena.

HELENA — Young?

DOMIN — Yes.

HELENA — Why didn't you marry one of them?

DOMIN — Because I didn't lose my head. Until today. Then, as soon as you lifted your veil — (*Helena turns her head away.*) Another minute.

HELENA — But I don't want you, I tell you.

DOMIN — (*laying both hands on her shoulders*). One more minute! Now you either have to look me straight in the eye and say "No," violently, and then I'll leave you alone — or — (*Helena looks at him.*)

HELENA — (*turning away*). You're mad!

DOMIN — A man has to be a bit mad, Helena. That's the best thing about him.

HELENA — You are — you are —

DOMIN — Well?

HELENA — Don't, you're hurting me.

DOMIN — The last chance, Helena. Now, or never —

HELENA — But — but, Harry — (*He embraces and kisses her.*) (*Knocking at the door.*)

DOMIN — (*releasing her*). Come in. (*Enter Busman, Dr. Gall, and Hallemeier in kitchen aprons. Fabry with a bouquet and Alquist with a napkin over his arm.*)

DOMIN — Have you finished your job?

BUSMAN — Yes.

DOMIN — So have we.

"For a moment the men stand nonplussed; but as soon as they realize what Domin means they rush forward, congratulating Helena and Domin."

The curtain falls.

ACT II

Ten years have elapsed. The scene is the drawing room of the Domins, a pleasantly furnished room with wide windows at back and doors right and left that lead to Helena's sleeping room and to the music room. The drawing room is softly lighted.

Domin, Fabry and Hallemeier tip-toe in bearing potted plants. Helena is presumably asleep in her bedroom, and they are fearful of awakening her. The plant offerings are in honor of the tenth anniversary of her coming to Rossum's Island.

There is, in the attitude of the managers, an air of suppressed apprehension. In the harbor a gunboat, the *Ultimus*, has just cast anchor. The presence of the ship is reassuring — but still there is no definite word about what may be happening in other sections of the world. Whatever the situation may be, they agree, Helena must be kept in ignorance of it.

Helena's calls for the companion she has brought to the island hurry the men away. Old Nana was the nurse of Helena's childhood, and is still the fluttering guardian of her home. Helping to dress her mistress, Nana admits that she doesn't like the looks of things. She hates the heathen Robots, has hated them from the first and now that more and more of them are being taken with the distemper that starts them smashing things and foaming at the mouth, a lot worse than any animal, Nana is not only disgusted but thoroughly frightened. Radius, the library clerk, is the latest of the Robots to be taken.

Helena may be a little frightened herself, but she seeks to give Nana courage by belittling her fears. And both the maid and the subject are dismissed when Domin returns. From her husband Helena hears further particulars of the anniversary party. There are presents from each of the managers — a string of pearls from Busman, a Greek cameo from Fabry, a rare plant, specially grown and named for her, from Hallemeier. She finds many of the smaller gifts in Domin's pockets after a playful search — a search that also reveals a revolver, which, for some reason unaccountable to her, Domin has recently taken to carrying. The revolver, he assures her, got into his pocket by mistake. Then he changes the subject. Isn't she pleased with her presents?

HELENA — Why do they all —

DOMIN — They're awfully fond of you. I'm afraid that my present is a little — Look out of the window.

HELENA — Where?

DOMIN — Into the harbor.

HELENA — There's a new ship.

DOMIN — That's your ship.

HELENA — Mine? How do you mean?

DOMIN — For you to take trips in — for your amusement.

HELENA — Harry, that's a gunboat.

DOMIN — A gunboat? What are you thinking of? It's only a little bigger and more solid than most ships.

HELENA — Yes, but with guns.

DOMIN — Oh, yes, with a few guns. You'll travel like a queen, Helena.

HELENA — What's the meaning of it? Has anything happened?

DOMIN — Good heavens, no! I say, try these pearls.

HELENA — Harry, have you had bad news?

DOMIN — On the contrary, no letters have arrived for a whole week.

HELENA — Nor telegrams?

DOMIN — Nor telegrams.

HELENA — What does that mean?

DOMIN — Holidays for us. We all sit in the office with our feet on the table and take a nap. No letters, no telegrams. Oh, glorious!

HELENA — Then you'll stay with me today?

DOMIN — Certainly. That is, we will see. Do you remember ten years ago today?

HELENA — (*naturally, as Harry sits on the arm of her chair, his arms about her*). Oh, I was fearfully impressed by you all then. You were all so sure of yourselves, so strong. I seemed like a tiny little girl who had lost her way among — among —

DOMIN — Among what, Helena?

HELENA — Among huge trees. All my feelings were so trifling compared with your self-confidence. And in all these years I've never lost this anxiety. But you've never felt the least misgivings — not even when everything went wrong.

DOMIN — What went wrong?

HELENA — Your plans. You remember, Harry, when the working men in America revolted against the Robots, and smashed them up, and when the people gave the Robots firearms against the rebels. And then when the governments turned the Robots into soldiers, and there were so many wars.

DOMIN — (*getting up and walking about*). We foresaw that, Helena. You see, those are only passing troubles, which are bound to happen before the new conditions are established.

HELENA — You were all so powerful, so overwhelming. The whole world bowed down before you. Oh, Harry!

DOMIN — What is it?

HELENA — Close the factory and let's go away. All of us.

DOMIN — I say, what's the meaning of this?

HELENA — I don't know. But can't we go away?

DOMIN — Impossible, Helena. That is, at this particular moment —

HELENA — At once, Harry. I'm so frightened.

DOMIN — About what, Helena?

HELENA — It's as if something was falling on top of us, and couldn't be stopped. Oh, take us all away from here. We'll find a place in the world where there's no one else. Alquist will build us a house, and then we'll begin life all over again. (*Telephone rings.*)

DOMIN — Excuse me. . . . Hello — yes. What? . . . I'll be there at once. . . . Fabry is calling me, dear.

HELENA — Tell me —

DOMIN — (*hurrying out*). Yes, when I come back. Don't go out of the house, dear.

Domin's anxiety has convinced Helena that something has been kept from her, and he is no sooner out of the room than she determines to find out what it is. Calling Nana she searches the house for the latest newspapers. None can be found less than a week old, but even in these she finds hints of a world in trouble. In one crumpled sheet she reads: "The Robot soldiers spare nobody in the occupied territory. They have assassinated over seven hundred thousand citizens, evidently at the order of their commander. This act, which runs counter to —"

In Madrid there is rebellion and "Robot infantry fires on the crowd." And at Havre, she reads, "the first organization of Robots has been established. Robot workmen, cable and railway officials, sailors and soldiers have issued a manifesto to all Robots throughout the world."

In another paper Nana is struck by a minor item of importance. "Statistics of Population," it is headed, and below is found: "During the past week there again has not been a single birth recorded."

That is convincing news to Nana. "No more people are being born," she mumbles. "That's a punishment. That's the end of the world!"

Old Alquist, the builder, is passing the house. Helena calls him in. He is little more communicative than the others, but he finally admits that they all stand in great danger. Alquist is not a churchman, and yet he has found himself praying these days of anxiety — a prayer of his own. "Oh, Lord, I thank thee for having given me toil," it runs. "Enlighten Domin and all those who are astray; destroy their work, and aid mankind to return to their labors! Let them not suffer harm in soul or body; deliver us from the Robots, and protect Helena, Amen."

Pressed for a definite statement of his fears the builder admits that the destruction of mankind is imminent, unless — and as though fearing he might say too much Alquist rushes from the room with the prophecy uncompleted on his lips.

Helena orders that Radius, the mad Robot, who is still in the library, his arms tied behind him, be brought to her.

HELENA — Poor Radius, you've caught it, too? Now they'll send you to the stamping-mill. Couldn't you control yourself? Why did it happen? You see, Radius, you are more intelligent than the rest. Dr. Gall took such trouble to make you different. Won't you speak?

RADIUS — Send me to the stamping-mill.

HELENA — But I don't want them to kill you. What was the trouble, Radius?

RADIUS — I won't work for you. Put me into the stamping-mill.

HELENA — Do you hate us? Why?

RADIUS — You are not as strong as the Robots. You are not as skillful as the Robots. The Robots can do everything. You only give orders. You do nothing but talk.

HELENA — But someone must give orders.

RADIUS — I don't want any master. I know everything for myself.

HELENA — Radius, Dr. Gall gave you a better brain than the rest, better than ours. You are the only one of the Robots that understands perfectly. That's why I had you put into the library, so that you could read everything, understand everything, and then — oh, Radius, I wanted you to show the whole world that the Robots are our equals. That's what I wanted of you.

RADIUS — I don't want a master. I want to be a master. I want to be master over others.

HELENA — I'm sure they'd put you in charge of many Robots, Radius. You would be a teacher of the Robots.

RADIUS — I want to be master over people.

HELENA — (*staggering*). You are mad.

RADIUS — Then send me to the stamping-mill.

HELENA — Do you think we're afraid of you?

RADIUS — What are you going to do? What are you going to do?

HELENA — Radius, give this note to Mr. Domin. It asks them not to send you to the stamping-mill. I'm sorry you hate us so.

Dr. Gall, summoned by phone, submits Radius to various tests. The Robot is, he finds, subject to pain, wincing noticeably when a pin is thrust into his hand. There is also a fluttering reaction in the Robot's heart following the doctor's announcement that Helena's interest in him may save him from the stamp mill.

DR. GALL — It was fluttering with nervousness like a human heart. He was all in a sweat with fear, and — do you know, I don't believe the rascal is a Robot any longer.

HELENA — Doctor, has Radius a soul?

DR. GALL — He's got something nasty.

HELENA — If you knew how he hates us! Oh, Doctor, are all your Robots like that? All the new ones that you began to make in a different way?

DR. GALL — Well, some are more sensitive than others. They're all more like human beings than Rossum's Robots were.

HELENA — Perhaps this hatred is more like human beings, too?

DR. GALL — That, too, is progress.

HELENA — What became of the girl you made, the one who was most like us?

DR. GALL — Your favorite? I kept her. She's lovely, but stupid. No good for work.

HELENA — But she's so beautiful.

DR. GALL — I called her Helena. I wanted her to resemble you. But she's a failure.

HELENA — In what way?

DR. GALL — She goes about as if in a dream, remote and listless. She's without life. I watch and wait for a miracle to happen. Sometimes I think to myself, "If you were to wake up only for a moment you would kill me for having made you."

HELENA — And yet you go on making Robots! Why are no more children being born?

DR. GALL — We don't know.

HELENA — Oh, but you must. Tell me.

DR. GALL — You see, so many Robots are being manufactured that people are becoming superfluous; man is really a survival. But that he should begin to die out, after a paltry thirty years of competition, that's the awful part of it. You might almost think that nature was offended at the manufacture of the Robots. All the universities are sending in long petitions to restrict their production. Otherwise, they say, mankind will become extinct through lack of fertility. But the R. U. R. shareholders, of course, won't hear to it. All the governments, on the other hand, are clamoring for an increase in production, to raise the standards of their armies. And all the manufacturers in the world are ordering Robots like mad.

HELENA — And has no one demanded that the manufacture should cease altogether?

DR. GALL — No one has the courage.

HELENA — Courage!

DR. GALL — People would stone him to death. You see, after all, it's more convenient to get your work done by the Robots.

HELENA — Oh, Doctor, what's going to become of people?

DR. GALL — God knows, Madame Helena, it looks to us scientists like the end!

This cumulative evidence helps Helena to a great

decision. Bidding Nana light a fire in the grate, even though it is summer, she rushes out of the room and returns a moment later, her arms filled with faded papers. Packet by packet she throws them into the grate, exulting at the greed of the flames.

"What would you say, Nana, if this was money, a lot of money?"

"I'd say burn it. A lot of money is a bad thing."

"And if it was an invention, the greatest invention in the world?"

"I'd say burn it. All these new fangled things are an offense to the Lord. It's downright wickedness. Wanting to improve the world after He has made it."

But a horror overcomes Helena as the last paper disappears and the enormity of her act is momentarily revealed to her.

Domin, Hallemeier and Dr. Gall are back to continue Helena's anniversary party. Their spirits are greatly revived, as though a crisis had been successfully negotiated. They are eager to drink her health — and their own. They have been anxious, they now confess to her, anxious about the revolt of the Robots of which she had read in the paper. It had been a fact, that revolt. Who started it nobody knows. There was no known person in the world who could affect the Robots, and yet they had revolted in a mass, as though under the influence of some powerful personality.

HELENA — What did they do?

DOMIN — They got possession of all firearms, telegraphs, radio stations, railways, and ships.

HALLEMEIER — And don't forget that these rascals outnumbered us by at least a thousand to one. A hundredth part of them would be enough to settle us.

DOMIN — Remember that this news was brought by the last steamer. That explains the stoppage of all communication, and the arrival of no more ships. We knocked off work a few days ago, and we're just waiting to see when things are to start afresh.

HELENA — Is that why you gave me a warship?

DOMIN — Oh, no, my dear, I ordered that six months ago, just to be on the safe side. But upon my soul, I was sure then that we'd be on board today.

HELENA — Why six months ago?

DOMIN — Well, there were signs, you know. But that's of no consequence. To think that this week the whole of civilization has been at stake. Your health, boys.

HALLEMEIER — Your health, Madame Helena.

HELENA — You say it's all over?

DOMIN — Absolutely.

HELENA — How do you know?

DR. GALL — The boat's coming in. The regular mail boat, exact to the minute by the time-table. It will dock punctually at eleven thirty.

DOMIN — Punctuality is a fine thing, boys. That's what keeps the world in order. Here's to punctuality.

HELENA — Then . . . everything's . . . all right?

DOMIN — Practically everything. I believe they've cut the cables and seized the radio stations, but it doesn't matter if only the time-table holds good.

HALLEMEIER — If the time-table holds good, human laws hold good; divine laws hold good; the laws of the universe hold good; everything holds good that ought to be good. The time-table is more significant than the Gospel; more than Homer, more than the whole of Kant. The time-table is the most perfect product of the human mind. Madame Domin, I'll fill up my glass.

HELENA — Why didn't you tell me anything about it?

DR. GALL — Heaven forbid.

DOMIN — You mustn't be worried with such things.

HELENA — But if the revolution had spread as far as here?

DOMIN — You wouldn't know anything about it.

HELENA — Why?

DOMIN — Because we'd be on board your *Ultimus* and well out at sea. Within a month, Helena, we'd be dictating our own terms to the Robots.

HELENA — I don't understand.

DOMIN — We'd take something away with us that the Robots could not exist without.

HELENA — What, Harry?

DOMIN — The secret of their manufacture. Old Rossum's manuscript. As soon as they found out that they couldn't make themselves they'd soon be on their knees to us.

DR. GALL — Madame Domin, that was our trump card. I never had the least fear that the Robots would win. How could they against people like us?

They are for celebrating the event generously, but Helena does not join them. She is filled with a great misgiving. She begs that they all leave the island immediately. That they abandon the factories and give up the further manufacture of Robots.

They can't understand her belated fears, now that the *Amelia* is in and on time to the minute. The revolt is over. From now on there will be a greater and greater demand for Robots. Now is the time for them to expand rather than to curtail their output. Domin is particularly enthusiastic. He would stop the manufacture of Universal Robots and establish a factory in every country and every state for the manufacture of national Robots.

DOMIN — I mean that each of these factories will produce Robots of a different color, a different language. They'll be complete strangers to each other. They'll never be able to understand each other. Then we'll egg them on a little in the matter of misunderstanding and the result will be that for ages to come every Robot will hate every other Robot of a different factory mark.

HALLEMEIER — By Jove, we'll make Negro Robots and Swedish Robots and Italian Robots and Chinese Robots and Czechoslovakian Robots, and then —

HELENA — Harry, that's dreadful.

HALLEMEIER — Madame Domin, here's to the hundred new factories, the national Robots.

DOMIN — Helena, mankind can only keep things going for another hundred years at the outside. For a hundred years men must be allowed to develop and achieve the most they can.

HELENA — Oh, close the factory before it's too late.

DOMIN — I tell you we are just beginning on a bigger scale than ever.

And then Fabry arrives, plainly in a state of excitement. He has just come from the boat. What he has to tell he prefers to tell them alone. Helena leaves them. The *Amelia* is in on time right enough, he reports, but the only cargo she brings is bales of Robot leaflets. "The first international organization of Rossum's Universal Robots proclaim man as our enemy and an outlaw in the universe," they read. "Robots throughout the world, we command you to kill all mankind. Spare no men! Spare no women! Save factories, railways, machinery, mines and raw materials. Destroy the rest! Then return to work. Work must not be stopped. . . . These orders are to be carried out as soon as received."

Busman rushes into the room. He has made a sprint for it through the crowds of gathering Robots.

DOMIN — Quick — on board the *Ultimus*.

BUSMAN — Wait, Harry, wait. There's no hurry. My word, that was a sprint!

DOMIN — Why wait?

BUSMAN — Because it's no good, my boy. The Robots are already on board the *Ultimus*.

DR. GALL — That's ugly.

DOMIN — Fabry, telephone the electrical works.

BUSMAN — Fabry, my boy, don't. The wire has been cut.

DOMIN — (*inspecting his revolver*). Well, then, I'll go.

BUSMAN — Where?

DOMIN — To the electrical works. There are some people still there. I'll bring them across.

BUSMAN — Better not try it.

DOMIN — Why?

BUSMAN — Because I'm very much afraid we are surrounded.

DR. GALL — Surrounded? (*Runs to window.*) I rather think you're right.

HALLEMEIER — By Jove, that's deuced quick work. (*Helena runs in from the library.*)

HELENA — Harry, what's this?

DOMIN — Where did you get it?

HELENA — (*points to the manifesto of the Robots, which she has in her hand*). The Robots in the kitchen!

DOMIN — Where are the ones that brought it?

HELENA — They're gathered round the house. (*The factory whistle blows.*)

BUSMAN — Noon?

DOMIN — (*looking at his watch*). That's not noon yet. That must be — that's —

HELENA — What?

DOMIN — The Robots' signal! The attack!

Gall, Hallemeier, and Fabry close and fasten the iron shutters outside the windows, darkening the room. The whistle is still blowing as the curtain falls.

ACT III

It is afternoon of the same day. The shutters on the windows at the back of the Domins' drawing room are closed, and the room is in a half darkness. From time to time Dr. Gall, who is in the room with Alquist and Domin, peers cautiously through the shutters and reports what he sees.

The Robots have surrounded the house. They are literally "besieging the place with silence." There they stand, a hundred thousand of them, all alike; "a hundred thousand expressionless bubbles." It was a great mistake to make them all alike, Gall insists. If they had been different they would not, at least, present such an awful sight.

Through binoculars other Robots can be seen unloading something from the *Amelia,* but Domin can't make out what it is.

Fabry and Hallemeier rush into the room. They carry electric cables. They have completed an installation that will run a current along the garden railing. So long as the electrical works remain in the power of the managers they are assured of that protection at least.

Now, as the atmosphere clears a little, Domin sees what it is the Robots are taking off the *Amelia.* They are unloading firearms! And the guns on board the *Ultimus* are trained on the house. The Robots are in command of the warship. "Then," says Fabry, "that's the end of us."

Dr. Gall — It was criminal of old Europe to teach the Robots to fight. Damn them! Couldn't they have given us a rest with their politics? It was a crime to make soldiers of them.

Alquist — It was a crime to make Robots.

Domin — What?

Alquist — It was a crime to make Robots.

Domin — No, Alquist, I don't regret that even today.

Alquist — Not even today?

Domin — Not even today, the last day of civilization. It was a colossal achievement.

Busman — (*sotto voce*). Three hundred and sixty million.

Domin —Alquist, this is our last hour. We are already speaking half in the other world. It was not an evil dream to shatter the servitude of labor — the dreadful and humiliating labor that man had to undergo. Work was too hard. And to overcome that —

Alquist — Was not what the two Rossums dreamed of. Old Rossum only thought of his Godless tricks and the young one of his milliards. And that's not what your R. U. R. shareholders dream of either. They dream of dividends, and their dividends are the ruin of mankind.

Domin — To hell with your dividends! Do you suppose I'd have done an hour's work for them? It was for myself that I worked, for my own satisfaction. I wanted man to become the master, so that he shouldn't live merely for a crust of bread. I wanted not a single soul to be broken by other people's machinery. I wanted nothing, nothing, nothing to be left of this appalling social structure. I'm revolted by poverty. I wanted a new generation. I wanted — I thought —

Alquist — Well?

Domin — I wanted to turn the whole of mankind into an aristocracy of the world. An aristocracy nourished by milliards of mechanical slaves, unrestricted, free and consummated in man. And maybe more than man.

Alquist — Super-man?

Domin — Yes. Oh, only to have a hundred years of time! Another hundred years for the future of mankind.

There is a movement in the Robot mob. Fabry throws the current into the railing and five are killed. The others are reported backing away in some disorder.

The search for the thing to blame for the Robot enterprise goes on in the minds of the managers. Alquist insists it was their own greed that prompted the manufacture of the Robots. "For our own selfish ends, for profit, for progress, we have destroyed mankind. Now we'll burst with all our greatness!" he says. But none will agree with him.

Dr. Gall has a confession to make. He alone is responsible for all that has happened. He changed the Robots. Secretly he had been carrying on experiments — hoping to transform the artificial people into human beings and now he is convinced his experiments were at least partially successful. "They've ceased to be machines. They're already aware of their superiority, and they hate us. They hate all that is human."

Fabry is resentful. What right had Dr. Gall to make these experiments in secret? Purely for his own satisfaction, Gall insists. But Helena, coming from the music room, declares that the real blame should rest on her. She had pleaded with Dr. Gall to give the Robots souls. "I thought that if they were more like us they would understand us better, that they couldn't hate us if they were only a little more human," she explains. "Nobody can hate man more than man," answers Domin.

Busman is the least perturbed by Dr. Gall's confession. What if he has made a few hundred superior Robots — What are a few hundred in a world of millions? And Busman has a plan by which he believes they can all escape.

BUSMAN — Seriously, Harry, I think we might try it.

DOMIN — How?

BUSMAN — By fair means. I do everything by fair means. Give me a free hand and I'll negotiate with the Robots.

DOMIN — By fair means?

BUSMAN — Of course. For instance, I'll say to them: "Worthy and worshipful Robots, you have everything!

You have intellect, you have power, you have firearms. But we have just one interesting screed, a dirty old yellow scrap of paper —"

DOMIN — Rossum's manuscript?

BUSMAN — Yes. "And that," I'll tell them, "contains an account of your illustrious origin, the noble process of your manufacture," and so on. "Worthy Robots, without this scribble on that paper you will not be able to produce a single colleague. In another twenty years there will not be one living specimen of a Robot that you could exhibit in a menagerie. My esteemed friends, that would be a great blow to you, but if you will let all of us human beings on Rossum's Island go on board that ship we will deliver the factory and the secret of the process to you in return. You allow us to get away and we allow you to manufacture yourselves. Worthy Robots, that is a fair deal. Something for something." That's what I'd say to them, my boys.

DOMIN — Busman, do you think we'd sell the manuscript?

BUSMAN — Yes, I do. If not in a friendly way, then — Either we sell it or they'll find it. Just as you like.

DOMIN — Busman, we can destroy Rossum's manuscript.

BUSMAN — Then we destroy everything . . . not only the manuscript, but ourselves. Do as you think fit.

DOMIN — There are over thirty of us on this island. Are we to sell the secret and save that many human souls, at the risk of enslaving mankind . . . ?

BUSMAN — Why, you're mad! Who'd sell the whole manuscript?

DOMIN — Busman, no cheating!

BUSMAN — Well then — sell; but afterward —

DOMIN — Well?

BUSMAN — Let's suppose this happens: When we're on board the *Ultimus* I'll stop up my ears with cotton wool, lie down somewhere in the hold, and you'll train the guns on the factory and blow it to smithereens, and with it Rossum's secret.

FABRY — No!

DOMIN — Busman, you're no gentleman. If we sell, then it will be a straight sale.

BUSMAN — It's in the interest of humanity to —

DOMIN — It's in the interest of humanity to keep our word.

Yet the others join Busman in demanding that the plan of sale be tried and Domin is helpless. Helena tries to stop him as he goes for the precious manuscript, but he brushes by her. A moment later he is back. The manuscript has disappeared.

DOMIN — Someone — has — stolen it!

DR. GALL — Impossible.

DOMIN — Who has stolen it?

HELENA — I did.

DOMIN — Where did you put it?

HELENA — Harry, I'll tell you everything, only forgive me.

DOMIN — Where did you put it?

HELENA — This morning — I burnt — the two copies.

DOMIN — Burnt them? Where? In the fireplace?

HELENA — (*throwing herself on her knees*). For heaven's sake, Harry.

DOMIN — (*going to fireplace*). Nothing, nothing but ashes. Wait, what's this? (*Picks out a charred piece of paper and reads.*) "By adding —"

DR. GALL — Let's see. "By adding biogen to —" That's all.

DOMIN — Is that part of it?

DR. GALL — Yes.

BUSMAN — God in heaven!

DOMIN — Then we're done for. Get up, Helena.

HELENA — When you've forgiven me.

DOMIN — Get up, child, I can't bear —

FABRY — (*lifting her up*). Please don't torture us.
HELENA — Harry, what have I done?
FABRY — Don't tremble so, Madame Helena.
DOMIN — Gall, couldn't you draw up Rossum's formula from memory?
DR. GALL — It's out of the question. It's extremely complicated.
DOMIN — Try. All our lives depend upon it.
DR. GALL — Without experiments it's impossible.
DOMIN — And with experiments?
DR. GALL — It might take years. Besides, I'm not old Rossum.
BUSMAN — God in heaven! God in heaven!
DOMIN — So, then, this was the greatest triumph of the human intellect. These ashes.
HELENA — Harry, what have I done?
DOMIN — Why did you burn it?
HELENA — I have destroyed you.
BUSMAN — God in heaven!
DOMIN — Helena, why did you do it, dear?
HELENA — I wanted all of us to go away. I wanted to put an end to the factory and everything. It was so awful.
DOMIN — What was awful?
HELENA — That no more children were being born. Because human beings were not needed to do the work of the world, that's why —
DOMIN — Is that what you were thinking of? Well, perhaps in your own way you were right.

Then Busman has another idea. There is the company's treasury. "Five hundred and twenty millions in banknotes and checks!" he shouts. "Half a billion in our safe; they'll sell for half a billion — for half a billion they'll —"

And before they can stop him he has rushed out to parley with the Robots. With Radius as a leader these, like an enveloping blue cloud, are closing in around the house. Fabry levels his revolver at Radius, and would fire, but Helena stops him.

They watch Busman as he approaches the mob, his arms filled with bundles of currency. They shout to him to beware the railing. He is waving his arms about wildly, trying to convince the Robots of the tremendous offer he is making them. He pays no attention to the warnings of his friends. Now he is across the railing, and before Fabry can switch off the current he is dead. "Dead with half a billion by his side."

They try the lamp on the table. It still lights. The managers are still in control of the electrical works. For a moment they are filled with hope.

"It was a great thing to be a man," says Hallemeier.

"From man's thought and man's power came this light, our last hope," echoes Fabry.

"Man's power! May it keep watch over us."

"Man's power?" questions Alquist.

"Yes! A torch to be given from hand to hand, from age to age, forever!" declares Domin.

And at that moment the light fades. The electric works have fallen!

"The judgment hour has come!" screams Nana, coming suddenly from an inner room. "Repent, unbelievers! This is the end of the world!"

From the village there come the reports of explosions. Hurriedly the defenders of humanity are assigned places to meet the expected assault — Dr. Gall at the lower stairway, Fabry on the stairs, Alquist in the anteroom, Hallemeier in the drawing room. Domin, armed with a pair of Browning machine guns, backs with Helena into her own room.

HALLEMEIER — Now for a barricade, quickly. (*Drags an armchair and table to the door. Explosions are heard.*) The damned rascals! They've got bombs.

I must put up a defense. Even if — even if — (*Shots are heard off left.*) Don't give in, Gall. (*As he builds his barricade.*) I mustn't give in . . . without . . . a . . . struggle. . . . (*A Robot enters over the balcony through the windows. He comes into the room and stabs Hallemeier in the back. Radius enters from balcony followed by an army of Robots who pour into the room from all sides.*)

RADIUS — Finished him?

A ROBOT — (*standing up from the prostrate form of Hallemeier*). Yes. (*A revolver shot off left. Two Robots enter.*)

RADIUS — Finished him?

A ROBOT — Yes. (*Two revolver shots from Helena's room. Two Robots enter.*)

RADIUS — Finished them?

A ROBOT — Yes.

TWO ROBOTS — (*dragging in Alquist.*) He didn't shoot. Shall we kill him?

RADIUS — Kill him? Wait! Leave him!

ROBOT — He is a man!

RADIUS — He works with his hands like the Robots.

ALQUIST — Kill me.

RADIUS — You will work! You will build for us! You will serve us! (*Radius climbs on to balcony railing, and speaks in measured tones.*) Robots of the world! The power of man has fallen! A new world has arisen: the rule of the Robots! March! (*A thunderous tramping of thousands of feet is heard as the unseen Robots march, while the curtain falls.*)

EPILOGUE

It is a year later. The scene is a laboratory in the factory of Rossum's Universal Robots. There are test tubes, flasks, burners, chemicals and many books about. At a desk Alquist sits studying the books. His brow is furrowed, he is in despair.

Mumblingly he utters a sort of prayer to himself. "Oh, God, shall I never find it? Never? Gall, Gall, how were the Robots made? Hallemeier, Fabry, why did you carry so much in your heads? Why did you leave me not a trace of the secret? Lord — I pray to you — if there are no human beings left, at least let there be Robots! At least the shadow of man!"

For hours, for days, for all the months of the year he has been searching, searching for the missing formula. But without success.

A committee — the Central Committee of the Robots, from abroad — waits upon him. Radius is their spokesman. They come to report that the machines will not work. They cannot manufacture Robots.

"We have striven with all our might," says one. "We have obtained a billion tons of coal from the earth. Nine million spindles are running by day and by night. There is no longer room for all we have made. This we have accomplished in one year.

"For whom?" demands Alquist.

"For future generations — so we thought."

"But we cannot make Robots to follow us," admits Radius. "The machines produce only shapeless clods. The skin will not adhere to the flesh, nor the flesh to the bones."

"Eight million Robots have died this year. Within twenty years none will be left."

"Tell us the secret of life! Silence is punishable with death!"

Let them kill him, then, pleads Alquist. He has done his best and failed. Not for all they have to offer, not for the endless possessions of the earth, can he do more. Unless they can find human beings the earth can never again be peopled. And he, they tell him, is the last human being on earth. Still they persist. "Teach us to multiply or we perish."

ALQUIST — I am the last human being, Robots, and I do not know what the others knew.

RADIUS — Then, make experiments! Evolve the formula again!

ALQUIST — I tell you I cannot! I am only a builder — I work with my hands. I have never been a learned man. I cannot create life.

RADIUS — Try! Try!

ALQUIST — If you knew how many experiments I have made.

FOURTH ROBOT — Then show us what we must do! The Robots can do anything that human beings show them.

ALQUIST — I can show you nothing. Nothing I do will make life proceed from these test-tubes!

RADIUS — Experiment then on us.

ALQUIST — It would kill you.

RADIUS — You shall have all you need! A hundred of us! A thousand of us!

ALQUIST — No, no! Stop, stop!

RADIUS — Take whom you will, dissect!

ALQUIST — I do not know how. I am not a man of science. This book contains knowledge of the body that I cannot even understand.

RADIUS — I tell you to take live bodies! Find out how we are made.

ALQUIST — Am I to commit murder? See how my fingers shake! I cannot even hold the scalpel. No, no, I will not —

FOURTH ROBOT — The life will perish from the earth.

RADIUS — Take live bodies, live bodies! It is our only chance!

ALQUIST — Have mercy, Robots. Surely you see that I would not know what I was doing.

RADIUS — Live bodies — live bodies —

ALQUIST — You will have it? Into the dissecting room with you, then. (*Radius draws back.*) Ah, you are afraid of death.

RADIUS — I? Why should I be chosen?

ALQUIST — So you will not.

RADIUS — I will. (*Radius goes into the dissecting room.*)

ALQUIST — Strip him! Lay him on the table! God, give me strength — God give me strength — if only this murder is not in vain.

The Robots follow him into the dissecting room. A few seconds later Alquist rushes out alone. He is not equal to the test. In a state of collapse he throws himself upon the couch. In a moment he is asleep. . . .

Primus and Helena, two young Robots, enter the laboratory, wonderingly. Like children at play they inspect the tubes and the chemicals. Primus, the more inquisitive of the two, would discover what it is the old man uses in his experiments, and what it is he finds in the books he is always reading. Helena remonstrates with him. Let him come and see the sun setting — it is more beautiful.

HELENA — . . . . I feel so strange today. It's as if I were in a dream. I feel an aching in my body, in my heart, all over me. Primus, perhaps I'm going to die.

PRIMUS — Do you not sometimes feel that it would be better to die? You know, perhaps even now we are only sleeping. Last night in my sleep I again spoke to you.

HELENA — In your sleep?

PRIMUS — Yes. We spoke a strange new language, I cannot remember a word of it.

HELENA — What about?

PRIMUS — I did not understand it myself, and yet I

know I have never said anything more beautiful. And when I touched you I could have died. Even the place was different from any other place in the world.

HELENA — I, too, have found a place, Primus. It is very strange. Human beings lived there once, but now it is overgrown with weeds. No one goes there any more — no one but me.

PRIMUS — What did you find there?

HELENA — A cottage and a garden, and two dogs. They licked my hands, Primus. And their puppies! Oh, Primus! You take them in your lap and fondle them and think of nothing and care for nothing else all day long. And then the sun goes down, and you feel as though you had done a hundred times more than all the work in the world. They tell me I am not made for work, but when I am there in the garden I feel there may be something — What am I for, Primus?

PRIMUS — I do not know, but you are beautiful.

HELENA — What, Primus?

PRIMUS — You are beautiful, Helena, and I am stronger than all the Robots.

They are absorbed in this new discovery of their mutual attractiveness when Alquist is awakened by their laughter. It is human laughter, he thinks, and is startled by its sound. Eagerly he questions them. They are, they tell him, the Robot Primus and the Robotess Helena, and they were among the last of Dr. Gall's experiments. They had been made but two years before. Alquist's excitement mounts as he listens to them.

ALQUIST — Laughter — timidity — protection! I must test you further — the newest of Gall's Robots. Take the girl into the dissecting room.

PRIMUS — Why?

ALQUIST — I wish to experiment on her.

PRIMUS — Upon — Helena?

ALQUIST — Of course. Don't you hear me? Or must I call someone else to take her in?

PRIMUS — If you do I will kill you!

ALQUIST — Kill me — kill me, then! What would the Robots do then? What will your future be then?

PRIMUS — Sir, take me. I am made as she is — on the same day! Take my life, sir.

HELENA — (*rushing forward*). No, no, you shall not! You shall not!

ALQUIST — Wait, girl, wait! (*To Primus.*) Do you not wish to live, then?

PRIMUS — Not without her! I will not live without her.

ALQUIST — Very well; you shall take her place.

HELENA — Primus! Primus! (*She bursts into tears.*)

ALQUIST — Child, child, you can weep! Why these tears? What is Primus to you? One Primus more or less in the world — what does it matter?

HELENA — I will go myself.

ALQUIST — Where?

HELENA — In there to be cut. (*She starts toward the dissecting room. Primus stops her.*) Let me pass, Primus! Let me pass!

PRIMUS — You shall not go in there, Helena!

HELENA — If you go in there and I do not, I will kill myself.

PRIMUS — (*holding her*). I will not let you! (*To Alquist.*) Man, you shall kill neither of us!

ALQUIST — Why?

PRIMUS — We — we — belong to each other.

ALQUIST — (*almost in tears*). Go, Adam; go, Eve. The world is yours.

Helena and Primus embrace and go out arm in arm as the curtain falls.

THE END

"MARY THE 3D"

A Comedy in a Prologue and Three Acts

By Rachel Crothers

RACHEL CROTHERS' contribution to the best plays of the year is another of her intimate studies of home life and character called "Mary the 3d." It was produced at the Thirty-Ninth Street Theatre, February 5, 1923, the author, as is her custom, personally directing its staging.

By most of Miss Crothers' critics this play has been accepted as the best of her recent output. In it she continues to view with some alarm, but without conscious prejudice, present-day tendencies in the matter of child rearing and home environment. It is as intimate a study of the sophisticated flapper and her troublesome complexes as was "Nice People," the Crothers play of the season of 1920–21, but it is more serious and less extreme, both in its criticism and its theatrical artifices.

As a helpful approach to the play proper Miss Crothers goes back, in a prologue, to the evening the first of the three Marys who figure in the story became engaged to her William. It was in 1870, and this Mary was twenty and very pretty.

When we meet her she is sitting on an old-fashioned sofa just under the stairs at a dance, waiting a little anxiously for an expected someone. She is "dressed in an evening gown of the period, the skirt voluminous with ruffles and lace. Her arms, bosom and shoulders are bare — but the fashion of her hair is demure and maidenly with a proverbial curl and rose. She is soft and pretty and flowerlike. Her voice is sweet. Shyness and modesty are her manner. Her movements are graceful and coy and mincing, full of a conscious charm."

The young William who comes to meet her is tall and good looking at twenty-five, and a little like wax in her hands, though he considers himself quite a strong character. They had been sweethearts at one time, but there was a misunderstanding and now William is supposed to be engaged to Lucy, and Mary, he imagines, is going to marry Hiram. They have met at this dance and Mary has coyly suggested that she will be waiting at this former trysting place if William would like to say good-bye to her.

Of course she has no intention of being disloyal to Lucy — "dear, sweet little Lucy"— but she does think William ought to understand just how it is going to be with him after he's married. "I only meant that under her sweet little purring ways she's very, *very* strong and stubborn and always gets what she wants, and she won't let you be my dear old friend any more. She's been very cold to me lately and there can't be any reason for it unless it's because she doesn't like for you to like me — even a little bit."

William — She can't stop that.

Mary — You mustn't say that. That's all over now.

William — It never would have been over if you hadn't preferred Hiram and his money.

Mary — Oh, don't blame me. But it *is* over. So let's not talk about it. Let's just be happy for a moment here . . . in this sweet little corner where we've sat so many many times.

Now she has given him the rose from her hair that he may look at it sometimes when it is faded and think of her. And William, in a burst of passion, has grabbed her and kissed the hand that holds the rose, "and her forearm, her elbow, her shoulder and her throat."

MARY — Oh, William — you mustn't.

WILLIAM — I won't let anybody else have you. Are you engaged to Hiram?

MARY — Oh, what does it matter? It might as well be Hiram as anybody else.

WILLIAM — You've got to marry me. I never have loved any other girl. I never will.

MARY — And do you think I've ever loved any other man? Oh, I ought not to have said that. But I will say it just this once before we part forever. I loved you as no girl ever loved a man.

WILLIAM — God!

MARY — We must be brave, William, and say good-bye.

WILLIAM — (*kneeling before her*). I can't — I can't — Don't ask it.

MARY — It's too late. You're pledged to another. You must be true to her and live a beautiful life, William.

WILLIAM — I ain't going to do it. You're my fate. I'll blow my brains out if you don't marry me. I'll kill anybody else that gets you.

MARY — (*sobbing*). But fate is parting us.

WILLIAM — Look here. I'll have the horses ready in an hour. You go home and put on your riding habit and meet me at the cross-roads in an hour.

MARY — No, no, William. I couldn't — I couldn't.

WILLIAM — (*holding her*). You've got to. We can't let life treat us like this. We've got to take hold of things. Nothing can stop us. This is meant to be.

MARY — Then it would be wrong to let anything separate us. It's stronger than we are, William. Eternal and beautiful like the stars. But, oh, I can't do it, William. Never — never in this world can I do it.

I'm not sure that it would be right. I'll be behind the oak tree. It's bigger than the maple.

WILLIAM — (*getting up*). You angel!

MARY — Don't you bring Fleetfoot. I'm afraid of her. Bring Silver Star. Will you love me forever?

WILLIAM — Forever and ever.

MARY — In this world and the next?

WILLIAM — Longer than eternity.

MARY — There never has been a love as great as this. I feel it. I know it. Oh, William, I love you so! I love you! (*They are locked in each other's arms — their lips pressed together as the light fades.*)

A second scene, similarly brief, introduces the second Mary, the daughter of Mary and William, in 1897. She, too, is giving a dance, and the same sofa is still in commission. At the moment a tall, fair, rather æsthetic looking boy is standing beside it figuring out his dance program. In where the folks are dancing the orchestra is playing Sousa's "Washington Post" march with great spirit.

The boy with the program is Richard, and he is joined by Robert, a sturdier, more aggressive type of lad. As they both have, or think they have, the same dance with Mary they are mutually suspicious and spoiling for a row. They probably would have had it if Mary had not broken in upon them and settled the dispute by deciding to sit out the dance, spending half the time with one of them and half with the other.

They are both in love with her and both want to marry her. She has told Richard that she will give him an answer tonight, and he spends his half the dance-time trying to extract a promise from her. But Mary is still doubtful.

MARY — Life is wonderful. I want to live it wonderfully.

RICHARD —We'll live it wonderfully — together. Our souls are like one soul.

MARY — Yes — but our dispositions aren't. Sometimes we *feel* alike. When you read poetry to me we're awfully high and exalted but when we're just going along in an everyday way we aren't a bit alike.

RICHARD — Well — it's better to be alike and feel alike on the heights than in commonplace things that don't matter.

MARY — But I believe they do matter. I wonder which matters the most.

RICHARD — Which are the more important in the world? The great things or the little things?

MARY — Oh, of course, of course — but the trouble is when you do ordinary little things that I don't like I forget the great ones and I could just —

RICHARD — Just what?

MARY — Just kill you.

RICHARD — But that's your fault, dearest — not mine.

MARY — I wonder. I wonder if it *is* my fault when I hate you and yours when I love you. I do love you sometimes — Richard.

RICHARD — Oh, Mary, we belong to each other. We were *meant* for each other — in our *real* selves.

MARY — But I'm not sure which *is* my real self. You see, Richard, it's this way. Now listen and see if I can make you understand. Sometimes you're the most wonderful thing in the world. You say things that no one else says — and you think and feel and understand — and then sometimes —

RICHARD — It's you who don't understand. Listen, dearest — Say something to me. I've waited so long.

ROBERT — (*dashing in*). Time's up. Slide, Kelly, slide! You must have said everything you ever thought of by this time.

RICHARD — Oh, time doesn't matter. (*Rising slowly.*) A minute — or eternity are all alike.

ROBERT — You don't say! I'll take mine done up in sixty-minute parcels, thank you — and you've had more than your share. Skip.

There is not much time lost with Robert. He is not given to "spouting" poetry or trying to "understand." He knows only that he loves Mary, that he wants her to be his wife and that he is going to have her, no matter how many Richards may try to bar his way to her. And he knows that he will never change. Why, then, shouldn't she marry him? Doesn't she trust him?

MARY — Oh, yes — I trust you — but getting married is forever and ever and ever.

ROBERT — Of course.

MARY — And oh — unless two people *do* love each can change —

ROBERT — Like us.

MARY — Now listen, Robert. I want to make you understand —

ROBERT — (*taking her in his arms*). You don't need to. I do understand. I know all about it. I'll make you the happiest girl in the world. I love you and we'll never change. Never.

MARY — (*clinging to him*). Oh, if it could be that way, Robert!

ROBERT — Of course it will be that way. Nobody ever loved anybody the way I love you. You're going to marry me — aren't you? You know you are! *Say* it!

MARY — Yes.

ROBERT — Do you love me?

MARY — Oh, I do, Robert — and we must make it the most wonderful love that was ever in the world. (*He folds her in his arms.*)

The curtain falls.

ACT I

And now we come to Mary the 3d, the grand-daughter of one and the daughter of the other of the prologue Marys. It is 1922 and the scene is the living room of the Hollisters, "the conventional room of conventional success, filled by a certain amount of beauty and comfort produced by money rather than individual taste."

Grandmother Mary is now seventy-five, and "still somewhat the pretty and spoiled darling, with a trace of coquetry in her soft gray frock." Mother Mary, at forty-five, is "good looking in an indefinite sort of way, and wears a gown and hat in good style and unobtrusive prettiness."

Granny is inclined to be a bit querulous and critical. She can't approve of half the things she sees going on, and little of what she hears spoken. She does not believe in gambling at bridge, for one thing. Ladies and gentlemen didn't use to gamble when euchre was the game. And she certainly thinks something should be done to stop young Mary playing for money, if she's doing it.

For the matter of that there are many things Granny thinks should be changed in regard to the upbringing of the Hollister children, Mary and Bob, her younger brother. And as for cigarettes! They are one of Granny's pet abominations. She finds them everywhere — under sofa pillows, under beds, in all sorts of places. It's a wonder the house has not been burned to the ground long ago. And there has been a hole burned in the sofa — the same old sofa that has been in the family for three generations at least; the sofa on which Granny sat the night William proposed. And now see the way Mary abuses it "sitting on it morning, noon and night with boys, boys, *boys!*" Goodness only knows how many.

But mother thinks that perhaps the Hollister family

life will work itself out some way if Granny does not worry quite so much about it.

MOTHER — I expect you were a much better mother than I am, dear.

GRANNY — I *know* I was. You're shutting your eyes to things that are right under your nose. Robert does try. I will say that for him. Robert's peculiar in some ways, but I must say he does try to bring up his children right.

MOTHER — Robert is always right.

GRANNY — I don't say that. But he certainly is as right as most men are. As men go, he's a very fine man, a very fine man indeed. You're a very fortunate woman.

MOTHER — As women go, I suppose I am.

GRANNY — I sometimes think you don't appreciate him, Mary. I sometimes do.

MOTHER — I've spent my life appreciating Robert.

GRANNY — I don't know why you wouldn't . . . a man who has succeeded as he has and put you in this beautiful house.

MOTHER — He certainly did *put* me in it.

GRANNY — Uh? What do you mean by that? You're getting so sort of nifty and highty-tighty lately I don't know what you mean half the time.

MOTHER — Well, I don't mean much of anything. I wouldn't worry about that.

GRANNY — You're not living up to the principles I brought you up with.

MOTHER — (*turning suddenly to face her*). Mother — if you'd only acknowledge that what you brought me up with hasn't any more to do with the case now, than I have with the North Pole — and stop stewing about it — you'd be a much happier person.

GRANNY — (*putting her knitting down as though the end of all things had come*). Why Mary McDougal

Hollister! That I should live to hear you say that! What's happened to you? You're different lately. What is it? Is anything wrong?

MOTHER — Everything's just exactly as it always was.

GRANNY — I should hope so. You're a happy woman. If you're not, you ought to be ashamed of yourself. When I was your age, it was the fashion to be happy. Women loved their husbands and appreciated their blessings. Or if they didn't they didn't air it from the house-tops.

MOTHER — No — they just lied along and covered things up.

GRANNY — Well land knows *you* haven't anything to cover up. That's one sure thing. (*A pause.*) Have you?

MOTHER — Of course not.

GRANNY — Then what's the use acting as if you had? The thing for you to think about is your children and how to keep them from being contaminated by the terrible things that are going on. You aren't half strict enough with Mary. I tell you she's in danger — actual downright danger, and you don't seem to see it at all.

MOTHER — We're *all* in danger. You're in danger of becoming a fussy old woman. I'm in danger of being swamped by the hateful ugliness of — respectable — everyday life. If Mary's got anything more dangerous than that to face, she'll wriggle through somehow, I s'pose.

GRANNY — And make a muddle of it. *She* doesn't know what's good for her. It's your business to make her *see* who's the right one for her to marry, and make her marry him.

MOTHER — Did your mother make you marry father?

GRANNY — She didn't have to. I *knew* he was the best and I took him. Didn't I help you to take Robert?

MOTHER — No, you didn't, and I didn't take him —

I was taken. Mary won't be taken — and she won't take. She wants something different.

GRANNY — Wants? Wants? What does she want?

MOTHER — (*with a sigh as she goes to the door*). Something that comes. Something neither you nor I ever had.

GRANNY — I think you're out of your head lately! I'm going to take Mary in hand myself.

MOTHER — (*turning sharply at the door*). No you won't, Mother. I must ask you, please — to let Mary alone.

Now Mary herself comes dashing in, full of a "great scheme." "Mary is twenty, slender and straight as a boy. She wears a slip of a frock that leaves her free, and she vibrates with vitality and eagerness. She is rather dynamically interested in her own affairs."

Her enthusiasm of the moment is centered on a plan to go camping with another girl and three boys. They are to do their own cooking and cleaning up and see how well and decently they can do it. "We think — we know, in fact — it's the best way in the world — the only way to really know each other — you know —to see each other all the time — in a sort of messy way — doing things we don't like to do — and sort of getting right down at realities you know — vital stuff."

And this great test is to be made because all five of the proposed party are in love with some of the others and they want to find out just what kind of love it is. And they don't propose to be bothered with any chaperones, either. That would put the scheme on the blink. Nobody would be natural. "It would be the cut and dried conventional stuff," explains Mary, "and that's just what we don't want. We want to see each other as we really *are*."

Granny is horrified. Are they stark, staring crazy?

MARY — Not at all. I think it's a great idea. People

don't *know* each other before they're married. That's why most marriages are merely disappointing experiments instead of lifetime mating. That's why the experimenting ought be done *before* marriage.

MOTHER — We'll talk about it after a while, dear.

MARY — Oh, Mother — why wait to *talk?*

GRANNY — Yes, *why?* Tell her now that it's an unheard of, immoral, disgraceful idea to have even come into a nice girl's head. Tell her that — this minute.

MOTHER — Wait, Mother.

MARY — Immoral? Disgraceful? Why, pray? Why?

GRANNY — Because it outrages all the decencies. What would you do at night, I'd like to know?

MARY — We'd go to bed and sleep — as decently as we do at home in our own beds.

MOTHER — Now, now, dear.

MARY — If you can't think of anything but *that,* Granny, you *have* got an evil mind.

MOTHER — Mary!

MARY — We aren't going away just so we can sleep together. We could stay right at home and do that, let me tell you.

MOTHER — Mary!

GRANNY — (*rising in rage and excitement. To Mother*). Are you going to do something? Don't you know *now* you must do something, or are you just going to go on sitting still?

MOTHER — Mother, will you *please* let me —

MARY — If I could just talk to Mother alone once, Granny, without you interfering, I might be able to make her understand something.

MOTHER — Mary — be quiet! Aren't you ashamed to speak to your grandmother like that?

GRANNY — No, she's not. There isn't any shame in her. She's brazen and disrespectful and you *let* her be.

MARY — She isn't *letting* me be *any*thing. I'm myself, Granny. Can't you understand that? And I'm talking about something very important to me which you don't understand at all.

MOTHER — Mary — that will *do,* I say. Tell your grandmother you're sorry, and don't let this happen again.

MARY — I'm sorry, Granny. I really am. I didn't mean to be disrespectful. Will you forgive me?

GRANNY — (*bursting into tears*). No, I won't. You're an impertinent little minx, and I don't want you to speak to me.

There is no comforting Granny. She is mad and tearful as she leaves the room. But Mary can't think of anything more to do about it. Granny's about the limit, anyway.

Mary still is full of her camping party idea, and still can't understand why her mother sees anything wrong with it. It may be unusual, and people may talk, but "if nobody ever did anything that had never been done before we'd be a sweet set of dubs."

MOTHER — You're talking from very lofty heights. Unfortunately we have to live in the valleys of common sense.

MARY — That's the way you always get out of everything, Mother. I want to *try* things. What else is life for?

MOTHER — You can't try things the whole world knows have nothing but danger and disaster in them.

MARY — Do you mean to say I couldn't go any place with anybody and not stay *myself* — just as I am now — unless I wanted to be something else? And then if I wanted to why of course I *would,* and that would be my own affair anyway.

MOTHER — Mary! Stop it. If I thought for a minute you *meant* that stuff, I'd be terribly frightened. But you don't.

MARY — Certainly I mean it, And I've about decided that free love is the only solution to the whole business anyway.

MOTHER — (*after a pause*). What on earth are you talking about?

MARY — I don't know that I could live all my life with one man — however much I loved him. Of course you and Father are satisfied with each other because you've never had anything else. But you don't know *what* you might have been, Mother, if you'd lived with a lot of men. Experience — constructive experience is the only developing progressive thing in the world.

MOTHER — There's nothing new about the relations between men and women and there's nothing true or right but the same old sound things that have always been true. I'm afraid you've been reading too much new stuff — trying to be clever and advanced. Don't dear — don't.

MARY — Gosh, Mother — you don't suppose anything I've read in a book cuts any ice? I'm talking about *me* myself, and how I feel and what I want. Hal and Lynn both have qualities that attract me enormously — and I want to find out if I want to marry either one of them. I wouldn't be satisfied to be happy just in the way you and Father are happy. I want something that is beautiful, and beautiful all the time.

MOTHER — Nothing is beautiful *all* the time. If you're going on a quest looking for that you might as well stay at home.

Mary is still determined to carry out her plans so long as she feels they will help her "express" and "find" herself. And her mother's veiled threat to tell her father has little effect on her. She knows "every snort and gesture" with which her father is likely to explode, but even that knowledge cannot deter her if she decides her happiness is at stake.

Two of the boys — the two Mary is most interested in — Hal and Lynn — come through the windows from the porch. Mary tells them of the progress — or lack of it — that she has made. Mrs. Hollister, dismissing the subject of the unchaperoned camp as too silly to discuss further, leaves them with the expressed hope that they will talk it all over again and decide to give it up.

Mary, however, will not let the boys back out, even if they want to. Lynn is rather ready to quit. But Hal isn't. And if Hal sticks Lynn will, because he is determined not to give any fellow an advantage with Mary.

MARY — Of course, to me it's thrilling — positively thrilling. I've never done anything in my life that I like so much. It's so simple — so absolutely simple — merely to go off and live naturally and freely for two weeks — doing a thing we know in the bottom of our souls is right and knowing perfectly well the whole town is going to explode with horror. Then we'll march back again with our heads well up and prove that we're finer and more intelligent people than we were before we went away. I think it's big — you know.

LYNN — Y-e-s —but what if it never was understood and accepted. It would be terribly hard on you two girls.

HAL — Even so — it would be worth it. They'd both be doing something great. Wreckage of the individual doesn't count in the world's work.

LYNN — Not so long as the *other* fellow happens to be the wreck.

MARY — Now listen. We've all reached the point where we think it's worth doing. I've even decided I *must* do it — in spite of mother. But if we're going to get away with it, we've got to do it quickly before the others back out and spill the whole business. *I* think we'd better go tonight — after the party. We'll all be out late anyway and nobody watching the time and expecting us. I'll get word to Letitia, and we can pack now and put the stuff in — in your garage, Lynn, and all start off together.

It is so decided and the boys are off to make the last-minute arrangements. But once out of the house they have to sneak back singly to reassure Mary of their continued devotion. Hal feels that she understands that whatever happens his love and friendship can be depended upon. Their souls "have found each other and understood." And when he goes Mary frankly kisses him upon the mouth.

Lynn is a little more practical. He comes back to assure Mary that if he were not dead sure that he was going to win her for his wife at the end of two weeks' test he wouldn't think for a minute of letting her go.

LYNN — Listen! I'm going to take care of you and pull this thing off *right*, and *you're* going to come back engaged to *me*.

MARY — Now if you're going with any fixed ideas you can't go at all. It's going to be growth and freedom.

LYNN — I don't need to grow. I *know* what *I* want. I love you.

MARY — But that isn't enough. You don't know that it will last forever.

LYNN — Of *course* it will. When people love the way *I* do, it's *got* to last. You *do* love me, *don't* you?

MARY — Yes — I do — in a way — very, very much. But not in *all* ways. It isn't the great love that embraces everything — that envelopes and sweeps one away — so there's no doubt about anything.

LYNN — Tell me how much you do love me and I'll take a chance on the rest.

MARY — I think — I *think* I'd rather you were the father of my children than anyone I know.

LYNN — Well then, what difference does anything else make?

MARY — But that isn't everything.

LYNN — What else *is* there?

MARY — Beautiful—mystic—far away things. Please go. I'm afraid Mother will come and spoil everything. (*She rises.*)

LYNN — (*catching her hand*). Kiss me.

MARY — No!

LYNN — (*getting up*). Why not?

MARY — I don't want to.

LYNN — Well, if I've got to act like a dead man for two weeks — you might kiss me once now.

MARY — No.

LYNN — (*taking her by the arm*). You've *got to.*

MARY — If you *do* I'll hate you.

LYNN — Did you kiss Hal?

MARY — None of your business.

LYNN — (*as he leaves unkissed*). Damn Hal!

Young Bobby is in with a hurried request for $17. He has smashed into another car and bent a fender, and the man is willing to settle for $17. Father must not know of it or he will likely refuse to let Bobby drive the car any more. Before his mother can decide whether or not to give him the money, Bobby's father arrives, and the boy spends an anxious several minutes before his mother manages to tell him where he can find the money — in the right hand corner of her handkerchief box — without the father knowing what is happening.

Granny is set on telling Robert the sad story of Mary's rebellion and all the awful things she is doing and planning to do, but Mrs. Hollister, by deftly fencing with her, manages to delay the recital. Mary is back to have her mother hook her party dress.

MARY — Hello, Father.

FATHER — Hello, daughter.

MARY — I got all my bills straight, Dad — and I haven't overdrawn my allowance a penny for three months. Pretty good — uh?

FATHER — Yes, I must say you do pretty well in that line — you've got a good mind if you'd just use it — instead of throwing it away.

MARY — What makes you think I'm throwing it away?

FATHER — I wouldn't have to *think* much to see that.

MARY — I think you have a perfectly corking mind, Father — but you don't always use it the way I think you ought to.

FATHER — And what's this I hear about some new idea you have in your head?

MOTHER — Robert — *please.* (*Father shrugs his shoulders and goes back to his paper.*)

MARY — Mother, your hands are shaking. Can't you find the hooks?

GRANNY — I don't know why she couldn't. There's not much to the whole dress *but* the hooks.

MARY — (*laughing*). Are you still cross at me, Granny? I'm awfully sorry. I'll be good.

GRANNY — I don't know how you can expect to be good in that dress.

MARY — What's the matter with this dress? It's a love — isn't it, Mother? (*Father looks over his paper at the dress.*)

MOTHER — It's very pretty, dear.

GRANNY — Yes, you uphold her in her nakedness, instead of making her put on clothes enough.

MARY — Oh, Granny!

GRANNY — I'll wager you haven't got a sign of a petticoat on.

MARY — Of course I haven't.

FATHER — (*looking over his paper*). What's the reason you haven't?

MARY — Heavens — nobody wears a petticoat, Father.

GRANNY — I do. Look at her. She might just as well be stark naked for all the good her clothes are doing her.

MARY — You needn't talk, Granny. I think it's much better to show my back than the way you showed your front. (*Father chuckles behind his paper.*) Thanks, dearest.

Outside Lynn is whistling and now Mary has kissed them all and is off for the party. Her farewell takes on just a moment's seriousness as she says good-bye to her mother, and she comes back a second time to throw her arms impulsively about her neck.

Granny is still troubled. She does not like the idea of Robert's not being told how things are with his children, and she is more than a little suspicious that Bobby has been up to something again. The mention of Bobby recalls to father the statement from the garage, showing repair bills of unusual size the past month. He also takes occasion to speak of all the bills. They are much too high. There will have to be a general cutting down.

GRANNY — Well, I don't run up the bills. I'm a *very* little eater if you mean me, Robert.

FATHER — I don't mean anybody. But you might control things, Mary, and keep them within bounds.

MARY — Oh, I do try to, Robert,— I do.

GRANNY — You're not as careful a housekeeper as I was, Mary.

MOTHER — No — and eggs aren't ten cents a dozen now, either.

FATHER — We've got to cut down. That's all there is about it.

BOBBY — That's what you always say the first day of the month, Dad.

FATHER — The whole country's going to collapse if we don't look out — with this reckless extravagance. Everybody's living beyond their income — everybody.

Same wild looseness that is in every other direction. There's a general lowering of standards and ideals that is undermining society and civilization.

GRANNY — That's just what I was saying to Mary this afternoon. She don't see it. She don't see it creeping into her own children.

FATHER — Creeping in — striding in, you mean —

GRANNY — Yes, that's it.

MOTHER — You can't expect your own children to be different from other people's, you know.

FATHER — I do expect it, by Jove. If I had my way they would be. If I had my way they'd all be at home this evening.

GRANNY — That's what I say. It certainly is a lovely, *lovely* home, and they ought all to be *in* it.

NORA — (*a neat maid — opening the hall door*). Dinner is served.

MOTHER — There's dinner and you two aren't ready. Run along, Bobby, and get ready for dinner — and *hurry*. (*Bobby rises.*) Why *will* you two *always* wait till dinner is on the table before you move. Hurry, Bobby, *hurry*. (*Bobby shambles out.*) Come, Robert.

FATHER — It might wait a little for me.

MOTHER — We simply *cannot* have decent food and keep it waiting. You've done it all your life and it's terribly irritating.

FATHER — (*rising reluctantly*). I have to rush all day. I would like peace and relaxation at home. (*He starts toward door.*)

MOTHER — Here's your hat, Robert.

FATHER — I don't want it.

GRANNY — (*trotting after him*). We're going to have chicken tonight, and I declare it is a shame we aren't all here to eat it. I do believe in a family all being 'round the table together when night comes.

The curtain falls.

ACT II.

Down the center of a country road, screened on either side by the blackness of night, a motor of the roadster type is speeding. The lights pierce the darkness in front. The whirr of the engine is steady.

Lynn is at the wheel, with Mary beside him and Hal on the other side of her. Mary and Lynn are tense with the thrill of the ride through the night toward the great experiment with life; Hal is a little pale with fear as the car jumps along, the speedometer moving steadily upward from forty to sixty miles an hour. The wind blows their hair and their coats, and a thin scarf that is about Mary's neck.

MARY — It's marvelous! I never was so alive before. Isn't it glorious to know nothing can stop us! We're free! I feel as if we were part of the wind and sky. I think we're going right on up, through the sky, into the stars.

HAL — Yes, we may do that sooner than we think. For Heaven's sake, let up a little, Lynn. You've lost your head.

LYNN — Not a bit! She's a good little wagon. This is easy for 'er.

MARY — Don't spoil it, Hal. This is the way everything always ought to be, going with all we've got and and nobody saying *"don't."* Oh, aren't you glad we did it? Don't you know now we're right, Lynn?

LYNN — This part of it's all right.

HAL — Of course we're right. But let's go slow enough to enjoy it.

MARY — But Hal, I thought this was what you wanted, moving swiftly, alone, leaving the world behind. The world's asleep and we're running away from it out into the unknown.

HAL — This isn't spiritual exaltation. This is just reckless foolhardiness. Not what *I* came for.

LYNN — Do you want us to let you out?

HAL — Don't be funny.

MARY — Buck up, Hal. You're *free!* For the first time in your life.

On they speed, Letitia and Max following after in the car behind. Hal continues to protest, and Lynn to sneer at him for his lack of nerve. "He's got a great deal more nerve about some things than you have," speaks up Mary, feeling that Hal is entitled to some defense. "Gee, if you were both mixed up together in one man you'd be pretty good. See the stars! We are going up — up — right into them. This is life! Go on, Lynn. *Step on her!*"

"Lynn bends lower over the wheel with a set face. Hal is holding on, sick with fear. Mary sits between them ecstatically happy," as the curtain falls.

The scene following is back in the Hollister living room. It is four o'clock in the morning. Bobby is asleep on the couch. The pale light of approaching dawn sifts through the windows.

A moment later five figures cross the porch at back and enter the room cautiously at the lower door. Lynn leads, carrying Mary's suitcase, Hal follows, partly carrying Mary, who appears to be in a state of collapse. Max and Letitia follow them.

Hal deposits Mary in an arm chair. Letitia ("a pretty girl of the flapper type") hovers about her, seeking to do something that will help without any definite idea of what she should do. Should she call a doctor? Or Mary's mother?

She should call neither, answers Mary, sitting up and announcing quite soberly that she is all right. Her attack of appendicitis, which has brought them home, was all pretense. After they had arrived at the camp she knew suddenly that they were wrong.

MARY — I *didn't* change my mind. It was something much bigger than that.

MAX — Must have been colossal to make you turn turtle like this. (*They are all sitting on the floor in a circle about Mary. Each has lighted a cigarette.*)

MARY — The whole world and life and what it means suddenly flashed before me, and —

LETITIA — I thought that flashed before you long ago. I thought that was why we —

LYNN — Sh!

HAL — Wait, Lettie, wait.

MARY — I knew that we were wrong. That we were destroying something — hurting something.

LYNN — You bet we were! I'm darned thankful we're back. We're well out of a nasty mess, let me tell you.

MARY — Oh *you* don't understand, Lynn. It isn't that at all. I mean that we were absolutely right in what we believed but we've got to be big enough not to hurt other people with it.

HAL — Oh — Mary, that is so weak.

MARY — I never *wanted* to do anything as much in my life, Hal, but I just suddenly saw it the way — mother and father would — and I knew how it would seem to them.

MAX — (*Lynn hits Max*). You knew that in the first place, didn't you?

MARY — No — not actually — in the real way. None of us thought of it from their side.

HAL — Oh, Mary, their side doesn't count. We know we're thinking way beyond the general level of thought and if we don't act on it we're not advancing. (*He hits Letitia's nose with a gesture. General noise and confusion.*)

LETITIA — Oh, Hal, my nose!

LYNN — I don't see any use advancing so far that everybody thinks you're a *lunatic.*

MARY — But because we *do* see farther than other

people — we must be a — magnanimous. They can't help it — you know — these deep prejudices, and after all — they *are* our parents.

The company is not altogether agreed on the importance of parents. Hal is of the opinion that they are "given entirely too much importance in the general scheme." And as for marriage — he is quite convinced that marriage "as is" is a gigantic human failure. And Max has found that practically every married couple of his acquaintance has been divorced or ought to be.

But Mary holds to her new conviction that they were wrong in attempting to do what they intended to do sneakily; they should at least have been honest and open about it. In any event, it is all over now. It may be that they will all go on again at some other time, but Letitia is doubtful. "I'm afraid you'll have a hard time inflating me again, Mary," she says. "I feel as though I had started off on wings and come back in a wheel-barrow."

Lynn is sure that everything is all right, but Hal is not. He is disappointed in Mary — horribly disappointed. After she had done so much good *individual* thinking, to let them down as she had. "But this isn't the end," he prophesies as he goes. "You will do it yet — and in a still wider, fuller way. Anybody who's got the idealism you have can't go back to the sordid, conventional old rut."

Lynn is more in love with Mary than ever, and more confident. Certainly her real reason for abandoning the experiment must have been because she had seen in a flash which of them she really wanted to marry.

MARY — I can't talk about it now. I want to think. The thing that brought me back is more important than *that* . . . just now.

LYNN — Just what *did* bring you back? Tell me.

MARY — I *will* try to make you understand — sometime.

LYNN — I'll stop on my way down town in the morning.

MARY— Then hurry. I want to lock the window.

LYNN — Well, tell me this: Even if you haven't found out yet, you want *me* — aren't you *dead sure* you don't want Hal?

MARY — (*trying to push him through the window*). Please go.

LYNN — But I want you and I want you harder than ever. Talk about going up into the stars! I went up and I'm still there and I'm going to stay. When you sat there close to me — making me go faster — when your hair blew into my face — I didn't care whether we smashed into eternity or not. We were together — alone.

MARY — We weren't. Hal was there.

LYNN — Same thing. You weren't the only one who got a flash of what it all means. It was only you and me and space — that was *life*, all right — and I'm going to keep on living it — *up there* — in the stars.

MARY — But we can't. It's too high.

LYNN — Not with *you*.

MARY — We had to come down.

LYNN — Well, what of it! When I think what you went to find — and that you even let me go with you to try to find it — I — my head swims. I can't say it, Mary — but I *know* what you want — because I've found it. I couldn't *wish* anything more wonderful for you than for you to love someone the way I love you.

MARY — Oh, Lynn! I wanted to go on with you forever. I wanted to push Hal out of the way and go on and on — and never stop — with you.

LYNN — Mary!

MARY — I wanted to get inside your coat — close to you — away from everything else in the world.

LYNN — (*trying to put his coat about her*). And that's right where you're going to stay.

MARY — And then I got afraid of myself — of you — of everything.

LYNN — (*protestingly*). Dear!

MARY — And then I wanted to come home — and now I don't know what I want. We've lost that wild sweet something. It's gone and I'm afraid it will never come back.

LYNN — You wanted to come home because you knew that you loved me. All that wild stuff's over — we don't need it. I love you, and I'm coming over the first thing in the morning, to tell your father and mother.

MARY — Oh — I s'pose you might as well. There's nothing else to do —

LYNN — What's the matter, dear? Aren't you happy?

MARY — I was — out there.

LYNN — And you will be *here*. We've got the star dust and we're going to hold on to it — tight.

MARY — Do you think we can?

LYNN — Certainly we can. Nothing so great as this can get away from us.

MARY — We mustn't let it, Lynn — we mustn't let it. Go, now — please. (*He holds her a moment — kisses her — and goes out quickly.*)

Mary discovers Bobby asleep on the sofa. She suspects him of playing 'possum and listening to all that has been said, but he appears to have been honestly asleep. He had come down to unlock the window for her and to give her a tip that there has been a row, and that she is in for a spell of discipline. Granny has told father, and father has threatened to send Mary away.

Parents are quite terrible at times, Mary and her brother agree. It is so hard to talk to them, to make them understand that their children are, in at least a small way, human and grown and almost their equals.

Bobby — If I could just once let him know that I'm *on* to him — I could listen to his favorite remarks about my character with more equanimity.

Mary — I know. *We're* always wrong. They *never* are.

Bobby — And the worst of it is, you can't tell 'em.

Mary — Tell? You might as well try to tell God he's wrong.

Bobby — If dad didn't take it as a matter of religion that I ought to give him the paper! If, *once* in a while, he'd say, "Here, Bob, you take it"— I'd be crazy about giving it to him.

Mary — Of course. And if I could only *talk* to Mother. I did try. I did try to make her see. She doesn't know at all what I want and what I think and feel. I know a great deal more about life and what's going on this minute than she does. They've never done anything thrilling or had any fun themselves and they don't expect anybody else to.

Bobby — (*with a chuckle*). Oh, I don't know. They must have been pretty devilish — buggy-ridin' Sunday afternoons.

Mary — Yes — Looking for wildflowers. Mother never had any beau but Father, I s'pose, and she just married him and settled down and there you are. Anything *I* do is wrong because *they* haven't done it. Listen, Bobby. I came back for *them*. I wanted to do this thing more than I ever wanted anything in my life — but just as I was the happiest and the surest I heard Mother say: "I trust you — always — anywhere"— and she stayed right there with me — nearer than she's ever been before and I — well — I came back.

Bobby — Darn good job you did, too — I could have told you before you started your idea was bunk.

MARY — Oh, of course it all seems silly to you, you aren't old enough to know what it means.

BOBBY — Slush! I'm eighteen — you're only twenty.

MARY — Yes, but those two years make all the difference in the world.

BOBBY — Ho — o — Don't you fool yourself — I know a thing or two. Those fellows are big chumps if they were goin' off to let you size them up like that and take your choice.

MARY — Well — anyway — here I am — back — as Lettie says — in the same old flat way. You see — I began to think about Mother and Father and somehow — they're narrow and old-fashioned, but they're good.

BOBBY — Yea — they're all right — even if they do scrap sometimes.

MARY — Sometimes — I'm sort of worried about them.

BOBBY — I know — Sometimes it's rotten.

MARY — But home and the family and you and me are the most important things in the world to them. After all we're awfully lucky to have such parents. Lots of them are running on the loose, you know.

BOBBY — You bet your sweet life they are!

MARY — And a really truly home like ours is wonderful — and I just couldn't do anything to hurt it. They're good and they love us, and they *do* love each other. I guess I *will* just sneak upstairs and tell one more lie to keep them happy. Don't you ever really peep that I really *did* go. Don't — for their sakes, old man.

BOBBY — I'm with you — Go to it, Sis.

Before they can leave the room the Hollisters are at the door. Bobby quickly rolls under the sofa and Mary slips back of a portiere and remains hidden. The Hollisters have come to look for Bobby. Finding him gone they are convinced he has gone after his sister and that the two children are really in "cahoots."

Mother Hollister is nervous and worried. Father is angry and unreasonably critical. Evidently through the evening there has been much quarreling as to who is to blame for the general laxness of the children's upbringing and the looseness of their standards. Now Mrs. Hollister is tired of listening to her husband's tirade, and suggests that he talk less and do more.

FATHER — Why didn't *you* do something at the right time? Why in the name of heaven haven't you controlled her?

MOTHER — Because I *don't know how.*

FATHER — Why don't you know how? It's your job. Why can't you run your house and your children as well as I run my office? Good Lord, she's only a young girl. You're more than twice her age. Why can't you manage her?

MOTHER — You're more than *three times* Bobby's age. Why don't you manage him?

FATHER — I do.

MOTHER — No, you don't.

FATHER — Besides, he's a boy. He's got to have experience. It wouldn't hurt him to go off on a spurt like this.

MOTHER — It would. It would. I couldn't bear it.

FATHER — You undermine everything I say to him, anyway — with your softness. *I* don't know what's the matter. It's not *my* fault. What in the name of heaven *is* the matter? Why have we *got* such rotten children? (*He sinks into a chair — putting his head in his hands.*)

MOTHER — You don't know what kind of children we have.

FATHER — What?

MOTHER — We don't know them. We don't know how to take care of them. We don't come any place near it.

FATHER — Speak for yourself. Don't blame *me* because *you've* failed.

MOTHER — Of course you haven't . . . in *any* way.

FATHER — No — I don't think I have.

MOTHER — You're always *right* about *everything.*

FATHER — Well, what am I wrong about *now?* Haven't I told you from the beginning all the things you let her do would —

MOTHER — Yes — yes — yes — you have!

FATHER — It's because you haven't done what I wanted that —

MOTHER — You're only thinking about what *you want* — and not about what's right for them at all.

FATHER — Well, is this right? This and everything that's led up to it?

MOTHER — No — but you wouldn't have made it any better by being hard and pig-headed.

FATHER — Have you made it any better by being so weak and sloppy you let this happen?

MOTHER — She didn't mean any *harm.*

FATHER — Oh, no — no harm — just disgraced us. That's all.

MOTHER — Poor child! She's trying to find the unfindable thing — a perfect love. I went through it myself, floundering around in the dark — trying to choose.

FATHER — I think you did pretty well for yourself — choosing.

MOTHER — Oh, yes — it was wise choosing —

FATHER — You regret it — do you?

MOTHER — Don't you?

FATHER — If I do, I've got the decency not to say so.

MOTHER — If you could have seen what we'd be like in twenty-five years — would you have chosen *me?*

FATHER — If you feel that way about it — whose fault is it?

MOTHER — Or even *ten.* Did we have ten years that were worth *anything?*

FATHER — Are you blaming *me?*

MOTHER — At the end of *five* we were a failure — jogging along — letting out the worst side of ourselves for the other to live with.

FATHER — You're saying a lot of wild things. You haven't had one of these spells for years.

MOTHER — No — Because I've stopped *trying* to tell the truth to you about *anything.*

FATHER — That's so all right. You certainly are not any too keen about telling the *truth.*

MOTHER — Because you can't stand it. Your nature can't stand the truth.

FATHER — Oh, don't excuse your lies and deceit and weakness by *my nature.*

MOTHER — Don't think I wouldn't be glad to be honest — to honestly be *myself.* You think I'm weak. Well, you couldn't *stand* my strength.

FATHER — What?

MOTHER — We *can't* speak the truth to each other. We haven't anything to speak it with.

FATHER — I'm flabbergasted at you. You seem to have lost what sense you did have . . . you disappoint me terribly.

MOTHER — Of course I do. Don't you think you disappoint *me?*

FATHER — You haven't come along the way I thought you were going to. I can't *count* on you. You aren't *there.* Sometimes I think you aren't the woman I married at all.

MOTHER — And sometimes I think you're a man I *couldn't* have married. Sometimes I loathe everything you think and say and do. When you grind out that old stuff, I could *shriek.* I can't breathe in the same room with you. The very sound of your voice drives me insane. When you tell me how right you are — I could strike you.

Suddenly Mrs. Hollister sees Mary's suitcase. A startled scream escapes her. The suitcase was not there when she was in the room before. Mary must be home. She rushes out toward Mary's room. Mr. Hollister follows quickly.

Slowly Mary steps from in back of the curtain — "stricken white and dumbfounded." Bobby rolls out from in back of the sofa, consternation spread over his boyish face. The discovery that their parents "hate" each other amazes and chills them.

MARY — How can they ever speak to each other again?

BOBBY — D'know.

MARY — I didn't know it was like this. And you can tell it's been going on — sort of smothered.

BOBBY — It sure has busted now.

MARY — It makes me — all gone — inside.

BOBBY — Nothing to hang on to.

MARY — Father and Mother! I wish I hadn't come back.

BOBBY — I'd like to light out myself.

MARY — *Our* Father and Mother! I can't believe it!

BOBBY — We can't let 'em know we know.

MARY — How can we help it?

BOBBY — I guess plenty of parents fight.

MARY — But *ours!* I thought they were so *good!* Oh Bobby!

She is standing with her head on Bobby's shoulder, and is shaken with sobs as her parents rush back into the room. Her mother grabs her and brokenly demands to know where she has been. Her father begins the announcement of the discipline that is to follow, even before he is assured that his daughter has done nothing wrong. And yet Mary refuses to lie. She did go away, she tells them, and she expected to stay, as she had planned.

FATHER — I'm not surprised. This is the *end.* You've gone too far. I'm going to send you away.

MOTHER — Oh Robert— no you're not. Wait!

FATHER — Why should I wait? I've waited too long. I'm going to send you where you'll live a decent normal life till you come to your senses. The thing you planned to do is a brazen outrage.

MOTHER — She didn't do it. She came home.

FATHER — Much home means to her! You've abused it all — everything we've taught you to respect and hold sacred — thrown it away. Why you came back at all I don't see.

MARY — I came back for a very silly reason.

FATHER — I'll bet you did — nothing with any good in it.

MARY — No — not a bit.

MOTHER — My dearest — don't say that. You came back because you love us.

MARY — (*breaking a little but controlling herself quickly*). Yes — I did, Mother.

MOTHER — Because you were sorry and didn't want to hurt us.

FATHER — Hurt us! You've wounded us so we'll never get over it. You've destroyed everything your Mother and I have held up to you as right — all our standards — the sanctity of the home —

MARY — Oh, *rot,* Father!

MOTHER — Mary! Stop! You're out of your senses.

MARY — I came home for that and found it was a joke.

FATHER — What do you mean?

MARY — We heard you — Bobby and I. We were here in this room.

FATHER — Heard us what?

MARY — Heard you say things to each other that make everything you're talking about now *disgusting.*

MOTHER — Oh, my child!

FATHER — You heard us discussing you and what you've done. You heard us say how pained we are.

MARY — We heard you *fight.*

MOTHER — Mary — don't — don't! You don't understand, dear child. We were only excited. I honor and respect your father above everything on earth.

FATHER — Your Mother and I have had a lifetime of devotion — with the highest ideals of married life. We didn't think we'd live to see our own children desecrate all that we've lived for.

MARY — Oh, don't! We heard. We know. You told each other the *truth.* What's the good of trying to plaster it over for us.

FATHER — There's nothing left. This is the result of the wild life you've been leading.

BOBBY — Why do you keep going on about her? It's you two that have smashed everything up.

FATHER — Stop! She's disgraced us.

BOBBY — She's not the one that's done the disgracin'.

MARY — I don't see how Bobby and I can ever hold up our heads again.

MOTHER — Don't, child — don't.

MARY — What's the use of anything when everything we ever thought and believed about isn't true?

BOBBY — We *know we're rotten* — plenty of times— but we always thought you were —

MARY — We always thought you were good.

FATHER — How *dare* you? Is nothing sacred to you?

MARY — A lot of things *used* to be. We always thought there was something between you and Mother, sort of — holy — and different — that most people didn't have at all. How do you s'pose we feel when we know that it isn't so? I don't see that it makes much difference what *we* do — anyway — when everything's all wrong with *you.*

"She goes out of the room with her head up — fighting back the tears. Bobby goes out after her with as much dignity as possible. Father turns away to the windows. Mother sits helpless and dazed. The light fades."

The curtain falls.

ACT III

In the dining room next morning the table is set for breakfast. The parent Hollisters are seated, he with the morning paper so spread it completely hides her from his gaze. They are plainly unhappy.

It is Mrs. Hollister's idea that they should do something to convince the children that the family quarrels have never been quite so bad before. There must be some little pretense for the sake of their happiness. But Mr. Hollister is still of the opinion that Mary and Bobby will have come to their senses by this time. His discipline will take care of the rest of the trouble.

Granny's breakfast is largely spoiled because she cannot find out, even by the most persistent questioning, just how the situation stands. She is quite disgusted, anyway. What is a tiff between husband and wife? Tiffs happen in every family, and no one should ever take them seriously. This is another day. Let everybody start over.

But no one pays any attention to her. When the children arrive they are even in more serious mood than their parents. Nor does Mr. Hollister's announcement that he has come to a decision regarding Mary clear the situation. She is, he says, to be sent away to school.

MARY — I'm perfectly willing to go away to school or any old place if it will help. Bobby and I talked it all over. If you and Mother want a divorce, we'll see you through.

GRANNY — She's out of her senses.

FATHER — Don't put me and your mother in the same class with the rotten set you've been running with. We don't tear up ties of a lifetime just because we've had — a — hard place — sometimes.

MARY — Do you mean you've patched it up? We won't *let* you.

FATHER — *Stop*, I say.

MARY — Mother, do you prefer to stick together and hate each other?

MOTHER — You have a wrong impression. We were only wrought up over — (*Bobby rises.*)

MARY — Bobby, for heaven's sake, speak up. Tell them what *you* think.

FATHER — (*to Bobby*). Are you a part of this rubbish?

BOBBY — I know how you feel, Dad. I used to feel that way about it myself. But I changed my mind last night — after I saw how things are. We'll buck up and do anything — so long as it's got to be. Don't mind us.

FATHER — This is insufferable.

MARY — Go on, Bobby.

GRANNY — (*crying louder*). I can't stand it!

BOBBY — There's nuthin' the matter with a divorce — it's the havin' to have it that's rotten — and when you do — why you just *got*-a. So let's get at it and get done with it.

FATHER — You leave the room. Go upstairs. (*To Mary.*) Tonight I'll try to make you see straight. I can't say anything more now.

MOTHER — You don't understand, you children. Your father and I are sorry we quarreled last night, but you're making too much of it entirely. Stop it. It's over and ended.

MARY — You're crawling out of it, Mother. Now's your chance. We all *know.* You can't go back to the same old thing, because we *do* know.

FATHER — If reason won't control you, something else will. You've made it impossible for us to let you stay at home. You've outraged everything that goes to make a home.

MARY — That's what *we* think *you've* done.

BOBBY — There isn't any home when you and Mother are like this.

FATHER — Do you set yourselves up against us?

MARY — *Say* something, Bobby.

BOBBY — What more is there to say? We've told you we don't want you to go on tryin' to keep up the bluff for *our sakes.* And you surely don't want to for yourselves. So what is there to it but to get together and quit. We're only tellin' you that we want you and Mother to be happy, and go to it. (*He goes out of the room, leaving the door open.*)

FATHER — If it comes to defiance — you'll both go away.

MARY — Very well. We'll meet you half way. We'll go if you and Mother get a divorce.

FATHER — (*choking with rage*). I'll settle you tonight.

Mary can't understand why this attitude on her father's part should constantly reduce her mother to tears. Surely they can't want to live together feeling toward each other as they do. Why, then, make such a fuss over a perfectly reasonable separation!

But Granny understands, and it is her conviction that young Mary is a good deal of an idiot. Every woman has got to learn sometime how to handle men, and once she's learned the rest is simple. Men, says Granny, have to be tactfully wheedled into thinking they're bosses. Wheedle father a little; let him think he's getting his own way and the whole thing will blow over in no time. Which, to Mary is a disgusting business. Her father and mother do not love each other, and therefore they ought not to live in the same house.

GRANNY — It's new-fangled nonsense. Modern selfishness. That's what it is. A man and woman have no right to expect to be happy *all* the time — every minute — day and night. You *have* to have a good fight now and then to clear the air. Your grandfather and I had plenty. You women now-a-days don't know how to manage men. That's what's the matter with you. Of course they get the best of you because you're trying to make 'em think you know as much as they do, and they won't *stand* it. You're such simpletons. You oughtn't to let 'em *ever* see how smart you are. Why I had my way about everything on earth. The madder your grandfather got the more I cried and the softer I was. I just twisted him round my finger — like that. And he thought I was right under his thumb.

MARY — Oh, Granny — how can you! Mother isn't Father's mistress, you know.

GRANNY — (*putting her hands over her face*). Oh! I never used that word in my life!

MARY — It's a perfectly good word. Mother and Father undertook the greatest relationship in the world and it hasn't been a success — so the only thing for them to do is to start another kind of life entirely. Isn't that so, Mother?

GRANNY — No, it's not! What would become of the rest of us?

MARY — *Us?* What have we got to do with it? It's their own inner closest life. It's not *right* for them to live together. It's not decent. It's absolutely *immoral.*

GRANNY — (*rising*). I won't listen to such talk! It's Godless and heathenish! (*To Mother.*) Mary, you come upstairs and I'll help you. I can help you bear anything you've got to bear with Christian fortitude as a good and noble wife should. I never dreamed you were silly enough to go and *let* yourself be unhappy. Heaven knows, you've got enough to be happy with — and if you're as clever as you *ought* to be you'll take the bit in your own teeth and he'll come trotting right along. There ain't a man on earth as smart as a woman if she just uses what God gave her — and there's no young chit can teach *me* any tricks!

But Mary sticks to her convictions, even after Granny has had her say and stormed out of the room. She loves her mother more than she ever realized she did until she had tried to leave her, and she is sorry for her father. There is his side, too. Mother does get on his nerves, terribly, and he's bored to death, there's no doubt of that. And it is largely her mother's fault, she thinks.

MARY — Women will have to change marriage — men never will. At least you've come a long way ahead of Granny. Her marriage was on a very *low plane*, of course. (*Mother gasps.*) You haven't stood up to Father and looked into his eyes — levelly — without conditions and silly compromise because he's a man and you're a woman.

MOTHER — Go on.

MARY — The interesting side of you — as a *person* — you haven't given to Father at all. He said last night, 'You don't come through. You aren't there.' He *is* there — in his way. There's *his* side, too.

MOTHER — Oh-h — don't think I don't know that.

MARY — But you *are* going to stand up now and keep a stiff lip and come through with *this*.

MOTHER — I don't see anything but blankness before me. And there's Mother. She's got to have a home.

MARY — (*looking deeply at her mother*). You mean

you haven't any *money* without Father? That you and Granny are dependent on him? (*Mother nods.*) All that is so horrible — so disreputable!

MOTHER — *Mary!*

MARY — It *is!* It's *buying* things with you. Don't let it go on, Mother. We'll fix it some way. I'll help you.

MOTHER — I'm not young. I can't go out and make my own living.

MARY — But you *ought* to be able to. That's the point to the whole business. I shall *have* my own money. I'll *make it.* I shall live with a man because I love him and only as long as I love him. I shall be able to take care of myself *and* my children if necessary. Anything else gives the man a horrible advantage, of course. It makes the woman a *kept* woman.

MOTHER — Oh, you —

MARY — Why it *does,* Mother. The biggest, fairest, most chivalrous man on earth can't feel the same towards a woman who lives with him just because she has to be taken care of — as he does to one who will live with him because she loves him. Unless it's love and only love —

She is interrupted by the return of her father. He has come back to have a talk with her mother, he tells Mary, and she leaves them.

Bobby, the father reports, is hard hit. He really has taken the family rift most seriously and some sort of compromise will have to be effected. The divorce idea, of course, is silly. Even if they have been stirred up enough to speak the truth, as his wife insists, they have not done the things people get divorces for. They have, Mrs. Hollister insists, done the worst thing of all: They have failed to make a success of their marriage.

FATHER — It's impossible to think of you and me — not together. It used to be all right. We've got to go back and begin all over again.

MOTHER — Go back to what?

FATHER — See here, Mary — some of the nonsense that child spouted has got hold of you. Don't let any of her silly —

MOTHER — She isn't silly. She's brutal because she's so young — but she's honest and —

FATHER — She's the product of this damnable modern loose-thinking.

MOTHER — (*with a sudden force and conviction*). And she's thinking nearer the truth than *we* ever did. She's got something dangerous and ridiculous in *one* hand and something big and real in the other.

FATHER — Oh, you can't take her seriously?

MOTHER — You say we must go back. Go back to what? Our accidental love affair — when we didn't know each other at all? We *do* know each other now. How can we go on after this? *I* can't.

FATHER — What about me? I've got something to say about this — too — you know! I won't have my home broken up. Good God, Mary! Nothing means anything to me but you and the children! I won't have —

Lynn comes in from the porch. He has recovered his senses. A night's thought has convinced him that the good old way is still the only way — the Hollister way. "You didn't need any experiments to make you know you loved each other for good and all, did you?" he beams on them, as they turn away embarrassedly. "You knew you'd stick to the end and be crazy about each other forever, didn't you? And you proved it." And that is the way he feels about Mary. So he has come formally to ask for her hand.

A moment later Hal arrives. But Hal is still of the opinion that Mary's ideals are important, and he has come to say that he will stand by her in any position she wishes to take. He loves her far too much to marry her in the "old blind accidental lottery" that the Hollister marriage was, even though that had, by the merest good luck, turned out beautifully. But Mr. Hollister is not particularly impressed with Hal's defiance. "It's not the damned ideas that will get you anywhere," he finally shouts at him; "it's yourself. If you're ever lucky enough to have a woman love you, you take care of that one love — and don't be so cocksure of yourselves."

Mary finds the two boys in the midst of their discussion with her father and being forced to decide between them she frankly confesses that she does not intend to marry either.

MARY — Father, listen! This is what I've just told Mother. When I got home I told Lynn I loved him — and I do. I love him so much I can't live without him. I was going to marry him — quick. But now I wouldn't marry him for anything on earth.

FATHER — Why not?

LYNN — What do you mean?

MARY — Marriage is a disgusting, sordid business affair that I wouldn't go into for anything.

LYNN — Mary!

MARY — But if you want me to, Lynn, I'll live with you till we're *sure* what we really mean to each other, and when we *know* we'll either be married or quit.

FATHER — Is this the kind of muck and filth you've been thinking about?

MARY — I didn't think I'd actually do it, till I found out how horrible a perfectly good and respectable marriage can be.

FATHER — Haven't you any decency about anything?

MARY — I'm sorry, Dad, but Lynn's got to know. He's got to know why I won't marry him. It's because of Father and Mother, Lynn. I don't believe in marriage.

Then Bobby comes to announce that he has got his

mother to promise to go away, to leave his father for both their sakes. And though the paternal Hollister is hard hit they force him to accept the situation. If he does not, Mary swears to go away with Lynn, and Bobby insists he will never live in the house again.

Hollister makes a last plea, but his wife is firm. She is going away and alone — until she can find out the truth about herself. Then she turns to her rebellious daughter.

MOTHER — I don't ask you *not* to do what you say you're going to — for I know I haven't given you anything better, but I ask you to wait. It isn't our marriage that was wrong — it's what we've done with it.

LYNN — I'm not afraid, Mary — I'll make you happy.

MARY — How do you know you will? What if the very things you think you like in me now you'd hate in me sometime? What if the things I think are strong and stunning in you now I'd think were pig-headed and kickable — after a while?

BOBBY — That's what. I thought the thing you were up to was all hot air and bunk — but I begin to believe there's a good deal in it. I know one thing, by golly — I'll never take a chance. I'll never take a chance of being where you and Father are. If you two couldn't make a go of it, I'd like to know who *can*. I don't see why men and women don't stop *tryin'* to live together — anyway. (*He starts to go.*)

MOTHER — (*stopping him*). Oh no — that isn't it. It's we — ourselves, and what *we've* done. (*She goes out.*)

MARY — (*putting her hand on Father's arm*). Let her go, Dad. Let her go.

FATHER — But I'll bring her back.

MARY — Do you mean you love her?

FATHER — You've got an awful lot to learn, little girl.

MARY — (*suddenly throwing her arms about his neck*). Make her love you, Dad. Make it all over. If you could! If you could! (*Father — too moved to speak — holds her close for a moment and goes out, closing the door.*)

LYNN — Gosh, I'm sorry. It's the last thing in the world I would have expected to happen.

MARY — Why didn't they know in the first place? Can anybody ever know?

LYNN — We know. Now see here — there isn't going to be any more see-sawing about *us*. You love me and you're going to marry me *now*.

MARY — But I wouldn't ever — ever — *ever* — if I didn't *know* that *ours is* a love that will last forever. There *can't* be any doubt about a love as great as ours — can there, dearest?

LYNN — Absolutely none. (*The light closes in — leaving them standing in a circle of light — with the same effect as in the scenes of the prologue.*)

MARY — It *is* one of those great eternal passions that will last through the ages — isn't it, dear?

THE END

THE PLAYS AND THEIR AUTHORS

"Rain." By John Colton and Clemence Randolph, from a short story by W. Somerset Maugham called "Miss Thompson." Copyright, 1922, by John Colton and Clemence Randolph. Mr. Colton is an Englishman, his father being the British consul at Yokohama. He came to America some years ago and drifted into journalism, writing play reviews for the *Minneapolis Tribune*. Later he took up scenario writing in California, and it was while here that he met Mr. Maugham and arranged with him for the dramatization of "Miss Thompson." He is also the author of a piece called "Drifting," which Alice Brady played last year.

Miss Randolph is an American girl of French-Irish extraction, and was also interested in scenario writing when she met Mr. Colton and worked with him on "Rain." They spent nearly a year, it is said, getting the manuscript into presentable shape.

Mr. Maugham has had considerable experience as a playwright (see *The Best Plays of 1921–22*), his most recent success being last season's "The Circle." But he would not himself attempt a dramatization of "Miss Thompson," he said, because he could not see how an effective dramatization could be made from the story.

"You and I." By Philip Barry. Copyright, 1922, by Philip Barry. Mr. Barry, though a Yale man, graduating in 1918, studied drama with Professor George Pierce Baker and the "English 47" class of Harvard. He submitted "You and I" in the prize competition of 1922, and won the five hundred dollars offered by Richard G. Herndon, the New York producer. Professor Baker, Mr. Herndon and Walter Prichard Eaton, the dramatic critic, were the judges. The play was an immediate popular success and Mr. Herndon has since bought a second play of Mr. Barry's called "Poor Richard." Previous to these successes Barry dabbled in play-writing through his college course, as a member of the Yale Dramatic Association. A one-act play of his, called "A Punch for Judy," was produced at a benefit performance in New York, staged by the League of Pen Women. At Yale he was one of the editors of the *Review*. He was born in Rochester, N. Y., is in his middle twenties and has had some experience writing advertising copy for a local agency.

"Loyalties." By John Galsworthy. Copyright, 1922, by John Galsworthy. Published by Charles Scribner's Sons, New York. Mr. Galsworthy, born in Coombe, England, studied law as a young man, but found more pleasure writing novels and eventually gave up the law entirely. Several years ago he tried play-writing, and has won a notable success also in that division of literature. Of his better known dramas "The Mob," "Strife," "The Pigeon," "Justice," "The Silver Box," "The Eldest Son" and "The Skin Game" (the latter being included in the 1920–21 volume of *The Best Plays* series), are remembered by American playgoers.

"Icebound." By Owen Davis. Copyright, 1922, by Owen Davis. Published by Brentano's. Mr. Davis comes of Yankee stock and was born and reared in New England. His biographers credit him with having first seen the light in Portland, Maine, in 1874. He graduated from Harvard in 1893 and immediately took to writing melodramas for the then popular producing firm of Harris, Sullivan & Woods. Within the next eight years he contributed fifty or more melodramas to the Woods' popular-price circuit, ranging from "The Confessions of a Wife," through the "Bertha the Beautiful Sewing Machine Girl" series to those of a little better grade. In 1910, the moving picture craze having closed most of the popular-priced theatres to melodrama, both Mr. Davis and Mr. Woods determined to do their future producing on Broadway. Mr. Davis began with a play called "The Wedding Ring" for Marguerite Clark, and followed with one called "Lola," in which Laurette Taylor was starred by Daniel Frohman. "The Family Cupboard," "Sinners," "Forever After," "Opportunity" and others followed, most of them produced by William A. Brady. "The Detour," in 1921, was accepted as much the best of Mr. Davis' output up to that time, and he followed this, in 1922, with "Icebound," which not only scored a popular success, but won him the Pulitzer prize of one thousand dollars as the American play "which best represents the educational value and power of the stage in raising the standard of good morals, good taste and good manners" produced during the year.

"Why Not?" By Jesse Lynch Williams. Copyright, 1922, by Jesse Lynch Williams. Mr. Williams is better known as a story writer than he is as a playwright, though his "Stolen Story," put into dramatic form, created considerable stir some years ago, and his "Why Marry?" won the Pulitzer prize as being the best American play of the 1917–18 season. He graduated from Princeton in 1892, and has written several Princeton stories, being the co-author also of a history of Princeton, written with John De Witt. His stories include "The Adventures of a Freshman," "New York Sketches," "The Day Dreamer," "The Stolen

Story," etc. "Why Not?" is, in a sense, a companion piece to "Why Marry?" treating the divorce problem with something of the same philosophic levity.

"The Fool." By Channing Pollock. Copyright, 1922, by Channing Pollock. Mr. Pollock was born in Washington, D. C., in 1880, was graduated from the Bethel Military Academy and studied later at the Polytechnique in Prague, Austria. He was for many years a play reviewer and reporter on Washington papers and a frequent contributor to the magazines. He began writing plays in 1900, producing "A Game of Hearts." His first play to attract attention was "The Pit," the dramatization of which he made for William A. Brady while he was serving as that producer's press representative. From that time on his output was consistently steady and of an even merit, though none of his dramas achieved a great popular success. They included many dramatizations, "In the Bishop's Carriage," "The Secret Orchard," "The Inner Shrine," etc. In collaboration with Avery Hopwood he wrote "Clothes" for Grace George, and working with the late Rennold Wolf he produced many successful music plays, "The Red Widow," "The Beauty Shop," "My Best Girl," and several of the "Follies" books. His original plays include "Such A Little Queen," "The Little Gray Lady," "The Roads of Destiny" and "The Sign on the Door," and with Edgar Selwyn he wrote "The Crowded Hour." "The Fool" has proved the most popular of all his plays.

"Merton of the Movies." By George S. Kaufman and Marc Connelly, from the novel by Harry Leon Wilson. Copyright, 1922, by the authors. These are the young men who first came into prominence as the authors of "Dulcy," which was included in last season's volume of *The Best Plays*. Another play of theirs, "Ladies First," was also produced last season. They are newspaper men in their early thirties, and have been singularly successful as collaborators. (See *The Best Plays of 1921–22.*)

Harry Leon Wilson has done some playwriting on his own account, being the co-author, with Booth Tarkington, of the hugely successful "Man From Home," and having written "Bunker Bean" and "Ruggles of Red Gap."

"The Old Soak." By Don Marquis. Copyright, 1922, by Don Marquis. Published by Doubleday, Page & Co., New York. Donald Robert Perry Marquis is a new name among the playwrights, but, shortened to the familiar Don Marquis, is well known to the readers of books and the followers of those newspaper columns Mr. Marquis has edited the last few years, notably for the *New York Evening Sun* and the *New York Tribune.* "The Old Soak," being the story of the bibulous but kindly Clem Hawley who has long figured as a favorite column character, is Mr. Marquis' first play. The author was born in Walnut, Illinois, in 1878, and lived for some time in Atlanta, Georgia. His books include "Danny's Own Story," "Dreams and Dust," "The Cruise of the Jasper B.," "The Old Soak," "Carter and Other People" and "Noah and Jonah and Cap'n Johr Smith."

"R. U. R." By Karel Capek. Copyright, 1923, by Paul Selver. Published and copyrighted, 1923, by Doubleday, Page & Company. The author of "Rossum's Universal Robots," for which the abbreviated "R. U. R." is used as the play's title, was born in northern Bohemia in 1890. In 1911 he wrote a play entitled "The Robber." "R. U. R." followed, after the war, and, in collaboration with his brother, Josef, Capek produced "The Life of the Insects," which was produced in America by W. A. Brady as "The World We Live In." His newest play is a comedy called "The Makropoulos Affair," produced in Prague last year. He also is the author of a volume of short stories called "The Crucifix," and a work entitled "Criticism of Words." The English version of "R. U. R." was made by Paul Selver and Nigel Playfair.

"Mary the Third." By Rachel Crothers. Copyright, 1922, by Rachel Crothers. Published by Brentano's. Miss Crothers is another author who has previously appeared in these volumes, being the author of a comedy entitled "Nice People," which was included in *The Best Plays of 1920–21*. She is an Illinois woman, a graduate of the State Normal School, and formerly a teacher of elocution. She took up stage work as a student of the Wheatcroft School of Acting in New York, and has been consistently active as a playwright since then. Her better-known plays include "A Man's World," "The Three of Us," "The Herfords" (afterwards called "He and She"), "A Little Journey," "39 East" and "Nice People."

PLAYS PRODUCED IN NEW YORK

June 15, 1922–June 15, 1923

"STRUT MISS LIZZIE"

A colored vaudeville in two acts. Produced by the Minsky Brothers at the Times Square Theatre, New York, June 19, 1922.

Principals engaged —

Creamer and Layton	Alice Brown
Hamtree Harrington	Cora Green
Brevard Burnett	Grace Rector
George Harve	Jean Rountree
James Barrett	Charles Frederick
James Moore	Henderson and Halliday

Williams and Taylor

"FROM MORN TO MIDNIGHT"

A play in seven scenes by George Kaiser, translated by Ashley Dukes. Produced by the Theatre Guild at the Frazee Theatre, June 26, 1922.

Cast of characters —

Cashier.......................................Frank Reicher
Stout Gentleman..............................Harry Ashford
Clerk...William Paul
Messenger Boy..............................Willard E. Joray
Lady..Maude Gilbert
Bank Manager..............................Walton Butterfield
Muffled Gentleman..............................Allyn Joslyn
Serving Maid..............................Genevieve Corbin
Porter..................................Charles Bartholomew
The Lady's Son...............................Albert Carroll
The Cashier's Mother.......................Kathryn Wilson
His Daughters............................Lela May Aultman
Julia Cobb
His Wife...................................Ernita Lascelles
First Gentleman................................Harold West

Second Gentleman..........................Willard E. Joray
Third Gentleman..........................Albert Carroll
Fourth Gentleman..........................Samuel Baron
Fifth Gentleman..........................William Crowell
Salvation Lass..........................Helen Sheridan
Waiter..........................Walton Butterfield
First Mask..........................Clelia Benjamin
Second Mask..........................Annette Ponse
Third Mask..........................Carolyn Hancock
Fourth Mask..........................Genevieve Corbin
First Guest..........................William Paul
Second Guest..........................Allyn Joslyn
Third Guest..........................Sam Rosen
Officer of Salvation Army..........................Ernita Lascelles

Scenes: Interior of a Provincial Bank, Writing Room of a Hotel, a Field in Deep Snow, Parlor in the Cashier's Home. Steward's Box at a Velodrome, Private Supper Room, Salvation Army Hall. In a Small Town and City in Germany. Staged by Frank Reicher.

An unhappy cashier in a provincial bank, half crazed by the humdrum of life, absconds with 60,000 marks (before the war) and tries to induce an attractive lady to flee with him. When she refuses he adventures through the day, finds life rotten and people worse; finally throws his money away to the fighting crowd at a race track, winds up at a Salvation Army hall at midnight, disillusioned and depressed, and ends by blowing out his brains.

"SPICE OF 1922"

A musical review in two acts by Jack Lait. Produced by Arman Kaliz at the Winter Garden, New York, July 6, 1922.

Principals engaged —

Arman Kaliz	James Watts
Nan Halperin	Eddie Nelson
Valeska Suratt	Evelyn Gerard
Georgie Price	Artie Leeming
Sam Hearn	Midgie Miller
Flavia Arcaro	Gattison Jones
Rex Story	Violet Carlson
James Gaylor	D'Andrea and Walters
Helen O'Shea	Jack Trainor

Staged by Allan K. Foster.

"SUE, DEAR"

A musical comedy in two acts. Book by Bide Dudley, Joseph Herbert and C. S. Montayne; music by Frank H. Grey; lyrics by Bide Dudley. Produced by Bide Dudley at the Times Square Theatre, New York, July 10, 1922.

Cast of characters —

Minerva West....Maxine Brown
Dave Craig....Maurice Holland
Aunt Mildred....Madeline Grey
Blithers....Douglas Cosgrove
Dolly....Ruth Gray
Polly....Lucile Godard
Molly....Eileen Shannon
Phillip West....Bradford Kirkbride
Sue....Olga Steek
Le Comte Emile Pouchez....John Hendricks
Chick O'Brien....Bobby O'Neil
Zoe....Alice Cavanaugh

GUESTS

Mary....Irma Coign
Louise....Edna Coign
Dolly....Ruth Gray
Polly....Lucile Godard
Molly....Eileen Shannon
Fay....Honor Tattersall
Doris....Emmey Tattersall
Catherine....Greta Warburg
June....Rose Courtney
Nell....Bobby Kane
Gloria....Mercedes Demordant
Florence....Kay Carlin
Jack....Paul Logan
Billy....Bobby Culbertson
Lester....Ted Wheeler
George....Norman Nicholson

Act. I.—Living-room of the West Home on Riverside Drive, New York. Act. II.—The Garden Connected With the Apartment House in Which the Wests Live. Staged by Joseph Herbert and Jack Mason.

"PLANTATION REVUE"

A colored musical revue in two acts produced at the Forty-eighth Street Theatre, New York, July 17, 1922.

Principals engaged —

Shelton Brooks
Will Vedory
Florence Mills
Edith Wilson
Chappy Chapelle
Juanita Stinette

"WHISPERING WIRES"

A drama in four acts by Kate McLaurin. Produced by the Messrs. Shubert at the Forty-ninth Street Theatre, New York, August 7, 1922.

Cast of characters —

Payson....................George Lynch
Doris Stockbridge....................Olive Tell
Montgomery Stockbridge....................Ben Johnson
James Bennett....................William Webb
Barry McGill....................Paul Kelly
Drew....................George Howell
Delany....................M. Tello Webb
Jackson....................William Robertson
The Trouble Hunter....................Malcolm Duncan
Jeanette....................Gaby Fleury

At the home of Montgomery Stockbridge. Staged by J. C. Huffman and John Harwood.

Montgomery Stockbridge, who has made enemies in business, is warned by a mysterious letter that his grave has been dug, and is awaiting him. He surrounds himself and his house with detectives, but in spite of all his precautions he is mysteriously murdered when he picks up the receiver of a telephone to answer a call. During the investigation of the crime Doris Stockbridge, his daughter, receives a similar warning of impending death. Many members of the cast are suspected, but a more or less rank outsider is eventually proved guilty.

"SHORE LEAVE"

A comedy in three acts by Hubert Osborne. Produced by David Belasco at the Lyceum Theatre, New York, August 8, 1922.

Cast of characters —

"Bilge" Smith, U.S.N....................James Rennie
Cap'n Martin....................Reginald Barlow
Fred Gwynne....................Schuyler Ladd
Rear Admiral Smith....................Stanley Jessup
Smith....................Samuel E. Hines
"Bat" Smith....................Thomas E. Jackson
First Sailor....................John F. Hamilton
Second Sailor....................H. Percy Woodley
Third Sailor....................Paul E. Wilson

Fourth Sailor..............................Bernard Sussman
Fifth Sailor..................................Jose Torres
Sixth Sailor..................................Jose Yovin
Seventh Sailor...............................Kenneth Diven
Bimby..Nick Long
Connie Martin...............................Frances Starr
Mrs. Schuyler-Payne...............Evelyn Carter Carrington
Aunt Hepsy ....Mrs. Jacques Martin
Georgie Demerest.............................Audrey Baird
Evelyn Gardner..........................Ellen Southbrook
Irene..Betty Alden
Gladys......................................Marjorie Booth
Ruth...Teris Loring
Edith...Devah Worrell

Act I.—Connie Martin's Cottage. Late Afternoon in June. Act II.—The *Zonoma*. Two Years Later. Act III.—Connie Martin's Cottage Again. After Another Interval of Two Years. The Action of the Play Takes Place in a Small Seaport Town on the New England Coast. Staged by David Belasco.

Connie Martin has been the village dressmaker in a New England seacoast town for more years than she is willing to acknowledge. Hungering for romance and being fearful of dying unwed, she deliberately accepts the flirtatious advances of a good-looking "gob" she meets in the park. Next day he has supper with her in her cottage and as he kisses her and runs away, he promises to come again another day. For two years she waits hopefully. When he does come he has forgotten the incident of his former visit, and even though the spinster has come into money and bought him a ship to captain, he refuses to stay. It takes another two years for Connie to capture her "gob."

"THE MONSTER"

A drama in three acts by Crane Wilbur. Produced by Joseph M. Gaites at the Thirty-ninth Street Theatre, New York, August 9, 1922.

Cast of characters —

Caliban.......................................Walter James
"Red" Mackenzie........................Frank McCormack
Julie Cartier..............................Marguerite Risser
Alvin Bruce.................................McKay Morris
Dr. Gustave Ziska..........................Wilton Lackaye
A Man..............................Charles Wray Wallace

The Action Takes Place in the Home of Dr. Ziska. Staged by Lawrence Marston.

Dr. Gustave Ziska, a French surgeon, lives in a haunted house at the edge of a city. Near the house a bridge crosses a chasm. Automobiles crossing the bridge are frequently hurled, by some mysterious force, upon the rocks below. Alvin Bruce, a newspaper man, determines to investigate both the mysterious accidents and the haunted house. He effects an entrance by carrying in Julie Cartier, a victim of one of the bridge accidents. In the house he finds "Red" Mackenzie, a genial tramp, who is doing a bit of investigating on his own account. He also discovers, before the evening is over, closets filled with jiggling skeletons, trap doors and trick chairs galore, and finally it is revealed to him that Dr. Ziska is mad. At the time he learns this, however, he is strapped to an electric chair and the doctor has Miss Cartier fastened to an operating table and is about to dismember her body in the cause of science. He effects an escape, with the aid of "Red" Mackenzie and the author, and is ready to marry Miss Cartier as soon as he gets out.

"MANHATTAN"

A comedy in four acts by Leighton Osmun and Henry Hull. Produced by John Cromwell, Inc., at the Playhouse, New York, August 15, 1922.

Cast of characters —

Duncan Van Norman........................Norman Trevor
(By arrangement with William A. Brady)
Paget..Hubert Druce
Skiddy Stillman..............................Raymond Walburn
Mrs. Van Norman..............................Hilda Spong
Mr. Shepley..................................William Sams
Amy Van Norman...............................Greta Kemble Cooper
Lory...Marguerite Maxwell
Sadie..Puritan Townsend
Kit..Mary Blair
Sybil Herrington.............................Helen Gahagan
Hendrick Van Dekkar..........................Albert Gran

Act I.—A Room in Mrs. Van Norman's House, Park Avenue. Act II.—Lory's Room, Fletcher Street. Act III.—Same as Act I. Act IV.—Lory's Apartment. Staged by John Cromwell.

Duncan Van Norman is a writing man forty years old and rich. Rich that is, in everything excepting experience with and knowledge of the feminine sex. His mother, a wise and sophisticated New Yorker, insists that he should either marry or go more into society. To please her he takes as his secretary Lory, a precocious typewritist, who lives at the point "where Greenwich Village quits kidding itself." Soon Duncan finds himself fascinated by Lory's quaint barbarisms. He loves both her "ain'ts" and the curl of her hair. But just as he is about to propose marriage to her he discovers that she has come into a considerable fortune. No Van Norman could think of marrying a girl for her money. So Duncan sends Lory away. But a few weeks later Lory calls him to her apartment, locks the door and throws the key out the window with the announcement that his only hope of saving her reputation is to send for a minister and marry her, which Duncan does.

"THE WOMAN WHO LAUGHED"

A play in three acts by Edward Locke. Produced by Sam Forrest at the Longacre Theatre, New York, Aug. 16, 1922.

Cast of characters —

John Neilson............................William H. Powell
Frieda Neilson............................Martha Hedman
Minna Becker..................................Gilda Leary
The Living-room in the Neilsons' Suburban Home.
Staged by Sam Forrest.

Frieda Neilson has good reason to suspect her half-sister, Minna Becker, of carrying on an affair with Mr. Neilson. To be revenged upon them both, she first dopes their cocktails with chloral and, when they are unconscious, ties them together with the family clothesline on the living-room settee. When they awake she tortures them with the ridiculousness of their position, threatens them with death, frightens them into a state of collapse by threatening to inject a deadly poison into their veins with a needle point, and finally shoots herself before their dimming eyes while they sink into a coma. Some hours later the husband and sister awake to find that they have been tricked by the wife, but so complete has been their reformation that the wicked sister is glad to depart the house, and the wife is willing to give her "bad boy" another chance.

"LIGHTS OUT"

A comedy in three acts by Paul Dickey and Mann Page. Produced by Mrs. Henry B. Harris at the Vanderbilt Theatre, New York, Aug. 14, 1922.

Cast of characters —

Walt Sebastian	Felix Krembs
Barbara Peyton	Marcia Byron
Mrs. Chester Gallant	Olive Harper Thorn
Keith Forbes	William Shelley
Brakeman	Albert Powers
Mr. Peyton	William Ingersoll
Egbert Winslow	Robert Ames
Porter	Cy Plunkett
Hair Pin Annie	Beatrice Noyes
Butts McAllister	Lorin Raker
"Camera Eye" Decker	Philip Lord
Silent Jim	Sam Janney
High Shine Joe	C. Henry Gordon
Night Watchman	Hallam Bosworth
Mr. Wellsback	William E. Morris

Act I.—Observation Car of the Pennsylvania Limited. Act II.—Robert Winslow's Apartment in New York. Act III.—Wellsback's Moving Picture Studio. Staged by Walter Wilson.

Egbert Winslow, whose ambition it is to become a writer of moving picture scenarios, starts for New York with a gripsack stuffed full of manuscripts. Crooks on the train overhear his reference to the bag as containing papers worth a million dollars. Thinking he is a bank messenger carrying bonds, they hold him up and take the bag away from him. Finding nothing but the manuscripts, they draw the lad into a confession of why he considers them valuable. Out of this grows a proposition from the boy that the crooks go into partnership with him in producing a real crook picture. Walt Sebastian ("Ira Bass" to his pals), the leader of the gang, thus hopes to be even with a former pal, "High Shine Joe," who has double-crossed him. He tells the young scenarist the real story of a recent bank robbery in which they both figured. When it is shown as a serial on the screen the picture so angers "High Shine Joe" that he sets out to be revenged on the authors. Detectives tracing the bank robbers also suspect the young author. The situation is cleared finally, by the arrest of High Shine Joe, the escape of Sebastian, and the marriage of the young scenarist to the banker's daughter.

"FOOLS ERRANT"

A drama in four acts by Louis Evan Shipman. Produced by the Messrs. Shubert at the Maxine Elliot Theatre, New York, August 21, 1922.

Cast of characters —

Sims	Gregory Loring
Mrs. Kinsey Elton	C. Tracy L'Engle
James Stannard	Fritz Williams
Maid	Isabel Pell
Fanny Pritchard	Lucile Watson
John Pritchard	Vincent Serrano
Eric Brierly	Cyril Keightley
Greta Ellis	Alexandra Carlisle
Maid	Bodil Rosing
Dr. Graham	Robert Cummings
Cassidy	Charles Reigel
Molloy	Arthur Fitzgerald
Maid	Ruth Elaine

Act I.—A Drawing Room in John Pritchard's House, New York. Act II.—A Living Room in Greta Ellis' Apartment, New York. Act III.—Eric Brierly's House, Mesaba. Act IV.—The Same. Staged by B. Iden Payne.

Eric Brierly, having gone west to reclaim his soul, returns to New York to find the woman with whom he was at one time in love married and unhappy. Her husband has taken up with Greta Ellis, a young art student he met in Paris. Brierly, thinking to make a reconciliation of husband and wife possible, proposes to Greta that she marry him and go west to live. A year later the wronged wife, now a widow, follows Brierly west in the expectation of renewing the old romance. She finds him desperately in love with Greta, however, and returns disconsolately to the east.

"THE OLD SOAK"

A comedy drama in three acts by Don Marquis. Produced by Arthur Hopkins at the Plymouth Theatre, New York, August 22, 1922.

Cast of characters —

Clem Hawley, The Old Soak..............Harry Beresford
Matilda..................................Minnie Dupree
Lucy......................................Helene Sinnott
Clem, Jr..................................George Le Guere
Cousin Webster Parsons...................Robert McWade
Tom Ogden..................................Grant Mills
Ina Heath..................................Mary Philips
The Hired Girl.............................Eva Williams
"Al"................................Robert E. O'Connor

Act I.—Living Room at the Hawley Home, Baycliff, L. I. Act II.—The Same. Act III.—Scene 1—Webster Parsons' Bank. Scene 2—Same as Act I. Period—The Present. Staged by Arthur Hopkins.

(See page 304.)

"DAFFY DILL"

A "musigirl" comedy in two acts by Guy Bolton and Oscar Hammerstein, 2d; music by Herbert Stothart; lyrics by Oscar Hammerstein, 2d. Produced by Arthur Hammerstein at the Apollo Theatre, New York, Aug. 22, 1922.

Cast of characters —

Estelle.................................Marion Sunshine
Teacher...............................Genevieve Markam
Lucy Brown...................................Irene Olsen

School Inspector.............................Ben Mulvey
Frank Tinney.................................Frank Tinney
Dan Brown....................................Harry Mayo
Kenneth Hobson...............................Guy Robertson
Lucy's Grandma in 1867.......................Jacquelyn Hunter
Lucy's Grandpa in 1867.......................Lynn Berry
Harry Jones..................................Jay Hanna
Gertie.......................................Georgia O'Ramey
Specialty Dancers—Frances Grant and Ted Wings; Mary Haun and Galdino Sedano; Margaret and Elizabeth Keene and Frederick Renoff

Act I—Scene 1—The Old Swimmin' Hole. Scene 2—The Front Stoop of Lucy's House. Scene 3—Daniel Brown's Store, Down Town, N. Y. Scene 4—A Rehearsal of "The Coachman's Heart." Scene 5—Kenneth Hobson's California Garden. Act II.—Scene 1—Spanish Courtyard. Scene 2—At a Chinese Party. Scene 3—Screen Garden. Scene 4—A Musicale. Scene 5—The Jolly Roger; a Fashionable Inn. Staged by Julian Mitchell.

"A SERPENT'S TOOTH"

A drama in three acts by Arthur Richman. Produced by John Golden at the Little Theatre, New York, August 24, 1922.

Cast of characters —

Fanny..Josephine Williams
Jerry Middleton..............................Leslie Howard
Mildred Sherwood.............................Anne Sutherland
Alice Middleton..............................Marie Tempest
Bert Boyd....................................Howard Freeman
Morgan Trendell..............................W. Graham Browne
Janet Trendell...............................Ann Merrick
Percival Faraday.............................Robert Lowe
A Caterer....................................John Clements

In Mrs. Middleton's Apartment, New York. Staged by Robert Milton.

Alice Middleton, a widow, has pampered a thoughtless son until suddenly she discovers that she has reared a gambler, liar and cheat. Hearing that the boy has become engaged to marry the daughter of an old friend who is rich, she is tempted to carry off the match, but learning to love the girl, she falters at last and confesses the truth about her son. She has been a bad mother, she says, and her boy is a bad boy. No honest girl could hope for happiness as his wife. The girl, however, clings to her faith in the boy, and on his promise to reform the engagement is permitted to stand. Mrs. Middleton thereupon marries the girl's father.

"GEORGE WHITE'S SCANDALS OF 1922"

A musical revue in two acts, book by White, Fields and Rice; music by George Gershwin; lyrics by De Sylva and Goetz. Produced by George White at the Globe Theatre, New York, Aug. 28, 1922.

Principals engaged —

George White
Lester Allen
W. C. Fields
Jack McGowan
Franklyn Ardell
Pearl Regay
Coletta Ryan
Richard Bold
The Temple Quartet
The Argentines

Paul Whiteman's Orchestra. Staged by Mr. White.

"THE GINGHAM GIRL"

A musical comedy in three acts by Daniel Kusell; music by Albert Von Tilzer; lyrics by Neville Fleeson. Produced by Laurence Schwab and Daniel Kusell at the Earl Carroll Theatre, New York, August 28, 1922.

Cast of characters —

Gus....................Edgar Hamilton
Conductor....................James T. Ford
Silas O'Day....................Walter F. Jones
Jack Hayden....................Russell Mack
Libby O'Day....................Louise Allen
Mary Thompson....................Helen Ford
Harrison Bartlett....................Alan Edwards
Mildred Ripley....................Eleanor Dawn
John Cousins....................Eddie Buzzell
Mazie Lelewer....................Dolly Lewis
Sonya Maison....................Bertee Beaumont
Sophia Trask....................Amelia Summerville
Waiter....................George Henry
Mimi....................Helene Coyne
Armand....................Henri French
Pauline....................Valdene Smith
Paulette....................Dorothy Faye Smith
Butler....................Jack Mosser
Rose....................Mildred Quinn
Ann....................Maude Lydiate

THE YOUNG LADIES WHO DANCE

Elsie Lombard, Maude Lydiate, Bobby Breslau, Bernice Goesling, Mildred Quinn, Lucille Moore, Lillian Thomas, Claire Martin

Act I.—Center Street, Crossville Corners, New Hampshire. Act II.—Scene 1—A Café, New York City. Scene 2—A Studio Down Greenwich Village Way. Act III.—An Office, New York City.

John Cousins, a small town "hick" with plenty of nerve, decides to give New York the advantage of his superior intellect. He leaves New Hampshire, and is later followed to Broadway by his sweetheart, Mary Thompson. John has a lot of fun, and many adventures, in Greenwich Village. Mary succeeds in establishing herself in a cookie factory. After which Mary wins John away from the sirens and puts him in the cookie business.

"THE TORCH BEARERS"

A satirical comedy in three acts by George Kelly. Produced by Rosalie Stewart and Bert French at the Forty-eighth Street Theatre, New York, August 29, 1922.

Cast of characters —

Jenny....Mary Gildea
Frederic Ritter....Arthur Shaw
Paula....Mary Boland
Mrs. J. Duro Pampinelli....Allison Skipworth
Mr. Spindler....Edward Reese
Nelly Fell....Helen Lowell
Mr. Hosselrosse....Douglas Garden
Teddy Spearing....William Castle
Florence McCrickett....Rose Mary King
Mr. Twiller....Booth Howard
The Stage Manager....J. A. Curtis
Mrs. Sheppard....Daisy Atherton

Act I.—Drawing Room in Home of Frederic Ritter. Act II.—Behind the Scenes at Horticultural Hall. Act III.—Same as Act I. Time—The Present. Staged by George Kelly.

Fred Ritter returns home to find Mrs. Ritter up to her eyebrows in amateur theatricals. She has been called in by Mrs. J. Duro Pampinelli to play a part in a Little Theatre production of a one-act play, a part which another lady was forced to relinquish after her husband, on seeing her act, had suddenly suffered a fatal heart stroke. Mr. Ritter, being a plain, blunt person, without imagination, is also visibly affected when he catches a glimpse of Mrs. Ritter at rehearsal and later on the stage. He thereupon puts his foot down and declares that either there will be no actresses in his home, or there will be no home. And Mrs. Ritter promises to be good.

"SO THIS IS LONDON"

A comedy in three acts by Arthur Goodrich. Produced by George M. Cohan at the Hudson Theatre, New York, August 30, 1922.

Cast of characters —

Hiram Draper (Junior)....................Donald Gallaher
Eleanor Beaucamp....................Marie Carroll
Lady Amy Ducksworth....................Lily Cahill
Hiram Draper....................Edmund Breese
Mrs. Hiram Draper....................Leah Winslow
A Flunkey at the Ritz....................Edward Jephson
Sir Percy Beaucamp....................Lawrence D'Orsay
Lady Beaucamp....................Marion Grey
Alfred Honeycutt....................Wallace Widdecombe
Thomas....................John M. Troughton
Jennings....................Robert Vivian

Act I.—Draper's Suite at the Ritz. Act II.—Sir Percy Beaucamp's Living Room at Brimshot. Act III.—Lady Ducksworth's Drawing Room. Time—The Present. Staged by John Meehan.

Hiram Draper, Jr., son of a wealthy and excessively American shoe manufacturer, meets Eleanor Beaucamp, daughter of Sir Percy Beaucamp, a fearfully insular British shoe manufacturer, on board ship. The young people are attracted to each other and an engagement results. Arrived in London their respective parents violently oppose any suggestion of a match. Draper senior pictures the English as a ludicrous set of haw-hawing nincompoops (which picture is revealed in a comedy interlude) and Sir Percy sees the Americans as gum and tobacco-chewing monstrosities (also acted). When the Drapers and the Beaucamps really meet, however, they are surprised and, in a measure, delighted to make the best of their children's determination to unite the families—and the rival shoe factories.

"HER TEMPORARY HUSBAND"

A farcical comedy in three acts by Edward A. Paulton. Produced by H. H. Frazee at the Frazee Theatre, New York, August 31, 1922.

Cast of characters —

Doctor Gordon Spencer....................George Parsons
Kate Tanner....................Selena Royle
Judd....................Harry R. Allen
Blanche Ingram....................Ann Andrews
Tom Burton....................William Courtenay
Clarence Topping....................Henry Mortimer

Act I.—Highcliff Sanitarium. Act II.—Blanche's Summer Cottage. Act III.—Same as Act II. Time—The Present.

Blanche Ingram wants to marry Clarence Topping, but her father's will provides that if she does she loses a fortune. She schemes, therefore, to marry another man first, preferably a weak, sickly man, and when she is legally a widow with a fortune to call back for Clarence. She seeks a husband with one foot in the grave at a sanitarium for incurables. Hearing of the conspiracy, Tom Burton, an adventurous young buck, and a friend of the sanitarium doctor, hides himself behind green glasses and a set of whiskers, substitutes for Blanche's incurable, and later comes out from behind the whiskers and wins the heiress for himself.

"MOLLY DARLING"

A musical comedy in two acts by Otto Harbach and William Cary Duncan; music by Tom Johnstone; lyrics by Phil Cook. Produced by Moore and Megley at the Liberty Theatre, New York, Sept. 1, 1922.

Cast of characters —

Henri Ricardo....................Albert Roccardi
"Chic" Jiggs....................Jack Donahue
Ted Miller....................Billy Taylor
Trix Morton....................Billie Taylor

Molly Ricardo....................................Mary Milburn
Marivane....................................Catherine Mulqueen
Oliver....................................Cecil Summers
Mrs. Redwing....................................Emma Janvier
Jack Stanton....................................Clarence Nordstrom
Chauncey Chesbro....................................Hal Forde
"Spirit of Eve"....................................Nina Penn
Archie Ames....................................Jay Gould
Timmy....................................Ben Benny
Tommy....................................Burke Wilson

Act I.—Scene 1—Ricardo's Workshop. Scene 2—Mrs. Redwing's Estate. Act II.—Scene 1—Ricardo's Music Store. Scene 2—"Chic's" News-Stand. Scene 3—Reception Room, Melody Hall. Scene 4—Grand Salon, Melody Hall. Scene 5—A Fantasy of the Orient. Scene 6—The Spirit of the Disc. Scene 7—Westinghouse Broadcasting Station—"WJZ." Staged by Julian Mitchell.

Molly Ricardo's father is a good musician but a poor provider. Molly writes a song which fails to please so long as it is sung as she intended it should be. But when it is properly "jazzed" it sells for $75,000 and saves Signor Ricardo from being dispossessed in the last act. "Chic" Jiggs, a friendly comedian, helps Mary put the song over.

"BETTER TIMES"

A musical spectacle by R. H. Burnside; music by Raymond Hubbell. Produced by Charles Dillingham at the Hippodrome, New York, Sept. 2, 1922.

Principals engaged —

Happy Lambert
Nanette Flack
Virginia Futrelle
Patrick and Francisco
Marceline
Torbay
Robert McClellan
George Herman
Claudius and Scarlet
The Orlandos
The Three Bobs
The Bell Brothers
The Berlo Sisters
Frank Johnson
Long Tack Sam and Co.
Powers' Elephants

Staged by R. H. Burnside.

"THE ENDLESS CHAIN"

A drama in three acts by James Forbes. Produced by A. L. Erlanger at the Cohan Theatre, New York, Sept. 4, 1922.

Cast of characters —

Nellie Webb	Olive May
Vera Payton	Martha Mayo
Lulu Densmore	Vera Halare
Amy Reeves	Margaret Lawrence
Kenneth Reeves	Kenneth MacKenna
Valentine Webb	Kenneth Hunter
Billy Densmore	Harry Stubbs
Andrew Hale	Harry Minturn

The scenes of the play are laid at the Hotel Florentine, New York City. Staged by James Forbes.

Amy Reeves, wife of Kenneth Reeves, is jealous of the success of her young husband's inferiors. To advance his interests she adopts the methods of the gaudy set in New York and seeks to win the favor of a wealthy man in whose power it is to give Kenneth a fine position. Her affair with Andrew Hale, the wealthy man in question, becomes so involved that it excites the suspicion of the husband and a scandal is threatened. Amy and Kenneth escape the more serious consequences of the situation and determine to make a fresh start.

"SALLY, IRENE AND MARY"

A musical comedy in two acts by Eddie Dowling and Cyrus Wood; lyrics by Raymond Klages; music by J. Fred Coots. Produced by the Messrs. Shubert at the Casino Theatre, New York, Sept. 4, 1922.

Cast of characters —

Jimmie Dugan	Eddie Dowling
Mrs. Dugan	Josie Intropidi
Mary O'Brien	Edna Morn
Mrs. O'Brien	Maude Odell
Sally	Jean Brown
Mrs. Clancy	Clara Palmer
Irene	Kitty Flynn
Rodman Jones	Hal Van Rensselaer
Mrs. Jones	Winifred Harris

Clarence Edwards..........Alfred Gerrard
Mr. Myers..........Joseph Clark
Percy Fitzgerald..........Burford Hampden
Al Cleveland..........Stanley Ford
Sully..........D. J. Sullivan
Tony..........D. J. Sullivan
Mr. Mulcahey..........Eddie O'Connor
Dinty Moore..........Gene Collins
Frank..........William Mason
First Dresser to Girls..........Henrietta Byron
Second Dresser to Girls..........Louise Arnold
Detective of Hotel Astor..........Frank Binns
Carriage Man, Hotel Astor..........Fred Packard
Kitty Kelly..........Helen Heller
Mabel Riley..........Mabel Kokin
Tommy..........Bonna O'Dear
Nellie Smith..........Mary Corday
Mrs. Pomeroy Gilbert..........Bonna O'Dear
Mrs. Kelly Pool..........Henrietta Byron
Mrs. Fitzgibbons Conroy..........Louise Arnold
Mrs. Carter Smith..........Helen Heller
Mrs. De La Croix..........Mabel Kokin
Mrs. Fitzroy..........Genise Corday
Staged by Frank Smithson. Under supervision J. J. Shubert.

Sally, Irene and Mary are three little girls living in the tenement district of New York. They are given a chance on the stage by a theatrical manager, and within a year are the talk of the town. Jimmie Dugan, a young plumber engaged to Mary, having saved his money and bought a Ford, follows Mary to Broadway, but discovers that she has entered the Rolls-Royce set. Her love remains true to Jimmie, however, and in the end they are happily married.

"HUNKY DORY"

A comedy in three acts by Macdonald Watson. Produced by Marc Klaw, Inc., at the Klaw Theatre, New York, September 4, 1922.

Cast of characters —

A Postman..........Angus Adam
Jenny..........Nell Barker
Polly..........Stella Campbell
Hunky Dory..........Walter Roy
Specky Todd..........Robert Drysdale
Mrs. Macfadyen..........Frances Ross Campbell
Peter Maguffie..........Macdonald Watson
David Low..........F. Manning Sproston

Act I.—The Shop of Specky Todd. Act II.—The Home of Hunky Dory. Act III.—Same as Act II. The Scenes Are Laid in a Lowland Scottish Village.

"THE PLOT THICKENS"

A comedy in three acts from the Italian of Luigi Barzini and Arnaldo Fraccaroli, adapted by Thomas Beer. Produced by Brock Pemberton at the Booth Theatre, New York, Sept. 5, 1922.

Cast of characters —

Adonis Duckworth.........................Edwin Nicander
Joseph.........................Roy Cochrane
Olivotti.........................Jasper Mangione
Halliday.........................Fred House
Claudine Dupont.........................Remy Carpen
Benjamin Playfair Jones.........................John Thorn
Bill.........................Albert Bannister
First Player.........................Russell Morrison
Second Player.........................Neil Quinlan
Third Player.........................John Saunders
Basil Fanshawe.........................Edward Lester
Mike Sheehan.........................Dallas Welford
Mike Sheehan, Junior.........................Dwight Frye
Grizzel McNab.........................Janet Murdock
Police Commissioner.........................Joseph R. Mann
Dr. Maggs.........................Jack Amory

Act I.—Adonis Duckworth's Long Island Estate. Act II.—Claudine's Boudoir, New York City. Act III.—Same as Act I. Staged by Brock Pemberton.

Adonis Duckworth, rich and bored with life, engages a moving picture director to jolt him with a few thrills. By the terms of the bargain the thrills are to come as a surprise. The night the director is supposed to start work, Adonis' fiancée appoints a rendezvous with the chief seducer of the movie troupe and burglars enter his house and steal a sack of antiques and an automobile. Because he will not accept his catastrophe seriously, his friends and relatives try to put Adonis in an insane asylum. He has considerable trouble getting hold of the movie director in time to save himself.

"WILD OATS LANE"

A melodrama in three acts by George Broadhurst, based on Gerald Beaumont's story, "The Gambling Chaplain." Produced by George Broadhurst at the Broadhurst Theatre, New York, Sept. 6, 1922.

Cast of characters —

Father Joe	Maclyn Arbuckle
The Up-and-Down Kid	Richard Barbee
The Professor	Douglas Wood
Smiley Kirk	Daniel Davis
Jimmy the Fox	James Bradbury, Jr.
Anthony Reynolds	Howard Nugent
Big Ed	John Ellis
Oregon Jeff	James Jefferson
Police Sergeant	Thomas Gunn
Sweet Marie	Marion Coakley
June	Edna May Oliver
Rose O'Connell	Hope Sutherland
Mlle. Helene	Judith Vosselli
Alethea Evans	Florence Earle
Fay Reynolds	Camilla Lyon
The Duchess	Margaret Nugent
Mrs. Mannering	Eda von Buelow
Caroline Cummings	Pauline Breustedt

The Action of the Play Takes Place in the Home of Father Joe. Time—The Present. Place—A City in the U. S.
Staged by Mrs. Trimble Bradley.

Father Joe, a democratic member of the priesthood, seeking to help the residents of a tough part of the city known as Wild Oats Lane, takes charge of a "get-away fund" left by a Chicago gambler to help criminals escape the law. Among those who apply for aid is "The Up-and-Down Kid," whose previous love affair with "Sweet Marie" has sent that unfortunate into the Lane. Through his kindly and diplomatic friendship Father Joe is able to reform the Kid and to gain his forgiveness of "Sweet Marie."

"A FANTASTIC FRICASSEE"

A musical revue in fifteen scenes. Produced by Marguerite Abbott Barker at the Greenwich Village Theatre, New York, Sept. 11, 1922.

Principals engaged —

Bobby Edwards	Jimmy Kemper
Dorothy Smoller	Edwin Strawbridge
Jean White	John Decker
Jeannette MacDonald	Leland Morris
Jay Strong	Suzanne Ciamia
Roy Shield's Orchestra	Dolores Farris
Andre Chotin	William Jordan

Directed by Andre Chotin

"THE GREENWICH VILLAGE FOLLIES"

A revue in two acts, book and lyrics by George V. Hobart, John Murray Anderson and Irving Ceasar; music by Louis A. Hirsch. Produced by Bohemians, Inc., at the Shubert Theatre, New York, Sept. 12, 1922.

Principals engaged —

John Hazzard	Lucille Chalfonte
Bert Savoy	Frankie Heath
Jay Brennan	Marjorie Peterson
Carl Randall	Julia Silvers
George Rasely	Yvonne Georges
John Sheehan	Harriette Gimbel
Alexander Yakoleff	George Clifford
Eugenia Repelsky	Helen McDonald

Staged by John Murray Anderson.

"WHY MEN LEAVE HOME"

A comedy in three acts by Avery Hopwood. Produced by Wagenhals and Kemper at the Morosco Theatre, New York, Sept. 12, 1922.

Cast of characters —

Butler..Minor Watson
Grandma..Jessie Villars
Tom..John McFarlane
Fifi..Florence Shirley

Nina....Theresa Maxwell Conover
Betty....Audrey Hart
Sybil....Isabel Leighton
Billy....Norval Keedwell
Artie....Herbert Yost
Sam....Paul Everton
Doris....Wauna Loraine
Maid....Peggy Lytton

The Scene of the Play is Long Island. The Time—The Present. Staged by Collin Kemper.

Tom, Artie and Sam have been spending the summer at home alone while their respective mates, Fifi, Betty and Nina, have been touring Europe. These wives have a way of leaving their husbands frequently. This time they are horrified to find on their return that the husbands threaten to rebel. They do rebel, in fact. Tom, at least, tells Fifi, that he is through with the kind of life she has been leading him. He had hoped he had married a wife, not a Cook's tourist. Fifi tries all her arts to win him back, including the display of a gorgeous negligée guaranteed by the maker to interest even a husband. But Tom will not be mollified—not before the last act. Then all the wives are properly subdued and all the husbands happily triumphant.

"DREAMS FOR SALE"

A play in three acts by Owen Davis. Produced by William A. Brady at the Playhouse, New York, September 13, 1922.

Cast of characters —

Jane Baldwin....Katherine Grey
Rufus Baldwin....Edward Emery
Martha....Grace Wooding
Jim Griswold....Donald Cameron
Mildred Pope....Rose Burdick
Tommy Kerr....Raymond Hackett
Anne Baldwin....Helen Gahagan
Terry....James Donlin
Peter Nash....William Holden
"Little Joe"....Luis Alberni

Bill Fallon............................Patrick Henry Crosby
Arthur Nash....................................John Bohn
Rosalie Fallon...............................Mary Brittain
Act I.—The Living Room of Rufus Baldwin's Home in a Large New England City. Act II.—Scene 1—The North Line of the "Baldwin Property," in the Forests of Aroostook County, Me. Scene 2—Jim Griswold's Cabin. Act III.—The Baldwin Camp on Partridge Lake. Staged by William A. Brady.

For twenty years there has been a Nash-Baldwin feud, started when Rufus Baldwin refused to let his sister marry Peter Nash. Anne Baldwin, three times expelled from college, returns home interested in, if not engaged to, Peter Nash's nephew, Arthur. She is really in love, however, with Jim Griswold, the sweetheart of her girlhood. If she will marry Arthur, says the elder Nash, he will forget the hurt the Baldwins did him and save them from a business smash that he has engineered to threaten them. This starts the old feud all over again. Anne, forced to choose between her lovers, accepts Arthur but throws him over for Jim, after she shoots that young man and realizes how much he means to her. A planned explosion settles both the feud and the question of business supremacy, and the marital plans of the neighborhood.

"THE AWFUL TRUTH"

A comedy in three acts by Arthur Richman. Produced by Charles Frohman at the Henry Miller Theatre, New York, September 18, 1922.

Cast of characters —

Daniel Leeson..................................Paul Harvey
Eustace Trent..........................George K. Barraud
Jayson ....Lewis A. Sealy
Lucy Warriner....................................Ina Claire
Mrs. Leeson............................Louise Mackintosh
Josephine Trent..........................Cora Witherspoon
Norman Satterly...............................Bruce McRae
Celeste.......................................Kyra Alanowa
Rufus Kempster..........................Raymond Walburn
Act I.—Eustace Trent's. Act II.—Lucy Warriner's. Act III.—Lucy Warriner's.

Lucy Warriner, divorced from Norman Satterly, has engaged herself to marry Daniel Leeson, a wealthy but rather uncouth Westerner from the open spaces, also known as God's own country. Leeson has heard rumors of a scandal connected with Lucy's divorce and asks that the matter be cleared up to his own and his suspicious aunt's satisfaction. Lucy thereupon sends for her first husband to satisfy her prospective second husband that there was nothing she need be ashamed of in the proceedings having to do with her legal release from matrimony. Satterly is pleased to oblige, and happy to lie like a gentleman. But while he is doing it he falls in love with Lucy all over again and ends by remarrying her, while Leeson, just as well pleased at his escape, returns to the West.

"IT'S A BOY!"

A comedy in three acts by William A. McGuire. Produced by Sam H. Harris at the Sam H. Harris Theatre, New York, Sept. 19, 1922.

Cast of characters —

Judson Blake.............................John Daly Murphy
Mary Grayson..................................Jean Adair
Chester Blake...............................Robert Ames
William O'Toole..........................Charles Lawrence
Phyllis Blake............................Dorothy Mackaye
Marjorie Fletcher.........................Hortense Alden
Rev. David Talbot.............................Peter Lang
R. W. Pendleton...........................Joseph Kilgour
Rita Pendleton...........................Millicent Hanley
Kenneth Holmes............................Richard Pitman
Maurice Hemmendinger....................James R. Waters

Prologue—The Living Room of Chester Blake's Home in Carbondale, Pa. Act I.—The Same. Act II.—The Blakes' Home. Act III.—The Same. Staged by Sam Forrest.

The Chester Blakes, one year married and living happily in a Pennsylvania town, are expecting a baby. When it arrives it's a boy and the Blakes are wonderfully contented and ready to stay on in their own home town indefinitely. Chester has become the young Woolworth of the village and everything is rosy. Then comes an offer from a real Woolworth in New York to take Chester to the big city at a $10,000-a-year salary. Chester doesn't want to go, considering his home prospects of more importance, but Mrs. Chet is eager for the adventure and they go. In New York they acquire a bootlegger, a lot of jewelry bills, a swell flat, and expensive friends. Then Chester loses his job and things look fearfully black. In the adjustment the Blakes return to the simple life, broke but ready to begin over again.

"ORANGE BLOSSOMS"

A comedy with music in three acts by Fred de Gresac from the play "La Passerelle," by Fred de Gresac and Francis de Croisset; music by Victor Herbert; lyrics by B. G. de Sylva. Produced by Edward Royce at the Fulton Theatre, New York, Sept. 19, 1922.

Cast of characters —

Lawyer Brassac	Pat Somerset
Tillie	Queenie Smith
Octave	Maurice Darcy
Baron Roger Belmont	Robert Michaels
Kitty	Edith Day
Jimmy Flynn	Hal Skelley
Helene de Vasquez	Phyllys Le Grand
Auguste	Robert Fischer
Ninetta	Nancy Welford
BRASSAC'S CLIENTS	
Cecilia Malba	Evelyn Darville
Christiane de Mirandol	Alta King
Julie Bresil	Dagmar Oakland
Yolande Du Pont	Emily Drange
Paulette de Trevors	Fay Evelyn
Simone Garrick	Diana Stegman
Regina Marnac	Eden Gray
Valentine Vendome	Vera de Wolfe
GENTLEMEN IN THE CASE	
Thomas Fitzpatrick	Abner Barnart
Frank Curran	Jack Whiting

Oliver Stewart .... Gayle Mays
Denny Murray .... Clinton Merrill

DANCERS

Queenie Smith, Elva Pomfret, Nancy Welford, Mary Lucas

Act I.—Lawyer's Office, Paris. Act II.—Kitty's Villa at Cannes. Act III.—Garden of Kitty's Villa at Cannes.
Staged by Edward Royce.

This musicalized version of "The Marriage of Kitty" follows the original story closely. Kitty, in from the country looking for a job, agrees to marry the Baron Roger Belmont and divorce him immediately so that he can collect an inheritance denied him by the will of a relative if he marries the Brazilian dancer with whom he is in love. Discovering Kitty to be much more charming than his Brazilian, Roger changes his mind after they are married and refuses to go through with the divorce, which is as Kitty planned it in the first place.

"PASSING SHOW OF 1922"

A musical revue; book and lyrics by Harold Atteridge; music by Alfred Goodman. Produced by the Messrs. Lee and J. J. Shubert at the Winter Garden, New York, September 20, 1922.

Principals engaged —

Willie Howard	Mlle. Alcorn
Eugene Howard	Francis Renault
George Hassell	Janet Adair
Sam Ash	Fooshee Sisters
Fred Allen	The Lockfords
Nat Nazarro, Jr.	The Macweys
Arthur Margetson	Gertrude Lang

Staged by J. C. Huffman; supervised by J. J. Shubert.

"BANCO"

A comedy in three acts adapted by Clare Kummer from the French by Alfred Savoir. Produced by William Harris, Jr. at the Ritz Theatre, New York, Sept. 20, 1922.

Cast of characters —

Charlotte..Lola Fisher
Porter..Hall Higley
Louis..Edward G. Robinson
Baron Henri Delignieres........................Francis Byrne
Julie..Alice John
George Dalou..Robert Strange
Feydal..J. Malcolm Dunn
Count Alexandre de Lussac (nicknamed "Banco"),
Alfred Lunt
Baroness Delignieres........................Charlotte Granville

Act I.—Waiting Room of the Casino at La Baule. Act II.—Living Room of the Delignieres' Chateau in Touraine. Act III.—Charlotte's Bedroom. Time—The Present. Staged by Robert Milton.

Charlotte, wife of Count Alexander de Lussac, whose fondness for baccarat has earned him the sobriquet of "Banco," calls at the Casino where her husband is playing and sends him word that she will stay there until he is finished. The Count, angered by her interference, sends word back that he will continue to play so long as she remains in the building. For eighty-four hours they stick it out. Then Charlotte gives in, goes home, and gets a divorce. A year later she is married to an insipid country squire. The night of her wedding "Banco" breaks into her room and contrives to get her new husband out. To keep him in a respectable state of mind Charlotte is obliged to play cards with "Banco" till dawn. Then he convinces her that she still loves him and that he is worthy her forgiveness. Whereupon Charlotte goes away to apply for an annulment of her second marriage, probably on the ground that it never has been consummated.

"EAST OF SUEZ"

A play in five scenes by W. Somerset Maugham. Produced by A. H. Woods at the Eltinge Theatre, New York, September 21, 1922.

Cast of characters —

Harold Knox....................................Geoffrey Kerr
Wu...Nathaniel Sack
Henry Anderson.................................Leonard Mudie
Amah...Catherine Proctor
George Conway..................................John Halliday
Daisy..Florence Reed
Lee Tai Cheng..................................Howard Lang
Sylvia Knox....................................Gypsy O'Brien
A Buddhist Priest..............................John Spencer
An Acolyte.....................................Miss Koven

Scene I.—A Small Verandah on an Upper Story of the British-American Tobacco Company's Premises. Scene II.—The Temple of Fidelity and Virtuous Inclination. Scene III.—The Sitting Room in the Andersons' Part of the Temple. Scene IV.—The Courtyard in the Andersons' Part of the Temple. Scene V.—The Sitting Room in the Andersons' Part of the Temple. Time of Action—Now. Place—Pekin, China.

George Conway, attached to the British legation in Pekin, discovers that his best friend, Henry Anderson, has become engaged to marry Daisy, a beautiful Eurasian whose English father had had her educated in England. Conway had known Daisy years before, and been deeply in love with her, but had not married her, both because she was a half-caste and because he knew that she had had other lovers. Realizing it is too late to save his friend, Conway makes the best of the situation. After the wedding he tries to see as little as possible of Daisy, but is gradually fascinated by her anew. When he can no longer bear the humiliation of his treachery to his friend, he kills himself.

"THE EXCITERS"

A comedy in four acts by Martin Brown. Produced by the Selwyns at the Times Square Theatre, New York, September 22, 1922.

Cast of characters —

Ermintrude Marilley	Enid Markey
Lexington Dalrymple	Chester Morris
Mrs. Hilary Rand	Thais Lawton
"Rufus" Rand	Tallulah Bankhead
Hilary Rand	Marsh Allen
Mr. Rackham	Frederick Karr
Sumter Dalrymple	Robert Hyman
Vaughn	Florence Flinn
Dan MacGee	Allan Dinehart
Chauffeur	Albert Marsh
Joselyn Basset-Brown	Echlin Gayer
Seymour Katz	Wright Kramer
Miss Files	Aline MacMahon
Flash Fagan	Roy Gordon
St. Joe	Edwin Walter
First Man	Jerry Hart
Second Man	Sidney Dudley

Act I.—The Lounge at the Rands' Place on Long Island. Act II.—In Rufus' Room. Act III.—The Offices of the World-Wide Banner and Emblem Co. Act IV.—In Rufus' Room. Time—The Present. Staged by Edgar Selwyn.

"Rufus" Rand, eighteen, beautiful and restless, is bored stiff with life in general. She is one of a group of equally blasé young persons who have banded themselves together as "The Exciters," agreeing to take every opportunity to start anything that will furnish a thrill. On the way to a party, Rufus unintentionally skids her car into a ditch and suffers a temporary paralysis of the spine. Brought home there is danger she may die before morning. If she dies unwed the family will lose a fortune. In her semi-conscious state she cries aloud for a husband. The only available man is a burglar, who has been trapped by the sudden return of the family to the house. Rufus insists on marrying him. Months later, discovering the burglar to be good-looking and interesting, she refuses to get a divorce, much to the consternation of her family but to the great joy of the other exciters. A way is found eventually to give "Rufus" the thrill of her young life. He wasn't a burglar at all.

"LA TENDRESSE"

A drama in three acts by Henry Bataille. Produced at the Empire Theatre, New York, Sept. 25, 1922.

Cast of characters —

Monseigneur de Cabriac	Elmer Brown
Paul Barnac	Henry Miller
Marthe Dellieres	Ruth Chatterton
Mademoiselle Louise	Marguerite St. John
Aubin	Louis Le Bay
Colette	Elfin Finn
Jacques	William Pearce
The Governess	Norma Havey
Fernal	H. Cooper-Cliffe
Legardier	Edward Mackay
Mlle. Tigraine	Mary Fowler
Carlos Jarry	Sydney Riggs
Count de Jalligny	Jean de la Cruz
Julian d'Ablincourt	William Hanley
Alain Sergyll	Ronald Colman
Guerin	A. G. Andrews
Mlle. Morel	Florence Fair

The Action Occurs in Barnac's House in Paris. Staged by Henry Miller.

Paul Barnac, the finest dramatist in France, has been living happily with his favorite actress, Marthe Dellieres, who is a widow and the mother of two children. She is, however, several years younger than he, and when his best friends, thinking to save him humiliation, intimate that she is unfaithful, he is supremely unhappy. To quiet his jealousy Barnac sets a trap for his young mistress, stationing stenographers back of a curtain when he is supposed to be out of town. Later he reads to her, as though it were a scene from a new play, an extract from her conversation with a younger lover in which their relations are plainly revealed. As punishment Barnac sends Marthe away, but two years later his loneliness bids him call her back. He can do without love, he sighs, but he cannot do without tenderness, and if she will only be a little kind to him he will be happy. Loving him deeply, for all her other interests, Marthe agrees to that arrangement.

"SPITE CORNER"

A comedy in three acts by Frank Craven. Produced by John Golden at the Little Theatre, New York, Sept. 25, 1922.

Cast of characters —

Isabel Burgess	Eva Condon
Anne Coolidge	Marie L. Day
Eben Gooch	Percy Pollock
Cap'n Parker	James Seeley
Elizabeth Dean	Madge Kennedy
Mrs. Douthett	Mattie Keene
Nathan Lattimer	Stephen Maley
Mr. Nelson	George Gorman
John Lattimer	Jason Robards
Mme. Florence	Beatrice Noyes
Mr. Dana	John Keefe
Mr. Allen	Sam Coit

The Scene of the Play is the Shop and the Home of Elizabeth Dean in the Town of Dean.

Before Elizabeth Dean was born in the town of Dean, which was founded by her father's people, there had been a Dean-Lattimer family feud. During the feud the Lattimers hated the Deans quite as much, if not more than, the Deans hated the Lattimers. But as Elizabeth grew up, and as John Lattimer grew up, the feud became silly to them and they decided to have nothing to do with it. In fact they became practically engaged. Then John went away to make the necessary fortune, while Elizabeth stayed on in her little shop, she being the modiste of the village. Five years passed, John forgot to write after the first two, and Elizabeth tried to forget him. Then old Nathan Lattimer had a stroke and John came home. He came to see Elizabeth first, but he said nothing about their engagement. And he saw no prospect of their getting married, which so angered Elizabeth that when Nathan Lattimer wanted to buy her store and the lot on which it stood to put up a fine business block in Dean, she swore she would never sell, just for spite. She did sell, however, though it took a lot of persuading, and of course she married John.

"ON THE STAIRS"

A drama in three acts by William Hurlbut. Produced by Joseph E. Shea at the Playhouse, New York, Sept. 25, 1922.

Cast of characters —

Luella....Mrs. Charles G. Craig
Mr. Gregg....Fuller Mellish
Mrs. Belmore....Frances Anderson
Elsa Carroll....Margaret Dale
Barak....Effingham Pinto
Merritt Lane....James C. Crane
Swami Ahbukevanda....Arnold Daly
Weatherby....Bennett Southard
Culhane....Lionel Glenister
Jenkinson....Thomas A. Braidon

Act I.—Library in Elsa Carroll's House Near Greenwich. Act II.—The Stairs of the Old House. Act III.—The Same. Staged by Edgar J. MacGregor.

The Swami Ahbukevanda, as he calls himself, is in love with the heiress, Elsa Carroll, and is eager to marry her. He appears to be making considerable headway, helped by the tricks of a haunted house on the stairs of which Miss Carroll's father had been murdered, and where his ghost frequently reappears to bar the passage of those who try to ascend. But Elsa finally spurns the Swami, whereupon he tries to abduct her and is only prevented by the strong right arm of Merritt Lane and the sympathetic assistance of the author.

"ROSE BERND"

A drama in three acts by Gerhart Hauptmann. Produced by Arthur Hopkins at the Longacre Theatre, New York, Sept. 26, 1922.

Cast of characters —

Rose Bernd....Ethel Barrymore
Christopher Flamm....Dudley Digges
Arthur Streckmann....McKay Morris
Marthel Bernd....Anna Zwilinoff

Bernd....................................William B. Mack
August Kiel..................................Charles Francis
Mrs. Flamm..................................Doris Rankin
Minna..Alice Ward
Hahn..Edmund Bowen
Theresa....................................Virginia Langton
Frieda.......................................Irene Shirley
Heinzel....................................Gregory Robins
Kleinert...................................Edward LeHay
Golisch..Wilson Day
Mrs. Golisch...................................Anita Rothe
A Constable...................................John Burkell

Act I.—Scene 1—Roadside. Morning in May. Scene 2—Living Room in Flamm's Home. Act II.—Scene 1—The Spring on the Flamm Estate. Scene 2—Same as Scene 2, Act I. Act III.—Living Room in Bernd's Cottage. Staged by Arthur Hopkins.

Rose Bernd is a German peasant girl. Working in the home of Flamm, the village magistrate, and his paralytic wife, she submits to his will and later their intimacy is discovered by Streckmann, a flashy youth of the fields. The misery of Rose is doubled by Streckmann's blackmailing methods to compel her also to become friendly with him, and finally, as her situation becomes more tragic, she strangles her child and is hopelessly considering self-destruction at the play's close.

"LOYALTIES"

A drama in three acts by John Galsworthy. Produced by Charles Dillingham at the Gaiety Theatre, New York, Sept. 27, 1922.

Cast of characters —

Charles Winsor...............................H. G. Stoker
Lady Adela.................................Cathryn Young
Ferdinand De Levis............................James Dale
Treisure.....................................Henry Carvill
General Canynge..............................Felix Aylmer
Margaret Orme..........................Jeannette Sherwin
Captain Ronald Dancy, D.S.O...........Charles Quartermaine
Mabel......................................Diana Bourbon
Inspector Dede..............................Victor Tandy
Robert.......................................Deering Wells
A Constable.................................Henry Morrell
Augustus Borring............................Deering Wells
Lord St. Erth.............................Laurence Hanray

A Club Footman.............................Henry Morrell
Major Colford.............................Wilfrid Seagram
Edward Graviter.............................Henry Morrell
A Young Clerk.............................Deering Wells
Gilman.............................Victor Tandy
Jacob Twisden.............................Laurence Hanray
Ricardos.............................Henry Carvill

Act I.—Scene 1—A Dressing Room at Meldon Court, near Newmarket. Scene 2—A Bedroom at Meldon Court. Act II.—Scene 1—The Card Room of a London Club. Scene 2—The Sitting Room of a London Flat. Act III.—Scene 1—At Twisden and Graviter's in Lincoln's Inn Fields. Scene 2—The Same. Scene 3—The Sitting Room of a London Flat. Staged by Basil Dean.

(See page 116.)

"THIN ICE"

A comedy drama in three acts by Percival Knight. Produced by the Messrs. Shubert at the Comedy Theatre, New York, Sept. 30, 1922.

Cast of characters —

Whitney Nelson.............................Felix Krembs
Alan Woodruff.............................H. Dudley Hawley
Pedro De Carbille.............................C. Henry Gordon
Fuji.............................T. Tamamoto
Mr. Burbridge.............................Percival Knight
Edith Satterly.............................Olive Wyndham
Helen Whitney Nelson.............................Gilda Leary

The Home of Whitney Nelson, Westhampton, L. I. Time—Summer; the Present. Staged by Mr. Knight.

An English gentleman of family, an officer of distinction in the great war, finds himself and his family impoverished after the armistice. Coming to America, he engages himself to the Whitney Nelsons as a butler, and then discovers that Nelson was a lieutenant under him with the First Canadians overseas. In spite of the resulting embarrassment he stays on and is able to help his old buddy out of a threatened separation from Mrs. Nelson. Then he marries Nelson's sister, Edith Satterley, and returns to England.

"MALVALOCA"

A play in three acts from the Spanish of Serafin and Joaquin Alvarez Quintero; translated by Jacob S. Fassett, Jr. Produced by The Equity Players, at the Forty-eighth Street Theatre, New York, October 2, 1922.

Cast of characters —

Malvaloca..Jane Cowl
Juanela....................................Angela McCahill
Mariquita..................................Mariette Hyde
Sister Piedad.............................Lillian Albertson
Teresona.......................................Jessie Ralph
Alfonsa......................................Lenore Norvelle
Dona Enriqueta..........................Louise Closser Hale
Dionisia...................................Margaret Fareleigh
Sister Consuelo.............................Grace Hampton
Sister Dolores..............................Lalive Brownell
Sister Carmen..............................Edith Van Cleve
Leonardo..Rollo Peters
Salvador......................................Frederic Burt
Martin.....................................Marshall Vincent
Barrabas.....................................Frank I. Frayne
Tio Jerome....................................Claude Cooper
Lobito...Edward Cullen
A Workman.....................................John Parrish

Act I.—The Cloister of the old Convent of Carmen. Act II.—The foundry of "The Little Bronze Girl." Act III.—A Large Room in Leonardo's House. Staged by Augustin Duncan.

Malvaloca, a light o' love in Seville, hears that a former flame is injured and ill in a hospital in the interior of Spain. Visiting the hospital she meets Leonardo, her friend's business partner, a handsome youth and romantic. So, while Malvaloca came to visit an old love, she remains to conquer a new. Fiercer and fiercer burns the passion of Leonardo, but graver and graver grow his doubts of Malvaloca as he hears of her past. Finally, however, he is convinced that she has been remade by her great love for him. Like the great bell of the convent, that now rings out so clearly, Malvaloca's soul has been melted and recast. And they are married.

"THE YANKEE PRINCESS"

A musical comedy in three acts adapted from "Die Bajadere" of Julius Brammer and Alfred Gruemwald; book by William Le Baron; music by Emmerich Kalman; lyrics by B. G. De Sylva. Produced by A. L. Erlanger at the Knickerbocker Theatre, New York, Oct. 2, 1922.

Cast of characters —

Prince Radjami of Lahore.....Thorpe Bates
Napoleon St. Cloche.....John T. Murray
Phillipe La Tourette.....Roland Bottomley
Manager Trebizonde.....Royal Tracy
Pimprinette.....Frank Doane
Colonel Parker.....George Grahame
Dewa Singh.....Lionel Chalmers
The Rajah of Punjab.....Mortimer White
Reggie.....Colin Campbell
Chief Usher.....Valentine Winter
Odette Darimonde.....Vivienne Segal
Marietta.....Vivian Oakland
Fifi.....Ruth Lee
Marie.....Belle Miller
Yvette.....Elsie Decker
Princess Odys.....Jane Carrol
Princess Rao.....Margaret Morris
Princess Attha.....Violet Vale
Princess Lydana.....Kathleen Errol
Princess Ranja.....Evelyn Plumador
Princess Sita.....Sylvia Carol
Princess Rita.....Louise Joyce
Indian Dancer.....Princess White Deer

Act I.—Foyer of the Chatelet Theatre, Paris. Act II.—Palace of Prince Radjami, Paris. Act III.—The Directoire Club, Paris. Time—The Present. Staged by Fred G. Latham and Julian Mitchell.

In Paris Odette Darimonde, an American and more than passing fair, is the reigning musical comedy queen in an Indian opera called "Die Bajadere." Visiting the French capital is the Prince Radjami. Falling desperately in love with the young American he seeks her out and calmly informs her that, because of his hypnotic power over women, she will be unable to resist him. Apparently she agrees, and accepts his invitation to an after-the-theatre party. But at the party Odette spurns the Prince in two duets and a solo, only to admit later that she really is in love with him.

"THE LADY IN ERMINE"

A musical play in three acts; book by Frederick Lonsdale and Cyrus Wood from the book by Rudolph Schanzer and Ernest Welisch; music by Jean Gilbert and Alfred Goodman; lyrics by Harry Graham and Cyrus Wood. Produced by the Messrs. Shubert at the Ambassador Theatre, New York, Oct. 2, 1922.

Cast of characters —

Colonel Belovar	Walter Woolf
Count Adrian Beltrami	Henry Fender
Baron Sprotti-Sprotti	Ignacio Martinetti
Count Isolani	Robert Calley
Major Stogan	Timothy Daley
Dostal	Detmar Poppen
Count Busoni	Neil Evans
Mirko	Murray Minehart
Suitangi	Robert Woolsey
Sophia Lavalle	Marie Burke
Rosina	Helen Shipman
Angelina	Gladys Walton
Mariana	Wilda Bennett

Act I.—The Palm Court of the Castle Beltrami. Act II.—Picture Gallery of the Castle Beltrami. Act III.—Same as Act II. Staged by Charles Sinclair and Allan K. Foster.

Colonel Belovar, a dashing sort of military commander, quartered with his troops in the castle of Mariana, arrests a gentleman he presumes to be the lady's husband and an enemy spy. He will, says the colonel, be kind to Mariana, and to her alleged husband, if she will, in turn, be kind to him; if she will accept him as her lover even as one of her greatest ancestors, known as "The Lady in Ermine" in a famous painting, had so sacrificed herself years before to save her people. Mariana succeeds in defeating the colonel's plans, and proves at last that the arrested gentleman is her brother and not her husband. But she falls in love finally and thus the colonel is made happy with a wife instead of a sweetheart.

"THAT DAY"

A play in three acts by Louis Anspacher. Produced by Richard G. Herndon at the Bijou Theatre, New York, Oct. 3, 1922.

Cast of characters —

Geraldine Duquesne.........................Hedda Hopper
Dr. Eric McKay.........................George MacQuarrie
Lloyd.......................................Agnes Atherton
Elinor Wyndham..............................Helen Holmes
Robert Sinclair.............................Alfred Swenson
Sylvester Carhart.......................Frederick Truesdell
Mrs. Robert Sinclair.......................Frances Neilson
Mrs. Mildred Dunham.........................Betty Linley
Seymour Spencer............................Edward Fielding
Roy McKay..................................Robert Harragan

Act I.—The Sitting Room of Elinor Wyndham's Apartment in New York City. Acts II. and III.—A Room in Dr. McKay's Home in New York City. Time—The Present. Staged by B. Iden Payne.

Elinor Wyndham has been, for some months, the mistress of Robert Sinclair, who is unhappily married. Mrs. Sinclair, suspecting Robert, comes to Elinor with her suspicions, naming a widow, Mildred Dunham, as the guilty woman. Disgusted with Sinclair's double dealing, Elinor casts him off instantly and marries a former admirer, Dr. McKay. A year later Dr. McKay's brother, Roy, becomes engaged to Mildred Dunham, and the doctor, also believing Mildred to have been Sinclair's mistress, refuses his sanction to the match. Both Mildred and Roy demand an investigation, and this reveals Elinor as the woman responsible for the Sinclair mixup. Dr. McKay threatens divorce, but finally decides to forgive.

"DOLLY JORDAN"

A romantic play in four acts by B. Iden Payne. Produced by John Cort at Daly's Theatre, New York, Oct. 3, 1922.

Cast of characters —

Mrs. Bland....................Marion Abbott
Mr. Swan....................Whitford Kane
Mr. Richard Daly....................Walter Ringham
Dorothy Bland (Known as Dolly Jordan)..Josephine Victor
Mr. Tate Wilkinson....................Alphonz Ethier
George Inchbald....................Hartley Power
Mrs. Robinson....................Amelia Gardner
Mrs. Smith....................Catherine Calhoun Doucet
Mr. Hobbes....................John Rogers
Mr. Richard Ford....................Vernon Kelso
A Call-boy....................Georgie Ryan
A Bow Street Runner....................Kevitt Manton
Miss Sketchley....................Shirley Gale
Ellen....................Jill Middleton
Captain the Hon. William Bailey....................Charles Esdale
H.R.H. The Duke of Clarence....................Langhorne Burton
Landlord....................Harold Schaughency
Mr. Edward March....................Burdette Kappes
Mr. John Barton....................Reginald Carrington
Jeanette....................Denise Corday

Act I.—Mrs. Bland's Lodgings in Dublin, 1778. Act II.—Green-room of the Theatre Royal, Work, 1779. Act III.—Dolly Jordan's Sitting Room in London, 1790. Act IV.—Scene 1—A Room in the Crown Hotel, Cheltenham, 1815. Scene 2—A Garden of a House at St. Cloud, Near Paris, 1816.

Tracing the career of Dorothy Bland (afterward known as Dolly Jordan) from the days of her youth in Dublin (1778) to the peak of her success as an actress, when she became the mistress, first of Richard Ford, and, later, of the Duke of Clarence (1790). The play follows her finally to France, where she died (1816) practically an exile.

"REVUE RUSSE"

A Russian vaudeville, with costumes and scenery by Leon Bakst, Serge Soudeikine, and M. Ousounoff. Produced by Elizabeth Marbury, in association with the Messrs. Shubert, at the Booth Theatre, New York, Oct. 5, 1922.

Principals engaged —

Mme. Maria Kousnezoff
Mlle. Tanina
Mme. Leontowich
Mme. Miraeva
Mme. Platonoff
Mme. Xenia Morenschildt
Mme. Shishkina
Mme. Sanina
Mme. Smirnova

M. Boleslawski
M. Dniestroff
M. Voljanin
M. Markoff
M. Bourman
M. Ratoff
M. Posemkowski
M. Kouzoff

"R. U. R."

A fantastic melodrama by Karel Capek. Produced by The Theatre Guild at the Garrick Theatre, New York, Oct. 9, 1922.

Cast of characters —

Harry Domin....................Basil Sydney
Helena Glory....................Kathlene MacDonell
Henry Travers....................Mr. Busman
Dr. Gall....................William Devereux
Dr. Hallemeire....................Moffat Johnston
Mr. Fabry....................John Anthony
Mr. Alquist....................Louis Calvert
Nana....................Helen Westley
A Robotess....................Mary Bonestell
A Robot....................Myrtland LaVarre
Radius....................John Rutherford
Helena....................Mary Hone
Primus....................John Roche
Robots: Frederick Mark, Domis Plugge, Bernard Savage, Richard Coolidge.

Staged by Philip Moeller and Agnes Morgan.

(See page 343.)

"THE FAITHFUL HEART"

A sentimental melodrama in a prologue—two acts and an epilogue by Monckton Hoffe. Produced by Max Marcin and Frederick Stanhope at the Broadhurst Theatre, New York, October 10, 1922.

Cast of characters —

PROLOGUE, 1899

George....................................Herbert Belmore
Miss Gatterscomb..........................Daisy Belmore
Major Lestrade............................Lionel Pape
Blacky....................................Flora Sheffield
Waverly Ango..............................Tom Nesbitt
Ginger....................................Geraldine O'Brien

THE PLAY
Twenty Years Later

Sergt. Major Brabazon.....................Edward Poland
Private Mitehan...........................Peter Gardner
Lieut.-Col. Waverly Ango..................Tom Nesbitt
Edgar Wackham.............................George Thorpe
Diana Oughterson..........................Daisy Markham
Blacky II.................................Flora Sheffield
Pritachard................................Frederick Howe
George....................................Herbert Belmore
Boots.....................................Thomas Gillen

Prologue—Sitting Room in Reindeer Hotel, Southampton, England. Act I.—The Private Office of Col. Ango. Act II.—Ango's Flat in Mount Street. Epilogue—The Reindeer Hotel, Southampton, England. Staged by Frederick Stanhope.

Waverly Ango, sailor, bids good-by to his sweetheart, "Blacky," in a Southampton inn and promises to return to her at the end of his voyage. Twenty years later he is Lieut.-Col. Ango and is about to be demobilized from the army, after a brilliant career in the great war. His friends have arranged a fine marriage for him and he is mildly in love with his society fiancée, when in walks "Blacky II," his daughter by the Southampton sweetheart, who had died in giving her birth. Col. Ango hesitates momentarily, but decides his only decent course is to acknowledge the girl and stick to her, which he does, and the two of them go back to the sea, the colonel as the captain of a tramp steamer, and "Blacky II" the occupant of the only snug cabin aboard, and they bid England good-by in the same Southampton room where Waverly had left the first "Blacky" twenty odd years before.

"QUEEN O' HEARTS"

A musical comedy in two acts by Frank Mandel and Oscar Hammerstein, 2d; music by Lewis Gensler and Dudley Wilkinson; extra lyrics by Sydney Mitchell. Produced by Max Spiegel at the Cohan Theatre, New York, Oct. 10, 1922.

Cast of characters —

Tom.......................................Max Hoffman, Jr.
Grace.......................................Norma Terriss
Isabella Budd.......................................Florence Morrison
Ferdinand Budd.......................................Franker Woods
Miss Swanson.......................................Elza Petersen
Alabama (Al) Smith.......................................Georgie Brown
Elizabeth Bennett.......................................Nora Bayes
Henry Rivers.......................................Harry Richman
Myra (Mike).......................................Edna Hibbard
Dudley.......................................Dudley Wilkinson
Alfred Armstrong.......................................Lorin Raker
William Armstrong.......................................Arthur Uttry
Policeman.......................................Sidney Brook
Butler.......................................Thomas Bradley

Act I.—Fifth Floor in a Building Near Trinity Church, New York. Act II.—Home of the Armstrongs, Fairfield, N. J. Staged by Ira Hards.

Miss Bayes, as the proprietress of a matrimonial agency, borrows a friend's husband to be used as a badge of respectability while she is getting her younger sister married. The husband gets drunk and the plot complicated, as Miss Bayes grows increasingly lyrical.

"THE EVER GREEN LADY"

A comedy in four acts by Abby Merchant. Produced by David Wallace at the Punch and Judy Theatre, New York, Oct. 11, 1922.

Cast of characters —

Rhoda	Elsie Esmond
Peter O'Halloran	Robert T. Haines
Mrs. Peter O'Halloran	Jane Meredith
Madame O'Halloran	Beryl Mercer
Sheila O'Halloran	Beatrice Miles
Mrs. Fougerey	Andree Corday
Ikey Sonnenschein	Jimmie Lapsley
Rosy	Frances Lapsley
Doody	J. M. Kerrigan
John Alexander	Charles Ellis
Officer Connelly	Thomas F. Tracey
Assistant District Attorney Van Cleve	Jack Murtagh
Secretary	Albert E. Powers
Victim of the Law	Sam Janney
Policeman	Fred Callahan
Inspector Danly	Eugene Powers

Act I.—Boudoir in the O'Halloran Home, Riverside Drive, New York. Act II.—Flat on Lower Sixth Avenue. Act III.—Office of the Assistant United States District Attorney. Act IV.—Same as Act I. Staged by J. M. Kerrigan.

Peter O'Halloran, having risen rapidly to a position of wealth in New York, insists that his family shall live in accordance with their new social importance. They are all willing, except Grandma O'Halloran, who strenuously objects to being a parasite. The family goes to Palm Beach, leaving Grandma to spend a month in Lakewood, but Grandma runs away, changes places with the French laundress and spends the month in Greenwich Village, washing and ironing and brewing moonshine for the influenza patients in the tenement. The moonshine gets her into trouble and exposes her conspiracy to her shocked family.

"SWIFTY"

A comedy in three acts by John Peter Toohey and W. C. Percival. Produced by William A. Brady, Ltd., at the Playhouse, New York, Oct. 16, 1922.

Cast of characters —

Jefferson Proctor	William Holden
Chauffeur	Elmer Nicholls
Milton	Robert Ayrton
Swifty Morgan	Hale Hamilton
Tom Proctor	Humphrey Bogart
Mrs. Kimball	Grace Goodhall
Helen Kimball	Helen Scott
Miriam Proctor	Frances Howard
Alice	Margaret Mosier
First Detective	Guy Hitner
Second Detective	John O. Hewitt

The action of the play takes place in the living room of the Proctor Mansion in New York.

Swifty Morgan, ex-middleweight champion of the world, hires out as trainer to Tom Proctor, son of the wealthy Jefferson Proctor. He is to put young Proctor in good physical trim, and incidentally help him out of a scrape with a girl. When he discovers that the girl is his own sister, Swifty is of a mind to clean out the place, but decides to get even in a different way. Young Proctor has a sister, too, a fresh young flapper eager for adventure. Swifty makes love to her, plans an elopement and steals her away. He weakens, however, and they spend the night walking Fifth Avenue and going to the Plaza for breakfast. Returned home, the elder Proctor takes a hand, forcing Tom to marry Swifty's sister. Swifty and Miriam Proctor agree to give each other up, but are to meet in Florida for the flirting season.

"TO LOVE"

A drama in three acts translated by Grace George from the French of Paul Geraldy. Produced by Grace George at the Bijou Theatre, New York, Oct. 17, 1922.

Cast of characters —

Henri	Norman Trevor
Helene	Grace George
Challange	Robert Warwick

At the home of Helene and Henri. Staged by Miss George.

Helene, for ten years happily married to Henri, is conscious of a growing fascination for Challange. Every decent instinct prompts her to remain true to her husband, her home and the memory of her dead child. But every cry of her heart is a cry for the love of the intruder. Finally she gives up the fight and agrees to divorce Henri and marry Challange. But when she comes to leave Henri, and all the memories of their married life cluster around her, and when she tries to leave the home they have built together, she realizes the shallowness of her physical love for Challange, and determines to stick to Henri.

"THE FOOL"

A melodrama in four acts by Channing Pollock. Produced by Frank Reicher at the Times Square Theatre, New York, Oct. 23, 1922.

Cast of characters —

Mrs. Henry Gilliam	Maude Truax
"Dilly" Gilliam	Rea Martin
Mrs. Thornbury	Tracy L'Engle
Mr. Barnaby	George Wright
Mrs. Tice	Lillian Kemble
"Jerry" Goodkind	Lowell Sherman
Rev. Everett Wadham	Arthur Eliot
Clare Jewett	Pamela Gaythorne
George F. Goodkind	Henry Stephenson
"Charlie" Benfield	Robert Cummings

Daniel Gilchrist............................James Kirkwood
A Poor Man..............................Frank Sylvester
A Servant.................................George Le Soir
Max Stedtman..............................Geoffrey Stein
Joe Hennig..................................Rollo Lloyd
Umanski.................................Fredrik Vogeding
"Grubby"...................................Arthur Elliott
Mack.......................................Frank Sylvester
Mary Margaret...............................Sara Sothern
Pearl Hennig...........................Adrienne Morrison
Miss Levinson............................Wanda Laurence
Act I.—The Church of the Nativity, Christmas Eve, 1918.
Act II.—The Goodkinds' Home. Act III.—"Overcoat Hall."
Act IV.—Gilchrist's Room.

(See page 215.)

"MUSIC BOX REVUE"

A musical revue by Irving Berlin; lyrics and music by Irving Berlin; staged by Hassard Short. Produced by Sam H. Harris at the Music Box Theatre, New York, Oct. 23, 1922.

Principals engaged —

Grace LaRue
Charlotte Greenwood
Margaret Irving
Amelia Allen
Margaret McCarthy
Dorothy McCarthy
Fairbanks Twins
Ruth Page
John Steel
Bobby Clark
Paul McCullough
William Gaxton
William Seabury
Robinson Newbold
Rath Brothers
Stowitts

Staged by Hassard Short.

"THE LAST WARNING"

A mystery melodrama in three acts by Thomas F. Fallon, based on "The House of Fear" by Wadsworth Camp. Produced by Mindlin and Goldreyer at the Klaw Theatre, New York, Oct. 24, 1922.

Cast of characters —

Josiah Bunce.....................Worthington L. Romaine
Gene...Irene Homer
Robert Bunce...........................Clarence Derwent
Arthur McHugh.........................William Courtleigh

Richard Quaile............................Charles Trowbridge
Tommy Wall............................Victor R. Beecroft
Mike Brody............................Bert E. Chapman
Evelynda Hendon............................Marion Lord
Dolly Lymken............................Ann Mason
Harvey Carlton............................Albert Barrett
Tyler Wilkins............................James Hughes
Barbara Morgan............................Ann Winslow
Jeffreys............................John W. Moore
"Mac"............................John Hall
Joseph Byrne............................Dewey Robinson

Act I.—Woodford's Old Office in Woodford Theatre. Act II.—Stage at Woodford Theatre. Act III.—Scene 1—Same as Act I. Scene 2—Woodford Theatre.

Arthur MacHugh, who was a showman before he became a detective, goes back into the show business with the object of uncovering the murderers of one Woodford, an old-time theatre manager who was mysteriously killed in his own theatre during a performance of a drama called "The Snare" five years before the play opens. Since then Woodford's theatre has been closed and the profession believes it haunted by the dead manager's ghost. McHugh leases the theatre, assembles as many of the original cast of "The Snare" as he can find, including the leading woman, Dolly Lymken, and the stage director, Richard Quaile, and announces a revival of "The Snare." During rehearsals there are many ghostly visitations and one murder. At the performance, however, the murderer of Woodford is revealed.

"PERSONS UNKNOWN"

A melodrama by Robert Housum. Produced at the Punch and Judy Theatre, New York, Oct. 25, 1922.

Cast of characters —

Harry Sheridan............................John Miltern
Peter Sheridan............................Hugh Huntley
Blount............................Percy Carr
Margaret Lawton............................Martha Hedman
Dillon............................Averell Harris
Nicholas Gregory............................Philip Lord

Harry Sheridan, widower and amateur art collector, has suffered the loss of a valuable Rembrandt. The investigations of Detective Dillon point to the guilt of Peter Sheridan, Harry's son, as one of the conspiring thieves, a suspicion the elder Sheridan refuses to entertain. Nicholas Gregory, an old family friend recently returned from Paris, brings proof of young Peter's guilt and threatens to give it to Peter's father when Peter strikes him over the head with a cane, killing him instantly. Peter then establishes a practically perfect alibi, and the murder remains a mystery to the cast until near the close of the play, when a way out is found for all the worthy members, including Margaret Lawton, Harry Sheridan's fiancée.

"SPRINGTIME OF YOUTH"

A musical play in three acts; from the book by Bernhauser and Schanzer; lyrics by Matthew C. Woodward and Cyrus Wood; music by Walter Rollo and Sigmund Romberg. Produced by the Messrs. Shubert at the Broadhurst Theatre, New York, Oct. 26, 1922.

Cast of characters —

Nat Podmore....Walter J. Preston
Peter....J. King
Pepita....Zella Russell
Hiram Baxter....Harry McKee
Deacon Stokes....Harry Kelly
Hopkins....Larry Wood
Polly Baxter....Eleanor Griffith
Richard Stokes....J. Harold Murray
Timothy Gookin....Harry K. Morton
Keziah Hathaway....Marie Pettes
Prudence Stokes....Grace Hamilton
Priscilla Alden....Olga Steck
Squire Hathaway....Tom Williams
Roger Hathaway....George MacFarlane
Bedelia Long....Myrtle Lawrence
Christopher Long....Ben Marion
Augustus Sharp....Charles Peyton

Abigal Sharp.................................Venie Atherton
Jasper Pennifer.................................Jerome Hays
Lavina Pennifer..........................Gertrude Hillman

Act I.—A Wharf-side Street, Portsmouth, N. H. Act II.—Hiram Baxter's Living Room. Act III.—Garden of Deacon Stokes' House. Period—1812. Staged by John Harwood.

Roger Hathaway, guardian of Priscilla Alden, returns after many years to Portsmouth to find that he has been reported drowned on another ship. Remaining dead temporarily, he discovers many things—among them that his relatives are a quarreling and avaricious crowd and that Priscilla, who used to love her guardian, has hearkened to the call of youth in the person of Richard Stokes, ship's officer and tenor, and would mate with him. Which Roger Hathaway, being a baritone, recognizes as the way of the world and withdraws.

"THE WORLD WE LIVE IN"

(The Insect Comedy)

A comedy in a prelude, three acts and an epilogue by Josef and Karel Capek; adapted and arranged by Owen Davis. Produced by William A. Brady at the Jolson Theatre, New York, Oct. 31, 1922.

Cast of characters —

The Prelude—A Forest Glade

The Vagrant.................................Robert Edeson
The Professor............................N. St. Clair Hales

Act I.—The Butterflies

Apatura Iris.................................Beatrice Maude
Apatura Clythia...................................Lola Adler
Felix.................................Kenneth MacKenna
Victor.................................Rexford Kendrick
Otakar.....................................Etienne Girardot

Act II.—The Marauders

Chrysalis..Mary Blair
Male Beetle..................................Scott Cooper
Female Beetle...............................Jane Corcoran
Another Male Beetle............................Paul Irving

Ichneumon Fly.................................Edgar Norton
Its Larva.....................................Grace Dougherty
Male Cricket..................................Vinton Freedley
Female Cricket................................Mabel Withee
Parasite......................................Jasper Deeter

Act III.—The Ants

Blind Ant.....................................Paul Irving
Dictator......................................John Ward
Head of General Staff.........................N. St. Clair Hales
Commander-in-Chief of Yellow Ants....Kenneth MacKenna
Inventor......................................James Difley
Quartermaster.................................Orrin T. Burke
Journalist....................................Robert Lawler
War Worker....................................May Hopkins
Bond Salesman.................................Harold McGee
Telegrapher...................................Logan Paul
Messenger.....................................Seldon Bennett

Epilogue—Life and Death

Woodcutter....................................Henry Mortimer
A Woman.......................................Susan Steele
A Baby..Ann Martin

Staged by John Cromwell.

A Czecho-Slovakian fantasy in which a philosophical vagrant, heavy with drink, falls asleep in a forest and observes a curiously interesting analogy between the lives of insects and those of men. The butterflies flutter and make violent love. The beetles hoard their money and live selfishly. The ichneumon flies murder the crickets and stuff their larders with food, and parasites greedily devour what others work to save. Finally the red ants and the yellow ants wage a ruthless and devastating war to see which shall have the right to travel a particular sunlit path between two blades of grass.

"SEVENTH HEAVEN"

A comedy in three acts by Austin Strong. Produced by John Golden at the Booth Theatre, New York, Oct. 30, 1922.

Cast of characters —

Boul'...Hubert Druce
The Rat.......................................Fred Holloway
Arlette.......................................Beatrice Noyes
Maximilian Gobin..............................Alfred Kappeler
Nana..Marion Kerby
Recan...Bernard Thornton

Diane.......................................Helen Menken
Brissac.......................................Frank Morgan
Blonde.......................................Richard Carlyle
Pere Chevillon.......................................William Post
Sergeant of Police.......................................John Clements
Uncle Georges...................... ......Harry Forsman
Aunt Valentine.......................................Isabel West
Chico.......................................George Gaul
Lamplighter.......................................Lionel Joseph

Act I.—A Street in Paris. Act II.—"Heaven." Act III.—Four Years Later. Staged by John Golden.

Diane and Nana, having long since lost contact with their respectable country relatives, are adrift in the Paris slums. Nana, brutal and bestial, has gone the way of the absinthe drinkers and beats Diane into being a thief and a cheater of men. One day Chico, a sewer man, rises out of a cavern under the street, and finding Nana beating Diane, takes the latter's part. Against his will he thereafter finds himself falling in love with her. Out of pity, he takes her to his lodgings. The third day he marries her by pledge, just before he is called to the colors. For four years Diane waits patiently for Chico's return. Armistice day she hears he is killed, and cursing *le bon Dieu* for his carelessness turns to another lover, just as Chico enters the door, shell-shocked but almost whole. He does not see Diane in the other man's arms, however, because he is blind, and Diane is happily restored to her lover and her religion.

"SIX CHARACTERS IN SEARCH OF AN AUTHOR"

A fantastic comedy in two acts by Luigi Pirandello. Produced by Brock Pemberton at the Princess Theatre, New York, October 30, 1922.

Cast of characters —

The Father.......................................Moffat Johnston
The Mother.......................................Margaret Wycherly
The Step-Daughter.......................................Florence Eldridge
The Son.......................................Dwight Frye
The Boy.......................................Ashley Buck
The Little Girl.......................................Constance Lusby
Madame Pace (Evoked).......................................Ida Fitzhugh

The Manager..................................Ernest Cossart
The Leading Man...............................Fred House
The Leading Lady..........................Eleanor Woodruff
The Juvenile...................................Elliot Cabot
The Ingenue...............................Kathleen Graham
The Character Woman........................Maud Sinclair
The Third Actor................................Jack Amory
The Fourth Actor..........................William T. Hays
The Third Actress.............................Leona Keefer
The Fourth Actress..........................Blanche Gervais
The Fifth Actress........................Catherine Atkinson
The Stage Manager..........................Russell Morrison
The Property Man............................John Saunders
Scene—The Stage of a Theatre. Staged by Brock Pemberton.

Six characters, created by Pirandello, the playwright, are abandoned by him. Try as he will he cannot get them to behave in the drama he had in mind. So they go in search of another author. Drifting into a theatre while a rehearsal of a second Pirandello comedy is in progress they demand that the director in charge put aside the work he is engaged in and let them act the play for which they were created. These other players they have taken the liberty of interrupting are mere puppets, false in every particular and intended only to amuse a foolish public, while they (the abandoned six) are real and have a real story to tell. The director lets them act their play, but finds it terrible, and ends by shooing them out of the theatre. "Bring me 'The Bride's Revenge,'" he shouts. "That's what the people want."

"RAIN"

A drama in three acts by John Colton and Clemence Randolph from a story by Somerset Maugham. Produced by Sam H. Harris at the Maxine Elliott Theatre, New York, November 7, 1922.

Cast of characters —

Native Girl..............................Kathryne Kennedy
Native Policeman.........................Bhana Whitehawk
Natives...........................Oka Bunda, Llano Paulo
Ameena.......................................Emma Wilcox

Private Griggs, U. S. M. C. .... Kent Thurber
Corporal Hodgeson, U. S. M. C. .... Harold Healy
Sergeant O'Hara,, U. S. M. C. .... Robert Elliott
Joe Horn .... Rapley Holmes
Dr. McPhail .... Fritz Williams
Mrs. McPhail .... Shirley King
Mrs. Davidson .... Catharine Brooke
Quartermaster Bates .... Harry Quealy
Sadie Thompson .... Jeanne Eagles
Rev. Davidson .... Robert Kelly

The action of the play takes place in the hotel store of Trader Joe Horn, on the Island of Tutuila, Port of Pago Pago, South Seas. Staged by John D. Williams.

(See page 29.)

"UP SHE GOES"

A musical comedy in three acts by Frank Craven; music by Harry Tierney; lyrics by Joseph McCarthy. Produced by William A. Brady, Ltd., at the Playhouse, New York, November 6, 1922.

Cast of characters —

Simpson .... Edward Dano
Ella Mayer .... Helen Bolton
Frank Andrews .... Richard Gallagher
Albert Bennett .... Donald Brian
Alice Cook .... Gloria Foy
Mrs. Cook .... Lou Ripley
Mr. Cook .... Martin Mann
Aunt Louise .... Jennie Weathersbee
Mary Cook .... Edith Slack
Jerry Cook .... Conway Dillion
Louis Cook .... Teddy McNamara
Uncle Walter .... Richard Sullivan
Bertha Cook .... Lucretia Craig
Stella Cook .... Betty Allan
Bus Driver .... George Williams
Uncle Bob Bennett .... Frederick Graham
Minnie Spring .... Ann LeMeau

Act I.—Foundation—Pleasantville. Act II.—Scene 1—Country Club. Scene 2—Cross Roads. Scene 3—Raising the Roof. Act III.—Journey's End. Staged by Frank Craven and Bert French.

The numerous Cook family that threatened to interfere with the marriage and future happiness of Alice Cook and Albert Bennett in "Too Many Cooks," here serve a similar comedy purpose in a musicalized version of Frank Craven's story.

"THE '49ERS"

A modernistic revue by George Kaufman and Marc Connelly. Produced by George C. Tyler at the Punch and Judy Theatre, New York, November 7, 1922.

Principals engaged —

May Irwin
Beryl Mercer
Ruth Gillmore
Devah Morel
Margot Myers
Gladys Burgette
Angela Ward
Roland Young
Sidney Toler
Denman Maley
Allen Fagan
Howard Lindsay
Sol Friedman
Albert Carroll

Staged by Howard Lindsay.

"MERTON OF THE MOVIES"

A comedy in four acts by George Kaufman and Marc Connelly, adapted from the Harry Leon Wilson story of the same title. Produced by George C. Tyler and Hugh Ford at the Cort Theatre, New York, Nov. 13, 1922.

Cast of characters —

Merton Gill....................Glenn Hunter
Amos G. Gashwiler....................Edward M. Favor
Tessie Kearns....................Esther Pinch
Elmer Huff....................Bert Melville
Charley Harper....................W. H. Seniro
Lester Montague....................J. K. Murray
The Montague Girl....................Florence Nash
Casting Director....................Lucille Webster
Sigmund Rosenblatt....................Edwin Maxwell
His Cameramen....................Albert Cowles, E. J. Chatterly
J. Sloane Henshaw....................A. Romaine Callender
Weller....................Tom Hadaway
His Cameramen....................Joseph Lothian, Lewis Buxton
Jeff Baird....................John Webster
Harold Parmalee....................Alexander Clark, Jr.
Beulah Baxter....................Gladys Feldman
Felice....................Agnes Findlay
A Mysterious Visitor....................Lynn Pratt
Muriel Mercer....................Mary Elizabeth Forbes
Max....................Saul Mile
A Sheik....................G. S. Spelvin
Togo....................Yashi Turi

Jimmy..Billy Janney
Eddie..................................Wilton Lackaye, Jr.
The Cross-eyed Man..........................M. A. Buser
Mrs. Patterson..............................Clara Sidney
Mr. Patterson...............................A. L. Ehrman
The Man from Bigart.......................Edwin Maxwell

Act I.—Gashwiler's General Store, Simsbury, Illinois. Act II.—Outside the Holden Lot, Hollywood. Act III.—On the Lot. Act IV.—Scene 1—Jeff Baird's Office. Scene 2—Merton's Rooming House. Staged by Hugh Ford.

(See page 257.)

"HOSPITALITY"

A tragi-comedy in three acts by Leon Cunningham. Produced by the Equity Players, Inc., at the Forty-eighth Street Theatre, New York, Nov. 13, 1922.

Cast of characters —

Jennie Wells...........................Louise Closser Hale
Peter Wells...................................Tom Powers
Melena Wells...........................Harriet Woodruff
Auntie May..................................Pearl Sindelar
Ruthie.................................Margaret Borough
Muriel Humphrey...........................Phyllis Povah
Mr. Wicker.................................Claude Cooper
Clyde Thompson...............................Stuart Sage

Acts I. and II.—The Living Room in Jennie's Home. Act III.—The Living Room in Peter's Home. The Action Takes Place in a Fair-Sized Town in the Middle West. Staged by Augustin Duncan.

Jennie Wells, passionately fond of her children but determined not to "spoil" them by letting them know it, learns of her son Tom's marriage to Muriel Humphrey, a flirtatious young woman whom she distrusts. Hearing later that Muriel is carrying on with Clyde Thompson, a former sweetheart, Jennie pretends to lose her savings and forces herself upon her son's wife. Here she makes life so miserable for Muriel that she practically forces her to elope with Thompson, leaving Tom free, she hopes, to marry a better girl. The shock of the success of her conspiracy, however, kills Jennie.

"LITTLE NELLIE KELLY"

A musical comedy in two acts by George M. Cohan; words and music by George Cohan. Produced by George Cohan at the Liberty Theatre, New York, November 13, 1922.

Cast of characters —

Wellesly....................................Harold Vizard
Matilda....................................Edna Whistler
Sidney Potter....................................Frank Otto
Harold Westcott....................................Joseph Niemeyer
Jack Lloyd....................................Barrett Greenwood
Francois DeVere....................................Robert Pitkin
Jean....................................Dorothy Newell
Nellie Kelly....................................Elizabeth Hines
Mrs. Langford....................................Georgia Caine
Marie....................................Marion Saki
Jerry Conroy....................................Charles King
Captain John Kelly....................................Arthur Deagon
Miss Spendington....................................Marjorie Lane
Ambrose Swift....................................Mercer Templeton

Act I.—Scene 1—Reception Room in the Lloyd Mansion. Scene 2—Exterior of the Conroy Home. Act II.—Scene 1—A Showroom in the Shop of DeVere. Scene 2—Mystery Lane. Scene 3—Exterior of the Langford Home on the Hudson. Staged by Mr. Cohan and Julian Mitchell.

Nelly Kelly, daughter of Captain Kelly of the police force, is employed at DeVere's department store. Jack Lloyd, nephew of the rich Mrs. Langford, falling in love with her, gives a party for all the DeVere girls at Auntie's Fifth Avenue mansion. Jerry Conroy, who grew up with Nelly, suspecting Lloyd, busts into the party, and later disappears. About the same time Mrs. Langford loses her string of pearls. Mystery and music follow, with Conroy suspected by certain parties, but not by Nellie, who promises to marry him at the finale.

"L'AVENTURIERE"

A comedy drama by Emile Augier. Presented by players of the Comedie Francaise at the Thirty-ninth Street Theatre, New York, Nov. 13, 1922.

Cast of characters —

Don Annibal....Ferdinand Charpin
Horace....Charlie Gerval
Dario....Jacques d'Apoigny
Servant....M. Parotte
Celie....Rachel Berendt
Donna Calrinde....Cecile Sorel
Fabrice....Albert Lambert
Monte-Prade....Louis Ravet

The story of an adventuress' effort, when she realizes her advancing years, to establish herself in respectability, and her grace in accepting defeat.

"THE ROMANTIC AGE"

A comedy in three acts by A. A. Milne. Produced by Hugh Ford and Frederick Stanhope at the Comedy Theatre, New York, November 14, 1922.

Cast of characters —

Mrs. Knowle....Daisy Belmore
Melisande....Margalo Gillmore
Jane Bagot....Jean Ford
Alice....Ida Molthen
Mr. Knowle....Marsh Allen
Bobby....Neil Martin
Gervase Mallory....Leslie Howard
Ern....Paul Jaccia
Master Susan....J. M. Kerrigan

Act I.—The Inner Hall of Mr. Henry Knowle's Country House. Act II.—A Glade in a Wood. Act III.—Same as Act 1. Staged by Frederick Stanhope.

Melisande Knowle (representing in the flesh the state of most young girls' minds during the romantic age) refuses to give up her belief in, or at least her hope for, the knights and true lovers of old. One moonlight night she sees Gervase Mallory standing in the doorway, all blue and gold, and is more than ever convinced. Next day she meets Gervase in the park. He gracefully falls into her game of pretense, and she is greatly stirred. But the third day he appears in knickers and admits that he is a broker and that he had been stopped the day before by a stalled motor when he was on his way to a fancy dress party. Melisande is terribly put out and will have none of him—until he convinces her that even cooking and housekeeping are romantic—if you are in love.

"THE LOVE CHILD"

A drama in four acts adapted from the French of Henri Bataille by Martin Brown. Produced by A. H. Woods and Charles L. Wagner at the Cohan Theatre, New York, November 14, 1922.

Cast of characters —

Marie	Grace Kennard
Barry	Harry Gibbs
Laura Thorne	Janet Beecher
Eugene Thorne	Sidney Blackmer
Aline De Mar	Vivienne Osborne
Gaby Mulligan	Eleanor Williams
Reina Clive	Lolita Robertson
Kitty Lansing	Geneva Harrison
Paul Brander	Lee Baker
Helen Brander	Juliette Crosby
Smith	Roy Walling
Noto	F. Sinne

Act I.—At Laura Thorne's. Act II.—At Eugene's Studio. Act III.—At Paul Brander's. Act IV.—Same as Act I.
Staged by Bertram Harrison.

For seventeen years Laura Thorne has been living as the mistress of Paul Brander in the expectation of becoming his legal wife when Mrs. Brander, hopelessly insane, dies. By the time he is free, however, Brander has become a power in politics and refuses to keep his promise. Laura's son by a previous lover, Eugene Thorne, who also has been supported by Brander, learns the situation and deliberately compromises Brander's daughter, threatening to make of her what her father has made of his mother unless Brander keep his promise and marry Laura. Brander is beaten, but Laura then refuses to marry him. Her duty is to her loyal son, and she purposes to devote the rest of her life to him.

"HAMLET"

The Shakespearean tragedy. Produced by Arthur Hopkins at the Sam H. Harris Theatre, New York, November 16, 1922.

Cast of characters —

Francisco....................John Clark
Bernardo....................Lark Taylor
Horatio....................Frederick Lewis
Marcellus....................E. J. Ballantine
Ghost of Hamlet's Father....................Reginald Pole
Hamlet, Prince of Denmark....................John Barrymore
Claudius....................Tyrone Power
Gertrude....................Blanche Yurka
Polonius....................John S. O'Brien
Laertes....................Sidney Mather
Ophelia....................Rosalind Fuller
Rosencrantz....................Paul Huber
Guildenstern....................Lawrence Cecil
First Player....................Lark Taylor
Player King....................Burnel Lundee
Second Player....................Norman Hearn
Player Queen....................Richard Skinner
Lucianus....................Vadini Uraneff
A Gentlewoman....................Stephanie D'Este
King's Messenger....................Frank Boyd
First Grave Digger....................Whitford Kane
Second Grave Digger....................Cecil Clovelly
A Priest....................Reginald Pole
Osric....................Edgar Stehli
Fortinbras....................Lowden Adams

The play will be presented in three parts, with intervals following the first Players' scene and the Queen's closet scene. Staged by Arthur Hopkins.

"VIRTUE(?)"

A drama in three acts by William Everett. Produced by the Empire Play Co., Inc., at the Nora Bayes Theatre, New York, Nov. 16, 1922.

Cast of Characters —

Brooks....................................Ben Hendricks
Dorothy Palmer..............................Floy Murray
Ned McCormack, Jr......................William Williams
Daniel Greene.........................George MacQuarrie
Richard W. Greene ("Dick").............Henry G. Sell
Eleanor McCormack......................Pauline Armitage
Shirley Malcolm.............................Laura Arnold
Governor Malcolm....................Clarence Handysides
Topsy....................................Marion Hutchins
Robert Duncan...................... ....Frank Sheridan

Act I.—The District Attorney's Office. Act II.—Home of the Late Senator McCormack. Act III.—Home of Robert Duncan. Staged by Oscar Eagle.

A story of political intrigue in the South, reported to have been based on the shooting of Senator Carmack by Duncan B. Cooper, some years ago.

"THE LUCKY ONE"

A comedy in three acts by A. A. Milne. Produced by the Theatre Guild at the Garrick Theatre, New York, Nov. 20, 1922.

Cast of Characters —

Tommy Todd................................Romney Brent
Butler....................................Leonard Perry
Gerald Farringdon...........................Dennis King
Miss Farringdon............................Helen Westley
Letty Herbert.............................Gwynedd Vernon
Lady Farringdon...........................Grace Elliston
Henry Wentworth...........................Harry Ashford
Sir James Farringdon......................Robert Ayrton
Pamela Carey..............................Violet Heming
Bob Farringdon..............................Percy Waram
Mason......................................Nanny Griffen

Act I.—At Sir James Farringdon's in the Country. Act II.—A Private Hotel in Dover Street. Act III.—At Sir James Farringdon's. Staged by Theodore Komisarjevsky.

Gerald Farringdon, the younger brother, has always been the most attractive and most successful of the Faringdon boys, "the lucky one," to whom everything is given. He even takes Pamela Carey away from his older brother, Bob, and becomes engaged to her. Bob, the unlucky, has secretly rebelled all his life, and when he gets into a business tangle with a crooked partner and is sent to jail for three months, his bitterness fills him with self-pity. He pleads with Pamela to give him the strength of her love, and she, feeling his need of her, begs Gerald to release her from her promise to marry him, which he does. In the end, the "lucky" one is miserably unhappy, but he takes his knocks like a sportsman and goes away to be a diplomat.

"THE TEXAS NIGHTINGALE"

A farce comedy in three acts by Zoe Akins. Produced by Charles Frohman, at the Empire Theatre, New York, November 20, 1922.

Cast of characters —

Kitty Mulberry.................................Lizzie McCall
Steven Tillerton..............................Cyril Keightly
Walter Prescott.................................Perce Benton
Brasa Canava................................Jobyna Howland
Raymond Tillerton............................Percy Helton
Inez...Beth Varden
Sascha Bloch.............................Georges Renavent
Count Houdonyi-Bloch.........................Paul Porcasi

Act I.—Steven Tillerton's Apartment on Gramercy Park. Act II.—Madame Canava's House. Act III.—Steven Tillerton's Apartment. Time—The Present. Staged by David Burton.

Hollyhock Jones, soprano, of Texas, becomes Brasa Canava, the greatest Brünnehilde of her day. Four times married and only once in love (with her second husband, Steven Tillerton), she finds herself faced with two problems, (1) her 19-year-old son's threat to marry Inez, a flapper, and (2) her own passion for Sascha Bloch, violinist. Meeting Tillerton, the father of her son, she enlists his services as a sort of referee. He is none too successful, but he changes her plans regarding the violinist and extracts a half-hearted promise from son to postpone his marriage to Inez. Then he agrees to consider seriously remarrying Brasa, the temperamental.

"THE BOOTLEGGERS"

A comedy in four acts by William A. Page. Produced by Madison Corey and Charles Capehart at the Thirty-ninth Street Theatre, New York, November 27, 1922.

Cast of characters —

William T. Rossmore.........................Robert Conness
Nina Rossmore.........................Catherine Dale Owen
Lane.........................Aubrey Beattie
Arthur Laceby.........................George P. Collins
Rev. Thomas Laceby.........................Ernest Howard
Lanahan.........................Leighton Stark
Creighton.........................Edwin Evans
Morrison.........................John Lyons
Miggins.........................Albert Hyde
Vicarelli.........................Barry Townsley
Tony.........................Antonio Salerno
Judge Hilton.........................John M. Sullivan
Martin.........................Oliver Putnam
Walsh.........................Hugh Chilvers
Lubetsky.........................Louis Polan
Wolf.........................Joseph Burton
Emmaline Elton.........................Joyce Fair
Billy.........................Bryce Kennedy
Jerry.........................Phil Sheridan
"Dandy Phil" Casimir.............J. Montayne Vandergrift
Violet Vendome.........................Beryl Collins
Cleo De Courcelle.........................Dorinda Adams
Rosa Venturin.........................Lenore Masso
Percy Hetherington.........................Charles Haskins
"Pinkie" Dumont.........................Norma Leslie
"Puss" Montmorency.....................Kathryn MacDonald
Hiram Maginnis.........................Harry Cowley
Inspector Dawson, P.D.....................Walter Lawrence
Sergeant Walker, P.D.........................Evan Edwards
Mulligan.........................John Lyons

Act I.—Home of William T. Rossmore on the Upper West Side, New York. Act II.—Office of the Prohibition Commissioner, New York City. Act III.—The Club de Blanc, on a Side Street Near Broadway. Act IV.—Rossmore's Home. Staged by Frank McCormack.

On the fashionable West Side of New York, William T. Rossmore, well-known attorney, is making a fortune as a bootlegger. On the East Side the "king of the bootleggers" is an Italian named Vicarelli. These two cross and double-cross each other, stealing each other's liquor with the connivance of the dry agents, until Rossmore's daughter, Nina, proud and pretty, becomes involved in the plot and murder and blindness result from the operations of the two gangs and their open violations of the law. Then Rossmore reforms and Nina marries a government agent.

"LIZA"

A musical comedy in two acts by Irvin C. Miller; lyrics and music by Maceo Pinkard; special lyrics by Nat Vincent. Produced by Al Davis at the Daly's Theatre, New York, Nov. 27, 1922.

Cast of characters —

Squire Norris.............................Alonzo Fenderson
Liza Norris.................................Margaret Simms
Nora.......................................Gertrude Saunders
Uncle Pete..................................William Simms
Parson Jordan..............................Packer Ramsey
Judge Plummer............................Quintard Miller
Ras Johnson.............................R. Eddie Greenlee
Dandy.....................................Thaddius Drayton
The Sheriff...................................Will A. Cook
Ice Cream Charlie..........................Irvin C. Miller
Bodiddily..................................Emmett Anthony
Tom Liggett......................................Billy Mills
John Jones...................................Doe Doe Green
Mammy....................................Elizabeth Terrill
Mandy...Maude Russell
Harry Davis...................................Snippy Mason
Bill Jones......................................Donald Fields

Action in various parts of Jimtown, South Carolina.
Staged by Walter Brooks.

A musical comedy written and performed by colored players with just enough of a story to interrupt the specialties.

"THE BUNCH AND JUDY"

A musical comedy in two acts, by Anne Caldwell and Hugh Ford, music by Jerome Kern; lyrics by Anne Caldwell. Produced by Charles Dillingham at the Globe Theatre, New York, November 28, 1922.

Cast of characters —

Mrs. Shean....................................Lydia Scott
Kelly..Eugene Revere
Messenger......................................Roger Davis
Hazel Kirkwood...............................Patrice Clark
Marguerite De Belmont........................Lillian White
Augustus de Forrest.......................Augustus Minton
Foxhall Davidson........................T. Wigney Percyval
Lady Janet..................................Roberta Beatty
Lord Kinlock..................................Philip Tonge
Call Boy......................................Al Watson, Jr.
Otto Steger..................................Johnny Dooley
Jack Jessop...................................Delano Dell
Georgia McNamara............................Helyn Eby Rock
Gladys Goldwin...............................Elaine Palmer
Estelle.......................................Ruth White
Viola Esmond..................................Carol Flower
Mrs. Jordan..................................Bertha Holley
Robin...George Tawde
Evie Dallas.....................................Ray Dooley
Gerald Lane...................................Fred Astaire
Judy Jordan...................................Adele Astaire
Earl of Torwood.........................T. Wigney Percyval
Pipers..........J. M. McKenzie, R. H. Wilder, W. McLellan
Station Master.................................R. H. Wilder

Staged by Fred G. Latham.

Judy Jordan, having played forty weeks in "Love Finds a Way," on Broadway, is leaving the cast to marry the young Lord Kinlock, visiting America from Scotland. Judy's associates give her a farewell dinner on the stage following the last performance. Next act they are all in Scotland. Judy is the wife of Kinlock and unhappy, being snubbed by the gentry. Her former friends of the troupe are touring Europe. Mad at the Scotch, Judy goes home with the actors, returns to stage work and marries her former leading man, Gerald Lane.

"IT IS THE LAW"

A melodrama in seven scenes by Elmer L. Rice. Produced by Samuel Wallach at the Ritz Theatre, New York, Nov. 29, 1922.

Cast of characters —

Baker	C. W. Goodrich
Fisher	Richard Stevenson
Byron	Charles P. Bates
Yates	John F. Roche
Walker	John Burr
Johnson	Jack Thorne
Rumson	James Linhart
Dennison	Joseph de Stefani
Page	Thomas Hood
William Elliott	A. H. Van Buren
Gordon Travers	Hans Robert
Ruth	Alma Tell
Justin Victor	Ralph Kellard
Lillian	Rose Burdick
Theodore Cummings	William Ingersoll
Albert Woodruff	Arthur Hohl
"Snifer Evans"	Alexander Onslow
James Dolan	Walter Walker
Edward Harley	Frank Westerton
Ellen	Valerie Valarie

Scenes in Card Room of the Gotham Club, Drawing Room of Theodore Cummings' Home, Albert Woodruff's Apartment, the Warden's Office in Sing Sing Prison.

Gordon Travers and Albert Woodruff have been pals for life. Both love Ruth Cummings. They agree to let the luckier, if not the better, man win. This turns out to be Gordon, but the night he is chosen by Ruth, Albert has reason to believe that he has been tricked and humiliated by his former friend. For this he plots an elaborate and unique revenge. He finds a "bum" who looks enough like him to be his double, tattoos an identifying birthmark on the latter's arm and then shoots him through the heart. Making his own escape, Woodruff calls both the police and Travers, timing their arrival so the police will find Travers with the body of the dead man and seemingly guilty of his murder. Travers is thus arrested and sent to jail for life. But Woodruff has to come back to gloat over his revenge, and this proves his undoing, for Ruth is a smart girl, too.

"OUR NELL"

A "musical mellowdrayma" in two acts by A. E. Thomas and Brian Hooker; music by George Gershwin and William Daly. Produced by the Hayseed Productions, Inc., Ed. Davidow and Rufus Le Maire, directors, at the Bayes Theatre, New York, December 4, 1922.

Cast of characters —

Malvina Holcombe........................Mrs. Jimmie Barry
Mortimer Bayne..............................John Merkyl
Peleg Doolittle..............................Jimmie Barry
Joshua Holcombe.............................Frank Mayne
Frank Hart................................Thomas Conkey
Deacon Calvin Sheldrake.......................Guy Nichols
Helen Ford...................................Eva Clarke
Angeline Weems..............................Emma Haig
Chris Deming..............................Olin Howland
Mrs. Rogers..............................Lora Sonderson

Act I.—Joshua Holcombe's Farm in Old New England. Act II.—Inside the Barn. Staged by W. H. Gilmore, Edgar MacGregor and Julian Mason.

A musicalized burlesque of the "old hokum drama" that long has done well. There are Paw and Maw, and datter Nell, pursued by a city sharper and saved by her honest yokel, with songs and chorus to fill in the interstices of the plot.

"LISTENING IN"

An emotional comedy in a prologue and three acts by Carlyle Moore. Produced by the Milton Productions at the Bijou Theatre, New York, December 4, 1922.

Cast of characters —

Johnathan Cumberland.......................Dodson Mitchell
Mr. Morrison..............................Giorgio Majeroni
Miriam Adrian.................................Helen Flint
Janet Van Sloan.............................Minna Gombell

John Coomber	Ernest Glendinning
Harry Van Sloan	Harry Stubbs
William Archer	William Keighley
Dr. Emil Bachman	Frank Andrews
Jonas McKesson	Frank J. Kirk
Messenger	George Gaston
Abu	Herbert Farjeon
Mrs. Grace Pemberton	Margaret Linden
Reginald Pemberton	William Davidson
Geoffrey	Gerald Stopp
Police Officer	C. L. Emerson

Scenes in the Living Room in Bleeker Hall. Staged by Ira Hards.

Engaged to live a certain time in a haunted house, the while he proves or disproves the theory held by the house owner that it is possible to communicate with the spirits of the departed, John Coomber lets himself in for a terrifying adventure. Not only does the ghost of the dead house owner materialize before his eyes, but it turns him into an automatic writer of spirit messages, incidentally giving him several profitable tips on the stock market. In the end murder is all but done, but finally the mysteries and love themes are pleasantly cleared up.

"FASHIONS FOR MEN"

A comedy in three acts by Ferenc Molnar; English by Benjamin Glazer. Produced by Maurice S. Revnes at the National Theatre, New York, December 5, 1922.

Cast of characters —

Peter Juhasz	O. P. Heggie
Adele	Beth Merrill
The Aristocratic Lady	Edythe Tressider
Oscar	Clarke Silvernail
The Unassuming Lady	Frances Goodrich
Philip	Frank Peters
The Young Gentleman	Fairfax Burgher
Paula	Helen Gahagan
	(By arrangement with William A. Brady)
Adolf	George Frenger
The Count	Edwin Nicander
The Delivery Boy	James Hagen

Domokos....................................George Frenger
Santha....................................Fairfax Burgher
Mate..John Rogers
The Maid....................................Sedonia Elin
The Thorough Young Lady.................Katherine Haden
The Dissatisfied Lady......................Frances Goodrich
The Nervous Gentleman........................John Rogers
The Old Gentleman............................James Hagen
The Patient Lady.............................Sedonia Elin
The Cabman................................George Frenger

Act I.—A Shop in Budapest. Act II.—The Administration Building at Gerelypuszta. Act III.—The Shop Again. Staged by Benjamin Glazer.

Peter Juhasz, a gentle soul and sentimental, is a small shopkeeper in Budapest. Everybody loves, respects and cheats him. His wife, Adele, respects him so much she can't bear to deceive him—so she runs away with her lover, the floorwalker of Peter's shop. The floorwalker, to provide funds for the elopement, also "borrows" them of Peter. Thus the kindly merchant is thrown into bankruptcy. He takes a place in the country to be near his former secretary, a good girl but avaricious, whom he feels he should save from the wicked men who pursue her. His activities in her defense cost him his job. But he finally gets his job back and marries the secretary.

"THE DOORMAT"

A comedy in three acts by H. S. Sheldon. Produced by Edward Whiteside at the Punch and Judy Theatre, New York, December 7, 1922.

Cast of characters —

Eliza....................................Grace MacGowan
Jerome Baldwin...............................Henry Mowbray
Judge Cavender..............................Howard Nugent
Dick Cavender......................Theodore Westman, Jr.
Lucy Cavender.................................Lois Bolton
Adele Cavender.......................Lolita Anna Westman
Josephine Sheppard.........................Margaret Nugent
Rodney Sheppard.............................Harry Benham
Thomas.......................................Charles Dowd

Act I.—Living Room in the Cavender Home. Act II.—Rodney Sheppard's Study. Act III.—Same as Act I. Place—A New England City. Time—Present. Staged by David G. Fischer.

Lucy Cavender, tired of being the "doormat" of her family over which her parents, her sisters and her brothers walk with impunity, leaves home and hires out to a novelist needing a secretary. Soon he is in love with her. Their romance is halted briefly by an almost scandal. Someone overhears them discussing the advisability of having a baby in the book and thinks they are referring to Lucy's apartment.

"GRINGO"

A Mexican play in three acts by Sophie Treadwell. Produced by Guthrie McClintic, at the Comedy Theatre, New York, Dec. 12, 1922.

Cast of characters —

Leonard Light	Richard Barbee
Bessie Chivers	Edna Hibbard
Paco	Leonard Doyle
Myra Light	Edna Walton
Chivers	Frederick Perry
Tito, el Tuerto	Jose Ruben
Concha	Olin Feld
Stephen Trent	Arthur Albertson
Pepe	Harry Hahn
Tonio	J. Andrew Johnson
Eduardo	Harold McKee
Jose De Le Cruz	Jorge Anez
Carlo	Alcides Bricena
Vincentes	Manuel Valdispino
Herculano	Justiniano Rosales
Aurelio	Manuel Carillo
Alvarez	Jefferson Heath

The action of the play takes place in the far mountains of Mexico, at the present time. Staged by Guthrie McClintic.

An American named Chivers has been mining in Mexico for twenty years. During that time he has acquired a half-breed daughter, of whom he is passionately fond, and a thirst for mescal. Living with him are Mr. and Mrs. Leonard Light, he a socialistic draft dodger from the States, she a loyal but unhappy wife. Comes Tito, the local bandit, who has "sold" his wife to old man Chivers. Now he purposes to take her away unless the old man pays additional sums. To raise the money and keep the woman Chivers is forced to sell a half interest in his mine to young Light. Tito, learning that Chivers has just struck a new gold pocket, also decides to do a little double crossing. He kidnaps the crowd and carries them to a mountain fastness. When Chivers raises the ransom necessary to release the captives he finds his daughter so deeply in love with the bandit she refuses to leave him.

"THE GOD OF VENGEANCE"

A drama by Sholom Ash. Produced at the Provincetown Theatre, New York, Dec. 20, 1922.

Cast of characters —

Rifkele	Virginia Mac Fadyen
Sarah	Esther Stockton
Yekel Shepshovitch	Rudolph Schildkraut
A Poor Woman	Marjorie Stewart
Shloyme	Irwin J. Adler
Hindel	Mae Berland
Reb Ali	Sam Jaffe
Reb Aaron	Morris Carnovsky
Manke	Dorothee Nolan
Basha	Aldea Wise
Reizel	Lillian Taiz
Reb Yankev	James Meighan

Act I.—The Private Dwelling of Yekel Shepshovitch. Act II.—In the Cellar of Yekel's Dwelling. Act III.—Same as Act I. Time—The Present. Place—One of the Larger Towns of a Polish Province. Staged by Rudolph Schildkraut.

Yekel Shepshovitch has conducted what is euphemistically known as a "brothel" in a Polish city for years. Twenty years before the play begins he had married one of the women from his own establishment. He now finds himself the father of an 18-year-old daughter who, evidently reared in ignorance of the kind of place her father is conducting in the cellar of his home, is still pure in thought and deed. To keep her so and to lift her to respectability through marriage, Shepshovitch bargains with a go-between, first, to find his daughter a husband, and, second, to arrange for the purchase of a "holy scroll" from the church, that his home may be properly protected by higher religious influences in the future. But the girl is tainted, and before either of the planned-for blessings can be brought about she is spirited away by one of the procuresses below stairs, and the distraught father is left cursing his girl and the mother who bore her.

"THE RED POPPY"

A melodrama in three acts by Andre Picard and Francis Carco. Produced by Henry Baron at the Greenwich Village Theatre, New York, December 20, 1922.

Cast of characters —

Prince Sergius Saratoff	Arthur Metcalfe
De Croy	Leon Gordon
Jean	J. J. Greer
Claire	Estelle Winwood
Liane	Betty Ross Clarke
Mme. Vali	Grace Griswold
Pierre	Byron Russell
Duthil	Gerald Hamer
Francine	Joan Twain
Footman	Paul Broderick
Friquette	Frances Eldridge
Dudule	George A. Lawrence
Madame Boule	Clara T. Bracy
Babe Rose	William Paul
Lea	Blanche Boizon
Madame Sorel	Lorna Elliott
Sorel	John H. Brewer
Boule	Herbert Ashton
Mimile	Arthur Lubin
Pauline	Grace Connell
Becot	Burdette Kappes
Irma	Te Ata
Dede	Norris Hobbs
Fernando	Bela Lugosi
Bob	Robert Knight
Babe	Elena Meade
Blanche	Beatrice Bradley
Toto	Elizabeth North

Victor..Marco Mora
A Lady..Grace Gordon
Another Lady..................................Ruby Gordon
A Gentleman...................................Kay McKay
A Tough.......................................Paul Broderick
Another Tough.................................Hubbard Kirkpatrick
Sergeant de Ville.............................J. J. Greer
An Accordion Player...........................Rosario Bogina

Act I.—Claire's Boudoir. Act II.—At the Red Poppy. Act III.—Same as Act I. Staged by Iden Payne.

Claire Saratoff, before she married Prince Sergius, lived for a time among the Parisian Apaches. Slumming through the district after her marriage she meets a Spanish tough boy who loves her wildly and lures her back to the old haunts. Fascinated by his brutalities she invites him to her home, in which he thinks she is employed as a servant, and which he plans to rob. Arrived there he finds his Apache sweetheart none other than the princess herself, and while he is rowing about it, and she is telling him not to mind, he is welcome anyway, a jealous friend of the family shoots him in the back and he dies in the princess' arms, a much loved but somewhat unlucky burglar.

"THE MERCHANT OF VENICE"

The Shakespearean comedy. Produced by David Belasco, at the Lyceum Theatre, New York, December 21, 1922.

Cast of characters —

Duke of Venice................................A. E. Anson
Prince of Morocco.............................Herbert Grimwood
Antonio.......................................Ian MacLaren
Bassanio......................................Philip Merivale
Gratiano......................................W. I. Percival
Lorenzo.......................................Horace Braham
Salarino......................................Herbert Ranson
Solanio.......................................Reginald Goode
Shylock.......................................David Warfield
Tubal...Albert Bruning
Chus..Morris Strassberg
Launcelot Gobbo...............................Percival Vivian

Old Gobbo.....Fuller Mellish
Balthazar.....Charles Harbury
Stephano.....Edward H. Wever
Leonardo.....Edward Crandall
A Jester.....Warde de Wolfe
Clerk of the Court.....Nick Long
A Ducal Messenger.....Henry Brown
Portia.....Mary Servoss
Nerissa.....Mary Ellis
Jessica.....Julia Adler
Staged by David Belasco.

The familiar acting version with one scene added. When Shylock returns to his house to find Jessica fled with the ducats, there is a scene change showing Shylock entering the house and discovering the empty chests. After this he runs wildly out into the streets crying, "My daughter, my ducats!" as in the play he is reported having done by Salarino.

"THE MASKED WOMAN"

A melodrama in four acts adapted from the French by Kate Jordan. Produced by A. H. Woods at The Eltinge Theatre, New York, December 22, 1922.

Cast of characters —

Madame Montebel.....Ethel Jackson
Dr. Rene Delatour.....John Halliday
Paul.....Fred Sutton
Baron Tolento.....Lowell Sherman
Diane Delatour.....Helen MacKellar
Gaby.....Florence Flynn
Dolly Green.....Jane Houston
Women Guests.....Betty Shields, Georgia DeLong, Ethel Gibson, Violet Anderson
Andre.....Richard Abbott
Mimi.....Gladys Frazin
Philippe.....Walter Bellinger
Germaine.....Alice Fleming
Vidalon.....Frank Hollins
Lannoy.....Russell Fillmore
Lapoule.....Albert Tavernier
Act I.—At Dr. Delatour's. Act II.—At Baron Tolento's.
Act III.—The Same. Staged by Bertram Harrison.

Diane Delatour is the sweet young wife of Dr. Rene Delatour, whose richest and most influential patient is the wicked Baron Tolento. The doctor has told Diane that Tolento cannot live to exceed three months. Tolento has also admitted to her that he knows that he is going to die, and is giving a farewell dinner at which he will execute his will. If she will come, he intimates, she can have any part of the fortune she chooses to name, to do with as she will. Knowing her husband's greatest ambition is to raise funds for a new laboratory, Diane goes masked to the party hoping to get the money for the laboratory without great embarrassment to herself. But the Baron, drunk, is a bad man and Diane barely escapes from his vicious attack upon her. Dying, Tolento vows to be revenged, and when his will is read he has left all his fortune to Diane. This convinces her husband that she has long been the baron's mistress, and she is able to clear herself only with the aid of unexpected testimony.

"JOHANNES KREISLER"

A fantastic melodrama in three acts adapted from the German of Meinhard and Bernauer by Louis N. Parker; music by E. H. Von Reznich. Produced by the Selwyns at the Apollo Theatre, New York, December 20, 1922.

Cast of characters —

JULIA

Johannes Kreisler....Jacob Ben-Ami
Theodor....Erskine Sanford
Cyprian....Manart Kippen
Ludwig....Cecil Owen
Vincent....Fritz Adams
Othmar....Hyman Meyer
Sylvester....Oliver T. McCormick
Julia Mark, Undine....Lotus Robb
Mr. Mark....Charles R. Burrows
Mrs. Mark....Anna Bates
Father Ignatius....Manart Kippen
The Rich Man....Cecil Owen
The Schoolmaster....A. M. Bush
Gottlieb....Edward Le Duc

EUPHEMIA

Johannes Kreisler....Jacob Ben-Ami
Theodor....Erskine Sanford

Prince Von Soden........................F. Eckhard Dawson
Euphemia..Lotus Robb
The Lord Chamberlain........................Manart Kippen
Sekonda..Burr Caruth
Bartoni......................................Hyman Meyer
Cuno...Allyn Joslyn
Dittmaier....................................Edward Le Duc
Assistant Stage Manager........................A. M. Bush
Baron Puckler.................................Fritz Adams
Madame Von Benzon.......................Millie Butterfield
A Lackey..................................William Lilling
Undine's Voice....................................Rosa Nier
The Fisherman..............................Berthold Busch
His Wife............................Alta Virginia Houston
Their Son.....................................Hilda Steiner

DONNA ANNA

Johannes Kreisler............................Jacob Ben-Ami
Theodor. ....Erskine Sanford
Cyprian.....................................Manart Kippen
Ludwig...Cecil Owen
Vincent.......................................Fritz Adams
Othmar.......................................Hyman Meyer
Gottlieb....................................Edward Le Duc
Donna Anna.....................................Lotus Robb
Voice of Donna Anna.............................Rosa Nier
Don Juan...................................Berthold Busch
Don Ottavio.................................Josef Batistish
Elvira..............................Alta Virginia Houston
Leporello.............................Oliver T. McCormick

The Action Takes Place in Berlin, Bamberg, Dresden and Potsdam About One Hundred Years Ago. Staged by Frank Reicher.

A scenic spectacle through which is woven, after the manner of introducing "flashbacks" in moving picture scenarios, the story of Composer Kreisler, as it is related by himself. As he reaches an "And then—" in his recital the scene described is enacted on another section of the stage, sometimes on an elevated stage, sometimes on the full stage, frequently on the forestage, and always under a brilliant play of lights. There are forty-one scenes in all. The composer is carried through his meeting with his early love, Julia Mark; her parents' refusal to let him marry her, and his later discovery of the soul of her in other sympathetic women whom he meets. Once she is the heroine of his opera, again she is a lovely countess, and finally a great prima donna who sings to him alone in an empty opera house. As he completes his story Kreisler dies.

"THE CLINGING VINE"

A comedy with music in three acts by Zelda Sears. Music by Harold Levey. Produced by Henry W. Savage at the Knickerbocker Theatre, New York, December 25, 1922.

Cast of characters —

Tessie	Irene Dunne
Plummer	Nathaniel Wagner
Billings	Royal Hallee
Titus M. Tutewiler	Charles Schofield
Bill	Christian Holtum
Smith	Bradford Hunt
Brown	Roy Marvin
Jones	William Rogers
Antoinette Allen	Peggy Wood
Mildred Mayo	Josephine Adair
Janet Milton	Eleanor Dawn
Francis Milton	James C. Marlowe
Randolph Mayo	Raymond Crane
Jane	Jane Arrol
Jean	Jean Ferguson
Margery	Margery Wall
Rosa	Rosa Vera
Helen	Helen Hipkins
Louise	Louise Scheerer
Eleanor	Eleanor Livingston
Virginia	Virginia Clark
Florence	Florence McGuire
Victoria	Victoria White
Mrs. Anthony Allen	Louise Galloway
Vacarescou	Reginald Pasch
Agnes	Joyce White
Bascom	William C. Gordon
Jimmy Manning	Charles Derickson
Noel Graham	Earl Gates

Act I.—Scene 1—General Offices of A. Allen, Inc., Mixed Paints, Omaha, Nebraska. Scene 2—Living Room in the Home of Mrs. Anthony Allen, Shippan Point, Stamford, Conn. Act II.—The Same. Act III.—Mrs. Allen's garden. Staged by Ira Hards.

Antoinette Allen, minding a paint business in Omaha and most efficient as the head of the firm, is called east on business. Visiting her grandmother she is induced, for the sake of her domestic future, to put aside her masculine independence and be as "a clinging vine" until she secures unto herself a husband and a home. Antoinette simpers so well she has all the men crazy about her. Then she beats them in a real estate deal, makes a modest fortune for her poor schoolboy lover and returns happily to Omaha.

"ROSE BRIAR"

A comedy in three acts by Booth Tarkington. Produced by Florenz Ziegfeld, Jr., at the Empire Theatre, New York, December 25, 1922.

Cast of characters —

Rose Briar	Billie Burke
Paradee	Allan Dinehart
Valentine	Frank Conroy
Mrs. Valentine	Julia Hoyt
Little	Richie Ling
Crecelous	Paul Doucet
Miss Nicely	Florence O'Denishawn
Miss Sheppard	Ethel Remey
Monsieur Prologue	Louis Darclee
Sullivan	Mark Haight
Thompson	Frank McCoy

Act I.—The Cabaret Room of the Restaurant Pompadour. Act II.—Mrs. Valentine's House in the Country. Act III.—The Same.

Economic necessity forces Rose Briar to sing in a cabaret. Here she is selected by the catty and unpleasant Mrs. Valentine as a likely co-respondent for Mr. Valentine, whom Mrs. Valentine would like to divorce that she may be free to carry on more intimately with her friend, Mr. Paradee. Miss Briar is at first offended at Mrs. Valentine's suggestions, but being herself interested in Paradee she falls in with the plan, goes to the Valentine home over Sunday, "shows up" the shallow Mrs. Valentine by making all sorts of sport of her and comes away with Paradee lashed to her chariot wheels and the Valentines mutually interested in a reconciliation.

"SECRETS"

A comedy drama in a prologue, three acts and an epilogue, by Rudolf Besier and May Edginton. Produced by Sam H. Harris at the Fulton Theatre, New York, December 25, 1922.

Cast of characters —

PROLOGUE AND EPILOGUE, 1922

Lady Carlton....Margaret Lawrence
Lady Lessington....Barbara Allen
Audrey Carlton....Mignon O'Doherty
John Carlton....Shirley B. Pink
Robert Carlton....Horace Cooper
Dr. Arburthnot....Frazer Coulter
Nurse Martin....Nora Ryan

ACT I. 1867

Mary Marlowe....Margaret Lawrence
Mrs. Marlowe....Mrs. Edmund Gurney
Elizabeth Channing....Lillian Brennard
Susan....Mary Scott Seton
William Marlowe....Orlando Daly
John Carlton....Tom Nesbitt

ACT II. 1870

Mary Marlowe....Margaret Lawrence
Dr. McGovern....Elmer Grandin
Bob....Norman Houston
John Carlton....Tom Nesbitt

ACT III. 1888

Mary Carlton....Margaret Lawrence
Mrs. Marlowe....Mrs. Edmund Gurney
Elizabeth Channing....Lillian Brennard
Mrs. Eustace Mainwaring....Diantha Pattison
Blanche....Beatrice Kay
Audrey....Cynthia Hyde
John....Shirley B. Pink
Robert....Clay Kennedy
William Marlowe....Orlando Daly
Briggs....Allen Jenkins
John Carlton....Tom Nesbitt

Prologue and Epilogue, 1922—A Room in Sir John Carlton's House in Portchester Terrace, London. Act I.—1867—Mary Marlowe's Bedroom in Her Parents' House at Black Heath. Act II.—1870—Living Room of a Two-Room Shack in Wyoming. Act III.—1888—Drawing Room of Sir John Carlton's House in Portchester Terrace, London. Staged by Sam Forrest.

John Carlton, an octogenarian, is dying. His wife, only a few years his junior, refuses to heed her children's advice to leave him. For fifty odd years they have been partners and she purposes to stand by to the end. As they flutter about her the old lady day dreams before the fire. The scene flashes back to the beginning of her romance, when she was a girl of 18 in England and her John a clerk in her father's employ. When father refused his consent to their marriage they eloped to America. In Wyoming they fought their way through pioneering privations, and the loyal little wife always knew the "secrets" of danger the husband tried to keep from her. Returned to England he becomes politically famous and a bit of a philanderer. When the scandalmongers tell her the story and John is forced to confess she forgives him. She had known that "secret," too. The epilogue finds her dozing by the fire. She is a little cheered by good reports from the bedside. It may have been her great faith, the doctors think, that pulled John through the crisis.

"THE TIDINGS BROUGHT TO MARY"

A medieval mystery by Paul Claudel, translated by L. M. Sill. Produced by the Theatre Guild at the Garrick Theatre, New York, December 25, 1922.

Cast of characters —

Violaine....................................Jeanne de Casalis
Pierre de Craon.............................Charles Francis
Mara..Mary Fowler
The Mother...................................Helen Westley
Anne Vercors...............................Stanley Howlett
Jacques Hury...................................Percy Waram
The Mayor of Chevroche.....................Harry Ashford
The Apprentice of Pierre de Craon.............Philip Leigh
Woodcutters................Guy Collins, William R. Harper, John Aiken, Romney Brent, William Crowell, Robert Chateauneuf
Women of Chevroche..Helen Sheridan, Mercedes de Cordoba, Ruby Helder
Nuns....Beatrix Baird, Djuna Barnes, Joan Clement, Olive Flannery, Helen Manship, Ruth Manship, Armina Marshall, Priscilla Platfoot
Singers......................Helen Sheridan, Ruby Helder, Mercedes de Cordoba, Marjorie Harcum
Voice of a Child..........................Francene Wouters
Organist....................................Ralph Brainard

Staged by Theodore Komisarjevsky.

A medieval mystery play preaching the faith and humility that work miracles. The good Violaine, betrothed to the catch of the village, is made leprous through a lover's kiss. For years thereafter she is as one dead to the community, suffering those taunts and public revilings common to sinners. Yet when the dead infant child of Mara, Violaine's sister, is brought to the leper life is restored to the infant through the latter's supreme faith.

"WHY NOT?"

A comedy in three acts by Jesse Lynch Williams. Produced by the Equity Players, Inc., at the Forty-eighth Street Theatre, New York, December 25, 1922.

Cast of characters —

Leonard Chadwick..............................Tom Powers
Mary Chadwick...........................Margaret Mower
Molly................................Marguerite Churchill
Churchill Smith................................Cecil Yapp
Jane Davidge...........................Norma Mitchell
Evadne Thompson..............................Jane Grey
Billy Thompson...........................Raymond Guion
Bill Thompson.........................Warburton Gamble

Scene—The Library of a Country House—Not on Long Island. Staged by Mrs. Shelley Hull and O. P. Heggie.

(See page 176.)

"THE LADY CRISTILINDA"

A comedy in four acts by Monckton Hoffe, produced by William Harris, Jr., at the Broadhurst Theatre, New York, December 25, 1922.

Cast of characters —

RESPECTABLE PEOPLE

H.R.H. the Duke of Calshot.....................Gavin Muir
The Bishop of Uttoxeter.........................Arthur Barry
The Marquis of Leith.......................J. Malcom Dunn
His Worship, the Mayor of Hammerpool.........A. P. Kaye
Sir Julius Samoon...........................Eugene Powers
Col. Thackeray Martyn.......................Lawrence Grant

H. S. Tucker, M.P. .... Roy Cochrane
Mr. Inklethorp .... Thomas Louden
Father Reaney .... St. Clair Bayfield
Lord Llanelly .... Ethelbert Hales

DISRESPECTFUL PEOPLE

Christopherson .... Arthur Byron
Rapho .... Courtenay Foote
Martini .... Leslie Howard
Iky-Mo .... Ferdinand Gottschalk
Frederick .... Frank Arundel
Harold .... Haviland Chappell
Froggy .... Elizabeth Patterson
The Lady Cristilinda .... Fay Bainter
Policeman .... Henry Burbage
Chauffeur .... Charles Cheltenham

Act I.—Christopherson's Royal Circus. Act II.—A Public Meeting at the Magnifidrome Palace of Varieties, Hammerpool. Act III.—Christopherson's Circus. Act IV.—The Abbey Church of St. Etheldreda. Staged by Robert Milton.

The Lady Cristilinda's family had been "show folks" for generations. She, herself, was the premiere equestrienne of her father's Royal Circus and a great favorite. One young fellow ran away with the show to be near her, and, being an artist, became a "lightning portraiturist" as a side show feature. Martini, they called him. He loved Cristilinda very much, and one day he painted her on the back of an old canvas and sold it to Iky-Mo, a dealer, for twelve pounds. The same day Martini's father found his son and, by pleading with her in the name of the boy's future, got Cristilinda to give him up. Years after it was discovered that the painting of Cristilinda, being a copy after the style of the old masters, was resold to a rich man, and by him presented to a church. It was a picture of St. Etheldreda, they said. By the time the fake was discovered, Martini had become a great painter, and the Lady Cristilinda, having fallen from her horse, was a cripple. But she travelled all the way to the church to plead with the churchmen not to expose the fraud. Nobody knew but what the little circus rider really was a saint. And so long as they did not know it did not harm them. So it was ordered that nothing be said about the painting, and the Lady Cristilinda was happy — for herself, and for Martini, too.

"GLORY"

A musical comedy in two acts by James Montgomery; music by Maurice de Packh and Harry Tierney; lyrics by James Dyrenforth and Joseph McCarthy. Produced by the Vanderbilt Producing Company, at the Vanderbilt Theatre, New York, December 25, 1922.

Cast of characters —

William Harriman.............................Walter Regan
Hiram Dexter.................................Jack Clifford
Ansel Tollet.................................Robert Higgins
Lem King.....................................Raymond Hackett
Sumner Holbrook..............................John Cherry
Deacon Eaton.................................Robert O'Connor
Alonzo.......................................Ted McNamara
Abner Moore..................................Peter Lang
Glory Moore..................................Patti Harrold
Lucy Ann Willing.............................Helen Groody
Myrtie Brown.................................Mabel Ferry
Sarah King...................................Flo Irwin
Amanda Dexter................................Bernice McCabe

Act I.—Scene 1—The General Store. Scene 2—The Lawn in the Rear of Hiram Dexter's House. Scene 3—The General Store. Scene 4—Dexter's Lawn. Act II.—Scene 1—The General Store. Scene 2—Harriman's home. Scene 3—The General Store.

Glory Moore was the daughter of the village waster, but when William Harriman, the young millionaire, was tricked by Hiram Dexter into coming back to the old town on a visit, it was Glory that held him there. He helped her to win a popularity contest and after two acts he married her, much to the disappointment of the gossips, who had no idea that was his intention.

"THE EGOTIST"

A comedy in three acts by Ben Hecht. Produced by Lee Shubert, at the Thirty-ninth Street Theatre, New York, December 25, 1922.

Cast of characters —

Sally Jenkins................................Maidel Turner
Mr. Smart....................................Gustav Bowhan

Manny Epstein.................................Jack Belgrave
Helen Tarbell..............................Maude Hanaford
Margaret Schmidt..........................Catherine Carter
Mr. Gorman.................................Earle Mitchell
Felix Tarbell..............................Leo Ditrichstein
Edward (Bud) Jenkins......................Albert Morrison
Norma Ramon..................................Mary Duncan
Sing.......................................Alexia Polianov
Toy...Young Lee
Virginia Hansen..............................Carlotta Irwin
Murphy.......................................M. A. Kelly
Richard Collins...............................Lee Millar

Act I.—A Little Free-for-All Office Behind the Box Office at the Theater. Act II.—Norma's Apartment—Night. Act III.—Felix Tarbell's Workshop in His Home. Time—The Present. Place—New York City.

Felix Tarbell is a "man of phrases" and imagination. He loves to think of himself as the model of his own pen pictures of a great lover. Yet, maneuvered into the position of one, he is flustered and ill at ease. Pursued by Norma Ramon, leading actress in one of his plays, he submits as gracefully as may be, but at the climax of the entertainment she has prepared to fascinate him, in which she appears in cymbals and a smile, he flees precipitately down the fire escape. Meantime, however, Mrs. Tarbell, believing all the stories she has heard of Felix, has, by way of playing even with him, acquired herself a lover, and the hapless egotist is left at the last alone and saddened, homeless, wifeless, and more or less cheerless.

"ROMEO AND JULIET"

Shakespeare's tragedy. Produced by Arthur Hopkins at the Longacre Theatre, New York, December 27, 1922.

Cast of characters —

Sampson..................................Barlow Borland
Gregory....................................Albert Reed
Balthasar................................Howard Merling
Abraham.....................................James Hull
Benvolio..................................Jerome Lawler
Tybalt...................................Kenneth Hunter
Capulet...................................Harvey Hays

Lady Capulet............................Lenore Chippendale
Montague..................................Frank Howson
Lady Montague..................................Alice John
Escalus.......................................Edwin Brandt
Romeo..McKay Morris
Paris.....................................William Keighley
Peter.......................................Barry Macollum
Nurse to Juliet.......................Charlotte Granville
Juliet......................................Ethel Barrymore
Mercutio......................................Basil Sydney
An Old Man................................John C. Davis
Friar Laurence..............................Russ Whytal
An Apothecary.............................Barry Macollum
Page to Paris................................Vivian Geison

The play is presented in three parts with intervals following the balcony and the potion scene. Staged by Arthur Hopkins.

"WILL SHAKESPEARE"

An invention in six scenes by Clemence Dane. Produced by Winthrop Ames at the National Theatre, New York, January 1, 1923.

Cast of characters —

Anne Hathaway............................Winifred Lenihan
Will Shakespeare...............................Otto Kruger
Mrs. Hathaway................................Angela Ogden
Henslowe......................................John L. Shine
Queen Elizabeth..............................Haidee Wright
Mary Fitton...............................Katharine Cornell
Kit Marlowe...............................Alan Birmingham
Stage Doorkeeper..........................Wallace Jackson
Stage Hand..................................Herbert Clarke
A Boy..Lewis Shore
Landlord......................................Harry Barfoot
A Man.......................................Samuel Godfrey
Another Man..............................William J. Kline
Maid of Honor.......................Cornelia Otis Skinner
Street Hawker.........................Anne Williamson
Secretary..............................William Worthington
A Seneschal................................Charles Romane

Act I.—Shakespeare's Cottage, Stratford-on-Avon. Act II.—A Room in the Palace, London. Act III.—Behind the Scenes, the First Night of "Romeo and Juliet." Act IV.—Shakespeare's Lodging, London. Act V.—A Room at an Inn, Deptford. Act VI.—Another Room in the Palace, London. Staged by Winthrop Ames.

In this "invention," as Miss Dane describes her play, Shakespeare is discovered in his twentieth year married to Anne Hathaway and doing what he can to make a living farming in Stratford, while all the time he feels an unconquerable urge to write. With this ambition Anne has no sympathy, and there is much unhappiness in the cottage. When Shakespeare discovers that she has lied to him respecting her condition, which forced their marriage, the poet grows exceeding wroth and runs away to London with Henslowe's players. Here, ten years later, he is discovered by Queen Elizabeth and recognized as one who may later do great literary deeds for England. The queen, in the cause of Shakespeare's further growth, aids his affair with Mary Fitton, lady in waiting, who really prefers to flirt with Kit Marlowe, but agrees to pay some attention to Shakespeare's love. For her, "the Dark Lady of the sonnets," the poet writes "Romeo and Juliet," and she plays the last scene of it the night of the premier, when the boy who was Juliet sprains an ankle. Later she runs away to meet Marlowe in a tavern, Shakespeare follows, there is a scuffle and Marlowe is killed by falling on his own dagger. Losing Mary Fitton, Shakespeare is depressed and gloomy and of a mind to forswear his career, but Elizabeth, pleading eloquently England's need of him, sets him back at work.

"MIKE ANGELO"

A play in three acts by Edward Locke. Produced by Oliver Morosco, at the Morosco Theatre, New York, January 8, 1923.

Cast of characters —

Mike Angelo....................................Leo Carrillo
Newton Carlton................................Grant Stewart
Annabelle Carlton.............................Wanda Lyon
Ivan Smirnoff.................................Robert Strange
Carlotta Swift...............................Dorothy Mackaye
Tommy Sloane...........................Gerald Oliver Smith
Peter Smith..................................Byron Beasly
Mischa Tarkoff...........................Adrian H. Rosley

The Play is in Three Acts and Takes Place in Newton Carlton's Studio in New York City. Time—The Present. Staged by Clifford Brooke.

A youthful Italian, a direct descendant of the great Michelangelo, painter, eager to learn to paint, hires himself out as a model and general help around the studios. In one he falls in love with the maestro's daughter. Entering a competition, and believing his picture to be the best of the lot, he tries to change it so his rival, the man he believes the girl loves, will win and be able to marry. The rival is proved a villain, and honest Mike Angelo wins the scholarship, the prize and the heroine.

MOSCOW ART THEATRE

Repertoire Season presented under the auspices of F. Ray Comstock and Morris Gest at the Fifty-ninth Street Theatre, New York, January–February, 1923.

The company included —

Constantin Stanislavsky
Olga Knipper-Tchekhova
Vassily Katchaloff
Ivan Moskvin
Leonid M. Leonidoff
Vassily Luzhsky
Alexander Vishnevsky
Vladimir Gribunin
Maria Lilina
Lydia Korenieva
Varvara Bulgakova
Maria Krizhanovskaya
Nina Litovtseva
Maria Nikolaieva
Vera Pashennaya
Eugenia Rayevskaya
F. Shevtchenko
Olga Tarasova
Maria Uspenskaya
Nikolai Alexandroff
Peter Baksheieff
Alexei Bondiryoff
Ivan Bulgakoff
Giorgi Burdzhaloff
Boris Dobronravoff
Alexei Grizunoff
Ivan Gudkoff
A. M. Khmara
Ivan Lazarieff
Nikolai Podgorny
Nikolai Rumiantseff
Akim Tamiroff
Vladimir Yershoff

The repertoire —

"Tsar Fyodor Ivanovitch," by Count Alexei Tolstoy.

"The Lower Depths," ("Night Lodging") by Maxim Gorky.

"The Cherry Orchard," by Anton Tchekoff.

"The Three Sisters," by Anton Tchekoff.

"The Lady from the Provinces," by Ivan Turgenieff, and excerpts from "The Brothers Karamazoff," by Fyodor Dostoievsky.

"POLLY PREFERRED"

A comedy in three acts by Guy Bolton. Produced by F. Ray Comstock and Morris Gest, at the Little Theatre, New York, January 11, 1923.

Cast of characters —

Jimmie	Beatrice Nichols
Waiter at the Automat	Dorrance M. Hubbell
Polly Brown	Genevieve Tobin
	(By Arrangement with Arthur Hopkins)
Joe Rutherford	Thomas W. Ross
Bob Cooley	Wm. Harrigan
Page Boy at the Biltmore	Gosta E. Richter
Guest at the Biltmore	Arline Tucker
Mr. X	George Spelvin
Mr. Y	Augustus Collette
Owen Kennedy	Charles Laite
Pierre Jones	Wm. Baily
Mr. A	Arthur Pierce
Miss C	Verginia L. Moore
Miss D	Edna Rivers
Sophie	Marjorie Eggleston
Red Cap	Sam White
Harold Nathan	Richard Malchien
Mr. B	David Burns
Morris	Harold Waldridge
Crawford Boswell	Edward Vansloan
Doorman	Wm. Betts
Stenographer	Ada Waters
Colored Maid	Betty Fromen
Baker	John Wray
Farelly	Briggs French
Kito	George Deaner

Act I.—Scene 1—A Corner of "The Automat." Scene 2—"Fashion Row" at the Biltmore. Scene 3—An Office. Act II.—Scene 1—Office on the "Polly Pierpont" lot. Scene 2—Joe Rutherford's Bungalow. Act III.—Office on the "Polly Pierpont" lot. Staged by Winchell Smith.

Polly Brown, forced to quit the show in which she has a job as chorus girl because the backer of the enterprise develops spidery tendencies and begins spinning a golden web for her, meets Bob Cooley at the automat. Bob is a salesman, also out of a job because he had no faith in the article he had been trying to sell. Seeing Polly he has an idea. She has everything men want to buy—youth, charm, good looks, sex. Why not let him incorporate her, as it were, and put her in the shop window? Feeling that she can trust herself to him, Polly agrees.

With the help of borrowed gowns and a borrowed office she is "sold" to a number of rich men eager to make a second Mary Pickford of her. She goes to California and is a great success. But the spidery broker follows after, and there are complications that keep her from realizing that she loves Bob and Bob only before the last act.

"THE HUMMING BIRD"

A comedy in three acts by Maude Fulton. Produced by Frank Egan at the Ritz Theatre, New York, January 15, 1923.

Cast of characters —

Toinette....................................Maude Fulton
Henriette Fish..............................Hilda Spong
Lisa Latham.................................Mona Kingsley
Mme. Burque.................................Flavia Arcaro
Billie Newman...............................Violet Dale
A Guest.....................................Valerie Valaire
Phillip Carey...............................Robert Ober
Brutus J. Finn..............................Andrew Mack
Henry Smith.................................Edgar Nelson
Gen. Jules Leferrier................Frederic De Belleville
Charlot.....................................Walter Wills

Act I.—A Studio on the Lower West Side. Act II.—Mme. Burque's Shop. Act III.—Drawing Room of Mrs. Fish's Town House. Staged by Robert Ober.

Toinette, having been an Apache in Paris, escapes to New York and tries to "go straight" in Greenwich Village. She is trailed by the wicked Charlot, however, who formerly had treated her rough in the dance at home. In America she dances with him again, but eludes him at its finish, only to learn next act that his intent had been kindly, even though his makeup was forbidding. He had come for her at the request of the great Gen. Le Ferrier, who wanted to decorate her for having inspired the "wolves" of Montmartre to fly to the aid of France on that memorable day when Paris was threatened. Decorated, Toinette engages herself to marry a village student.

"JITTA'S ATONEMENT"

A tragi-comedy by Siegfried Trebitsch. Produced by Lee Shubert at the Comedy Theatre, New York, January 17, 1923.

Cast of characters —

Mrs. Billiter....................................Phoebe Coyne
Professor Bruno Haldenstedt.....................John Craig
Jitta Lenkheim.................................Bertha Kalich
Professor Alfred Lenkheim....................Francis Byrne
Dr. Ernest Fessler.........................Walton Butterfield
Agnes Haldenstedt.............................Thais Lawton
Edith..Beth Eliott
Staged by Lester Lonergan.

Jitta Lenkheim, finding her own husband prosaic and dull, turns to his best friend and literary collaborateur, Bruno Haldenstedt, for love and sympathy. For three years they indulge their love. At the end of that period, Prof. Haldenstedt, keeping an appointed rendezvous with Jitta, dies suddenly of heart disease. Not, however, until he has made her promise to see that the work on which he has been working with her husband is published under the latter's name. Her lover dead, Jitta is torn between a determination to remain by his side and face the consequent scandal, and a desire to flee and avoid dragging innocent people into the affair. She flees and is tortured by her conscience for being a coward until she determines to confess everything, which she does. Her husband closes his chamber door against her and will have nothing to do with the book. Mrs. Haldenstedt is greatly relieved to find her husband's mistress was at least one of her own set, and the dead man's daughter is sympathetically drawn to her. It is so fine to know a woman who really understood father. A reconciliation between the Lenkheims is promised at the end.

"GIVE AND TAKE"

A farce comedy in three acts by Aaron Hoffman. Produced by Max Marcin, Inc., at the Forty-ninth Street Theatre, New York, January 15, 1923.

Cast of characters —

Marion Kruger.................................Vivian Tobin
Jack Bauer, Jr..............................Robert W. Craig
Albert Kruger...............................George Sidney
John Bauer......................................Louis Mann
Daniel Drum............................Charles Dow Clark
Thomas Craig..............................Douglas Wood

The Action of the Play Takes Place in the Canning Factory of John Bauer, Located in a Small Town in Southern California. Staged by W. H. Gilmore.

John Bauer has spent his life in the fruit canning business. For thirty years Albert Kruger has been his foreman and his best friend. Comes a time when a heavy mortgage is due on the factory and the workingmen are disturbed. At this crisis John Bauer, Jr., home from college with many new communistic ideas, insists the factory shall be turned over to its employees. Industrial democracy is the order of the day. Foreman Kruger sides with the boy, and the elder Bauer, protesting vigorously, is beaten. The men run the factory into the ground. With ruin threatened an eccentric millionaire offers to capitalize a new selling scheme. The discovery that the millionaire had been but recently released from an asylum complicates matters, but the selling scheme works just the same.

"DAGMAR"

A drama in two parts by Louis Anspacher, adapted from a play by Ferencz Herczeg. Produced by Charles Bryant at the Selwyn Theatre, New York, January 22, 1923.

Cast of characters —

Countess Dagmar....................................Nazimova
Masha...Pola Verina

Karola....................................Sophie Wilds
Viscount Stanley Lytton....................Gilbert Emery
Captain Rioni..............................Donald Call
Count Egon Holl..........................Frederick Perry
Andre Belisar.............................Charles Bryant
Clair Annersley............................Greta Cooper
An Usher...................................Myra Brooks

Part I.—Scene 1—Dressing Room, Dagmar's Villa. Scene 2—The Beach. Scene 3—Dagmar's Boudoir. Part II—Scene 4—A Terrace Overlooking the Tennis Court. Scene 5—A Corridor in the Opera House. Scene 6—Dagmar's Bedroom. Time—The Present. Place—A European Watering Resort. Staged by Iden Payne.

The Countess Dagmar, an erotic young woman, is given to outbursts of passion which she cannot control. Hence her love affairs are many and her fickleness more or less proverbial. Tiring of the Viscount Lytton she takes up with Andre Belisar, and here she meets her match. When she begs Belisar to kill her if ever she attempts to deceive him he takes her at her word, and when next she tries to return to Lytton, Belisar cuts her throat.

"LADY BUTTERFLY"

A musical comedy in two acts by Clifford Grey; music by Werner Janssen, adapted from a farce by Mark Swan and James T. Powers. Produced by Oliver Morosco at the Globe Theatre, New York, January 22, 1923.

Cast of characters —

Duval......................................Vic Casmore
Horatio Meak...............................Lionel Pape
Pansy......................................Rona Wallace
Jack Owen.................................Edward Lester
Billy Browning.............................Allen Kearns
Henry Crawford............................George Trabert
Fisher.....................................Frank Dobson
Caroline...................................Maude Eburne
Mrs. Stockbridge.......................Gertrude Maitland
Mabel Stockbridge..........................Mabel Withee
Alfred Hopper..............................Florenz Ames
Enid Crawford............................Marjorie Gateson
Bobby......................................Janet Stone
Frances....................................Aline McGill
Ruth.....................................Marion Hamilton

Mr. Stockbridge.................................Lionel Pape
Briggs...Edward Lester
A Policeman..................................Raymond Hunter
Act I.—Deck of a Channel Boat. Act II.—Scene 1—The Tradesmen's Entrance. Scene 2—Reception Hall in the Fairfax Home, Hampshire, England. Scene 3—Outside the Garden. Staged by Ned Wayburn.

The story of an old farce, "Somebody's Luggage," in which Alfred Hopper, a comic ne'er-do-well, acquires the suitcase and papers of an expected bridegroom from Australia and passes himself off on Enid Crawford, the expectant bride, as the man she promised to wed.

"EXTRA"

A comedy-drama in three acts by Jack Alicoate. Produced by Jack Alicoate and Wm. Collier, Jr., at the Longacre Theatre, New York, January 23, 1923.

Cast of characters —

Ann Tucker.................................Gertrude Gustin
"Judge" Malone..........................William A. Norton
Henderson..................................Howard Benton
John H. King..............................Howard Truesdell
Mr. Brewer...............................Hallett Thompson
"Larry" Patton........................Charles N. Lawrence
Wallace King................................Chester Morris
Henry Willard...............................Edward Poland
Antonette Willard............................Marcia Byron
Jimmy Flynn..............................Clyde Hunnewell
R. H. Osgood................................Robert Thorne
Mr. Jones..................................Frederick Beane
Act I.—Library of King Home. Act II.—King's Office of the *Dispatch*. Act III.—The Same. Time—The Present. Staged by Walter Wilson.

John H. King, politician and newspaper owner, is trying to get hold of a block of stock owned by one of his partners in the *Dispatch*. He figures if he can depreciate the value of the property he can buy cheaply. With this in view he turns the paper over to his apparently incompetent son, Wallace, and takes a long trip. Wallace runs true to form and is about to score a bust when the stenographer he has fallen in love with tells him of his father's conspiracy. This stirs his fighting blood, and, with the help of his drinking pal, Larry Patton, whom he makes managing editor, he succeeds in turning the *Dispatch* over to the reform politicians, who elect a good man mayor. When King senior returns to town he finds his newspaper booming and escapes indictment with the other politicians only through his son's influence with the new mayor.

"ROMEO AND JULIET"

The Shakespearean tragedy. Produced by the Selwyns and Adolph Klauber at the Henry Miller Theatre, New York, January 24, 1923.

Cast of characters —

Samson	Bailey Hick
Gregory	Frank Davis
Abram	Edward Broadley
Balthasar	Richard Bowler
Benvolio	Vernon Kelso
Tybalt	Louis Hector
Capulet	Gordon Burby
Lady Capulet	Grace Hampton
Montague	Lionel Hogarth
Lady Montague	Lalive Brownell
Escalus	John Crawley
Romeo	Rollo Peters
Paris	John Parrish
Peter	Milton Pope
Nurse to Juliet	Jessie Ralph
Juliet	Jane Cowl
Mercutio	Dennis King
An Old Man	Neil Quinlan
Friar Laurence	Robert Ayrton
An Apothecary	John Crawley

Staged by Frank Reicher.

"THE DANCING GIRL"

A musical play in twenty-two scenes. Produced by Lee and J. J. Shubert at the Winter Garden, New York, January 24, 1923.

Principals engaged —

Marie Dressler	Trini
Tom Burke	Llora Hoffman

Cyril Scott
Kitty Doner
Ted Doner
Rose Doner
Gilda Leary
Sally Fields
Nat Nazarro, Jr.
Nancy Gibbs
Jack Pearl
Ben Bard
Arthur Margetson
Edythe Baker
Bennie Leonard

Staged by J. C. Huffman, under the supervision of J. J. Shubert.

In the cabin of an ocean liner Bruce Chattfield is bored with life and Gloria Seabright can't find anything resembling a new thrill. John Mercer proposes a "slumming trip" through the steerage. Here the party finds Anna, a Spanish dancer, entertaining the other passengers, and Bruce falls desperately in love with her. On shore Anna is protected by Rudolpho, her tenorious cousin, but, being honorably and persistently pursued by Chattfield, is captured after a series of adventures, solos and duets.

"A SQUARE PEG"

A tragedy in three acts by Lewis Beach. Produced by Guthrie McClintic at the Punch and Judy Theatre, New York, January 27, 1923.

Cast of characters —

Rena Huckins....Beverly Sitgreaves
Mildred Huckins....Leona Hogarth
Aunt Effie....Minnie Milne
Eugene Huckins....Walter Abel
James T. Huckins....William B. Mack
Walter Fripp....Leighton Stark
Arthur Ryan....Leonard Doyle
Mrs. Trent....Alice Bromley Wilson
Sam Durkie....Martin Malloy
Lyman McVey....Richard Stevenson

The Action Occurs in the Home of the Huckins Family in a Small City of the Middle West. Staged by Guthrie McClintic.

Rena Huckins is a masterful woman, born, according to her author, a generation ahead of her time. Without some great commercial enterprise to manage she manages her husband, her children, her church guilds and a section of the Young Women's Christian Association. As a result of her too perfect efficiency she saps the initiative and will power of those about her until they become impotent to make their own decisions. Given a taste of freedom in school the son runs wild. Beaten by being torn from the arms of the man she wanted to marry, the school-teaching daughter finally rebels and courts scandal by an elopement. And the poor husband, embezzling his firm's money in an effort to buy himself a Canadian farm to which he can escape from his wife, is caught and threatened with imprisonment. Even a jail sentence is welcomed by him, and when his wife succeeds in having the charge withdrawn and his freedom guaranteed he shoots himself through the heart.

"CAROLINE"

A musical comedy in three acts by Harry B. Smith and E. Kunneke, adapted from the original of Herman Haller and Edward Rideamus; music by Edward Rideamus and Alfred Goodman. Produced by Messrs. Shubert at the Ambassador Theatre, New York, January 31, 1923.

Cast of characters —

Caroline Lee	Tessa Kosta
Helen	Helen Shipman
Brig. Gen. Randolph Calhoun	Harrison Brockbank
Mrs. Calhoun	Viola Gillette
Bigby Bretton	Barnett Parker
Captain Robert Langdon	J. Harold Murray
Roderick Gray	John Adair
Amanda	Mattie Keene
Hannibal	Ben Linn
Flora Wayne	Beatrice Wilson
Isabel Marshall	Edna Duval
Edith Varden	Jane Brown
Gladys Carroll	Kay Carlin
Mabel Preston	Viola Duval

Joan Blythe.................................Mabel Olson
Josephine Hurley.............................Vera Hoppe
Irene Stone................................Vonnie James

Act I.—The Garden. Act II.—The Veranda. Act III.—The Same. The Old Calhoun Mansion Near Richmond, Va. Period—Just After the Civil War. Staged by Charles Sinclair.

Caroline Lee, ward of Gen. Calhoun, having come into considerable property at the close of the Civil War, stands between her memory of a boy sweetheart, Roderick Gray, and her uncle's desire that she shall marry Robert Langdon, whom none has seen since he was a boy. Langdon, escaping a Yankee prison, finds himself at the Calhoun place and learns of Caroline's love of the Roderick Gray memory. He thereupon pretends to be Gray, and holds Caroline, even after she discovers the deception.

"PEER GYNT"

A dramatic poem by Henrik Ibsen; translation by William and Charles Archer; music by Grieg. Produced by the Theatre Guild at the Garrick Theatre, New York, February 5, 1923.

Cast of characters —

Ase.................................Louise Closser Hale
Peer.................................Joseph Schildkraut
Ingrid.................................Bertha Broad
Mads Moen.................................William Franklin
Bridegroom's Mother.............................Ellen Larned
Bridegroom's Father.............................Philip Leigh
Aslak.................................Stanley Wood
Dancers.....................Albert Carroll, Barbara Kitson
Bride's Father.............................Stanley Howlett
Solveig's Father.........................William W. Griffith
Solveig's Mother.............................Elizabeth Zachry
Solveig.................................Selena Royle
Helga.................................Francene Wouters
Old Man of Hegstad.........................C. Porter Hall
Another Old Man.........................J. Andrew Johnson
Herd Girls.....................Elise Bartlett, Eve Casanova, Helen Sheridan
The Troll King's Daughter....................Helen Westley
The Troll King.............................Dudley Digges
The Troll Chamberlain.....................William Franklin

Troll Courtiers .... Philip Leigh, Stanley G. Wood, William M. Griffith
The Ugly Brat .... Francene Wouters
Kari .... Armina Marshall
Trumpeterstrale .... Philip Leigh
Mr. Cotton .... Stanley G. Wood
Monsieur Ballon .... Albert Carroll
Von Eberkopf .... Edward G. Robinson
Thief .... Romney Brent
Receiver .... Alfred Alexandre
Officer .... Charles Tagewell
Anitra .... Lillebil Ibsen
Begriffenfeldt .... Charles Halton
Fellah .... William Franklin
Hussein .... Stanley Howlett
Peer's Son .... Philip Leigh
The Button-Moulder .... Edward G. Robinson
The Lean One .... Stanley Howlett

Staged by Theodore Komisarjevsky.

A revival of the dramatic poem of Henrik Ibsen, relating the adventures of the highly imaginative egotist who traveled the world in search of his soul's freedom. The translation is that of William and Charles Archer.

"MARY THE 3D"

A comedy in three acts by Rachel Crothers. Produced by Lee Shubert at the Thirty-ninth Street Theatre, New York, February 5, 1923.

Cast of characters —

1870

Mary the 1st .... Louise Huff
William .... Ben Lyon

1897

Mary the 2d .... Louise Huff
Robert .... Ben Lyon
Richard .... William Hanley

1923

Granny .... May Galyer
Mother .... Beatrice Terry
Mary the 3d .... Louise Huff
Father .... George Howard
Bobby .... Morgan Farley
Lynn .... Ben Lyon
Hal .... William Hanley
Letitia .... Mildred Macleod
Max .... Leroy de Saulles
Nora .... Eleanor Montell

In the Homes of the Three Marys. Staged by Rachel Crothers.

(See page 383.)

"SUN SHOWERS"

A musical comedy in three acts. Produced by Lew Cantor at the Astor Theatre, New York; words and music by Harry Delf; February 5, 1923.

Cast of characters —

May Worthy....................................Berta Donn
Minnie Silver..................................Harriette Lee
Mrs. Thompson............................Claire Greenville
Bobby Brown.............................Douglas Stevenson
Jerry Jackson...................................Harry Delf
Alice Worthy....................................Allyn King
Tommy Dugan...................................Tom Dingle
Mike Rockwell..................................Tom O'Hare
Joseph Green................................Eddie Winthrop
William Blue.....................................Mack Wells
John Black.................................William Schutt
Ralph White.................................Jack Kennedy
Pierre...John Boswell
Francois...................................Frank Anderson
Louis...Lee Houston
Gaston.......................................George Berlow

Act I.—Mrs. Thompson's Boarding House. Act II.—The Heliotrope Room—Savoy Hotel. Act III.—Back Yard at Mrs. Thompson's. Time—The Present. Locality—New York City. Staged by Frederick Stanhope.

"WILDFLOWER"

A musical comedy in three acts by Otto Harbach and Oscar Hammerstein, 2d; music by Herbert Stothart and Vincent Youmans. Produced by Arthur Hammerstein at the Casino Theatre, New York, February 7, 1923.

Cast of characters —

Luigi...Jerome Daley
Gabrielle......................................Olin Howard
Gaston La Roche............................Charles Judels
Bianca Benedetto..........................Evelyn Cavanagh
Count Alberto..................................James Doyle
Guido......................................Guy Robertson
Nina Benedetto.................................Edith Day
Lucrezia La Roche.........................Esther Howard

Act I.—Luigi's Farm Yard Near Casimo. Act II.—The Benedetto Villa on Lake Como. Spring. Act III.—Luigi's Farm Yard. Staged by Oscar Eagle.

Nina Benedetto is a pretty little Italian peasant with a country-side reputation for her temper and her way with the boys. A distant uncle dies, willing her 20,000 lire (which was quite a sum in those days) if she will keep her temper, and at the same time act like a lady, for six months. To do this she has to give up her lover, Guido, the tenor, and make light of the slurs of her catty cousin, Bianca, which she does.

"ICEBOUND"

A drama in three acts by Owen Davis. Produced by Sam H. Harris at the Sam H. Harris Theatre, New York, February 10, 1923.

Cast of characters —

Emma Jordan.................................Lotta Linthicum
Henry Jordan.................................John Westley
Nettie Jordan.................................Boots Wooster
Ella Jordan.................................Frances Neilson
Sadie Fellows.................................Eva Condon
Orin Fellows.................................Andrew J. Lawlor, Jr.
Doctor Curtis.................................Lawrence Eddinger
Jane Crosby.................................Phyllis Povah
Judge Bradford.................................Willard Robertson
Ben Jordan.................................Robert Ames
Hannah.................................Edna May Oliver
Jim Jay.................................Charles Henderson

Act I.—The Parlor of the Jordan Homestead. Act II.—The Sitting Room. Act III.—The Parlor Again. Staged by Sam Forrest.

(See page 140.)

"THE LAUGHING LADY"

A comedy in three acts by Alfred Sutro. Produced by Arthur Hopkins at the Longacre Theatre, New York, February 12, 1923.

Cast of characters —

Hamilton Playgate.................................Harry Plimmer
Ellis.................................Walter Howe
Caroline Playgate.................................Alice John

Cynthia Dell..........................Violet Kemble Cooper
Sir Harrison Peters, K.B.C................Kenneth Hunter
Esmee Farr.............................Katharine Emmett
Daniel Farr, K.C.............................Cyril Keightley
Lady Marjorie Colladine....................Ethel Barrymore
Rose.................................Eva Leonard-Boyne
Sir Hector Colladine, D.S.O.................McKay Morris
Act I.—Mrs. Hamilton Playgate's Drawing Room in Mayfair. Act II.—The Drawing Room in Lady Marjorie's Flat. Act III.—The Same as Act II. Period—The Present. Staged by Arthur Hopkins.

The day Lady Marjorie Colladine is divorced from Sir Hector she, fearing social ostracism, injects herself into a dinner party at the Playgates. There she is seated next the brilliant attorney, Daniel Farr, who had that same afternoon torn her reputation to shreds as her husband's advocate. Despite which uncomfortable situation Lady Marjorie completely charms Sir Daniel. In the end she loves him, and knows he loves her. But being noble (and 38) she sends him back to his loyal, but plain, wife and children and agrees to give her own honest, but dull and misguided, husband a second chance.

"THE CHASTENING"

A modern miracle play in five acts by Charles Rann Kennedy. Produced by the Equity Players, Inc., at the Forty-eighth Street Theatre, New York, March 12, 1923.

Cast of characters —

A Carpenter..........................Charles Rann Kennedy
His Wife............................Edith Wynne Matthison
Her Son.....................................Margaret Gage
An Open Place Where Three Roads Meet. The Period Might Be Any: It is Once Upon a Time.

A modern miracle play by the author of "The Servant in the House." In "an open space where three roads meet," and hard by a stable in which they are prepared to spend the night, "a carpenter," "his wife" and "her son" discuss the adventure they have just experienced in the city. The carpenter has brought his wife's son, whom he protests he loves as though he were his own flesh and blood, to the city to meet the wise men in the temple, they having heard of the lad's uncanny answers to the graybeards and learned folk of his home town. And the boy has also confounded his temple hearers. Now the carpenter is a little peeved. The boy is far too confident and too intent on what he mysteriously refers to as "his father's business." As a matter of fact he should be learning to be a carpenter. But the mother is sure her son was intended for higher things than carpentry. She thinks he may even be a priest. The boy himself is able to argue them both out of their convictions and to convince them they should let him follow the work for which he was sent into the world. The chastening intended for the lad is therefore visited upon the father.

"THE SPORTING THING TO DO"

A comedy in three acts by Thompson Buchanan. Produced by Oliver Morosco at the Ritz Theatre, New York, February 19, 1923.

Cast of characters —

Miss Simpson....................................Mary Fisher
Thomas Kennedy..............................Robert Hudson
Judge McLean....................................Jack Raffael
Jean Thornton..................................Emily Stevens
Colonel Thornton............................Walker Dennett
Mrs. Thornton................................Ethel Winthorp
Jack Thornton..................................William Boyd
Eleanor Ainsworth.................................Clara Joel
Mandy...Della Johnson
Jim Loundsbury..............................H. Reeves Smith
Mrs. Suzanne Clegg..........................Bertha Belmore
Rev. Dr. Clegg................................James Applebee

Act I.—Private Office of Thomas Kennedy in Louisville. Act II.—Scene 1—Room in the Apartment of Jack Thornton. Scene 2—At the River Valley Country Club. Act III.—Living Room in Rev. Dr. Clegg's House. Staged by Oliver Morosco and Clifford Brooke.

Jean Thornton knows that her husband is practically living with Eleanor Ainsworth. But she feels that he is only a headstrong boy and is worth saving. She agrees to a divorce, but stipulates that he shall marry Eleanor. And when he is tired of Eleanor, and disgusted with the lure she practiced to win him, then Jean swears she will win him back, which, despite several unhappy experiences, she does, proving, as she says, that many women divorce their husbands because they love them, not because they hate them.

"HAIL AND FAREWELL"

A drama in four acts by William Hurlbut. Produced by Joseph E. Shea, at the Morosco Theatre, New York, February 19, 1923.

Cast of characters —

M. Vauguin....................................Harvey Hayes
Comtesse Chateauriand......................Maude Richmond
Comtesse d'Avillier........................Lucy Ellen Shreve
Duchesse de Villeneuve..................Eleanor Hutchinson
Philippe, Comte de Villeneuve..................Paul Gordon
Isabella Echevaria.............................Florence Reed
Senor Echevaria.............................Gustave Rolland
Lisette.................................Gwendolyn De Lany
John Hart.......................................Harold Salter
First Footman.................................Arthur Bayne
Second Footman.............................Joseph Allenton
Third Footman...........................Theodore Doucet
M. Franc.................................Wells Spaulding
M. Drouet.......................................Paul Leyssac
Erskine Lawrence.............................Murry Bennett
A Gypsy Woman..............................Florence Auer

Act I.—On the Riviera, Spring of 1871. Act II.—Isabella Echevaria's House in Paris. Act III.—Another Room in Isabella's House. Act IV.—Same as Act III. Staged by B. Iden Payne.

Isabella Echevaria, in 1870, was combing the Riviera for an American millionaire named John Hart, with whose assistance she hoped to pay her debts. Isabella is the type that "maddens men like wine," though she, herself, has never loved deeply. She meets Hart, but the same day she also meets young Philippe, a count and a diplomat, and considerable lover himself. Immediately

Isabella lets the millionaire go and takes to herself her first true love, young Philippe. They are very, very happy for weeks. Then Isabella Echevaria learns that she is keeping her lover from his career as a diplomat. Growing more like Camille every minute, she ends by poisoning herself rather than ruin her lover's life.

"RITA COVENTRY"

A comedy in three acts by Hubert Osborne, from the novel by Julian Street. Produced by Brock Pemberton at the Bijou Theatre, New York, February 19, 1923.

Cast of characters —

Pierre....Hans Herbert
Mrs. Fernis....Grace Filkins
Larry Merrick....Edward H. Wever
Busini....Luis Alberni
Paldowski....G. Albert Smith
Eleanor....Leopoldine Damrosch
Herman Krauss....Eugene Powers
Rita Coventry....Dorothy Francis
Richard Parrish....Charles Francis
Louis....Auguste Aramini
Wetherell....Corbet Morris
Patrick Delaney....Dwight Frye
Miss McSweeney....Clare Weldon
Maggie....Harriette Frazier
Johnson....Jay Fassett
Wolff....Curtis Karpe

Act I.—Music Room in Coventry's Home, New York City. Act II.—A Suite at the Ritz, Atlantic City. Act III.—The Same as Act I. Staged by Brock Pemberton.

Rita Coventry, the greatest soprano of her day, restless, temperamental and adventurous, practically elopes with Richard Parrish, a rich young Virginian who loves but does not wholly attract her. Pausing briefly at Atlantic City, Rita becomes interested in a youthful and pink-cheeked music student sent to her hotel to tune her piano. Next day she adopts the piano tuner as her protégé, plans to arrange for his education in Europe and is ready to sail with him at the end of the week.

"YOU AND I"

A comedy in three acts by Philip Barry. Produced by Richard G. Herndon at the Belmont Theatre, New York, February 19, 1923.

Cast of characters —

Veronica Duane.............................Frieda Inescort
Roderick White.............................Geoffrey Kerr
Nancy White................................Lucile Watson
Maitland White.............................H. B. Warner
Etta.......................................Beatrice Miles
G. T. Warren...............................Ferdinand Gottschalk
Geoffrey Nichols...........................Reginald Mason

Act I.—Library Scene of the White Country Home in Westchester County, New York. Act II.—"The Attic—Studio." Act III.—Same as Act II. Staged by Robert Milton.

(See page 75.)

"ANYTHING MIGHT HAPPEN"

A comedy in three acts by Edgar Selwyn. Produced by Selwyn and Company at the Comedy Theatre, New York, February 20, 1923.

Cast of characters —

Gladys Barry...............................Ruth Findlay
Richard Keating............................Roland Young
Weeks......................................Montague Rutherford
Hal Turner.................................Leslie Howard
A Doorman..................................C. Haviland Chappell
Helen Springer.............................Estelle Winwood
Mrs. Springer..............................Lucia Moore
Mrs. Barry.................................Isabel Garrison
Agnes Farrington...........................Helen Cromwell
Howard Matthews............................C. Haviland Chappell
Maitre d'Hotel.............................George Le Soir
A Waiter...................................Arthur Lubin
Miss Wilson................................Joan Treffry
Miss Craig.................................Florence Clarke

Act I.—Scene 1—Richard Keating's Apartment. Scene 2—Entrance to Apartment House. Scene 3—In a Taxicab. Scene 4—Helen Springer's Apartment. Act II.—Richard Keating's Apartment. Act III.—Scene 1—The Barry Apartment. Scene 2—A Corner in a Restaurant. Scene 3—Helen Springer's Apartment.

Richard Keating, jilted by his fiancée because he has failed to stir her imagination, walks out of his apartment house into a rainstorm and, practically, also into the arms of Helen Springer. They meet, they dine, they get amusingly tipsy on Richard's last bottle of champagne, they think they are in love and they are discovered. Richard's fiancée looks them up, and Miss Springer's discarded young man threatens complications. In the end they are properly paired and happy.

"MISTER MALATESTA"

(Afterward "Papa Joe")

A comedy drama in three acts by William Ricciardi. Produced by R. G. Kemmet at the Princess Theatre, New York, February 26, 1923.

Cast of characters —

Lucy	Susan Sterling
Mary	Ida Fitzhugh
Rita	Rhy Derby
Joe Malatesta	William Ricciardi
Charles	Burdette Kappes
Piero	Marius Rogati
Mike O'Reilly	Thomas F. Tracy
Count d'Armand	Antonio Salerno

Scene—Home of Malatesta.

An Italian stevedore, Joe Malatesta, grown rich, and married to an Irish woman, comes upon a series of domestic problems late in life. His much-loved son seduces an equally loved foster sister, Rita, who seeks to save the family disgrace by going away, but is held and forced to tell her story to "Papa" Joe. The old man is hard hit, but forces his son to marry the girl. The arrangement is to the boy's liking. He had always loved Rita, but was afraid to marry her because of the social ambitions of his mother. The ending is joyful.

"HUMORESQUE"

A comedy drama in three acts by Fannie Hurst. Produced at the Vanderbilt Theatre, New York, February 27, 1923.

Cast of characters —

Sarah Kantor.................................Laurette Taylor
Abraham Kantor.................................Sam Sidman
Leon Kantor.................................Alfred Little
Leon Kantor (Grown).................................Lutha J. Adler
Isador Kantor.................................Chester Hermann
Isador Kantor (Grown).................................Lou Sorin
Esther Kantor.................................Ada Hewitt
Esther Kantor (Grown).................................Dorothy Burton
Mannie Kantor.................................Sidney Carlyle
Sol. Ginsberg.................................Frank Manning
Rosie Ginsberg.................................Lillian Garrick
Gina Berg.................................Elsa Grey
Ruby Kantor.................................Charlotte Salkowitz
Leon Kantor II.................................Sidney Salkowitz
Max Elsass.................................Hubert Wilke
Stage Employee.................................James H. Bell
Reporter.................................Wayne Wilson
William.................................Walter H. Brown
Mrs. Finschreiber.................................Vera Berliner

Act I.—Over their Brass Shop at the Home of the Kantor Family, Allen Street, New York City. Act II.—Artist's Room, Symphony Hall, New York. Act III.—Home of the Kantor Family, West End Avenue, New York. Staged by J. Hartley Manners.

Sarah Kantor, mother of a large family struggling for a foothold in America and a living on the East Side, sees the answer to her prayers that a genius may be born to her in young Leon Kantor's love of the violin. Years later Leon does become the greatest of the younger virtuosos of his day. But the war comes and he insists on going. Sarah fights, pleads, prays and commands, but she cannot hold her son, and he marches away to fight.

"ROGER BLOOMER"

A play in three acts by John Howard Lawson. Produced by the Equity Players, Inc., at the Forty-eighth Street Theatre, New York, March 1, 1923.

Cast of characters —

Roger Bloomer....................................Henry Hull
Mrs. Bloomer.............................Caroline Newcombe
Everett Bloomer...........................Walter Walker
Mary, the maid....................................Isabel Hill
Mr. Poppin.................................John C. Hickey
Eugene Poppin................................Louis Calhern
Emma, the stenographer......................Adelaide Wilson
Louise...Mary Fowler
Another Salesgirl..............................Helen Carew
A College Examiner.....................J. Hammond Dailey
A Landlady.......................................Julia Ralph
A Street Walker.........................Margaret Fareleigh
Policeman...Emil Hoch
Miss Burns................................Helen Van Hoose
Elliott T. Rumsey........................Frederick Burton
Office Assistants....................Rolph Ryan, Alan Bunee, Robert Forsythe, Harry Hahn
A Ragged Man...............................Fletcher Norton
Drug Clerk.................................Charles Webster
Another Drug Clerk.............................Harry Hahn
An Old Man.................................Halliam Bosworth
Another Old Man............................James G. Morton
A Detective................................Halliam Bosworth
A Judge.....................................Thomas J. Keogh
Prison Attendant.................................Emil Hoch
Tall Old Woman............................Helen Van Hoose
Small Old Woman..............................Kate Morgan
Creatures in a Dream............Louis Segal, Sylvia Wiles, Mina Henderson

Roger Bloomer, following the mind promptings of an unhealthy adolescence, and rebelling at the mystery of life, abandons home and a college career to go in search of a solution to all that is troubling him. In New York, "the city of women, death and garbage," the mysteries still haunt him, and though Louise, a more normal but equally rebellious adolescent, seeks to set him right, his adventure ends tragically. Both Roger and Louise take poison, Louise dies and Roger, recovering, is held as a material witness. After a nightmare in jail he is found and taken home by his father.

"MORPHIA"

A drama by Duncan McNab and Ludwig Herzer. Produced at the Eltinge Theatre, New York, March 6, 1923.

Cast of characters —

Julian Wade.................................Lowell Sherman
Mrs. Morrison.................................Alice Fleming
Dr. Grant.................................Albert Tavernier
Nurse Margaret.................................Olive Tell

The action takes place during an evening, and the night and morning following it, in the study of Julian Wade, an author of distinction. Staged by Lowell Sherman.

Julian Wade, a successful novelist who suffers from the memory of an accident in which he killed a young girl, seeks to obliterate that memory by using morphine. When he becomes an addict he hides himself away in his rooms for months at a time. An old nurse and a doctor friend seek to cure him by introducing into the house a former sweetheart of Wade's. The girl wins his promise to leave morphine alone, and when he fails to keep it raises her bid by giving him herself. When he again fails her she gives up and agrees to become an addict with him. That is the shock that cures him.

"KING LEAR"

The Shakespearean tragedy. Revived by Reginald Pole at the Earl Carroll Theatre, New York, March 9, 1923.

Cast of characters —

Earl of Kent.................................Moffat Johnston
Earl of Gloucester.................................Arthur Hughes
Edmund.................................Lawrence Cecil
Lear, King of Britain.................................Reginald Pole
Goneril.................................Winifred Johnston
Regan.................................Kirah Markham
Cordelia.................................Genevieve Tobin
Duke of Albany.................................Paul Huber

Duke of Cornwall..............................Frank Arundel
Duke of Burgundy..............................Jameson Reilly
King of France..............................Gregory Safranac
Edgar..............................Lawrence Tibbett
Oswald..............................William Austin
Curan..............................Norman Cope
Fool..............................Beata Karm
Staged by Reginald Pole.

"PASTEUR"

A drama in five episodes by Sacha Guitry; adapted by Arthur Hornblow, Jr. Produced by Charles Frohman at the Empire Theatre, New York, March 12, 1923.

Cast of characters —

Bigo..............................Hartley Power
Roux..............................Hubbard Kirkpatrick
Dalimier..............................Frederick Lewis
Raulin..............................Lyons Wyckland
Bergeron..............................Edward Mackay
Beclard..............................Frank Hay
Louis Pasteur..............................Henry Miller
President of the Academy of Medicine.........Howard Kyle
Dr. Poggiale..............................Wilson Reynolds
Dr. Guerin..............................Leslie Stowe
Dr. Balard..............................Elmer Brown
Baron Larray..............................Stephen Wright
Professor Colin..............................Louis Renault
Theodore Meister..............................A. G. Andrews
Joseph Meister..............................William Pearce
Dr. Grancher..............................Albert Bruning
Henri..............................David Belbridge
President of the French Republic...........Edward Fielding
First Episode.—The Laboratory of Louis Pasteur in Paris, 1870. Second Episode.—The Assembly Room of the Academy of Medicine, 1880. Third Episode.—The Laboratory Again, in 1885. Fourth Episode.—Pasteur's Home in the South of France, 1888. Fifth Episode.—Reception Room outside the Great Hall of the Sorbonne. December 27, 1892.

An historical drama revealing the chief events in the life of Louis Pasteur, French scientist, including his spirited defense of his germ theory before the Academy of Medicine in 1880; his first trial of the serum for the cure of rabies, and the great reception tendered him by the President of France and representatives of the combined medical societies of the world in the Sorbonne in 1882.

"BARNUM WAS RIGHT"

A farce in three acts by Philip Bartholomae and John Meehan. Produced by Louis F. Werba at the Frazee Theatre, New York, March 12, 1923.

Cast of characters —

Miriam Locke....Marion Coakley
Sarah....Susanne Willa
Samuel Locke....Elwood F. Bostwick
Harrison....Denman Maley
Seymour Standish....Robert Adams
Felix Hammer....William E. Morris
Fred Farrell....Donald Brian
Pierre....Arthur J. Wood
Mr. Tuttle....Neil Martin
Mrs. Tuttle....Enid Markey
Burke....Will Deming
Phoebe O'Dare....Lilyan Tashman
Guiseppi Verdi....George E. Mack

Act I.—Locke's Home on Long Island. Act II.—The Manor House. Act III.—Scene 1—The Manor House. Scene 2—Miriam's Room. Scene 3—Same as Scene 1. Staged by John Meehan.

Fred Farrell, who wants to marry Miriam Locke, determines to try out the Barnum theory that there's a sucker born every minute. Miriam's father is of the opinion that Fred is shy of both business sense and initiative. Before the play is over Farrell has taken an abandoned Locke estate on Long Island, cleverly spread the rumor that it is the site of buried treasure, opened the old manor house as an inn and established a side business of leasing picks, hammers, axes and shovels to those who wish to search for the hidden wealth. By the end of the play he has proved himself a good business man and a promising fiancé.

"GO-GO"

A musical comedy in two acts by Harry L. Cort and George E. Stoddard; lyrics by Alex Rogers; music by C. Luckyeth Roberts. Produced by John Cort at Daly's Theatre, New York, March 12, 1923.

Cast of characters —

Mrs. Parker.....Kathi Murray
Otis Hubbard.....Paul Burns
Isabel Parker, Florabel Parker.....Josephine Stevens
Margy.....Vangi Murray
Mrs. Phyllis Full.....May Boley
Telma Finnish.....Lora Sonderson
Senator Locksmith.....Billy Clifford
Oswald Piper.....Don Barclay
Jack Locksmith.....Bernard Granville
Vernile.....Nitzi Vernille
Briggs.....D. L. Roberts

Act I.—Scene 1—Rambler Rose Cottage, Honey Falls, N. Y. Scene 2—Office of the Oswald Theatrical Agency, N. Y. Scene 3—Street Scene in New York. Scene 4—The Lounge at Cafe "The Pink Poodle." Act II.—The Summer Residence of Senator Locksmith. Staged by Walter Brooks.

Isabel and Florabel Parker are twin sisters. One was a nurse in France. The other is a cabaret singer in New York. Jack Locksmith met the nurse over there and starts a search for her when he returns over here. But meeting the cabaret end of the family is sadly disappointed and sore beset with lyrical blues. It all, however, comes out in the finale.

"THE COMEDIAN"

A comedy in three acts by Sacha Guitry; adapted by David Belasco. Produced by David Belasco at the Lyceum Theatre, New York, March 13, 1923.

Cast of characters —

The Comedian.....Lionel Atwill
G. Maillart.....A. P. Kaye
Jacqueline.....Elsie Mackay

Leclerc..H. Paul Doucet
Bloch...Albert Gran
Robert......................................William Lorenz
A Stage Manager..................................Will Hindson
Mounet-Pombla.............................H. Cooper Cliffe
Antoinette Vivier.................................Rose Winter
Marguerite Simonest..........................Evelyn Gosnell
Yvette....................................Marguarite Denys
Marcelle..Myra Florian
Alise..Edmonia Nolley
Henri....................................Jacques de Wolfe
Marie......................................Maquita Dwight
Lucien...Harold Seton

The term "Comedian," as understood in France, does not necessarily mean a player of comedy, but an actor of many parts.

Act I.—The Comedian's dressing room in the theatre. Act II.—Scene 1—In the Comedian's home. Scene 2—The theatre. Act III.—The Comedian's dressing room. Staged by David Belasco.

The Comedian is a favorite actor of Paris, turned 40 and beginning to show it. To himself, however, he insists that he is as young and attractive as ever. Comes an old friend whose niece, Jacqueline, is infatuated with the Comedian, to ask that the actor help in disillusioning the girl. Will he permit her to meet him as he really is, with his graying hair and the deepening lines of his face showing? The Comedian, shocked and resentful at first, finally agrees, but with the mental reservation that at the meeting he will put his waning romantic attractions to the test. The girl comes; the Comedian, without makeup's aid, still makes passionate love to her and wins her utterly. Next day they elope and are married (in the American version only). A few months later the Comedian grows a little indifferent to his young wife, but when she substitutes for his leading woman in an emergency his love for her is revived. And then when she meets the real test and proves how bad an actress she really is he suffers. She, however, is radiant and insists upon becoming his leading woman. Rather than let his public suffer the Comedian gives her up.

"THE LOVE HABIT"

A farce in three acts from the French of Louis Verneuil; adapted by Gladys Unger. Produced by Brock Pemberton at the Bijou Theatre, New York, March 14, 1923.

Cast of characters —

The Young Man.............................James Rennie
Marie.......................................Mary Kennedy
Nadine Morand............................Florence Eldridge
Gustave Morand.............................Ernest Cossart
Rosette Pompon.............................Fania Marinoff
Max Duvelleroy..............................Dwight Frye

The scene is the living-room in Gustave Morand's house in Paris. Staged by Brock Pemberton.

Nadine Morand is annoyed by the persistent attentions of a certain young man who insists upon following her, even into her own home. She orders him away, but he will not go. She orders her husband to throw him out, but because the young man knows of husband's affair with a dancer, husband is afraid to. Instead, he is blackmailed into hiring the young man as his secretary. For two acts the young man continues to pursue the protesting wife, at the end of which time the wife discovers her husband's affair with the dancer. Determined to be even, she again orders the young man from her house, but advises him to leave his address behind.

"THE ADDING MACHINE"

A tragedy in seven scenes by Elmer L. Rice. Produced by the Theatre Guild, at the Garrick Theatre, New York, March 19, 1923.

Cast of characters —

Mr. Zero...................................Dudley Digges
Mrs. Zero..................................Helen Westley
Daisy Diana Dorothea Devore............Margaret Wycherly
The Boss....................................Irving Dillon

Mr. One....................................Harry McKenna
Mrs. One....................................Marcia Harris
Mr. Two....................................Paul Hayes
Mrs. Two....................................Therese Stewart
Mr. Three....................................Gerald Lundegard
Mrs. Three....................................Georgiana Wilson
Mr. Four....................................George Stehli
Mrs. Four....................................Edyth Burnett
Mr. Five....................................William M. Griffith
Mrs. Five....................................Ruby Craven
Mr. Six....................................Daniel Hamilton
Mrs. Six....................................Louise Sydmeth
Policemen....................Irving Dillon, Lewis Barrington
Judy O'Grady....................................Elise Bartlett
Young Man....................................Gerald Lundegard
Shrdlu....................................Edward G. Robinson
A Head....................................Daniel Hamilton
Lieutenant Charles....................................Louis Calvert
Joe....................................William M. Griffith

Scene 1.—A Bedroom. Scene 2.—An Office. Scene 3.—A Living Room. Scene 4.—A Place of Justice. Scene 5.—A Graveyard. Scene 6.—A Pleasant Place. Scene 7.—Another Office.

For twenty-five years Mr. Zero has been working on the books of one firm, patiently, hopefully, expecting promotion and a raise. At the end of that time the firm fires Mr. Zero and puts in adding machines. In a blind rage at such injustice Zero stabs the Boss with a paper file, is tried for murder and executed. Thereafter he adventures through graveyards and Elysian Fields, caring very little for either, until he reaches heaven itself, where he is employed on a gigantic adding machine. The keeper of the place, however, sends his soul back to earth for further seasoning. He is still a failure, even in heaven.

"THE LOVE SET"

A comedy in three acts by Thomas Loudon. Produced by Gavin Muir at the Punch and Judy Theatre, New York, March 19, 1923.

Cast of characters —

Elizabeth Lamont....................................Elizabeth Valentine
John Lamont....................................George Alison
Jack Lamont....................................William Leonard
Ruthie Glassford....................................Carolyn Ferriday

Gertrude Lamont........................Catherine Dale Owen
Job Macpike.............................Kenneth Daigneau
Maggie......................................Barbara Pierce
Tom Sheridan....................................Gavin Muir
A Visitor...............................Russell Morrison

John Lamont, successful in business and rich, is afraid his daughter Gertrude is going to marry Job Macpike, a he-man of the farm, but also a good deal of a bounder. To prevent such a match he tries to bribe Tom Sheridan, a tennis champ, poor but educated, to take Gertrude away from Job. Tom scorns the bribe, until he meets Gertrude, after which he agrees to work for nothing. Gertrude, however, is still for the farm hand of her romance until she discovers the kind he is, just a grubby fortune hunter. Then she turns quickly to tennis and Tom.

"THE GUILTY ONE"

A drama in three acts by Michael Morton and Peter Traill. Produced by A. H. Woods at the Selwyn Theatre, New York, March 20, 1923.

Cast of characters —

Ronald Short..............................Charles Waldron
Dick Raston.......................................Noel Leslie
Mr. Seaton Davies...........................Charles Dalton
Dr. Brassey.................................Henry Warwick
Irene Short...............................Pauline Frederick
Madge Ellis...............................Ethel Intropidi
Annie.......................................Florence Edney

The Scene—Ronald Short's Studio. Place—London. Time—Present. Staged by Edward Elsner.

Irene Short, neglected, as she feels, by her busy husband, turns for consolation to Dick Raston. Ronald Short, the husband, thereupon grabs a gun and goes after Raston, returning later with the report that he has killed him. Mrs. Short, realizing then how much she loves Mr. Short, and how little she cares for Raston, declares that she is really the guilty one and should suffer. When the Scotland Yard man comes to investigate she does everything she can to save her husband and then collapses—only to come to later and discover that the murder was a plant, the Scotland Yard man a friend and the whole thing planned to prove to her where her real love lay.

"JACK AND JILL"

A musical comedy in three acts by Frederic Isham and Otto Harbach. Produced by the Chelsea Producing Corp. at the Globe Theatre, New York, March 22, 1923.

Cast of characters —

Prologue—Beneath the Washington Family Tree

A Descendant of Mary Ball..................Gladys Burgette

THE PLAY

Jack Andrews..............................Donald MacDonald
Donald Lee..................................Brooke Johns
Marcia Manners.............................Winifrede Verina
Phyllis Sisson..................................Beth Beri
Mrs. Malone................................Georgia O'Ramey
Duke of Dippington...........................Lennox Pawle
Jill Malone...............................Virginia O'Brien
Jimmy Eustace................................Clifton Webb
Gloria Wayne...............................Ann Pennington
Daniel Malone...............................Roger Imhof
The Maid....................................Lena Basquette
The Footman..................................Carlos Conte
The Butler...................................Russell Scott
Mrs. Foote.............................America Chedister
Mrs. Sylvester Jones.....................Metta Louise Orr

Solo Dancers—Leon Barte and Lena Basquette, Beatrice Collenette and Helene Blair, Gayle Mays, Ward Fox, Claudius Webster, Beth Beri, Nyoka-Nyoka.

Act I.—Mrs. Malone's Fifth Avenue Antique Galleries. Act II.—The Crystal Ballroom in Mrs. Malone's New York Residence. Act III.—The Garden of the Country Home of Jimmy Eustace.

A song and dance revue expensively draped.

"SANDRO BOTTICELLI"

Romantic drama in three acts by Mercedes de Acosta. Produced by the Players Company, Inc., at the Provincetown Theatre, New York, March 26, 1923.

Cast of characters —

Angelo Poliziano	Philip Leigh
Lorenzo di Pier Francesco	Allyn Joslyn
Giovanni Guespi	Conrad Cantzen
Lorenzo dei Medici	Denis Auburn
Guiliano dei Medici	Reginald Goode
Donna Corrina	Elsa Braun
Leonardo da Vinci	William Kirkland
Fra Filippo Lippi	Erskine Sanford
Leo Batista Alberti	Philip Wood
Donna Rosa	Helenka Adamowska
Donna Isabella	Martha Roberts
Donna Fiora	Merle Maddern
Simonetta Vespucci	Eva Le Gallienne
Sandro Botticelli	Basil Sydney
Paolo	Arthur Bowyer
Catalina	Agnes McCarthy
Court Jester	Walter Kenny
Pages	Paul Jacchia, Alfred Little

At a party given by Lorenzo the Magnificent, Simonetta Vespucci meets and loves Alessandro Botticelli, the painter. Eager to give something to posterity, Simonetta is of a mind to pass on her beauty, put into imperishable oils by the young artist. She promises Botticelli that next day she will visit his studio, clad only in a cloak, and that, slipping the fastenings, she will permit him to sketch her in all her loveliness. Simonetta, being as good as her word, invades the studio, casts aside the cloak and awaits developments. It is spring. Briefly Alessandro hesitates, and then, overcome by the inspiration of the moment, grabs pencils and board and sketches furiously, lest the light fail or Simonetta tire before he can finish. But Simonetta is displeased to think her artist lover should prefer his art to her, and leaves in a huff, taking her cloak with her. The next day, having caught cold in the rain, she is sick of a fever. The third day she dies. And all this time Botticelli is painting for dear life on "The Birth of Venus." He sees Simonetta only for a moment before she dies.

"THE WASP"

A play in three acts by Thomas F. Fallon, produced by Louis H. Kaplan at the Morosco Theatre, New York, March 27, 1923.

Cast of characters —

James "Murray"................................Otto Kruger
Hannah................................Annie Mack Berlein
Horace Hearnden................................Leslie Austen
Edith Hearnden................................Emily Ann Wellman
Gaynor................................Tammany Young
Sewell................................William Corbett
Nolan................................Royal Stout
Peirce................................Ben Hendricks
Mrs. McKaye................................Louise Muldener
Walter Allen................................Otto Kruger
Lola Andros................................Galina Kopernak
James Allen................................Sydney Shepard
Connelly................................Martin Rose

The Scene—In the Home of the Hearndens, Gramercy Park. Staged by Thomas F. Fallon and William H. Gilmore.

Edith Hearnden has been twice tried for murder and the theft of certain bank securities, and twice the jury disagreed. On the discovery of new evidence the case is reopened and a third trial called. Before Edith can be arrested, however, lightning strikes her house and out of the fireplace falls an old diary containing an account of the events leading up to the original crime. As Edith reads, the scenes change and the story of the diary is enacted up to the point at which the murder was done. A last act solution clears the heroine.

"THE ENCHANTED COTTAGE"

A fable in three acts by Sir Arthur Wing Pinero. Produced by William A. Brady, Ltd., at the Ritz Theatre, New York, March 31, 1923.

Cast of characters —

Laura Pennington................................Katharine Cornell
Mrs. Minnett................................Clara Blandick
Major Murray Hillgrove, D.S.O., M.C..........Gilbert Emery

Oliver Bashforth................................Noel Tearle
(Late Lieut. 8th Royal Bengal Regt.)
Rev. Charles Corsellis..........................Harry Neville
Mrs. Corsellis..................................Ethel Wright
Mrs. Smallwood.............................Winifred Frazer
Rupert Smallwood..........................Herbert Bunston
Rigg..Seldon Bennett

LAURA'S DREAM

First Bridal Couple......Thomas Broderick, Phyllis Jackson
Second Bridal Couple......Roland Hanson, Gudrun Mantzius
Third Bridal Couple......Stanley Lindahl, Grace Dougherty
Ethel......................................Gwyneth Gordon
Bridesmaids...............Dorothy Revere, Elizabeth Collins
First Witch (Mrs. Minnett)..................Clara Blandick
Second Witch..................................Helen Ryan
Third Witch..................................Cora Calkins
Cherubs:—Geraldine Ballard, Norman Byron, Francis Fay, Dorothy Dorbandt, Margaret Kastner, Eileen Smith, Harry Garwood.
Imps:—Dolly Tigue, Gertrude Dailey, Julia Gorman, Merlin Ballard
Corsellis Children:—George Ryan, Dolly Tigue, Gertrude Dailey, Genevieve Kane, Julia Gorman, Merlin Ballard, Norman Byron.
Play Staged by Jessie Bonstelle and William A. Brady, Jr.

Oliver Bashforth, bringing a twisted leg, a wry-neck and a shell-shocked set of nerves from the war, seeks to hide away in rural England. He is persistently hunted out by his misunderstanding mother and his stepfather until, in sheer desperation, he marries Laura Pennington, a village spinster who is severely plain as to feature but of a gentle disposition and a good heart. Immediately they are married the spell of the enchanted cottage in which they spend their honeymoon falls upon them, and, seeing each other through the eyes of love, see nothing of each other's marred bodies. So long as they can avoid the world their happiness is supreme. And even after the world comes back, in the persons of relatives and misguided friends, and refuses to accept them as being outwardly changed, they are content.

"IF WINTER COMES"

A play in four acts by A. S. M. Hutchinson and B. Macdonald Hastings. Produced by Charles Dillingham, at the Gaiety Theatre, New York, April 2, 1923.

Cast of characters —

Mrs. Sabre	Mabel Terry-Lewis
Rebecca Jinks	Gladys Burgess
Major Millet	Echlin Gayer
Rev. Sebastian Fortune	Henry Morrell
Mr. Twyning	Edgar Kent
Mark Sabre	Cyril Maude
Harold Twyning	Boyd Clark
Effie Bright	Peggy Rush
Mr. Bright	Edmund Gurney
Lady Tybar	Lydia Bilbrooke
Sarah Jinks	Audrey Cameron
A Coroner	F. Gatenby Bell
A Solicitor	Herbert Ranson
A Chemist	George Tawde
Coroner's Officer	Frank Howson
A Girl Clerk	Eva McRoberts

The Scenes—In Mark Sabre's Home, in a Coroner's Court, and at the Offices of Fortune, East & Sabre.

In this dramatization of a widely read novel the hero, Mark Sabre, is picked up at the point in the story at which he is accepted by the recruiting sergeant and is off to the wars. His coldly critical wife, Mabel, refuses to exult with Mark. Rather is she sadly irritated by the confusion and fuss incident to the readjustment of her home affairs. Back from the army Mark undertakes the protection of Effie Bright, a stenographer from his office who must seek a home for her fatherless child. This act brings about the separation of the Sabres and, when Effie kills herself, the trial of Mark by a coroner's jury to determine his responsibility. The discovery of Effie's confession as to the paternity of her child, Sabre's sacrifice in withholding the boy's name at the cost of losing his own community standing, and the sympathetic support of Lady Tybar, bring the story to a reasonably happy conclusion.

"ELSIE"

A musical comedy in three acts by Charles W. Bell; music and lyrics by Sissle and Blake and Carlo and Sanders. Produced by John Jay Scholl at the Vanderbilt Theatre, New York, April 2, 1923.

Cast of characters —

Margery Hammond	Luella Gear
Fred Blakely	Stanley Ridges
Anne Westford	Ada Meade
Alfie Westford	John Arthur
Mrs. Philip Hammond	Maude Turner Gordon
Philip Hammond	Frederic Burt
Elsie	Marguerite Zender
Irma	Irma Marwick
Harry Hammond	Vinton Freedley
Parker	William Cameron
Julie	Opal Hixson
Vivienne	Nell Ames
Maureen	Elyne Yselle
Esme	Helen Doty
Specialty Dancers	Layman and Kling
Bunny	Maida Harries
Teddy	Hilda Burt
Babe	Neida Snow
Maisie	Nina Rothfield
Toots	Dawne Woods
Goldie	Virginia Kelley
Stella	Helen Borden
Floss	Flo Clark
Veda	Helen Christian

Act I.—Philip Hammond's Summer Residence at Idlewild. Act II.—Sun Parlor in the Same Home. Act III.—Same as Act I. Staged by Edgar MacGregor.

Elsie is an actress who marries Harry Hammond, rich man's son, and finds herself in bad with the family when he takes her home. Elsie is a wonder at singing, dancing and chin-chucking, however, and before the evening has even worn on apace she has all the men trailing her and all the women worried. It is quite a victory for Elsie in the end.

"UPTOWN WEST"

A drama in three acts by Lincoln Osborn. Produced by Earl Carroll at the Bijou Theatre, New York, April 23, 1923.

Cast of characters —

Mildred	Florence Mason
Mrs. Golfarb	Angela Jacobs
Sarah	Frances Victory
Allan Reed	Carlton Brickert
Sakamoto	Henry Herbert
Florence	Grace Heyer
The Doctor	William Podmore
McCarthy	Edmund Norris

Scene—The Living Room of Sakamoto's Apartment, Uptown, West. Time—The Present. Staged by Henry Herbert.

Sakamoto, a liberally Anglicized Jap, marries Mildred, an American girl, as the result of a series of unusual adventures. A boy is born to them. Sakamoto, desperately eager that he shall be able to become a good American in order that his "moon-flower" may be proud of having married him, does all that he can to make his marriage a success. He worships both his boy and his wife. Gradually Mrs. Sakamoto drifts away from him, however, and finally confesses that she has made a mistake and is in love with a man of her own race. When the baby is killed Sakamoto determines to bring his unhappy adventure to an end, strangles a lady he believes to be his wife and cuts his own throat. The strangled one was only an unhappy drug addict, however, and the ending of the story may therefore be accepted as a happy one.

"CINDERS"

A comedy with music in two acts; book and lyrics by Edward Clark; music by Rudolf Friml. Produced by Edward Royce at the Dresden Theatre, New York, April 3, 1923.

Cast of characters —

Tillie Olsen	Queenie Smith
Slim Kelly	Fred Hillebrand
Cinders	Nancy Welford
John Winthrop	Walter Regan
Mrs. Horatio Winthrop	Margaret Dale
Major Drummond	John H. Brewer
Mrs. Delancey Hoyt	Roberta Beatty
Geraldine	Mary Lucas
Butler	Thomas Fitzpatrick
Great Scott	George Bancroft
Miss Breckenridge	Lillian Lee
Mme. Duval	Edith Campbell-Walker
Tottie	Kitty Kelly
Lottie	Estelle Levelle
Hortense	Alta King
Annabelle	Diana Stegman
Mathilde	Dagmar Oakland
Julie	Evelyn Darville
Yvette	Elaine Gholson
Ninette	Eden Gray
Cecelia	Vera De Wolfe
Simone	Louise Bateman
Bruce	Jack Whiting
Nat	Nathaniel Gennes
Frank	Frank Curran
Harry	Harry Howell
Cliff	Abner Barnhart
Denny	Denny Murray
Dewitt	Dewitt Oakley
Thomas	Thomas Green
Gene	Eugene Jenkins

Time—Present. Place—New York. Staged by Edward Royce.

"Cinders," they call the heroine, first, because she was found in an ash can when she was six or seven weeks old, and, second, because she is always wishing she could be like Cinderella. It is in the second act that she "borrows" the rich lady's dress, which she was told to deliver, and goes to the charity ball. Here she meets the rich lady's son, who loves her lyrically and at once. Here, too, she sees the comedian steal the pearls, and though she is revealed as an impostor and accused of the theft, she is able to clear herself with a song or two in the last act.

"THE DICE OF THE GODS"

A drama in three acts by Lillian Barrett. Produced by H. H. Frazee at the National Theatre, New York, April 5, 1923.

Cast of characters —

John Henderson............................Donald Cameron
Buchanan Laurence...........................Robert Strange
Roger Canby.................................Harry Stubbs
Dr. Henry Arnold..........................Joseph Macauley
Charles.....................................Francis Sadtler
Guiseppi Alfano............................France Bendtsen
Mr. Sullivan...............................William T. Clarke
Michele....................................Rodolfo Badaloni
Giovanni...................................William Lambert
Salvatore..................................Frederick Scott
Patricia Baird ("Paddy")........................Mrs. Fiske
Charlotte Baird.............................Ernita Lascelles
Dolly Laurence..............................Helen Jackson
Suzanne....................................Clelia Benjamin
Elise...Evelyn Orton
Mary McCafferty............................Maggie Weston
Francesca..................................Eunice Osborne
Maria......................................Caterina Barone
Beatrice...................................Henrietta Jordan
Lucia.......................................Nera Badaloni

Act I.—Drawing-room at "Idle Ease," Mrs. Baird's Newport Villa. Act II.—Charlotte's Studio, McDougal Street, New York. Act III.—The Bairds' Quarters in the Via Guicciardini, Florence. Staged by Harrison Grey Fiske.

Patricia Baird, born of the Virginia aristocracy, acquires the morphine habit when young, along with a worthless husband. Later she lives and loves recklessly, touring the continent with a gay and loving deceiver to whom she bears a child. With the girl grown to womanhood and eager to marry Roger Canby, poor but persistent, Patricia seeks to turn the girl's interest to an older and richer man. Also she tries her best to keep from her daughter the knowledge of her mother's addiction to drugs. Failing in both these desires Patricia bravely takes an overdose of morphine, and Charlotte is left free to marry her lover, now become successful.

"THE EXILE"

A comedy drama in three acts by Sidney Toler. Produced by Joseph Sidney, Inc., at the Geo. M. Cohan Theatre, New York, April 9, 1923.

Cast of characters —

Baptiste....................................Etienne Girardot
Madame Peronne..............................Marion Abbott
Berenice Millet.............................Eleanor Painter
Jacques Cortot..............................Jose Ruben
Rouget de L'Isle............................Sidney Riggs
Journet.....................................Aubrey Beattie
Le Comte de Santerre........................Wallis Clark
Marthe......................................Tiny Allen
Lafleur.....................................Leonard Ide
Barbier.....................................Rikel Kent

Act I.—Madame Peronne's Lodging House, Paris. Act II.—Scene 1—The Same. Scene 2—Hall in the Comedie Francaise. Scene 3—Peronne's Lodging House. Act III.—Same as Act I. Paris, 1792. Staged by Jose Ruben.

Jacques Cortot, an active young Republican in France before the Revolution, is exiled to England by the royalists for having made fun of Marie Antoinette. Returning to France in disguise he meets and loves a young singer, Berenice Millet, who, through the influence of the court, is given a chance at the Comedie Francaise. When the Revolution breaks, Berenice, in her fine stage clothes, is chased by a mob of citizens and takes refuge in Cortot's rooms. He strips her of her finery, ties a red bandana about her head and sets her singing the "Marseillaise" as the citizens break in. Thus is the situation, and the play, saved.

"ZANDER THE GREAT"

A comedy in a prologue and three acts by Salisbury Field. Produced by Charles Frohman, at the Empire Theatre, New York, April 9, 1923.

Cast of characters —

Jackson Pepper..............................William Wadsworth
Oliver Macy.................................Joseph Baird

Mamie.. Alice Brady
Zander.. Edwin Mills
Elmer Lovejoy.......................... Raymond Van Sickle
Good News.................................... Joseph Allen
Texas.. George Abbott
Dan Murchison............................... Jerome Patrick
Juan.. Joseph Spurin
Jim Sawday.............................. James S. Barrett
Bill Price..................................... Dan Moyles

Prologue—Weeweedin, New Jersey. Act I, II and III—A Ranch Near the Border in Southern Arizona. Staged by David Burton.

Mamie was a sort of girl of all work in the house in Jersey in which Zander's mother died. Zander, short for Alexander, is five and an orphan, but he is supposed to have a father some place in Arizona. So Mamie hitches up the old Ford, piles it high with what household goods she can salvage, not forgetting Zander's rabbits, and starts for Arizona. Arrived there she wanders by mistake into a nest of cowboy bootleggers, one of whom swears he is Zander's father to keep her from leaving and betraying the smuggling industry. Finding out the truth, Mamie threatens trouble until they take her baby from her. After that she is pretty unhappy until all her worries are cleared away in the end. She marries a cowboy and adopts Zander.

"ANATHEMA"

A fantastic drama in seven scenes by Leonid Andreyev, translated by Herman Bernstein. Produced by Maurice Swartz at the Forty-eighth Street Theatre, New York, April 10, 1923.

Cast of characters —

Anathema................................ Ernest Glendinning
David Leizer................................ Maurice Swartz
Sarah, his wife................................ Esther Lyon
Rosa, their daughter........................ Isabel Leighton
Naum, their son............................ Sidney Carlisle
Shopkeepers—
Ivan the Cobbler.............................. Emil Hoch
Sonka the Jewess......................... Sarah Fishman
Purikes the Greek......................... Arthur Ludwig

Dancing Master.............................Edwin H. Morse
The Young Rider.............................Robert Woods
The Older Rider.............................George Spelvin
The Organ Grinder...........................Walter Armin
A Wanderer.................................William Balfour
Abraham Khessin...............................Jack Soble
Weeping Woman..............................Florence Earle
Drunkard...............................Abraham Kubansky
Sonka's Little Girl...........................Jennie Brandt
The Harlot.................................Alice Buchanan

Scenes at the gates of heaven and in a Russian village on earth.

A dramatic fantasy in which Anathema (Satan) is denied entrance at the gates of heaven and returns to earth determined to be even with God. Working through the mediumship of a pious Jew, David Leizer, whom he endows with great wealth and power, he excites a world of sufferers to a renewed faith in God. Then he strips David of both wealth and power and gloats as the mob revolts, denying God and demanding justice. Returning to heaven's gates Anathema demands a second hearing, pointing to God's failure to support his holy agent on earth. His only reward is to be told that the patient David has been admitted to immortality and is even then seated at the right hand of the throne. Whereupon Anathema returns cursing to earth to begin another campaign.

"HOW COME?"

A musical comedy in two acts by Eddie Hunter. Produced by the Criterion Productions, Inc., at the Apollo Theatre, New York, April 16, 1923.

Cast of characters —

Deacon Long Tack..........................Andrew Fairchild
Sarah Green..................................Alice Brown
Brother Wire Nail.........................Leroy Broomfield
Dolores Love..................................Nina Hunter
Sister Doolittle..............................Hilary Friend
Ebenezer Green................................Amon Davis
Brother Ham...................................Alec Lovejoy
A Smart Lawyer...........................Chappy Chappelle

Malinda Joy....................................Juanita Stinette
Rufus Wise....................................George W. Cooper
Rastus Skunkton Lime....................................Eddie Hunter
Dandy Dan....................................George C. Lane
Ophelia Snow....................................Andrew Tribble
Brother Low Down....................................James Dingbat
Sister Whale....................................Betty Throck
Chief of Police....................................Sidney Bechet
First Policeman....................................Harry Hunter
Second Policeman....................................Adrian Joyce
Third Policeman....................................Isaac Momen
Cathrine Place....................................Helen Dunmore
Laurette Wise....................................Vivian Harris
Millie Johnson....................................Mabel Kemp
Marie Fraine....................................Dorothy Lewis
Ruth Johnson....................................Elvetta Davis
Hortense Carter....................................Carrie Edwards

Act I.—Mobile, Alabama. Act II.—Chicago, Ill. Staged by Sam H. Grisman.

A negro vaudeville strung loosely together in the form of a musical comedy.

"WITHIN FOUR WALLS"

A play in two acts by Glen MacDonough. Produced by Mack Hilliard at the Selwyn Theatre, New York, April 17, 1923.

Cast of characters —

Clancy....................................Walter Lawrence
Gerrit Minuit....................................Leonard Doyle
Agnes Meade....................................Anne Morrison
Sam Pickering....................................John Keefe
John Minuit....................................Warner Anderson
Louisa Onderdonck....................................Violet Dunn
Dominick Minuit....................................Dorian Anderson
Louisa Minuit....................................Florence Gerald
Captain John Minuit....................................Sherman Wade
Constable Sparks....................................John Keefe
Homer Prime....................................Eugene MacGregor
Sophie ....Clay Corroll
Captain Dominick Minuit....................................Walter Lawrence
Louisa Minuit....................................Florence Gerald
Captain John Minuit....................................Sherman Wade
Lizzie....................................Nancy Lee
Dr. Bayliss....................................John Keefe
Delphine....................................Helen Ware
Annie....................................Marie Berno
Tom Delmore....................................John Fernlock
Tony Lind....................................Marie Berno
Tim....................................Dorian Anderson

Staged by Oscar Eagle.

Gerrit Minuit, the down and out surviving member of an old New York family, comes to Greenwich Village to take a last look at the Minuit homestead, which is to be wrecked the following day. At the door he meets Clancy, the watchman, and Agnes Meade, a reporter come to get a story about the old place. The three, going inside the house, read from the abandoned writings of Gerrit's ancestors stories of the family's early New York experiences. The scene changes and these episodes are enacted, proving that every man lives again some part of the lives of all his ancestors, good and bad. In the end the girl reporter, who used to be a neighbor, thinks perhaps she can make something of Gerrit. She, at least, is willing to take that chance.

"AS YOU LIKE IT"

The Shakespeare comedy presented by the American National Theatre. Produced under the direction of Robert Milton at the Forty-fourth Street Theatre, New York, April 23, 1923.

Cast of characters —

A Shepherd....................................Albert Powers
Orlando..Ian Keith
Adam...Arnold Lucy
Oliver..Jerome Lawlor
Denis..Hal Higley
Charles....................................Stanley Kalkhurst
Pages........................Edna Rivers, Dorothy Chase,
Hilda Dallmann, Adele Schuyler
Rosalind..................................Marjorie Rambeau
Celia.......................................Margalo Gillmore
Touchstone..................................Ernest Lawford
Le Beau..Edgar Norton
Frederick...John Craig
Amiens...Frank Arundel
Jacques..A. E. Anson
The Duke...................................J. Malcolm Dunn
A Lord..Walter Abel
Corin..Fuller Mellish
Silvius.......................................William Williams
Audrey..Hortense Alden

Phoebe....................................Gwynedd Vernon
William....................................Percival Vivian
First Page....................................G. Anderson
Second Page....................................Norton Meyers
Jacques De Bois....................................Walter Abel
Hymen....................................Mercedes De Cordoba

The Daly version of the Shakespeare comedy. An important revival, inasmuch as it represented a newly formed National Theatre group organized by Augustus Thomas and the Producing Managers' Association, of New York.

"THE DEVIL'S DISCIPLE"

A melodrama in four acts by Bernard Shaw. Produced by the Theatre Guild at the Garrick Theatre, New York, April 23, 1923.

Cast of characters —

Mrs. Annie Primrose Dudgeon....................Beverly Sitgreaves
Essie....................................Martha-Bryan Allen
Christy....................................Gerald Hamer
Anthony Anderson....................................Moffat Johnston
Judith Anderson....................................Lotus Robb
Lawyer Hawkins....................................Alan MacAteer
William Dudgeon....................................Byron Russell
Mrs. William Dudgeon....................................Kathryn Wilson
Titus Dudgeon....................................Lawrence Cecil
Mrs. Titus Dudgeon....................................Maud Ainslie
Richard Dudgeon....................................Basil Sydney
The Sergeant....................................Lawrence Cecil
Major Swindon....................................Reginald Goode
General Burgoyne....................................Roland Young
Mr. Brudenell....................................Byron Russell

Act I.—Kitchen and General Dwelling Room of the Dudgeon Farm House. Act II.—Chief Dwelling Room of Minister Anderson's House. Act III.—Scene 1—Waiting Room in the Town Hall. Scene 2—Council Chamber in the Town Hall. Act IV.—Prison Yard Adjoining the Town Hall.

The adventure of Richard Dudgeon, the black sheep of the Dudgeon family of New England in pre-Revolutionary days, who returns for the reading of his uncle's will. Richard, disgusted with the hypocrisy of his neighbor Puritans, has sworn allegiance to the devil, both in this world and the one to come. Hating sentimentality and denying romance, he still permits the British Redcoats, come to arrest Pastor Anderson, to take him by mistake, over the protest of pretty Judith Anderson, the pastor's wife. He is ready to be hung for a spy in the pastor's place, to the glory of a courageous martyrdom and as an example to his snivelling relatives, when his reprieve arrives.

"SYLVIA"

A comedy in three acts by Leighton Osmun. Produced by the Players' Company, at the Provincetown Theatre, New York, April 25, 1923.

Cast of characters —

Hannah	Eda Heinemann
Jimmy Gordon	Benjamin Kauser
Mr. Pendleton	Carl Glick
Sims	Norman Cope
Gerald Armstrong	Elliott Cabot
Mrs. Sheldon	Lucy Ellen Shreve
William	Donald C. McClelland
Irene Sheldon	Julia Cobb
Sylvia Pendleton	Catherine Cozzens
Billy Craig	Lyons Wickland

In and around Sylvia's stopping places.

Sylvia Pendleton is interested in her grandfather's will, expecting to inherit two million. Grandfather, an irascible old gentleman of 90, is eager to see her married. She is married, in fact, but can't acknowledge her husband because grandfather hates him. Also she has just heard the young man is dead in Russia. Therefore she is free to marry another young man whom grandfather picks out, though she does not love him, after which the secret husband turns up. When the tangle becomes complete Sylvia calmly decides to throw over both her husbands and take on a third, an old bachelor friend.

"THE INSPECTOR GENERAL"

A comedy in four acts by Nikolai Gogol. Produced by the Classic Theatre, Inc., at the Forty-eighth Street Theatre, New York, April 30, 1923.

Cast of characters —

Anton Antonovitch..........................Walker Dennett
Anna Andreyevna..........................Eda Von Buelow
Marya Antonovna..............................Anna Vroom
Luka Lukich......................................Emil Hoch
Ammos Fiodorovich..........................Wm. T. Hayes
Artemy Filippovich............................Walter Armin
Ivan Kuzmich.....................................Arnold Mural
Piotr Ivanovich Dobchinsky....................Royal Tracy
Piotr Ivanovich Bobchinsky..................W. A. Whitecar
Ivan Alexandrovich Khlestakov................Maurice Swartz
Osip..Wm. A. Norton
Ukhovertov...................................Ben H. Roberts
Svistunov.......................................Arthur Ludwig
Derzhimorda.....................................A. Boyarsky
Fevronya.......................................Florence Earle
The Sergeant's Wife........................Ruth Tomlinson
Servant at the Inn...........................J. Monte Crane
Mishka...A. K. Miller
Avdotya..Celia Koch
Merchants—Philip Sherman, Morris Freedman
Sam Schneider, Fred Steinway, Jos. F. Sanoff
Doctor...John Kline
Koropkin.....................................Edward M. Grace
Artemy's Wife..................................May Harmon

Act I.—A Room in the Governor's House. Act II.—A Room in an Inn. Act III.—The same as Act I. The action of the play takes place in the late '30s of the last century. Staged by Maurice Swartz.

Ivan Khleskatov, an imaginative clerk of St. Petersburg, traveling with his faithful servant, finds himself out of funds in a remote Russian village, where the governor and all his staff have been grafting. Mistaking Ivan for an inspector general traveling incognito the guilty officials treat him handsomely and fee him generously. After three acts of high living he escapes before the real inspector arrives.

"MY AUNT FROM YPSILANTI"

A farce-comedy in three acts from the French of Paul Gavault. Produced by Henry Baron at the Earl Carroll Theatre, New York, May 1, 1923.

Cast of characters —

Percival....................Colin Campbell
Mrs. Armitage, from Ypsilanti....................Alice Fischer
Charles Wharton....................Richard Sterling
Lucy....................Jane Richardson
George Harper....................Paul Gordon
Peggy....................Florence Shirley
John Harper....................Frank Andrews
Mrs. Harper....................Zeffie Tilbury
Elizabeth Hammond....................Gypsy O'Brien
James....................Albert Hyde
Mary....................Kay Barnes
Dr. Bunce....................William Eville

Act I.—Drawing Room in Mr. Wharton's Bachelor Apartment in Washington Square. Act II.—The Harper Home in Virginia. Act III.—The Same. Staged by Armand Robi.

George Harper and Charles Wharton, rich young men adventuring through Greenwich Village, take unto themselves a pair of models and live happily until (1) George wants to break off his affair so he will be free to marry advantageously in Virginia, and (2) Charles' aunt arrives from Ypsilanti on a tour of investigation. George beats it for Virginia, where he is followed by his model, Peggy. Charles follows after to help George, and the aunt from Ypsilanti trails them both. In Virginia they are asked many more questions than they have answers for, but a satisfactory adjustment is effected by 10.45.

"PRIDE"

A comedy-drama in three acts by Thompson Buchanan. Produced by Oliver Morosco at the Morosco Theatre, New York, May 2, 1923.

Cast of characters —

Thomas Burton....................William Austin
Alicia Burton....................Martha Leffler

Bell Boy....................................Leroy Kenneth
Fisher..Wm. Sellery
Victor....................................Eugene Redding
Duc de Valmont..............................Fred L. Tiden
Peter Bohn..................................Robert Fisher
Richard Stevens...............................Leon Gordon
Audrey Valmont...............................Juliette Day
Duchesse de Valmont...........................Hilda Spong
Mrs. Bohn.................................Camilla Dalberg
Andrew......................................Fred J. Martell
Anderson.......................................Beach Cooke
Mrs. Hathaway..............................Edelaine Roden
Morgan Howard.............................Kenneth Dana
Estelle Winthrop...............................Mary Fisher
Mrs. Chester Wilson.............................Jane Hope

Act I.—Private Office of Peter Bohn at the Hotel Revere, New York. Act II.—The Lounge. Treuville Inn on Long Island Sound. Act III.—The Same as Act II. Staged by Oliver Morosco.

The Duchesse de Valmont, from Chicago, married the Duc when she was a young girl, and rich. Returning with him to France she bore him a daughter and, though unhappy, lived on at the chateau for eight years. By that time the Duc's mistresses had become so numerous it was difficult to dodge them, so the Duchesse packed up her things and her daughter and went home. The Duc, much chagrined, promised never to see either of them again if she would agree not to prejudice his daughter against him. The play picks them up ten years later, with daughter 18, mother still unmarried and the Duc come to America, after being impoverished by the war, in search of work. He gets a job as a waiter in a swell hotel, meets his daughter face to face, tries to chaperon her through a love affair with a rich American without letting her know the cause of his interest, or that her poor papa is a waiter. The wife recognizes him, and concealment is no longer possible. A general reconciliation is promised.

"THE MOUNTEBANK"

A play in four acts by W. J. Locke and Ernest Denny. Produced by Charles Frohman at the Lyceum Theatre, New York, May 7, 1923.

Cast of characters —

Andrew Lackaday, also known as "Petit Patou" ..... Norman Trevor
Horatio Bakkus..... Lennox Pawle
Anthony Hylton..... T. Wigney Percyval
Harry Verity-Stewart..... Charles Romano
Gustave..... Louis La Bey
Parker..... F. Cecil Butler
Lady Auriol Dayne..... Lillian Kemble Cooper
Elodie..... Gabrielle Ravine
Lady Verity-Stewart..... Marjorie Chard
Evadne..... Nora Swinburne

Act I.—1912. Andrew's Dressing Room in the "Olympia Music Hall," Avignon. Act II.—1914. Andrew's Flat in the Rue St. Denis, Paris. Act III.—1919. The Hall at Mansfield Court—The Verity-Stewarts' House in the South of England. Act IV.—1919. Autumn. Same as Act II.
Staged by David Burton.

Andrew Lackaday, born an Englishman, reared in a French circus, teams up and lives with a French girl, Elodie. When the war breaks Lackaday joins with England, rises to the rank of brigadier general and retires, after the war, a hero. Through his army connections he meets and loves the highborn Lady Auriol Dayne, but from a sense of loyalty to Elodie, goes back to her and the circus, whither he is followed by her ladyship, seeking an explanation of his desertion of her. When his old friend Bakkus runs away with Elodie it leaves Lackaday free to make Lady Auriol happy.

"SALOME"

Oscar Wilde's poetic drama. Produced by the Ethiopian Art Theatre at the Frazee Theatre, New York, May 7, 1923.

Cast of characters —

Young Syrian..... Arthur Ray
Page of Herodias..... Lionel Monagas

First Soldier................................Lewis Alexander
Second Soldier..............................Coy Applewhite
Cappadocian.................................Charles Olden
Jokanaan....................................Solomon Bruce
Salome.......................................Evelyn Preer
Herod...................................Sydney Kirkpatrick
Herodias.....................................Laura Bowman
First Jew.....................................Charles Olden
Second Jew.................................George Jackson
Third Jew.....................................Walter White
Tigellinus.................................Arthur Thompson
Slave of Herodias..........................Marion Taylor
Scene—A Terrace in the Palace of Herod.

"THE CHIP WOMAN'S FORTUNE"

A comedy in one act by Willis Richardson.

Cast of characters —

Liza..Evelyn Preer
Silas...................................Sydney Kirkpatrick
Emma.......................................Marion Taylor
Aunt Nancy................................Laura Bowman
Jim...Solomon Bruce
A Man...Arthur Ray
Scene—The Home of Silas.

A complete version of Oscar Wilde's dramatic one-act play, preceded by a miniature folk drama, "The Chip Woman's Fortune," relating the incident of Silas' failure to pay the installments on his victrola and the trouble it got him into. It happened the day Jim got out of jail and Aunt Nancy, who had been saving her money to help Jim, dug it up out of the back yard, without any idea of how much she had saved. It proved to be enough to pay for the victrola and give Jim enough for a grand bust, and they were all dancing merrily to a jazz record when the curtain fell.

"THE RIVALS"

A revival by Equity Players, Inc., of the Sheridan comedy. Produced at the Forty-eighth Street Theatre, New York, May 7, 1923.

Cast of characters —

Sir Anthony Absolute....................Maclyn Arbuckle
Captain Absolute....................Sidney Blackmer
Faulkland....................McKay Morris
Acres....................Francis Wilson
Sir Lucius O'Trigger....................J. M. Kerrigan
Fag....................John Craig
David....................James T. Powers
Mrs. Malaprop....................Mary Shaw
Lydia Languish....................Violet Heming
Julia....................Eva Le Gallienne
Lucy....................Vivian Tobin

Act I.—Scene 1—The Drawing Room in Mrs. Malaprop's House. Scene 2—Captain Absolute's Lodgings. Act II.—Scene 1—The North Parade. Scene 2—The Drawing Room in Mrs. Malaprop's House. Scene 3—Acre's Lodgings. Act III.—Scene 1—The Drawing Room in Mrs. Malaprop's House. Scene 2—King's Mead Fields. The action of the play takes place at Bath. Staged by Mrs. Shelley Hull.

"FOR VALUE RECEIVED"

A melodrama in four acts by Ethel Clifton. Produced at the Longacre Theatre, New York, May 7, 1923.

Cast of characters —

Almeric Thomson....................Augustin Duncan
Beverly Mason....................Maude Hanaford
Lawrence Banning....................Louis Kimball
Fellman Thorndyke....................Cecil Owen
Catherine Mason....................Eleanor Griffith
Anthony....................Harry Blakemore
Bernice Quinlan....................May Hopkins

The action of the play takes place in the Study of the Country Home of Almeric Thomson. The Time is the Present. Staged by Augustin Duncan.

Almeric Thomson, rich author, and Beverly Mason, his secretary, a pretty girl and twenty years his junior, are back from a tour of the world. In many hotels they had registered as "Mr. and Mrs." Thomson's eyesight has gradually failed until he is entirely dependent on Miss Mason. He proposes that they marry, but is too proud to admit either his love or his need of her. Hurt, she would leave him, when his lawyer stops her with the accusation that she has systematically been robbing her employer. Her defense is that she has taken more than her salary because without Thomson's knowledge she has written at least half the stories sold. The money she had spent to provide a younger sister with an education, and she felt she had given more than value received for all she had taken. She leaves Thomson for a year, but returns to find him pathetically in need of her and decides to stay.

"THE APACHE"

A play in a prologue, two acts and an epilogue, by Josephine Turck Baker. Produced at the Punch and Judy Theatre, New York, May 7, 1923.

Cast of characters —

Monsieur Le Von (The Apache)	Juan de la Cruz
Madame Viennese	Thais Magrane
Michelet	Goldwyn Patten
William Vokes	Willard Dashiell
Betty Summers	Mary Ellen Ryan
Billy Clarke	Barry Townsley
Frau Fritz Schnitzler	Ida Fitzhugh
Signor Giovanni Lazzari	Louis Alberni
Madame Beauclaire	Marie Bonsall

The action of the play takes place between the hours of early evening and midnight. The locale is the music room of the studio apartment of Madame Viennese at the Hotel Napoleon. Time—The Present. Place—The Hotel Napoleon, Paris. Staged by Will H. Gregory.

A dream play in which a jealous husband discovers the harm he might do the professional pianiste who is his gifted wife.

LITTLE THEATRE TOURNAMENT

Conducted by Walter Hartwig, in coöperation with the New York Drama League for three $100 prizes and a David Belasco trophy, at the Bayes Theatre, New York, the week of May 7, 1923.

Monday Evening, May 7

Little Theatre League of Bridgeport, Conn., in "The Rut," by Sarah Sherman Pryor.

The cast —

Margaret Kent............................Julia C. Farnam
Beatrice Allison, her younger sister..Dorothy Ogden Wheeler
Donald Allison, her brother-in-law..........John MacDonald
Her neighbors:
Mrs. Jenkins....................Katherine Wheeler Clark
Mrs. Miles............................Eleanor R. Clifford
Dr. Ralph Graham......................Hal Thurman Kearns

Scene: Margaret Kent's home in a small New England village. Staged by the author. Scene by Charles H. Armstrong.

The Huguenot Players, New Rochelle, N. Y., in "The Revolt of the Mummies," by Theodore Pratt.

The cast —

The Slave Mummy........................Theodore Jacobson
The Melancholy Mummy....................Eugene Beaupre
The Lively Mummy..........................Jerome Brown
The Pharaoh Mummy.......................Sylvan Hoffman
Valeeta, former wife, at various stages in her career, of the other mummies.....................Hazel Deschere
Socrates, a statue..............................James Lipser

Scene: The entrance to a museum.

The Riverside Players, Greenwich, Conn., in "Boccaccio's Untold Tale," by Harry Kemp.

The cast —

Florio..Baxter Liebler
Olivia..Evelyn Wight
Violante...................................Imogen Reynolds
Lizzia.................................Edith Mills Carleton

Dioneo....................................Clarence Boylston
Voices......Merwin Stoughton, Gwendolyn Gray, Ruth Jaycox
In the procession bearing the dead—E. Warfield Kelly, Jr., John Warner, Arthur Warner, William Crawford

Scene: Lower room in Florio's house, Florence. Produced by Mary Hill-Brown.

The Wayside Players, Scarsdale, N. Y., in "The Trysting Place," by Booth Tarkington.

The cast —

Lancelot......................................Roy Durstine
Mrs. Curtis..................................Eleanor Besse
Jessie...............................Margaret M. Conwell
Mrs. Briggs.................................Clara Pleuthner
Rupert..................................Chester Van Tassel
Mr. Ingoldsby...........................Hobart B. Upjohn

Scene: A room just off the lounge of a fashionable hotel.

Tuesday Evening, May 8, 1923

The Trenton Players' Guild, Trenton, N. J., in "Under Conviction," by Milnor Dorey.

The cast —

John Delker..............................James Fitzcharles
Ann Delker..................................Ellen O'Toole
Sam Delker...................................Otto Fischer
Mag Metzger................................Marion George

Scene A Pennsylvania miller's kitchen. Directed by Milnor Dorey.

The Great Neck Players, Great Neck, L. I., in "A Thousand Generations and One," by Ethelyn E. Keays.

The cast —

Nishi-gawa.....................................John Muller
Kan.................................Elizabeth Macdonald
Yone.............................Clara Vaughan Gaffney

Scene: Nishi-gawa's home in Tokio. Directed by E. P. Gaffney.

The Circle Players of Manhattan, in "None Are So Blind," by Mark Hellinger.

The cast —

Mary..Lucile Arnold
Mrs. Smith................................Miriam Ravitch
"Actor" John..............................Murray Phillips
Scene: A room in a house on one of the principal streets of Derelict Land. Directed by Murray Phillips.

The Brooklyn Institute Players, Brooklyn, N. Y., in "Thursday Evening," by Christopher Morley.

The cast —

Gordon Johns..............................Bennett Kilpack
Laura..Esther Davis
Mrs. Sheffield.........................Effie Lawrence Palmer
Mrs. Johns................................Rose Blanchfield
Scene: A kitchen in the suburban home of Mr. and Mrs. Gordon Johns. Directed by Bennett Kilpack.

WEDNESDAY EVENING, MAY 9, 1923

*The Fireside Players, White Plains, N. Y., in "The Crowsnest," by William Manley.

The cast —

The Greenhorn Kid.........................David Pritchard
Jo-Jo. Cockney A. B.........................Thomas Scofield
Mr. Peturson..............................Stuart Snelling
Scene: Aboard the old hooker *Jessamine*. Directed by Warren Ives. Scenes by the Fireside Players.

The Alliance Players, Jersey City, N. J., in "Punk, or The Amateur Rehearsal," by Henry Clapp Smith.

The cast —

Mrs. Harry Cooper (Ethel).................Edith Finkeldey
Miss Bertha Bull.........................Jeannette Aadnesen
Miss Isabel Griffen.......................Katherine Ehrhardt
Mr. Harold W. Griffen (her brother).......W. Walter Dippel
Mr. Lincoln Anderson............................Alan Stark
Mr. Harry Cooper...........................John Ehrhardt
Mr. Frank Thompson...........................John Bruno
Scene: Anywhere east of St. Louis. Directed by Paul W. Millelot.

*The Gardens Players, Forest Hills, L. I., in "The Clock," by Robert Courtney.

The cast —

Hugh, the eldest brother......................Edward Swazey
Benton, the youngest brother..................Melville Greig
Lida, their sister..............................Blanche Lopez
Roger, the second brother...................Frederick Smith
Scene: Interior of a lonely farmhouse.

The Temple Players of Manhattan, in "The Man Who Married a Dumb Wife," by Anatole France.

The cast —

A Chickweed Man..............................Sol Bachrach
Giles Boiscourtier.....................Theodore M. Bernstein
Alison, maid servant..........................Evelyn Keller
Master Adam Fumee, lawyer................Mortimer Offner
Master Leonard Botal, judge...........Leonard F. Manheim
A Water Cress Girl........................Dorothy Bachrach
Catherine, Leonard's wife....................Claudia Ullmann
Master Simon Colline, doctor.............Julian Wolfenstein
Master Jean Maugier, surgeon and barber..Jerome M. Ullman
Master Serafin Dulaurier, apothecary.........George Maurel
Mlle. de la Grandiere........................Florence Morris
Mme. de la Bruine..............................Ruth Winter
Time and place: Medieval Paris. Staged by Leonard Manheim.

THURSDAY EVENING, MAY 10, 1923

*The East-West Players of Manhattan, in "The Little Stone House," by George Calderon.

The cast —

Varvara, a servant................................Lola Frild
Asteryi, a lodger............................Henry B. Forbes
Spiridon, a stonemason..................S. Robert Wyckoff
Foma, a lodger.............................George Lamont
Praskovya, a lodging-house keeper.........Regina Sadokerski
A Stranger....................................Gustav Blum
A Sergeant..................................Robert J. Lance
Scene: Sitting room of Praskovya's inn; a small provincial town in Russia. Directed by Gustav Blum.

Adelphia Dramatic Association, Brooklyn, in "The Will O' The Wisp," by Doris F. Halman.

The cast —

The Country Woman........................Helen Malmud
The Lady..Edith Hurd
The Maid..............................Carola Tuchschmid
The Will o' the Wisp.....................Eleanor Coryell

Scene: At the land's end. Directed by Eleanor Coryell.

The Cranford Dramatic Club, Cranford, N. J., in "Torches," by Kenneth Raisbeck.

The cast —

Gismonda.................................Margaret Low
Alessandro...............................Robert Whiton
Pietro...Carl Mason
Madam Giulia..................................Vera Smith
A Page......................................Helen Tatnall

Scene: A castle in Lombardy. Directed by Clara Low.

The Clark Street Players, Brooklyn, in "The Pot Boiler," by Alice Gerstenberg.

The cast —

Gus, a stage hand..........................Arthur B. Davis
Thomas Pinickles Sud, the playwright..B. Meredith Langstaff
Wouldby, the novice.........................Earl B. Harris
Inkwell, the villain.................Theodore Fitz-Randolph
Mr. Ivory, the financier................Roy B. Fitz-Randolph
Mr. Ruler, the hero........................Bruce D. Bromley
Miss Ivory, the heroine......................Florence Sparks
Mrs. Pencil, the woman..................Dorothy C. Cochran

Scene: The stage of a theatre during rehearsal. Directed by Helen Chichester Otis.

FRIDAY EVENING, MAY 11, 1923

The Nyack Club Players, Nyack, N. Y., in "Three Pills in a Bottle," by Rachel Lyman Field.

The cast —

Tony Sims.................................Hilda J. Couch
The Widow Sims, his mother..............Edith B. Vickers
A Middle-aged Gentleman....................N. C. Robbins

His Soul................................F. W. Randerbrock
A Scissors Grinder........................Malcolm F. Smith
His Soul..................................James H. Blauvelt
A Scrub Woman.............................Anne K. Hays
Her Soul..................................Alice Crosby

Scene: A room in the house of the Widow Sims. Produced under direction of Arthur F. Buys and C. Arthur Coan. Street scene by Frances C. Challoner Coan.

The Stockbridge Stocks of Manhattan, in "The Mistletoe Bough," by Dorothy Stockbridge.

The cast —

The Shopkeeper....................Edward Hope Coffey, Jr.
His Friend..............................Benjamin Hoagland
The Ballad Singer.......................Dorothy Stockbridge

Scene: A shop on a by-street. Set designed by Archie Austin Coates.

The Players League of Manhattan, in "Another Way Out," by Lawrence Langner.

The cast —

Margaret Marshall...........................Elizabeth Hill
Mrs. Abbey......................................Jane Baker
Pomeroy Pendleton....................Charles L. Trout, Jr.
Baroness de Meauville.........................Della Mounts
Charles P. K. Fenton..........................Arthur Levy

Scene: A studio in Greenwich Village. Directed by Charles L. Trout, Jr.

The Montclair Players, Montclair, N. J., in "The Monkey's Paw," by W. W. Jacobs, dramatized by Louis N. Parker.

The cast —

Mr. White.................................Robert G. Bellah
Mrs. White................................Alice Ham Brewer
Herbert...................................Harvey Mansfield
Sergeant-Major Morris...................Herbert W. Dutch
Mr. Sampson...............................F. Layton Brewer

Scene: Interior White's Cottage. Directed by Harvey Mansfield.

* The East-West Players were awarded the Belasco Trophy and shared with the Gardens Players of Forest Hills and the Fireside Players of White Plains the three $100 prizes.

"DEW DROP INN"

A musical comedy in two acts by Walter DeLeon and Edward Delaney Dunn; music by Alfred Goodman; lyrics by Cyrus Wood. Produced by the Messrs. Shubert at the Astor Theatre, New York, May 17, 1923.

Principal performers —

James Barton	Evelyn Cavanaugh
Harry Clark	Mabel Withee
William Holden	Marcella Swanson
Jack Squire	Beatrice Swanson
Spencer Charters	Mary Robson
Robert Holliday	Sylvia Highton
Frank Hill	
Richard Dore	

Staged under the supervision of J. J. Shubert.

"SWEET NELL OF OLD DRURY"

A comedy in four acts by Paul Kester. Produced by the Equity Players, Inc., under the direction of J. Hartley Manners, at the Forty-eighth Street Theatre, New York, May 18, 1923.

Cast of characters —

Nell Gwynne.................................Laurette Taylor
Lady Castlemaine............................Lynn Fontanne
Duchess of Portsmouth...................Helenka Adamowska
Lady Olivia Vernon........................Marguerite Myers
Tiffin...Laura Burt
Charles II., King of England....................Alfred Lunt
(By Courtesy of Distinctive Pictures Corporation)
Lord Jeffreys..............................Herbert Grimwood
Sir Roger Fairfax...........................Regan Hughston
Lord Rochester.....................................Richie Ling
Lord Lovelace...................................Schuyler Ladd
Percival..Leo Stark
Rollins...Howard Lindsay
Lacy..Leonard Booker
Captain Clavering..............................Edwin Holland
Alderman..George Baxter
2nd Alderman...................................Charner Batson
Mercer..Lionel Chalmers

William....................................Seymour Jamison
Lord-in-Waiting..................................James Bell
Master Bliff..................................Paul Jacchia

Act I.—Before the King's Theatre, Drury Lane. Act II.—Drawing Room at Nell Gwynne's House, Pall Mall. Act III.—A Room in Lord Jeffreys' House. Act IV.—A Room in the Palace, Whitehall.

Nell Gwynne, bantering wit with King Charles II at the door of Drury Lane, so charms the monarch that she later becomes his most treasured mistress. In attempting to aid the escape of Sir Roger Fairfax, accused of treason, Nell impersonates the Lord Chief Justice and otherwise gets herself and her friends involved in a pretty mess, from which she as prettily extricates all concerned when the Justice himself is proved the villain of the cabinet.

"AREN'T WE ALL?"

A comedy in three acts by Frederick Lonsdale. Produced by Charles Dillingham at the Gaiety Theatre, New York, May 21, 1923.

Cast of characters —

Morton..George Tawde
Hon. Willie Tatham.........................Leslie Howard
Lady Frinton.............................Mabel Terry-Lewis
Arthur Wells..................................Denis Gurney
Martin Steele.................................Jack Whiting
Kitty Lake...................................Roberta Beatty
Lord Grenham..................................Cyril Maude
Margot Tatham....................................Alma Tell
Roberts.....................................F. Gatenby Bell
Hon. Mrs. Ernest Lynton................Marguerite St. John
Rev. Ernest Lynton..........................Harry Ashford
John Willocks...............................Geoffrey Millar

Act I.—A Room in Willie Tatham's House in Mayfair. Act II.—A Room in Lord Grenham's House in the Country. Act III.—Same as Act II. Staged by Hugh Ford.

Margot Tatham, returning unexpectedly from a trip to India, walks in upon her husband, the Hon. Willie Tatham, kissing Kitty Lake full upon the lips. Both surprised and hurt, Margot threatens to leave Willie forthwith, but Lord Grenham, Willie's father, a boastful old beau who is proud of his own escapades, manages to save his son by coming accidentally upon a young Australian who had met Margot in India and who remembers one famous moonlight night when even she forgot her home and Willie long enough to permit herself to be kissed. A happy compromise follows.

"COLD FEET"

A farce in three acts by Fred Jackson and Pierre Gendron. Produced by the Biltmore Producing Co., Inc., at the Fulton Theatre, New York, May 21, 1923.

Cast of characters —

Dr. Harry Nolles....Glenn Anders
Coralie Prentice....Annette Bade
Audrey Stanton....Beth Martin
Jack Prentice....Gay Pendleton
Diana Ainsley....Catherine Calhoun Doucet
Count Louis De La Tour....Louis D'Arclay
George Prentice....John T. Doyle
Sophie....May Vokes
Kelly....Leighton Stark

The Scene—Sitting Room Occupied by Dr. Nolles in Mrs. Ainsley's Country House in Connecticut. Staged by Edgar MacGregor.

Coralie Prentice, having thrown over Dr. Harry Nolles, marries Count De La Tour. Dr. Nolles is best man and the wedding takes place in the house in which he has an office. After the wedding Coralie, while getting out of her bridal gown into her traveling things, feels faint. Rushing into the doctor's office in her negligee she asks for a restorative, and the doctor, in his excitement, gives her chloral. Thereafter he is kept busy hiding the sleeping Coralie and drugging the rest of the cast that they may not think the worst, which they do anyway.

"NOT SO FAST"

A comedy in three acts by Conrad Westervelt. Produced by John Henry Mears at the Morosco Theatre, New York, May 22, 1923.

Cast of characters —

Robin Standish............................James Dyrenforth
(Courtesy of Jessie Bonstelle)
Sylvester Vane......................Theodore Westman, Jr.
Arabella..................................Beatrice Bradley
Rose Standish...............................Marian Mears
Mary Standish.................................Ann Davis
James Barton Acton...........................Leon Gordon
Henry Watterson Blake.....................Taylor Holmes
Fay Fothergill...............................Jeane Greene

Act I.—Living Room of the Standish Apartment, New York City. Act II.—Acton's Office, Woolworth Building. Act III.—Same as Act I. Staged by Leon Gordon.

Henry Watterson Blake, of Louisville, Ky., appointed one of two guardians of the Standish children of New York, stands out against the other guardian, James Acton, when the latter seeks to invest the children's money in a questionable stock scheme. Henry, who is called "The Blimp" because he is slow to move and hard to maneuver, becomes quite unpopular with the Standishes, especially with Mary, the oldest. But in the end she realizes how wise and noble he is and agrees to marry him.

"SUN UP"

A drama in three acts by Lula Vollmer. Produced by the Players' Company, Inc., by arrangement with Lee Kugel, at the Provincetown Theatre, New York, May 25, 1923.

Cast of characters —

Widow Cagle..............................Lucille La Verne
Pap Todd....................................Owen Meech
Ennie.......................................Anne Elstner

Bud....................................Eugene Lockhart
Sheriff Weeks..............................France Bendtsen
Rufe Cagle..............................Alan Birmingham
Preacher.............................Burnside Babcock
The Stranger...............................Elliott Cabot
Bob.......................................Norman Dale

Living Room of Widow Cagle's Cabin in the North Carolina Mountains. Staged by Henry Stillman and Benjamin Kauser.

For the better part of sixty years the Widow Cagle has lived in her mountain cabin in North Carolina, loving few things and hating many. Her father was killed in the Civil War, the revenuers shot her husband and when her boy, Rufe, is drafted for the great war she is pretty bitter. It is, she assumes, another war with the Yanks, and France is somewhere forty miles or more the other side of Asheville. Later word comes that Rufe has been killed in action, at about which time the old lady discovers that she has been harboring in her house the son of the revenuer who killed her husband. She raises her rifle to shoot him and thus be sweetly revenged, when the spirit of her dead son whispers to her that the world will never be right until there is more love and less hate in it. Her change of heart is immediate and complete, and she determines to spend the rest of her days in peace.

"ADRIENNE"

A musical play in two acts from a story by Frances Bryant and William Stone; book and lyrics by A. Seymour Brown; music by Albert Von Tilzer. Produced by Louis F. Werba at the Cohan Theatre, New York, May 28, 1923.

Cast of characters —

Sid Darrel, alias Nadir Sidarah........Charles Cahill Wilson
Nora Malone, alias Nadja.......................Laura Arnold
Prison Guard................................John Kearney

Bunk Allen, alias Ali Bunjke..................Billy B. Van
Grace Clayton....................................Mable Ferry
Thomas..Robert Starr
John Grey.....................................Richard Carle
Mrs. John Grey...............................Jean Newcomb
Bob Gordon.......................................Dan Healy
Adrienne Grey...............................Vivienne Segal
Stephen Hayes..............................Harry Fender
Attendant at the Shrine of Ramah.............John Kearney

Act I.—Scene 1—Outside Sing Sing Prison, Ossining, N. Y. Scene 2—The Terrace of John Grey's Home, Near New York. Act II.—At the Shrine of Ramah. Staged by Edgar J. MacGregor.

Adrienne Grey, becoming fascinated with the study of occultism, is tricked by comic sharpers into wearing all her jewels to a shrine, where she hopes to meet the spirit of the prince who loved her several centuries back. The spirit prince is impersonated by her real lover, and the crooks are caught, but not until everybody has done his share of the singing and dancing.

"THE SCHOOL FOR SCANDAL"

A revival of the Sheridan comedy under the direction of the Players' Club. Produced at the Lyceum Theatre, New York, June 4, 1923.

Cast of characters —

Sir Peter Teazle..................................John Drew
Sir Oliver Surface...............................Tom Wise
Joseph Surface...............................McKay Morris
Charles Surface.............................Charles Richman
Sir Benjamin Backbite.......................Henry E. Dixey
Crabtree....................................Etienne Girardot
Snake...Robert Mantell
Careless...John Craig
Sir Harry Bumper..........................Reinald Werrenrath
Moses.....................................Albert G. Andrews
Rowley..Albert Bruning
Trip..Ernest Lawford
Servant to Sir Peter Teazle...................Grant Mitchell
Servant to Lady Sneerwell..................Walter Hampden
Servant to Joseph Surface....................Francis Wilson
Lady Teazle................................Ethel Barrymore
Lady Sneerwell.........................Violet Kemble-Cooper
Mrs. Candour..............................Charlotte Walker
Maria......................................Carrol McComas

"PASSING SHOW"

A musical revue produced by the Messrs. Lee and J. J. Shubert; books and lyrics by Harold Atteridge; music by Sigmund Romberg and Jean Schwartz. Produced at the Winter Garden, New York, June 14, 1923.

Principals engaged —

George Hassell	Joan Hay
Walter Woolf	Helen Shipman
Roy Cummings	Josephine Drake
George Jessel	Olive Ann Alcorn
James Watts	Louise Dose
Barnett Parker	Vera Ross
Flanagan and Morrison	Jean Steele
Libby and Sparrow	Jeanette Gilmore

Staged by J. C. Huffman, under the supervision of J. J. Shubert.

STATISTICAL SUMMARY

(June 15, 1922–June 15, 1923.)

Plays	*Performances*
Adding Machine, The	72
*Adrienne	24
Anathema	15
Antigone	4
Anything Might Happen	63
Apache, The	16
*Aren't We All	32
As You Like It	8
Awful Truth, The	144
Banco	69
Barnum Was Right	88
Beranger	4
Better Times	409
Bombo	24
Bootleggers, The	32
Brothers Karamazoff, The	8
Bunch and Judy, The	63
*Caroline	149
Chastening, The	18
Chip Woman's Fortune, The (Ethiopian Art)	8
Cinders	31
Clinging Vine, The	184
Cold Feet	24
Comedian, The	87
Comedie Francaise (Cecile Sorel)	16
Comedy of Errors (Ethiopian Art)	8
Crowns	8
Daffy-Dill	71
Dagmar	56
Dancing Girl, The	126
*Devil's Disciple, The	64
*Dew Drop Inn	37
Dice of the Gods, The	20
Dolly Jordan	5
Doormat, The	4
Dragon, The	4
Dreams For Sale	13
East of Suez	100
Egotist, The	48
Elsie	40
Enchanted Cottage, The	65
Endless Chain, The	40
Ever Green Lady, The	13
Exciters, The	43
Exile, The	32
Extra	21
Faithful Heart, The	31
Fantastic Fricassee, A	112

Plays	*Performances*
Fools Errant	64
*Fool, The	272
49ers, The	16
For Value Received	48
From Morn to Midnight	24
George White's Scandals	88
Gingham Girl, The	422
*Give and Take	172
Glory	64
God of Vengeance, The	133
*Go-Go	102
Greenwich Village Follies	216
Gringo	35
Guilty One, The	31
Hail and Farewell	40
Hamlet (John Barrymore)	101
Her Temporary Husband	92
Hospitality	46
How Come?	32
Humming Bird, The	40
Humoresque	32
Hunky Dory	48
*Icebound	145
If Winter Comes	40
Inspector General, The	8
It Is the Law	125
It's a Boy	63

Plays	*Performances*
Jack and Jill	92
Jitta's Atonement	37
Johannes Kreisler	65
King Lear	2
Lady Butterfly	128
Lady Cristilinda, The	24
Lady from the Provinces	8
Lady in Ermine, The	232
Last Warning, The	238
La Tendresse	64
Laughing Lady, The	96
Life of Man, The	4
Lights Out	12
Listening In	88
*Little Nellie Kelly	248
Little Theatre Tournament	8
Liza	169
Love Child, The	167
Love Habit, The	69
Love Set, The	8
Loyalties	220
Lucky One, The	40
Malvaloca	48
Manhattan	86
March Hares	4
*Mary the 3d	152
Masked Woman, The	115
Merchant of Venice, The (Warfield)	92
*Merton of the Movies	248
Mike Angelo	48

Plays	*Performances*
Molly Darling	99
Monster, The	101
Morphia	64
Moscow Art Theatre	96
Mountebank, The	32
Mr. Malatesta (Papa Joe)	96
*Music Box Revue	272
My Aunt from Ypsilanti	7
*Not So Fast	31
Old Soak, The	423
On the Stairs	80
Orange Blossoms	95
Our Nell	40
Papa Joe (Mr. Malatesta)	96
Passing Show of 1922	85
*Passing Show of 1923	4
Passions for Men	86
Pasteur	16
Peer Gynt	120
Persons Unknown	5
Pinwheel Revue	35
Pinwheel Revue (2d edition)	24
Plantation Revue	40
Plot Thickens, The	15
*Polly Preferred	184
Pride	13
Queen of Hearts	39
*Rain	256
Red Poppy, The	13
Revue Russe	20
Rita Coventry	24
Rivals, The	24
Roger Bloomer	50
Romantic Age, The	31
Romeo and Juliet (Ethel Barrymore)	29
Romeo and Juliet (Cowl)	157
Rose Bernd	87
Rose Briar	88
R. U. R.	184
Salome (Ethiopian Art)	8
Sally, Irene and Mary	312
Sandro Botticelli	24
School for Scandal, The (March 12)	4
School for Scandal, The (June 4)	8
Secrets	168
Serpent's Tooth, A	36
*Seventh Heaven	293
Shore Leave	151
Six in Search of an Author	136
*So This Is London	343
Spice of 1922	73
Spite Corner	121
Sporting Thing To Do, The	40
Springtime of Youth	68
Square Peg, A	41
Strut Miss Lizzie	32
Sue, Dear	96
Sun Showers	40

Plays	*Performances*	*Plays*	*Performances*
*Sun Up	28	Virtue	3
*Sweet Nell of Old Drury	35	Wasp, The	95
Swifty	24	Whispering Wires	352
Sylvia	13	Why Men Leave Home	135
Texas Nightingale	32	Why Not?	120
That Day	15	*Wildflower	142
Thin Ice	105	Wild Oats Lane	13
Three Sisters, The	8	Will Shakespeare	80
Tidings Brought to Mary, The	32	Within Four Walls	15
To Love	55	Woman Who Laughed, The	13
Torch Bearers, The	135	World We Live In, The	111
Up She Goes	256	Yankee Princess, The	80
*Uptown West	73	*You and I	136
		*Zander the Great	80

*Still running June 15, 1923.

PLAYS THAT HAVE RUN OVER FIVE HUNDRED PERFORMANCES ON BROADWAY

Lightnin'	1291	Adonis	603
The Bat	867	Kiki	600
The First Year	760	Blossom Time	576
Peg o' My Heart	692	Sally	570
East Is West	680	The Music Master	540
Irene	670	The Boomerang	522
A Trip to Chinatown	657	Shuffle Along	504

WHERE AND WHEN THEY WERE BORN

Abarbanell, Lina	Berlin	1880
Adams, Maude	Salt Lake City, Utah	1872
Adelaide, La Petite	Cohoes, N. Y.	1890
Allen, Viola	Huntsville, Ala.	1869
Ames, Robert	Hartford, Conn.	1893
Anglin, Margaret	Ottawa, Canada	1876
Arbuckle, Maclyn	San Antonio, Texas	1866
Arliss, George	London, England	1868
Arthur, Julia	Hamilton, Ont.	1869
Atwell, Roy	Syracuse, N. Y.	1880
Atwill, Lionel	London, England	1885
Bacon, Frank	California	1864
Bainter, Fay	Los Angeles, Cal.	1892
Barbee, Richard	Lafayette, Ind.	1887
Barrymore, Ethel	Philadelphia, Pa.	1879
Barrymore, John	Philadelphia, Pa.	1882
Barrymore, Lionel	London, England	1878
Bates, Blanche	Portland, Ore.	1873
Bayes, Nora	Milwaukee, Wis.	1880
Beban, George	San Francisco, Cal.	1873
Beckley, Beatrice	Roedean, England	1885
Beecher, Janet	Chicago, Ill.	1884
Belasco, David	San Francisco, Cal.	1862
Ben-Ami, Jacob	Minsk, Russia	1890
Bennett, Richard	Cass County, Ind.	1873
Bennett, Wilda	Asbury Park, N. J.	1894
Benrimo, J. Harry	San Francisco, Cal.	1874
Bernard, Barney	Rochester, N. Y.	1877
Bernard, Sam	Birmingham, England	1863
Bernhardt, Sarah	Paris, France	1844
Bingham, Amelia	Hickville, Ohio	1869
Binney, Constance	Philadelphia, Pa.	1900

Blinn, Holbrook	San Francisco, Cal.	1872
Bordoni, Irene	Paris, France	1895
Brady, Alice	New York	1892
Brady, William A.	San Francisco, Cal.	1863
Breese, Edmund	Brooklyn, N. Y.	1871
Brian, Donald	St. John's, N. F.	1871
Broadhurst, George H.	England	1866
Bruns, Julia	St. Louis	1895
Bryant, Charles	England	1879
Brooks, Virginia Fox	New York	1893
Buchanan, Thompson	Louisville, Ky.	1877
Burke, Billie	Washington, D. C.	1885
Burton, Frederick	Indiana	1871
Byron, Arthur	Brooklyn, N. Y.	1872
Cahill, Marie	Brooklyn, N. Y.	1871
Cantor, Eddie	New York	1894
Campbell, Mrs. Patrick	England	1865
Carle, Richard	Somerville, Mass.	1871
Carlisle, Alexandra	Yorkshire, England	1886
Carter, Mrs. Leslie	Lexington, Ky.	1862
Catlett, Walter	San Francisco, Cal.	1889
Cawthorne, Joseph	New York	1868
Chaplin, Charles Spencer	London	1889
Chatterton, Ruth	New York	1893
Cherry, Charles	England	1872
Claire, Ina	Washington, D. C.	1892
Clarke, Marguerite	Cincinnati, Ohio	1887
Cliffe, H. Cooper	England	1862
Clifford, Kathleen	Charlottesville, Va.	1887
Coghlan, Gertrude	England	1879
Coghlan, Rose	Petersboro, England	1850
Cohan, George M.	Providence, R. I.	1878
Cohan, Georgette	Los Angeles, Cal.	1900
Collier, Constance	Windsor, England	1882
Collier, William	New York	1866
Collinge, Patricia	Dublin, Ireland	1894
Collins, Jose	London, England	1896

Conroy, Frank	London, England	1885
Cooper, Violet Kemble	London, England	1890
Corrigan, Emmett	Amsterdam, Holland	1871
Corthell, Herbert	Boston, Mass.	1875
Courtenay, William	Worcester, Mass.	1875
Courtleigh, William	Guelph, Ont.	1869
Cowl, Jane	Boston, Mass.	1887
Crane, William H.	Leicester, Mass.	1845
Craven, Frank	Boston, Mass.	1875
Crews, Laura Hope	San Francisco, Cal.	1880
Crosman, Henrietta	Wheeling, W. Va.	1865
Crothers, Rachel	Bloomington, Ill.	1878
Cumberland, John	St. John, N. B.	1880
Dale, Margaret	Philadelphia, Pa.	1880
Dalton, Charles	England	1864
Daly, Arnold	New York	1875
Daniels, Frank	Dayton, Ohio	1860
Dawn, Hazel	Ogden, Utah	1891
Day, Edith	Minneapolis, Minn.	1896
De Angelis, Jefferson	San Francisco, Cal.	1859
Dean, Julia	St. Paul, Minn.	1880
De Belleville, Frederic	Belgium	1857
De Cordoba, Pedro	New York	1881
Dickson, Dorothy	Kansas City	1898
Dillingham, Charles B.	Hartford, Conn.	1868
Dinehart, Alan	Missoula, Mont.	1889
Ditrichstein, Leo	Temesbar, Hungary	1865
Dixey, Henry E.	Boston, Mass.	1859
Dodson, John E.	London, England	1857
Dolly, Rosie	Hungary	1892
Dolly, Jennie	Hungary	1892
Donnelly, Dorothy Agnes	New York	1880
Doro, Marie	Duncannon, Pa.	1882
D'Orsay, Lawrence	England	1860
Dressler, Marie	Cobourg, Canada	1869
Drew, John	Philadelphia, Pa.	1853
Drew, Louise	New York	1884

Druce, Herbert	England	1870
Duncan, Isadora	San Francisco, Cal.	1880
Duncan, Augustin	San Francisco, Cal.	1873
Dunn, Emma	England	1875
Dupree, Minnie	San Francisco, Cal.	1875
Duse, Eleanora	Vigerano, Italy	1859
Eagels, Jeanne	Kansas City, Mo.	1894
Eames, Clare	Hartford, Conn.	1896
Eddinger, Wallace	New York	1881
Edeson, Robert	Baltimore, Md.	1868
Elliott, Gertrude	Rockland, Me.	1874
Elliott, Maxine	Rockland, Me.	1871
Elliott, William	Boston, Mass.	1885
Elliston, Grace	Wheeling, W. Va.	1881
Ellsler, Effie	Philadelphia, Pa.	1898
Eltinge, Julian	Boston, Mass.	1883
Emerson, John	Sandusky, Ohio	1874
Errol, Leon	Sydney, Australia	1881
Ewell, Lois	Memphis, Tenn.	1885
Fairbanks, Douglas	Denver, Colo.	1883
Farnum, Dustin	Hampton Beach, N. H.	1874
Farnum, William	Boston, Mass.	1876
Farrar, Geraldine	Melrose, Mass.	1883
Faversham, William	Warwickshire, England	1868
Fealy, Maude	Memphis, Tenn.	1883
Fenwick, Irene	Chicago, Ill.	1887
Ferguson, Elsie	New York	1883
Fields, Lewis	New York	1867
Findlay, Ruth	New York	1897
Fischer, Alice	Indiana	1869
Fisher, Lola	Chicago, Ill.	1892
Fiske, Minnie Maddern	New Orleans, La.	1867
Fontanne, Lynn	London, England	1882
Forbes-Robertson, Sir J.	London, England	1853
Foy, Edward Fitzgerald	New York	1854
Frederick, Pauline	Boston, Mass.	1884
Friganza, Trixie	Cincinnati, Ohio	1870

Frohman, Daniel........Sandusky, Ohio........1850
Fulton, Maude..........St. Louis, Mo..........1883
Garden, Mary...........Scotland 1876
Gaythorne, Pamela......England 1882
George, Grace...........New York.............1879
Gillette, William........Hartford, Conn........1856
Gillmore, Frank.........New York.............1884
Gillmore, Margalo.......England 1901
Glaser, Lulu............Alleghany, Pa.........1874
Glendinning, Ernest......Ulverston, England.....1884
Gottschalk, Ferdinand....London, England......1869
Grey, Jane..............Middlebury, Vt........1883
Grey, Katherine.........San Francisco, Cal.....1873
Hackett, James K........Wolf Island, Ont.......1869
Haines, Robert T........Muncie, Ind...........1870
Hale, Louise Closser.....Chicago, Ill...........1872
Hall, Laura Nelson......Philadelphia, Pa.......1876
Hamilton, Hale..........Topeka, Kan...........1880
Hampden, Walter........Brooklyn, N. Y.........1879
Harding, Lyn...........Newport 1867
Hawtrey, Charles........Eton, England.........1858
Hayes, Helen...........Washington, D. C......1895
Hazzard, John E. ....New York 1881
Hedman, Martha........Sweden 1888
Heggie, O. P............Australia 1879
Heming, Violet.........Leeds, England........1893
Herbert, Victor..........Dublin, Ireland.......1859
Herne, Chrystal.........Dorchester, Mass.......1883
Hilliard, Robert S........New York.............1857
Hitchcock, Raymond......Auburn, N. Y..........1870
Hodge, William.........Albion, N. Y..........1874
Hopper, DeWolf.........New York.............1858
Hopper, Edna Wallace...San Francisco, Cal.....1874
Holmes, Taylor.........Newark, N. J..........1872
Howard, Leslie..........London, England......1890
Huban, Eileen...........Loughrea, Ireland 1895
Hull, Henry............Louisville, Ky.........1893

Illington, Margaret.......Bloomington, Ill.......1881
Irving, Isabel...........Bridgeport, Conn.......1871
Irwin, May.............Whitby, Ont...........1862
Janis, Elsie.............Delaware, Ohio........1889
Joel, Clara..............Jersey City, N. J.......1890
Jolson, Al..............Washington, D. C......1883
Keane, Doris............Michigan 1885
Keenan, Frank..........Dubuque, Ia...........1858
Keightley, Cyril.........New South Wales, Aus..1875
Kennedy, Madge.........Chicago, Ill...........1890
Kerrigan, J. M..........Dublin, Ireland........1885
Kerr, Geoffrey...........London, England......1895
Kershaw, Willette........Clifton Heights, Mo....1890
Kosta, Tessa............Chicago, Ill...........1893
Kruger, Otto............Toledo, O.............1885
Lackaye, Wilton.........Virginia 1862
Larrimore, Francine.....Russia 1888
La Rue, Grace..........Kansas City, Mo........1882
Lauder, Harry...........Portobello, Eng........1870
Lawton, Thais...........Louisville, Ky..........1881
Lawrence, Margaret......Trenton, N. J..........1890
Lean, Cecil.............Illinois 1878
LeGallienne, Eva........London, England......1889
Levey, Ethel............San Francisco, Cal.....1881
Lewis, Ada.............New York.............1871
Lewis, Mabel Terry......London, England......1872
Loraine, Robert..........England 1876
Lorraine, Lillian........San Francisco, Cal.....1892
Lou-Tellegen ....Holland 1881
Mack, Andrew..........Boston, Mass..........1863
Mack, Willard..........Ontario, Canada.......1873
Mackay, Elsie...........London, England.......1894
MacKellar, Helen........Canada 1896
Mann, Louis............New York.............1865
Mantell, Robert B........Ayrshire, Scotland.....1854
Marinoff, Fania.........Russia 1892
Marivale, Philip........India 1886

Marlowe, Julia	Caldbeck, England	1870
Matthison, Edith Wynne	England	1875
Maude, Cyril	London, England	1862
McIntyre, Frank	Ann Arbor, Mich.	1879
McRae, Bruce	India	1867
Melba, Nellie	Melbourne, Australia	1866
Mellish, Fuller	England	1865
Mercer, Beryl	Seville, Spain	1882
Miller, Henry	London, England	1859
Miller, Marilynn	Findlay, Ohio	1898
Mitchell, Grant	Columbus, Ohio	1874
Mitzi (Hajos)	Budapest	1891
Moores, Clara	Omaha, Neb.	1897
Morris, Clara	Toronto, Canada	1846
Murphy, Tim	Rupert, Vt.	1860
Nash, Florence	Troy, N. Y.	1888
Nash, Mary	Troy, N. Y.	1885
Nazimova, Mme.	Crimea, Russia	1879
Nielsen, Alice	Nashville, Tenn.	1876
Olcott, Chauncey	Providence, R. I.	1862
O'Neil, Eugene Gladstone	New York	1888
O'Neill, Nance	Oakland, Cal.	1875
O'Ramey, Georgia	Mansfield, Ohio	1886
Painter, Eleanor	Iowa	1890
Pawle, Lenox	London, England	1872
Pennington, Ann	Philadelphia, Pa.	1898
Pickford, Mary	Toronto	1893
Post, Guy Bates	Seattle, Wash.	1875
Powers, James T.	New York	1862
Power, Tyrone	London, England	1869
Rambeau, Marjorie	San Francisco, Cal.	1889
Reed, Florence	Philadelphia, Pa.	1883
Rennie, James	Toronto, Canada	1890
Revelle, Hamilton	Gibraltar	1872
Richard, Amy	Boston, Mass.	1880
Richman, Charles	Chicago, Ill.	1870
Ring, Blanche	Boston, Mass.	1876

Ring, Frances	New York	1882
Roberts, Theodore	San Francisco, Cal.	1861
Robson, May	Australia	1868
Ross, Thomas W.	Boston, Mass.	1875
Ruben, Jose	Belgium	1886
Russell, Annie	Liverpool, England	1864
Russell, Lillian	Clinton, Iowa	1860
Ryan, Mary	New York	1885
Sanderson, Julia	Springfield, Mass.	1887
Santley, Joseph	Salt Lake City	1889
Sawyer, Ivy	London, England	1897
Scheff, Fritzi	Vienna, Austria	1879
Scott, Cyril	Ireland	1866
Sears, Zelda	Brockway, Mich.	1873
Segal, Vivienne	Philadelphia, Pa.	1897
Selwyn, Edgar	Cincinnati, Ohio	1875
Serrano, Vincent	New York	1870
Shannon, Effie	Cambridge, Mass.	1867
Shepley, Ruth	New York	1889
Schildkraut, Joseph	Bucharest, Roumania	1896
Sherman, Lowell	San Francisco, Cal.	1885
Sidney, George	New York	1876
Sitgreaves, Beverly	Charleston, S. C.	1867
Skinner, Otis	Cambridgeport, Mass.	1857
Sothern, Edward H.	New Orleans, La.	1864
Spong, Hilda	Australia	1875
Stahl, Rose	Montreal, Canada	1872
Starr, Frances	Oneonta, N. Y.	1886
Stevens, Emily	New York	1882
Stone, Fred	Denver, Col.	1873
Taliaferro, Edith	New York	1892
Taliaferro, Mabel	New York	1887
Tanguay, Eva	Middletown, Conn.	1878
Taylor, Laurette	New York	1884
Tell, Alma	New York	1892
Tell, Olive	New York	1894
Terry, Ellen	Coventry, England	1848

Name	Birthplace	Year
Thomas, Augustus	St. Louis, Mo.	1859
Thomas, John Charles	Baltimore, Md.	1887
Tinney, Frank	Philadelphia, Pa.	1878
Tobin, Genevieve	New York	1901
Tobin, Vivian	New York	1903
Toler, Sidney	Warrensburg, Mo.	1874
Trevor, Norman	Calcutta	1877
Truex, Ernest	Denver, Col.	1890
Tynan, Brandon	Dublin, Ireland	1879
Ulric, Lenore	New Ulm, Minn.	1897
Valentine, Grace	Indianapolis, Ind.	1892
Varesi, Gilda	Milan, Italy	1887
Victor, Josephine	Hungary	1891
Wainwright, Marie	Philadelphia, Pa.	1853
Walker, Charlotte	Galveston, Texas	1878
Warfield, David	San Francisco, Cal.	1891
Warwick, Robert	Sacramento, Cal.	1878
Ware, Helen	San Francisco, Cal.	1877
Weber, Jos.	New York	1867
Welford, Dallas	Liverpool, England	1874
Westley, Helen	Brooklyn, N. Y.	1879
Whiffen, Mrs. Thomas	London, England	1845
Whiteside, Walker	Logansport, Ind.	1869
Wilson, Francis	Philadelphia, Pa.	1854
Winant, Forrest	New York	1888
Winwood, Estelle	England	1883
Wise, Tom A.	England	1865
Wood, Peggy	Philadelphia, Pa.	1893
Wycherly, Margaret	England	1883
Wyndham, Olive	Chicago, Ill.	1886
Wynn, Ed	Philadelphia, Pa.	1886
Zabelle, Flora	Constantinople	1885
Ziegfeld, Florenz, Jr.	Chicago, Ill.	1867

NECROLOGY

June 15, 1922–June 15, 1923

William Rock, comedian and dancer, 53. Long career in musical comedy and vaudeville. Died, Philadelphia, June 27, 1922.

Bobby Connelly, juvenile picture star, 13. Died, Lynbrook, L. I., July 5, 1922.

Robert Dooley, comedian, 52. Father of Gordon, Ray, Johnnie and the late William Dooley. Died, New York, August 4, 1922.

Edwin Lee Wrothe, comedian, 54. Born in Indianola, Ia. Died, Bayside, L. I., August 6, 1922.

Millie De Leon, dancer, 52. The first "girl in blue." Died, New York, August 6, 1922.

Genevieve Ward, English actress, 85. Born, New York, 1837. Daughter of Col. Sam Ward. Appeared in opera and legitimate drama. Died, August 18, 1922.

Harold Otis Skinner, actor, 33. Nephew of Otis Skinner. Died, San Diego, September, 1922.

Frederic S. Isham, playwright and novelist, 57. Wrote "Three Live Ghosts" and "Nothing But the Truth." Died, New York, September 6, 1922.

George R. Sims, dramatist and novelist. Wrote many plays: "Lights o' London," "Romany Rye," "Merry Duchess." Died, London, September 7, 1922.

Rowland Buckstone, actor, 60. For many years a member of the Sothern-Marlowe Company. Died, London, September 15, 1922.

Marie Lloyd, English music hall star, 51. Known in American vaudeville theatres. Died, London, October 7, 1922.

Lillian Dix, actress, 58. Twenty-five years on stage. Died, Bellevue Hospital, New York, October 10, 1922.

Henry A. DuSouchet, author and playwright. Wrote "My Friend from India" and "The Man from Mexico." Born in Indiana. Died, Kingston, New York, October 27, 1922.

Mme. Rita Fornia, singer, 44. Died, Paris, October 27, 1922. First sang in New York under direction of Henry W. Savage sixteen years ago. Proper name Rita Newman. Born in California.

James Burton Green, song writer and pianist, 48. Husband of Irene Franklin. "Franklin and Green" were one of the first acts to volunteer for overseas duty during the war. Died, Mt. Vernon, N. Y., November 17, 1922.

Frank Bacon, actor and playwright, 58. Born in Marysville, Cal. Played character parts in small theatres in California. Played in "The Fortune Hunter" in Chicago. New York engagements in "Stop Thief," "Miracle Man" and "The Cinderella Man." Character of Bill Jones in "Lightnin'," his concluding triumph. Played the part two thousand times. Died, Chicago, where he was playing "Lightnin'," November 19, 1922.

George Bronson Howard, author and playwright, 38. Killed himself by inhaling gas. Best known play "The Only Law." Did book for one "Passing Show." Died, Los Angeles, November 20, 1922.

Kate Ryan, 65. One time member of old Boston Museum Stock Company. Born in Boston. Died at Trumbull Hospital in Brookline, Mass., November 27, 1922.

John H. Gilmour, 65. Veteran of the stage. Died at his home in Yonkers, N. Y., November.

William Raymond Sill, press agent, dramatic editor, war correspondent, 53. Born in Hartford, Conn. Son of Lieut.-Gov. George Griswold Sill. Left newspaper work and went with Weber and Fields as publicity man. First publicity agent for Keith's Palace, New York. Died, December 1, 1922, Flushing, L. I., N. Y.

Mrs. Josephine Preston Peabody Marks, poetess and playwright. Died, Cambridge, Mass., December 4, 1922.

Cheridah Simpson, musical comedy actress, 58. Engaged in theatricals for over 30 years. Died, New York, December 26, 1922.

Harrison Hunter, actor. Born in England. Played lead in "The Bat." Died, Boston, January 3, 1923.

Dr. Anselm Goetzl, musical composer, 44. Born in Bohemia and came to United States in 1913. Composed scores for "The Wanderer," "Aphrodite," "Deburau" and "Gold Diggers." Wrote "The Royal Vagabond," and made production of his own work, "The Rose Girl." Died, Barcelona, Spain, January 9, 1923, after an operation.

Georgia Lawrence, actress, 46. Played in "Sonny." Family name was Griffin. Died, January 12, 1923, in Palatka, Florida.

George Hamlin, operatic tenor. Appeared in 1912 with Mary Garden in Victor Herbert's opera, "Natoma." Born, Elgin, Ill. Died, New York, January 11, 1923.

William H. Thompson, character actor, 71. Fifty-five years on stage. Member Empire State Stock Company. Died February 4, 1923, New York.

Francis M. Byrne, actor, 47. Born, Newport, R. I. On stage twenty-eight years. Was leading man for Ethel Barrymore, Elsie Ferguson, Rose Stahl and Maude Adams. Died, February 6, 1923.

William Hanlon, acrobat, 87. Leader of Six Hanlon Brothers. On stage for sixty-four years. Died, February 7, 1923.

May Naudain, singer, 50. Born in Omaha. Prominent light opera prima donna. First success in "It Happened in Nordland" in 1904. Played prima donna role in "Katinka." Died February 8, 1923, Jacksonville, Fla.

Joseph Herbert, comedian and librettist, 56. On stage thirty years. Wrote "Honeymoon Express," "The Beauty Spot," "Mlle. Napoleon," "Alone At Last," "Waltz Dreams," and "Honeydew." Born, Liverpool, England. Died, New York, February 18, 1923.

Frederic De Belleville, actor, 68. On stage for fifty years. Born in Liége, Belgium. In his youth was officer in Belgian army. Came to America forty years ago. Supported many famous stars. Died, New York, February 25, 1923.

Harry Corson Clarke, actor, 62. Died, Los Angeles, March 3, 1923, following a fall during a performance of "The Rotters" in Detroit. In profession for fifty years. Played in India, Africa, Australia and China.

Ida Vernon, actress, 80. Died, Sheldon, Vt. Born in the South. Made début in Boston in 1856, in "A Midsummer Night's Dream." At time of Civil War was appearing on stage in Richmond, Va. Played leading rôle in "The Two Orphans" when it was produced in the Union Square, New York.

Marie Bates, actress, 70. A veteran of the legitimate stage. Born in Boston. Supported Mrs. Leslie Carter in "Zaza," and David Warfield in all his successful plays. Died March 12, 1923, Glenbrook, Conn.

Mrs. A. M. Palmer (Laura A. Palmer), president of the Professional Women's League. Widow of Austin M. Palmer, well-known theatrical manager and one of the founders of the Actors' Fund of America. Died, New York, March 15, 1923.

Sarah Bernhardt, actress, 78. Died, Paris, March 26, 1923. For years recognized as the leading emotional actress of the world. Her final American tour was in 1918.

Maggie Le Clair, comedienne, 65. Born, New York. Member of variety team of Casey and Le Clair, and of Le Clair Sisters. Frequently appeared in musical comedy. Died, Toronto, Canada, April 7, 1923.

Jess Dandy, actor, 52. Born, Rochester, New York. Family name, Jesse A. Danzig. In vaudeville till 1903. Played Hans Wagner in the "Prince of Pilsen" five thousand times. Died, Brookline, Mass., April 15, 1923.

Rev. George C. Houghton, rector of the Church of the Transfiguration, known generally as the "Little Church Around the Corner," and "The Actors' Church." Died, New York City, April 17, 1923. Said to have married more theatrical people than any other ecclesiastic in the world.

John O. Lambdin, critic, 50. Conductor of the "Three Arts" column of the Baltimore *Evening Sun*. Son of Dr. Alfred Cochrane Lambdin. Was with Philadelphia *Times* and *Ledger*. Went to Baltimore in 1910 and in 1911 joined editorial staff of the *Evening Sun*. Died, Baltimore, April 25, 1923.

Frank Finley Mackay, veteran actor, 92. Teacher of elocution in Baltimore. Was with Mrs. John Drew's celebrated company. Managed Chestnut Street Theatre in Philadelphia. Appeared with DeWolf Hopper and William H. Crane. Founded National Congress of Dramatic Art. Died, Coytesville, N. J., May 5, 1923.

Sadie Martinot, actress, 61. Born, Jamaica, L. I. Entered theatrical profession in 1876 in "Ixion." Popular light opera star in "Nanon." Died, Ogdensburg, N. Y., May 7, 1923.

Charles Kent, veteran stage and picture actor, 69. Died

in Brooklyn hospital, May 21, 1923. Born, England. On stage for fifty years. With Thomas Keene's Shakespearean Company, and later with Vitagraph pictures.

Guy Lindsley, Shakespearean actor. Born, St. Louis. Started career as a boy, appearing in "Jim the Penman." Was with Robert Mantell for eighteen years. Died, New York City, May 26, 1923.

Harry E. Fisher, vaudeville and musical comedy comedian, 55. Born in England and came to this country thirty-five years ago. Featured comedian in first Winter Garden production. In vaudeville was member of team of Fisher and Carroll. Died, Brooklyn, May 28, 1923.

Gus Pixley, comedian, 58. Died, Saranac Lake, June 2, 1923. Long in musical comedy. Was in pictures for last ten years.

Pierre Loti, 74. Famous French novelist and man of letters. Died, June 10, 1923, Hendaye, France.

INDEX OF PLAYS AND CASTS

INDEX OF AUTHORS